THE LOCUST JOB

CRAIG SCHAEFER

Demimonde Books

Cover Design by James T. Egan of Bookfly Design LLC.
Author Photo ©2014 by Karen Forsythe Photography
Craig Schaefer / The Locust Job
ISBN 978-1-944806-19-4

Contents

The Story So Far

Daniel Faust has a foot in two worlds. In Las Vegas he carries a gun—and an enchanted deck of cards—as an enforcer for the criminal underworld. He's also one of the rare humans to ever receive a knighthood in the courts of hell, an honor he didn't want or ask for.

The Enemy, a living nightmare from the first story ever told, has targeted Daniel and his crew for destruction. Not long ago, the Enemy brought in a little extra help. He made an alliance with the Network, an interdimensional crime syndicate, and its Vegas representative: Elmer Donaghy, a necromancer from a plague-blasted parallel world. With the aid of his friends, Daniel defeated Elmer's plans, escaped a deadly trap, and managed to reconcile with his long-lost brother.

Now Daniel and his nemesis are racing for the same prize, artifacts belonging to a dead 1940s stage magician named Howard Canton. Daniel doesn't know why the Enemy wants them so badly, or why he's dispatched thieves around the globe to snatch up Canton's legacy, but he's determined to find out.

Other characters from the first story are revealing themselves at last, as Earth hurtles toward its inescapable climax. Just like they have been on so many other parallel worlds, the Enemy and the Paladin are due for a showdown. The winner takes all, and if the Enemy wins—as he usually does—the planet dies, consumed by horror and fire. And nobody knows who, or where, the Paladin is.

The machinations of an ancient coven recently pushed Daniel into the path of two other reincarnated characters, the Witch and her Knight. What ensued was a cross-country scramble against a ticking clock and a small army of assassins, as Daniel fought to keep his charges alive and help them find a lost treasure: Wisdom's Grave, the resting place of the first witch who ever lived and, they hoped, a key to breaking their endless cycle of death and reincarnation.

That story ended on a dark night in upstate New York, at an abandoned zoo, where friends and foes came together to fight a greater enemy. Among the denizens of the occult underground the "Wisdom's Grave incident" is the stuff of whispers and legends. Some say that a king was killed that night. Some say that God himself died at the hands of a vengeful witch. Some say that the very fabric of magic was changed forever.

Daniel Faust was there. He doesn't talk about it, save to say that he fought alongside some of the bravest people he's ever known. And when that long and terrible night was over, and the smoke cleared, not all of his friends came home again.

1.

The mortician did a good job. Carolyn Saunders was a sleeping beauty on quilted white satin, eyes closed, and a deft hand with a makeup brush had left her radiant. She glowed with the kind of peace I knew she never found in life. Then again, do any of us? I remembered her last words as she lay pinned in the alien wreckage, half-crushed under a slab of fallen steel. *Did we win?*

We told her we did. Then she died. I was still trying to figure out if we lied or not.

Caitlin's hand, manicured nails glistening like dark cherries, curled on my shoulder. We were twins in funeral black. I turned to one side, met her questioning glance, then looked behind us. Small turnout today and most of the softly whispering mourners in the parlor were part of my crew, members of my family of choice. The only unfamiliar faces were locals. Blood relations, I thought at first. Then I made enough small talk to find out that Carolyn had her own family of choice. A couple of librarians, the clerk at the grocery store, her mailman. They came with their memories, their funny anecdotes, their questions. They'd leave with them, too. As far as they knew, she'd died of a sudden and inexplicable heart condition.

"I don't like it," I said.

Caitlin understood what I meant. She always did.

"We can hardly print the truth on her gravestone," she said.

I knew she was right, but I needed to argue anyway. "She deserves better than this."

"We know." Her fingers tightened on my shoulder. "The people who matter know. And *she* knew."

The casket was lined with trinkets and tokens to be buried with her body, coffin gifts. A few cards. A small antique iron key caught my eye; it hadn't been there when I first arrived, and I didn't see who left it. Or the oval cameo, onyx on Victorian pewter, bearing the silhouette of a horned owl. My lips went tight.

We'd brought a going-away present of our own. An airplane bottle of Dewar's scotch, the neck tied with a bow of green ribbon. We weren't the only people to send Carolyn to the afterlife with booze—the casket looked like a well-stocked minibar—but I knew she would have appreciated the gesture. I nestled it next to her cold and pale hand. Our fingers brushed, skin to skin; she felt like a wax doll.

"Funny," I said, keeping my voice low. "I mean, she's not in there. We know better than most people, that's not...that's not *her*. It's just the leftovers."

"Rituals matter," Caitlin told me.

"It just seems silly. And you know, I say that, but here I am, doing it, and I don't know—"

"Rituals," she said, "matter. You're here to say goodbye, love. Do it in your own time and in your own way."

She gave me some space, punctuating her words with one last squeeze before drifting off across the parlor to talk to Bentley and Corman.

I had to swallow my words before my voice broke on them, like waves over a jagged rock. Grief was a dirty fighter. It came up from behind and sucker punched me right when I thought I had a handle on things. I took a few deep breaths. I wasn't going to get teary-eyed, not here. My refusal wasn't some misplaced machismo; it was a gesture of respect, because nothing would have pissed Carolyn off more than people weeping over her dead body. She'd want us to honor her memory by getting roaring drunk and looking for trouble.

That I could manage.

I felt a shadow at my back. Two shadows, with waves of platinum blond hair and little black cocktail dresses. Justine and Juliette stood side by side, Juliette clutching a paperback with a lurid cover to her chest.

"I didn't know you knew Carolyn," I said.

"*Knew* her?" Justine gaped at me. "We were, like, the stars of her books."

"We're totally famous," Juliette added.

I glanced down to the paperback in her arms. *The Killing Floor*. Of course. I wasn't sure why it took me so long to make the connection.

"Right," I said. "We had a threesome."

Juliette's jaw dropped. "We *did*?"

Justine shook her head. "I think we would have remembered that."

"No," I said. "In the novel. She wrote you in as the leather-clad vampire vixens."

"And?" Justine said.

"And," I said, "you know, there was...that scene."

"That wasn't you," Justine said. "That was Donatello Faustus."

"Right. Who is a fictional version of me."

"I'm pretty sure he isn't," Juliette said.

"No," Justine said. "Donatello is cool. And hot. He's a thief, and a sorcerer, and he goes on adventures. He's nothing like you."

"He's *the guy*," Juliette added.

I stared at her. "You have got to be messing with me right now."

Justine glanced at her sister. "Sidebar. Need to talk in private."

They took half a step back. They did not lower their voices in any appreciable manner.

"Danny is very confused," Justine said. "Did we maybe, just maybe, have sex with him and then completely forget about it?"

"Because he was really, really bad?"

"Exactly."

Juliette looked my way. "Danny? Are you bad at sex? We are your friends and you can confide in us."

"We can get you help," Justine said, "but only if you admit you have a problem."

I looked past them, hunting for a lifeline, and spotted a conversation on the other side of the funeral parlor that needed my immediate intervention.

"Ladies, if you'll excuse me."

As I brushed past them, I heard Juliette stage-whisper to her twin: "He actually thinks Donatello Faustus was based on him. I mean, it'd be funny if it wasn't so sad."

"Where would he even get that idea?" Justine asked.

On the far side of the gathering, Melanie's mop of neon-blue hair contrasted with her graveyard-black frock. The teenager's ensemble was mismatched, more fit for a goth party than a funeral, but that was her style. Not unlike the woman who was talking to her, in her late forties with a delicate, heart-shaped face and the first traces of crow's-feet around her eyes. Melanie was hanging on her every word, and I didn't like it. I didn't like it even before I got close enough to eavesdrop.

"—watching over all of us, but she also needs our help. If you have faith—"

"Hedy," I said. "Didn't know if I'd see you here."

"Of course," she replied. "We all came."

She gestured to the tall window at her back. I glanced out over rolling lawns, flat Midwestern grass ending at the edge of a cornfield. There were people in the field. Distant, still figures, watching us.

"Just in case," Hedy said.

Just in case of an attack. The possibility had occurred to me, and Caitlin had dispatched watchers of her own, security operatives from her infernal court. We had done more than give the Network a black eye; we'd chopped one of its limbs off and left the syndicate bleeding. Bleeding too badly to rally and come back for another round this soon, I figured, but it was bound to happen eventually.

"Melanie? Do me a favor, give us a second here? I need to have a word with your new friend."

I had thought about coming up with some excuse to send her out of earshot, but the kid was too smart for that. She read my tone, nodded, and took a hike. I eased into Hedy's personal space.

"She's not yours," I said.

"I don't have to tell you," Hedy replied, "that Melanie has stunning magical potential. She radiates with it—"

"She's. Not. Yours."

Her delicate eyebrows lifted. "You should let me teach her, Daniel. I can equip her in ways that you can't."

"I made a promise. To her mom, to Caitlin, and to myself, that I'd keep Melanie safe."

"Which is exactly why you should place her in my care."

There was that bastard grief again, slapping me across the face and making my eyes sting right when I thought I'd shaken him off.

"Carolyn was my friend," I said, "and she got involved with you people and now she's in a goddamn box."

"Carolyn was a martyr to the cause," Hedy replied, "and she made her own choices. I can help Melanie find her true potential. She would learn to shine in my coven."

"Half your coven is *dead*," I told her.

The second the words left my mouth, seeing the way the last bit of color fled from her cheeks, how her lips parted, I would have done anything to take them back.

"I'm sorry," I said.

A hand, gloved in delicate black lace, fluttered at her side. "No, it's fine."

She started to turn, to walk away.

"No. Hedy. Please, listen. I'm sorry. That was a fucking asshole thing to say—"

"You aren't wrong," she said, her voice trembling with a forced laugh. The kind of laugh that rides just ahead of tears.

"I'm still an asshole. And I'm sorry. I know you're a good teacher."

We lingered on the edge of the room, silent, while she waited for the rest of the words to find their way out of the twisted tangle in my guts.

"I had an apprentice once before," I said. "I lost her. She took on a fight she wasn't ready for, trying to impress me, and I was just...a second too late."

"I know," Hedy said.

I squinted at her. "Who told you?"

Her smile was gentle. She put her hand on my arm.

"Pain recognizes pain," she said.

"It's not that I think you'd be a bad teacher, or that she wouldn't be safe with you. It's..."

I trailed off, gazing across the room to Carolyn's open casket. What was it, then? Making sense of my own emotions was like doing a jigsaw puzzle with all the edge pieces gone. Fuzzy borders and mismatched connections. Hedy gave me the time I needed to sort it out.

"I reconnected with my kid brother recently. Then the Network found out about him. He's safe, for now. I've got people watching him and his wife and kid around the clock, while I try to figure out a long-term solution."

"I think the Network has more pressing problems at the moment," Hedy observed.

"For now. But he's only in their sights because he's my brother, and that makes this situation my responsibility. Then Melanie asked me to teach her. Her mom's a big shot in Prince Sitri's court, so she was pretty much born with a target on her back. And now, because I said yes, my enemies are her enemies too."

"I don't hear anyone saying it was a bad decision."

"I'm not used to having this kind of skin in the game," I said. I could see it now, the light of clarity at the heart of the knot. "Not used to having people depend on me like this. Honestly, Hedy, I think you'd be great for Melanie. Probably a better teacher than I'd ever be."

"I have a little more practice at it," she said.

"And part of me...part of me is aching to say yes. Fine, fuck it, you take the reins." I looked her in the eye. "But that's a cop-out, because Melanie is my responsibility. And when you step up and take on a responsibility, that's that. You have to follow through. If I can't do that, I'm nothing at all."

I looked back to the window, to the silent watchers in the field.

"It's all moving so fast now. Like we're on this ramp lined with knives and just one stumble, that's all it's going to take. And if I screw up now, it's not just me who gets hurt."

"You know," Hedy said, "it's okay to be scared."

I stared at the horizon. A thin gray line in the distance, between farmers' fields and an overcast sky.

"Didn't say I was scared," I said.

"No, but it's still okay if you are. Few things are more frightening than watching history unfold, and we've been blessed with front-row seats. The world—the *worlds*—have changed. And will continue to change. Finding Wisdom's Grave wasn't the end of the journey. Only the beginning." She eyed me, thinking. "There's something you might keep in mind."

"Yeah?"

"When I have a particularly gifted student on my hands, I'm not shy about recruiting a little help, to ensure she receives the full education that she deserves. That's not an abdication of my responsibility as a teacher; it's *part* of my responsibility. Many skilled hands make for lighter work."

"It takes a village?"

"Or a coven," Hedy replied. "Just think about it. For that matter, she's not the only one who could benefit from a bit of extra tutelage."

I didn't follow her at first. Then I chuckled. "I'm turning forty next week. I'm a little too old to be anyone's apprentice."

"Is that your confidence talking," she asked, "or your pride?"

The funeral director was on the move, cradling a clipboard in his hands. I checked my watch.

"I think they're about to get started," I said and nodded to the open casket. "I'm going to go up there. Want to say one last goodbye before they shut the lid."

2.

We put Carolyn's body in the ground, and that was that. Some people said a few kind words, mostly her local friends; my people couldn't say much at all without giving away the truth.

"That," I told Melanie as the sparse crowd dispersed, drifting to the parking lot at the cemetery's edge, "we'll do later tonight. Memorial party at the Bast Club."

"Didn't she get banned from there?"

"She did," I said. "That's why we picked it. Sort of a middle finger from beyond the grave."

"Didn't *you* get banned from there?"

"Remains to be seen. I mean, yes, I technically held the club's owner at gunpoint and tried to force him to swim through a flooded tunnel that was infested with venomous snakes, but no one has officially told me I'm persona non grata. Yet."

"Now I wish I could come," Melanie said. "Wait. Can I come?"

I had gone back and forth on that decision, and I gave myself time for one last flip-flop before I answered her. I'd just started her training in earnest, and making her apprenticeship status public—public as far as the occult underground went—could draw some bad heat in her direction.

On the other hand, it had to happen sometime, and I couldn't ask for a better event for her social debut. Most of my friends would be there, and every one of them would be keeping an eye on her. Many hands, light work, it takes a village, etcetera.

"You can come," I said. "No drinking. You get caught with booze and your mom'll kill me."

"She'll have to get in line," Caitlin said, passing by. "Are you taking the rental?"

"Is that okay? We should just be a couple of hours behind you."

She leaned in, quick, and her pomegranate lips pecked against mine.

"I'll catch a ride with Freddie and Halima." She pressed a set of keys dangling from a hard plastic Avis tag into my open palm. "Be safe."

Melanie looked between us. "Wait. What are we doing?"

"We're taking a field trip," I told her. "Time for a fundamental part of your education; not the kind you can plan for, just have to grab the opportunity if and when it happens. I'm going to teach you how to pull a locust job."

* * *

Melanie and I took the rented sedan. I drove, hugging backwater curves that cut between farmers' fields, rolling golden seas of wheat under the hard afternoon sun. The endless flat nothing of the American Midwest, on a road pinned between two empty horizons.

"This has been a tradition since...pretty much forever," I told her. "Bentley found a reference to it in a book from the Renaissance once, and they made it sound like it had been a thing for centuries even back then."

The radio was turned down low. All I could get out here was a bluegrass station or a fire-and-brimstone preacher. I'd opted for the bluegrass and a banjo strummed, jangling at the far edge of my hearing, an undercurrent chasing the steady rumble of the tires.

"So," Melanie said, "someone in the community dies, then we just go in and...take all their stuff? Anything magical, I mean."

I nodded. "Books, journals, artifacts, it all has to go."

"So the muggles don't find it."

I drummed my fingers on the steering wheel. Then I gave her the side-eye.

"What?" she said.

"What's the rule?" I asked her.

She sank in her seat.

"No Harry Potter references."

"Ever," I said.

"Ever." She tilted her head at me. "They're not easy to avoid."

"Easier than you think. Try it. Anyway, yes, part of it is a keeping-the-secret thing, but that's really not all that important. If somebody finds a book filled with occult glyphs in their grandmother's bookshelf, they're going to assume grandma *believed* she was a witch, not that she actually had magical powers. A higher priority is keeping cursed or dangerous relics out of outsiders' hands."

"Do a lot of magicians keep that kind of stuff just...lying around their house?"

I thought about my personal stash, courtesy of my elevation to knighthood in Prince Sitri's infernal court. Giving out cursed gifts was a rite of passage for Caitlin's people, and thanks to my debut party I had inherited a sea chest filled with lethal fun. Among other curios, I'd been given a poppet that would come to life and eat my eyes if I ever left it out after midnight and a tie clip that could induce death via explosive bowel movements.

Never say that demons don't understand comedy.

"Happens more often than you might think," I told her. "But a locust job isn't just a smash-and-grab. It's a chance for people who were friends of the dead to come together, say goodbye, make connections. Always friends of the dead, tight ones. After all, you can end up finding journals, diaries, personal stuff that's nobody's business to see. Think of it like...rushing over and clearing the porn off your buddy's laptop before his mom finds it."

"Wow, classy analogy."

"I try," I told her.

"So you and Carolyn were tight?"

I had to think about that.

"Carolyn was a complicated..." I paused, my voice catching on the cliché. "She really wasn't. She was a functioning alcoholic who made more enemies than friends, especially once she started writing real occult-underground gossip into her books. And she was kind of an asshole. Thing is, she wasn't...a mean asshole, if that makes any sense. She wasn't malicious, and she never went out of her way to hurt anybody. She just wanted to tell her stories and entertain people. And drink. Sometimes I wonder what she was like before she found out what she was."

Melanie studied me. "You mean one of the characters? From the first story."

"The eternal Scribe," I said. "Doomed to relive her life again and again and again. She told me that when the cycle repeats, the Enemy usually keeps the Scribe alive until the very end, so she can record his glorious deeds. That was the future she was looking forward to. Chained to some asshole's throne with a pad and a pen while she watched the world die, so she could spend her last years stroking his ego. I think the booze was just her way of trying to check out early."

"But it's over, right? The first story is done."

I wasn't sure about that. *Something* had happened at the Vandemere Zoo that long and bloody night, something that changed the cosmic order, but I was still piecing together the details. Maybe the story died with its author, or maybe it was too baked into the fabric of reality to ever unravel.

Either way, we still had to deal with the fallout, here and now. The Enemy was out there. And he knew my name.

I must have gone silent longer than I meant to. I saw Melanie in the corner of my eye, watching, lips bending in a small, tight bow.

"You okay?" she asked.

"I think finding out, learning what she was...I think it broke her a little bit." I stared at the road ahead, the endless flatland, the gray horizon. "She was always blustery, bold. She'd stick both fingers in the devil's face and tell him to fuck off if she had a drink or two in her. But there were times, quiet times, just the two of us, and she was..."

"What?"

"Sad," I said.

Her voice drifted back to me, a sigh carried on a gust of whiskey-tinged breath. *All those books, written by other mes. Scattered across countless dead worlds, lost and unread forever. I wonder if any of them were any good.*

Melanie repeated her question: "Are *you* okay?"

I focused on the road ahead. We had work to do. Grief, the sneaky bastard, circled around me and looked for an angle of attack, but the call of duty was enough to shore up my defenses for now.

"Business at hand," I said. "Okay, so. Normally, obviously, it wouldn't just be us on this job. But everybody knows you need to learn how this works, so they're standing down and we've got an exclusive claim on Carolyn's house. I'll tell you right now that there may not be anything to find. I came out this way during the whole Wisdom's Grave mess, looking for her. So was a squad of government agents—from the spooky, extralegal side of the government—and they were busy raiding the place. Very possible they stripped it bare. Did I tell you—"

I paused. Melanie's lips had started moving, mimicking my last few words in silence like she knew them by heart.

"About how they stole your car?" she asked. "You may have mentioned it once or twice in passing."

"'One day,' Bentley told me, 'I hope you have an apprentice just like you when you were young.' At the time, I didn't realize it was a curse."

"So we're going to break into a probably empty house," Melanie said.

"No. *You* are going to break into a probably empty house while I watch. Have you been practicing?"

Bentley and Corman, proud fathers that they were—though I don't know why I deserved much pride—never threw anything out. Corman had scavenged up the old locksmith's board they used for teaching me back in the day, a standing sheet of plywood inlaid with a dozen different flavors of your common household lock. Once I got over the rush of nostalgia, I'd passed it along to Melanie with a set of starter picks.

She waggled her hand from side to side. "Eh. I mean, I'm practicing, I just don't know if I'm getting any better."

"Keep working at it. You will. I'll check your technique today and see if I can give you some pointers. Then we get into the fun stuff: how to toss a house and cover any trace that you were ever there. Nobody's actually going to come around, so it's a perfect learning environment."

"I hate to sound like I'm in algebra class," Melanie said, "but how often am I actually going to use this stuff in the real world?"

As little as possible, if I had anything to say about it. For most of us, the magic life and the criminal life went hand in hand. I didn't want that for her. Melanie was a good kid. I wanted her to stay that way. I couldn't put blinders on, though, and pretend people wouldn't be trying to pull her into the shadows left and right. Hell, they already were. Starting with her own mother.

"These are survival skills," I told her. "The whole point of survival skills is that you may not use them every day, but when you need them, you really, *really* need them. Picture this: something goes horribly wrong, off the rails in a way you never planned for. Now, through no fault of your own, you're in a strange house with a dead body on the floor and the cops are on their way."

"Through no fault of my own," she echoed, dubious.

"A situation I have found myself in more than once, yes."

"A dead body, through *no* fault of your own."

"A victim of cruel fate," I said.

"You or the dead guy?"

"Does it matter? So there you are, time's running out, your fingerprints are all over the house and you've got to cover your tracks. Knowing how to do a full forensic wipe—preferably with household chemicals found in your average kitchen—is the difference between freedom and twenty years in prison. You may only need to do it once in your entire life, but when that day comes you'll be damn glad you know how."

She took that in. I saw the place up ahead, a ranch house so far off the beaten path there was barely a ghost of a dirt road tethering it to the world. My eyes narrowed.

"The hell is this?" I breathed.

Melanie turned in her seat, following my gaze. Carolyn had visitors.

There were two SUVs in the driveway. Not the spooky-government type, this time, mismatched and off-color, caked with road dust. Her front door hung wide open.

"I thought it was just us," she said.

"It is. It's supposed to be."

"Are you going to pull in?"

"No."

I kept driving, overshooting the house, keeping my speed steady in case someone was watching from the gingham-curtained windows. Just another passing stranger. I scouted up ahead, looking for a spot to turn the car around and double back once we'd slipped out of sight.

"Could she have friends you didn't know about?" Melanie asked.

"No. Civilian friends, yes. Our kind of people, not a chance. Those aren't friends."

She kept her eyes on the mirror, watching the farmhouse fade behind us. "So what do we do?"

Good question. My first instinct was to drop Melanie off somewhere, out of harm's way, and come back with reinforcements. No time for that, and besides, I knew I wouldn't be doing her any favors. Melanie lived in a dangerous world, and teaching her how to take it on was my job now. A simple truth that rubbed up against the simmering anger in the pit of my stomach.

Whoever had broken into Carolyn's house, they weren't allies. They were thieves, looking to rip off my dead friend.

They were going to answer for that.

3.

There was a farm a quarter mile down the road. Barns, silos, a broken-down tractor gathering dust, and a two-level house that had seen better days, windows webbed with cracks. A hot wind blew battered metal chimes around, jangling in the arid stillness.

I pulled over at the side of the road. My tires kissed the edge of a muddy ditch.

"Careful when you get out," I told Melanie.

Her eyes widened. "You're not making me stay in the car?"

I checked my arsenal. I'd flown in for the funeral; my gun stayed at home. A fresh deck of enchanted playing cards, gently brushed with the aroma of spicy desert oils anointing their faces, nestled in my breast pocket. Under my jacket, on my left arm, I wore the custom spring-loaded sheath Caitlin had bought for me. It cradled the long, slim tube of Howard Canton's wand.

Canton the Magnificent, a stage magician and occultist, had left behind a legacy of oddly gimmicked relics. Relics the Enemy desperately wanted to get his hands on, and the wand was at the top of his shopping list. We still didn't know why. Canton's heyday was in the 1940s, when the Enemy was securely locked away in a dead, barren prison world called the Pessundation. They had never met, never crossed paths, and Canton was long in the grave by the time the Enemy escaped.

I was still learning all the tricks embedded in Canton's wand. It was a powerful little thing with one big caveat: he'd purposefully designed the wand so that it wouldn't help the person wielding it. Its powers only activated in the defense of the innocent, and the wand stubbornly refused every attempt to fool it or to game the system.

Believe me, I tried a lot. And I'm good at gaming the system.

"Stay behind me, stay low," I told Melanie as I shoved my door open. "New lesson plan: how to adapt to the unexpected and think on your feet. This is one you *will* use every day."

My polished leather shoes crunched in grass hard as straw, then squelched, sinking into the loam as I led the way along the edge of a wheat field. The rippling golden stalks made a natural curtain, covering our approach. As we closed in on Carolyn's lonely ranch house, I cut a path through the wheat and moved in a smooth, fast crouch. I heard Melanie right behind me, rustling footsteps and nervous breath.

I found a spot with an angle on the driveway and two of the windows, got down on one knee, and froze.

"What are we—" Melanie started to ask.

"Watch," I said.

I caught movement inside. People—three at least, though with a pair of SUVs in the driveway I figured there had to be more—rummaging through the house. Moving quick, like they were pressed for time. *Like they know what a locust job is all about,* I thought, *and they're expecting Carolyn's real friends to show up any minute.*

"Are we going in there?" Melanie whispered.

I shook my head. "Don't know how many there are or what they're carrying. If you're expecting trouble, always tilt the odds in your direction as much as you can before the fight starts. Choosing the battlefield is a big advantage."

"How do we—" She paused. "Oh. We don't have to go in there. But they have to come out here."

"Unless they're moving in, yeah." I pointed, drawing a line from our perch in the wheat to the driveway. "Looks like about fifteen feet of open ground between Carolyn's door and the SUVs. No cover, and they don't know we're here. Yet."

I felt Melanie's eyes burning a hole in my back. The question she wanted to ask, unspoken.

"I'm not going to kill them unless I have to," I told her. "I want answers, not bodies."

"What if their answers aren't good enough?"

"One step at a time," I said.

Someone was coming out. A figure in a dirty flannel hoodie, head bowed and arms tucked in, body language tight as a coiled spring. Hands empty. She was a young woman, a wisp of a thing, maybe a couple of years older than Melanie. I caught a glimpse of her face under the hood as she turned. Pale skin, sharp features, and bright eyes glaring from a raccoon mask of smeary charcoal makeup. She said something. I couldn't hear the words, but the way her finger jabbed at the SUVs told me two things. She and her buddies were leaving, and whatever they hoped to find here, they didn't get it.

"Now?" Melanie whispered.

I held up my open hand. *Wait for it.* Patience rewarded me a few seconds later, when a trio of men emerged from the house. One carried a holster on his hip, and the other two toted shotguns on shoulder slings. Sleek black Mossbergs that could cut through a wheat field—and us—without missing a beat.

Another two, a man and a woman, followed in their wake. So six in all—no, seven, another woman was late to the party and getting the brunt of their leader's ire—a mixture of older teenagers and people in their twenties. Young crew, and their youth was the only thing they had in common besides the hardware they were packing.

Not the only thing. I relaxed, breathing deep, and sent out my psychic tendrils. They wavered through the open air, invisible to the untrained eye. In my second sight, though, they glowed royal violet and squirmed like sea anemones, their tips licking at the intruders' faces. I felt their presence as much as saw them, getting a sense of their souls. A catalog of symbols flickered in my mind's eye, translating feelings to thoughts to bone-deep knowledge.

"Melanie," I breathed. I waved her a little closer, and the wheat rustled as she scooted up alongside me. "Reach out, like I taught you. Gentle and smooth. Tell me what you see."

She put her fingertips to her temple and squinted, hard. The fingertip thing was a bad habit I was going to have to train her out of. Posing like a superhero when you're using your psychic senses is like touching your ear when you're talking on a concealed earpiece: a rookie move guaranteed to draw heat. I kept quiet about it for now, though; I didn't know how much longer the home invaders would stick around, and I wanted to find out if Melanie could see what I saw.

She didn't let me down. Her lips parted in soft surprise.

"They're like me," she said. "Cambion."

Humans born with demonic blood. Their malformed souls were twists of rusty barbed wire in my second sight, speckled with ruby droplets. Humans and demons were never intended to reproduce, as far as I knew—they were two different species with two very different designers—but nature always found a way to surprise us. The pack was breaking up, splitting into the two vehicles, and the sullen young woman with the hoodie and the raccoon makeup hopped behind the lead car's wheel.

"Except her," Melanie whispered, nodding to her blurry form through the sun-smeared windshield. "She's...different."

Good word for it. Hoodie girl was a purebred human, but her soul blazed like a hot white diamond. My mental tendrils quivered around her, afraid to get too close, and her heat washed over my cheeks like I was standing with my face next to an open oven door.

"Remember what I showed you when we were practicing last week? How every magician feels different, depending on how strong they are and the style of magic they practice? You were able to see the alchemical symbols dancing around Bentley's aura and smell the herbs he last used."

"Sure. And the blood on Jennifer's hands." Melanie's shoulders tightened. "So what is *she*?"

I wasn't sure, but I knew a wrecking ball when I saw one.

"Trouble," I said.

"Are we going to stop them?"

The engines revved to life. I stayed put.

"No," I said. "Between the guns and whatever flavor of magic she's packing, that's a fight we don't need. Two against seven is a sucker bet."

I took out my phone and pulled up a notepad app, copying down the lead car's license plate number. And the second car's, as they rolled out together and turned hard, kicking up dirt and bouncing along the rough dirt road.

"Assuming those rides aren't stolen," I said, "and maybe even if they are, there's a good chance we can do some digging and figure out who these people are. Then I'll arrange an introduction under better circumstances."

"Better circumstances?"

"The kind where all the guns are on my side of the room." I rose and swatted dirt from the knee of my trousers. The motion sent a reflexive ache up the small of my back. "C'mon, looks like the coast is clear. Let's do what we came for."

"They all came out empty-handed," she said, following me as I broke from cover.

"They don't know Carolyn like I do. She had a special hiding spot for the good stuff, and I don't mean the expensive liquor." I paused. "I mean, not just the expensive liquor. I figure either the feds found her stash when they raided the place or it's still there, waiting for us."

We were coming up on the front door. It dangled, pushed by a stray gust of warm wind. They hadn't even bothered closing up after themselves. The disrespect rankled me, but I heard Melanie's sigh of relief.

"Well, at least the door's still—" she started to say.

I darted ahead of her, reached in, flicked the lock, and pulled the door shut.

Melanie came to a dead stop. "Really? We caught a lucky break, and you're just tossing it out?"

"Really." I stepped aside and gestured her up to the plate. "Any other day, I'll take any win I can get, but you're not going to learn anything from a lucky break. Get your picks out and do it the hard way."

If there were an Academy Award for overacting, her melodramatic sigh and the expansive roll of her eyes would have won her the nod. All the same, she approached the door, crouched down, and studied the lock as she prepared for the challenge.

"Could have done it the easy way," she said, unrolling her soft case of picks. A twin to mine, a coil of green oilcloth, only smaller and equipped with the bare essentials.

"The only easy day," I told her, "was yesterday."

"Great. I get extra work *and* clichés."

"There are no clichés in this dojo." I crossed my arms. "Only pain."

She grumbled a little more, but the complaining stopped as her concentration kicked in. I knew why Melanie was a straight-A student, and her mom being a demon prince's personal accountant was only part of the reason. She had a knack for locking onto a problem, squaring it in her mental sights, and taking it apart one piece at a time. A good quality in any student, a great one in my line of work. She selected her picks, slid a tension rake through the narrow keyhole, and leaned close. Her gaze went distant. She was learning to let her fingers do the interpreting, feeling the rasps and bumps of the lock, and her ears played a distant second as she hunted for the tumblers' whispering click.

She was learning. So was I, slowly remembering how to teach. Her basic picking technique was sound, nothing more practice couldn't make perfect in time. When I saw little errors or things she could do better, I bit my tongue. Back when I was teaching Desi, my first apprentice, she wanted—needed—instant feedback. But everyone learned in their own way, and I'd soon found that Melanie benefited more from a little breathing room. I'd give her pointers after the lesson was done, so she could stay focused in the moment. She usually took copious notes.

The lock clicked. The knob turned, door groaning open on tarnished hinges. She was getting it. I helped, some. My instruction, her practice, and she was getting it. When I was a kid—and definitely anything but a straight-A student—I could never understand why anyone would want to become a teacher.

I was starting to get it, too.

"And now?" she asked.

"To the victor go the spoils," I said. "Lead the way. Let's see if Carolyn left any secrets behind for us."

4.

"This is messed up," Melanie said.

I couldn't disagree, and I wasn't any less angry now, seeing the condition of Carolyn's house. Her rustic furniture was in pieces amid piles of torn stuffing; someone had taken a knife to her sofa cushions and gutted them, hunting for hidden treasure before tossing them across the living room. Vacation photos lay facedown in puddles of broken glass, most ripped from their frames, crumpled, discarded like bits of trash.

Melanie had paused just inside the doorway. Before she took one more step, she tugged on a pair of thick blue latex gloves and offered me a couple from a fresh pack. The rest went back into her purse, a chrysanthemum-adorned Japanese design on a vinyl strap.

"They must have been tearing the house up all morning, while we were at the funeral," she said.

"Not necessarily." I prowled through the wreckage, eyes sharp. "Carolyn got herself kidnapped at the start of the whole Vandemere mess. Then the feds raided this place while she was out. Then she came back, almost immediately got kidnapped again, and then this morning happened. Suffice to say, a lot of people with bad intentions have tromped through here recently. Anyone could have done the remodeling work."

I nudged a broken chunk of wood, part of a shattered chair, with the mud-spattered toe of my shoe.

"She deserved better than this."

Melanie looked back over her shoulder at me. "Should we clean up?"

It felt like the decent thing to do. Pointless, though. Carolyn didn't have any family, not the flesh and blood kind who might stumble in here and get upset. The next people to pass this way would be men from the bank, here to foreclose when the mortgage payments stopped showing up. I don't have a lot of sympathy for banks.

"Let's just finish the job and hit the road," I said.

"Is it still here? Her cache, I mean."

I wasn't sure. We were in the wrong room. All the same, I tried to look inscrutable.

"I don't know," I said. "*Is* it?"

I'm not that mean. I gave her pointers as she explored the house, showing her typical places a magician—or anyone else with a secret to hide—might conceal their stashes. I showed her how to hunt for fresh plaster and paint, the telltale signs of drywall carved away and carefully replaced, and how to tap for hollow spaces. She probed the edges of a shag carpet, studied tacks, and ran a ruler along the tops of shelves to feel for unseen latches.

"Always use a long object for that, never your hand," I said as we passed through the kitchen. Empty bottles of Glenlivet sat at the top of an open garbage can, the trash composting in the stifling heat and choking the room with a stench like sour milk.

"I've got gloves on," she said, wriggling her blue-sheathed fingers.

"Not for fingerprints," I said. "Traps."

Now she looked at her fingers. "Is that...common?"

"No, but it only takes one time. I've seen people tie doorknobs to a shotgun propped on a chair or put a dummy pile of drugs on a pressure switch wired to a block of C4. Never underestimate how far a person will go to keep what they've got, even if what they've got isn't a lot. *Especially* if it isn't a lot. Steal a million dollars, you might get sued. Steal ten dollars and you'll probably get stabbed."

Melanie cracked a smile for the first time all day. "So only steal really expensive things."

"I like your attitude," I told her. "The best kind of score is expensive, small, and heavily insured. You get the loot, the mark gets reimbursed, and the insurance company writes off the loss. Everybody walks away in one piece."

"What's the worst kind of score?" she asked.

I thought about that as we left the kitchen behind, stepping into Carolyn's office. I wasn't surprised to see her computer gone, nothing but a dust-free rectangle where it once sat on her desk. The feds had grabbed that, I figured. I wondered what would happen to all of her work. Unfinished books, chapters half-written.

"The sentimental kind," I decided. "Money is money. Steal something that *means* something though, something personal to the mark, and you can bet they'll come gunning for you."

I watched Melanie as she prowled the small office, scrutinizing the floor, occasionally glancing my way. Her blue-sheathed finger scooped up a long trail of dust along the abandoned desk.

Then she marched to the back wall and rapped her knuckles against it, listening to the hollow response from the far side of the wood-grain panel. I couldn't help laughing as she started feeling for the hidden seams.

"How'd you know?" I asked.

She gave me a wicked grin. "You have a tell."

That was news to me. "Really?"

"Well, it was a couple of things. When we first started searching, you steered me toward the bedroom and bath."

"Okay," I said. True enough.

"Going the other way passes through the kitchen, utility room, and this office. It's a tiny house and this is pretty much the end of the tour."

"Still following."

"We're going to be late for the party, and it's a two-hour drive back to Chicago, probably longer since now we're going to hit rush-hour traffic. Which you hate, so you want to hurry me up. I also knew that you know exactly where Carolyn's hiding place is. If we passed through the room it was in, and you found it empty...well, first of all, considering the state of the house, whoever found it first would have left an obvious trace. A big hole in the wall, an open safe, something like that. They wouldn't trash the whole house and then tidy up the one thing they were searching for."

Sharp instincts. I nodded my approval. "Good. And?"

"And if I missed it, you'd give me some sort of hint. Otherwise we could be here all night. You didn't. Leading me to suspect we just hadn't been in the right room yet."

She put her cheek to the wall, both hands feeling along the grain, fingernails digging into faded grooves.

"This is a game," she said. "I wasn't playing against the house. I was playing against you. Since this is the last room, I took my time. Pretended to be searching when I was really studying your expressions."

Her fingertips curled in an almost invisible seam. The thin panel of wood let out a hollow pop as she pried it loose.

"And you kept glancing at this stretch of the wall. Micro-glances. Quick, but I caught it."

I gave her a heartfelt golf clap. Then I helped her heft the panel out of the way, exposing Carolyn's inner sanctum. We leaned the panel against the neighboring wall.

"You impress me more every day," I told her.

A faint blush colored her cheeks. "You're just saying that."

I really wasn't.

One tug of a dangling string clicked a bare overhead bulb to life, shining down stark white across Carolyn's wall of paranoia. Well, in hindsight, it's not paranoia if it's all true. Colored pushpins decorated a sprawling map, and newspaper clippings and notes were bound in a spiderweb of bright string. Threads zigzagged across the nation, leaping from article to seemingly unrelated article. Day-Glo highlighter slashed across key phrases framed margin notes scribbled in a cramped hand.

"Whoa," Melanie said.

"Whoa indeed. I think she had half this much last time I was here."

Some of the clippings were old, familiar because I'd been involved in the first story years before I knew there was a first story to be involved in. A yellowed column about the Enclave Casino brought back a surge of memories, some good, some painful, sort of like this entire day so far.

"What was she trying to do?"

"Learn," I said. "Carolyn was a pack rat when it came to knowledge about the first story. She hoarded anything that might be connected to it, anything that might give us some insight on how to stop the ball rolling once it started."

A strip of paper attached to the map listed names of the characters in a rainbow of colors—the Enemy, the Paladin, the Witch and her Knight, and others—with "in play" scribbled next to three-quarters of them and "confirmed dead" beside a couple others. Pushpins tracked their last known locations. Melanie pointed to the map.

"The Enemy doesn't have a pin."

"She couldn't find him," I said. "Closest we've gotten was tracking him to a ranch down in Texas, but he was only there to finish a ritual: the sacrifice of a year king. See, when he knew he was going to get locked up and he couldn't stop it from going down, the Enemy put ninety percent of his power into a reliquary and gave it to his right-hand woman for safekeeping. To get it back, he's got to pop the locks, and each piece is sealed behind some kind of grand ritual gesture. Something only he can accomplish. So he thinks, anyway."

"So who locked him up in the first place?" Melanie tilted her head. "Better question: how?"

"If I knew, I'd be trying to learn that trick for myself. All we know is that he was sealed away for a long time. No Enemy, no repeating cycle, no mass planetary extinctions. All good. Then some dumbasses from a pharmaceutical company started cooking up fertility drugs with plant clippings taken from the Garden of Eden. One of the aforementioned dumbasses, wanting an insurance policy, went looking for a parallel Earth. What he found was the Pessundation, the Enemy's prison world. He opened a doorway and accidentally set him loose."

"Overkill," Melanie said.

"Sort of like hunting a rat with a rocket launcher. He had no idea what he was doing. And now we've got to clean up his well-intentioned mess, which is how these things usually tend to go. Consider it an object lesson."

I took a step back. Then another, until my shoulders bumped the wall of the nook. I tried to take it all in at once. The spiderweb of rainbow thread, twisting from scrap to scrap, tying twenty years of newspaper clippings and maps into a unified whole. An outsider would see a conspiracy theory; I saw the life's work of a woman trying to make sense of the role she'd been written for. And a way out.

There was something here. Something I could use. I just couldn't spot it yet.

"Do me a favor," I said. "I think I saw some cardboard boxes in the bedroom. Grab 'em for me? We're taking everything with us."

I needed more eyes on this and bigger brains than mine. Thankfully, I knew just where to find a few. While Melanie went hunting for boxes, I texted the license plate numbers of those two SUVs to Pixie. She had access to the LexisNexis database—well, she had access to the password of somebody who had access to the database—and she could run a lookup for me. I kept thinking about the girl in the gray flannel hoodie and the smeared mask of mascara. Shining like a white diamond and leading a pack of cambion with barbed-wire souls.

How did you know Carolyn? I wondered. *And what exactly were you hoping to find here?*

5.

The last time I went to the Bast Club, things didn't go so well. In my defense, I was trying to do a good deed at the time. You'd think by now I'd have learned my lesson about those.

We rolled into downtown Chicago after dark, winding our way through back streets and alleys, down one-way arteries with barely enough room to scrape by between ramshackle fencing and crumbling brick walls wearing jackets of old graffiti. The way to the club was a thing you felt more than a thing you knew, a map drawn by instinct. A single streetlamp cast a puddle of sodium light across the parking lot pavement. There were no signs, no windows, just a single door covered in battered sheet metal. If you didn't know where you were, you didn't belong here.

I hammered my knuckles on the door. Melanie stood next to me, fidgeting.

"You nervous?" I asked her. The metallic echoes faded.

"Little bit," she said.

"Don't be." I stretched, stifling a yawn behind my hand. "You're with me, and I'm a pretty big deal around here."

The door swung open. A gust of warm air scented with sandalwood drifted through the doorway, carrying the faint strains of chamber music. The doorkeeper looked like a Vegas croupier in a prim black vest and pressed burgundy button-down. The way he wrinkled his nose made me wonder if I'd stepped in something.

"Oh," he said. "It's...*the guy*."

"With guest," I replied.

He looked Melanie up and down, getting a little of his decorum back.

"Good evening, madam. Is this your first visit to the Bast Club?"

"First time," she said, ducking her head.

"And you're with him, why?"

"She's my apprentice," I said. I was starting to sense a slight lack of hospitality here.

He tuned me out and gave Melanie a graceful bow.

"Welcome, madam. Please remember our simple rules. Take nothing that does not belong to you and lay no hand on another, save by their invitation." He paused just long enough to shoot me a dagger-pointed glare. "Speak no true names and tell no secrets, save those which are yours to tell."

"I can manage that," Melanie said.

"That's a relief," he replied.

He stepped aside for her. Just for her. He wasn't quite stopping me from coming in, and he wasn't quite barring the path, like he was figuring out how much trouble he wanted to make for me. I had five words to help him decide.

"You aren't getting paid enough," I told him.

He cleared the way.

The club had a familiar feeling, like slipping into a comfortable and worn-in sweater. Motes of stray magic danced at the corners of my eyes, neon crackling along the varnished puzzle-piece floor. Incense hung in the air, echoes of ancient temples, mixing with the aroma of aged whiskey. The corridor opened up onto the main room, swinging tonight, from the chrome-railed bar to the velvet-curtained conversation nooks. Piped-in violins muffled the din of low conversation. I was catching looks, here and there, and getting stared at by a couple of yellow-eyed strangers at the pool table, but if anyone had a problem with how my last visit ended, they weren't inclined to say it to my face.

I didn't see the intruders from Carolyn's place in the crowd. Didn't expect to, but considering the Bast Club was the Midwest's premier hot spot for the occult underground, I figured it was worth a look. I did see Corman, the big man waving to me from a corridor off by the coat check.

"Hey, kiddo," he said, pulling Melanie into a one-armed bear hug. "How'd she do?"

"Better than I did my first time out. I've got a couple boxes stuffed with Carolyn's notes in the trunk. Think you and Bentley could take a look once we get back to Vegas? I could use some fresh eyes on this."

"Of course. C'mon, we rented one of the party rooms."

He steered Melanie around and led us up the hallway. I saw what he was doing; Melanie had looked like a deer in a truck's headlights since we walked in the door, which didn't surprise me. The Bast Club was a little over the top. Corman's beefy arm stayed in place around her shoulder, protective and reassuring, until she found her footing again.

That'd be a little easier to do in the relative sanity of the Juilliard Room. With the exception of a cocktail waitress on the roam, dressed like a refugee from a Victorian cosplay convention, most of the people here were family. Caitlin, Freddie, Halima, and Mama Margaux were holding court in one corner of the green-velvet-draped room; Halima had her usual club soda, the rest sipping some kind of frosted purple concoction. Tiny knots of conversation mingled and milled under dangling lights, their orbs shrouded beneath elaborate curtains of antique stained glass. The ones who weren't part of my crew were all locals, regulars at the bar who drank with Carolyn, people I knew only by their face or their reputation. I exchanged a few casual nods on my way across the room.

Jennifer and Bentley were a party of two, Jennifer keeping one watchful eye on the room as she studied an open folder in Bentley's arms. She was still wearing her dress from the funeral, under a black cargo jacket that didn't bother hiding the bulge of a shoulder holster.

"Oh, he ain't gonna like that," she was saying, her Kentucky twang pitched low.

"Who's he, and what's he not going to like?" I asked, pulling Bentley close. He was so thin these days, a frail bird. I held on to him just long enough to make sure he was okay. Then Jennifer clasped my hand and hauled me in close, thumping my back while she gave me a peck on the cheek.

"He's you, sugar, and...oh, I'll just let Bentley tell it. I wanna see the look on your face."

Bentley cleared his throat and clutched his folder to his chest. "We've, ah, been doing some research."

"Normally that's a prelude to good news," I said.

"And it might be. Possibly. I think we're in agreement that we have two priorities right now: removing the mantle of the Thief, before it takes over your life, and finding a way to deal with the Enemy."

Every character in the first story lived their lives on repeat. The same broken road and the same unhappy ending. After I got saddled with the Thief's role—swapping it with the real guy, a cat burglar named Marcel Deschamps—I finally found out how that particular chapter ends. The Thief comes home from a successful heist and his lover murders him for the loot. At first I laughed off the danger; Caitlin's the best thing that ever happened to me. But the story is baked into the fabric of the universe. If you don't fulfill your role, eventually it starts rearranging the world to *make* you play along.

That hadn't happened to me, though. Yet.

"Enemy's the priority," I said. "For all we know, whatever he did to stick me with the Thief's role was purely symbolic and I'm immune to the story's power. We're all agreed that Caitlin's not trying to kill me, right?"

Bentley tugged the knot of his slender black tie. He usually didn't hedge like this.

"Yes, well, agreed. And since we know the story always ends in a confrontation between the Enemy and the Paladin, finding the

Paladin and ensuring their success may be our best hope. I've been going over my correspondence with Carolyn before she passed. She was quite certain, based on her own research, that the Paladin always reincarnates as a woman."

"Okay." I glanced over my shoulder, hunting for the waitress. Maybe it was the influence of the dearly departed, but I was too sober for this party. "So that rules out half of the human race. Still leaves us with a few billion possibilities, but it's a good start."

"Then I checked my notes about your...vision when you were behind bars."

The Prophet, a guy named Buddy with a slightly sunbaked brain, had put me in a trance with the aid of some magically spiked prison wine. He kicked my consciousness into the world next door, where I got a front-row look at what happens to a parallel Earth when the Enemy wins. It wasn't pretty. Another one of the Prophet's incarnations had been there to greet me, and she told me everything that went wrong that time around.

"*He barely had to lift a finger to win,*" she said. "*Tragedy never visited the Paladin's doorstep, and she ended up a backwoods sheriff's deputy; that one needs pain to drive her ambition.*"

"I'm building a profile," Bentley explained. "A woman, with a defining tragedy in her early life, civic-minded and possibly inclined toward a career in law enforcement."

That made sense to me. "Plus some kind of occult underground connection, right? Otherwise she'd never figure out what she is."

Jennifer's lips were quivering. I knew that look; she was fighting with everything she had to keep a smirk off her face.

"Bentley," I said. "What's in the folder?"

He handed it over. Inside, pages torn from a yellow legal pad were flooded with Bentley's careful cursive, his notes and observations. On top rested a single newspaper clipping from over twenty-five years ago; the headline blared *Local Sheriff Murdered by Home Invader*. I kept reading.

TALBOT COVE, Mich. — The community of Talbot Cove was stunned by a combination murder and child abduction late Tuesday night. Sheriff Harry Black was home with his wife Elise and his daughters, Angie and Harmony, when...

"Oh, are you *fucking* kidding me—" I was cut off by the electronic *snap* of a cell-phone camera, as Jennifer captured my expression for posterity.

"And that's going on Instagram," she said, tapping her screen.

I took a breath and tried again. "Are you telling me Harmony Black is the Paladin?"

"No," Bentley said. "I'm saying she's a Paladin candidate. The criteria are fairly strict, but I can't imagine she's the only woman on earth who fits the bill. I'm hunting for others. What we really need is some kind of test to identify a first-story character. As it stands, the only way we know for certain is, well, once they've met their demise. Which is a bit late."

I spotted the waitress and flagged her down.

"Could I get some alcohol, please?" I asked her.

"What kind?"

"The kind that will get me drunk," I said. "Quickly and efficiently."

She came through, bringing me two fingers of amber in a tulip-shaped Glencairn whiskey glass. It smelled like rich firewood, burned down my throat like gasoline, and left an afterglow that eased the tension I'd been carrying on my shoulders. The room was gathering together now, talking, giving eulogies for Carolyn, and I ordered a second glass.

I was a little loose by the time it was my turn to say something, but I guess I needed to be. Every eye was on me.

"There's always a disconnect at these things," I said, "between what you're supposed to say and what you really think. Ultimately, we're supposed to lie."

My words sank down into a cushion of curious murmurs while I sipped my drink.

"And that's okay. We're here to celebrate someone we cared for, someone we lost. And it hurts. And it sucks. So if I got up here and talked about how Carolyn was a kind and loving soul who fostered homeless puppies, it might make us feel a little better. But here's the thing: if she valued anything, she valued honesty."

The crowd parted, glasses clinking, to make way for a rolling cart. Caitlin and Margaux were bringing in a long cake, fluffy and white, the ornate frosting ringed with black candles. I wasn't sure whose tradition the idea of funeral cake belonged to, but my stomach was growling and I could get behind the idea.

"Carolyn was kind of an asshole," I said. "She was abrasive, rude, and a certified drunk. She'd steal your life and put it between the covers of a book and she never asked permission. Not for that, not for anything else either."

Off to the side, Bentley was setting out paper plates and silverware. Margaux passed Caitlin a long-handled knife for cutting the cake. People were looking my way, nodding a little, hearing me. My throat went tight. It took me a second to force the next words out.

"And she was my friend. She was a good person where it counted. She tweaked noses that needed tweaking—including mine when I deserved it, though I never would have told her so—and she never backed down from a fight. And in her final hour, she died the same way she lived: on her own terms and like a goddamn boss."

I raised my glass.

"Thanks, Carolyn. I'm going to miss you."

Glasses went up all around me, catching the light, glistening off the sudden dampness in my eyes. Someone patted my shoulder.

Then Canton's wand, nestled in its spring-loaded sheath against my forearm, kicked.

The tiny nudge sent a shock of adrenaline coursing through my veins. Canton's wand only woke up in the presence of a lethal threat. I looked left, right, saw Caitlin bringing down the knife to make the first cut of the cake—

I wasn't sure, after, what happened in what order: everything fell together in a heart-lurching jumble. The wand jolted a second time. My knees went out from under me. I tumbled to the parquet floor, dropping my whiskey glass, watching it shatter in slow motion as the blade of Caitlin's knife broke loose from the wooden handle. Momentum flung the sharpened steel straight for me, slicing the air, parting my hair as it whistled just above my head and plowed into the curtain-draped wall.

The blade hung there, quivering, buried in the green velvet. If I hadn't dropped, it would have punched a hole in my sternum.

The room fell silent. Caitlin stared down at the broken handle.

"Oh," she said.

Oh.

6.

We didn't have to look far to get help. The room already played host to the best and brightest of Las Vegas and Chicago's magical communities; everybody had an area of expertise and everybody had an opinion. The blade and the broken handle were laid out on a table, studied, photographed, ringed with a circle of salt and smudged with an incense that smelled like musty gym socks.

They hunted for traces of a curse, of mechanical sabotage, of anything that could explain my near-death experience. Caitlin mostly just clung to me, one hand on my arm, the other rubbing my back in slow circles like I was the one who needed reassuring. I pretended to be shakier than I was, so she could distract herself by taking care of me.

Not that I wasn't plenty shaken up.

"We've ruled out a curse on the knife itself," Bentley was telling me, "but we'll need to examine both you and Caitlin."

"Bentley." I shook my head. "We know what this is."

"We have to consider all possibilities."

"We know," I repeated, "what this is. I thought, I mean, I hoped I was immune. I'm not."

Melanie hovered nearby, keeping her distance like I might be contagious.

"The Thief's story," she said, putting it together. "You just came home from a heist. I mean, it wasn't much of a heist but—"

"But it counts, for the purposes of the story," Caitlin said. Her lips pursed. "And I almost...Daniel, I'm so sorry. It was an accident—"

I pulled her close, holding her shoulders, murmuring in her ear.

"Hey. Hey. I know. It's okay." I nuzzled her neck, then looked over her shoulder to Bentley. "Could you find the waitress for me? I was going to cut myself off, but I could really use another drink right now."

Melanie squinted at us, uncertain. "So...you lived, right? You survived. So it's over."

"Doesn't work like that. When the first story decides it's time for your exit, you can dodge the bullet but you can't outrun it. It'll try again. And again." I gently pulled free from Caitlin's arms, still keeping her close, so I could talk to both of them. "The story just manipulated the world to try and kill me. The question is, how long do we have before it can take a second shot?"

"I should go," Caitlin said. She turned toward the door.

I took hold of her wrist. She looked back and our eyes locked.

"Stay," I said. "Please."

"Daniel, *I'm* the vector for this bloody thing. The lover who kills the Thief. If we're not in the same room together, it's a bit harder for me to accidentally murder you."

"If the story wants to try hard enough, it'll find a way. Besides, I wasn't exactly a virgin when we met. I have plenty of former lovers who have reasons to want me dead. Valid, defensible reasons that even I couldn't argue with. If one of them is on her way over with a shotgun as we speak, I'll feel safer with you at my side. And, you know. If anyone's going to do it..."

Caitlin's lips parted. Her fingers rose, and she touched her heart.

"Daniel. Are you saying...you want me to be the one who murders you?"

"I'm saying I want to remain unmurdered. But if I had to pick? You're my one and only choice."

Melanie looked from me to Caitlin and back again, head cocked like a confused puppy.

"I don't know if this is romantic or disturbing," she said.

The waitress didn't come back. A trio of bouncers did, arms

flexing under tight dress shirts, looming over me and standing in a perfect triangle like they were about to bust out a dance routine.

"You're banned, Faust," the guy up front said with a thumb jerk over his shoulder. "Out."

I had expected this. That said, I didn't have time for it. Not ever, and especially not at the moment.

"No, I'm not," I said, barely looking at him.

"Orders from Management. Al-Farsi says you're no longer welcome in his establishment after that shit you pulled last time. You're banned."

"No," I said, stroking Caitlin's hand. "I'm not."

The bouncers shared an uncertain glance.

"But you are," one said.

"But I'm not." I waved my other hand, taking in the room. "See? I'm right here, waiting for my drink. Clearly not banned."

The leader tried again. "Management says you have to leave."

"Ah, see, there's the mistake. He says many things, but you have to read between the lines to understand what he really wants."

He had my full attention now. I gave Caitlin's hand a squeeze, gently let go, and turned to face him. Inching into his personal space, I lowered my voice.

"See, al-Farsi has a credibility problem. This is supposed to be a safe haven for the underground, but when a demonic bounty hunter rolled in here and demanded he hand over two of his paying customers, he bent over backwards to cooperate. Well, tried to. That's a bad look. Now, I'm both a representative of Vegas's New Commission and a knight in Prince Sitri's court, so it's safe to say my opinion—especially since I was there—holds some water. I've got people calling me, asking, 'Hey, is the Bast Club still safe? Is it even cool anymore? Is it...'" I snapped my fingers. "Melanie, what's the thing the kids are saying online these days?"

"Canceled?" she said.

"Canceled," I echoed. "That was it. 'Is the Bast Club *canceled?*' And I'm just not sure what to tell them. So here's what you're going to do. You're going to go up to al-Farsi's office, and you're going to convey my thanks."

"I...I am?" the bouncer said.

"You are." I leaned in close and murmured the rest in his ear. "You're going to thank him for remembering that I go wherever I goddamn please and that I don't answer to him. He answers to me. You're also going to thank him for picking up my party's bar tab tonight. It was a generous gesture and it means a great deal to me. In fact, since he was so kind, I can consider bygones to be bygones and leave it at that. And if he doesn't agree...I'll be happy to come up and speak to him personally about it."

The bouncers left. Three minutes later, the waitress showed up with my drink.

* * *

The crowd cleared out. Carolyn's local friends—except for Freddie and Halima, who hung back—drifted to the front lounge or out into the Chicago dark. My crew stayed behind. We gathered around a long table in the party room, Caitlin close at my side, and hashed out our strategy over another round of drinks.

"Change in priorities," I said. "This...curse, this cosmic wrinkle, whatever you want to call the first story, it's officially gunning for me. From what we know, once it starts, it doesn't stop. Ever. Not until the story's been told the way it wants to be told."

Mama Margaux raised her hand, her brow furrowed. I gave her a nod.

"So there's no spirits behind this thing, nothin' we can bind or bargain with?"

Bentley shook his head. "Entirely baked into the structure of the universe. The first story isn't a sentient force. It just...*is*."

"Could try to outrun the sucker," Jennifer suggested. "Look, one way or another, it all ends when the Enemy and the Paladin square off, right? So let's bust our butts and arrange their dance ticket, pronto."

Corman snorted. "Sounds like nine times out of ten, the fight ends with the Enemy going scorched-earth on the whole planet. That's not something we want to rush."

Freddie raised her cocktail glass. Something frosted and peppery, as red as her fire-engine hair. She coughed, cheeks flushed.

"Darlings, if I may? I have a very nice lair right here in town—"

"*Lair?*" Melanie whispered.

"It's secure. Extremely secure. Built for holding people who don't want to be held. Let's just lock Daniel inside for the duration and keep him safe while the rest of us take care of the threat. Simple. Done."

Halima gave her friend a sidelong glance. "I don't think he would enjoy that much."

"It's not about enjoyment, my sunshine; it's about keeping our BFF Daniel alive. I'm perfectly willing to chain him to a wall and seal him inside a windowless cell to make that happen, even if I have to keep him there for years and years."

"Thanks," I said.

"I'm a giver," Freddie replied, tossing back the last of her cocktail.

Caitlin held up a finger. "Point of order? Nobody chains Daniel to a wall but me. And while I'm grateful for the offer of assistance, everything we've seen suggests the first story is...implacable. Relentless. I'm not sure anywhere is safe, no matter how secure it is."

I had an idea. Not a sure-fire plan, but it was the best angle of attack I could muster.

"Marcel Deschamps," I said.

"The original Thief," Bentley said.

"The *real* Thief. Look, we don't know how the Enemy stuck his title on my head, but we know this much: the characters of the first story aren't like us. They don't have mortal souls. When they die, the story wipes their memory and rewrites them onto some other parallel world so they can start all over again. We had a theory a while back. Just a theory, but I think it's time we gave it a shot."

Corman remembered. "That when Deschamps croaks, he'll be reborn elsewhere, and he'll take the title with him. No more Thief. Not on this world, anyway. Could work. Maybe. But what if taking him out means you're stuck with the job forever?"

"And that's why I haven't tried. I put the whole problem on the back burner because there are too many unknowns, too much risk, and we had other fish to fry. As things stand, though? I can either wait around to die, or I can get proactive and roll the dice. I'll take that bet, if you're all with me."

They were with me. One look around the table, seeing the light in my family's eyes, and I felt ready to take on the world.

"Whatever you need," Jennifer said, "you got it. So what's the game plan?"

"We know that Deschamps has been on the Enemy's payroll for at least two years. That's when the Canton artifacts started going missing. There was a string of high-profile cat burglaries fitting his MO, targeting auction houses, private museums, historical archives from Rome to Dubai. Interpol's been chasing him for ages, but the man's a ghost. Arguably, befitting the role he was written for, he's one of the best thieves in the world. He's been silent for the last few months, maybe setting up the groundwork for another big heist."

I laid my hands flat on the table.

"We're going to do what no one else can," I said. "We're going to hunt down Marcel Deschamps. And then we're going to kill him."

7.

I didn't go home to Las Vegas. I flew east, to Boston, on a four-and-a-half-hour flight with a plane change in Cincinnati. I touched down at Logan International under a slate-gray sky, heavy with rain.

I wanted Caitlin to come. She stood her ground. We didn't know exactly what rules the first story operated under, but until a little more time had passed since my last "successful heist," she insisted I was safer without her. I didn't believe that. Melanie, on the other hand, volunteered for the job. I told her it was a school night. One of the rules, when I'd agreed to take her on as my apprentice, was that her grades came first.

That was an excuse. I knew what kind of dirty shoulders I'd be rubbing against back here. Lockpicking, breaking and entering, those were survival skills any halfway decent magician should know, and I was fine teaching her the basics. But you could skirt the edge of the gangster life without diving in headfirst, and the way I saw it, part of my job was keeping her out of those shark-infested waters. In Boston, I'd be going all in.

And I'd be doing it alone. I had Canton's wand up my sleeve, a new deck of cards in my pocket, and a freshly dry-cleaned suit. There was nothing to do on the flight and no one to talk to, so I read one of Carolyn's pulp novels on my phone. I couldn't call it reading, really, just brushing up against the words and hearing her voice, like a chat with an old friend.

Meanwhile, Pixie had gotten back to me about the break-in crew. The two SUVs were rentals, picked up—and dropped off later that day—at O'Hare Airport. Not locals, then, and they'd driven down from Chicago on the morning of the funeral just like the rest of us. She was working on getting the details of the credit card they'd paid with, but that would take her more time and require a bit of creative social engineering. I wired her some cash and told her to keep digging.

Then there I was, standing alone on a soot-blackened stretch of wet pavement outside the airport, breathing diesel exhaust and watching a line of cabs inch along. Their brake lights glistened like open wounds. A plane rumbled overhead, cutting through stormy clouds on its way to anywhere but here. Boston was a stranger to me.

When you're in the life, you learn to see cities as layers of systems. First there's the top layer, where civilians live. Street grids, public transportation, arteries made of train tracks and asphalt. The places you can go are clearly marked, with signs and conductors to show you the way.

Look deeper.

Look deeper and you start to wonder about the unmarked doors at the subway station or the narrow, dark alleys you normally walk by without a second glance. You start watching the maintenance workers, the janitors, the people with jangling rings of keys on their cracked leather belts. These are the invisible people who keep society running, and if you go where they go, and if you're clever about it, you can learn their secrets.

Forget about pentacles and Latin invocations: this is the beginning of real magic. Magic is when you discover how to navigate, how to get from point A to point C and never touch ground in between. Or never come up from the underground. Magic is knowing which doors are unlocked, which can be jimmied, which ones are unguarded, and which security cameras are never watched. It's knowing the forgotten infrastructure of a city, the tunnels and utility stairs and systems abandoned by law-abiding citizens long ago but still there, still accessible to people who are willing to break the rules.

Look deeper.

Look deeper and you learn to read the street like a page of ancient scripture. Graffiti becomes guideposts, marking boundaries you won't see on any official map. You grow a gunslinger's antennae and a nose that can catch the black-powder smell of violence five minutes before the blood starts to spill. A new layer of systems unveils itself: doors you can only find if you're not looking for them, streets you can only navigate by following a crow or marking a sigil on the sidewalk with a stick of blue chalk.

I've been to a gourmet restaurant in Los Angeles where the rich and famous dine on human flesh. I've been to a speakeasy in Manhattan where they mix drinks by mood, and the labels on the bottles don't resemble anything from this world's liquor stores. These are the doorways you can darken if you know the territory.

Out west, I knew the territory. In Boston I had a beginner's eyes, green as some teenage runaway fresh off a Greyhound bus. I also had a business card that might open a few doors if I used it just right, and a single lead to chase. Marcel Deschamps wasn't in Boston.

But he had been here.

* * *

"We've found nine thefts related to Howard Canton's belongings and memorabilia," Bentley had told me. I met up with my adoptive dads on the Chicago lakeshore, in an Irish pub called the Galway Arms, taking up a wooden four-seater in the back. He spread out a paper map, city names called out in emergency-orange highlighter.

I was on my way out of town one way or another, destination still unknown, and I wasn't sure when I'd eat again. I decided to fuel up with a half slab of baby back ribs, served over a bed of french fries with homemade coleslaw on the side. My drink was a dark pint of Guinness, the stout so thick it went down like a bitter milkshake.

"Seven," Corman said, musing over his own pint, "are Marcel's jobs. The last two are after he went quiet."

I had been at ground zero for one of those later heists. The same night I went after Canton's top hat, sleazing my way into a private museum of stage magic, the Enemy made his own move. Instead of Marcel, he sent his right-hand monster, Ms. Fleiss, and a hit team of rifle-toting commandos.

"Still doesn't make sense," I muttered into my drink. "Hitting David's museum would have been a milk run for Marcel; he would have been in and out like a ghost. After seven successful jobs, why suddenly switch tactics and call in Fleiss and her brute squad?"

"Any chance the Enemy knew you'd be there?" Corman asked. "Or her? I mean, they both want you dead. That'd be enough reason to bring the firepower."

No. I had considered that angle myself, walking back through the night, wondering if I might have told the wrong person or let something slip, and I'd come up empty. Fleiss had tried to kill me when we locked horns at the museum, but only after she recovered from a moment of surprise. *You,* she told me, *are a deviation from the plan.*

"They weren't expecting trouble. What was the other one?"

"About two weeks later." Bentley unfolded his reading glasses and slipped them on before checking his notes. "In Detroit. An art dealer. A security guard was killed during the break-in, and the gallery was extensively damaged, possibly vandalized."

Definitely not a Marcel job. Marcel was a cat burglar from the old school. No violence, nothing broken, and nothing taken but the exact loot he came for. It was a matter of pride.

"What was the score?" I asked.

"Several pieces of artwork, collectively valued in the high-six-figures range, and a pocket watch once belonging to Howard Canton. The dealer had just bought the watch at an auction a few days prior." Bentley squinted behind his glasses. "The thieves weren't connoisseurs. They stole some cheaper pieces while either abandoning or damaging much more expensive ones. The gallery had a Murakami on display and they walked right past it."

"Fleiss doesn't strike me as an art lover," I said. "Could have stolen whatever was easily portable, to cover the fact that they were only there for the watch. I've used that trick myself. Okay, so out of the thefts we know Marcel committed, exactly what was taken?"

"From the top: a set of Chinese linking rings, three copper-plated cups for the cup and ball trick, a scotch-and-soda gimmick..."

"Keep going," I said.

Corman eyed me over his glass. "What are you hunting for, kiddo?"

Seven heists meant seven starting points to choose from, all at the bottom of a cold trail. That didn't mean they were all created equal or that the most recent snatch would be the warmest on the list. I sifted through the facts. Marcel was a globetrotter. He traveled for his jobs, crossing oceans for a single score. That told me the Enemy was paying him what he was worth. It also told me he knew the territory from here to Saudi Arabia.

It doesn't matter how good of a thief you are, though, when it comes to world travel. Checkpoints, border crossings, airport security lines—there were a dozen ways to get busted *after* you took the score and slipped into the night. That was where a heister needed a little extra help.

That was where I'd nail him.

"On that list," I said, "what's the biggest item? Physically the biggest."

Bentley ran his fingertip down the notepad, then tapped the next-to-last line.

"A substitution trunk, used for performing his version of Houdini's Metamorphosis routine. Police report says it was made of lacquered three-quarter-inch birch wood, with iron fittings."

There were a dozen ways to build a sub trunk, depending on what kind of illusions you had in mind, but they all had two things in common: they were big, big enough to hold a body or two, and they were heavy as hell. Hard score, for a burglar working alone. Even harder to deliver.

"That's the one. Where'd he steal it?"

"Boston," Bentley said.

* * *

I went looking for a map of the city, down in the bottom of a glass. The beer was domestic, served from a cracked plastic pitcher that hadn't been washed in a week. The rim of my glass tasted like Windex. I couldn't complain; I was drinking for business, not pleasure. I lost my tie on the way to East Boston, popped a button on my collar, and rumpled up my jacket before carelessly slipping it back on again. My shoes and the hem of my slacks went on a date with a mud puddle.

I hadn't had a chance to shave that morning, and I was glad. The stubble on my cheeks helped sell the story. It was a story about the kind of guy who went from flush to busted and back again on the regular, the kind who went to dive bars—real dives, not the cultivated hipster kind—day-drinking in a wrinkled Versace dress shirt.

From there it was all fishing, all afternoon, as I drank and listened and hunted for my way in. I cast my line in a saloon gone to seed, where the once-shining brass lay buried under grubby fingerprints and the bar collected dead flies. No bites, so I tried my luck at a Latino dive near Shay's Beach. The joint was frozen in time, tinsel and cardboard shamrocks from the last St. Patrick's Day still dangling like dream catchers over the bar and a two-foot Santa gathering dust in the corner near an empty tip jar. A Spanish station played on a tinny radio, the music swallowed by the steady roar of planes taking off from Logan, close enough to make the floor tremble.

Come sunset I was sitting down to a meal of soft pretzels at a bar and grill in Eagle Hill, washing down boulder-sized chunks of salt with another flat beer. The fading light beyond the front window was a tidal wave of dirty molten gold, glinting off the battered hood of a parked car and stabbing icepicks into my eyes. I turned away.

This was an older crowd. Rough hands, noses shot with blown-out veins, stooped shoulders loaded down with invisible burdens. They drank the cheapest stuff on tap and waited for the inevitable. Not the guy two seats down from me, though. He was in his eighties, could have been a retired teamster or a fisherman, but his faded cuffs were clean and the silver signet ring on his pinkie finger didn't come from a garage sale. The regulars drank beer or bottom-shelf booze, neat. He had a cocktail with a chunk of withered lime balanced on the glass's edge by the prong of a red plastic sword.

"Whatcha drinking?" I asked with a nod at his glass. "Looks good."

He looked away from the TV and gave me a cigar-yellowed smile.

"Cuba Libre, my friend. You can never go wrong with the classics."

I gave the bartender the high sign.

"One for me too," I said. "Put 'em both on my tab."

The old man chuckled like he knew a secret. When the bartender brought my drink over, he raised his glass.

"Cheers."

I mirrored him. The bartender had skimped on the rum, the cola was off, and he'd used too much lime juice, but it was still the best drink I'd had all day. The old man was right: you really can't beat the classics.

"Used to drink these like water, back in Havana," the old man said.

"You don't look Cuban."

He chuckled again. "Nah. When I was a kid, still wet behind my ears, I was in the import-export trade. Cuba was open for business back then. And business was good. Castro rolled up with the army in '59 and kicked everybody out. I didn't even have time to pack a suitcase."

"Doesn't sound like a good memory," I said.

"Everything ends, sooner or later." He studied his glass, rolling it in his hand, the overhead lights shimmering in the amber broth. "But when Havana was hot, it was *hot*, my friend. Bright days and long, sweet nights. So what do they call you?"

"Emerson." I leaned across the empty stool and offered him my hand. His grip was tight, firm.

"Fazio." He had a gleam in his eye, reading my open pages. "You aren't from around here."

"The accent give me away?"

"Not just the accent," he said. "You got the look of a man who doesn't stay in one place for too long."

"Like they taught me in science class, a body in motion tends to stay in motion."

His lips curled. "Wear out your welcome?"

"Looking for fresh opportunity," I said.

"And you came to Boston? Kid, you don't know the territory."

"You said it. Bet you could point me the way, though."

He considered me over his drink.

"Once, I could have drawn you a whole damn map. Nowadays I'm mostly out of the game." He raised his glass. "Enjoying my semi-peaceful semi-retirement here in this opulent splendor. But once upon a time..."

"Yeah?"

"I was an operator," he said, giving me a knowing nod. "Like you."

I had found my way in.

8.

I kept the Cuba Libres flowing. Once Fazio decided he could trust me, and once he passed the line from booze-fuzzy to lit, he opened up like a faucet. I migrated stools, sidling alongside him. I could have listened to his war stories all night.

"—and that's how the Italians ended up running three-quarters of this town," he was telling me. "The Accardos and the Patriarcas split it down the middle."

"How about the Irish?" I asked.

"They got the rest. Then you got your freelance crews, mutts, the occasional out-of-towner, all working for table scraps. Hell, the biggest gunrunner in Mattapan's a goddamn Dominican." He studied his glass like it contained the secrets of the universe. "The times are changing, my friend. So what's your line?"

"Removals, mostly."

"Ah, I see your angle."

"Am I that obvious?" I asked.

"You got a line on something juicy, and you want to make sure you're not stepping on anybody's toes."

"I try to walk with a light step," I said. "A little respect up front saves a lot of pain later on."

Fazio waved his empty glass at the bartender.

"Bill! Another round. And stop using so much lime juice, you prick. You're gonna give me a permanent pucker." He turned back to me, swiveling on the barstool. "I knew I liked you. Respect's a rare commodity these days."

"I was wondering—" I paused, then waved off my own

question. "Forget about it. I don't want to put you on the spot or anything."

His bushy eyebrows scrunched up with amusement. "Hey, ask what you want to ask. I'll answer if I want to answer. No sweat off my balls."

"I got a line. It's a custom request, actually, from a reliable buyer out west. He's into antiques, wants me to boost a vintage writing desk, supposedly dates back to the court of Louis the Fourteenth."

"Fancy," he said. "Hell, in my day, we mostly jacked cigarette trucks. We'd run 'em down to New York and sell 'em with fake tax stamps. You could make good money in cigarettes."

"Sounds a lot easier to move, which is my problem. I cased the target already. I can do the job, that's not an issue. What I can't do is get a three-hundred-pound antique desk from here to Sacramento. Can't exactly check it with my luggage, you know? So do you maybe...know anybody reliable who could help me out for a reasonable fee?"

Fazio gave me a long, hard look in the eye. Deciding. This kind of introduction was always a risk. If he pointed me at somebody and I turned out to be a bum or, worse, a cop, it could blow back on him in all kinds of unpleasant ways.

So he thought about it. And decided I was neither a bum nor a cop.

"Joe Peretsky," he said. "Young blood. Not a lot of respect for the old ways and he's got a real hot head on his shoulders, but if you need something moved and you need it done right, he's the one to talk to. Now, ain't gonna lie, it'll cost you a pretty penny. Worth it, though; he's the best transporter on the East Coast."

In other words, exactly the kind of help Marcel Deschamps would look for.

* * *

The old man had a map in him after all. It pointed me true north, straight to the rolling gates of Peretsky and Sons. Joe had the best cover a transporter could ask for: his own independent trucking company with a pair of angle-roofed storage bays and an open lot, all ringed by a fence topped with coils of barbed wire. Spotlights blazed down, lighting up the asphalt, and a freezer truck was rolling out as I walked up to the deliveries door. I wasn't surprised to see workers in flannel and denim gassing up trucks and hustling cargo pallets along at this hour; a legitimate shipping company was a twenty-four seven operation, and I figured that had to go double for an outfit like this.

I caught the attention of one of the drivers, raising my voice over the throaty growl of a semi's engine. "Looking for Joe. Seen him?"

He pointed me toward the storage sheds. A guy in his twenties, with a beak of a nose and acne scars cratering his cheeks, was giving his men their marching orders. He held his clipboard like a blunt weapon. I raised a friendly hand as I walked up, showing him it was empty. He still didn't look happy to see me.

"Non-employees can't be back here in the yard," he told me. "It's an insurance liability. Go up to the front office, talk to my receptionist."

"Actually, that's sort of why I'm here," I said.

I had decided on a change of tactics and a change of story. I handed him my bogus business card, cooked up special for occasions like this one. His frown dropped another two notches.

"'Paul Emerson, Private Investigator,'" he read. Then he shoved the card back at me. "I don't need a PI for anything."

"I'm not looking to drum up business," I said. "I'm working a case for the Wilcox Insurance Group."

"Never heard of 'em. What's that got to do with me?"

"A few months ago, an antique dealer in Davis Square was hit by a burglar. They only took one thing: an old trunk. Lacquered three-quarter-inch birch wood, iron fittings?"

I phrased it like he knew what I was talking about. The look in his eyes, hard as gunmetal, told me I was right.

"I'm going to ask you one more time," he said. "What's that got to do with me?"

"Wilcox insured that trunk for...well, between you and me? For a hell of a lot more money than it's worth. They've asked me to approach the person who took it and see if he'd be willing to return it for a fair price. No cops, no questions asked, all off the record and everybody wins. But I can't make my offer, or pay the man, until I track him down."

Joe's gaze flicked left, then right. I felt a shadow closing in and tilted my head, just far enough to see one of his guys flanking me with a crowbar dangling in his grip. I figured there was one on my other side, too. Waiting.

"You can leave now," Joe told me.

"I'm not going to waste your time," I said. "Marcel Deschamps hired you to move that trunk out of Boston. I'm not looking to make any trouble for him or for you. More like I'm the Wilcox Insurance Santa Claus, and I've got a sack full of tax-free cash for all the good boys and girls. All you have to do is tell me where you shipped the trunk, and I'll put money in your hand."

Joe moved in, so close I could smell the rancid garlic on his breath.

"I don't *have*," he said, "to do a goddamn thing. You walk onto my lot and accuse me of, what, being some kind of thief? You can either get the hell out of here, or you can leave in an ambulance with a split skull. Your choice."

A heavy hand clamped down on my shoulder from behind. "Time to go," the guy with the crowbar told me.

He wasn't wrong. It was definitely time to go.

They walked me out through the gate and locked up behind me. I kept walking. I jammed my hands in my pockets like a sullen kid and breathed the night air. An insurance-ransom scam was always a risky gamble, and this time it went sideways on me. It worked like a charm on people who were hungry for quick cash or just plain gullible, but Joe was too careful to fall for a line like that. After all, I could have been an undercover cop, a bounty hunter, or a half dozen other flavors of trouble. I would have kicked me out, too.

But I wasn't walking away empty-handed. His words said one thing, but the guilty look on his face said something else: he knew that trunk. He'd seen it, moved it, and he could tell me exactly where it went.

And if he didn't want to cooperate, his shipping records would.

* * *

I found an all-night diner. I watched the clock, and I ordered coffee and eggs. Around two in the morning, I'd had enough coffee. I drank the last bitter dregs of my third cup, straight black, and watched a squad car prowl along a rain-slicked and lonely street.

Time to get back to work.

I closed in on the far side of the fence circling the Peretsky and Sons lot. Quiet now, perimeter lights still on but the engines gone silent. I kept my distance and stayed in the shadows, watching for security guards. This was going to be a touch-and-go kind of job, nowhere near the level of preparation I normally demanded, but time wasn't on my side here.

Joe was running a classic transporter operation, moving contraband nestled in with perfectly legal cargo. I knew what day the trunk had been stolen; all I had to do was get a look at the company's shipping manifests, line up the dates, and I'd have a short list of addresses.

One of those addresses, if my hunch was right, would lead me to the Enemy's doorstep. And Marcel.

The nice thing about trespassing in criminal territory is that they usually don't call the cops when they catch you. The bad thing is, they'll do a lot worse than toss you into a holding cell. I was only here to look and learn, not take. If I pulled this off without a hitch, Joe would never even know I'd been here. I mentally composed my exit strategy just in case. A fast escape from Peretsky and Sons and then a fast escape from Boston, out on the first plane that'd get me closer to home.

Ten minutes passed, crawling along in the drizzle, and I hadn't seen a flicker of movement inside the compound. No footsteps, no telltale flashlight beams. That felt hinky. No reason a place like this would be left unguarded for a second. Under normal circumstances, I'd scrub the job and go home empty-handed. But these weren't normal circumstances, so I circled the fence and looked for a blind spot, out behind the brick wall of the storage depot.

I snapped my fingers and conjured a spark of magic. The deck of cards in my pocket shivered to life, waking up, and the three of spades leaped into my waiting fingertips. I took a few steps back, eyed the fence, and flicked my hand.

The card lanced through the air, a steel-edged hornet, and sliced through the coil of barbed wire. The wire snapped with a guitar-string *twang*. Tension broken, the frayed ends of the wire fell limp along a five-foot stretch of fencing. More than wide enough. I hooked my fingers between the chain links, dug the toe of my shoe in, and climbed. Up and over, dropping down in a low crouch to the asphalt on the other side.

I followed the depot wall, padding along under the shadows of wide and dark windows set high in the old red brick. Too high for me to reach. I hunted for a back door instead.

And I found one, right around the corner. It was wide open.

Someone had used a fresh corpse as a doorstop.

9.

The dead guy holding the back door open, slumped on the ground halfway in and halfway out, wore the uniform gray of a security guard. His eyes were open, catching the glow of an angled light above the steel door, and blood flecked his pale lips. His throat looked like someone had crushed a rotten apple.

I stepped over his corpse and made my way inside.

The depot was a maze of stacked pallets and boxes, crates with destination labels for all fifty states. I couldn't tell what was legitimate cargo and what was disguised contraband. Then again, I was more focused on making sure I didn't get any blood on my shoes. That and hunting for the killer who had arrived ahead of me.

Over to my left, electric light shone through a gap in the wall of boxes. I saw the windows of an office. Joe's office, I figured, exactly where I'd find the shipping records. Before I found a way to get there, I came across another body, sitting slumped and pale with his back to a crate stamped *Fragile*. All his blood was on the outside. I couldn't tell what killed him at first, until I noticed how his tight uniform shirt caved in over the crater someone left in his chest.

Footsteps caught my ear. Soft as mine, rustling like a mouse the next aisle over. I stepped right, turning, moving to cut them off.

I knew the killer. Well, I'd seen her face before. The young woman stopped dead in her tracks, eyes blazing, surrounded with a raccoon mask of dark, smeared makeup. She was wearing the same shabby flannel hoodie from when she'd led the break-in at

Carolyn's house. And she still burned like a white diamond in my second sight. She had a courier's backpack slung over one shoulder and a laptop under one arm. Fingerless gloves sheathed her hands, faded brown leather adorned with spidery designs in copper wire.

A bit of glinting brass caught my eye. A vintage pocket watch dangled from her studded belt, hooked to an antique chain that snaked through denim loops and disappeared into her jeans pocket.

"I've got two questions," I said.

"I'm in a hurry," she replied.

"That laptop. Is that from Joe Peretsky's office?"

By way of response, she slipped it into her backpack, tugged the zipper shut, and shouldered the pack again. Freeing her hands up.

"I'm going to need that," I told her.

"That wasn't a question."

"No. But I'm still going to need it. How do you know Carolyn Saunders?"

That rattled her. She with a question. "Who *are* you?"

Normally I answered that question with a quip or a lie. I thought about it and made a rare decision to tell the truth. If she didn't know who I was, she'd be finding out soon enough.

"The name's Daniel Faust. And Carolyn was a friend of mine."

She didn't know my face, but she knew my name. I watched her expressions flicker—surprise, hostility, a touch of fear—like she was deciding which one suited her.

"You," she breathed.

"Oh, you *have* heard of me."

She got her composure back. She relaxed a little, hips swaying where she stood, like a cobra ready to strike. I kept my guard up. She looked like I could lift her in the air with one hand, but I'd seen the damage she'd inflicted on her way in. I still didn't know what had caused the wounds on those bodies.

"You did me a favor once," she said, "and you didn't even know it. That's good news for you. Means I'm not going to kill you. Not tonight, anyway. Turn around, walk away, and you get to live."

"You know, that's usually my line. So you know my name, what's yours?"

She smiled. The tip of her tongue brushed her front teeth.

"Ada," she said. "Ada Lovelace."

"Lord Byron's daughter? The mother of modern computing?" I squinted at her. "You look younger than I expected."

She laughed. "My dad was a science geek. And look at you, knowing history. I thought you were just a cheap, ruthless thug."

"Now you're hurting my feelings. I'm not *cheap*. And I'm a man of many skills."

"Really?" she asked.

I nodded. Then I flexed my wrist, and Howard Canton's wand dropped into my open hand. My fingers caught it, twirling the bone-tipped wand with a flourish.

"I know a few magic tricks," I said.

Her expression changed in a heartbeat. What little color I could see in her pale cheeks drained away. Her eyes went wide, locked onto the wand like a targeting laser.

"Where did you get that?"

"Long story," I said. "It involved a top hat and a mummy."

"That," she said, her throat tight, "is *mine*."

"Considering it was stashed away by its creator about...oh, I'm going to guess fifty years before you were born, I don't think you can back that up."

She squared her footing.

"Change of plans," she said. "I'm going to take that from you. And I may or may not kill you, depending on how hard you make me work for it."

"I don't think you can back that up either."

Her hands began to move in slow circles, serpentine, like a tai chi move. Then they rippled, leaving blurry and dark trails in their wake. The copper wire adorning her fingerless gloves took on a deep red glow, like a branding iron heating in a bed of coals.

I knew how the security guards had died now.

"Nice gloves," I said.

"Thanks. Made 'em myself. Inlaid transmutation glyphs channel curse-energy along the electromagnetic spectrum."

"Sounds complicated."

"I'm a complicated woman," she said.

Then she came at me. She charged down the aisle with inhuman speed, her body a blur of shadow as she drew back her fist for a lethal blow. I was ready for it. A card was already leaping to my fingertips and then blazing like a bullet straight toward her. Card and shadow collided in a burst of blinding sparks. She screeched, her body wavering in and out of sight as she tumbled to the concrete floor. Before I could follow through she was already rolling, scrambling on her hands and knees like a cat, propelling herself toward a break in the wall of boxes.

I didn't chase her. Instead, I slowed my breath, relaxed, and opened my third eye.

There she was. I couldn't see her physical body, but her spirit gleamed white-hot. She was perched just behind the wall, motionless. An ambush waiting to happen.

"You can't hide from me," I called out. "Look, I don't want to hurt you. I just need the data on that laptop. It's a matter of life and death."

Mine, mostly. Her laughter echoed off the bare girders overhead.

"I can't hide, huh?"

I moved sideways, easing on light footsteps through the labyrinth and keeping her glowing beacon in sight. I figured I could work my way around and come up behind her.

Then I heard the ticking of a watch.

It crackled, reverberating off the depot walls, rolling along the gloomy aisles. Steady and strong at first, then slower, slower, and her light faded with it. The watch gave one final, pendulous *tick* and fell silent. She vanished from my second sight.

Now her giggle seemed to come from every direction at once, as impossible to pinpoint as she was.

"Canton's Hibernation," she said.

I knew the Enemy was hot to recover Howard Canton's relics. I had assumed, until now, that I was the only person who had figured out how to *use* any of them. I had just enough time to realize how wrong I was before a blur hit me from the left, Ada leaping into sight and snapping her heel out. An explosion of pain billowed in my gut and I went flying, crashing into a standing crate shoulder-first, hard enough to shatter the wood. I toppled over with it, landing hard, buried in a bed of broken planks and packing straw.

I was dazed, head reeling, and all I could think was *move*. I pulled myself out of the wreckage and tumbled onto the floor. Then I got back on my feet, clutching the wand in a death grip as I turned, hunting for any sign of her—

—and she boiled from the darkness, a living shadow, and thrust both of her palms out. Her gloves connected with my chest like a pair of defibrillator paddles set on high blast. Something tore inside me, wet, as the world erupted in purple sparks, and then my back slammed against the concrete.

I couldn't move. I was seeing double, images overlapping and then sliding out of focus, my head pounding like a five-tequila hangover. She sauntered toward me, her light footfalls booming like cannon-shots.

"This wasn't personal," she told me.

She clenched her fists, gathering hungry oil-slick shadows as they slowly spun, building force for a death blow. My back was locked, wouldn't let me sit up. I tried to shove myself back along the floor, but my knee buckled and spasmed.

Then light shone off to one side, an angel's halo in my blurred vision as bay doors rattled open. There were footsteps, fast, heavy, and Joe Peretsky's voice, loud and strident.

"I don't care who these assholes are, you find 'em, and you take them *out!*"

"Crap," Ada hissed. She twirled like a ballerina and darted out of sight. I couldn't copy that move. I rolled onto my belly, fighting to hold my churning stomach down, and groaned as I shoved myself up on all fours. Standing was a harder trick to master; I grabbed a heavy crate and pulled until I stood on wobbly feet. I didn't know how many guys Joe had brought to the party, but I wasn't in any shape for a fight.

Out. The way I came in. I tried to retrace my footsteps, doubling back, shouting voices rising over the ringing in my ears. I turned one corner and confronted a familiar face, the driver with the crowbar who had escorted me out the first time. Now he had a gun. The fat revolver swung up in his grip and I threw myself down, hitting the floor as two shots rang out and chewed holes in packing crates, raining down splinters. I found the strength to run, and scrambled just ahead of another bullet.

"Here! He's over here!" shouted another voice as I crossed an intersection between pallets. A squat-looking bruiser was pointing his finger with one hand and his gun's muzzle with the other. I sent an ace card flying. His head snapped back as it carved into his skull, burying itself red-diamond deep between his eyes. His body buckled and I was on the move, running the other way, before his knees hit the concrete.

I saw the back exit, Ada's first victim still slumped in the doorway. A shot rang out behind me. The bullet went high into the wall and ricocheted off the crumbling red brick. I loped over the corpse, broke hard left, and angled for the stretch of fence where I'd cut the barbed wire on my way in.

From the far corner of the depot, the beam of a flashlight shone in my face and another gunman shouted. I responded with a pair of cards, not even aiming. I heard him yelp, falling back, the flashlight clattering to the asphalt. That bought me just enough time to grab the fence and haul myself up and over, barely catching my balance before I plummeted hard on the other side. My leg twinged, a muscle yanking taut.

I forced myself to keep moving, keep running, breaking down

alleys and across darkened backyards. I ran until my chest was a burning brand, searing with every labored breath, and the chaos had faded to the soft trill of crickets in the still hours before dawn.

10.

"Is it safe to be near you?" Caitlin asked.

That was a loaded question if I'd ever heard one.

She picked me up at McCarran Airport, idling at the curb in her snow-white Audi Quattro. I fell into the passenger seat, still aching after seven hours in the air and two changeovers, and leaned my head against the buttery leather seat. It was early afternoon in Las Vegas, the desert sun high, hot enough to steal my breath and make the air above the highway shimmer.

"Consider the Thief's story," I said. "He comes home from a successful heist, and his lover murders him."

"Right," she said.

"Well, I just got my ass kicked, so we should be fine."

I gave her the gory details as we headed north on Paradise Road. The slumbering beast of the Vegas Strip loomed in the distance, dirty concrete castles and glass pyramids and money-green palaces all waiting for nightfall when they could come to life. When I finished, Caitlin fell into a gloomy silence. I made a few phone calls.

We were a block away and her hands were tight on the leather-wrapped steering wheel, tight enough that I could see them going white from the strain.

"You're going to break that thing," I told her.

Usually that'd get at least a tiny smile. No reaction.

"What is it?" I asked. "And don't say nothing because we both know it's something and I'm going to pester you until you talk to me."

"This," she said. "This...situation."

"So we're in danger. It's also a Thursday. Know what those two things have in common? They both happen once a week, and we always get through it together."

"That's the *problem*," she seethed, eyes on the road. "Give me an enemy I can battle, a throat I can seize, a heart I can tear out, and all's well with the world. Not only are you under attack by a force of...cosmic malice, a process we can't see or touch or kill, but it's trying to turn *me* into the murder weapon. I can't fight it. And I can't stop it. All I want is to be at your side, helping you, but the longer we're together the more likely I am to hurt you."

That wasn't all of it. I heard the rest, dangling unspoken. I gave her the time she needed to wrestle it out.

"It wasn't that long ago," she said, "that I broke your trust. And you forgave me."

Double or nothing, I thought. That was the bet I made with Naavarasi, after the shape-shifting trickster trapped us both. I gambled my eternal freedom for Caitlin's. It was the best way I could rebuild a bridge that had almost burned down.

While I was hunting for a way out of Naavarasi's trap, I met one of Caitlin's old lovers. He warned me that I was under her sway—that she'd used her demonic powers to make me fall in love with her. I asked Caitlin for the truth. She gave it to me. She also told me that she'd stopped using them a long time ago; my emotions were all mine now. I just had to decide if I could take her back, knowing what she'd done when we first met.

In the end, it was an easy choice.

"And it's killing me," Caitlin said, her voice on the edge of breaking, "that now you can't trust me again. And there's nothing I can do about it."

The Audi coasted to a stop at a red light. She sat rigid, stone-still and eyes forward. I put my hand over hers.

"Hey."

She met my gaze, her eyes glistening.

"Double or nothing," I said.

She leaned against me and rested her head on my shoulder until the light turned green.

*　*　*

The art-deco nightclub, its curved walls shimmering under a fresh coat of ice-white and sapphire-blue paint, stood in the shadow of the Strip. A narrow VIP parking lot looped in and out of the road out front like a squat horseshoe, dark asphalt laid firm but still waiting for painted stripes. A sign read, *The American, where Old Vegas meets New, coming this summer.*

It was starting to look like a real club. I let us in with my keys, hit the lights, and watched the overheads flicker to life with a satisfying hum. The dance floor was finally in place, pristine parquet leading up to the lip of an elevated and scalloped stage, just the right size for a brass band. Chromed tables and stools topped with pearl-colored leather sat shrouded under plastic, waiting to make their debut, and pale blue LEDs shone under the glass shelves of an empty bar.

The American had gone from a late-night drunken fancy to an idea to a plan. I'd grown it like a gardener raising a bonsai tree, trimming and carefully cultivating, overseeing every detail from the first round of financing to the endless real estate hunt to the architectural design. And then a million other details after that, every step of the way.

To be honest, if I'd known how much work was going to be involved, I might have left it at the "drunken fancy" stage. But this was something I'd built, my own piece of the city, and I was proud of it.

Now I just needed to live long enough to see the grand opening.

The cellars were still under heavy construction. There were extra security concerns in play, given what I was planning to use them for. One room, though, just off the wooden shell of a staircase, was almost finished. It was a dedicated conference room, with a long oval table carved from a slab of black Italian marble and ringed with ergonomic leather-backed chairs. The entire wall opposite the door was a sheet of sleek porcelain steel, one giant canvas for dry-erase markers.

Bentley and Corman were right behind us. I'd asked them to bring their files on the Canton heists. All of them and anything Pixie could scrounge up with her hacking skills on short notice. "Pay her whatever she needs," I told them. "I'm good for it. We don't have time to negotiate."

What she could get was a full internal police report, courtesy of the Detroit PD, on the most recent theft. Bentley spread out the photographs, fresh from his printer, across the marble slab. One shot of the murder victim, an art gallery security guard, was the last piece of confirmation I needed. He'd been taken apart by a professional, his gun arm snapped and his rib cage turned into a broken, bloody crater.

"There's a new player in town," I said. "Let's figure out what we know."

I uncapped a dry-erase marker, stood at the porcelain wall, and wrote, *Ada Lovelace.*

"If that's an alias," Bentley said, "she has excellent taste."

I started at the beginning, thinking back to the break-in at Carolyn's place. On the next line I wrote, *Has team of shooters, at least six, all cambion.*

"But she's definitely a pure-blooded human?" Caitlin asked.

"And a magician. Damn strong one."

"If you've already got the occult underground connections," Corman reasoned, "ain't exactly hard to round up some cambion muscle who'll do anything for a buck."

He wasn't wrong. Cambion like Melanie, who actually had a supportive environment and family to lean on, were a rare exception. Most grew up abandoned, abused, left to the mercies of the erratic rages in their tainted blood. Not a formula that made for well-adjusted and law-abiding citizens. I hesitated before writing the next line, but it felt significant. Just one word: *Killer.*

Felt like a value judgment, too, from a man who had no business pointing fingers. It wasn't like I had any hesitation pulling a trigger when I needed to, and I almost never lost sleep over it. I turned to the table, trying to explain.

"She's not a professional," I said.

Corman nodded, gruff, and rapped his knuckles on the crime scene photo. "Didn't have to do that. Dozen ways to take care of a security guard without killing 'em. I oughta know, we taught you how. I would've kicked your ass if you pulled a lazy stunt like that."

"And last night she killed another two guards at Peretsky's depot. Ada's a powerhouse, but *not* using that power doesn't seem to occur to her. Besides, any professional heister knows you never hurt civilians on the scene if you don't absolutely have to. Sure, scare 'em into compliance, smack one around if you have to, but you don't kill them. Basic decency aside, it's stupid to add a murder rap to a burglary charge. That's just common sense."

Bentley sat on the edge of his chair, elbow propped on the marble conference table, chin resting on the heel of his hand as he pondered.

"On the phone," he mused, "you said she tinkered together her own weapon?"

"Channeling gloves, mixed with a little kung fu. The martial arts she could have picked up from any decent dojo. The magic end...I don't know. She's obviously smart, some kind of occult-engineering prodigy. *I* couldn't build something like that. But her style feels rough, unpolished. I think she might be self-trained."

"So someone taught her how to fight," Bentley said, "but they didn't necessarily teach her anything else. Nothing about how to live in our world, nothing about responsibility. She's a toddler with a loaded gun. I think, Daniel, you will find that this incident in Detroit was her very first theft. And she knew how to use the pocket watch?"

I added a fresh line to the porcelain wall. *Canton's Hibernation.*

"It made her invisible on a psychic level," I said. "She just wasn't there, like her body was dead. The effect fits the pattern—all of Canton's magic was defensive, from what we've seen—but the relic doesn't. Until now, all of the Canton relics were used in his stage act. Not sure how a pocket watch ties into that."

Corman leaned back. He tapped his chin.

"The milk-can escape," he said.

A twinkle shone in Bentley's eyes. He reached over and squeezed Corman's arm. "The milk can. Of course."

Caitlin glanced between them. "Not following."

"It was one of Harry Houdini's signature escapes," Corman explained. "He'd be handcuffed and stuffed inside a three-foot-high steel milk can; then his assistant would flood it with water. He'd have to get out before he drowned."

Bentley beamed. I could tell he was happy to be in his old wheelhouse, playing historian. "In the forties, Howard Canton performed the same feat. On at least two occasions, he was in the can for over eight minutes—much longer than anyone could possibly hold their breath. Ironically, the audience didn't care for it. It was so blatantly impossible that the thrill was lost. That's the difference between an escape routine and a magic trick."

"Not impossible," I said, staring at the porcelain wall. "Not if you have the right tool for the job. The pocket watch. Canton's Hibernation doesn't just make a person look like all their vital signs have stopped; they actually *do* stop. Suspended animation."

"Hell of a gimmick," Corman said. "Kiddo, if you go toe to toe with this girl again and you have to take her out? You'd better make damn sure she's really dead."

"I just want to know who she is and where she came from. Which leads me to..."

I added a line: *Did her a favor?*

"She didn't know my face, but she knew my name. Said I did her a favor once and I didn't know it. She was willing to part peacefully, but her tune changed once she got a look at my wand. She's chasing the Canton relics, same as us."

"Same as the Enemy," Caitlin said. "Could she be on his payroll, just like Marcel and Fleiss?"

"Considering where we crossed paths and what she stole? No.

She wanted Joe Peretsky's shipping manifest, same as me, and for the same reason: she's hunting for Marcel. I need him dead to break this curse; she wants him so she can get her hands on the rest of the Canton relics."

"That," Bentley said softly, "could end very badly for her."

No question. Ada's fists could deliver a magically fueled beatdown, but the Enemy could rewrite a person's history with a touch of his ghostly hand. I saw him erase a man's entire adult life once, murdering him with a train that had stopped running twenty years ago. He left ragged holes in the fabric of history and sowed deadly paradoxes wherever he walked.

Some problems could be solved with brute force. The Enemy wasn't one of them.

"Could another player be backing her up?" Corman asked. "We haven't heard a peep out of Elmer Donaghy since you ruined his day down in Boulder City."

"Or Naavarasi," Caitlin said, with a reflexive wrinkle of her nose.

I had thought about that on the flight home. Elmer and Naavarasi had three things in common: they were both self-styled chess masters who loved layering plans inside plans, Caitlin and I had wrecked their schemes and left them bleeding, and it was absolutely, positively, one hundred percent inevitable that they were both coming back for revenge sooner or later.

"I'm ruling out Elmer," I said. "The Network is having problems with a capital P right now. Adam is missing, probably dead, and their communication and supply lines have been cut. I wouldn't be surprised if Elmer's just scrambling around trying to figure out what the hell is going on. Or jockeying for position and taking out his competitors. Either way he's going to be busy for a while."

"And...her?" Caitlin asked.

Naavarasi. The rakshasi "mistress of illusions" had lived up to her name more than once. From the moment she came into my life she'd used me as a pawn in the longest con I'd ever seen. It went beyond playing the sucker, making us all believe she was a show-off who was incapable of doing anything clever without bragging about it; she kept that act up for ages, never breaking character, until the jaws of her trap slammed shut and we found out just how smart and self-controlled she really was.

Years ago she'd sent her son Kirmira—a son she insisted didn't exist—to serve the Chicago Mob. One orchestrated gang war later, she lured him in and snapped his neck to win our trust. When I landed behind bars, she dangled her help in front of me, in exchange for a pair of favors I couldn't refuse. And all of it, years of groundwork and manipulation and blood sacrifice, ended in a plot to enslave Caitlin and destabilize Prince Sitri's entire court.

But I wasn't so sure.

Everybody said I was being paranoid, that I was letting Naavarasi live in my head without paying rent, but I couldn't shake the feeling that capturing Caitlin and me wasn't her endgame. It was just one more piece of the plan. I still thought about the first time we met. Naavarasi had tried to recruit me then, telling me we were both outcasts, outsiders, that we were made for each other. She told me that she had been watching me for years. I asked her why.

I can't tell you that, she replied with a jade-lipped smile. *It would ruin the surprise.*

At least I knew Ada wasn't her in disguise or another one of her children. A rakshasa's power to shape-shift only works until you figure out the trick. Their souls smell like peat and musk, wild jungle and raw, bloody meat. Catch the psychic scent once and you'll never forget it. That was one way, maybe the only way, Naavarasi would never be able to fool me again.

Before I could answer Caitlin—and *too soon to tell* was the best reply I could muster anyway—we had a visitor. Pixie appeared in the conference-room doorway, looking winded, casual in her ripped jeans and a faded WrestleMania T-shirt. She lugged the silver clamshell of a vintage laptop under one arm, adorned with stickers for bands I'd never heard of, and plopped it on the table.

"I kept digging on the Detroit thing," she said. "Found something you should see."

"Did...I give you a key for the front door?"

She shoved her Buddy Holly glasses higher on her nose and fired up the laptop, barely glancing at me.

"No, I borrowed a key from one of your construction guys, cut my own copy, and put it back before they noticed. Hi. I'm a hacker. We do more than computers."

I glanced at Caitlin. "'Borrowed,' she says."

"I gave the original back. So yes. Borrowed."

"Caitlin, tell her that's a sin."

Caitlin waggled her hand from side to side. "Eh. There's leeway in these matters."

"See?" Pixie said. "She gets it. Okay, so, the break-in and murder at the Becker Gallery is still officially unsolved, but the Major Crimes squad had a suspect. Suspects. An organized gang working in the area. But they never brought any of them in for questioning."

"Why not?" I asked.

"Because they're dead," Pixie said. She swiveled her laptop around and showed me the carnage on the screen. "Three days after the Becker Gallery got hit, somebody went on a killing spree."

11.

The first victim had been caught with his pants down. Literally. He was facedown dead on a filthy bathroom floor, trousers around his ankles, abandoned in a puddle of his own piss.

"Meet Kornel Foster," Pixie said. "Thirty-two, suspected money launderer and fence, murdered in the men's room of the A-Bomb. Thrash club on Gilbert Street. He was the first to die that night."

"Wait," I said. "That night?"

"It all happened on one night. Somebody had a hit list and some very good intel. According to Major Crimes, the gang responsible for the gallery job was led by somebody called 'the Madrigal.' No idea how many people were involved, but every single person on the cops' short list of suspects—except the boss—was murdered in the span of about eight hours. Mostly strangled with a garrote, then mutilated postmortem."

"Did you say 'madrigal'?" Bentley asked.

"Weird, right? Usually crime bosses go for scarier aliases. Like 'the shark' or 'the wolf.' Or 'the guy.' That one's *super* intimidating."

I let that slide. I was more bothered by the number of nodding heads, forcing me toward an uncomfortable realization. I was the only person in the room who didn't know what a madrigal was.

"I really hate to ask—" I started to say. Then I caught Bentley's schoolmaster glare. "*But* asking questions is the only way to learn, and learning is a lifelong process. What's a madrigal?"

"A sort of choral composition that originated in the Italian

Renaissance," Bentley explained. "A proper madrigal involves many voices, singing as one. Perfect unison."

Something bugged me about that, but I couldn't put my finger on it. Caitlin was more focused on Pixie's screen. She pointed to a spray of digitized scarlet.

"Can you magnify that a bit?"

"Just a little," Pixie said, zooming in on the wet red ruin of the dead man's neck. "More than that, it'll be too blurry to see anything. That help?"

Caitlin leaned closer.

"Did all the victims have wounds like this?"

"Exactly the same," Pixie said. "Back of the neck torn open, vertebra cracked."

"What do we know about the gallery's owner?"

Pixie swiveled her laptop around. Her fingers rattled on the keyboard, sifting through files.

"Not a lot. Armand Becker, emigrated from Switzerland about a decade ago, has a reputation as a tastemaker. If he features you in his gallery, you're pretty much guaranteed to make a splash."

"And evidently, he has infernal connections." Caitlin glanced my way. "These were Order of Chainmen killings."

Hell's bounty hunters. "How do you know?" I asked.

"The wounds. A human soul stays with the body for a very brief period after death, maybe a minute, give or take. Chainmen use a specialized tool to dig into their victims' necks, extract the soul, and capture it." Her gaze slid up and to the left as she hunted for an analogy. "It's a bit like a melon baller. But for people."

Pixie stared at her. "And on the list of things I did *not* want to learn today..."

"So he called out the big guns to get his stuff back," I said. "Ada has the watch, so either she's the Madrigal, or she was part of the Madrigal's crew and managed to fly under the radar. There could still be an active bounty on her head."

"The Order's records aren't public," Caitlin said. "Discretion is part of the service. That said, I might have a way in."

She rose, drifting to the far edge of the room as she made a phone call. I looked to Bentley and Corman.

"How are we doing on tracing Canton himself?"

"Bupkis," Corman said.

"We know what we *don't* know," Bentley elaborated. "'Howard Canton' was definitely a stage name. Not at all uncommon, especially in his era. For instance, the so-called 'original Chinese conjurer' Chung Ling Soo was actually a man named William Robinson. He dressed in Mandarin clothes, painted his face to appear more Asian, and only spoke in broken pidgin English whenever he was in public. He kept the charade going until his dying day."

"That's only slightly horribly racist," Pixie said.

"There were a *lot* of mysterious 'Chinese' and 'Arabic' magicians running around London in those days," Corman said. "Point is, 'Canton the Magnificent' could have been anybody offstage, and if he left a mark in the occult underground, it was under a different name."

Caitlin finished her call. She came back to the table, eyes like razors. I knew that look. It was the look she got when she knew somebody was lying to her and she was deciding how much she was going to have to hurt them.

"Bad news?" I asked.

"Oh, not at all. I just spoke to Fontaine. He confirmed this was an Order contract. In fact, he confirmed that he did the job."

"Then why..." I trailed off, not sure if she knew her murder face was showing.

"He confirmed it with a string of stammering denials. To hear him tell it, not only does he know nothing, he's never set foot in Detroit. He hemmed and hawed like a child caught with his hand in a cookie jar and chocolate smeared all over his face."

I squinted at her. "I thought you two were friends."

"We are. Allies, at least, and when Fontaine is on a tear it's hard to make him *stop* talking about his exploits. Something was unique about this hunt. Something special, and he's afraid to tell me about it." She curled her hand and studied her manicured nails. "I can't put pressure on him, real pressure, without burning our bridges, and I don't want to do that. So that's the best we're going to get out of him unless he has a change of heart."

These pieces didn't fit. As far as we knew, the infernal courts—current company excluded—were in the dark when it came to the Canton relics. Who would call out the Chainmen to track one down and punish the thieves? All I knew for certain was that Ada and her gang had hit the gallery, and she had skipped town with her life and the pocket watch, just ahead of hell's vengeance. I couldn't be a hundred-percent positive that she was the Madrigal, but considering she was obviously in charge of the crew that raided Carolyn's house, it felt like a safe bet.

Madrigal.

Then it clicked. I pressed my palms to the table. "Many voices singing as one."

"Hmm?" Caitlin said.

"Ada. Her alias. A madrigal is a chorus of many voices, singing as one. A chorus of souls, of lives, all expressed in unison. What does that remind you of?"

A sly smile rose to her lips. "A chorus of identical lifetimes. Ada is a character from the first story. And she knows it."

"Either she's after the Canton relics for the same reason we are, because we know the Enemy wants them—"

"Or better yet, she knows *why* he wants them," Caitlin said. "And she can tell us."

"But which character is she?" Bentley asked.

"She can tell us that, too." I looked to Caitlin. "We're going to Detroit. I can't find Marcel without the shipping records Ada stole, so we need to track her down. Let's start at the scene of her first crime and work the trail from there."

"We, though?" Caitlin shifted in her chair, uneasy. "Is that safe, given present circumstances?"

"I don't see another option. If the Chainmen were involved, that means demonic politics are in play, and Detroit is Prince

Malphas's territory. I'm not exactly on his list of favorite people. Thanks to my knighthood he can't just straight-up kill me, but that doesn't mean he can't make my life difficult."

"His people won't be much happier to talk to me," Caitlin said.

"No, but they're afraid of you, and that always helps. Like Al Capone said, 'You can get much further with a kind word and a demon than you can with a kind word alone.'"

Pixie glanced up from her laptop. "Wait. Did he actually say that?"

"Please? Come with?" I rubbed Caitlin's arm in pleading circles. "Don't make me go to Detroit alone."

"When you put it that way," she said, "it seems like it would be cruel not to accompany you."

"That's the spirit. C'mon. We'll go to Detroit, pick up Ada's trail, track her down, and then...well, I guess we'll have a long discussion about why stealing is wrong." I paused. "And then I'm going to steal that laptop from her and probably Canton's watch, too. I am *really* not good at imparting moral lessons."

12.

Detroit was a city in flux. Moving, reinventing, building up and tearing down. Towering orange cranes marked a border between a dead neighborhood and another coming back to life, like the band of shadow along the dark side of the moon. Crumbling brick, broken windows, and overgrown, abandoned lawns bordered a desolate corridor of road, while up ahead, skyscrapers caught the setting sun on their mirrored faces and turned to towers of gold.

The Becker Gallery stood in a resuscitated stretch of town, where leaning tenements had been gutted and turned into corporate lofts overlooking the river. The gallery's facade, a curling wave of glass and chrome frozen in mid-crash, rubbed shoulders with a jazz club and a Tesla dealership. The air just inside the sliding doors was museum-cold and tinged with a faint herbal scent, like camphor.

We'd discussed our approach on the plane. Given that the Chainmen had avenged the gallery's theft, there had a good chance Armand Becker had connections in low places. And considering this was Malphas's territory, he didn't have any reason to be open and friendly with us. The "cold peace" between the infernal courts guaranteed a bare minimum of civility and not much else. We decided to go in casual and keep our credentials and our real names close to the vest.

It was half an hour before the gallery's closing, last light dying outside the curving, scalloped windows, and only a few other patrons wandered the pristine ivory hall. Some stood clustered around a van-sized canvas, murmuring and making notes. It looked like an explosion in a paint factory to me, but I heard snatches of words like "visionary" and "seven figures."

Art theft is a specialty business. Cash is cash, gemstones can be stripped of their provenance, precious metals can be melted down, still valuable in their anonymity. An artwork's uniqueness makes it hard to move; if you're trying to fence a hot Rembrandt, it's kind of impossible to argue it isn't the identical portrait that just got stolen from the museum down the block. So I never got into that line, too much work, too much risk. Unfortunately, that also left me with a gap in my education, and my understanding of modern art could fill a very short pamphlet.

"Tell me something," I whispered to Caitlin. As we strolled along, the buttery-tan wooden flooring captured pools of light from the track fixtures overhead. "Should I be impressed?"

"Highly," she said, taking in the displays. "Becker has an excellent eye. He knows what's good, and he knows what sells."

I couldn't miss the gaps here and there, empty spots along the walls waiting for fresh art after Ada's crew ransacked the place. The gallery didn't just display paintings; Becker dabbled in sculpture here and there, with stark white pedestals bearing metallic swirls, inscrutable machined designs. Nothing caught my eye until we rounded a corner and stopped cold in our tracks.

A discreet plate, set into the base of a foot-tall rounded dais, read *Sacrament*. The sculpture was nine feet tall at its brutish shoulders, a vaguely humanoid figure crouched on all fours with club-like stumps for limbs. I wasn't sure what the artist had made it out of; it looked like rotten meat covered in lacquer, shot through with veins of gray mold. Its blind, featureless face craned toward the overhead lights on a serpentine neck, frozen in a posture of mute agony and supplication.

"I don't get it," I said.

"It's...trying to pray," Caitlin mused. She slowly circled the dais, studying it from every angle. "With no mouth. This is a challenging piece. I think I like it."

"You have good taste," said the man striding our way. From

the Swiss accent and the pressed gray suit, I figured we'd found Armand Becker. He took Caitlin's hand with a light touch. "*Sacrament* is a debut piece from a promising new artist, Delia Sauveterre. Just got it in last week, and it's already gathering buzz."

"Sounds like a good time to get in on the ground floor," Caitlin said. "I love discovering new artists. I'm Madeline, and this is my partner—"

"Peter," I said, stepping in for a brisk handshake. My Peter Grayson alias had been dead and buried since my last arrest, but old practiced lies are the best kind. They roll right off the tongue.

"Armand Becker," he said. "So pleased to meet you both. Are you looking to acquire anything in particular?"

He wanted to know if we were window shoppers or a potential sale. Fair enough. Caitlin took the lead, just like we rehearsed on the way over.

"We are," she said, then pointed to the looming rotten-meat man. "Not this one, though it would make for a nice conversation piece. Not enough room for it at home. What we'd like to find is a pair of works from established artists, with long-term investment potential..."

While she kept him talking, I cased the gallery. Security was good, not great, especially for a place that had been knocked over less than a month ago. In my experience, businesses that got bit tended to overreact, armoring themselves with more protection than anyone would ever need. For a little while, anyway, until the painful memory faded and natural human laziness took over.

I didn't spot any cameras, but tan plastic boxes set high in every corner of the gallery sported a steady green light. Motion detectors, quality ones. Nothing I could get past without shutting down the entire security system. I looked to the mutant sculpture; the sheer size of it had me thinking.

"Sorry to interrupt," I said. "Could I use your washroom?"

Armand pointed the way. "Up the hall, on your right."

I thanked him and ambled along a side passage, pausing to check the windows for breakage sensors that might trigger an alarm. They were all wired, as expected, but I had to look. My real hunt started in the back hallway, wide and tall enough for the kind of pieces that couldn't fit through the gallery's main entrance. I had to smile when I came upon the back doors. Any professional gallery wouldn't take chances with breakage; a propped-open door coming free at the wrong moment could do a million dollars in damage. These doors were precision models with automatic swing arms, designed to open wide on demand and stay that way. And just like I hoped, they were fitted with Honeywell REX sensors. The long, slender bars above the doors were passive thermal readers, designed to save employees some hassle. On the outside, you'd need a key card or a code to activate the doors. On the inside, all you had to do was walk right up and the request-to-exit sensor would unlock the door for you.

I loved REX sensors. They made my job so much easier.

My next stop was Armand's office, conveniently marked with a brass nameplate on the door. The handle didn't budge. I glanced up the corridor. I was sure Caitlin could keep him talking as long as I needed her to, but I was exposed here and anyone wandering along would spot me trying to finesse the lock. It would keep for later. I'd already decided to make a second visit after the lights went out.

*　*　*

Escape took a little longer than expected. I thought Caitlin was selling her prospective-customer role to the hilt, until I realized she had actually found some pieces she liked. Thankfully, not the giant rotting-meat man. She talked pricing, narrowed her interest to a single painting, and gave Becker her decoy contact information as he put it on reserve for her.

"Are you really buying that thing?" I asked as the gallery doors whisked shut behind us.

"Not out of pocket, no. Once we get home I'll ask Emma if the treasury will cover it."

"It looked like a paisley necktie printed on a canvas. It looked like one of *my* paisley neckties."

She lifted an eyebrow. "It's a Heidecker. Trust me, in ten years it'll be worth twice what we pay for it. In a hundred, it could be worth millions. Or the equivalent, after inflation."

When you're immortal, all investments are long-term.

"I'm thinking dinner," I said. "But first I need to find an office-supply store before everything closes for the night."

"Gloves?" she asked. I hadn't told her about my plan for a break-in yet, but she knew me well.

"Brought those from home," I said. "I need to find a very specialized piece of equipment."

Two hours later, I was coasting on the glow of a fried-chicken dinner from Pollo Chapin and a side dish of mac and cheese mixed with slivers of jalapeño pepper. That and a glass of bourbon from a bar down the block. Just one drink, to cut the pregame jitters.

"If you want to sit this out, we can meet up afterward," I said to Caitlin. She looked at me like I'd insulted her mother.

"As if I'd miss it. When's the last time we went burgling together, hmm?" She curled her arm around mine as we walked along the moonlit sidewalk. "I enjoy our little jaunts. Besides, I want to see what you're going to do with *that*."

That was nestled in a plastic bag from Staples. We scouted the block, staying on the far side of the street from the darkened facade of the Becker Gallery and keeping it casual as we watched for signs of movement. No guards on the site, armed or otherwise. Either Becker was being amazingly lax in the wake of Ada's robbery, he had incredibly good insurance, or he believed that lightning never struck the same place twice. We turned down a side street and angled toward the back of the gallery, where a small patch of pavement connected to an alley just wide enough for a delivery truck.

I crumpled the bag, tossed it in a dumpster, and brandished my prize: a can of Dust-Off. I untaped the long red plastic nozzle from the side and screwed it into place as we approached the back doors, holding the can in an upside-down grip. A test squeeze of the trigger let out a hissing cloud of white vapor, like hot breath on a cold winter's day. It billowed and vanished, leaving a faint cleaning-chemical smell in its wake.

"Dust-Off is a fluorocarbon," I explained. "When you use it the right way, only the pressurized vapor shoots out. Turn the can upside down, you get the actual liquid, which boils off as soon as it contacts open air. Hence, the cloud of vapor."

"And that gets us into the gallery how?" she asked.

The twin doors were joined by a fine gap, the space filled with furry black insulation. The mosquito nose of the can pierced through the insulation with ease. I stood on my toes, angling the inverted can upward.

"The Honeywell REX is a passive thermal sensor. It's accurate, but it's not *smart*. It watches for any sudden shift in temperature—in other words, a warm-bodied human approaching from the other side—and politely unlocks the door for them."

I squeezed the trigger and spat boiling vapor into the sensor's eye. Two seconds later, the door clicked. I pulled it open and gestured toward the threshold with a flourish and a bow.

"Sometimes the old tricks are still the best ones," I said.

"Can't believe it was that easy," Caitlin said. "Though I am impressed."

"Technically, we're only halfway in, and that was the only easy part. The entire gallery floor is wired for motion; someone could break in like this and start grabbing artwork, but they'd set off an alarm the second they set foot in there. All *we* need is access to Becker's office. We do this right, nobody will ever know we were here."

The office door barely put up a fight. I pressed one gloved hand to the wood, ears perked as I pushed it open. We had no way of knowing if he'd set up another motion detector inside. If he had, we'd have to grab whatever we could and bolt before the cops showed up.

I flicked the light switch. A desk lamp flooded the windowless room with a warm, soft glow, glinting off Victorian wallpaper in wintergreen and ivory stripes. The lock on his filing cabinet was easier than the door. I flicked through rows of tight-packed folders, rifling across his receipts and invoices, while Caitlin sat down at the desk and clicked his PC's mouse. A screen lit up in the corner of my eye.

"Anything good?" I asked.

"He left it unlocked," Caitlin said, "which suggests there's nothing particularly nefarious to find here. What am I looking for, exactly?"

"Wherever they smuggled the art they stole, Ada and her buddies are going to have to find a specialty fence. There aren't many of those, and even fewer who'll do business with amateurs. Remember, they killed a security guard during the heist; the paintings they took have some serious weight now. Anyway, if we can find Becker's insurance report, we can get the names and artists of the pieces. That'll help us track them down."

That errant detail bugged me. Becker *had* live, on-site security here once. Why hadn't he brought in a replacement? Maybe he was the kind of perfectionist who insisted on three rounds of interviews before making a hire, but one phone call and he could have a temp-heavy outfit like Gold Star Northwest in here, filling the gap in the meantime. Careless. My mind started wandering, thinking about how maybe I could go a little above and beyond as long as we were already here, and snatch Caitlin that painting she liked.

The rules of the first story stood like a wall in my path. The Thief's lover kills him after a successful heist. If I didn't want to tempt fate, I couldn't take anything from this place, not so much as a stray scrap of paper or the green marble coaster on the edge of Becker's desk. I'd have to rely on my memory if we found what we were looking for; taking *notes* felt like too much of a risk.

"Curious," Caitlin murmured. I glanced over my shoulder. She had Becker's email open, scrolling through his correspondence.

"Whatcha got?"

"Do you see any sales to a woman named Dima Chakroun?"

He had an entire manila folder with her name on the tab. I opened it up and started reading. She had made six high-dollar buys in the last two years. Chakroun was in LA, but all the art ended up on a truck bound for Chicago.

"She's spent over a million bucks in here, yeah. What about her?"

"She's Nadine's financial advisor," Caitlin said. "And look at this."

I sidled around the desk to stand at her shoulder. I didn't recognize the incoming email address—it was a cryptic jumble of letters and random numbers—but I knew the signature by heart.

To say I'm disappointed is an understatement, old chap. The theft of Stegall's Journey to the Sea *wasn't a random accident; the thieves knew damn well that I had just paid you for it, that I WANTED it, and they stole it to give me—and my prince—the proverbial middle digit. Stegall's star is already on the rise, exactly as scheduled, and I was supposed to have a lock on his entire first wave. Clearly you have an information leak. You've always been a reliable servant until now, and I urge you not to give us any more reasons to be concerned. —Royce*

Royce was Caitlin's counterpart in the Midwest, the hound and right-hand man to Prince Malphas. Between him and Nadine's agent showing up in the invoices, it wasn't hard to figure out Becker's real line of business.

"He's not just a dealer to the rich and famous," I said. "He's the art hookup for Malphas's court. Long-term investments for demons with a lot of money to throw around."

Caitlin tapped her burgundy fingernail against her chin. "Considering his reputation as a tastemaker, and how many fledgling artists blossom after being featured here? Plus this mention of a star being on the rise 'as scheduled'? I'd have to call Calypso and see what he knows, but I'd be willing to bet quite a few of those up-and-comers paid a visit to the crossroads."

"So artists sell their soul for success, Malphas's agents tell Becker to showcase their work and promote it right away, then those same agents buy up the art and sit on it. The bargaining demon makes the artists famous, and suddenly those early pieces are worth a mint."

I had to admire the sheer audacity of the scheme; it was kind of brilliant. Caitlin's expression turned sour.

"*We* should have thought of that," she said. "I'm having a word with Emma as soon as we get home."

I pointed to the screen. "This explains the Order's involvement, too. It had nothing to do with Canton's pocket watch. The Chainmen were called out because Ada and her crew got greedy and stepped on Royce's toes. If they had just stolen the watch and left the art alone, none of this might have happened."

She clicked through to Becker's response. All apologies and contrition, plus a promise to refund Royce's money and keep an eye out if the piece resurfaced anywhere. Despite who he was dealing with, the dealer couldn't resist getting a little snippy by the end.

All due respect, I was given to believe that your authority was unquestioned. My security was hardly prepared for an organized attack directed at you and your people, and if I'd been properly informed, I would have taken steps to prevent it.

Fair enough, Royce conceded. *We were surprised ourselves. I doubt they'll hit your gallery again, but just in case, I'm sending you a gift to help prevent further problems. At my behest the Order is hunting and exterminating every thief that local law enforcement has placed under suspicion. Hopefully, we'll recover the art in the process. I have no doubt that some will escape—we're still trying to identify the leader of the gang—but they'll find my prince's region quite inhospitable from now on. We thought these people had been eliminated long ago. We won't make that mistake twice.*

The last line of the email sent a chill down my spine, a gust of winter wind carried on a bad memory.

They call themselves the Redemption Choir.

13.

I'd made the same mistake Royce did. Then again, I could be forgiven for making assumptions. I'd been standing at ground zero the night Caitlin and her loyalists faced down the Redemption Choir and their leader, a deranged incarnate demon named Sullivan. Sullivan was born to the demonic Choir of Envy, and his twisted nature led him to covet the two things he could never have: humanity and salvation. So he'd banded together a ragtag army of cambion, taught them to hate themselves just like he did, and turned them into budding terrorists.

His master plan was to lay hands on the Ring of Solomon, a relic capable of commanding demons, and forge Caitlin into his personal weapon. Would have worked, too, if I hadn't swapped it out for a fake.

Caitlin beat Sullivan to a pulp and buried him under ten tons of rock. His final resting place is a parking lot now. As for his followers, that was Melanie's turn to shine. She stood up and she stood tall, calling to his cambion to lay down their guns, turn away from Sullivan's lies, and take a chance on a new way of life. Most of them crossed the line and stood with us. The few who couldn't, the ones he'd indoctrinated down to the bone, were allowed to leave in peace. Leaderless, directionless, we figured they'd drift off into the sunset.

Caitlin was on her phone, talking in a hushed whisper. I hustled back to the filing cabinet. I could feel the clock ticking, time weighing on me like a pressure front rolling in ahead of stormy weather while I rummaged for Becker's insurance filing.

Caitlin hung up. "Emma conferenced me in with one of her people at the Silk Ranch. The parking lot hasn't been touched."

"Sullivan's dead," I told her. "His diehards went back east, looking for a new leader, someone to guide them. And they found Ada."

It made sense now—our first confrontation, when she told me I'd done her a favor without knowing it. By helping to take Sullivan out, I'd paved her path to the top of the food chain. I took a deep breath. Fighting the Redemption Choir had pushed me to the edge, left me busted and broke and homeless, sending me on a downward spiral that took months to pull myself out of. Sometimes, when the wind blew the wrong way, I could still feel the aching aftermath of the whipping I took from Sullivan's cane when they held me hostage. Or see the shocked look in the eyes of the teenage kid I murdered, slicing his throat with a shard of broken mirror to escape.

But a name was just a name. Sullivan was dead and gone, Ada was the target, and this job hadn't changed. The stolen art would lead me right to her doorstep, and then...and then I'd have to make some hard choices.

My gloved fingertip scrolled down a list of recent acquisitions. Becker bought art from brokers in four countries, but most of the recent buys were from the days after the break-in, so they weren't the pieces I wanted.

"Hon?" I said. "What was the name of that sculpture you liked?"

"*Sacrament*, why?"

"It's not on the list."

The alarm went off. It trilled, loud and strident, echoing through the darkened halls. I didn't know if we'd done something, missed a trigger, or if it was just sheer bad luck, but we needed to get the hell out before the cops showed up. I shoved folders back into place, slammed the filing cabinet shut, and led the charge out into the hallway.

Sacrament was waiting for us.

The sculpture stood at the open archway of the gallery. We hadn't triggered the alarm; it had, when it woke up and set off the motion detectors on its lumbering way toward us. I remembered Royce's email. *I'm sending you a gift to help prevent further problems.*

The creature had eyes after all. They had been closed before, while it posed motionless on the dais and pretended to be a work of art. Now they blossomed in a set of six, black and piggish and swallowing the shadows as they erupted from its misshapen rotting-meat face. It had a mouth, too. The creature showed us, its hinged jaw opening wide, displaying a maw lined with jagged and broken teeth. A wave of stench blew down the corridor, the reek of an open sewer main on a hot summer day. Caitlin skidded to a stop at my side.

The beast's roar was louder than the alarm, earsplitting and shrill, the sound of a train whistle on the express ride to hell. It galloped down the double-wide hall on its four elephant legs, almost filling it with its rotten bulk. I threw myself clear as one of the glistening cannon-thick limbs swung at me. Dropping low, I rolled on the tile and covered my face as plaster and paint chips rained down from the ruptured wall.

"Need room!" Caitlin shouted. I couldn't argue, but I had to dart backward as another pillar of meat slammed down where I'd just been standing. The tiles buckled under its stump, erupting in a spray of shattered ceramic. My back hit the wall, cornered, literally, and the creature's six eyes squinted with feral malice. Its boneless neck curled, elongated head rearing back as its jaws opened wide. A rivulet of gray drool dripped from a tooth the size of my fist, spattering the floor at my feet.

No room to go around. That only left me one option, and as the beast's head plunged, maw wide and hungry, I crouched low and dove. *Under* it, hitting my belly on the floor and scrambling on hands and knees, hearing its steam-whistle roar as its teeth gnashed against thin air. Its lacquered rotten-meat bulk trembled and roiled a foot above me, pillar-legs shaking. I scrambled free just as its entire weight plummeted to the floor, crushing tiles to dust. I stumbled across the threshold and burst into the main gallery.

It was already back on its legs, tromping around and locking onto me with a frustrated wheeze. Caitlin was at my side, breathless but grinning now, as eager to fight as the beast was to feast. She brandished a brass tube engraved with serpentine glyphs and clutched it high above her head.

"Keep it distracted, would you, pet?"

A stream of playing cards riffled through the air, flowing from my hip pocket to my open palm.

"I can manage that," I said.

It barreled toward me, head bowed, ramming speed. I held my ground as long as I could and flung card after card, enchanted pasteboard sizzling through the air and carving into its bulk. Cards lodged in its meaty hide, bristling quills leaking trickles of black blood. I dove left at the last second and it shot past me, plowing headfirst into a display wall. The ivory wood crashed down, taking a quarter-million dollars of art with it. One rotten pillar-foot pounded down onto a broken frame, cracking wood and ripping canvas as the beast wheeled around, hunting for me.

Caitlin gave the brass tube a shake and it erupted, sprouting a telescoping haft, the business end blossoming into a wickedly barbed spear tip. She twirled the spear above her head then braced it against her hip, sidestepping in a fast circle and hunting for an angle of attack. The beast noticed her, catching the glimmer of infernal brass, and its head swung around. I stole a second to take a breath and find my focus, lined up the ace of hearts, and let it fly.

The card carved along the creature's face, slicing it from one black eye to another and gouging a furrow in the meat between. Black ichor sprayed, the beast stomping and whistle-howling, wheeling toward me. I'd distracted it, all right. It roared in, a mad stampede, every fall of its elephant feet splintering the gallery's wooden floor and leaving shattered potholes in its wake. My heel hit the wreckage of the display wall and I fell, landing hard as the creature loomed over me. As I scuttled back on my hands, desperate, fighting for room to get my balance back, it raised one foot to crush me under its killing weight.

Caitlin was an airborne ballerina, frozen for a moment under the gallery lights as she sailed above the creature's back, spear spinning gracefully in her hand. Then she braced the haft in both fists and came plunging down.

She landed on its back and the spear drove home, spitting a torrent of black blood. The creature screamed. It rose up on its hind legs, trying to buck her loose, and I scrambled clear just as its forelegs came down with the sound of an earthquake. Caitlin clung fast. The beast shook and thrashed and she wrenched her grip from side to side, digging the spear in deeper as a fresh gout of ichor splashed her face. Her eyes were bright diamonds under the midnight blood spatter, her laughter like an angel at play.

The beast gave one last screeching bellow and collapsed onto its belly, legs sprawling and broken beneath it. The thunderous crash reverberated through the gallery then faded away, swallowed by the trill of the burglar alarm.

Caitlin jumped down from the monstrosity's back. With a flick of her wrist, her spear telescoped inward, snapping inch by inch until it was back to a foot-long cylinder of brass. The back of her other hand wiped across her eyes, flicking droplets of goo to the floor.

"Changed my mind," she panted, breathless. "I don't like this sculpture one bit. I'm inclined to find the artist and deliver a scathing critique."

"I don't know. I think I've got a new appreciation for the power of modern art." I pushed myself to my feet and pointed a shaky hand at the fallen display wall. "But I think it stepped on that painting you wanted."

"Some things just weren't meant to be. Time to go?"

I heard sirens in the distance, their trembling rise and fall playing a jailhouse harmonica counterpart to the gallery alarm. It was definitely time to go.

14.

Every good-sized town has a hangout or two where the clued-in come to mingle and talk shop. Back home it's the old reliable Tiger's Garden: cozy, good drinks and even better food, and a very exclusive guest list. You can only find the door if you're not looking for it, and you can only get in if the Garden wants you to. In Chicago there's always bright chaos and top-shelf booze on tap at the Bast Club. In New York—if you absolutely have to, and you know the right passwords and gestures to open the elevator door—you can find a pretentious sanctuary at Dashwood Abbey.

St. Louis, I wasn't sure about. And it looked like St. Louis was our next stop. I made some phone calls that night. We'd ended up at a roadside motel a half mile from the Becker Gallery, the end of the line after a dead sprint through twisting, turning alleys and side streets, careful to throw off any scent we might have left behind. Caitlin hid in the shadows while I booked our room. When I came back, she made a beeline for the shower, intent on washing off the black ichor that clung to her face like a mask of spattered volcano mud.

I sat on the edge of a flowered bedspread from the fifties and watched TV until she called out to me, telling me she needed help scrubbing her back. To be honest, I wasn't sure she really did, but I was willing to be lied to. If you've never showered with your lover after sharing a near-death experience, I highly recommend it.

I washed her back; then she washed mine. Her hands slid upward, across my shoulders, fingers curling around my throat as her breath gusted over the nape of my neck. Then one thing led to another. Later we held close to one another, flesh to flesh and cheek to cheek. The steaming water sluiced down and her long scarlet hair clung to my skin like it would never let go. I pressed my palms to the cool, damp tile to steady my trembling legs.

"St. Louis?" I said again.

"That was the Redemption Choir's first home, its spawning ground before they moved west, and Sullivan's old stomping grounds," she whispered in my ear. "Good odds that's where its remnants fled to. Familiar territory."

"Then that's where they met Ada."

I had hoped to find Becker's insurance claim. All I had, thanks to Royce's email, was a single stolen piece: *Journey to the Sea*, by a fledgling painter named Stegall. The first thing I did, once we finally clambered out of the shower and toweled each other off, was put out feelers to all the specialty fences I knew. If that canvas showed up for sale anywhere, I wanted to be the first bidder they reached out to. Next on my list was Bentley, and I hoped I wasn't calling too late, waking him up.

I had, but he muffled a yawn behind his hand and pretended I hadn't.

"If there's a gathering place on the level of the Bast Club, I haven't seen it," he told me. "St. Louis tends to pitch younger in its occult community. Less organized, more ad hoc."

"Perfect spot for a guy like Sullivan to gather up disaffected kids." *Or Ada*, I thought.

"Quite. There is one venue you might find worth investigating. It's not purely for the underground, more of a mixed bag, but I can give you a few pass-phrases to get you through the door. Assuming those phrases are still in use, which...they may not be. It's been a very long time."

"Worth a shot," I said, reaching for a motel-branded pad and a pen.

Caitlin and I went to bed after that. We went to sleep a couple of hours later. Then it was up at first light, catching a shuttle flight from Detroit to St. Louis. I watched the side mirrors all the way to the airport and didn't relax until we were in our seats, buckled in and taxiing to the runway. Caitlin made a few discreet calls in the taxi once we landed. The bad news was that word spread fast, Becker was losing his mind, and Royce was furious, looking for someone to tear apart with his bare hands. The good news was nobody had any idea we had even been in town—yet—and we weren't even on the short list of suspects.

The nice thing about the Redemption Choir was that they were a bogeyman for all occasions. No matter how unlikely it was that Ada and her crew would come back for another shot at Becker's gallery, everyone seemed happy to put the blame square on their shoulders. Royce and company assumed, naturally enough, that "the Madrigal" had inherited Sullivan's crusade against the powers of hell.

I wasn't so sure.

I could understand stealing art for cash, especially as a target of opportunity, but everything else I'd seen from Ada so far—boosting the pocket watch, stealing the shipping records to track Marcel, the break-in at Carolyn's house—had been laser-focused on the first story and Howard Canton's legacy.

Now I just needed to figure out how those two things were connected.

The address Bentley had given us, nestled in a suburb, wasn't our usual kind of haunt. The Everyday Grind perched on the edge of the Maryville University campus, a coffee shop snug along a quiet, sunny street. It shared a row of one-floor storefronts with a college bookshop and a music store that specialized in vintage vinyl and cassette tapes. I felt like I needed my hair in a man bun for this trip, or at least some flannel.

If I looked out of place when we stepped through the door, nobody gave me a second glance. No one but the young, freckle-faced barista behind the counter, who gave us a cheerful wave. She was twenty going on fifteen, with her hair in bright blond pigtails. There were two people ahead of us in line, both college kids, so I drifted over to an overstuffed corkboard and scoped the room out.

In the violet light of my third eye, the room shifted like the subtle roll of the sun at noontime. Shadows slid and pointed in opposite directions. The two twentysomethings in a warm patch of sunlight, genially arguing over a chessboard, had barbed-wire twists for souls. A balding man hunched over his laptop lifted a mug to his lips, the coffee burbling with frothy white light. I saw the light slide down his gullet beneath skin gone transparent, spreading out along his arms to his fingertips, then setting off sparkles of inspiration as he typed. On my right, the corkboard became a labyrinth of secrets. Tiny glyphs, inked in the corners of concert flyers, took on new meaning. Sigils in the margins of an ad for an English tutor offered entirely different teaching services—if you knew how to read them and how to ask for what you wanted. A lost-dog notice became an offer to sell exotic ritual tools; the board was an entire secret marketplace standing in plain sight.

As for the barista, I wasn't sure what she was. Older than twenty, add a zero, maybe two. She shimmered the way ice catches sunlight on the skin of a winter pond. I caught the scent of cinnamon, and honey, and the pages of an old and musty book. She caught me looking. She peered past the shoulder of the guy she was talking to and gave me an impish wink before turning back to him.

"Interesting," Caitlin murmured under her breath.

I glanced sidelong at her, wondering if she felt like elaborating. She didn't. We got in line together and waited until the last customer had shuffled off with his drink. The pigtailed barista showed us her teeth, too perfect, even, and white to be real. I remembered the words Bentley had given me.

"We are pilgrims, from a lonely lane," I said.

She put her fingertips to the bow of her lips.

"Oh, honey," she said, "we haven't used that line around here in years. Don't worry, though. I think the three of us can see each other just fine, yeah? What can I make for you?"

"Is there a local specialty?"

"You look like you didn't get enough sleep last night. How about a nice caramel latte?"

"Sold," I said.

"I'll have the same," Caitlin added. Her body language was reserved, and she eyed the woman behind the counter like a bomb that might be primed to blow.

As we waited, hanging back a bit, I leaned in close.

"So what exactly—"

"Nothing I've ever seen before," Caitlin replied, eyes locked on the barista. "And that bothers me."

The Grind served its coffee in genuine ceramic mugs, broad and deep and mud-brown. She gently slid our drinks across the counter, the foamy tops adorned with intricate latte art. I could feel the latent magical charge nestling between the molecules of milk, laid out in a trio of tangled, baroque glyphs. Symbols meaning *fortune, vitality, life.*

"Question for you," I said, handing her a twenty.

She leaned toward the cash register. "Maybe. What's your name?"

One other thing Bentley had told me last night: *if the barista has blond hair, give your true name. If dark, lie.* That was the thing about the occult underground. Strange places had strange rules. And just like the laws of the civilian world, sometimes you could do an end run around those rules...but only once you knew why they existed in the first place, and the punishment if you got caught breaking them.

"Daniel," I said, playing it safe. I didn't ask for hers.

"You're looking for someone."

"A woman, around your age," I said, keeping up the polite fiction that she was anywhere near as young as she looked. "Calls herself Ada. Ada Lovelace."

Something flashed behind the barista's eyes, a moment of displeasure eclipsed by a fresh smile. She pointed toward a low wooden stage set into the corner of the room, custom-built for soulful acoustic jams and poetry slams. A young man sat on the edge of the stage, shaggy, with a ruff of long brown hair and a goatee. He had a cheap guitar balanced on his knee, and he gave it an experimental strum as he tightened a string.

"You should talk to Dylan," she said.

She didn't offer me change for the twenty, and I didn't ask. Caitlin and I eased across the room, mugs in hand. I sipped from mine, gingerly, trying not to break the milk-foam sigil until it tingled against my lips. The drink was strong and sweet, perfectly balanced, with a dash of caramel and a spark of false nostalgia; I swallowed down the fleeting memory of a warm summer day in childhood that never really happened.

"Hey," Dylan said, glancing up from his guitar as we approached.

"Hey. Mind if we ask you some questions?"

He tensed up like we might be cops, looking to run him downtown for some buried sin. Then he looked from me to the front counter, seeking a sign from above. Whatever he saw in the barista's eyes, a little stiffness drained from his shoulders.

"About?" he asked, still wary.

"A local, maybe a regular. Ada." I had a fix on Dylan now, up close and personal. There was no mistaking the pulse of tainted blood in his veins, the energy stretched tighter than his fresh guitar string. I decided to take a chance. "Runs with the Redemption Choir."

From the way he winced, I could tell he wasn't one of Sullivan's crew. Or Ada's. He gestured to a table and the three of us took a seat.

"Used to be a regular," he said. "She was a student at Maryville, engineering track. Dual major, I think. Chemical and mechanical."

"Talented," I said.

"One way to put it. She hasn't been there for a month, though, from what I hear. Hasn't been here either."

A month was long enough to regroup with the remnants of the

Choir and set off on her crime spree. Not long enough to have been running with Sullivan's original crew. I could tell Caitlin was working the timeline, same as me.

"And before that?" she asked.

"Before that, she was around. Hung out with those guys, sure, before they went west. I didn't. Not my crowd."

He waved a hand and I saw a glimmer in his eye, a telltale shift from white to runny-egg yellow as his demonic blood strained to show itself. A blink and it was gone.

"I'm *fine* with who I am," he said. "And Sullivan was a two-faced jerk. I never fell for his preacher bullshit."

"Did Ada?" Caitlin asked him.

"No. She was way too smart for that. And, y'know, human. All the way human, so his whole 'blood tainted with hell's corruption' jive wouldn't work on her. She just hung out with him. Dangled on his every word, followed the pack around like she was some kind of human mascot."

I shook my head, not following.

"So...she didn't believe in him, but she still followed him around?"

Dylan snorted. "You ask me? She was *learning* from him. Not learning the stuff he was trying to teach, either. She was studying him, his moves, how he talked, how he thought."

"For what purpose?" Caitlin asked.

"You gotta understand. Ada is...let me put it this way. If I had to settle on one word to describe her? Just one?"

He leaned back and thought about it, but not for too long. He already knew the word he wanted.

"Dangerous," he said. "That girl is dangerous."

15.

Dylan propped his guitar on his lap and tuned it while we talked, frowning at his memories and one stubborn string.

"Ada always came in hot, no halfway with her, you know? Whatever she was excited about, it was the most important thing in the world. Until the next thing she decided to get excited about."

"Flighty?" I asked.

"More like she was a rebel looking for a cause. One week it was saving the eroding ice caps, then it was equal rights, then it was the rain forests. All good stuff, don't get me wrong, but sometimes it felt like the actual cause wasn't as important as...looking for something to define herself by. She wasn't hunting for a righteous fight; she was hunting for *her* fight, trying them on one after another until she found one that fit just right."

I shrugged. "She's what, twenty or thereabouts? Sounds like a lot of twenty-year-olds. Myself included, at that age."

"Not this intense," he said. "Like, if you weren't one hundred percent on board with her passion du jour? You were dead to her, at least until the wind shifted. So she was running with Sullivan's crew, and I noticed little bits of...friction. She never openly contradicted him, but I could feel her pushing. Tiny pushes. Testing the edges of his authority to see just how far she could go."

Even then, she'd been angling for a takeover. "Did Sullivan notice?"

Dylan laughed. "Oh, he noticed. Same deal on his end: he never called her on it, but I saw him icing her out. Passive-aggressive vibes all around. When the Redemption Choir saddled up and went west, he made it very clear that she wasn't invited to tag along. She left about a week after that on her own, disappeared for a couple of months, then started showing up around the coffeehouse again. She was different after that."

"Different how?" I asked.

He thought about that. He strummed his guitar, testing it with a low and rumbling chord.

"Intense. I mean, she was always intense, but it wasn't the same. Used to be you couldn't shut her up about whatever her latest obsession was. Once she came back, she barely talked at all. She'd get her coffee, sit and read all night. She faded from the social scene and then...well, I guess she left again. And she hasn't been back since."

Caitlin tilted her head, eyes sharp. "Reading? What sort of books?"

"Might sound weird, but they were all about stage magic. I remember she mentioned having some kinda low-key interest as a teenager, but that all fell by the wayside once she decided she was out to save the world. After, though? It was all she was interested in."

Wherever her exodus had taken her, she'd come back with a fresh obsession—and not long after that, she rallied the remnants of the Redemption Choir and launched a crime spree. I looked to Caitlin; she was a step ahead of me, following the same trail.

"But when she left that first time," Caitlin said, "she definitely didn't follow Sullivan?"

Dylan shook his head. "Nah. I heard, and this is all friend-of-a-friend secondhand, that she told somebody she was going home for a while. Between her workload at school and getting swept up in Sullivan's orbit, she said she needed to clear her head and get her priorities in order."

"Where's home?" I asked.

He glanced to the ceiling, eyes in a squint. "It was...lemme think, somewhere in Michigan."

"Detroit?"

"Small town, real small. What was it?" He snapped his fingers. "Talbot Cove. That was it."

* * *

Detroit was radioactive until the heat settled down, so we booked a shuttle flight to Chicago, rented a car, and drove for the border. We followed the curve of Interstate 90 east along the bend of Lake Michigan's shore, curling down and then up again, as the metropolitan sprawl receded and broke against rolling hills and endless faded green. This was sportsman country, ripe fly-fishing waters and hiking trails, and backwoods houses set a mile apart from their closest neighbors.

The seclusion appealed to my larcenous sensibilities. The number of doghouses I saw, not to mention the gun racks on every mud-spattered pickup, not so much. There are two things I hate dealing with on a break-in job: shotguns and dogs.

"This is...rustic," I said as I held the wheel tight. Rough road jolted against the rental coupe's tires.

"Damned with faint praise," Caitlin murmured.

"I like cities," I said. "I can operate in cities. That's my natural habitat."

"There's something to be said for occasional diversity."

I gave her the side-eye. "You can't be enjoying this."

"Darling, the first time I ever set foot on this world, I spent years living at the edge of a Scottish moor. Before the discovery of electricity, or flushing toilets."

"No TV, no movies, no casinos," I said, "just haggis. That sounds horrifying."

"It was delightful. We created our own fun. And we ate more than haggis." She paused. "There was *also* mince and tatties. Anyway, didn't really experience a city until my second visit. That was New York."

"Had to be some culture shock."

"It was the summer of 1775. Everyone had culture shock."

There was a sign up ahead, forest green on aluminum struts. *Welcome to Talbot Cove: The Town That Works! Population 2,032.*

"I do not like this," I said.

"As you've made abundantly clear."

"No." I gestured at the sign as we rolled on by. The edge of town loomed up at the crest of the next hill. "This. I keep thinking about that newspaper clipping Bentley dug up. What are the odds that Harmony Black and Ada Lovelace were both born in the same podunk backwater town in Michigan? It's a small world, but it's not *that* small."

"What's the saying in magic?" Caitlin asked. "No such thing as a coincidence?"

"Bingo. Not always true, but in this case...I'm thinking there's something very weird afoot in Talbot Cove."

Not that you could tell by looking. Talbot Cove was just another blink-and-miss-it postage stamp town, like a hundred others I'd driven through before. At best, a stop for gas and grub on the way from point A to point B. One long main street cut through the heart of town. I slowed to a steady cruise, hunting for a vacant parking meter, and studied the crawl of progress. Half of the storefronts had been there since the 1950s, judging from the dusty, faded awnings and the vintage fonts on their signs, but now a mom-and-pop pizza joint awkwardly rubbed shoulders with a Verizon franchise.

One of the busiest shops on the main drag was a video rental place. A sign in the window said they also did affordable VCR repairs. I was tempted to ask Caitlin if this was what hell was like, but I was afraid of what she might tell me.

"Where shall we start?" Caitlin asked.

I swerved up to the curb and put the car in park. The spire of a clock tower rose up a block away, whitewashed clapboard frozen in time.

"If the kid with the guitar was right," I said, "whatever happened when Ada came home set her on a collision course with the Canton relics. So we've got a lead to chase. Let's hit up the town hall, see if they've got some kind of public registry or maybe a local newspaper archive we can sift through."

Progress marched on, eventually. The listless clerk lit up once I slipped him a folded twenty, and he ushered us through a door marked *Community Records*.

"You're in luck," he said. "Time was, we kept every issue of the *Talbot Eagle* in hardcopy. Stored 'em all in packing boxes; if you didn't know the exact date you were looking for, forget it."

"And now?" Caitlin asked.

"New mayor's pushing a green initiative. Sprang for new computers, wants everything, whatchamacallit, digitized. We've spent the last two months working our way through, page by page. Now, the whole archive isn't available just yet—got a ways to go—but most of it's searchable and I should be able to help you run down anything you can't find."

He ushered us to a pair of PCs, old fat terminals with amber text and expectant, strobing cursors on the screen, nestled in side-by-side library carrels. This felt like the kind of town where everybody knew everybody; I stopped him as he turned to go, thinking I might save us some time.

"Out of curiosity, do you know a family that lives around here, the Lovelaces? They'd have a daughter in college now."

He scratched his chin. "Can't say it rings a bell, no."

There was a good chance that "Ada Lovelace" was an alias. Even if the name came up empty, we had the Canton connection to follow. I thanked him, gave him another twenty bucks, and he made himself scarce. Caitlin and I sat down and got to work.

I hit the newspaper archives, municipal records, even a phone directory; there was no record of a Lovelace family living in Talbot Cove. I was about to give up, declare it a dead end and move on to hunting for Canton, when Caitlin tapped me on the shoulder.

"Found them," she said.

"Who?" I asked, leaning in. "Ada or Canton?"

"Both."

Her screen displayed a grainy scan of an *Eagle* column, dated three years ago. *Students Wow at Annual Talent Show.* I was about to make a quip about every day in Talbot Cove being a slow news day, when she pointed at the top paragraph.

—*Cove High School, and this year didn't disappoint. Top honors went to class president Ada Lovelace Canton, who electrified judges (literally!) with her science-based take on a traditional magic show—*

Caitlin tapped the space bar, and a file photograph sprang open in a new window. It was her, all right. Younger, more clean-cut—she hadn't adopted the smeared-mascara look yet—and standing onstage dressed in a tuxedo and tails. A pair of welder's goggles adorned her magician's top hat, and a familiar pair of fingerless gloves sheathed her waving hands.

"Lovelace is her middle name," I murmured. "But that means…"

We had a solid trailhead now. That was all we needed. I set my phone on speaker and got Pixie on the line, drawing her into the hunt as we searched for births, deaths, property records, all the bits and pieces of data that make up a lineage.

Twenty minutes later, I was staring the truth dead in the eye. *Ed Canton (wife: Louise Canton), born 1926, died 1954.* I saw his family tree spread out beneath him: his son, and then his son's son, and then Ada.

The timeline fit perfectly. We knew "Howard Canton" was a stage name, but all he'd changed was the first half of it. Flimsy now, but a good enough disguise in the days before mass media and the Internet. Ed Canton was Canton the Magnificent, born and raised right here in Talbot Cove, the kind of place where a man could vanish whenever he needed to. And Ada was his great-granddaughter.

16.

Jim and Dora Canton were Ada's grandparents. They were also, as far as we could tell, her sole legal guardians. Her parents were out of town and out of the picture, no records anywhere, and it was Jim and Dora's name on all of Ada's old high-school paperwork. They lived in a snug little house on the east side of town, complete with a white picket fence. We did a slow drive-by, scoping it out. Jim had his chin up, whistling, eyes bright as he mowed the front lawn without a care in the world. The scene didn't look right to me, not after what I'd already learned. Armed with Ada's full name, I had called up Maryville to do a little digging.

"This is Paul Emerson from Chase Bank's student-loan processing department," I said, putting on my best call-center voice. "I just need to verify a student's enrollment, please."

Ada was enrolled. She was also terminally truant. The records clerk told me, sounding vicariously embarrassed, that as far as she knew Ada hadn't been to any of her classes in over a month.

"Tell me something," I said to Caitlin as we cruised past the Canton house. "You're the proud grandfather of a college student who has, for all intents and purposes, dropped out and vanished. Would *you* look that happy?"

"I'd be all teeth and claws," she muttered.

"Either they're mixed up in all this, which I doubt—"

"Or they have no idea their precious darling granddaughter is running with a bad crowd," she said.

"With? She's *running* the bad crowd."

"Should we break the grim news to them?"

"I'm thinking the opposite," I said. "We need to know what happened to Ada last time she was here. She found something that set her onto her great-grandfather's trail. Something that sent her over the edge. I mean, she might have been obsessive before, but I'm pretty sure that security guard at Becker's gallery was her first actual murder. And at the depot in Boston, she took out two more guards like it didn't mean a thing."

"She developed a taste for blood," Caitlin observed. "When an animal does that, we put them down."

"Nobody turns into a killer overnight. Not unless something—or someone—pushes them down that road. Ada came home, and she got that push."

* * *

Dora Canton had rosy apple cheeks. She stood at her husband's side just inside the front door of their house, both of them vacillating between bewilderment and glowing pride.

"Ada didn't tell us she'd won an award," she said.

"Well, she doesn't know yet," I replied with a conspiratorial wink. "I do hope you can keep a secret, at least until the announcement is made on Friday. Did she tell you she'd been nominated?"

Her grandparents shared a glance.

"Not a peep," Jim said. "I talked to her just last week. All she said was that her classes were going fine."

Ada was covering. Calling home from wherever she was hiding, pretending everything was fine. That wasn't a long-term plan; eventually the college would get in touch with her grandparents, or her grades would show up. Something would give her away. I wondered if she even had a real plan or if she was just spinning plates, trying to hold the pieces of her life together. Everything I'd seen Ada pull so far told me she was reckless. A danger to herself and others, and getting more dangerous by the minute.

"They're going better than fine, I should think," Caitlin said. "She's a rising star. It's time she was recognized for it."

"And you are with...?" Dora asked.

"The National Engineering Merit Foundation," I said. "We seek out the best and brightest young engineering students for special recognition each year. It's a shortlist of twenty, nominated by their professors, and then voted on by a body of professionals."

"And Ada landed in the top three," Caitlin said. "*Very* prestigious."

"We like to do a brief interview with people who are close to our winners, so we can get a sense of who they are outside the classroom. The human-interest angle. That is, if you have a few minutes."

The lie got us inside, a seat on the Cantons' afghan-draped sofa, and two glasses of freshly squeezed lemonade. On the way in, I checked the photographs on the fireplace mantel. Lots of pictures of a younger Dora and Jim, along with a man and woman who, from their ages and the infant cradled in the woman's arms, I suspected were Ada's parents. One big happy family until they suddenly weren't. I stepped carefully around the question, making small talk until I was on solid enough footing for it.

"So you're...her grandparents?" I asked, checking my notes on a spiral pad. I'd picked up the pad at a local convenience store on the way over. The notes were mostly my shopping list.

"Ada's parents, well—" Dora gave Jim a pained look. He was stoic, but he didn't meet my eyes. "It's still hard to talk about, I'm sorry."

"I'm sorry, I don't mean to intrude."

"No, it's all right. When Ada was five years old, there was a...a car accident. Thank God she was strapped in, she was fine, but our son and our daughter-in-law were killed in the collision. We've raised her ever since."

I made sympathetic noises and steered the conversation, hunting for something we could use. I was already convinced that Jim and Dora didn't know a thing about their granddaughter's secret life. I was also dying to ask Jim about his father, but "did you know he toured as Canton the Magnificent?" was too far out of left field under the circumstances. Caitlin, sharp as a razor, found a backdoor entrance to the question.

"Going over her high school records," Caitlin said, "we noticed she won first prize at a...talent show, I believe?"

The corners of Dora's eyes crinkled as she savored the memory. "Oh goodness, I remember. She worked on her performance for months. Always a perfectionist, our Ada. Not sure where she got the idea to do magic tricks, but it was a lovely show. Of course, I'm biased."

"No other magicians in your family, then?" I asked.

Jim waved his hand. "Not a one. Ada's father was an engineer—I figure that's where she got the brains—and my old man was a long-haul trucker. Not a lot of time for pulling rabbits out of hats."

I bit down on the obvious follow-up question, but one glance at Caitlin told me she was thinking the same thing I was. Long-haul truckers could be away from home for weeks at a time. A perfect cover, if Canton was hiding his theater life from his own family. Even in the modern age, the outside world had a hard time finding a foothold in Talbot Cove; back in the forties and fifties, it would have been a fortress of isolation.

After that they wanted to gush a little, telling us about Ada's achievements, her academic record, the time one of her experiments set the garage on fire. I let them talk and pretended to take notes. I knew one thing right off the bat: Ada was their kid. The gulf of a generation, the pages of the chapter torn out between them, only brought them closer together. They'd raised her, and they talked about her with the kind of pride reserved for parents whose child had climbed higher, blossomed brighter, than they ever had.

Sometimes I wondered what that felt like. Then I thought about all the ways parenthood could go wrong. Like how I was sipping these nice folks' lemonade, listening to their warm memories and their hopes for the future, knowing full well that their beloved child was racing headfirst for a mortuary slab. I could only hope it wasn't me who ended up putting her there.

Not that she was short of volunteers for the job. Her first outing, she and her buddies managed to piss off Royce and draw the wrath of the Chainmen. Her second, she ripped off a transporter for the Boston mob and killed two security guards on her way in. I didn't know what she was planning for her third act, beyond tracking down Marcel Deschamps—and if that trail led her to the Enemy's doorstep, she was as good as dead. My best hope was finding Ada before it was too late. Do that, and maybe I could figure out a way to save her from herself.

Dora offered to show us Ada's old room. I said a couple of photographs might be perfect for the newsletter. We followed her up a narrow flight of steps to the first room on the left. I never would have pegged it as a budding killer's room, but then nothing lately was turning out the way it first appeared. Appropriate, under the circumstances. Her room was white and pink, a poster of a horse on one candy-colored wall, a dresser lined with trophies. Science fair, math camp, debate team. While Caitlin snapped a photo with her phone, I was scouting for anything that might betray the source of her obsession.

All three of my eyes came up empty. In my second sight, the room was as null as the rest of the house, a magical void. If she ever studied her craft in this room, she'd been smart enough to take her tools and books with her when she went off to college.

"Looks like she never left," I said.

"Well, she comes home whenever she can." Dora clasped her hands together, her gaze distant as it fell upon the empty bed. "Feels like she was just here."

"Recently?" I asked.

"She visited over break. Not that we got to see her all that much."

"Girl never stops moving," Jim said, looming in the doorway behind her. "Not for a second."

"Coursework?" I asked.

"Volunteer work." Jim chuckled. "I told her, you're already in college, you don't need to pump up your resume with that stuff. Just get good grades, people'll be falling all over themselves to offer you a job once you graduate. But that's our Ada. She's not happy unless she's making other people happy. She's always been that way."

"What sort of volunteer work?" Caitlin asked.

"Up on the north side of town there's this old theater, the Rialto. It's been boarded up for God knows how long, decades, I think. Anyway, the town wants to rehab the place, turn it into a community center. Ada got herself on the cleanup crew, and she was out there every waking hour for two weeks straight."

Dora bunched up the droopy neck of her sweater in a nervous fist. "I'm just glad she didn't get tetanus. All that old rusty junk in there, I was *sure* she'd get tetanus."

Caitlin and I shared a glance. I flipped my notebook shut.

"A conscientious and civic-minded young lady," I said. "We'll be sure to note that in the press release."

17.

The Rialto had been a palace once. I had never seen her in her prime, but her art-deco corpse had beautiful bones. Plaster swells rose up along hard angles and embraced the theater's body like the rib cage of a whale, bleaching in the sun. A long and tall marquee hung out front, lined with cracked and burned-out bulbs. A ten-yard dumpster stood at the curb. It was piled high with splintered wood and rotten upholstery stretched over the husks of old, broken seats.

"Town's website says this is one of the oldest buildings in Talbot Cove," I said as we circled around the side of the theater. "This, the town hall, and the old paper mill. Every other founders' structure in town has been rehabbed or demolished and rebuilt at least once, but these were the originals. Historical landmarks."

Caitlin craned her neck, looking up to the eaves of the theater. We eased down a narrow strip of alley, more an accident of architecture than actual planning, where scraggly weeds grew wild between the cracked paving stones.

"And this alone was the apple of Ada's inquisitive eye," Caitlin purred. "She found something here. Something that transformed her from a righteous crusader to a murderous one."

An off-the-rack hardware-store padlock and a length of bike chain secured the bar on the backstage door. Kid stuff. Caitlin kept a casual lookout while I jimmied it open, jamming the cheap combination wheel and popping the hasp. The chain slithered free and coiled in the weed-choked dirt at my feet. The door opened with a groan, yawning into darkness.

I tapped my cell phone and turned it into a window of white light. I held it high in my grip, strobing the beam across antique wooden floorboards smeared with arcs of gray dust. Caitlin didn't need the help; her pupils blossomed, motes of copper dancing in the black as her eyes adjusted to the gloom. The stale smell of sawdust and mothballs hung in the musty air.

The boards of the stage creaked under my shoes. I stood at the edge of dead footlights, shining my beam across the empty chasm of the theater. Most of the seating had been stripped away, leaving bare floor and rusted bolts behind, the first stage of renovations to come. I lingered there for a bit. Imagination painted the gallery full, spectators in evening clothes shuffling down the ghostly aisles, filling the seats, the velvet-draped walls catching the din of anticipation and bouncing it off crystal chandeliers. I saw Caitlin in the corner of my eye, staring at me. Must have been something on my face.

"You've never performed for an audience, have you?" she asked.

I twirled my left hand. A playing card, the jack of spades, popped up between my thumb and index finger. Then it danced, spinning across the back of my knuckles, and I caught it before it fell. With a snap of my fingers, the card vanished from sight. No sorcery there, just practice and muscle memory.

"Never did," I said. "Learning stage magic and escape techniques was part of Bentley and Corman's curriculum, though. It's tradition, teaches you discipline and gives you some moves that come in handy long before you get into the real stuff. By the time I hit my mid-twenties, I could have put on a hell of an act if I ever wanted to go straight."

"Did you ever want to?"

I arched an eyebrow. "Go straight? Never. Not even once."

"I know *that*," she said with an impish smile. "Did you ever want to tread the boards?"

I looked out across the imaginary audience.

"I don't know. Always thought it might be fun. I'd probably be too anxious, though. All those eyes watching me?"

"Really. Daniel Faust. Afflicted with stage fright. We've literally killed monsters together."

"Hey, there's scary, then there's *really* scary." I looked her way. "How about you? Ever miss it?"

Caitlin wandered to the edge of the stage. She stretched, languid, as her copper-flecked eyes gazed out into the dark.

"It's been a long, long time," she said. "Last time I stood on a stage was...1926? Or '27? Did a silent film with my friend Lulu. I think there's still a print floating around out there somewhere. I'd like to track it down someday."

"Bet you were a hell of a flapper."

Her laughter echoed in the cavernous gloom.

"I took my tips on style from the very best. Lulu used to say, 'A well-dressed woman, even though her purse is painfully empty, can conquer the world.' And back then, mine was empty indeed."

"Look at you now," I said. "Hound and heir to a prince."

Caitlin played that off with a chuckle as she strolled past me. "The latter means less than you think, pet. I fully expect Prince Sitri to hold his throne until the heat-death of the universe. There will be no royal crown upon my brow. I'm not affronted by that; I rather enjoy being his hound. I'd be bored silly, sitting on a throne all day."

"Workaholic," I said.

"Guilty. Besides, Earth is where the fun is."

Whatever Ada found here, it wasn't on the stage. My phone's light marked a path beyond the proscenium arch and down a sagging flight of stairs that groaned dangerously under our feet. A dead and silent boiler room stood below the theater. Then a long, narrow hall lined with abandoned dressing rooms, most of the doors stripped from their hinges. The furniture was gone too, presumably sold off long ago or junked as scrap by the rehab team. All that remained were solitary cells, thin and moldy carpet, discolored rectangles on the walls where mirrors once hung.

But something still lived here, in the lonely heart of the Rialto.

I wasn't the only one who felt it. At my side, Caitlin's eyes narrowed to slits. There was magic here, old magic, baked into the crumbling brick and haunting this place more than any ghost or roaming phantom. If the spell once cast upon the Rialto was a symphony, what remained was the last fading echo of the final chord. Or the background radiation left behind in the wake of a leaking nuclear bomb.

Fat orange cords ran the length of the hallway; the rehab team had brought in a pair of generators and standing lights to guide their work. They'd been down here. *Ada* had been down here. I paused as a lumpy shadow inside a dressing-room caught my eye. A forty-pound yellow sack of Quikrete slouched three-quarters deflated, next to a plastic bucket, a couple of trowels, and a crumpled plastic tarp.

"Repair work," I murmured.

"That's the plan, no? They're going to have to remodel this place from top to bottom if it's ever going to reopen."

"Yeah, but...not yet. Look at this place; they're still stripping it down, moving the old junk out. And once they are ready to start repairs, it's going to take a heck of a lot more than one bag of mortar and a couple of hand tools."

I led the way down the corridor, checking every doorway, my phone's beam slowly panning across every bare surface.

"This was somebody's personal project," I said.

And there it was, last dressing room on the left. An uneven patch of wall untouched by a speck of paint, where new bricks filled the ghost of an old doorway. Sloppy gray mortar oozed between the slabs, frozen and drooling, an amateur do-it-yourself job by someone who had never worked a day on a real construction site.

"They were in a hurry," Caitlin mused. "Didn't want anyone stumbling upon their discovery. This is the child of panic, not planning."

I pressed my fingers against the rough face of the makeshift wall. It held firm.

"I'll need something to break it down," I said. "I'll scout around upstairs. Maybe they left a crowbar or something—"

"Pet?" Caitlin said. "Step back."

I stepped back. So did she, measuring the distance from the wall to the dressing-room doorway. Then she shot at the masonry like a bullet from a gun, lunging and snapping one foot out in a kick that could crush bones like glass. Bricks shattered under her heel, spitting a cloud of chips and dust as they jarred loose. Two more kicks brought the makeshift construction down in a rumbling cascade, leaving a jagged and gaping hole behind.

"Or," I said, "we could get it open that way."

She gestured to the hole with a courtly bow. I gingerly stepped across the pile of rubble, shining my light into the darkness beyond. The hidden space was smaller than the dressing room, some kind of walk-in storage closet judging from the antique steamer trunks lining the wall. They stood open and empty on their corroded brass hinges, stripped bare of whatever treasures they once held. A projector sat on a dusty wooden table, alongside a trio of aluminum film canisters.

Two of the canisters were empty. The third, still cradling a thick spool of old celluloid, wore a strip of faded yellow tape across its face. Black ink in a feminine hand read *Watch Me*.

That sounded like solid advice. While Caitlin carefully threaded the reel, I ventured back upstairs, hunting for the generators the rehab crew left behind. One still had a cup of gas in the tank. I got it chugging after a few false starts, then spooled down one of the endless snaking extension cords.

The projector rattled to life. A rectangle of light blossomed onto the back wall of the storage room. Black and white numbers counted down, covered in scratches and cigarette burns.

Then we were looking at a dressing room, possibly one of the ones we'd just been standing in, back in the Rialto's heyday. I knew the man in the top hat and tails in a heartbeat: Howard Canton himself, fresh from the stage. He dropped his top hat—the same one I'd held in my hands, the hiding place for his magic wand—onto a makeup vanity and stripped off his tuxedo jacket.

Then came a transformation I didn't expect. Canton's pencil-thin mustache peeled off. So did his bushy eyebrows, revealing the real, slender ones beneath. The dress shirt came unbuttoned, exposing a tight-laced binder before the magician donned a casual robe and tugged the belt snug around her waist.

"Howard Canton...was a woman?" Caitlin whispered.

I'd gotten the generation right, the magician wrong. Ed and Louise Canton were Ada's great-grandparents, and I thought that Ed had taken to the stage under an assumed name. *Louise* was Howard Canton, hiding her identity twice over. Her voice, deep and resonant, warbled across the room on the tinny audio as she addressed the camera's eye.

"If you're watching this..." She trailed off, wearing half of an amused smile. "Well, if you're watching this, I'm dead. Hopefully after a long and happy life, passing peacefully in bed and surrounded by my loved ones, but I don't think that's in the cards. I've run afoul of a man named Damien Ecko. Well, not a—not a *man*, exactly, not anymore. The point is, a confrontation is inevitable, and only one of us is going to survive it. I can't guarantee it'll be me."

That prediction was right on the money. The last time Ecko and I faced off, he'd casually bragged about murdering Canton back in the fifties. At least I could find some pleasing irony in the fact that Canton's own wand, lost for decades, had helped me put the undead bastard down once and for all.

"My name is Louise, but if I do my job right, history will only know me as Howard Canton. I've taken pains you can't imagine to maintain the deception. It's funny. When I was just starting out, I was told—again and again—that audiences wouldn't take a woman seriously upon the stage. I could be the magician's assistant, just not the star of the show. And I would love to tell you that's the reason for my charade. But believe me, if it were an option, I'd rather languish in obscurity as Louise than shine as

Howard. It's galling, working so hard, perfecting an act, never to be recognized or applauded for it."

Louise sat down at the vanity. She paused, gathering her thoughts.

"But someday, most likely when I'm long dead, most likely when you're watching this very recording, a creature is going to come hunting. Hunting for my legacy, and for your inheritance. You see, the Paladin...the Paladin always reincarnates as a woman. And so I've concealed my true identity, in the hopes that the Enemy doesn't pick up my trail. At least not before you do."

18.

"I'm getting ahead of myself," Louise Canton said, her black-and-white image flickering on the wall. "I'll make another recording after this, with all the information you need, all the lore I've gathered. Suffice it to say that a singular story lies at the heart of creation and I am a part of it. And, if I've done my job properly, so are you."

I looked to the empty film canisters on the table. And then to the empty steamer trunks along the wall. *Ada*, I thought. *This is what she saw. This is the moment that changed her life forever.*

"I didn't know what I was, not at first," Louise said. "Ed and I went to Tibet, for our honeymoon. Trip of a lifetime, we thought. I had no idea. Once my eyes were opened to the real world, once I started searching for knowledge—using my touring performances for cover—I learned a few essential facts. First and foremost, the cycle is broken. The Enemy was imprisoned in a pocket world; his captors meant well, they really did, but it's a flawed cage. Eventually, he will break free, and the story will resume as it always has. What the jailers' efforts bought me was time. A life's worth, at least, and that's a luxury I don't think I've ever had."

I was still trying to wrap my head around Canton being the last incarnation of the Paladin. Or, for that matter, the fact that her wand was nestled in a sheath against my inner arm. Did explain why the thing was so goddamn stubborn, though. It knew what I was.

"My plan is in two parts," Louise explained. "The first is perhaps unprecedented, but necessary. Our memories are burned away with every fresh incarnation and I've found no way around that obstacle. My response is a more subtle bit of spellwork. I am attempting to dig a channel for my own...spiritual signature, I could say. A snare—a trap, really—for myself. If it works, and I can only pray it does, then my next incarnation will be born right here in Talbot Cove. More than that, she will be drawn, one way or another, to the psychic beacon I've placed in this room."

She spread her open hands, looking resigned.

"And that, sadly, is the burden I now lay upon your shoulders. If my work is true, then you...well, you're me. The Paladin, reborn. And if the Enemy has been unleashed, it is your destiny to face him in battle. If you fail, this world and everyone in it will die. The fate of countless billions—everyone alive, everyone who *will* ever live—depends on you now."

I felt a ghost at my side. I could almost see her in the corner of my eye: Ada, standing behind the crackling beam of light, watching her great-grandmother on the silver screen. Ada, who had spent her entire life hungering for a crusade, aching for a righteous war to fight.

It was too much. The Paladin's burden was monstrous, too heavy for anyone to carry, let alone a kid like Ada. Most people would break under a weight like that.

"Which brings us to the second part of my plan," Louise said. "With a lifetime to prepare, a life of unexpected peace, I've set myself to solving the problem of the Enemy. Not just defeating him—which means we do this all over again, on some other world, just as we've done since the dawn of time—but *ending* him. My aim is to craft a series of occult devices, devices imbued with my own power and knowledge. I will arm you for victory, and together? Together we will eradicate the Enemy and write the final chapter of this story at long last. We're going to save the multiverse."

A cigarette burn erupted in the heart of the projection, blossoming, igniting Canton's image and swallowing the film until nothing was left but black scratches on silver and the metronome tick of the projector. The tail of the film slipped free of its spool and spun, slapping the air. I flicked a heavy switch and powered the projector down.

"Fuck my life," I muttered.

Caitlin gestured to the empty film canisters. "Presumably, the rest of her brilliant plan was on those. Which Ada took with her, along with anything she found in those two steamer trunks."

"She got the crusade she always wanted. And a license to kill. This explains her newfound thirst for violence. When you're fighting to save the lives of billions, a few random security guards are a small price to pay. My hunch is Ada was always a budding killer; what she needed—what she *wanted*—was an excuse."

"She may spill far more blood before she's finished," Caitlin said.

"And she could be wrong. Look, yes, hell of a coincidence that she's the last Paladin's great-granddaughter. And *if* Louise Canton's ritual worked, if she really got herself to reincarnate in the same tiny backwater town and pull herself toward the messages she left behind, maybe Ada really is her."

"But," Caitlin said.

I held up two fingers. "Ada Lovelace Canton and Harmony Black. Both of them born in Talbot Cove. Both of them drawn to the occult underground. When Ada was five years old, a car wreck killed her parents; when Harmony was five, a home invader killed her father and stole her sister."

"They're both Paladin candidates. And if Harmony is the Paladin..."

"Then Ada's fighting a crusade she can't win. And worse, if Louise really did embed a way to destroy the Enemy into her magic kit, and Ada's running around gathering up all the stray pieces—" I pressed my fingers to my forehead, wincing at a stab of pain behind my eyes. "Jesus, she might as well gift wrap it for him. He'll kill her with a wave of his hand, literally, and scoop it all up from whatever's left of her corpse."

"He's already made some progress on that front," Caitlin

observed. "Considering he's sent Marcel all over the globe to snatch up anything and everything connected to Canton's legacy, clearly the ruse wasn't as airtight as Louise hoped. He knows, and he has a head start on all of us."

Ada might not be the Paladin. Or she might be, and I wasn't sure which possibility I liked less. I was back at that coffeehouse in St. Louis, hearing her old buddy's voice. *If I had to settle on one word to describe her? Just one?*

Dangerous. That girl is dangerous.

I was more or less ready to accept that our world's entire future hinged on a showdown between the Paladin and the Enemy. I was less prepared to face the possibility that the Paladin was a psycho. In the end, though, it didn't change what needed to be done.

"First things first," I said. "We stay the course. We find Ada, get the shipping records, track Marcel down before she does, and kill him. Once I'm not the Thief anymore, I'll have a little more breathing room."

"Agreed," Caitlin said. "And then?"

"The fact is, we've got two strong candidates for the Paladin, but no proof. Hell, it might not be either of them. When it's time for the final showdown, we'll only have one shot, and if we're wrong, bye-bye planet. We *have* to be right about this."

"So we need...some sort of test." Caitlin pursed her lips, thinking. "Which requires knowledge we don't have. Yet."

"I'll rope in Hedy and her people. They might have some insight."

"Have they heard anything from...?" She flicked her gaze skyward.

"From what I gather, everybody on that end of things is working on the Network angle. Pulling Adam off the board—not to mention taking out the King of Rust—opened up one hell of an opportunity. The kind that may not come around for another few thousand years. They're focused on taking advantage while they can and making the most of it. I can't blame 'em, but it means we can't expect any help from on high; they're dealing with a few hundred other problems at the moment."

"The usual state of affairs. Which leaves this matter on our shoulders."

"On the *Paladin's* shoulders," I said. "Which brings us to step three. Once we figure out who she is, we need to make damn sure she wins the big game. If Canton's relics are the key to making that happen, I want them. All of 'em."

"What about the ones already in the Enemy's possession?" she asked.

"Especially those."

"He can rewrite history with a touch of his hand, and you...want to rob him."

"Hey, I did tell Melanie we were going to pull a locust job. I figure Louise Canton's is about seventy years past due." I looked to the silent projector. "The Paladin might have to fight fair. We don't."

"Which doesn't change our present impasse," she said. "The girl is long gone, and I don't see any reason for her to return anytime soon."

Ada was covering, calling home, trying to keep her grandparents in the dark and pretend that everything was fine, a short-term solution at best, and it was only a matter of weeks, days maybe, from coming apart at the seams. A woman with a serious plan would know that. The backlash from the art heist in Detroit, losing five of her crew in a single night, must have rattled her hard.

What else did we know? She'd taken over the Redemption Choir and the last of Sullivan's half-demon flock, and while their aim was different, the methods were the same. She'd learned Sullivan's entire playbook and studied his style before we buried him. If she wasn't sure of her own next move, she'd fall back on his.

"Let's go home," I told Caitlin. "It's just a hunch, but I think I know where she is."

19.

The heavy-metal thrum of the helicopter's blades drowned out the world, even with bulky cans over my ears. The swing arm of the headset hovered in front of my lips as I told the pilot where to fly.

"Little more east. Couple of miles, maybe."

"You got it." His voice crackled in my ears, tinny and muffled. He pulled the stick and our chopper veered out into the desert, toward painted red rocks and distant mountains, the skyline of Las Vegas a remote memory at our backs. We had left the highway, and civilization, soaring through a cloudless blue sky as the morning sun battered down and sent all the night creatures scurrying for cover. All of them except for me, anyway.

Normally if I needed a pilot I'd call the twins. Reluctantly, but I'd call them. The federal dragnet that targeted their old boss and sent him on the run had frozen all of Nicky's assets, including the Vegas sky-tour franchise. Fortunately, the feds auctioned it off for pennies on the dollar and the new owner was open to unusual business proposals. Five hundred bucks bought me two hours of flight time, anywhere I wanted.

I was chasing an old, bad memory. I was pretty sure I knew the way.

A man-made speck rose up in the distance. I lifted a pair of binoculars to my eyes. The shuddering chopper turned the lenses into smeary blurs of light.

"Can you hold her steady?"

"This *is* steady," he said.

Fine. Hovering was a bad idea anyway; there was no justification for it, not out here in the middle of nowhere. I lowered the binoculars to my lap.

"Do me a favor," I said. "Fly that way. Not toward it, but *past* it, like you're on your way somewhere and your flight path's just a coincidence. Pass by close, so I can take a good look real quick, but keep going and don't slow down."

"One flyby, comin' right up." The helicopter leaned as he pulled right, setting his course.

I cupped my hand over my eyes to cut the glare. We'd only get one shot at this; coming back for a second pass would make anyone on the ground suspicious, and I didn't want them any more paranoid than they already were.

The distant heat mirage took on shape and form. Sunbaked adobe walls, wooden struts, a compound ringed with a tall iron fence. The Spanish mission, once long-abandoned, had become Sullivan's base of operations back when he took the Redemption Choir west.

Ada's base now.

A row of pickups gathered dust in the compound lot, sturdy four-by-fours built for the rigors of the desert. A handful of people were offloading wooden crates from a back bed, lugging them into the main building. From this distance, I couldn't make out faces, let alone tell if they were the same thieves who hit Carolyn's place, but in my second sight they glistened like fresh blood on twisted barbed wire. Cambion. Unless there were two packs contending for the Redemption Choir's name, I'd found Ada's home away from home.

* * *

"A handful of rogue cambion are hardly a threat," Caitlin sniffed, following me around the bedroom as I tossed gear onto my storm-gray duvet. "Not to me, and especially not in my father's territory. If they're not entirely feral, there's a good chance they'll stand down at my command."

"I'm not questioning your skills or your authority," I told her.

I ran a fast mental inventory: black turtleneck, black jeans, black running shoes with good padding on the soles. Grappling hook. Where was my grappling hook?

"Then why is this even in question? I should go with you."

The worry at the edge of her voice yanked me from full throttle to a dead stop. I turned to face her, jolted out of my hustle, and looked her in the eye.

"It's not them I'm worried about."

She got it now. Her lips tightened.

"It's me," she said.

"In Michigan, we were just digging for intel. Nothing taken, so no harm, no foul. Tonight is a heist. I'm going in there to steal that shipping laptop, plus any Canton relics I can get my hands on—"

"And your part of the first story is in play," she said. "The Thief returns home victorious, and his lover murders him."

I closed the space between us. One hand slid around Caitlin's hip, pulling her close. My fingertip traced the tight curve of her jaw.

"I know you would never hurt me on purpose," I said. "But we also know the first story is a real fucker when it comes to arranging accidents and twisting people's fates around. So this is the safe way to play it. I'll go in alone, grab the shipping data, and hightail it to wherever Marcel Deschamps is hiding. I put two in his head, boom boom, he's reborn as the Thief on some other planet, and I come home and take us out for a nice dinner to celebrate. Deal?"

She still looked dubious, but her hard edges softened. She reached up, took hold of my finger, and gave it a squeeze.

"Vetri Cucina?" she asked.

"I'll call and make reservations. Do two things for me?"

"Name it."

"Kiss me goodbye?"

"No," Caitlin said.

Then she pulled me in close, our lips met, and the world melted around us until I ran out of breath. Her arms folded around me, hands holding me tight.

"But I'll kiss you goodbye for now," she murmured in my ear. "Just for a little while. What else?"

Reluctantly, slowly, I pulled away. I opened my closet door and dodged to one side as a pair of cardboard boxes, precariously balanced at the top of a mountain of junk, came sliding down to crash at my feet.

"Help me find my grappling hook?"

* * *

Parting took longer than expected. There were more semi-goodbye kisses in between finding the rest of my gear. Then a drive across town to the car-rental place, where I picked up an SUV and drove southwest on I-15. Four more hours on the highway would land me in Los Angeles. My destination was less than halfway there, in the wilderness of the Mojave National Preserve and down twenty minutes of beaten back road. The GPS could only do so much—"secret cambion terrorist hideout" wasn't on the list of destination options—but memory and the flyover would take me most of the way.

The sun sizzled down at the highway's edge, painting the horizon in dirty pink neon. Then came the turquoise blue, and the darkness beyond. I flicked on the SUV's headlights, beams shaking over every bone-jolting lump in the road. More a suggestion of a road now, a trail carved back in the days when only horses rode out this way. A desert pilgrimage for priests and outlaws, looking for redemption or looking for Spanish gold.

I didn't expect to find either one tonight, but I'd take any gold I could get. I'd settle for Marcel's address.

Close enough. The SUV rumbled to a stop and I killed the engine. The headlights died, plunging the world into shadow. My duffel sat on the passenger seat; it rattled as I shouldered it. Then I jumped out and my running shoes touched down on pale hard-packed sand, an astronaut landing on the moon.

Frigid as the moon, too. The desert turned arctic by night. I was thankful for it as I rolled a black ski mask down over my face. The ninja look would be sweltering—and impractical—in the heat of the day, but now I blended with the landscape, a fast-moving shadow. We were far enough from the electric pollution of urban sprawl for the stars to come out; they were a spray of chipped ice, glinting in the black, and thin cold light shone down from a merciless sliver of bone-white moon.

Night critters scurried ahead of me, vanishing into the scrub, off on their own nocturnal missions. A fist-sized spider perched on a rust-red rock and slowly unfolded its furry forelegs, stretching itself awake.

I followed a glow on the western horizon. The glow became standing floodlights. One cast a wide and pale arc across the compound, framing the sleeping trucks. Another illuminated the approach to the iron gates. I went wide, leaving the road and circling the mission grounds.

The beam of a flashlight dropped me to my knees. I froze, low in the sand as a pair of men strolled a slow and lazy patrol just inside the fencing. I held my breath, didn't move, didn't blink until they turned their backs and moved on. Even then, I didn't start moving again until the distant crunch of their footfalls faded to silence.

I studied the mission as I circled around. The main building had inner lights on, shining behind the frosted glass windows. Occasional shadows moved in and out of sight, but I couldn't get a real idea of how many followers Ada had now—or how many of them, like the two on patrol outside, were packing heat. I had brought an insurance policy of my own, a .45 automatic in a calfskin shoulder holster, but trading bullets was a last resort. My goal was the usual on a score like this: get in, get out, and be long gone before anyone figured out they'd been robbed.

That said, a "score like this" usually had more prep time and research involved. Normally I'd want blueprints, multiple angles of surveillance, at least three nights and preferably a week of constant watch on the target. When it came to breaking-and-entering jobs, intel was king; the more you knew before you went in, the more likely you'd come out in one piece.

Time denied me that luxury. Ada wanted Peretsky's shipping

manifest for the same reason I did: to track down Marcel Deschamps. If she hadn't gone after him yet, she was getting ready to, and I couldn't risk losing her trail. Worse, I couldn't risk her running into the Enemy before she was ready. And she was a long way from ready.

I circled to the back, took a knee in the scrub, and waited. I had one eye on my watch. Not the fancy one Caitlin had bought me, but an old workhorse of a Seiko Chronograph on a black leather strap. I had started the stopwatch at the sentries' last pass, and now I waited for their footsteps to return. Eventually they plodded along, and I clicked the stopwatch as they vanished once more.

Twenty minutes. That was how long it took them to make a full circuit of the compound, and how long I had to get over that fence, find a door, finesse the lock, and get inside and out of sight. I was already on the move, keeping low as I eyed the first challenge in my way.

The fence was wrought iron, a good nine feet tall with stout bars and ornamental spikes at the top. I waited ten minutes and burned half my lead as I got ready. Time I couldn't afford, but sound carried in the desert deeps. I wanted the sentries to be as far away as possible, on the opposite side of the compound, before I made my move.

My grappling hook was a three-pronged model for professional climbers, lightweight aluminum and tethered to ten feet of thick hazard-yellow rope. I stepped back a foot, judged its weight in my hand, considered the distance, and gave it a throw. The hook sailed up in the air, came down—and lodged between two spikes with a hard metal *clang* that set my teeth on edge. The sound reverberated like a gunshot, washing out into the darkness as its last throbbing echoes faded into silence.

I froze, ears perked. Listening for voices, running feet, barking dogs. Nothing. I grabbed the dangling rope with both hands, braced one shoe against the thick iron bar, and began to climb. Slow, hand over hand, feeling the clock counting down with every step toward the top. I ignored the stubborn ache in the small of my back. Mantling the fence slowed me down; I slung one leg over, bracing myself with both arms and vividly picturing what a hard landing on those spikes would feel like.

Then came the other leg, and I curled the crook of one arm between the fencing as I pulled the hook free. Then I dropped, free-falling for one breathless stomach-lurching second and landing in a crouch on the hard-packed earth. The rope slithered along with me. One good tug and the far end snaked over the top. I gathered it up as I moved, coiling it around my forearm to keep it from tangling up.

Somewhere off to my right, maybe a hundred yards, I heard voices and footsteps. The tail of a flashlight beam strobed across a stretch of fencing. I cursed under my breath. Either they'd heard something after all or maybe they'd just picked up their pace a little, spurred along by the cold. Either way I had three minutes less than I thought, and now I was jogging as fast as I dared, escaping along a stretch of faded adobe wall and hunting for a way inside.

I found a door, not the one I would have chosen. No window, solid oak, simple lock, but that didn't matter. If I got in and found a cambion convention sitting on the other side or even just a single guard with a fast trigger, blood was going to spill. Nothing I could do about that now, not with the sentries closing in fast. I shouldered the coiled rope, took out my picks, and held my breath. I worked by feel, struggling to roll the tumblers as the flashlight beam loomed closer. They were almost around the corner. I had ten seconds, maybe less, and—the stout iron knob turned in my leather-gloved grip. The door swung inward and I moved with it, flowing like water. I pulled the heavy oak shut behind me, trying not to make a sound, and turned to face whatever was waiting on the other side.

Hopefully not a bullet.

20.

I pressed my back to the oak door and took slow, deep breaths. I eyed the knob, waiting to see if it would jiggle. It held fast. Outside, the sentries moved on by.

I stood at the end of a long, narrow hallway. Dour brown stucco rose up to wooden struts like mine-tunnel supports, decorating the bend of an eleven-foot ceiling. Soft light flickered from wall sconces, bulbs sheathed under old and dusty tulip-petal glass. Voices drifted down the hall, too muffled to make out the words, and thumping electronic music. As I eased closer, one hand drifting toward my holster, gunshots rang out.

Every muscle in my body went tight. I darted to one side, up against the wall and trying to escape the circular glow from the wall sconce, and my automatic was halfway into my hand before I realized the shots weren't real. Hollywood bullets from Hollywood guns, too uniform, too much bass. The clatter of an imaginary submachine gun covered my footsteps as I eased closer, edging toward a wide, open archway halfway down the hall.

Back in his day, Sullivan had converted one of the old chapels into a common room for his cult. That hadn't changed, though the mood had. Last time I'd been here it was all silence, religious pamphlets, and hard-eyed cambion stripping and cleaning their guns. This time the heavy weaponry was up on a sixty-inch television screen. Four of Ada's followers, the oldest in his early twenties and the youngest somewhere north of fifteen, lounged on an L-shaped sectional with their heads turned away from the archway. Their eyes were fixed on the screen, and they passed a big plastic tub of popcorn around, drinking off-brand soda while they watched an alien war unfold. Digital soldiers went down screaming in a trench explosion as one of the cambion showed off his video-game mastery.

Not that they were unarmed. A shotgun sat out on an end table next to a red Solo cup and a half-empty two-liter bottle of Big Fizz Cola. One of the cambion wriggled on the couch, getting comfortable, baring a holstered revolver on his hip.

"Owned," said the cambion with the controller, downing another target. "Owned, owned, *also* owned—"

"You could let one of us play," his buddy with the belt holster groused. He reached for the popcorn bowl.

"Or maybe you could get good, scrub."

"Can't get good if you hog the Playstation all night, now can I?"

I was getting ready to creep past, picking my direction. I could keep moving down the hall or opt for a second passage angling opposite the open archway. Down the hall felt safer, but—

Footsteps. Clicking loud off the weathered floorboards, coming fast from the side passage. Nowhere for me to hide. I jogged back, steps light, and pressed myself flat against the wall.

The new arrival was a woman in her early twenties dressed in a pale pink bathrobe. Not Ada, another of her half-blood followers. She steamed right past me, intent on her target, and stood in the open doorway with her hands on her hips. I quickly took another two side steps to the left, getting out of sight before the gamers turned around.

"You need to turn it down," she said. From her tone, not for the first time tonight. "Ada's trying to sleep."

"Sorry, sorry," someone said. I heard them fumbling for the remote; the gunfire and dramatic music dropped a few notches. Not good. I was counting on the sound to cover my escape. For that matter, the second the new arrival turned around, she'd see me plain as day.

Don't leave, I thought, hunting for a solution. *Not yet.*

I worked the lines of sight. I was behind her now, but if I crossed the archway, the cambion looking her way would spot me. I was safe where I was, but only until she turned. From where I stood I could see the oaken door I'd entered from—too far down the hall to reach, too dangerous to try it—and the end table at the edge of the sofa.

"You should all be asleep," she said. "Tomorrow is a big day."

"You're not sleeping," one of them protested.

She folded her arms across her chest. "*I'm* not sleeping because my room is right above this one, and someone is up past midnight playing *Call of Dumbass* with the speakers cranked up. Gee, I wonder who that could be."

Great. I was already worried about her turning around. Now she was about to lead an entire parade right past me. I had one idea. Desperate, a long shot, but it was all I had. I snaked a single playing card from the deck in my hip pocket, drawing off the top.

"We're not even leaving until, like, noon," the one with the controller protested. I heard a wilting electronic dirge as the distraction brought his electronic alter ego down. "And we can sleep on the plane."

The whole clan was going on a trip together. I had to bet that Ada had gone over the shipping records with a fine-toothed comb and found Marcel's home address. That sealed it: leaving empty-handed wasn't an option. I ran my thumb over the face of the playing card, rousing it awake with a tiny spark of magic, and calculated angles like a billiards player going for a championship-winning shot.

The girl took one angry step into the room, just like I needed her to.

"We are going to *war* tomorrow," she said, "and if you don't take this seriously—"

I flicked the card. It flew high in a blur, arcing past her back and up toward the top of the open arch. Then it sparked off the stucco wall and fired downward. The razor edge of the card sliced through the two-liter bottle of cola. It burst with a bang, spraying soda in a jet across the cambion on the sofa, knocking the big

Solo cup over and spreading a dark amber river across the old floorboards.

"What did you *do?*" one shouted. I heard feet hitting the floor, people jumping up, a remote control clattering.

"Nothing, I didn't even touch it!"

Now it was all muffled curses and scrambling and that was my shot. I held my breath, got low, and lurched past the open archway. I was halfway down the hall, heart pounding louder than the sound of my footsteps, before I was sure they weren't coming after me. They were shouting—at each other, everyone looking to lay blame for the mess on someone else's shoulders—and the noise muffled my retreat until I rounded the next corner and slipped out of sight.

I had counted five cambion so far. I knew she had more than that from the crew at Carolyn's alone, and I had to figure most of the compound was sleeping. I aimed to keep it that way. I passed a few closed doors and eyed the dark cracks beneath the old, warped wood. The slightest creak or groan would give me away if anyone was a light sleeper, so I had to be picky about where I went digging. Where would Ada rest her head?

Easy. If she stayed true to form, she'd be in Sullivan's old quarters. The suite that once belonged to the mission's monsignor. I knew the way.

Through the kitchens, cluttered, counters packed with bulk-sale crackers and chips and an industrial-size tub of generic peanut butter. The revitalized Redemption Choir was feeling more and more like a cash-strapped frat house by the minute. The dining room changed my opinion. Maybe it was the careful row of automatic rifles, new and shiny and clean as a whistle, lining the antique table. Or the open crate at the far side, with some of the artwork from Becker's gallery standing on end and shrouded under rolls of bubble wrap.

An open spiral notebook next to a burner phone told me the score. Phone numbers, checkmarks, and occasional notes like "*wants the Currin, offering $26K.*" Another page listed details of a bank transfer, with routing numbers and a confirmation string. They were slowly moving the stolen art, turning what they could into cash—and from the look of the hardware on display, turning the cash into weapons.

I studied one of the guns. It was a Belgian F2000, a stubby bullpup rifle with a profile straight out of a sci-fi movie. The piece was new, fresh-off-the-assembly-line new, straight from an arms dealer's briefcase. If I was reading the numbers in the ledger right, they'd also paid about ten times what it was worth. I couldn't get a weapon like this from Winslow; then again, he'd be the first to remind me that I didn't need one.

Amateur hour. If they were taking a score, guns were a liability for anything but crowd control. If they were looking to make a kill, they could get just as much done with a few silenced .22s as they could with the action-movie hardware. Don't get me wrong, there's a time for shock and awe, and I'd gone that route a few times myself—but I knew how to do it with a fraction of the budget. I hoped that comment about "going to war tomorrow" was just hyperbole, something for Ada to pump up the troops with.

The alternative was that they'd dug past Marcel already and found the Enemy's lair. And no matter how they imagined that fight was going to go, they were dead wrong.

I kept moving. Up a tight, curving back staircase, winding around lacquered wooden banisters, and up to the second floor.

My destination was the last bedroom at the end of the hall, flanked by closed and darkened doors on either side. I inched along, listening to the floorboards groan under my feet and someone's soft and steady snore. The noise of the television downstairs had faded to silence, and I hoped that didn't mean they were all on their way upstairs. I moved as fast as I dared to, padding my way to the final door.

The cold, antique handle turned in my grip. The threshold drew a line of shadow across the faded wood grain. I eased my way inside.

I stood by the door until my eyes adjusted to the gloom. This was a two-room suite, wide but spartan, with antique furniture that was probably handmade by the monks who once lived here. Sanded, heavy, with Gothic details. Everything smelled like church: old incense smoke and the musk of forest resin. A heavy purse dangled over the back of a chair by its strap. Clothes, eclectic and punk, were draped over a table. More outfits slouched on their hangers, leaning from a half-open wardrobe.

I listened to Ada's shallow breath. She was asleep in Sullivan's old bed, on the far side of an open doorway. Fifteen feet away. I made my way to the writing desk, taking it one slow step at a time.

21.

As I crept toward the desk, a dull glint of metal from the wardrobe caught my eye. Canton's brass pocket watch dangled on a chain from a herringbone vest. The wardrobe was right next to the open doorway and I could see the silhouette of Ada's body under thin covers on the bed just beyond the threshold. Her slender shoulders rose and fell with her sleeping breath.

I took another step. The sanded wood groaned under my heel.

Ada rolled over. She dragged the sheets with her as her legs shifted, and she let out a tiny sigh of discontent. I turned into a statue, crouching down in the dark, straining to see if her eyes were open. After a long, frozen minute, the rasp of gentle snoring washed through the doorway.

I tried again, holding my breath and counting the footsteps. Three, two, one last dangerous step and I was close enough to touch the dangling watch. I gingerly unclipped the chain and took hold of my prize. The metal pulsed against my palm; it was warm, too soft for brass, like the reassuring feel of a friend's hand in mine.

Not the prize I'd come for, though. That was over on the antique writing desk amid a clutter of stray paper and crumpled receipts. I recognized the scratched-up gunmetal clamshell of Peretsky's laptop. I eased my way over, still slow, careful, and added it to my haul. A memo pad sat beside it, with letterhead from a Holiday Inn in Detroit. Nothing written on it, but I peeled off the top couple of pages and took them with me. If she'd been using it to make notes or give her people their marching orders, some quick work with a light pencil might unveil the impressions her words had left behind.

The thin mattress crinkled. Ada rolled under the covers again, going fetal. She whimpered in the dark. It was a tiny, quavering sound, like it should have come from a girl half her age. *Nightmare*, I thought. *What do paladins have nightmares about?*

But she wasn't a paladin, not yet, even if the first story had plans for her. She was too young, too green, too eager, and she was going to get herself and her followers killed. I told myself that I couldn't let that happen; if she really was the capital-P Paladin, going off half-cocked wouldn't just be the end for her, it'd be the end of the world. Watching out for her was just good business on my part. Looking out for my own self-interest.

That was bullshit, though.

If someone handed me ironclad proof that Ada wasn't the Paladin, it wouldn't change a thing. I still wasn't going to let her throw her life away. She was a dumb mixed-up kid who had gotten roped into a destiny way too big for her shoulders—too big for anyone's shoulders—and she didn't deserve that. She'd also earned herself a taste for blood—nothing I could do about that, but maybe I could pull her away from the path she was on before it was too late.

Canton's wand pulsed against my forearm. Not a warning this time. More of an...approving nod?

"Nobody asked your opinion," I breathed, reaching for a stray ballpoint pen. "Jerk-ass wand."

I uncapped the pen and wrote a quick note on the hotel stationery.

Ada,

Hopefully taking the laptop will slow you down a little, but I have to figure you already cracked it open and you know where Marcel is. We're on the same trail, for slightly different reasons. I need you to stand down. I know you think you've got a destiny to fulfill. Maybe you do, but you aren't ready for this fight.

I touched the pen to the pad, thinking, trying to come up with anything that might break her stride. I decided on the truth.

Look up the name Cameron Drake. You'll find a boy who died in Derry, PA, when he was twelve, killed by a freight train. But I knew him. I knew him last year, when he was a lottery winner living on a ranch in Texas. The Enemy laid one hand on him and rewrote his entire life's history. Edited him out of reality, and now people who were his friends for years can't remember that he ever existed. That is the kind of power you're up against.

I know you won't like hearing this. When I was your age, once I decided on something, nobody could tell me a damn thing to change my mind. And I got hurt, a lot, because of it. And I got other people hurt. You don't have to make my mistakes.

I stared at the words on the page. More of a confessional than I planned on writing, but there it was.

Anyway, I added, *I stole your watch.*

If you want it back, come and find me. We can sit down and have a talk about your higher calling. I'll be waiting.

—D.F.

I left it at that. She whimpered again as I slipped out of her suite. The dreaming Paladin fighting some invisible war, all alone on the battlefield.

Getting out was easier than getting in. The common room downstairs was dark, all the choirboys and girls gone to sleep, and even the sentries outside had tucked in for a few hours' rest with no one taking their place on patrol. That gave me a moment's pause. Could have just been sloppy procedure, which wouldn't surprise me, but another possibility came to mind: whatever they had planned for tomorrow, this impending "war," Ada needed all hands on deck.

The sun had returned to the desert, tangerine rays of dawn breaking over the rust-red mountains. I navigated across the scrub on my way back to the rental car, listening to the warbling trill of morning birds and the leather-winged rustle of insects. My duffel bag had gotten twenty pounds heavier on the walk, just like my eyelids. I thought about curling up in the back seat and catching a quick catnap, but sleep was a luxury right now. My work for the day was only getting started.

* * *

The Tiger's Garden didn't look like much. Rickety tables, a three-seater bar lit by dangling paper lanterns, thin and cigarette-burned carpet—it was a shoebox of an Indian restaurant trapped somewhere in the early 1970s. All the same, it was the most exclusive club in town. The rich aroma of tandoori chicken and fresh-baked naan threw a lasso around my sleepy brain and tugged me inside. Corman and Mama Margaux were already there, sitting down to breakfast and drinking their first cocktails of the day. Amar, the Garden's sole visible employee, swung by with one for me, too: the Bloody Mary I was just about to order.

"And the pencil you'll be wanting, sir," he said. He handed over a bright green #2, sharpened to a dagger point.

Corman gave me a wave. "Hey, kiddo. Grab some grub. Bentley can't make it; he's watching the bookstore this morning. It's inventory day. So how'd you do out there?"

I fell into a chair and dropped my duffel at my feet. Amar had laid out four place settings, and I glanced to the restaurant door. I'd been hoping to see five or six.

"Jennifer on her way?" I asked. "And good. It went good. I think."

"Jennifer's with Caitlin," Margaux said. "She asked us to tell you to call her. *Call* her, not go see her—said that was important. What's the pencil for? And have you been sleeping any? You look dog-tired."

I leaned over, unzipped the duffel, and pulled out the stolen pages from Ada's hotel stationery. The tip of the pencil whisked lightly in my hand, drawing a slow and steady charcoal arc across the blank paper.

"Old trick to pick up impressions on a notepad," I said. "If somebody writes with a heavy enough hand, sometimes you can get lucky."

I wasn't going to, not today. The pencil etching highlighted faint grooves in the page, the traces of Ada's pen, but nothing I could use. Stray numbers, part of an address, mostly too blurry to make out. I put the pages aside and took out Peretsky's laptop.

"Didn't answer my second question," Margaux said.

I lifted my glass. "I did not answer it. This is true. Hey, get ready to celebrate."

She squinted at me. "Celebrate what?"

"If it's not for Bentley or Jennifer, I think we're about to celebrate that mysterious fourth place setting."

The jingle of the bell above the front door didn't disappoint me. Melanie stumbled in, blinking, a little wobbly on her feet.

"This," she said, "is not exactly what I expected."

"Hey, that's our girl," Corman called out. "Sit down, get yourself some breakfast. Best food on Fremont Street, hands down."

Margaux looked between Melanie and me. "Her first time?"

"Her first time," I said.

Amar swooped in with his brass-rimmed tray and held it out to her.

"Your Mountain Dew, miss."

Melanie took the tall glass, uncertain, ice cubes bobbing in a fizzy sea of green. "But how did you know I wanted—"

He was already gone, vanishing through the swinging door behind the bar. I pulled out the fourth chair for her.

"Don't ask. He won't tell. Nobody really knows how it works."

"Jennifer says she knows," Margaux observed.

"Jennifer just waves her hands and says 'quantum mechanics' a lot." I looked to Melanie. "Two rules in here. No violence, and never try to open the windows."

Melanie cast a nervous glance to the back wall and the row of closed wooden shutters, each one latched tight.

"I get the no-fighting rule," she said, "but what's with the windows?"

"This place isn't exactly *on* Fremont," Corman said. "And

seeing as the Garden doesn't show up on any map of the city, not to mention being a little unstuck in time..."

"Whatever's out there, the story goes, it's nothing decent folk want to see," Margaux said. "*Or present company.*"

I clinked my glass against Melanie's. "The important thing is, this is a milestone. The Tiger's Garden chooses its own clientele. You only get in if it wants to let you in. And nobody's a hundred-percent certain how it picks the guest list, but one thing is always true: only real, practicing magicians ever find the place."

"Congrats, kiddo," Corman said. "You made the grade. Now keep studying."

I opened up the stolen laptop. Margaux got her phone out and rested it alongside the tandoori dish. It rang twice before Jennifer's drawl crackled over the speaker.

"Hey, y'all."

"Jen," I said. "Mama says you're with Cait?"

"Girls' day out," Caitlin chimed in. I heard traffic noises on the other end of the line and the steady purr of her car's engine.

"Doing what?"

"Not being anywhere near you," Jennifer said. "Sugar, the Thief's story is in play and you just came back from a heist. Unless you got your keister kicked again—"

"I did not," I said, trying not to sound as indignant as I felt. "Things went pretty well, actually."

"—then you're radioactive until proven otherwise. We're tryin' to keep you alive right now."

"Yeah," I said, "radioactive around Caitlin. What are you worried about?"

"Did you forget that we used to date?"

"Sure. For, like, two weeks before we broke up."

"Well, 'the Thief's lover' doesn't specify a time frame or an active relationship status," Jennifer said, "and you and me did more than share a milkshake and draw hearts on a frosted window. Until you break this thing, you gotta stay away from anybody you ever did the devil's dance with."

I stared at the phone. "The devil's dance?"

"You know. Bumping uglies? Extreme heavy petting? Holding a joint session of Congress and establishing a bipartisan resolution?"

"Hold up," Melanie said. "So this curse can affect any woman he ever slept with?"

"Anyone he ever slept with," Caitlin said.

"On that note," Jennifer added, "you should steer clear of the twins, too."

"I never slept with the twins," I said.

"They're tellin' everybody you did. Allegedly they were *not* impressed."

I felt a headache coming on.

"No, they're confused about a conversation we had at the funeral—you know what? Not even relevant. Let's move on. Please?"

Ada had done the hard work for us. Whatever kind of security Peretsky had on his laptop, she'd cracked it wide open. I paged through shipping manifests, read along copies of labels, hunting along a slender window of time. It wasn't hard to match up Marcel's heist of the antique trunk in Boston with the two-hundred-pound package Peretsky had transported three days later.

A home address would have been nice, but I knew better than to hope for miracles. Canton's old trunk had been shipped to a private box at a franchise called Mailboxes and More in a Scottsdale, Arizona, strip mall. I checked a map, then I checked my watch.

"About a five-hour drive," I said. "If we leave right now, we can make it by early afternoon."

Melanie perked up. "You're bringing me with?"

"We know what box Marcel rented. Now we need all of his customer information: what address and phone number he signed up with, his credit card receipt, the works. I'm sure most of it is bogus, but if he made a single slip, we'll have him dead to rights."

"What about Ada and her gang?" Corman asked.

"They've got the same intel we do, and they're on the same hunt. Have to assume they'll be paying a visit." I looked to Melanie. "We just have to get there first."

22.

My best-laid plans didn't account for a tractor-trailer crash on US-93. We sat in motionless traffic, the rented SUV's engine making clunky little ticking sounds as I drummed my fingers on the steering wheel.

"If we're lucky, they took the same road," I said. "If we're *really* lucky, Ada took my note to heart and decided to stay home."

Melanie shifted in the passenger seat. She shot a look at the side mirror, gazing back at the sea of cars behind us. "And if we're not?"

It sounded like Ada was bringing her entire crew. Overkill for a job like this, but if she expected to find Marcel's hideout somewhere nearby, like I did, it made sense. Get it all done in one trip.

"We'll scope it out when we get there and play it by ear."

I drummed louder, like the rhythm could jolt my thoughts into order. I had filled Melanie in on almost everything. Almost. An unspoken part of the conversation had been lurking around the edges of our drive, an obligation waiting to be fulfilled. I needed to stop putting it off.

"It probably won't even come up," I said, "but if it does, I don't want it to hit you by surprise, okay?"

Her eyebrows furrowed. "What's that?"

"Ada's crew. They're calling themselves the Redemption Choir."

Melanie's pale cheeks faded one shade closer to eggshell white. She sank in her seat.

"But they're not—I mean, they're not really..." She trailed off.

"Near as I can tell, Ada studied Sullivan's bag of tricks back in St. Louis. Took a master class from him, call it Demagoguery 101. When we broke the Choir up, she gathered the diehards and started hunting for fresh recruits."

"So everything that happened back then," she said, her voice softer now. "We didn't even win. It was for nothing."

"No." I reached over and took her hand. She looked like she was trying to shrink to nothing, to fade into her seat and vanish. I needed to pull her back. "*No.* It wasn't for nothing. Sullivan is dead and gone."

And so was Melanie's father.

He'd betrayed us all, turning double agent and working to deliver the Ring of Solomon into his master's hands. All for Melanie. Trying to "save" his half-demon daughter. Turned out she didn't need saving from anyone but him.

Only three people alive knew what happened that night, behind closed doors in an abandoned brothel. Me, Caitlin, and Emma, Melanie's mom. The official story was that I killed the man. He jumped me from behind with a knife, and I took him out in self-defense. That was the story we decided on, to save Melanie from the truth.

The truth was he died empty-handed and down on his knees, begging for mercy. Emma snapped his neck. Melanie didn't need to know, didn't need to see her mother like that, and I could take the weight of the kill. So I took it.

"The people you convinced that night," I said, "the cambion who turned their backs on Sullivan—they're doing all right now, yeah? Their lives are better now."

Melanie nodded, slow. "Yeah. I mean, I check in on a few of them. Sometimes."

I knew for a fact that she checked on every single one of them once a month, like she was their self-appointed social service worker.

"So not for nothing," I said.

It took another hour before emergency crews hauled the rolled-over semi off to the shoulder. We eased on by, the rubberneckers ahead of us leaning on their brakes for a better look. I saw all I needed to: smashed windows, a plume of gray smoke drifting from the twisted guts of the engine, a fleck of something rusty on the back of an empty driver's seat. Some trucker had gotten up that morning, maybe eaten breakfast, and gotten on the road and down to business just like he'd done a thousand times before. Nobody expected random violence, random death out of nowhere.

Hopefully that wasn't a sign of things to come.

We rolled into Scottsdale just after dark. I put Melanie on lookout duty as I cruised past the strip mall. Then I drove two more blocks, turned around, and did it again. On the third pass I pulled into the parking lot. Plenty of spots to choose from; the place was dead, a few of the shops still open for another couple of hours, but only a pizza parlor a few doors down was doing any kind of real business. No signs of trouble, no red flags. If the Redemption Choir had already been here, they'd come—and gone—in peace.

I parked close but not too close, midway up the lot with Mailboxes and More in sight. The glass box, lit from within, gave us a diorama-perfect picture of what waited inside. A long curving customer-service counter, a bank of mailboxes, and a bulky copy machine rounded out the front. It looked like half the space was concealed behind the front desk, dedicated to storing packages and sorting mail. Two employees, a young woman in overalls and an older, white-haired man, were on duty. "On duty," in this case, meant the man mostly puttered around in back while the woman hovered behind the register and played a game on her cell phone. I gave it ten minutes, watching for anything hinky, and they didn't have a single customer.

"So what's the plan?" Melanie asked. "Will they give us Marcel's info if we, you know, offer them some money or something?"

Bless her heart, she didn't even want to say the word "bribe." For the thousandth time I wondered if I was going to ruin her. Then I thought about the kind of teacher her mother would have insisted on hooking her up with if I hadn't stepped in. I could give Melanie the survival skills she needed without dragging her that far down into the dark. Just far enough to get the job done.

"Normally that would be our best and easiest bet," I said. "They're retail employees in a strip mall. Whatever they're getting paid, it's not enough to buy loyalty. But. That's not going to work in this situation. Can you guess why?"

I gave her time to think about it. I followed her line of sight; she was focused on the two clerks, taking in their patterns, their body language.

"They're keeping each other honest," Melanie said. "We wouldn't be able to approach either of them without the other one overhearing. And if one takes the money and the other narcs to their boss, they'll get fired."

That little rush of pride hit me just right. A man could get hooked on softer drugs than that.

"And that's a bingo," I told her. "Even if someone's willing to take a bribe, they'll never go for it if it feels like too much of a risk. If you're angling to deliver a payoff, always get your target alone before you make the sales pitch."

"Which we can't do. So what now?"

I glanced at the dashboard clock. "They close in about an hour and change. How do you like your pizza? You don't get any weird toppings on it, do you?"

"Is pineapple weird?"

"I think you know the answer to that, and you should be ashamed of yourself. Okay, so we'll get *two* pizzas, take our time eating dinner, and come back after they lock up for the night. As B&E jobs go, this shouldn't be too hard. First, though, we need recon. You up for a little challenge?"

Trick question. I knew she was up for it. She squared her shoulders and gave me a steely nod.

"Go on in," I told her, "and make like you're interested in opening a box. Chat 'em up, get the details, keep them talking for a few minutes. And while you do—"

"Locks and alarms?" she asked.

"Locks and alarms. Cameras, too, if they have any. Figure out what we'll be dealing with in there. If you happen to get a look in back, even better, but don't break your neck. It's always better to leave a place empty-handed than to leave looking suspicious."

"On it," she said. I watched her go.

Through the glass, she looked like a natural. All smiles at the front desk, cool and casual, animated as she asked questions. She pointed at one of the displays; the clerk turned around and Melanie's gaze lifted to carefully scan the walls. Breaking the job down into pieces, covering every angle, just like I taught her.

The absence of headlights caught my attention. A dirt-brown Toyota van cruised through the parking lot, dusty and running dark, too late at night for the driver not to notice their beams were off. I slouched low in my seat. The van reached the far end of the lot, paused, and then circled back for another pass.

I was already dialing Melanie's number. Time to scrub it and go. I didn't know if the van was a threat, couldn't even see the driver's face, but it was out of place and that was all the reason I needed to call things off. Noticing smaller details than that had saved my life more than once.

She didn't answer, didn't even reach for her purse. She was in the zone, quizzing the desk clerk and casing the place with stolen glances. I got her voicemail, hung up, and tried again.

The van stopped out front, cutting off my line of sight.

"Hello?" Melanie answered.

I had my phone cradled between my shoulder and my cheek, freeing up my hands so I could check the load in my .45 automatic.

"Get out," I said. "Tell the clerk this call is a family emergency and get out of there *now*. Don't ask questions. Just do it."

The back doors of the van opened up. Ada was the first to jump down, her slender frame draped in a bulky brown leather duster adorned with studs and brasswork, like a cowboy who read too many Jules Verne novels. Her hands clenched and unclenched, sheathed in her homemade fingerless gauntlets. Three choirboys backed her up. Their overcoats bulged with too much hardware and too much nervous energy.

The van took off the second the doors slammed shut. It rolled to the end of the strip mall and pulled a hard left, down an alley for delivery traffic. Circling around to the back doors, I had to figure. I reached up, killing the dome light so it wouldn't ignite when I opened the SUV's door, and slid from the driver's seat in a crouch.

Melanie almost made it out. She ran into Ada at the door. Ada turned her around, showing her something under her duster, and ushered her back inside. The desk clerk put her hands in the air. The last of the choirboys locked the door behind him, flipped the Open sign to Closed, and reached up to grab hold of a security grate. A wall of chain rattled down, sealing off the front entrance.

I was right. They were planning to go out the back door. The question was whether they'd do it with their hostages alive or dead. So far, Ada's death tally included an armed guard at an art gallery that catered to the infernal elite and two more security thugs at a mob-owned storage depot. Unnecessary kills, but I could see some wiggle room for a self-defense argument. Big gulf between that and shooting a pair of unarmed retail clerks.

And Melanie.

I wanted to think Ada was better than that, that *she* wanted to be better than that, but I couldn't shake one undeniable fact: she and her crew weren't wearing masks. Either she didn't care about the cops getting her description, she was too sloppy to have thought about it...or she wasn't planning on leaving any witnesses behind.

Ada and her men were herding everyone into the back of the shop. I broke into a dead sprint. Faster than I should have, reckless as I veered down the side alley and past a sleeping delivery truck.

I had sent Melanie into the lion's den. Whatever happened to her tonight, that was on me. I'd already lost one apprentice, and I could still see her dying moments when I closed my eyes. That was my limit, all the ghosts I could carry with me.

I couldn't lose Melanie, too.

23.

The van was parked out back, lengthwise along a loading dock. The back door of Mailboxes and More stood propped open, held fast with a loose brick, a long rectangle of light streaming out into the alley. The driver was puttering with the rear doors of the van, rummaging around inside.

I forced my legs to stop. My heart kept running, hammering. I took a deep breath and moved in a loping panther stride, footfalls light on the rough asphalt, finger on the trigger of my .45.

The choirboy heard me coming at the last second. Too late. He had just started turning around when I snaked my arm around his neck and pressed the barrel of the gun to his temple. I squeezed his throat in the crook of my arm, not hard enough to choke him out, just enough to get his undivided attention. My voice was a whisper in his ear.

"You make a sound, you die. Nod if you understand."

He nodded, fast.

"Do you know who I am?" I breathed.

Another nod. Good.

"You're going to do exactly what I tell you, exactly how I tell you to do it. And if I suspect, for even a second, that you're *thinking* about not cooperating, I'll kill you where you stand. Got it?"

He got it. More important, he believed me. A bad reputation could be an asset sometimes. I pulled him back from the van and steered him toward the spill of light. As we neared, I heard voices from inside. Voices and cardboard-tearing sounds.

"—anything we can sell," Ada was saying. "Electronics, jewelry—if we can put it on eBay, add it to the pile."

"Got a car stereo over here," one of her choirboys called out.

I didn't hear Melanie or the clerks. Then again, I didn't hear any gunshots either. Yet. My jaw clenched so tight I could feel it starting to tremble. I kept my own hostage right in front of me, a full-body shield as I nudged him over the threshold and into the storage room beyond.

Ada was supervising, pacing, while one of her boys looted the mailboxes and another brandished a box cutter, halfway into gutting a small mountain of packages. The third cradled a sleek bullpup rifle in his hands, standing over the captives. They'd lined up Melanie and the two clerks, putting them down on their knees against the cinder-block wall, fingers laced behind their necks. Melanie looked stoic, eyes hard, scared but keeping it together. The clerks had sweaty faces, the old man looking like he was about to lose his dinner.

"Let's not be stupid," I announced. "Weapons on the ground. Now."

The cambion with the box cutter pointed it at me. Then at Melanie.

"I told you," he said to Ada. "I *told* you I recognized this bitch. She was there, the night they murdered Sullivan."

"Please," gasped my hostage, straining to breathe with the crook of my arm tight around his throat. "Do what he says. He'll kill me."

"No, he won't," Ada said.

She made the tiniest gesture, a flutter of her gloved hand. The choirboy with the rifle brought it to his shoulder. Not aiming at me, aiming at Melanie's head, point-blank.

"He's going to let you go," she said, "and then he's going to lower that gun."

The cambion at the letter boxes tossed a sheaf of envelopes to the floor and unholstered his pistol. The one with the box cutter traded his blade for another bullpup rifle, scooping it up off the service counter. I ran the math. Three visible firearms, and Ada could do more damage with her bare hands.

But the only weapon I cared about was the one trained on Melanie. And Ada knew it.

Giving up wasn't an option. For all I knew, they'd gun us both down the second I surrendered what little leverage I had. For now I needed to keep Ada talking and look for another way out.

I needed to get into her head.

I nodded to the wreckage, the pile of broken cardboard boxes and packing peanuts strewn around her buddy's feet. "I thought you were here to get Marcel Deschamps's address. What's with the smash-and-grab?"

"It's called seizing an opportunity." Ada wrinkled her nose at me. "We need operating capital and we're already here, so why wouldn't we take what we can?"

I glanced at the haul by the door. A stereo, a generic Blu-ray player, a couple of video games in glossy shrink-wrap.

"Oh, yeah, this is a regular Fort Knox," I said. "Bring all that crap to a pawn shop and you'll walk out with *maybe* fifty bucks in cash."

"Every little bit counts," she said.

"And to get that fifty bucks, you just committed at least a dozen counts of mail theft. You know what that is? That's federal. Felony offense, five years per count. The local cops don't come after you for mail theft; the Postal Inspection Service does, and don't let the name fool you. *I* don't fuck with the Postal Inspection Service, and I've crossed the actual FBI before."

I couldn't read her. Not yet. Ada's face was a blank mask, a wall of detachment.

"What's your point?" she asked me.

"My point is that you don't know what the hell you're doing. Same as in Detroit. You just had to grab some free art when you broke in to steal Canton's watch, didn't you? And the blowback from that 'seized opportunity' got five of your followers killed by the Chainmen. Your fighting skills are great. Strategy, not so much. Did you even know who you were robbing?"

"Of course we knew," snarled the gunman standing over Melanie. He was talking to me but his eyes were on her, targeting her upturned face down his iron sights. "We were striking a blow against the infernal courts and their boot-licking lackeys. Lackeys like you."

"Well, as long as your friends died for the revolution, I guess that makes it all right, comrade."

His rifle swung up. So did the other one, ten feet away on the opposite side, bracketing me in their sights. Good. I wanted them aiming at me, not Melanie. That was a start. My prisoner squirmed as much as he dared with my pistol's muzzle pressed tight against his forehead. He wasn't much of a shield—I suspected the ammo in those rifles would chew right through his body on its way to mine without even slowing down—but I could still hope the choirboys wouldn't murder one of their own.

"They died," Ada said, "doing the right thing. Something you know very little about."

"I know about Talbot Cove," I said.

Her brow furrowed. Uncertain now.

"I know about Louise Canton," I continued, pressing the advantage. "I know that you think you're the Paladin—"

"I *am* the Paladin."

"What about Harmony Black?"

Her head gave a little twitch. "Who?"

"My point exactly. Okay, try this on for size: you know certain things are always true in every incarnation, right? The Paladin is always a woman and always touched by some kind of family tragedy as a child. If Louise's ritual actually worked, we also know she was reborn in Talbot Cove."

"And I qualify, on every point," she said.

"So does a woman named Harmony Black," I said. "On every point. Maybe you should meet up and find out if you really are who you think you are. And believe me, I've met her. If anybody gets to call herself a paladin, it's her goody-two-shoes ass. At least she doesn't go around killing innocent people."

"Innocent?" Ada stared at me. "I've never hurt an innocent person in my life. I'm the *hero* of this story. Literally."

My gaze flicked, pointedly, to the hostages along the cinder-block wall.

"They're fine," she said.

"For now. You honestly expect me to believe you busted in here to strong-arm the place, showed these people your faces, and you were going to let them live to talk about it?"

"We were going," she said, "*are* going to take them with us. Unharmed. Once we find Marcel, we'll find the rest of the Canton family artifacts. Once we do that, the Enemy's days are numbered. And yes, I got your note. Don't you understand? I planned for this in my last life, when I was my own great-grandmother. All of this. I'll be unstoppable. And then I'll save the world."

Her delusions of grandeur aside, I was stuck on the first part.

"You were going to take three hostages," I said, "kidnap them—"

"As insurance, just in case the law tries to stop us. Leverage. They aren't going to be hurt under any circumstances."

"Kidnap them, and take them *across state lines*. Do you even..." I had to search for the words to express how floored I was. "So you took what could have been a simple in-and-out ten-minute burglary and turned it into a situation that's going to bring the state cops, the postal inspectors, *and* the FBI down on your heads. All at the same time. For three hostages you don't need and fifty bucks worth of stolen crap. You know, I'm trying to save you from yourself here, but you're making it *real* hard."

Something changed in her demeanor. Her eyes went soft, her shoulders down, the aggression draining away. Her gaze met mine, unblinking, a silent command to hold eye contact.

"But I don't need to be saved," she said. "You do."

"Me," I said.

"You."

She took a step toward me. One hand gracefully lifted, the circuitry on her fingerless glove gleaming as she curled her fingers in a gentle beckon.

"I studied up on you," she said. "I know where you came from. A broken home, a broken life."

"I found a home," I told her.

"You've lived a life of violence, of crime, of depravity. But it isn't your fault."

"Of course it is," I said. "I don't pawn my shit off on other people."

"No." Her head swayed, slow, serpentine, as she stared into my eyes. "It isn't your fault. You've been manipulated, pushed into the gutter, denied the opportunities that would have made you a better man. But I can change all of that."

"Really," I said.

The word didn't come out right. I meant to say it with bravado, maybe a little scorn. It sounded like more of a question.

"Really," she echoed. "And you *want* to be a better man. I know this about you. Tell me: you've been fighting against the Enemy on your own, haven't you?"

"That's got nothing to do with being 'a better man,' whatever that even means. The Enemy's looking to turn this planet into a smoking cinder. You'd have to be crazy *not* to fight."

"Crazy. Yes." She wagged a finger at me. "And you aren't crazy. You're smart. Logical. I like that about you."

I didn't understand what was happening here. I just knew I didn't like it. In the corners of my vision I could see her cambion followers standing transfixed, hanging on Ada's every word.

And so was I.

"You know how the first story works," she said. "And you know that the Paladin is this world's only hope. You're strong. Strong magic, strong will. You could be a game changer. Logic tells us that you should throw your support behind the Paladin. Logic says you have no other choice. Join me. Let's work together. We'll beat him. Together. Don't you want that? All you have to do is put the gun down. Put the gun down and say *yes*."

She said all the right things. She delivered patter more polished than a sideshow barker while her big soft eyes roped me in and pried my heart open wide. She was reasonable, kind, tender even. I wanted to believe her. God, I wanted to believe her.

"You aren't responsible for the things you've done," she said. "But even you can be redeemed. You can be saved. Let me save you."

And suddenly it wasn't hard to look away. It wasn't hard because Melanie was on her knees against the wall with her hands behind her neck, trying to hide her fear, and I knew what the truth was. I was absolutely responsible. For myself, and for her. For my family, for everyone who counted on me to make the right call when the world went dark and sideways. I looked back to Ada.

"You're good," I said. "Better than Sullivan ever was. But like I told you, I don't pawn my shit off on other people. I'm responsible for everything I've ever done."

"You can still be redeemed," she told me.

"Ada, if I was a hundred-percent certain you were the Paladin—and I'm not—I still wouldn't join you. Because you aren't ready. You're going to die out there, and your followers are going to die with you."

"Then *help* us."

"I'm trying to. But before I can do that, you've got to slow the hell down, stop going off half-cocked, and listen to me. You have to be prepared to accept that you might not be the chosen one, okay?"

Her beckoning hand fell limp to her side. Her voice was softer now, as if her words were meant for me alone.

"I spent my entire life looking for my crusade," she said. "Not a crusade. My crusade. I knew it was out there. I knew that I was born to a higher purpose. Can you imagine what that's like? God, can you? Always restless, hunting, aching for that one...that one ray of light from the heavens, to point you in the right direction. Then, one day, I saw that ray come down. I saw the light, Daniel."

Her eyes glistened, damp under the flickering lights.

"And I know," she said, "as surely as we are standing here, as surely as I live and breathe, that I am the Paladin. I am who I say that I am."

"Even if you are," I said. "You're still not ready for this fight."

Doubt. That was the weapon I needed right now. I didn't want to break her, didn't want to tear her down, but if I didn't throw her off her relentless stride she'd march right off the side of a cliff. I had a plan, a desperate hazy shred of a plan, and only one shot at pulling it off.

"What if I could prove it?" I asked. "What if I could prove, right here and now, that you aren't prepared to face the Enemy? Would you listen then?"

She tilted her head, eyes a little sharper now. The tip of her nose twitched like she was trying to smell my intentions.

"Show me," she said.

Carefully, I uncoiled my arm from my hostage's neck. I gave him a little push, nudging him to go and stand with the rest of the choirboys.

Then I pulled back the flap of my jacket and holstered my gun.

24.

My former captive made his unsteady way across the room. He rubbed his throat and stood at Ada's shoulder. I had three guns pointed at me—two military-grade rifles and a stubby little pistol that could kill me just as dead, just as fast—but that was exactly how I wanted it. I looked to Melanie. Then I pointedly flicked my gaze toward the two hostages, pale and trembling, lined up on their knees beside her.

Melanie's eyes narrowed, and she gave me an almost imperceptible nod. Message received. She knew I was about to make a move, and she knew what I wanted her to do.

I flexed my wrist. The spring-loaded sheath up my sleeve released, and Canton's wand dropped into my outstretched hand. I caught it, the ebony shaft cool and smooth in my grip. Its ivory bone caps glinted under the lights. Ada stared at it like a dragon spotting a juicy pile of gold.

"My wand," she said.

"Louise Canton's wand."

"I am Louise Canton. I mean was. You know how this works." She held out her hand. "I need that back. And my watch. Please."

"Do you know what the wand does?"

Not entirely a rhetorical question. I'd sussed out a few of its tricks—when it felt like working for me, which it usually didn't—but I suspected I hadn't seen everything it was capable of yet.

"Marvelous things," Ada said.

"Not sure if you're aware of it, but you can't just use this thing anytime you like. Louise put a sort of...safety protocol on it. The wand won't do anything to protect the person who wields it. When she went to face Damien Ecko, she didn't even bring it with her."

"Of course," Ada said, like I'd just stated the obvious. "Most of the relics work that way, the ones that aren't purely defensive, like my pocket watch. I had to make sure they wouldn't be misused if they fell into the wrong hands before I reincarnated. Do you know what someone with bad intentions could do with that kind of power?"

I might have had an idea or two.

Ada put her hands on her hips, chin high, proud as a peacock. "The wand was built for a champion, someone born to fight the powers of darkness. Like I told you, I'm the hero of this story. I'm here to save the world."

I kept my free hand low, tilted toward Melanie. I flashed five fingers. Then, after a slow deep breath, four. In my peripheral vision I saw her shift on her knees, getting ready to move.

"Then I've got one question," I said to Ada. "And I hope you'll take it to heart."

"Ask me anything," she said.

Three. Two. One.

My fingertips rippled with magic as I mentally *pulled*, and my deck of cards streamed from my pocket into my open palm. Then I flung them out, sending them scattering across the room far and wide, and twirled Canton's wand.

Canton's Multiplication wove fifty-two cards into a hundred, two hundred, five hundred and twenty as the pasteboard danced and flurried in a whirlwind. Melanie jumped to her feet, grabbed the shell-shocked hostages by their arms, and hauled them toward the back door. I held my ground and played conductor of the fluttering orchestra. One of Ada's men took a knee, struggling to see through the hail of flying cards, and targeted the fleeing hostages through his scope. I flicked the wand toward him. A fresh storm blew in, diamonds and hearts spinning in a tornado to block his line of sight.

"If you're the good guy," I shouted over the ocean-wave crash of the cards, "why is the wand protecting these people from *you*?"

Before I turned to run, just for a moment, the storm of cards parted and I saw Ada's face. She stood there, frozen, trembling like my question had speared her to the core.

Then the moment passed and her eyes went cold. Her chin lifted and her lips formed a tight, hard line. I'd seen that face before. On Sullivan. I knew what it meant. It meant she'd decided that she couldn't be wrong because she *wouldn't* be wrong, and all the proof in the world would only make her dig her heels in harder.

I'd done all I could. I fell back, out the door, into the alley, turning and breaking into a run as the card-storm shattered. I heard the waterfall cascade as it all tumbled down. Then shouts and pounding footsteps. I drew my .45, spun, and fired off a wild shot. One of Ada's men, halfway out the door, stumbled back and fell behind cover.

At the alley's edge, headlights strobed across my face, blinding me for a split second before the oncoming SUV swerved hard and screeched to a stop. Melanie clutched the steering wheel in a death grip, while the two hostages huddled in the back seat. I jumped in on the passenger side. I hadn't even shut the door before Melanie stomped on the gas, shoving me back against the seat as we rocketed across the strip-mall parking lot.

"Good apprentice," I gasped. "Take a right at the access road."

Melanie nodded to the rearview mirror and the two clerks, clutching each other in the back seat. "What about them?"

Excellent question.

* * *

Melanie drove like a pro, once I got her to ease off the gas. She took a winding course across town, doubling back, making sure Ada didn't manage to put a tail on us. Then we found an all-night diner. I sat the clerks down at a booth and told them to order whatever they wanted.

In the aftermath of the adrenaline rush, hunger flooded in to fill the void. I ordered hash browns and scrambled eggs, and coffee, black. Probably the first of several. I still had to drive us back to Vegas tonight, another four or five hours on the highway to look forward to. Hopefully not empty-handed, but I wasn't feeling optimistic. We'd left Ada and her crew occupying the store, which meant they had all the time they needed to ransack the records and find Marcel's address.

I hoped Ada would do a little soul-searching. I wasn't optimistic about that, either.

The younger clerk, the woman whose hands hadn't stopped fidgeting since we sat down, finally asked the inevitable question. "What...happened back there?"

"Here's what's going to happen," I told her. "When we're done here, you and your pal are going to call the police. You're going to tell them that three men forced their way into your store at closing time with guns. They were wearing ski masks and gloves, so you don't have any idea what they looked like. The back door was open, you saw an opportunity, and you ran for it."

"That's it?" the older man asked.

I reached for my mug of coffee. "That's it. Minimal details. Nothing's more suspicious than a witness who remembers too many details or remembers too clearly. You were traumatized, it's all a blur, end of story. Those people won't be back; nobody's going to bother you again."

"Who are you?" the woman asked.

Melanie had ordered a stack of chocolate-chip pancakes, and she was wolfing them down like she hadn't eaten in a week. She looked up from her syrupy mountain. "We're the *other* thieves."

I kicked her under the table. Lightly.

"We were hoping to find some information about one of your customers," I said, leaving aside the specifics. "We'd be willing to offer some financial compensation for your time and trouble."

My earlier lesson about bribery still stood, but the circumstances had changed. Both clerks had been roped into a conspiracy of necessity—at least if they wanted to tell a story the authorities would believe—and neither was going to be ratting the other one out. They shared a nervous glance.

"You saved our lives tonight," the man said. "Whatever we can do for you, just say it."

I reached for the pepper. Coal-dark flakes rained down across a bed of hash browns.

"Unfortunately," I said, "those other folks wanted the same info, and they've got a few reasons to stop us from following their trail. I have a feeling all the paperwork from your shop is burning in a garbage can as we speak."

The young woman shook her head. "Not a problem. We're a franchise. All the Mailboxes and More stores have terminals connected to a central mainframe. Nothing's really stored on-site. They could burn the whole place down, and I can just log in from another location. What do you need?"

I needed a glimmer of hope, and she'd just handed me one. I snatched it close and held it tight.

"You would have received a large delivery a couple of months back," I said, "from a shipping company in Boston called Peretsky and Sons. Crate about the size of a dresser, about two hundred pounds—"

The woman laughed. "Oh, we remember that one."

"Yeah," her partner said, wincing. "I, uh, sustained a work-related injury lugging it into the back room."

"He had to wear a truss for a month."

"Not the sort of thing you forget," he said.

"We're looking for the guy it was shipped to," I said. "I assume he came in to pick it up. Might have been in his late twenties, early thirties? French accent?"

She shook her head. "Nope. It sat in back for a week, taking up space, then the customer called. Corporate client. Not a French guy, though. A woman. British, I think."

Ms. Fleiss, then. The Enemy's right-hand monster. I leaned a little closer to the table, feeling like a bloodhound on a fresh trail.

"Corporate client? What company?"

She frowned, combing her memory. "Northern...something, I think. I can find out in the morning. Anyway, she gave us an out-of-state address and paid us to have it shipped there."

Scottsdale wasn't the final destination. It was a stopover, just another link in the chain in case someone came after the stolen property. Nice and compartmentalized: if Marcel got nabbed on a heist or his buddies in the Boston mob turned informant, the most they could give up was an address at a mailbox store. Once it was safely delivered, Fleiss stepped in and moved the goods along the pipeline.

A pipeline with two things waiting at the end: the mother lode of Canton relics, and the Enemy himself.

* * *

I gave the clerk the number of a burner phone, one of a half dozen sitting in my top dresser drawer back home. Then I gave her and her partner fifty bucks each, over their protests, and sent them packing. Nothing I could do after that but wait. That and have a second cup of coffee for the road. We got back on the highway just past midnight, cruising northwest under a canopy of stars and chasing a strobing white line across the desert flats.

"You did good tonight," I said to Melanie. "You did damn good."

"I didn't do anything," she said, sheepish.

"You kept your head and stayed cool under pressure."

"That's easy, though."

"No," I said, "it really isn't. Most people can barely manage that skill on a good day, and you had some pissed-off dudes pointing guns at you. So...you okay?"

She thought about that.

"She's not like him," she said.

"Hmm?"

"Ada," Melanie said. "She's not like Sullivan was."

"She's got his whole preacher routine down pat."

She shook her head. "Yeah, but Sullivan hated himself, and he wanted everyone to feel the way he felt. I think Ada wants…"

Melanie stopped talking. I offered my own interpretation to fill the gulf of silence.

"To be a hero?"

"Not exactly." Melanie looked out into the dark, the distant mountains drifting by like monoliths of shadow. "That's part of it, but…I think she wants to feel like she matters."

"Everybody matters," I said.

"Easy to say. Harder to feel. Sometimes…you know, yeah, Ada had a good home, and did great in school, and had the whole world going for her, but that doesn't always matter as much as people think it does. You can have all that stuff and still feel empty inside."

"You ever feel that way?" I asked her.

She gave me the ghost of a smile. "Not as much as I used to. Not anymore. So…do you think she's the Paladin?"

"Flip a coin. Our options are her, Harmony Black, or somebody else entirely. Admittedly, I'm just listening to my gut here, but I think it's either Ada or Harmony. Which means we've got to keep them both alive and breathing until we know for certain."

"Fifty-fifty odds," Melanie said.

"Well, they've both demonstrated deeply un-Paladin-like behavior. Ada kicked my ass with magic kung fu, and Harmony stole my car—"

"Not the car again," Melanie groaned.

"I'm just saying, these are acts of aggression that cannot stand unanswered."

"I know the real problem between you and Harmony," she said. "See, you're a Slytherin and she's a Ravenclaw."

"Goddamn it, Melanie."

* * *

I dropped Melanie off and tried not to look at the clock as I aimed my headlights for the east side of Vegas. I didn't want to think about how long I'd gone without any sleep. The sun did its best to remind me, as false dawn shimmered on the horizon. I trudged up the stairs, letting myself into my apartment over Della's Pool Hall, and collapsed face-first onto the mattress.

I swam back to the land of the living sometime around one in the afternoon. Razor blades of light sliced through the gaps in my venetian blinds, drawing lines across the bristle on my cheek. I was still wearing last night's outfit, and my mouth tasted like something had crawled onto my tongue and died there. I stumbled to the bathroom, leaving a trail of rumpled clothes on the floor in my wake, and turned the shower on full blast. Eventually I felt like I could pass for human again.

Once I toweled off, my first stop was the bedroom dresser. Top drawer, where a clutter of phones—all different models, burners bought with cash and kept on hand for a rainy day—sat piled in a lidless shoebox. One had a text message waiting for me.

I read it. Then I stood there, transfixed, staring at the screen. I had to smile.

"Found you," I whispered. "*Found* you, you son of a bitch."

25.

"Canton's substitution trunk was shipped to a company called Northlight," I said. "Their HQ, Northlight Tower, is in the heart of Seattle. And that's where we'll find the Enemy."

It was a little after 4:00 p.m. All hands on deck, down in the conference room below my club, after I sent the construction crews home early. Bentley and Corman, Mama Margaux, and Melanie sat around the black Italian marble, while Pixie perched at the table's far end with her laptop and a portable projector designed for business presentations. Caitlin and Jennifer still weren't safe to be around me, not with the first story's rules in play, so they listened in on a conference call.

Pixie hit a key. The projector, pointed toward the wall of white porcelain steel, flashed a photograph. Northlight Tower was a sleek silver spike, thirty-seven stories of brutal elegance.

"And that's our next score," I said.

"Leaving aside my immediate misgivings," Bentley said, "and they are *severe* misgivings...you're certain you've found the Enemy's lair?"

"He's in there," I said. "And more importantly, that's where he's keeping all the Canton relics that Marcel stole for him."

"What about Marcel himself?" Margaux asked.

"Trail's gone cold," I said, "but if he's not hiding out at Northlight, that's where I'll pick his scent up again. Look, the Enemy and Ms. Fleiss both know how to get in touch with him, right? If there's a way to find him, it's somewhere in that tower."

"That's a damn big 'somewhere,'" Corman grunted, folding his arms. "So what makes you so sure this is the place?"

Pixie tapped another key. The photograph was replaced with the yellowed, faded scan of a corporate charter. "For starters, Northlight was founded back in 1957. Corporate attorney of record? One Hildegard Fleiss."

"That was back when she was bouncing from world to world, protecting the reliquary while she waited for her boss to bust out of interdimensional prison," I said. "There are probably a lot of Northlights out there. This one started booming about twenty years ago, right around the time the Enemy went free."

"What do they make?" Bentley asked.

"Nothing but money. And I mean that literally. They do some nominal trading in real estate, some hedge-fund management, but it all looks purpose-driven to support the Enemy's personal projects. Their corporate website is word salad, lots of 'focusing on cross-lateral enrichment to build brand synergy.'"

"Their most recent line is defense," Pixie said. "Northlight took a twelve-million-dollar contract from the Pentagon last year to research improved radar imaging systems."

Caitlin's voice purred over the speaker at the heart of the table. "I'm presuming no such products have been delivered?"

"Nope. Money goes in, nothing comes out. Your tax dollars at work." Pixie paused. "Well, not like any of us pay taxes."

"Hey, I pay my taxes," I said. "I mean, I pay taxes for my minimum-wage job at the bookstore. Come to think of it, I'm supposed to get a refund this year."

Jennifer's whistle trilled over the phone line. "Twelve mil, though? I'll say this for the Enemy, he ain't no halfway crook. But is that all we got to go by, Fleiss's name showing up back in the fifties?"

"Can I show them the weird stuff?" Pixie asked me.

"Show 'em the weird stuff," I said.

The next slide was from Northlight's corporate website. An employee profile, highlighting their head of human resources.

The photograph depicted a portly man whose suit and tie matched his surname, his hair a U-shaped ring around a premature bald spot. He gave the camera a nervous smile.

"Percy Blue," Pixie said. "He's been with the company for three years. But the internet never forgets. I fired up the Wayback Machine and found a picture of his predecessor."

Another click. Same webpage, same text, new photograph. Jordan Blue was thin, short, still nervous, wearing an identical blue suit and blue tie.

"They related?" Corman asked.

"No," Pixie said. "No relation, and while I was digging into that, I ran the new guy's photo through a reverse image search and found his former place of employment."

Next photograph. Same man, smiling bright, wearing a smock and a paper hat as he squirted mustard onto a hot dog.

"Meet Lubomir Barzcak," she said. "First-generation immigrant and food-cart vendor who set up shop one block from Northlight Tower, until he disappeared one morning. Still considered a missing person by Seattle PD. One week later, he became Percy Blue."

"He changed his name?" Margaux asked.

"He *became* Percy Blue," I said. "Complete with a six-figure bank account, a degree from the Wharton School of Business, and a native's mastery of the English language. In one week. Now check out the rest of Northlight's executive branch."

Pixie scrolled through the next few photographs, more screen-grabs from the corporate site.

"Ms. Green, director of the accounting department," she said. "And here's Mr. Purple, head of client relations."

Corman squinted at the projection. "This an employee directory or a box of crayons?"

"We've tied at least one other senior executive at Northlight to an active missing-persons case," I said. "They weren't hired so much as assembled from scratch, custom-built, and all within the last five years or thereabouts."

"This goes beyond altering a person's actual history," Bentley said. "The Enemy...*rewrote* these people. Changed them into something completely new."

I gestured to the image on the wall. "Editing reality. Like how he stuck me behind bars and gave everyone memories of a trial that never happened. My best guess? This isn't part of some grand scheme; it's practice. The Enemy's been unlocking his old powers one by one, getting his mojo back. Scooping up victims off the street and turning them into color-coded servants with imaginary lives is just a way to stretch his wings. He can keep an eye on his creations and make sure they don't come unraveled."

"And if they hold fast..." Bentley said, his voice trailing off.

"Then he knows he's ready for bigger and badder things," I said. "The Enemy is getting stronger."

"And you want to go in there," Jennifer said. "The eye of the reality-twisting hurricane."

"Want to? No. But Louise Canton spent a lifetime designing relics to take the Enemy out. Not just this one time, on this one planet. She was pretty damn sure she could wipe him out for good."

"And seeing as he's been scooping them up all over the world," Margaux mused. "Well. He believes it too, doesn't he?"

"Making it even more likely that the entire tower is one giant magical death trap," Caitlin added.

Jennifer's drawl joined her on the phone line. "Seems to me you're cruisin' for a bruisin' if you go in there blind. You need recon for this gig."

"Agreed," I said. "I need to get in there twice. Once to learn the lay of the land and figure out exactly what kind of security they've got—mechanical, magical, and otherwise—and find where the Canton relics are being held. Then we make a final plan and pull the heist."

"The Enemy and that...creature Fleiss both know your face," Bentley said. "If they so much as get a whiff of your presence—"

"That's something we need to brainstorm, then. We know

Fleiss goes on errands all the time, and we know the Enemy *can* leave the tower, seeing as he showed up down in Texas. What we need is some serious motivation, something we can dangle to draw them both out and keep them distracted."

"What else can we do?" Pixie asked.

"For now? I need as much intel as we can gather safely and without drawing attention. Neighborhood demographics, street layouts, access routes. Police and EMT response times. I only need one plan for getting in; I want at least three for getting out."

"I assume Northlight has a private security force," Caitlin said.

"Well, that's...what I'll be working on next," I said. "Turns out, at least as far as our preliminary research goes, they outsource their guards. Tall Pines Security holds the contract."

Bentley and Corman shared a glance. Bentley turned back to me, head slightly tilted.

"Your brother's company," he said.

"Well, not *his* company exactly, but he did get a recent promotion."

"You okay with that, kiddo?" Corman asked.

I knew what he meant. I had a way in, a route to get all the inside dirt I needed on Tall Pines. And to lay hands on it, I'd have to hustle my own brother. The same brother who just came back into my life—and promptly became a Network target for his troubles.

"I'm fine," I lied. "It's only a matter of time before Ada follows the same trail I did, and if she goes charging into Northlight Tower with guns blazing—which she will, because the Redemption Choir doesn't know the meaning of the word 'subtle'—she's going to get herself killed. Best way to stop that from happening is if I steal the Canton relics first and tell her so."

"Then she'll be comin' after you," Jennifer pointed out.

"I'm fine with that, too."

26.

Teddy and I hadn't talked much lately.

We'd had our surprise reunion at Mayor Seabrook's office. She'd called in Tall Pines for protection after a string of credible threats. Called me in, too, and we'd bumped into each other by cosmic chance. He was more surprised to see me than I was to see him, considering as far as he knew, I'd died in a prison riot at Eisenberg Correctional.

Teddy was a fast study. Maybe it was his military background, his stint in the Navy, that made him quick to adjust and adapt. He was fine with his big brother being a fugitive ghost living under an assumed name, and when it came time to talk about what I did for a living...well, he said the word "gangster" before I did, and he didn't really care. He was just happy to have me back in his life.

I didn't understand that, but I was thankful for it.

Then he'd gotten swept up in the plot against Seabrook, bound and held hostage at the Neon Museum by a pack of Ms. Fleiss's thugs. He saw me yank Fleiss into a mail sack and vanish. Then he saw the sack ripple and erupt as I burst back into reality with my crew behind me, half rescue mission and half killing spree. He saw me conjure a whirlwind of razor-edged playing cards, and watched my girlfriend climb a neon sign like a spider before ripping a man's throat out with her teeth.

He didn't call me after that. Didn't blame him. I figured he had some thinking to do.

When he finally did start texting again, he didn't ask any hard questions. Small talk, mostly. Asking about local events and places to eat like a recent transplant would, and I steered him toward the hidden gems of the city. Every now and then he gave me a tentative reminder that his dinner invitation was still open. I'd been putting him off. After so many years apart, I'd messed up his world and nearly managed to get him killed just by coming into casual contact; the last thing his life needed was more of me in it.

And here I was, dropping him a text, setting up that dinner. Not out of brotherly love, but because I needed something from him. *And if there was any other way*, I told myself. I didn't bother finishing the rationalization. It wouldn't make me feel like any less of an asshole.

His place was over in Henderson, on a quiet suburban street dotted with palm trees. I double-checked the address and parked at the curb. Teddy was doing all right for himself; he'd moved into a two-level ranch with an expensive address, new construction, bone-white stucco, and a pebble-bed front yard. Modern architecture with a little south-of-the-border style and artisanal driftwood details. Two cars in the driveway, a workhorse of a silver Ford pickup and a Porsche Cayenne.

The front door opened when I was halfway up the walk. Teddy loomed in the doorway, halfway between eager and nervous. Felt like I was looking into a mirror.

"Hey," he said.

"Hey." I met him on the stoop. His arms made an awkward quarter-reach, then fell to his sides.

"Are we—" he said. "Are we a hugging family?"

Our boundaries were a tangled mess of distance and lost time. Things other families just *knew*, we had to figure out, like we were starting all over again. I thought about it, then reached out and pulled him in. It felt good.

"Yeah," I said, slapping his back. "Why the hell not?"

He looked past me, to the curb. "New ride?"

"Rental," I said. "My car is...it's a long and complicated story. I'll tell you later."

"Wasn't sure if you were bringing your, uh..."

"Girlfriend?"

I could see all the questions he was afraid to ask, swirling behind the forced eagerness in his eyes.

"Yeah," he said. "I mean, we've got tons of food if she wants to come on by."

"She's got a thing tonight," I said.

"Well, c'mon in! Let me introduce you."

Teddy's home was air-conditioned perfection and ivory tiles, more driftwood and calculated Tex-Mex atmosphere, but with the clutter of a life well lived. Toys littered the hallway, crayons and books lay scattered across a glass living-room table, and food crumbs flecked the ivory sofa cushions.

"Careful where you walk," Teddy said. "We just started getting her into Legos. She loves 'em, but my feet may never heal. And speaking of—"

A six-year-old tornado came gusting down the stairs, nearly tripping over her own buckled shoes. Her blond pigtails flew out behind her until she skidded to a stop.

"Dan, this is Stacy. Stacy, this is your Uncle Dan. Say hi?"

She had big, bright eyes and a gap-toothed smile. "Hi," she said, staring up at me.

I wasn't sure how to deal with kids. Or the flood of emotions that hit me from both sides at once, twin gale-force waves slamming the sides of my ship and rocking me off-balance. I had a niece. Teddy had told me that, when we first talked on the steps outside Mayor Seabrook's office, but actually seeing her in the flesh was something else entirely. This small and innocent creature, with my family's blood in her veins.

Stacy.

I had a history with that name. The Stacy Pankow job had changed my life forever. She was a porn star and a junkie, murdered and dumped in the storm tunnels under the city by her abusive boyfriend. I had been hired to find the truth and deliver payback. I did what I was paid for, and then I freed Stacy's restless spirit from where she'd been trapped. I freed her, so she could go straight to hell.

That Stacy had been innocent too, once. The world had a way of fixing that.

But here was this perfect child, family, innocent, and suddenly I wanted to build a tower a hundred stories tall and keep her at the very top, and build a wall around that tower, and ring that wall with electric fence and—

—and you can't do any of those things. Sooner or later, we all get our turn on the anvil of the world. You bend or you break, but either way you don't come back the same.

Another new arrival breezed in through an open archway, a cluttered modern kitchen at her back. Short blond hair, wearing a sauce-stained apron over her T-shirt and jeans. I could see where Stacy got her eyes.

"You must be Daniel," she said and threw her arms around my shoulders. "I'm Peg. Teddy's told me *so* much about you."

"About your plumbing business," he offered, saving me from having to ask. I shot him a look over his wife's shoulder. *Plumbing?* My fault, we should have coordinated stories before I showed up. Hopefully she wouldn't ask me to help fix anything around the house.

"Potato salad is underway," she said. "Hon? You want to put the burgers on?"

"The grill master is in the house," Teddy said.

"Yes, dear," Peg replied, "but the grill is in the backyard."

"The grill master is leaving the house. Dan? Come and witness poetry in motion."

"Poetry?" I said. "I thought we were having burgers."

Peg tapped my shoulder. "This one I like. We're keeping this one."

The yard out back, ringed by a picket fence, was another expanse of groomed white pebbles. Prickly cactus provided a splash of green, springing up around the fence's inner edge, and a picnic table stood beside a bright pink plastic playhouse. Teddy grabbed a couple of brown glass bottles from the overstuffed fridge, some kind of local IPA, and passed me one. The sliding glass door rumbled shut behind us.

He brandished a bottle opener and popped my cap, then his. The beer had a rich, nutty smell, mingled with an aroma like fresh-baked bread. We clinked bottles and drank.

"Seriously," I said. "You told her I'm a plumber?"

Teddy gave the patio door a sheepish look. "I was on the spot, didn't really have time to think about it. Besides, I thought all you Mafia guys say that you're plumbers."

"That's more of a New York thing, but there is some truth in the stereotype. So how's work going?"

He reached for the lighter fluid and rolled back a stainless-steel hutch. I didn't know much about grills, but I could tell he'd spent some serious cash on his. It looked like a fixture in a gourmet restaurant.

"Regional manager, can't complain," he said. "Tall Pines is expanding all over the place. They offered me a raise last week if I'd move out to Akron, take the lead on a new franchise there."

I wasn't sure which way to feel about that. On one hand, my gut instinct was to send Teddy as far away as possible—Akron was fine, Singapore or Beijing would be better—to keep him out of my orbit and clear of my damage. On the other hand, as long as he was in Vegas I could keep an eye on him.

"You taking it?" I asked.

He spritzed the grill. A wave of heat wafted over us, joining the afternoon sun and carrying the earthy smell of charcoal.

"Nah. I mean, it feels like we just got here, and I can't be pulling Stacy from school to school, especially at her age. Kids need roots to grow. That's what the self-help books tell me, anyway." He gave me a sidelong glance and reached for a tray of hamburger patties. "I swear, she's six years old and it still feels like we're just making this parenting thing up as we go along."

"I imagine it's like that for everybody."

"Probably. I read a fatherhood-advice manual and the first thing it told me was that there's no such thing as a manual for being a good father. I mean, they were being metaphorical, but I probably could have saved my twelve bucks."

"We didn't have a great role model," I said.

"We did not." He stared at the grill. Patties sizzled as they landed on the slats. "Usually I just ask myself what Dad would have done in any given situation. Then I don't do that. Seems to be working out so far."

"Amen." I saluted him with my bottle. "So with all this new business coming in, does Tall Pines offer a one-size-fits-all kind of package? Like, pay a certain amount and you automatically get a set number of guards working a set number of hours?"

He shook his head and flashed a smile, amusement mingling with the pride in his voice. "We aren't Gold Star, Dan. Nah, half my job is on the customer-service end, arranging custom-tailored packages. We meet with the client, find out where their weak spots are and how much they're willing to spend, and come up with a comprehensive solution. I never upsell. Which ticks my boss off a little, but we built our name on quality service."

I edged my way toward the real question, each word testing the ice under my feet.

"So these security plans," I said, "I imagine they have to get updated on a regular—"

The glass door slid open and we had company. Peg emerged with a plate of buns in one hand and a plastic bowl of potato salad precariously balanced in the other. I rushed up and grabbed it before it could fall. Stacy zoomed between us, charging through the swinging door of the plastic playhouse.

"In case you're wondering," Peg said, "no. She never stops moving. I don't know where the energy comes from."

"I just want to know where I can get some of that," I said.

I tried to make myself useful. Peg and I ferried out the obligatory staples, the ketchup, the mustard, more bottles of beer all around, pinning napkins under a bottle of relish to keep them from blowing away in the bone-dry desert breeze. I got Peg talking about her job—she was a physical therapist who specialized in sports injuries—which saved me from having to make up too many details about my alleged plumbing company. Stacy swung by to show me the plane she'd built from a rainbow riot of Legos. At least, I think it was a plane. It was a damn fine effort anyway. Then the burgers were ready and the first bite, slathered in onions and a slab of American cheese, was juicier than my last porterhouse steak.

At some point I ended up crouched in Stacy's playhouse, listening intently to the deep and complex lore involving Miss Ruby Spaceman and Princess Poodle, who were vying for the Lego throne of New Town City. Personally, I felt I had to pledge allegiance to Miss Ruby Spaceman, which sparked no little controversy among the miniature courtiers. Stacy reassured me with a confidential wink that both princesses were actually best friends and working together on a super-secret plot to weed out traitors in the ranks.

The afternoon rolled on by with good food and casual conversation, and mostly, it was just a comfortable place to be.

We cleared plates, Stacy went inside to watch videos on her mom's tablet, and the sky slowly took on an azure glow. Night was coming. I still had a job to do.

27.

Teddy and I were out back, side by side, leaning against the fence and drinking the last couple of beers. At some point we'd fallen into a companionable silence. Insects trilled in the gathering dark.

"I figure you'd tell me if I needed to worry," he said.

I eyed him over the neck of the bottle as I brought it to my lips. "About?"

"I mean, you've had my family under round-the-clock watch for over a month now." Something must have shown on my face. He broke into a grin. "C'mon, bro. I work in security for a living. Did you really think I wouldn't notice? I gotta tell you, your guys look tough, but they're not good at playing inconspicuous. I can recommend some courses they could take. Probably get you a group discount."

"They're mostly a deterrent," I said.

"Yeah, well." His smile faded. "They're following Peg when she takes Stacy to school, and when she picks her up in the afternoon. My wife and kid, Dan."

"I know. I told them to." I contemplated my bottle and chose my next words. "If I thought you needed to worry, I'd tell you to worry. Like I said, they're a deterrent."

"Against?"

"That whole deal that went down, with Mayor Seabrook's kidnapping. They didn't just grab you because you were protecting her. I've been butting heads with a...let's call it a gang, called the Network. And they found out that you're my brother."

He didn't answer at first. Then he breathed his response into the mouth of his bottle.

"Fuck."

"They tried to use you to put the squeeze on me. So I squeezed back."

"What'd you do?" he asked.

"You really want to know?"

He held my gaze long enough for me to read the answer in his eyes.

"I squeezed back," I said, "in a manner that left no question about how I felt. And I sent them a message: they want to come after me, that's fair ball. But nobody touches you or yours. You're not a part of this."

"You think they got the message?" he asked.

"They got the message. Besides, we had another run-in not long ago. The Network...let's just say they've had better days. They're going to be licking their wounds for a while."

"So," he said. "This have anything to do with why you were pumping me for information earlier?"

"Was I?" I asked, all innocence.

He contemplated his bottle.

"You know, if you're going to be robbing one of my company's properties, I should really report it to somebody."

"You going to?"

"I said 'should.' Just ease my conscience? Tell me nobody's going to get hurt. Lie if you have to, so I can sleep tonight."

"You can sleep like a baby," I told him. "Truth is, this is kind of a Robin Hood gig. A very bad individual has some things that don't belong to him. I aim to reunite these objects with their rightful owner."

Once I figured out who the rightful owner was, anyway. And if it turned out to be Ada? Only once I knew she was ready to handle them, and not one second sooner. Until then, Canton's relics were safer in my hands than anyone else's.

Teddy went quiet. I could hear his gears turning in the dark.

The night air went cool, then cold, heavy with the weight of his unspoken questions.

"At the Neon Museum," he said.

"Yeah?"

He looked me in the eye. "I saw some things."

"I imagine you did," I said.

"Next day, this guy, one of Mayor Seabrook's aides, pulled me aside and put an envelope in my hand. One thousand dollars, in cash. Then he told me what I *really* saw—Commissioner Harding busting loose and taking on the terrorists like a one-man army—and said that if I got my memories right, there was another envelope waiting for me."

"What'd you do?"

He shrugged. "Collected my two thousand dollars. I've got a bank account set up for Stacy's college fund."

"Good man."

I drank my beer and listened to the insects trill and waited for the inevitable question to drop.

"Where'd you learn how to do...the things I saw you do?" he asked me.

"I was out on the streets," I said. "Fell in with a bad crowd. Then I fell in with a good one. Learned some tricks from both of 'em. They're just tricks, that's all."

I wasn't being cagey for no reason. I was standing on treacherous ground here. A lifetime of experience had taught me that opening people's eyes to the real world was the fastest possible way to ruin them beyond any hope of repair. Questions led to more questions, and that led to answers about humanity, the universe, the afterlife. People could either handle those hard truths or they couldn't. I had already pulled Teddy too close to the edge of that cliff, just by stepping back into his life.

"No," he said. "I took Peg and Stacy to the Strip last weekend, to see David Gosselin's magic act. Those were tricks. What you did, and your friends—that was real."

"Teddy, I need you to trust me when I say there are things you don't want to know."

"How can you be so sure?"

"Because you care about sleeping at night." I tilted my bottle back. "I stopped sleeping at night a long time ago. I can tell you this: you're not crazy, and what you saw was real. You remember the woman who was there, called herself Ms. Fleiss? She works for the guy I'm angling to take down. That's the job I'm planning."

There was a glint in Teddy's eye, some strange recognition. I figured it was post-traumatic stress. I gave him a second to put his thoughts together.

"I remember her threatening to shoot me in the kneecaps," he said. "So, you pull off this...job, my family will be safer, right?"

And the entire planet, but I wasn't going to get into that tonight. I settled on a halfway truth.

"A lot of people will be. Like I said, he's a very bad individual."

"I'm in," he said.

"Pardon?"

"Tell me what you need. I'm gathering this guy uses Tall Pines for security, right? Give me the details. I'll pull his records for you: employees, shift timing, protocols, all of it."

"I don't want to get you in trouble," I said.

He laughed. "I won't be. I'm, like, one level of access away from having the run of the company database. All I need is five minutes with my boss's computer, which he never locks. And the man takes two-hour, three-martini lunches every single afternoon. There's no risk involved here."

I had come here to use him. I should have been happy to have him on board. Still, I'd hoped I'd be able to get the intel I needed and leave him none the wiser. I didn't need him getting sucked into my orbit. People who did that tended to never leave. That or hit terminal velocity, burning up in the atmosphere as they crashed down.

But he was offering. And he had what I needed. And I'd come here to use him.

"Northlight," I said. "The company's called Northlight; their HQ is in Seattle."

"Done and done," he said.

* * *

I called up Caitlin on the drive home. Ostensibly to give her an update. Really, I just needed to hear her voice.

"Miss your face," I said.

"Miss yours," she purred over the line. "If it was safe, if there was any way—"

"I know," I said.

Streetlamps reflected pale orbs of light across the dusty windshield, smears in the suburban darkness. The Strip was a distant carnival, pulsing, shifting, the call of electronic sirens from a concrete reef.

"How are you holding up?" she asked me.

I was touch-starved and tired and lonely and "I'm fine," I said.

"Did you get what you needed?"

A glimpse into another life. A house in the suburbs, a family, burgers on the grill and craft beer in the fridge. The life I could have had, if I hadn't gone down the left-hand road.

"Teddy's on board. He's going to call me tomorrow afternoon. Then...well, then we move. No sense waiting. The longer the first story is in play, the more chances it gets to rearrange the world and set up an accident."

"Jennifer and I are both keeping our distance."

"Sure, but there are other candidates for 'the lover who kills the Thief.' Roxy's dancing in Reno, last I heard, and Peach was going to try out for NASCAR, and that leaves..." I paused, not sure how much detail I wanted to get into.

"Daniel? Though it's a card I rarely need to play these days, I was born into the Choir of Lust. You're not going to shock me."

"There were...maybe one or two others."

"You dirty little slut," she said, utterly deadpan.

"But I did *not* sleep with the twins."

"You know," she said, "hopefully this excursion—assuming we

all survive it—leads to freeing you from the first story's curse. But we need to consider alternatives."

"Alternatives?"

"What happens if we can't find Marcel Deschamps, if he's too far underground to reach? Or what happens if he dies and leaves the mantle of the Thief on your shoulders?"

I rolled up to a four-way intersection. Red light, dead silent, no action in sight. My fingers drummed the steering wheel, a pressure valve letting out a little nervous energy. The road home was to my right. The light strobed green and I rolled straight through instead, heading toward the Strip.

"First of all," I said, "nobody is so far underground that *we* can't get at them. Not even the Enemy can hide him that deep."

"And if the curse is well and truly stuck? If killing Marcel doesn't free you?"

I'd been thinking about that. I'd been thinking about that a lot.

"Then it's business as usual," I said.

"Meaning?"

"You can't cheat the first story," I said. "When it decides it's your time to go, it's your time to go. Eventually, sooner rather than later, it's going to kill me. If it needs to, it'll put one of my exes on a plane and then crash it right on top of me."

"We *do* know two women who escaped the cycle."

"Yeah, and they took some once-in-all-human-history measures. I can't duplicate that trick. I'm not going to spend the time I've got left running, Cait. I want to spend it with you."

She fell silent for a moment. I drove, merging with the gridlock on Tropicana Avenue. A sea of scarlet brake lights, horns splitting the air, the neon cacophony of the Strip rising up all around me. The flashing glow and the noise gave my brain something to latch on to. Soothing chaos.

"You meant what you said, at the Bast Club."

"If anyone's going to take me out," I said, "I'd rather it be you than anybody else. Hell, if nothing else, it'll piss all my enemies off. But let's not plan my funeral just yet, okay? Not until Marcel's in the ground. Then we'll see what happens and take it from there."

"I hear traffic," she said, changing the subject.

"Don't think I'm going to be able to sleep at home tonight." *And I can't come over to your place.*

"Wherever you do sleep," she said, "dream of me? And I'll dream of you."

I pulled into the parking garage at the Metropolitan, cruising past pop-art murals, hunting for an open spot. Fifteen minutes later I was up at a piano bar, nursing a Jack and Coke and listening to an obligatory medley of Billy Joel songs. The people swirling around me, the noise, the energy, acted like a balancing weight against the turmoil in my gut. It all evened out, smooth as the liquor.

28.

"There's a problem," Teddy said.

The problem at the moment was the heavy sunlight straddling my chest and stabbing ice picks into my eyes. I shifted under strange covers, on a mattress wider and softer than mine, and had a momentary *where-am-I?* panic. Then it all came flooding back. Drinks, more drinks, at some point I think I stole a tourist's wallet. At another point I'm pretty sure the piano player shifted from Billy Joel to doing instrumental versions of Fall Out Boy's greatest hits.

No. I had taken the cash from the tourist's wallet, stuffed it in his fishbowl of tips, and *paid* him to play Fall Out Boy. My motives were a mystery, lost in a bottle of Jack Daniels. Teddy was in my ear, still talking on the phone, and I had to stop him in mid-breath.

"Wait," I said, forcing myself to sit up. The hotel suite lurched around me and I anxiously slid my legs over the side of the bed, touching down on groomed carpet. "Wait, sorry, I just woke up."

"It's almost two in the afternoon."

"Yeah, I decided to get up early. What's the problem?"

"I used my boss's account to check out Northlight's profile. Beyond the basic staffing details, their entire set of security protocols is binder-only."

"Meaning?"

"Meaning it's literally in a binder," he said. "Physical copies, kept on-site. It's not terribly uncommon. Basically, once you get hired as a guard, they sit you down and have you read the hard copy on your first day to learn the rules and regulations."

"None of it's online?"

"None of it," he said. "So it's harder for people like...well..."

"Like me," I said.

"To learn the shift timing and stuff like that. But I've got a solution."

I took my first wobbly step away from the bed. I was surrounded by pale blue and white, comic pop-art prints on the wall, sunlight streaming through every window and offering a panoramic view of the mountains in the distance. I was mostly looking for the bathroom.

"All ears," I said.

"I can get us in."

I stopped in mid-stumble.

"In?" I said.

"I do have access to their staffing details. After all, everything's got to run through the Tall Pines payroll system. And I can edit those details."

"Go on," I said.

"Like most of our clients, Northlight always has some degree of churn. Security is a temp gig for a lot of our guys, not something they're trying to make a career out of. I've also got access to programmable ID cards, and I'm pretty sure I've got a uniform in your size."

"You can get me in," I said.

"I can get *us* in."

"Uh-uh," I said. "I appreciate the help, but that is way too dangerous."

"It's too dangerous if I send you in alone. I've worked for Tall Pines for years. I know our basic operating procedures, how things are done, how to pass like I belong on the team. You don't. Without me, they'll make you in five seconds flat."

The room listed again. I found a convenient wall to lean on.

"I'm not volunteering to do anything crazy," Teddy said.

"Believe me, I'm not looking for any more excitement in my life. But if you just need to get into that security room, get a copy of the manual, and leave? That I can arrange."

That was exactly what I needed, along with the general lay of the land. I could scout the building while he grabbed the security protocols. If we were fast and quiet, no one would ever know we were there...and I knew, even as I did it, that I was talking myself into a bad idea.

"Still too dangerous. Teddy, these people are...I mean, you saw Ms. Fleiss."

"I saw you yank her into a mail sack and make her disappear."

"It was temporary," I said.

"We'll keep a low profile. In and out in twenty minutes, and I'll cover our tracks in the staffing system once we're done. You and me, bro. We can do this."

I told him I'd think about it. I told him I'd call him back. It was a foregone conclusion, though. I needed what he had, and given a little more time I could come up with every justification in the world to go through with it. I stumbled back to the bed, picked up the house phone from the nightstand, and dialed room service.

"I'd like the eight-ounce burger, cooked medium, with sriracha aioli, bacon onion marmalade, white cheddar, and spicy pickles. Also, could you add a fried egg to that?"

"On the side, sir?"

"No. As a topping. Just fry an egg and slap it right on the patty."

"Can do, sir. Anything else?"

"Three bottles of water," I said, "and a selection of your finest artisanal Ibuprofen."

* * *

Later that afternoon, I transferred Teddy the cash for the trip. We made our flight plans separately. Separate hotels, too, nothing to connect us at any point in the line. I flew in to Sea-Tac on the tail of a gray and drizzly sunrise. My .45 stayed at home; traveling with guns was a pain, and I didn't need to give the law any reason to look twice at my Paul Emerson alias while I was still breaking it in.

I had my wand, a fresh deck of cards, and Canton's pocket watch. That would have to be enough. I wasn't looking for a fight, anyway; this was purely recon and intelligence-gathering, laying the groundwork for the real heist. If anything went wrong today, we'd have to scrub the entire plan.

I booked a room at a Motel 6 by the airport. Teddy's flight wasn't due for another half hour, so I had a little time for prep work. I slid my sleeve back, taking the spring-loaded wand sheath from my carry-on bag and buckling it around my forearm. Then I turned my attention to the watch.

Canton's wand had helped me out in times of trouble, unveiling bits and pieces of what it was capable of. No such luck with the watch. It sat stubborn and silent, and the only time I'd seen it in action was when it was in Ada's hands. I laid the watch on the TV stand and poked at it, prodding with my fingertips and my psychic tendrils, trying to wake it up. Whispered incantations bounced off its dull brass shell. It didn't want anything to do with me.

"Have I not figured out the trick here?" I asked the watch. "Or are you just being pissy because I stole you?"

The watch's hand ticked along in sullen silence.

A knock sounded at the motel-room door. I let Teddy in, and he laid a garment bag out on the bedspread. He'd come dressed for work, in pressed uniform gray with a Tall Pines patch on his shoulder. I glanced to his heavy leather belt, the open loops and empty holster on his hips.

"You look..."

"Suave? Dashing?" he asked

"Underequipped."

"Armory's on site," he said. He rapped his knuckles on the garment bag. "Get changed or we're going to be late for work. Speaking of, what I *couldn't* get were the standard key-lock access cards we'd normally be assigned on our first day."

I wriggled into slacks so starched they could stand up on their own. This wasn't going to be one of my favorite disguises.

"So what's the plan?" I asked. "New-hire orientation?"

He shook his head. "Too dangerous. Orientation means the on-site manager double-checks a new employee's credentials and plays twenty questions. Plus you're assigned a minder for training, meaning you're under constant watch, and I figured you wouldn't want that. I put us in the staff database retroactively. Officially, we started work a week ago last Tuesday."

"And how do we sell that story when nobody there is going to recognize us?"

Teddy beamed at me. I recognized the look on his face. It was the one I get when I figure out something clever.

"According to the payroll records," Teddy said, "Northlight Tower currently has a staff of twenty-four full-time security guards and another thirty-two part-timers."

I squinted at him. "For an office building? That feels like overkill."

"Not," he said, "if you have around-the-clock coverage. Three shifts, and a lot of regular staffing shuffles, not to mention the turnover rate."

I saw where he was going with this. "So if anyone asks, we just got transferred from the night shift."

Teddy snapped his fingers. "Exactly. Worst-case scenario, the shift supervisor calls it in to verify. Well, thanks to me, according to the home office our papers are in order. And if he wants to check with the night supervisor, he'll have to wait until the guy wakes up and returns his call. You said we going to be in and out fast, right?"

"Quick like bunnies," I said. I stopped buttoning my uniform shirt long enough to lean in for a fist bump. "Nice going."

"It must run in the family."

I hoped not. I liked the idea of Teddy in suburbia, living my mirror life. All the same, dipping a toe in the pool, just once, couldn't hurt him too much.

I hoped.

* * *

We made our way downtown, along winding and narrow streets, cold rain rippling down the windshield of a rented hatchback. Northlight Tower was dead ahead. The chrome and glass spire, a wet spear capturing the murky daylight, froze the breath in my throat.

The path to finding Marcel Deschamps was in that building. The stolen Canton relics were in that building.

And judging by the aura of raw and seething malice, radiating from the upper floors like a miasma of black storm clouds and snapping, ravenous squid beaks, I knew one other thing for certain.

The Enemy was here.

Teddy pulled into an underground parking garage, rolling down a concrete ramp. "If anyone stops us, let me do the talking," he said.

"One thing," I told him.

We prowled along a gallery of silent cars, angling for a sign marked *Employee Parking*. He gave me a sidelong glance, uncertain now, like he'd caught something in my voice.

"If I tell you to run," I said, "you run. If I tell you to run, it's because something has gone very, very wrong, and you do not hesitate, you do not ask questions, you just *run*. Leave me behind, get out any way you can, and call that phone number I gave you. Tell them what happened."

"Dan, I don't care what happens in there, there's no way I'd leave you behind."

I didn't say another word until he pulled into a parking spot. The engine died with a faint rattle. I waited until he looked me in the eye.

"If I tell you to run," I said, "you run."

A cleaning crew was halfway through an employee entrance, propping open windowless double doors to wheel a supply cart inside. I rushed up and held the door for them. Then Teddy and

I let ourselves in, following in their wake. The card-locked door clicked behind us.

The bowels of Northlight Tower were aggressively mundane. Beige walls, fat piping, corkboards with employee schedules and flyers, nothing different from a dozen other office buildings I'd explored before. Teddy was a step ahead of me, walking with a practiced authoritarian stride. While he watched for human trouble, my senses were on high alert, sniffing for trails of stray magic.

Sniffing as much as I dared, anyway. Theoretically, Canton's pocket watch could shield my psychic presence like it had for Ada, but only if I figured out how to use it. The Enemy was here—maybe thirty-seven floors above our heads, maybe a heartbeat away—and if he sensed me in his lair we'd be good as dead. Or rewritten. For that matter, there was a good chance Fleiss was prowling the halls. I'd tried to get through to her the last time we faced off, to reach the woman she still was under the shackles of the Enemy's lies and open her eyes to the truth. All I'd managed, I was pretty sure, was to make her that much more eager to tear me apart.

If there's one cosmic truth, it's that no good deed goes unpunished. That's why I avoided them whenever possible.

"*Hey*," a hard voice snapped from a side corridor, stopping us in our tracks. "You two. Over here. *Now.*"

Teddy said he'd done all the groundwork, planted us on the staff roster and ensured our cover was all but bulletproof. I was about to find out if he was right.

29.

I didn't like this guy.

He was standing in my way, which was enough of a reason to want him gone, but he was going the extra mile. Stubble from a recent buzz cut, hands on his hips and chest puffed out like a drill sergeant, and a pair of mirrored sunglasses dangling from the breast pocket of his uniform shirt. One look and I knew if he could get away with wearing them indoors, he would.

"Who the hell are you two?" he demanded. "And what are you doing on my floor?"

"Sir," Teddy said, standing at attention. "Smith and Jones, sir. We were just transferred from the third shift, starting today."

I tried not to wince. Those were the names he went with? A natural instinct for deception did not run in the Faust family blood. All the same, the man staring us down didn't bat an eyelash.

"I didn't request any new hires. My schedule's full up as it is."

An ID card dangled from a sky-blue lanyard around Teddy's neck. Mine, too. He'd printed and laminated them at the home office. He handed his card over for inspection and I followed his lead.

"Don't know about that, sir," Teddy said. "Above our pay grade. We just follow orders, you know? They said, 'Your schedule's changing, be here at nine tomorrow,' so we're here at nine sharp."

"Should have been here at *seven* sharp." He shoved the cards at us with a scowl. "Follow me. We're going to get this sorted out.

Telling you right now, you can assume you're going straight back to third shift."

He led us up a short, unmarked flight of stairs and down an access hall with a discreet placard marked *Security Room One*. Implying there was a room two, maybe more, elsewhere on the premises. He unlocked the door with his key card—I was going to need one of those to get anywhere in this place—and we followed him into a long and narrow command suite. Banks of monitors lined the walls on either side; I'd been in casino security rooms with fewer electronic eyes than this. A quartet of guards watched the steady and constant feed, sliding on the casters of their swivel chairs to check this screen or that, fiddling with overcomplicated consoles, filling out shift paperwork on sturdy steel clipboards.

The drill sergeant shoved open a door on the opposite end of the room. Small office beyond, barely larger than the desk and chair inside, military medals and service ribbons pressed under glass on a wall display.

"Wait here," he grunted. "Let me get Juan on the phone, ask him what the hell he was thinking."

Teddy seemed placid, but my alarm bells were going off. He was on a first-name basis with our supposed shift supervisor. Not good. That told me he'd have a better-than-average chance of actually getting him on the phone. If he did, our cover was blown.

"It wasn't Juan who reassigned us, sir," I said, trying to catch him before he shut his office door. He caught it in mid-swing and glared at me. "It was...oh, what was his name? Guy from the Nevada office."

I looked at Teddy, hoping he caught my drift. We needed someone this guy wouldn't be able to reach, at least not until we were long gone. My brother didn't let me down.

"Schubert," he said. "It was a Mr. Schubert, in payroll."

The drill sergeant stared at us, incredulous. "The hell are you dimwits talking about? Nevada doesn't decide how we handle staffing. They're a different sales region."

I spread my hands wide, helpless. "Like he said, sir, above our pay grade. They told us to be here, so we're here. Sorry, we don't mean to cause you any trouble."

He sighed and shook his head. "Forget it. Not your fault. Just cool your heels a second and I'll get it sorted out."

The office door shut. Teddy leaned close, dropping his voice to a murmur.

"Schubert's on his honeymoon in Cancun. He won't be back until next week."

"Anyone checking his voicemail?" I breathed.

"Yeah. Me."

I gave him the most discreet of fist bumps. Then I turned my attention to the monitors. Four men to cover twenty-four screens, each feed automatically shuffling between cameras on a ten-second timer. The coverage was a mixed bag. On one hand, that was too many electronic eyes for a crew this small to handle. On the other, no reasonable security grid expects constant overwatch. Nine out of ten feeds showed empty hallways, quiet office floors.

Humans are a predator species. We're attuned to movement. I noticed, as a pack of suited employees walked down a hallway, one of the guards instantly flicked his gaze to follow them. He watched with the bored curiosity of a veteran security professional. His buddy at the far end of the desk was absorbed in writing up a report, ignoring the feeds just above his line of sight.

Final verdict: the building had one hell of a security net, with twenty-four seven coverage. I'd need a disguise to let me slip past the cameras unnoticed, or a way to take the grid down. If I went in during the daytime, a disguise could be as simple as one of my tailored suits, blending in with the professional crowd. Then again, smuggling Canton's relics out while the building was full of people would be a challenge in its own right. *Nighttime maintenance crew?* I thought. *Cleaners?* Lots to consider.

I noticed one more thing. Each feed had a status line with a time stamp—suggesting the footage was being recorded and backed up somewhere in the building, another potential problem—and a floor number. None of the cameras recorded anything above the thirty-third floor.

Teddy gave me a nudge. I followed his line of sight to a gray plastic binder, sitting on a pile of loose folders halfway down the left-hand console. I wandered over and got the attention of the closest guard.

"Hey, mind if I use your binder real quick? Need to check something."

"Sure," he said, barely glancing my way.

I felt my final seconds slipping away as I leafed through the manual. Speed-reading the first few pages confirmed what I already suspected: around-the-clock surveillance, no notable gaps in coverage where I could slip through between shifts, security camera footage backed up to an off-site server owned by Tall Pines. The security room and the staffing desk at every point of entry had a bank-style panic alarm; hitting the button would summon heavy response from Seattle PD, plus fire and rescue teams.

Guards were cleared to carry Tasers and pepper spray. No mention of firearms until I hit a section in a different font, the text offset, clearly an insertion into the usual company boilerplate. *12.8—Jaguar Teams. Guards approved for Jaguar clearance may carry discretionary tools as needed pursuant to their special duties as defined in section 19—*

I was already tearing through the manual, hunting across a paper jungle. Section 19 covered "extraordinary protocols in the event of a building-wide emergency."

19.2—Team JAGUAR ONE will move the patient in room 3603 using the provided gurney to the medical transport. Medical transport will then carry ONE + patient to off-site facility Alpha. Survival of the patient is an absolute imperative.

19.3—Teams JAGUAR TWO and THREE will move the collection in room 3712 to waiting armored vehicles. Vehicles will ferry the collection to off-site facilities Alpha, Beta, and Gamma for secure storage.

The office door opened and the boss loomed in the doorway, glowering.

"I got no idea," he said. "Can't get hold of anyone at the Nevada office, at least not anybody who knows anything about anything. You two, go home. Somebody'll call you when we get the schedule sorted out."

"We gonna get paid for coming in today?" I asked. Pushing it, but a little irritation would be expected under the circumstances.

"Call it a surprise vacation day," he told me. "Just get going. I got nothing for you to do here."

He vanished back into his office. The other guards ignored us, nothing but background noise in the business of their ordinary routine. Teddy and I headed for the door. I paused on the threshold. No chance I could snatch anybody's key card; the only one I saw out and on display was dangling from a lanyard, secure around its owner's neck.

A spare metal clipboard hung from a peg on the wall. That I grabbed on my way out. Never underestimate the value of a clipboard.

Once the door closed behind us, Teddy looked my way. A bead of sweat glistened on his forehead. "Well?" he said.

He'd already done enough, taken more risks than I could have asked for. I wanted to send him home, here and now. That said...

"One last thing," I told him. "Take a walk around the ground floor. There might be some kind of vehicle bay, with a medical transport on standby. See if you can find it."

He squinted at me. "Like an ambulance?"

"Exactly. I don't think it'll be part of the parking garage. It'll be in its own spot, probably near the main elevators. Just see if you can find it. If not, no big deal. And if anybody questions you, you got turned around on your way out. Just leave and we'll meet up back at the motel."

"What about you?" he asked.

"I'll be right behind you."

I needed a closer look upstairs. The "collection" on the

penthouse floor wasn't hard to figure out; that was where the Enemy was keeping his stolen relics. To have any chance at a decent plan, I'd have to get an idea of the security in play. The lack of cameras on the upper floors, and a special armed security detail to handle evacuation duty, told me I could expect something nastier than pepper spray.

Then again, it was the penthouse floor. The Enemy himself was the best security anyone could ask for.

I was more curious about the other proviso in the emergency protocols. Who was the patient in 3603?

We split up. A swinging door opened into the civilian wings of the tower. My polished shoes clicked on smooth marble as I strode through the crisp air of the lobby, clipboard in hand. Nobody questioned a man with a clipboard. The rain was coming down harder now, cold and thick, turning the glass wall of the lobby into an oily blur. Employees clustered around a bank of elevators. I watched a door chime open, a few suits get on, and one waved a key card past the wall of buttons before hitting their floor.

I wasn't going anywhere fast without one of those cards. I put on my game face and made my way to the check-in desk. One of the guards, a lanky guy with a short-cropped Afro, traded casual nods with me.

"Hey," I said. "Know who I talk to about getting a replacement access card? They just moved me over from the night shift and, man, I'm so sleep-lagged, I totally forgot mine at home."

He winced. "Ouch. Yeah, you can go over to HR and they'll issue a temp card, but they're gonna dock your pay for it."

And, if they had any brains at all, verify my access with the drill sergeant in charge of security. Too risky.

"If they gotta, they gotta," I said. "How much are we talking? Twenty bucks?"

"*Eighty.*"

I clenched up like my wallet was burning in my hip pocket. Then I hit him with the puppy-dog eyes.

"You've got to be kidding me," I groaned. "I've just got to go upstairs and verify cleaning-supply inventory for, like, fifteen minutes. I'm on camera duty downstairs the rest of the day. I don't even *need* the damn card after that."

He gave me a hard look, thinking. Then he slid a glossy white card across the desk.

"Borrow mine. *Don't* tell anybody. And bring it right back. I go to lunch in half an hour."

I bowed and walked backward and heaped praise on the man's shoulders all the way to the elevator doors.

The elevator was a rounded cage of glass, clinging to the skin of the tower. I waved the card, hit the button for the thirty-sixth floor, and it rewarded me with a chime as the door shuddered tight. Then I was airborne, watching the blurry ghost of Seattle fall down around me in the morning rain. I thought about my vision behind bars, my jaunt to the world next door: buildings capsized, Tropicana Boulevard turned to a wasteland of burned-out cars, a scrap of newspaper with a headline that simply read *GOODBYE*.

Seattle would be the epicenter when the Enemy was ready to start burning our world to the ground. Northlight Tower was where it would all begin.

This was where it would end, if there was anything I could do to stop it.

The elevator glided to a standstill. The door slid open and I stepped out into the hallway. Cautious now, still keeping up my "I belong here" stride and brandishing the clipboard but keeping my eyes and my senses wide open. There were no cameras on the upper floors, which told me the Enemy had business he didn't want the peons watching.

And I could feel him now. A pressure on my sinuses, a ruinous weight, a living cancer hunting for healthy cells to infect. I pulled my psychic tendrils inward. Canton's pocket watch sat in my hip pocket, still stubbornly useless.

Like the corporate floors below, nothing about this place screamed "lair of a world-devouring monster." Open doorways looked in on empty galleries, cubicle farms without chairs or employees, sitting under dead lights. I kept my ears perked for the sound of approaching footsteps, but I was utterly alone. Theseus, taking his first steps into the labyrinth of the Minotaur.

I followed the numbers on the walls. All the way to 3603. The door clicked, unlocking under a wave of my borrowed card, and swung wide. I heard the strains of an old instrumental, some big-band waltz, heavy on the violins. A short hallway was draped in plastic sheeting. CDC plastic, for sterile containment.

I brushed aside the dangling tarp and stepped into a hospital room. A picture window on the wall looked out over the streets of Paris.

I stood there, transfixed for a moment, staring at the rise of the Eiffel Tower just a few blocks away. An antique radio sat on a rustic window-side table, the source of the soft warbling music. A body lay upon a hospital bed, frail and blurred under a tent of heavy plastic. Its head was turned away from me on the pillow, motionless, gazing at the impossible vista beyond the window.

30.

"Hello?" I called out, my voice barely more than a whisper.

The figure under the plastic tent didn't move. I eased into the room, still keeping an eye on the view of Paris. I stepped past the closed door of a supply closet. An empty gurney stood alongside it, ready to evacuate the patient in case of emergency.

The big-band tune swelled and died, fading to silence. The old recording crackled as a new song began. A torch song: Vera Lynn, crooning to the boys as they headed off to war, promising they'd meet again someday.

The figure on the bed moved. Its shoulders shook, trembling once and then going still. Like a man in silent tears.

I circled the bed and pulled the tarp back.

I knew him. We'd never met, but I knew him from his profile, from the grainy photographs in his Interpol jacket. The thing on the thin mattress had been Marcel Deschamps once.

Before his left arm had been severed at the shoulder. Or his right hand reduced to a stump of slug-white scar tissue. The flowered bedsheet fell short of where his legs should have ended; both of them had been amputated at the knees, leaving him with helpless nubs. Half of his face was a mutilated twist of burns that flowed downward like a waterfall of melted flesh, curling around his throat.

His one good eye fixed upon me. His voice was nothing but a wheezing rasp, squeezing through severed vocal cords.

"Jesus," I whispered. "What did they do to you?"

I already knew the answer. He'd been rewritten, his life's history edited by the Enemy's time-defying magic. And I could guess why.

One of the locks on the Enemy's reliquary had a simple requirement: the ritual sacrifice of the Thief. But that wouldn't do, not once he learned the truth about Louise Canton and her plans. Not while Marcel was running all over the globe on his payroll, pulling off impossible heists and snatching up the Canton relics. He needed Marcel to finish his hunt. That's where I came in, the proxy sacrifice.

But I'd ruined the scheme. I lived, and escaped Eisenberg Correctional with my life intact and the mantle of the Thief stuck to me. If anything happened to Marcel before the Enemy could deal with me, well…it looked like he agreed with my own hunch on that one. Marcel would reincarnate on some other world, taking the role of the Thief with him, and good luck ever finding him again.

So he'd put Marcel on ice. Keeping him alive for the duration, alive and suffering and powerless to die.

Marcel's pale lips twitched. I didn't need to be a lip-reader to make out what he was trying to say.

Kill me.

I wanted to. I could end it right here. Smother him with his own pillow, two rough minutes and it would all be over. He'd be gone and so would the curse on my head. The Enemy would take a major hit, a chunk of his old power still sealed behind an impossible lock. It was a win on all counts.

Except.

Except one floor above me, somewhere, there was a vault. And in that vault were all of the Canton relics he'd collected from around the world. Relics that—if Louise was right, if this wasn't some hopeless crusade—could kill the bastard for good.

If I ended Marcel here and now, the Enemy would know I'd been here. He'd relocate the artifacts and triple his security. No chance I'd pick up the trail, let alone get another shot at stealing them back.

The Paladin intended for her next incarnation, whoever it was, to carry her relics into battle. The fate of the Earth, maybe *every* remaining Earth, might depend on it. This was bigger than me and my problems.

"I'll come back for you," I told Marcel. I let the plastic tarp flutter down, a wall between us. Leaving him with that promise was the best I could do.

*   *   *

I got off the elevator on the penthouse floor.

The air wasn't right. The careful climate control of the lower floors was gone, replaced by muggy heat imported from some other part of the world. It smelled like swamp gas and old leather. Clammy sweat spread between my shoulders, the stiff fabric of my uniform shirt clinging to my back.

The corridor twisted left, then right, canary paint on the walls giving way to eggshell white and then pastel blue, every bend a new color. A bit of corporate art hung on the wall to my right, a bland pastoral, a house at the edge of a tranquil wheat field.

I paused in mid-step and looked again.

I was sure, just for a second, that a figure had been painted in the farmhouse's window. Hands pressed to the glass, the impossibly long black O of its mouth screaming in silence.

It was gone now. Just a square of pale yellow. I kept moving.

The halls didn't make sense and the office numbers were out of order. Most were empty and dark, like the floor below. Another was filled with employees. They sat at desks, typing, papers occasionally rustling. Not a word spoken between them. I realized, as I was about to move on, that every man in the room had the exact same pinstriped suit and blue polyester tie. They also had the exact same fresh shaving nick high on their left cheekbones.

The pressure in my sinuses flared. Something scrabbled behind my eyes, like someone had opened a bag of spiders inside my skull.

He was coming.

I ducked through the open doorway and off to one side, my

hip bumping the plastic pillar of a water cooler. The water in the tank rippled. None of the silent, cheek-scratched typists glanced up from their work. I fumbled in my pocket and dug out Canton's watch.

Now, I told it. *You need to start working NOW.*

There were footsteps up the hall, coming this way. The pocket watch held its cold silence.

"I don't understand." The Enemy's voice drifted from the hallway. "What's the damn problem?"

Closer now. I fought to hold my focus, to fold my senses inward, to make myself a mouse, a speck of dust, as I pressed my back to the wall. But this was his dominion. He was going to sense me, and here I was trapped in a room with only one way out.

Two, I supposed, but throwing myself out a thirty-seventh-floor window was just a faster way to die.

The watch had concealed Ada's presence when we battled in Boston. Why? Because she was Louise's great-granddaughter? Couldn't be it. None of the other relics were keyed to Canton's blood, and she had no guarantee the Paladin would reincarnate in her own family. The wand worked for me, albeit reluctantly. So did Canton's top hat. There had to be a trigger mechanism.

"I've gotten hold of a local Network cell," Ms. Fleiss said, her tone clipped and cold. "They're sending a representative with explanations and apologies."

"Tell them to bring the explanations and leave the apologies at home."

Ada wasn't protecting anyone when we fought. She was the aggressor, killing two guards before she took a shot at me, so the wand's conditions weren't in play. All the same, Canton's fail-safes were supposed to ensure the relics only worked in the right hands. What would Ada have been thinking about?

The footsteps were twenty feet away, coming in swift as a breeze. In a few seconds they'd be on top of me. Close enough to touch.

She'd be thinking about the cause. Ada only thought about the cause. Becoming the Paladin, defeating the Enemy, leading the Redemption Choir to glory.

I pressed the brass shell of the watch to my heart and thought about my people. I thought about Teddy, downstairs, alone. I thought about how if the Enemy caught me here, he'd lock the building down. My brother would never leave this place alive.

My brother.

The watch *ticked*.

A single sound, like a gunshot, as the world shifted out of focus. Colors faded to sepia and then gray, everything sliding an inch to the left and leaving newsprint blurs behind. My pounding heartbeat slowed to a gallop, to a trot, to a crawl.

Then the watch ticked one more time, and my heart stopped.

I was a dead man with his back to the wall. The pressure and scratching sensations in my head faded, muffled in gauze. I felt something pulling at me, tugging at the core of my being, and I vaguely realized it was my soul. My body was dead and my soul was trying to leave, to move on.

Not yet, I thought.

I watched the hallway through the open door. The Enemy loomed into sight, a black-etched negative on the skin of the world. He flickered and flowed, filmstrip lightning-scratches across his shadow echoing his irritation.

"And what about you?" he snapped.

Fleiss walked alongside him, eyes shielded behind onyx lenses, impassive and facing straight ahead.

"Me, my lord?"

"You can't even open a damned gateway. Which you were *built* for."

Fleiss curled one hand in the air. In a blur, her nails had become black iron claws, long and curved and sharper than razors. She swiped her index finger downward.

Her claw tore a line in the air. The fabric of the world came undone, fraying, and beyond it shone a light like liquid gold. The

Enemy flung an arm over his eyeless face, his eternal pearly smile twisting in a grimace of pain.

"*Close it.*"

She snapped her fingers and the wound whipped itself shut. Nothing remained but the faint scent of roses.

"Not my fault," she said. "As I said, the Network emissary will explain—"

"Remains to be seen," he said. "You're clearly malfunctioning."

In the split second before they turned, slipping out of sight, I saw the look on her face. Her pursed and bloodless lips, the tension in her jaw.

"I am not—" she said, her voice halting.

Say it, I thought, cheering her on. *Tell him you're not an object. You're a person, not a thing. Not HIS thing. Say it.*

"I am not certain what's gone wrong," she said. "Something in the Shadow In-Between. I'm sorry. We'll attend to it."

"See that you do," he seethed.

I stayed frozen in a world of gray, heart stalled, lungs empty of breath, with my back to the wall. The tugging at my soul was a constant, insistent pull, like an unscratchable itch deep in my bone marrow. When I was finally certain they were gone, when there was no sound but the rustling of pages and the typing of the silent employees, I pulled the watch from my breastbone.

The world lurched back into focus and color and light. My veins burned as blood coursed along oxygen-starved limbs, flaring with the sensation of poking needles. I gave the cold brass shell a trembling pat.

"Good watch," I breathed and pushed myself away from the wall. I ambled up the hallway, continuing my hunt for room 3712.

I found it down another stretch of corridor, one that backtracked in a way that seemed to overlap with the one I'd just crossed. The geometry of this place defied any logic, any attempt to blaze a rational trail. The Enemy had been flexing his muscles up here. The suite's door was closed tight, reinforced steel, with the hinges on the inside. Instead of a card reader, a numerical keypad secured the lock.

I felt time pressure bearing down. I had promised I'd bring my borrowed card back in fifteen minutes, and I was pushing the envelope. If the guy on desk duty got suspicious, he could blow this entire recon operation with a single phone call to the drill sergeant downstairs. All the same, I gave myself a solid two minutes to study the workings of the vault.

The keypad was an Allegion. Heavy-duty, with optional biometrics. Of course, with no fingerprints and no eyes, any lock the Enemy could open had to be simpler than that. I knew these models could store a code up to twelve digits long and trigger an alarm on an unsuccessful attempt. Brute force wasn't going to get me past this obstacle.

Not past the door, either. One rap of my knuckles and I knew it was solid. I'd have an easier time carving through the wall beside it, and that was assuming the vault beyond didn't have a reinforced shell. Nothing I could crack without professional-grade safe-peeling tools, a few hours to spare, and the freedom to make plenty of noise. None of which I was going to have.

I worked the problem as I hustled back to the elevator. Maybe I didn't have to get through that door. According to the security protocols, the resident "jaguar teams" would evacuate the vault in the event of a building-wide emergency. That said, they were also heavily armed and, presumably, if they were allowed on this floor, they'd been edited by the Enemy's touch. I could trick them into opening the vault for me, but actually getting my hands on the goods would mean one hell of a firefight. Too dangerous. Subtle and quiet was the only way to play this.

I wanted to be in, out, and long gone before the Enemy ever knew I was here.

I held my breath and didn't exhale until the elevator door shut. Then I was gliding down to solid ground, the rain-licked city rising up outside the glass cage. My phone vibrated against my hip. I had a message from Teddy, marked five minutes ago;

apparently cell phones didn't work on the penthouse floor. I made a mental note.

Found a vehicle bay, he wrote. *Waiting for you. Take left at employee cafeteria then right through double doors. You should see this.*

I dropped the borrowed card off back at the front desk—just in the nick of time, from the antsy, irritated look on the man's face—and followed the signs for the cafeteria. I was ready to find my brother and get out while we still could.

31.

Big bay doors, open to the rain, looked out upon a stretch of back alley. This cavernous room technically wasn't a vehicle bay. It was the building's garbage room, where double-wide dumpsters collected the corporate tower's refuse and waited for pickup. Off to one side of a loading dock, though, on a span of oil-stained concrete, a quartet of vehicles stood with their silent grilles turned toward the exit.

An ambulance—branded with a private label I'd never heard of, probably fake—stood beside a trio of identical armored trucks. Brinks livery, most likely also counterfeit or just stolen from a depot somewhere, intended to blend into city traffic. Nothing fake about the armor, though. I circled around, checking out the gun ports and the run-flat tires. I was still stuck on the intercept-the-relics plan, but it was looking more and more like a nonstarter. Each of the three trucks was bound, in case of emergency, for a different remote site. *If* I stationed people at every possible escape route, and *if* each one was equipped to ambush and take down an armored car filled with armed combatants...

Teddy trailed behind me, watching, pensive. "What do you think?" he asked.

"I think I have to get inside one hell of a serious vault on the penthouse floor. Without setting off any alarms."

"Can you do it?"

I glanced back at him. "Any security system can be cracked."

"That didn't sound like an answer."

I circled the ambulance. On top of the relics being evacuated, a building-wide alarm meant they'd sprint Marcel on board and whisk him off to parts unknown. And now that I knew the measures the Enemy had taken to ensure he stayed alive until I could be dealt with...

I couldn't let him slip away. No matter what else happened, Marcel Deschamps couldn't leave this building alive. One more item on an impossible to-do list.

"Any security system can be cracked," I told Teddy. "You just have to figure out the trick."

"And...have you? Figured out the trick?"

I stared out at the rain, drizzling along the dirty stonework.

"I'm starting to get an idea," I said. "C'mon, let's go."

He drove. We sat in traffic a block from the tower, gridlocked at lunchtime, and the warren of streets surrounding Northlight offered more congestion in every direction. A string of ideas clicked together like puzzle pieces. A way in, a way out, what I'd need to get the job done. That old familiar elation crept up on me, the confident surge of a plan coming together.

It wasn't impossible. Just...ninety-five percent impossible. I could work with those odds. I called Jennifer on the way back to the motel.

"Just finished recon," I said.

"And?"

"And this locust job is a go. We're going to steal Canton's stuff back."

"You got the ways and means, sugar?"

"Getting there. One thing I know for certain." I craned my neck, peering around a stalled-out delivery truck at the red lights and construction up ahead of us. "Do me a favor and call Winslow, tell him I need a meeting as soon as I land back in Vegas."

"Shoppin' for a new ride?"

"I think I know how to get inside the Enemy's vault. Getting out and getting clear is going to be harder. I need a wheelman."

* * *

"I got somebody," Winslow said. "Solid with a cage, reliable. Mostly legitimate, these days."

"Mostly," I echoed.

"I find 'em work about once a year. Enough to keep a hand in."

A good wheelman wasn't just a driver. Anybody could drive. I'd been behind the wheel of a getaway car—a *cage*, in Winslow's derisive parlance—myself more than once, and I'd done fine, but that didn't make me a wheelman. A wheelman knew the territory, knew the roads, felt a map like it was made of his own veins and arteries. They were creatures of clockwork timing and Swiss watch precision. Normally I preferred to recruit locally; nobody knew a city's streets better than a native. That said, time was short and I couldn't risk putting out feelers for hired help in the Enemy's own city. One whisper getting back to Northlight Tower and the job would be blown before we even started.

So Winslow sent me to the Palomino Run, a dirt track two miles past the Vegas city limits. It was a sketch of an oval in the sage-littered scrub, ringed by bright orange construction barrels. Rickety wooden stands a few decades past their prime stood skeletal along one long side of the track, flanked by checkered pennants that caught the arid wind. Once a month, a local crowd would come out for dirt-bike racing, the occasional rally, or even a demolition derby now and then. The rest of the year it was strictly a practice track, a secluded spot for racers to push their limits and their engines.

My driver-to-be, Pecos, was alone on the track. A mud-spattered car shot past as I walked up to the construction barrels. It was a Frankenstein collision of east and west, Ford and Nissan parts grafted together to create a low-slung beast that caught on the eye like a fishhook. Meshwork and roll bars protected its ungainly hard angles, and it slouched on one brick-red shoulder as it leaned into a curve. The car wouldn't win any beauty pageants, but it was forged for handling and speed.

I reached high and gave a wave, hoping the driver spotted me. Pecos rounded the far bend and the curve slung the mutant sedan my way like a slingshot. I kept waving. Pecos tapped the brakes, coming in for a landing.

In a heartbeat, everything went wrong.

The rear tires fishtailed, kicking up a shower of dirt as the car went out of control, still shooting toward me at eighty miles an hour, veering sideways on the track. I threw myself out of the way, landing hard on my shoulder and rolling in the scrub as it hit the first orange barrel with a *bang* of ruptured plastic, ballast water spraying in all directions. The car jolted and spun a full one-eighty, wiping out two more barrels and sending them flying, finally juddering to a stop.

The engine growled, then died.

"*Fuck*," shouted a muffled voice. The caged door slammed. "I swear to God, I have no idea how that just happened."

As the driver, a woman in a scarlet one-piece racing suit, pulled off her helmet, I shoved myself up to my hands and knees in the dirt. One look and I knew exactly how it happened.

"Peach?" I said.

She cradled her helmet under her arm. "Dan? Winslow didn't tell me you were the client. This...this is embarrassing."

She offered her gloved hand and pulled me to my feet. She looked good, just like I remembered her. Same freckles, same high blond ponytail. She had tried to run me over the last time I saw her, too, but that had been on purpose.

"Embarrassed because it's me, or embarrassed because you wiped out?"

"Mostly the latter," she said. "I don't know what—"

I waved a shaky hand. "Forget it. Not your fault. Seriously, it really isn't your fault. There's a...thing going around. It's a long story. You're calling yourself 'Pecos' now?"

"Had a 'too many people knowing my name' situation. I figure you know what that's like."

I did. "I'm Paul Emerson now."

"Boring, but effective," she said.

"I thought you were headed off to NASCAR."

"I was. Came back."

She didn't offer details and it wasn't my place to press. I felt her quills rising, so I changed the subject.

"Winslow says you're looking for work."

She looked me up and down. "Could be. What's the score?"

"Corporate office in downtown Seattle."

"Size of the crew?"

"Me and a plus-one. We infiltrate on our own. Just need you standing ready to pull us out."

"What kind of trouble are we looking at?"

"Depends," I said.

"Depends," she echoed.

"Truth is, if things go south, I won't make it to the extraction point. Second the alarm sounds, your job is to hustle my plus-one out of there. Leave right on the buzzer, don't look back, and you'll be halfway out of Seattle before the cops show up."

"Who's your plus-one?" she asked. "New girlfriend?"

"My brother."

She arched an eyebrow at that.

"Shouldn't take scores with blood in the mix," Pecos said. "That's a good way to get hurt."

"So's bringing your girlfriend along, but I keep doing it." I spread my open hands. "Forty minutes of driving, maybe an hour, tops. Pickup spot to a drop-off a few miles outside city limits. Also, you don't need to bring your own wheels; the mark will provide, and I've already got a ride picked out for you. All you have to do is hotwire it."

Her short-cropped fingernail tapped her pursed lips. "And after?"

"Dump it, burn it, sell it to a chop shop, doesn't matter to me. Consider it an added bonus or don't."

"Let's talk about that," she said. "What's my cut of the score?"

"No cut, the loot isn't going on the market. I'll pay you a flat fee up front; just name your price."

"Not going on the market? So either this is a cash-money job, or you're grabbing something for yourself. What's the score?"

"Vintage magic tricks," I said.

"Weirdly enough," she told me, "I believe you."

The rest came down to negotiation, and we still knew each other too well, even after all these years, to waste much time. I gave her a number, she gave me another, and we met three-fourths of the way toward the middle. Then I told her the plan. I still had my doubts about bringing an ex-lover onto the crew, given my current predicament, but this was a self-correcting issue.

I wouldn't see Pecos again, face-to-face, until my work at Northlight Tower was done. If the killing of Marcel Deschamps freed me from the Thief's story, she wouldn't be any danger to me on the way out.

If it didn't free me, she was the least of my problems.

*   *   *

The stockroom of the Scrivener's Nook had become a construction site. Plastic tarp covered the floor and bookshelves, while power tools lay in a ragged row on a bench by the back door. I dragged a heavy sheet of plywood in from the alley, laying it atop a pile of its siblings. Bentley had a two-inch square swatch of wood to experiment with, and he peered at it through safety goggles as his latex-gloved hands rubbed it down with a sponge. The treated wood darkened, fading, taking on a tone like dried leaves in the dregs of a teacup.

"This should do nicely, I think," he said as he studied his handiwork.

Corman walked past him, unrolling a blueprint and stretching it wide in his beefy hands.

"First things first," he said, "gotta see if I still remember how to build one of these suckers. It's been a while."

Melanie came in behind me, lugging a heavy plastic sack with the rest of the shopping list. She dropped it by the power tools and the sack plopped down with a metallic clatter, a couple of loose steel hinges sliding free.

"What are we making?" she asked.

"When people look at a security system," I told her, "they see locked doors, motion detectors, cameras. The physical bits and pieces."

She tilted her head at me. "Well...that's what security is, right?"

"Only on the surface level. Look deeper and you see that every security system is created by people. And people make mistakes. Show me the most flawless network of locks and cameras in the world, and I'll show you the very flawed person who engineered it. If you want to get into someplace you're not supposed to be, you start with the people who are paid to protect that place. Crack them, you crack the system."

"Okay," Melanie said, uncertain. "So...what's with the DIY project?"

"When you get down to it," Corman told her, reaching for a hacksaw, "some heists aren't much different from pulling a short con. Step one is figuring out what your mark wants more than anything in the world."

"What's step two?" she asked.

"You go fishing. Cast it out there like a baited hook and wait." He tested the saw's blade on the pad of a callused thumb. "And once they bite? You reel 'em in."

"I'll show you what we're working on," I told Melanie, "but first you and me have an appointment across town. Have to go see a man about the final piece of the plan. And you have to master a new and important apprentice skill."

My tone tipped her off. She gave me a suspicious look. "Which is?"

"It's called, 'Taking one for the team.'"

"I'm not going to like this, am I?"

"Probably not," I said, "but look at it this way: you're a theater geek, right?"

"That's...one way to put it," she said.

"Consider this to be valuable practice." I wriggled jazz hands at her. "*Acting*."

32.

Melanie clutched her hands to her chest. Her fingertips fluttered like the pitter-patter of her heart as her eyes went starry and wide.

"I...*love* your work," she said.

There was an apparatus on the darkened stage, some kind of Spanish Inquisition torture device mated with a giant industrial mixer. David Gosselin dangled from a stainless-steel bar in mid chin-up. He bucked his hips and swung his lean body, landing on the stage in a graceful crouch, and slicked his coal-black hair with his fingertips while he rose to his full height. His white poet's shirt ruffled as he walked to the stage's edge. His slacks were tight enough to be painted on.

"Beautiful words," he said, "from a beautiful young lady."

His fingertips twirled. Now he held a fresh red rose blossom, and he offered it to Melanie, bending low in a courtly bow.

We were front row at the David Gosselin Theater, the best place in Vegas to see magicians named David Gosselin perform. Four hours to showtime. His security team didn't want to let us in, not until Melanie put on the kitten eyes and batted her eyelashes.

"You're an inspiration," she told David. "When you made the Great Wall of China disappear? Or when you made the White House disappear? Or when you made the Leaning Tower of Pisa disappear? I watched that one twenty-seven times and I still can't figure out how you did it."

He leaned closer. I could smell his aftershave. Drakkar Noir, I was almost certain.

"That's because it was..." He dropped his voice to a purr and flared out his other hand. Motes of glimmering light followed his fingertips, becoming a rainbow before fading to darkness. "*Magic.*"

"Amazing." Melanie said, on the verge of swooning.

David looked my way. "This is your new apprentice? I have to say, Faust, she's a lot smarter than I would have expected. More charming, too. Out of your league, really."

"Gee," I said, "thanks."

He gestured to the mechanical monstrosity at his back.

"This little thing? Glad you asked."

"I didn't—"

"It's my new illusion," he said, talking over me as he paced the stage. "The Conundrum! I must simultaneously face being cut to pieces in a giant blender, set on fire, and drowned in boiling oil. Only the greatest magical mind the world has ever known and the greatest escape artist of our time could hope to survive such a spectacular stunt. Yes, only those two men could do it."

He struck a pose, flashing two fingers in a V. Then he joined them together.

"Or should I say...the *one* man...who is *both* of those men."

"You really need to work on your stage patter," I said.

"Hey," he said, "when you own your own theater and a private island, you can give me performance notes."

I had to admit, I couldn't really argue with his logic.

"We need a favor," I said.

Stress on *we*. He looked from me to Melanie, his interest piqued.

"Of course you do. But how can I, a humble entertainer, be of service?"

"Two things," I said. "First, we have to borrow Canton's top hat."

His expression curdled like roadkill on a hot day. I'd already "borrowed" the hat once before, just ahead of Fleiss and her hit squad, and wrecked half of his private museum in the process. To be fair, Fleiss had done most of the wrecking, but he still blamed me for the damage.

"And I just finished paying for repairs," he muttered. "Insurance wouldn't cover it, called it an act of God. Tell me, why would I let you within a mile of that hat ever again?"

"Because I found the mother lode."

He froze on the stage in mid-stride.

"You mean..."

"The stolen Canton relics. All of them."

"And...you're willing to share?"

In truth? He'd be damn lucky if I even gave him the hat back. But without his cooperation I was going to have to break into his museum—again—and steal it, and I was already pressed for time.

"There's a big picture in play," I told him. "Those relics have a purpose. Once that purpose is fulfilled...we can talk."

"Okay, okay." His head bobbed and he made reassuring sounds, but I could tell he was a world away, already arranging a museum display with all the Canton memorabilia he ever dreamed of owning. "I'm on board. Theoretically. Maybe. What's the second favor?"

I told him the details while Melanie told him how much she admired him for helping us out. Without her help, I don't know if I would have sold him on it. We still didn't leave with an absolute commitment, but I figured we got as close as we could.

"Once the apparatus is ready," he said, "if you really think you can pull this off—and I want to hear that from Bentley and Corman, too, because I actually trust *their* judgment—I think I can lend a hand."

"We'll reimburse you for the damage," I told him.

"At the very least. And as for you, young lady..." David bowed low. He reached out, graceful as a swan, and curled his fingers behind her ear. Two powder-blue tickets sprouted in his fingertips. "For Friday night's performance. Front-row seats, for you and a friend."

"I wouldn't miss it for the world," Melanie told him. She was so sincere I almost believed her.

*   *   *

"When you told me what you wanted," Melanie said, "I figured he was going to try to sleep with me—"

"I wouldn't put you in a situation like that," I said.

"He just...wanted me to tell him how awesome he is."

We were side by side on Flamingo Road, walking fast under a shimmering desert sun, surrounded by the sleeping monoliths of the Vegas Strip. A hot dry breeze ruffled my hair.

"Sex appeal is easy," I told her. I tapped the side of my head. "Ego appeal is powerful."

She clutched her hands to her chest. "You're so good at this. I mean, watching you work, it's amazing. I'm learning so much."

"Well, thank you. I mean, I've had a lot of prac—"

I paused. Then I gave her the side-eye. Melanie's lips were squeezed tight, trembling, fighting off an impending smirk.

"Smart-ass," I said.

Back at the Scrivener's Nook, a cordless screwdriver whined and ratcheted hinges into place. The rough hull of a cabinet—or maybe a coffin—stood in the heart of the sawdust-littered tarp.

"I still got the old knack," Corman said. "We're on schedule for tonight. Could use an extra hand, though."

Melanie held up her open palms. "I have two of those."

I headed out alone for the next leg of the setup. Down to Paradise Road, snug against the outer fencing of McCarran Airport. The Paradise All-Suites was technically a tourist motel; that said, if you couldn't afford to stay elsewhere, you couldn't afford to visit Las Vegas. In practice the All-Suites was a hangout for transients, pushers, hard-luck locals, and the occasional mob of teenagers looking for a place to party. Last time I visited this place, I ended up chasing a dealer out a window and down the street, both of us waving guns. The regulars didn't even bat an eyelash.

Now I strolled through the courtyard, watching windows,

checking lines of sight. The motel was a three-floor horseshoe, ringing a concrete pavilion and a swimming pool with a patina of dead gnats. The reek of chlorine, poured in by the gallon, singed my nose hairs. I glanced east, then west, measuring the distance across as a jet roared overhead.

This'll do, I thought.

I walked into the front office and laid my money down.

"Room on the third floor, please," I said. "Facing the courtyard."

The clerk raised a bushy eyebrow. "You sure? Gets noisy at night."

"I'm a heavy sleeper."

He took my cash and gave me a key on a fat plastic tag. The room was just what I expected: chipped particleboard furniture, paper-thin carpet with dubious stains, and a jail-grade mattress I wouldn't touch without a full battery of vaccinations. I pulled aside the musty curtains and let the sun stream in on a pillar of dancing dust.

Pixie showed up twenty minutes later, twirling a second key on its tag. "I grabbed 208, on the opposite side," she said. "With binoculars I could see just about everything. You want me to set up the sound equipment?"

"Not yet," I said. "Any of the locals see you lugging expensive-looking electronics in, they won't be there much longer. Let's get this room ready first."

She had scavenged up a standing corkboard from somewhere, and we propped it up at an angle to the window so that anyone in front of it would be visible through the glass. Then it was time to decorate with pushpins and printouts. I tacked up a map of the city, anointing roads with a streak of yellow highlighter, and circled a final destination in blood-red ink. Next up were the printed emails, big blocks of Courier font. I put my highlighter back to work, making key phrases pop.

"These look real," I said.

Pixie was over by the TV stand, arranging more set dressing. A couple of cardboard coffee cups, drained to their ice-cold dregs, joined a faded receipt from a Starbucks across town.

"Mocked 'em up in ten minutes with a word processor, but they won't know that." She held up a crumpled fast-food bag and another receipt. "Think this is overkill? Will they even check the addresses?"

"If they do, they do," I said. "Every piece tells a story."

I took a step back and studied our handiwork, looking for any whisper of the inauthentic. The room told a story, all right. It was a story about long hours of surveillance, painstaking planning, an opportunity in the making.

I looked a little longer. I was stalling. I knew that.

"Time for the hard part," I said.

Pixie slid her chunky glasses low on her nose, eyeing me over the rims.

"Hard to do, or hard on your pride?"

Hard all around, really.

"Just my pride," I told her. "Is your end all set for tonight? You can definitely shut the generator down?"

She crossed her arms. "For three seconds. Three seconds before the backup kicks in, and I can't do anything about that. You'd better make it count."

I was aware. Meanwhile, I had a text from Jennifer: *Got the boom-boom prepped and ready. Waiting on you, sugar.*

I hadn't talked to Detective Gary Kemper for a while. He'd helped us yank a corrupt cop off the streets, something I considered a mutual win but he felt a little angst over, considering he knew we were taking his colleague to a soundproof room with plastic-sheeted walls. I'd been giving Gary some time to cool off in the interim.

When I called him up and told him my plan, though, he was all on board. Not just because of the bigger picture, the whole trying-to-save-the-world angle. He was on board because he got to do something he'd always dreamed of.

The doors of the Clark County Detention Center whisked

open. A churning crowd parted as Gary led me in with my hands cuffed tight behind my back. The desk sergeant, distracted, barely glanced up from his computer screen as we reached the front of the line.

"Whatcha got?" he asked Gary.

Just like Corman told Melanie, sometimes staging a heist isn't all that different from pulling a con. Step one: figure out what your mark wants more than anything in the world. I walked right up to the desk, eyes hard, chin high.

"The name's Daniel Faust," I said, "and I'd like to confess to a couple of crimes."

33.

I smiled for my mug shots, until they told me to stop.

Name? Daniel Faust. Address? No permanent abode, currently living in a room on the third floor of the Paradise All-Suites, overlooking the pool. Fingerprints? On file. Each of my fingertips rolled against the ink pad, leaving curling black labyrinths on a fresh index card. In half an hour those prints would be scanned, fed into the Clark County database, and then shared with the federal IAFIS system. And then they'd ping back with a rap sheet a mile long and a warning flag in screaming red neon.

Daniel Faust, convicted of multiple counts of first-degree homicide and grand larceny, sentenced to life imprisonment in Eisenberg Correctional Penitentiary without the possibility of parole. Presumed dead in a riot that left half the prison in flames.

I had intended to stay dead forever. As long as my ashes lay buried in a potter's field, I could operate like a free man. "Paul Emerson" was a solid citizen with credit and papers, and nobody—not the local cops, not the feds—was even looking for me. In one fell swoop I'd brought my real name back to life, turned myself into a dirty-winged phoenix, and ensured the law would hound me all the way to the gates of hell.

If I survived the next twenty-four hours, I'd have consequences to face. In the short term, though, it had to be done. *I'm still in control*, I told myself as the pastel yellow bars of the holding cell rattled shut at my back. It wasn't true, but it made me feel better. I had promised myself, after Eisenberg, that I'd die before setting foot in another prison. If we didn't pull off this plan with absolute precision, every step of the way, soon I'd be headed straight for solitary lockdown in a supermax. For the rest of my natural life.

At least I wasn't alone. A motley crew of scumbags loitered along the benches, and two of them were mine: a pair of thickset Cinco Calles bangers who had staged a fight outside a bar just an hour ago, ensuring they'd be picked up and brought to holding. We exchanged subtle nods, and one flashed me a sign: four fingers, then one, pointing downward. I echoed the gesture against my hip.

Across from the holding cell, a reinforced window shot through with chicken mesh offered a view of the parking lot and the street beyond. Just an average afternoon, sunny and clear, people out enjoying life and taking their freedom for granted. I felt a stomach pang.

I'd started taking it for granted again, too. Maybe this was the reminder I needed. All I had now was time. Time to stew, to wait, to walk through my choices and think about what I could have done differently. I leaned against the wall and watched the world go by.

This was taking too long. No clock in here, the decor designed to strangle my sense of time—sort of like a casino, but trading cigarette smoke for the stale odor of fear-sweat and piss. I took deep breaths, pushing down against my nerves with a firm but gentle hand.

I heard movement in the hallway. Gary loomed behind the bars, wearing the most punchable smirk I'd ever seen.

"Come to gloat?" I asked him.

"Damn right," he said.

I walked up to the bars with a panther stride, slow, reading his eyes. His real eyes, under the mask he was wearing.

"Been waiting a long time for this," he said.

"Enjoy it while it lasts. I won't be here much longer."

"Even if some judge was dumb enough not to hold you on remand, who do you think's gonna pay your bail? I just got word your brother left town. Got on a plane half an hour ago. Your own blood, and he doesn't want anything to do with you."

Perfect. Gary's taunts were a status update in disguise. Teddy and Pecos were off to Seattle, getting ready for their part of the heist.

"I do just fine without him," I said.

"Sure. Look at you now. You don't get it, do you? Your prints lit up the Bureau like a slot machine hitting triple sevens. Oh, and *somebody* might have leaked the news of a notorious fugitive's capture to the media."

"Can't imagine who," I said.

"Can't imagine."

Gary had spread the word all right. Just like I told him to. There was a method to my self-destructive madness. The louder Gary bugled my arrest to the rooftops, the faster the Enemy would hear about it.

The sooner the Enemy heard about it, the sooner he'd come for me.

The next lock on his reliquary wouldn't pop until he fulfilled the needed sacrifice: the torture and death of the Thief as he languished behind bars. And here I was, all gift-wrapped and waiting. A few twists of a literal knife and the bastard would get a fresh rush of power for his trouble. Maybe enough to return him to his old world-burning glory.

You'd have to be a saint to resist temptation like that, and I didn't know any saints. Any other time, this bait would have been *too* good to dangle, but I had an advantage: the disruption in the Shadow In-Between had—for now, at least—shut down Ms. Fleiss's power to carve doorways and leap across worlds. She couldn't teleport herself into my holding cell, so once the Enemy handed out her marching orders, she'd have to fly to Nevada on a plane like everybody else.

A private jet, fueled and ready, could make it from Sea-Tac to Vegas in two and a half hours. I had to figure she'd be here with a tactical squad in three, at most. And if I was still here when they arrived, they'd massacre every living person in this police station just to get at me.

"You must be having the time of your life," I said to Gary, pouring on the fake anger. "Standing on the other side of those bars like you think you're better than me."

He knew what was coming. I saw his body shift, getting ready for it. One hand dropped low to his hip, palm cupped and turned inward.

"I don't think," he said. "I know I'm better than you."

Every con in the holding cell could read my caged-lion tension. They fell silent, anticipating, the air electric as I got nice and close. My right hand curled into a fist.

"This isn't a petting zoo, Detective. You should be more careful. Get this close to the cages...one of these animals might *bite*."

My fist loomed high and fired down like a hammer between the gaps in the bars. He dodged back, my punch missing him by inches. He still played it rattled, staggering back until he bumped the corridor wall. There were hoots behind me, snickers, my fellow inmates enjoying the show.

"The feds are already sending their people to collect your ass," Gary snarled. "You know what that means? Extradition. You know where? To a state where they're real needle-happy. And I'm going to be there when they stick it in your arm."

One last bit of intel, as he charged off and out of sight to the lazy applause of the men behind me. The FBI was moving fast, eager to have a word with the surprise survivor and maybe instigator of the Eisenberg riot. That was an added complication I didn't need.

Gary had left me one more present, too, in a split second of distraction. When everyone was looking at my raised right fist—including, hopefully, anyone manning the closed-circuit camera—nobody paid attention to my left hand as it brushed past the bars. Or his right, as it pressed a bit of contraband into my palm.

I cradled it close, chancing a momentary glance into my cupped fingers to make sure it was intact. It was a broken arc of white plastic about the length of my middle finger, curled like a crescent moon. The inside edge was sharpened to a razor sheen, the tool of a jailhouse assassin. When all was said and done, reconstructing the impending crime, the authorities would assume I smuggled it in somehow. Sure, I'd been searched on my way in, with aggression and a cold rubber glove, but accidents did happen.

I gazed across the corridor and out the chicken-wire window. The sun was going down. The feds were on their way to claim me and Ms. Fleiss was on her way to kill me. Time to take this show on the road.

A new arrival rolled into the parking lot, taking it slow like he was hunting for a space up front. The rusted-out panel van was an old junker, the kind you'd see on a lot that offered cash deals with no insurance checks and no questions asked. The driver, brim of his brown hoodie pulled low, hopped out and speed-walked toward the corner. Heading across the street.

My arms prickled with the first blush of a cold and clammy sweat. My distraction was ready, but it came with a caveat: under my orders, they were only supposed to use it if the parking lot was clear. That part of the plan was out of my control. All I could do was hope for the best and prepare for whatever came next.

The barred door up the hall rattled open, accompanied by a shrill buzzer. I turned the plastic shiv with my thumb, angling it against my palm.

Gary came back with a uniformed officer and a clipboard. The holding-cell door made a stubborn grinding sound as remote servos triggered the lock release. It rolled open on a rust-flaked track.

"Prisoner Garcia, Miguel J.," Gary barked. "Step up, your lawyer's here."

One of my Calles friends pushed himself off the bench, striding toward the open gate with a gunslinger's swagger. I wasn't far behind him. Not close enough to alarm the uniformed cop, but close enough to make my move when the time was right.

Then everything happened at once.

The murky sky beyond the glass turned to high noon as the panel van erupted in flame. Its sides bulged, windows exploding, as shaped charges blasted the roof open like a volcano and a pillar of screaming fire burst loose, blazing bright. The shock wave thumped the ground and punched me in the heart as car alarms squalled, headlights flashing, a symphony of confusion while twisted debris rained down in a burning-metal storm.

Pixie—dressed in her Sunday best, posing as the Calles's lawyer and sitting alone in a reception room—heard her cue. With the tap of a button, the generator died. The overhead lights flickered once and went dark, the only illumination coming from the fires raging beyond the cracked glass of the corridor window.

Miguel coldcocked the uniformed cop and sent him sprawling to the concrete. I lunged past him, grabbed Gary by the wrist, spun him around, and pressed the business end of the plastic shiv to his throat. Prisoners were already running up behind me, boiling out of the holding cell like fire ants from a burning mound. Riot psychology: start the violence, stand aside, and a pack mentality takes hold. People will do things they never would in their right mind, like try to break out of jail when they're only in for a misdemeanor or two. Guards were flooding in from the front of the station, ready to restore order, facing down a wave of bare-fisted cons.

The first of the escapees hit the floor, flopping bonelessly as the barbs of a Taser delivered fifty thousand volts. I pulled Gary back in the opposite direction, away from the melee.

"Nobody follows me," I shouted, "or this pig gets it!"

I shouldered open an access door. The lights flickered back on, backup generator whirring to life. Gary pretended to struggle as he hustled backward with me.

"'Pig'?" he whispered. "Seriously?"

"Hey, I'm trying to be convincing here."

I shot a glance over my shoulder. Clear sailing, at least for another twenty seconds or so. We hit a steel-clad door and I spun him around to face the lock.

"Open it!" I said. "No funny business, or your wife's gonna be a widow tonight."

"You know I'm divorced," he muttered as he fumbled with a heavy ring of keys.

Out in the back lot, the air crackled with flame and the distant, looming wail of sirens. There were shouts, the echo of a single gunshot, doors slamming and horns blaring as pedestrians charged for cover across a congested intersection. I moved Gary five steps to the right. The cameras here had a blind spot.

Gary pressed his car keys into my hand and nodded toward the gate. "The blue Mazda. Do me a favor and don't wreck it. I just paid off the bank last month."

"I'll treat it like it was my own."

"I said *don't* wreck it." He shot a glare at me. "This plan is suicide. You're going to die out there. You know that, right?"

"Then this is the last time you'll ever see me. I figured you'd be happier about it."

His frown stayed put, but his glower went soft.

"Lot of people counting on you," he said. "Don't fuck this up."

"I'll try my best."

"Try harder than that."

Gary sighed. The sirens were louder now, coming in hot.

"Okay, let's do this." He tapped his cheekbone. "Right here. Make it look good, gimme an ugly bruise for the cameras."

I didn't insult him by asking if he wanted a three-count first. His head snapped back as my fist connected. He wobbled on his feet, wincing.

"Oh, no," he said. "I've been knocked unconscious by your mighty blow. I've never been hit so hard in my life. My senses are reeling."

"You don't need to be like that," I said.

He lowered himself to the concrete with deliberate care, making himself comfortable.

"How could anyone stand before such a sheer muscular powerhouse?" he said. "I will surely be out cold for at least five minutes, maybe six, but who knows what kind of long-term damage I've suffered from my brutal beating at the hands of Daniel Faust?"

"Bye, Gary," I said, stepping over his legs.

"If only he had become a boxer instead of turning to a life of crime," Gary moaned at my back. "Those iron fists would have made him a world champion."

I flipped him off at the edge of the camera's blind spot. Then I broke into a run, gripping the keys and hunting for my getaway ride.

34.

I drove southbound with flames at my back and a convoy of emergency-services trucks rolling north, firing past me in the gathering dusk and painting the cloudless sky with flashes of blood red and arctic ice. As the wailing sirens faded, I clicked the radio on. I was already the talk of the town. Most of the dial was breathlessly reporting on an explosion at the detention center and an attempted escape, warning people to stay clear of the area until the fire teams got everything under control. One of the AM stations was ahead of the game.

"...were all recaptured save for one prisoner, a convicted murderer and prison escapee named Daniel Faust. Faust is believed to have orchestrated the violent breakout, his accomplices using a homemade bomb to destroy one wall of the detention center. Faust took an officer hostage at gunpoint and is now on the run. He is considered armed and extremely dangerous..."

Well, at least they tried. I didn't mind all the wrong details. If people were looking for a con and his hostage, they'd ignore a man driving alone. I figured my mug shot would be on every TV station in the city within thirty minutes; unless I hit bad traffic on the expressway, I'd only need twenty. Gary would buy me time, playing groggy when his buddies found him and only "noticing" his car keys had been stolen once he'd gotten his senses back.

I was still playing it down to the wire. I dumped the car in an alley one block from the Paradise All-Suites, left the keys in the glove box, and made the rest of the trip on foot. Now the hardest part was staying cool, walking smooth and casual while every muscle in my body screamed at me to run. My stomach clenched as a metro cruiser streaked by, lights flashing. The cop behind the wheel didn't give me a second glance, but I still kept my head on a swivel, making sure he didn't double back.

I didn't return to my room at the All-Suites. Instead I headed across the pavilion, past the gnat-flecked swimming pool and up a flight of white concrete steps littered with cigarette butts. I knocked on the door to room 208: two long, two short.

A deadbolt clicked. Bentley let me in, his frail hand protective on my shoulder. The lights were doused, curtains wide, all the better to see across the way. A folding chair and a pair of binoculars faced the grimy window. On a side table, a digital speaker bristling with a rainbow tangle of wires let out faint hissing static.

Melanie jumped up from the chair. "How'd it go?"

"Well, the world knows I'm alive now. Also, everybody wants to put me in prison, murder me, or both. How's your night going?"

"Nothing so far," she said. "But before she left, I helped Pixie test the sound equipment. We're good to go."

"David just phoned," Bentley added. "He's ready when you are. Shall we?"

I stared at the distant horseshoe bend of the motel and the glowing rectangle of light in my rented room. I weighed my next move.

"Wait for it," I said. "I want to be sure."

Bentley had my gear. I had carried an old wallet to my arrest, stocked with odds and ends from my first life: my original driver's license, some frequent-shopper cards, all in my real name. I wouldn't be getting it back, but that was fine. Bentley handed me my Paul Emerson wallet, fat with spending cash. I unbuttoned my sleeve and he helped me buckle my wand sheath along my forearm, cinching the leather straps tight. Next was Canton's pocket watch—the key to my unfolding plan, if it didn't decide to quit working—and a fresh pack of playing cards. Now I was ready for a fight.

"One last thing," Bentley said. "She couldn't be here, for obvious reasons, but Caitlin wanted me to make sure you had this."

It was the heavy cardboard stub of a train ticket. Amtrak, the 11 Coast Starlight, leaving from King Street Station. A twenty-hour trip from Seattle to Vegas, in a Superliner roomette for two.

"Caitlin and Jennifer have already left," Bentley said, "and they'll be waiting for you at the rendezvous point. Your Emerson alias is intact, but given that your photograph will be...uncomfortably public for a while, taking the train home seemed safer than flying."

And driving would be safer than the train, but that wasn't the point. I got Caitlin's message, loud and clear. The second Marcel Deschamps breathed his last, if this worked how we thought it would, I'd be free from the curse of the Thief once and for all.

If.

I tried not to think about the alternative. She was trying too, and that was the message printed on the ticket. Hope. Hope and the promise of twenty hours alone in a private cabin with the shades drawn low, where we could make up for lost time together. Caitlin could have waited to give it to me, held the ticket until we met again after the job was done. No, she wanted me carrying it into battle, like a knight with his lady's favor. And so I would. I slid it into my breast pocket, right up against my heart.

"We got movement," Melanie said.

I padded to the window at her side. I didn't need the binoculars to pick up the flurry of motion down in the parking lot. Two dark sedans swung into side-by-side parking spots, rolling with military precision. So did the men who clambered out, six of them, with dark glasses over their eyes and bulges under their tailored jackets. And then came Fleiss, imperious, pointing as she strode toward the steps on the opposite side of the motel.

My orchestrated arrest, as much as it might end up screwing me in the long haul, had a dual purpose. First, to lure Ms. Fleiss out into the open and along a path of my design. Once she heard about my jailbreak, she wouldn't dare go home to the Enemy empty-handed, especially not after she'd lost me twice before. Pride and terror and misplaced love would keep her on my footsteps like a bloodhound.

That was why, when the cops booked me, I made sure they recorded my rented room at the Paradise All-Suites as my current address. Arrest records were easy to lay hands on, and that's how I wanted it. A nice and simple trail for her to follow, all the way to my carefully staged hideout.

When they kicked in the door, the bug in the room picked up the noise and blared it over Pixie's jury-rigged speaker with a pop of static and the crackle of shattered wood. Melanie passed me the binoculars.

"Clear!" called out one of Fleiss's men, dipping low to poke the nose of a silenced pistol under the mattress. The same shout echoed from the dingy bathroom, over the rustle of a shower curtain ripping aside.

Fleiss trailed in their wake. She paused in the heart of the room, framed in the lenses of my binoculars. Her nostrils flared. She stared at the window, seeming to look directly at me, and my breath caught in my throat. Could she see me, this far away, lurking in the shadows? Fleiss had been human once, but that had been a long, long time ago, before the ordeal that transformed her into a Cutting Knife. One of only nine in the multiverse; seven, now that I'd helped to free two of her sisters. Between what the Network had done to her and what the Enemy had done to her after that, brainwashing and corrupting her power to their own ends, I still wasn't entirely sure what she was capable of.

All I knew was that she was damn near unstoppable, a juggernaut of iron claws and rage. And if she figured out the truth, this entire plan was sunk here and now.

The moment passed. She turned away from the window, looking to the litter on the credenza, then the standing corkboard. Her voice was a sinuous whisper, drifting through the speaker on the table.

"So that's why you came back."

I watched her study the map. Her fingertip traced a road, the imaginary route I'd marked in highlighter, groundwork for a heist that didn't exist. Then her gaze drifted to the printouts, the emails supposedly stolen from a hacked account.

"Ma'am?" one of her men asked, standing at her shoulder.

"I didn't think he'd dare return to Vegas, not after the last time we crossed paths. He'd know I'd be hunting. But if he found the perfect target, one he couldn't refuse..." She tapped her black fingernail against a tacked-up printout. "This is what he was after when he ran afoul of the law. Now, the vital question: will he flee the city, aiming to save himself while he still can? Or is he so rash, so arrogant, as to think he can still steal his prize on the way out?"

"That's our cue," I told Bentley. "Melanie, hang out here for at least half an hour after they leave, just to be safe."

She took the binoculars back and gave me a salute. Fleiss had fallen into a thoughtful silence. On our way out the door, I heard her speak once more.

"Of course he is," she said. "Of course he's that arrogant. And I'll take great pleasure in punishing him for it. More to the point, even if he flees, we won't be going back empty-handed. We'll finish his little heist ourselves. My lord will be very, very happy when he sees the surprise gift I'm bringing him."

Bentley's old silver Caddy waited downstairs, pulled up snug by the foot of the motel stairs. I dove in back, lay flat, and pulled a blanket over my head, just a little extra precaution in case some eagle-eyed motorist had seen my mug shot on TV. Bentley drove like a man possessed.

35.

When I put my plan together—or at least the random scraps and thoughts that I'd eventually hammer into a plan—I took Melanie aside. This was a good learning opportunity.

"The heart of all magic," I said, "is deception."

She was standing at the checkout counter at the Scrivener's Nook, the bookstore dead quiet as usual. With her left hand she spread a fan of cards on the grainy wood, slid them back together, then cut the deck. I noticed her slip a card from the bottom of the stack and shuffle it to the top. Most people wouldn't have caught it. The kid was good. She'd been learning card tricks from Bentley and Corman for a while now, and I had her on a refresher regimen to keep her skills sharp.

"You mean this kind of magic or the real thing?" she asked.

"*All* magic. Raw power is nice to have. Skill is better; you can accomplish a lot with a little, if you know how. But when you're going toe-to-toe with an opponent, whether that opponent is an audience you're trying to fool, a mark you're trying to con, or a magician who wants you dead, power and skill don't count for jack if they see you coming. Look at it this way: who's more dangerous, the Enemy or Naavarasi?"

Melanie started flipping cards. Red, black, red, black, in perfect synchronicity. She glanced up from the deck.

"The Enemy, duh. He can literally change reality."

"That's power," I said. "But what's he actually done with it? He's so focused on his personal finish line—popping the rest of the locks on his reliquary and getting even *more* power—that he comes at every problem like a sledgehammer. Sending out Fleiss and a carload of shooters is usually his first reaction, when it should be his last. He's predictable, and a predictable mark is an easy mark."

"And Naavarasi?" she asked.

"Illusions. That's all she's got. Well, that and a mean right hook, but Caitlin still kicked the snot out of her. Her shape-changing schtick doesn't even work on us anymore, not since I figured out how to catch her psychic scent. And yet? She backed both of us into a corner and damn near won."

"And that's skill," Melanie said, following along. She waved her hand and discreetly slid one card over another, squaring them carefully to hide her ruse. With a flip, a red diamond appeared to turn into a spade.

"That's skill plus deception. I'm worried about the Enemy. I respect Naavarasi."

"You are going to kill her though," Melanie said, giving me a curious look.

"Oh, we're going to kill her, dig up the body, and then kill her again. She's got it coming. Just...as soon as I can figure out how, without breaking any infernal laws. This knighthood thing is a bitch. I assume Prince Sitri is getting a good laugh out of it, which is exactly why he gave it to me." I shrugged. "My point being, deception does what brute force can't. And step one of any good con is to know what your mark wants. What does the Enemy want?"

"To destroy the multiverse?"

"True," I said, "but that's long-term. A good con focuses on the here and now. Something concrete and tangible, like an easy payday."

"Well, he wants to get the rest of his old power back—" She thought about it. "Which means, in the short term, he wants you."

"Excellent. What else?"

She flipped another card, turning the ten of clubs into...the seven of clubs. She frowned at the misstep, gathered up the deck, and started the trick from scratch, shuffling.

"Well, he wants all of the Canton relics. He figured out what Louise Canton was up to, and he knows they've got the power to beat him. Or at least he thinks they do. If the new Paladin is armed with Louise's gear when they fight, and they are bound to fight eventually, she's going to wreck his shit."

"Language," Bentley called from the back room.

"She is going to wreck his shit, though," Melanie murmured, shooting a glance toward the open doorway.

I nodded. "That's the operating theory. For our purposes, it doesn't matter if it's true or not. What matters is what the mark believes. So, we know two things: presented with the opportunity, the Enemy will go after me, and he will go after a stray Canton relic. He can't *not* do it."

"Which one are we going to use as bait?"

"Both," I said.

*   *   *

The silver Cadillac screeched to a dead stop under a stray streetlamp. I threw back the blanket and lurched for the door handle before Bentley had a chance to kill the engine. Time was not on our side.

Along with his theater and at least one private island, David Gosselin had parlayed his magical fortune into his own private museum. It was an urban castle, a refurbished factory on the edge of town, red brick with steel crenellations. No signs out front, nothing to mark the wonders kept within; the museum allowed visitors by appointment only.

David stood in the doorway. He waved us inside, shooting a nervous look over our shoulders like he could see Fleiss and her hit squad closing in.

"Did they buy it?" he asked.

"Hook, line, and sinker," I said. "Fleiss is on her way, so let's hustle. I want you and Bentley out of here in five minutes."

"Everything's ready. We can do it in three."

Vintage posters in underlit frames marked his collections, gathered from across the world. Houdini, Thurston, Blackstone, their memorabilia and magical apparatuses on elegant pedestals, framed in moonlight from the panes of glass overhead. Trick tables and rods of glass, devices to manifest the impossible. And at the heart of the museum, a new space set aside for the marvels of Canton the Magnificent.

Wishful thinking on David's part, considering his last Canton collection had gone the way of the Vandals sacking Rome. His new version, rebuilt from the bullet-riddled rubble, only featured a single exhibit.

* * *

"We know that Marcel was running all over the globe, snatching up Canton relics," I had explained to Melanie. "Then, once I escaped Eisenberg and ruined the Enemy's proxy-Thief plan, he put Marcel on ice to keep him alive and breathing until I could be dealt with. Since then, Fleiss and her hand-picked shooters have been on recovery detail."

"They haven't gotten a whole lot," Melanie said. "Just the substitution trunk, right? Ada stole the pocket watch before they even found out about it."

"There's not a lot left to get. That's the problem. Not sure how he figured it out, but the Enemy had one hell of a head start on all of us. He was hunting those relics long before we had even heard of Canton the Magnificent." I held up a finger. "But. The thing about rare collectibles is, there's generally not some master checklist that tells you when you've found them all."

I showed her my notepad, scribbled with the rough draft of a fictitious email chain. Once I was happy with the wording, I'd forward it to Pixie to be transformed into believable printouts.

I've had it privately authenticated and will include the chain of custody paperwork with the cabinet, wrote David Gosselin in a message to Christie's New York. *This is unquestionably the prop used by Howard Canton to perform the Sunrise Majestic routine, as seen at*

King's Hall in his 1949 benefit performance. The original swords are missing, but otherwise the cabinet is intact and in near-mint condition.

The auction house—or at least my imitation of the auction house—promptly replied.

Can include in Sale 18408, pending authentication by our own experts. Please forward documentation for initial examination.

Consider me highly motivated to sell, David replied. *Given what happened last time I had Canton memorabilia in my museum, I want this thing gone ASAP.*

"So you're going to fake your own arrest—" Melanie said, walking through the plan.

"Nothing fake about it," I said. "Not if I want to grab the Enemy's attention."

"Then you're going to break out, vanish, and leave a trail to a motel room where it'll look like *you* were planning to steal the relic."

"Presenting Fleiss, assuming she's the one he sends to kill me, with a golden opportunity," I said. "She's terrified of disappointing her boss, and she'd dread the idea of heading back without anything to show for it. But all she has to do is finish the job I started, and she can fly home with a new relic for the collection."

"What's this 'Sunrise Majestic' routine?" she asked, tapping the notepad. "I've never heard of that trick."

"Because it doesn't exist. I made it up. A solid con banks on what your mark knows and what they don't know."

I flipped the notepad shut.

"The Enemy wrote the book on real magic, and Fleiss is almost as good as he is," I said. "But I'm willing to bet that neither of them knows a damn thing about *stage* magic."

* * *

The cabinet awaited. Built by hand in the back room of the Scrivener's Nook and artificially aged by Bentley's alchemical and stagecraft know-how, it was a prize the Enemy couldn't refuse. The Sunrise Majestic was a little deeper than a coffin, dressed in faded nightingale-blue paint and adorned with stars and a sun in flaking gold leaf. The tall wooden shell stood thick and sturdy, plywood disguised as solid oak with careful varnish and detail work, and its antique hinges bore a patina of artfully applied tarnish.

It awaited a corpse. White funeral satin lined the inside of the box, quilted and yellowed with age.

"We sourced the satin from a vintage shop over on Bonneville," Bentley said.

He was pleased with his handiwork. I couldn't blame him. If I hadn't known better, I would have believed this was some dusty artifact, lost for years in a storage locker. My fingers ran over the buttons in the quilting, feeling for a hidden catch.

A button turned between my fingertips. The satin-lined panel swung open on a concealed hinge. Beyond the false bottom awaited a tiny, unadorned space, cruelly thin.

"Can you even fit in there?" David asked, looking on with his hands on his hips.

"Going to find out," I said. I stepped into the compartment, so narrow I'd have to turn my head and feet sideways to fit. Bentley stepped up to seal me in.

"The release catch is by your left hand," he said and waited until I'd found it.

He shut the lid and we tested it, twice, just to be safe. The mechanics were sound. There were plenty of ways to hide a body in a substitution trunk, like the one Marcel had stolen in Boston; most amounted, one way or another, to playing games with a viewer's depth perception and concealing a compartment for some hapless, scantily clad assistant to hide in before the big reveal.

The tightness in my gut against the wood reminded me that I was a long way from the size of a scantily clad assistant. Same principle, though. All we'd done was build a standard sub trunk with a standing-coffin shape, to make it look like a different trick. Any professional magician's stagehand would know it at a glance.

I was gambling—my life, just for starters—that Fleiss wouldn't. My recon trip to Northlight had left me with one obstacle I couldn't crack: the vault on the penthouse floor. I wouldn't be able to guess the door code, wouldn't have the time or the tools to drill my way in. That left me with one desperate solution.

David handed me Canton's top hat. It nestled in the crevice at my side, collapsed nearly pancake-flat for the trip ahead.

"One Trojan horse coming right up," I said. "Seal me in and hit the road."

36.

I thought I was prepared for the ordeal ahead of me. Not even close.

The second lid swung shut under Bentley's reluctant hand and locked with a metallic *click*. I stood squeezed between two hard sheets of plywood, pinned so tight I couldn't take a deep breath. My lungs swelled halfway and then stopped, frozen by the walls of wood. Shallow breaths made my pulse race faster, made me want to breathe deeper, a cycle of sudden anxiety that fed itself like a perpetual-motion furnace.

Sweat broke out on my face, soaking my shirt, the tiny space trapping the Vegas heat and baking me alive. A bead trickled down my temple and my cheek, tickling, leaving a burning itch in its wake. My arms were pinned at my sides. No way to scratch, no way to move at all. Now I was itching between my shoulders, all along my legs, like ants were marching in prickly waves across my skin.

I had to focus. If I didn't focus, I was going to die here.

My left hand, down at my side, pressed the hard bulge in my hip pocket. My fingertips traced the curve of Canton's pocket watch.

Muffled, distant, I heard the sound of breaking glass. A burglar alarm squalled once, then died, whining into deflated silence. Boots tromped against the hardwood floor.

Now, I told the watch. Nothing happened.

The outer lid of the cabinet creaked open on its artfully distressed hinges. "There it is," said a man's voice.

"Yeah, but...what's it do?" another asked.

"It's...well...it's the Sunrise Majestic. I mean, everybody knows that. It's famous."

"Quiet," Fleiss snapped.

I wasn't alone in my shallow prison. An alien consciousness probed at the edges of my mind as Fleiss's hands and her power both searched the cabinet for any signs of a trick. I focused on the watch and my trapped, shallow breath. Faces flickered through my mind: my friends, my family, everyone counting on me to survive and bring Canton's relics home. I thought about Ada.

My heartbeat slowed. My heartbeat stopped. With a final thunderous *tick* of the watch, a crashing cymbal only I could hear, my body died.

Fleiss's presence passed over me, then through me, and pulled away.

"Bring in a dolly and wheel it to the truck," she said. "*Carefully.* Not one scratch, or you won't enjoy the consequences."

I was weightless, hoisted up in the air, and I heard one of the men grunt.

"Goddamn, this thing is heavy."

"It's oak," one of the others said. "My wife's got a solid oak hutch. Smaller than this, and the thing weighs three hundred pounds. Lift with your knees."

Five minutes later I was flat on my back, listening to the groan of a diesel engine as the road rumbled against my shoulders. I held very still.

The stillness merged with the thrumming of the tires and I sank into the vibrations. I felt like I was slowly drifting out of my own skin, like I'd slip loose and tumble free, through the cabinet, through the truck bed, down below the road and deep into the quiet core of the earth. I caught myself, mental fingers scrabbling to keep hold.

The truck jolted to a stop, bumping my head against the top of the cabinet. The little shock of pain was good for me. It kept me sharp. I felt Fleiss's men lifting my coffin, unintentional pallbearers, and ferry me for about fifteen feet in their wobbly grip. Then I was on a solid surface again and listening to the rising roar of a private jet's engine.

My ears popped as we lifted into the sky, pressure building in my sinuses. And the vibrations of the plane pulled at me again, a gentle but relentless tug. Maybe it was the confinement, the fear, the shortness of breath from my oxygen-starved lungs, but I thought I heard a voice. Felt it, more than heard it, calling to me from a dark and shining horizon.

Why do you linger? it asked. *That body is dead. It will rot and feed the world and you have no place there anymore. Come away. Come away.*

Canton's Hibernation was a short-term disguise. I doubted Louise had ever tried using it for more than ten minutes at a time, just long enough to pull off her milk-jug escape and prepare her future incarnation to use it against the Enemy's senses. I was going on nearly two hours now. The perfect illusion of death could fool anyone, even my own soul. I clung tight to myself, my senses, my identity, dangling above a chasm. There were rocks below in the dark, rocks that would dash me to pieces if I let go.

A fresh fear joined the rest, forming a siren chorus. What if I *hadn't* fooled Fleiss? She'd been deceived and manipulated by the Enemy, but she wasn't stupid, far from it. If she sensed me hiding in the cabinet, then pretending she hadn't noticed—and delivering me to the Enemy, gift-wrapped and ready to die—would be the natural choice.

And I wouldn't know until we arrived at the heart of Northlight Tower, cut off from any hope of a rescue.

I couldn't play the what-if game. There wasn't enough breath in my lungs to waste any on maybes. I dug my fingernails into the plywood against my back. The rough sensation was a distraction from the itching, the sweat, the heat, the claustrophobic and devouring darkness. A tiny one, but I'd take anything I could get. Anything to help me hold it together until the end of the line.

* * *

The jet came down rough in Seattle, bouncing me against the plywood sheets as the wheels slapped the runway, rose up, then bounced back down again. The engine screamed in my ears. We'd barely stopped when the cargo bay door dropped open with a clang. Time went fuzzy around the edges, and I still felt the vibrations of the plane long after they'd hauled the cabinet out and loaded it onto another truck.

There was a slow drift upward in a cargo elevator. Then a long, shivering silence, before two voices broke the stillness.

"*Beautiful*," the Enemy purred.

"I brought it just for you," Fleiss said.

I felt them both, looming just on the other side of my hiding space. Two black suns, throbbing with malevolent power, and nothing between us but a quarter inch of cheap wood and quilted satin.

"But you *didn't* bring me Faust," he replied.

Her voice went tight.

"He...escaped from custody before we landed in Nevada, my lord. There was nothing I could have done."

"Excuses," he muttered, his voice muffled by the wood. "Nothing is more tedious. Or pathetic."

"I—" she started. Whatever she was going to say next, she stumbled over the words, going silent for one heartbeat too long. "I apologize, my lord."

The Enemy was silent too for a moment, reflective.

"This," he said, "does please me, though."

I heard a static rustling sound, his voice fading a bit as he moved away from the cabinet.

"Imagine. Wasting an entire lifetime tinkering with these little toys, thinking they'd give her an advantage against me." He raised his voice. "You aren't smart, Louise. Not very smart at all, are you?"

"If I may—" Fleiss said.

"How many of her incarnations have I killed, Fleiss? How many, on how many worlds?"

"I...wouldn't venture to guess."

"Not this time. No, not this time. She thought she was going to end *me* for good?" His voice arced to a half-mad shout. "*You aren't smart, Louise!* Not like me. No. I've learned from my mistakes. Things are going to be different this time."

"My lord? I hate to interrupt, but if I may remind you, you do have a meeting."

"Hmm?" he said, jolted from his reverie.

"Mr. Smith is waiting for you in the conference room on thirty-four. He's brought an olive branch from the Network and, one hopes, an explanation for the recent...irregularities."

"Oh? Oh. Of course. Accompany me, would you? I'll come back when we're done. I'd like to spend a little...personal time with my new acquisition."

A door whispered shut. Then silence. I counted backward from twenty and when I hit zero, I yanked my fingers away from the husk of Canton's pocket watch.

My veins were on fire. I tried to buck, to inhale, but the tight wood trapped me. I fumbled at the release latch, fingers slipping, caught it—

—the hidden compartment slammed open and I crashed to a hard white ceramic floor, my eyes wide, gulping down air like a newborn baby. My knees buckled, arms and legs seizing up with muscle cramps, and I rolled onto my side as I rubbed life back into the burning tissue one flare-up at a time. Slowly the waves of agony receded and color returned to the world. I was here. Alive.

And alone, inside one of the Enemy's personal vaults.

I pushed myself to my feet, unsteady, and reached for Canton's top hat. I held it by the brim and gave it a shake. The collapsed hat sprang to its full height, glossy black and ready to help put on a show. I had just the routine in mind.

It was a vanishing act.

37.

The walls of the vault, as I'd expected, were reinforced against anyone cutting or drilling their way inside. I watched my hazy reflection, a carnival fun-house blur, waver across sheets of stainless steel. White marble pedestals ringed the room, each one bearing a red velvet pillow, each pillow bearing a stolen treasure. All but two by the door, empty and expectant; I figured those were waiting for Canton's wand and hat. The door itself had a bank-vault-style wheel lock. It held the reinforced door securely shut, but it was never intended to keep someone on the inside from getting out.

I studied the room while I weighed the conversation I'd just overheard. I wasn't sure what bothered me more: the fact that the Enemy was even more of a raving lunatic than I had realized, that despite my best efforts Fleiss was still firmly under his spell, or that they were both on their way to meet with Mr. Smith, a Network agent who I had personally shot right between the eyes. He looked dead enough the last time I saw him.

If I got the chance before I left Northlight Tower, I'd kill him again and make it stick. First things first, though. I was surrounded by Louise Canton's legacy, a treasure trove of devices handcrafted and designed to ensure the Enemy's final demise.

I had no idea how any of them worked.

For that matter, I wasn't sure why he'd kept any of this stuff around instead of tossing it all into the nearest furnace. If someone created an artifact designed for the express purpose of killing me, smashing it to pieces and then melting those pieces to slag would be at the top of my to-do list. Instead, the Enemy built a museum. I supposed I could chalk it up to an out-of-control ego—you could chalk most things in life up to somebody's out-of-control ego—but I had a nagging suspicion there was more to it than that.

And I didn't like how he talked about Canton. Like he had a bigger plan, this time around, than fighting the Paladin and starting the story's cycle all over again.

I scooped up a pair of brass linking rings from the closest velvet pillow. Something roused against my fingertips, a wary and cold spark of magic warming to my touch. Cagey and distant, but there. The Chinese linking rings were one of the most time-honored, classic, and boring tricks in stage magic history. I hoped the Paladin didn't have to go into battle with these; win or lose, that'd just be embarrassing.

I held the brim of Canton's top hat with my other hand, turned it upside down, and slid the rings inside. They sank into the hat, tapped the satin—and then slid through. My wrist followed them in, then my arm, enveloped by a sensation like warm pudding and then icy, airless cold.

Canton had enchanted some sort of dimensional pocket into her top hat, a secure hiding place for her wand when she was preparing to face Damien Ecko. I'm pretty sure she never intended it to be used as a loot sack. Then again, she never anticipated me, either. A sturdy cotton rope with a knot tied on one end was the next relic into the hat. Then a trio of steel cups and a squishy red foam ball. I recognized a vintage poster on the wall from David's own collection, stolen when Fleiss hit his museum the first time around. I took it down, popped it free from the frame, rolled it up, and slid it into the hat lengthwise.

All the while I was giving sidelong glances to the substitution trunk that Marcel stole in Boston, sitting in a place of pride at the heart of the room. That wasn't going to fit. I had no way of getting the thing out with me, which left one crucial decision: leave it behind, or wreck it? If the Enemy had found some means of perverting Canton's relics to his own ends, I'd be leaving a potentially powerful piece of magic under his control. On the other hand, if I set the thing on fire or took an ax to it, I could be ruining a key piece of Canton's original plan.

I stared at an Arabian brass lamp, plucking it from its pillow, and gave it a wistful rub with my thumb.

"I don't suppose you want to provide some insight here?" I asked it. "Anything? Any guidance at all?"

The lamp refused to offer up any advice. Or a genie, for that matter. I stuck it in the hat.

The last of the stolen relics—a set of trick coins, hollow silver Peace Dollars stamped in 1927—joined the lamp and the rest. The top hat spun in my hands, almost weightless, and I put it on with a flourish. Then I took hold of the vault door's wheel, stiff under my hands, and tugged it into motion.

The trunk could stay. I wanted to make a clean sweep, but I still didn't know the full scope of Louise Canton's master plan or how all of this gear was supposed to take the Enemy down. Leaving the trunk in play might not have been the safest choice, but it felt like the smartest move I could make. Everything else in the vault was coming with me.

"For my next trick," I said as the door swung wide, whispering on its oiled hinges, "the murder and reincarnation of Marcel Deschamps."

So far, the plan was good. The plan was holding. I'd smuggled myself into the Enemy's vault and rounded up his artifact collection; all I had to do now was go down one floor, put Marcel out of his misery, and make my getaway. Teddy and Pecos should be quietly blending in near the lobby, waiting to put their part of the heist into motion. Meanwhile, assuming everybody was on schedule, Caitlin and Jennifer would be staging the last part of the plan at the far edge of the city. We'd all gone over the fine details, rehearsed as much as we could, and we knew our jobs.

Which didn't explain why I turned right instead of left, heading in the opposite direction of the elevator banks.

This was my one and only shot at piercing the mysteries of Northlight Tower. Once the Enemy came back and found his ransacked vault, the counterfeit cabinet and its secret compartment, he'd know exactly how he'd been hit. And exactly who hit him. He'd probably double his security, at least. Zero chance I'd ever be able to slip in under his nose a second time. Still wouldn't matter, under normal circumstances; the prospect of wandering the halls and running straight into the Enemy, or Ms. Fleiss, was all the motivation I needed to get the hell out of here.

But thanks to what I'd overheard, I knew exactly where they both were. In a conference room three floors below. No telling how long the meeting with Smith would last, but I assumed they had a lot to talk about. Enough that I could risk a few minutes—five, maybe—and poke a little deeper.

I regretted my decision almost immediately. The farther I walked, the less sense the penthouse floor made. Corridors doubled back onto themselves, branching in impossible intersections. Beige and blue and sunflower yellow warred at every turn, as if the floor had been formed by a half dozen office buildings colliding in a dimensional nexus. Mismatched office chairs lined the wall outside a door marked "Waiting Room." Beyond the door was an identical hall with identical chairs. And through it all, not a single living soul. Just me, a mouse in a lunatic's maze.

Double doors silently opened onto a reception area, shadowy under amber-tinted lights. A stone fountain burbled on a receptionist's curved desk, and more rows of seats—some canvas, some leather, a few rickety aluminum folding chairs—sat vacant. A chemical tang hung in the air, like the fluoride smell of a dentist's office.

The receptionist had a plastic smile and blank eyes, like painted glass. "Can I help you?" she asked.

I had an idea where the windowless doors beside her desk would take me. Not anywhere I wanted to go. All the same, if I didn't take a peek, I knew I'd wonder what I might have found there. I'd never get an opportunity like this again.

"Dropping off a sales report from Mr. Blue," I said. I strode toward the door, unstoppable, a model of smooth confidence. Inside, I was bracing for a fight.

She didn't even notice that my hands were empty. "Okay," she said and went back to smiling blankly at the wall.

The door yawned onto darkness. I let it fall shut behind me, sealing me in.

38.

I clicked the light on my phone.

It was an office. *The* office, with a sleek glass desk and a high-backed executive chair. Floor-to-ceiling windows would have offered a billion-dollar view of the Seattle skyline but they'd all been blacked out, coated in onyx paint. The darkness around me was a hungry thing, devouring the glow of my phone, swallowing sound. My footsteps were silent on the thin black carpet, like I was walking on an alien moon. All I could hear was the steady drumbeat of my own pulse.

I circled the desk. Antique tarot cards lay in a horseshoe spread on the glass. I couldn't divine anything from their pattern; it was a mishmash of predictions, jumbled futures, and what-ifs. Beside them was a book. Thick, with heavy and yellowed pages between blank hard covers. I opened it.

I meant to start from the beginning. My hand disobeyed me. I opened the book somewhere around the halfway point, my fingers ruffling the pages like they knew exactly where to go.

It was a play.

My light fell upon stage instructions in crisp type. When I saw my own name on the page, somehow I wasn't even surprised. Everything about this felt normal, natural.

DANIEL FAUST stands in the ENEMY'S inner sanctum, it read. *As he follows the stage instructions, he suddenly realizes exactly what he has discovered.*

The rest of the page—the rest of the book, as far as I could tell—was blank. Then it hit me. Fresh text appeared on the page as if an invisible typewriter was hard at work.

FAUST: *It's the reliquary.*

I whispered the words, reading them from the page. Or the page typed them out as I spoke them. Everything was happening at once.

Faust has found the vessel of the Enemy's essence, the narrative continued. *Is the play documenting events as they unfold, or is it dictating them, weaving reality to suit its needs? He isn't certain. He only knows, with the fearful instinct of a prey animal in the presence of an apex predator, that this is the most powerful magic he has ever witnessed. His pulse quickens.*

"You're not the boss of me," I muttered.

It wasn't wrong, though. I could hear my own heartbeat in the heavy silence, a war drum echoing in my ears. Faster now, as my mouth went dry.

His immediate instinct is to burn the book. Of course, just as quickly, he realizes that such an attempt would be fruitless.

"Yeah, have to figure he'd have warded this thing against—" I paused as my own words spilled out on the page, a fresh line of dialogue.

FAUST: *Yeah, have to figure he'd have warded this thing against—stop that. That. Stop doing that. Stop writing down everything I say.*

I gave up. So did the open page, until a fresh suspicion loomed in the back of my mind. More type blossomed under my phone's beam of light.

Then it hits him. This is no mere receptacle, a system of locks to keep the Enemy's power safe. The reliquary, the play, is a sentient being.

When the Enemy knew he was about to be banished, he stashed away as much of his magic as he could, trusting Fleiss to keep it safe until he found a way to bust out. It only occurred to me now that he'd lost more than a few spells in the process. The Enemy wasn't even a man: he was a shadow negative, the flickering, erratic outline of a human being with nothing but a pearly white smile. I'd assumed, wrongly, that it was his natural state.

"You're...him, aren't you?" I said to the book. "Not just his magic. Parts of his mind, his personality, even his body. No wonder he's so damn crazy. He's *incomplete*."

The reliquary holds its silence, read a new line of type.

All the more reason to stop him from putting himself back together. As it was, the Enemy could twist reality, rewrite history, play with the laws of physics. He was limited by range—he had to get his spectral claws on somebody to alter their past, and the space-warping weirdness of the penthouse floor hadn't leaked to the tower below—but at his full potential there was no telling what he'd be capable of.

"Tell me this much," I said. "How'd he figure out what Louise Canton was up to? And why is he hanging on to her artifacts instead of destroying them?"

Faust reflects, the play said, *on the possibility that Canton worked with people who knew her secrets. Stagehands, an assistant or two. One of those people may have kept a diary, which found its way into the Enemy's hands.*

I could see it happening. Didn't mean I necessarily believed it, though. "What about his Canton museum? Why hang on to magical relics that are designed to kill him? Don't tell me it's just his ego."

Faust considers the role of the ego when it comes to occult operations. A strong sense of self is often the only thing that keeps a mortal mind from fracturing into splinters when exposed to reality-altering magic.

Not an answer. Not wrong, but not an answer. Before I could muster another question, type unfolded on the page. Fresh directions for me to follow.

Faust thinks he knows who the current incarnation of the Paladin is. He pictures her in his mind's eye.

No. My gut clenched. I threw up a brick wall, blanking my thoughts. When the Enemy returned to his office, he'd read every word of this. This wasn't just a reliquary. It was a trap, and I'd walked right into it.

He pictures her name, the play commanded.

I cursed at the page and my words became a line of dialogue. Or it gave me my line and I parroted it out loud. I was swept up in the wave of black ink, on the page instead of reading it, a character in the Enemy's play. I thought about walls, about the blue glow of a dead television channel. I filled my mental ears with the memory of hissing static.

He is remembering her face and her voice, the play wrote, *and he pictures her name.*

There is nothing harder, in the entire world, than trying *not* to imagine something. The perversity of our minds demands it. And in a heartbeat, in one faltering second of will, I knew what I'd done. The evidence of my treason unfolded before my eyes.

Ada Lovelace Canton

Harmony Black

Faust believes that one of these women is the Paladin. In truth, they may both be innocent, but the possibility alone is enough to seal their fates. He has betrayed these women. And when they die, their blood will be on his hands.

"Fuck you," I said. "You know, I've got a real easy way to keep you from snitching."

His plan is obvious, the page read. *He will steal the reliquary and take it with him. Before he shuts the cover, though, he realizes that won't work. The reliquary is a fixed point in the multiverse, existing on multiple parallel Earths, absorbing and harnessing the very powers of creation. It is stronger than the Enemy himself, older than the Enemy, and it is fully capable of defending itself from harm.*

"What are you going to do?" I said. "Give me a paper cut?"

The reliquary will be forced to defend itself, it replied.

"And if you could do that, you would have already done it. I'm calling your bluff. Let's go."

I slammed the cover shut, scooped the book up under my arm,

and charged out of the office. The glassy-eyed receptionist didn't say a word.

I found an access stairwell. Unlocked, no alarm. I took the stairs all the way down, three floors to the street. A battered utility door opened onto a side alley. I burst out, heart pounding, my prize in hand. I'd gotten away clean.

I forced myself to slow things down. Walking casual, blending in, making my way toward the riverfront. A gossamer mist clung to the water tonight. The air smelled of salt and diesel fumes. Up ahead rose the towering limestone bend of the Stettle Arch. Both moons were blooming tonight, one full and ice blue, the other a bone-white curve in the starless sky.

I'd gotten away clean, but a nagging sense of worry dogged my footsteps. Something was wrong. I just couldn't put my finger on it.

Tangerine.

I took the bullet train home. The Argisene Grimoire was stowed away in my carry-on bag, and customs didn't give me a second glance. I wasn't tempted to read the thing; the grimoire had a long, sordid history of madness and death, and I didn't feel like joining that particular party. Whatever the client wanted it for, that was his business. Getting paid was mine.

Noir York City was where I rested my head. Deep in the cyclopean caverns of Oswald Heights, under endless ribbons of skyway concrete and the black, roiling storm clouds. You couldn't see the moons from here on a good night, and it was never a good night in this burg.

My office was on the eighty-third floor of a building that forgot its own name around the same time it forgot to pay the janitors: a long, long time ago. Black block letters on the pebbled glass let my visitors know the score. *Danielle Faust Investigations*, it read. *Private Inquiries, Occult Consultations, Discretion Assured.*

That was for the friendly visitors. For the rest, I had a bloodthorn sigil etched into the doorframe, a line of brick dust across the threshold, and a sawed-off shotgun taped to the underbelly of my desk.

I clicked on the lights and caught a glimpse of my reflection in the mirror by the door. Tired. Mostly tired. Still, I didn't look half bad for a dame pushing forty. I wore a long blazer over my corset top, fishnets with a leather skirt, and boots that could kick a man when he was down and make him beg for more. Chestnut bangs poked out under the brim of my top hat. A tarot card nestled in the hat's deep purple band: the Tower, my personal favorite. I figured the art of a fortress crumbling in a cataclysm was ample warning for anyone who might get too close to me.

I needed two things, whiskey and cocaine. I was all out of whiskey. I stashed the spell book in my safe, where it would sit until the client called me back. Then I tossed my hat onto the rack by the door and tapped out a line of neon-green powder on my desk blotter.

I tried to keep my eyes off the bulletin board. It was dressed in old glories, faded newspaper clippings I kept around to torture myself over times gone by. *Magic Detective Unmasks Cabal*, one read. Another blared, *Psychic Shocker! Hero Cop Battles Ghosts at Museum of Industry!*

Better days.

And better lays, I thought, my gaze drifting to the framed hologram on the edge of the cluttered credenza. Me and Connor, out on a night stroll across the Cornelius Bridge. I was leaning back in his strong, muscular arms, and he flashed the camera his Irish rogue smile. I should have known it wouldn't work out for long. I drank bourbon, he drank blood. Still, it was only a matter of time before I got wasted enough for a two-in-the-morning phone call, and we'd be in my bed or his by three. Might as well get it over with. I wondered what he'd give me first: a climax or a deep sense of regret.

"The shit I put up with," I muttered, reaching for the desk phone. It rang before I touched it. "Faust Investigations."

"It's Harding," said the gruff voice on the other end. "You in town?"

A phone call from the chief of police was never good. A phone call from the chief of police after midnight was even worse.

"I might be."

"I might have a job, then."

"Are you asking in my capacity as a private investigator," I said, "in my capacity as a state-licensed de-animator, or in my capacity as the *prima domina* of the Sanctum Rouge?"

That threw his stride. "Do...I have to choose one?"

No. But when you're a magic detective, it helps to lay your credentials on the table right up front. I didn't want Earl forgetting who he was dealing with, especially when we got around to discussing my fee.

"Talk to me," I said.

"There was a breakout at Corum Asylum earlier tonight—"

"Of course there was." I leaned over my desk blotter, chopping the green powder with a razor blade and making a nice, tight line. "Might want to fix that revolving door."

"Trigger Mortis and Damsel escaped. Now we've got a hostage situation on our hands."

"Trigger doesn't take hostages. He takes heads."

"Him we've got cornered across town. It's Damsel. She's at Wonder Pier, and my guys can't get anywhere near her. You need to save those people."

I shoved my chair back. No rest for the wicked.

* * *

"You aren't supposed to be here," Damsel cooed at me.

She had long wispy mermaid hair, spun like gold, and kaleidoscope eyes. Baby-blue fractals whirled and broke inside her irises like the fragments of her own waylaid sanity. We faced off under the Ferris wheel, a monument of violet and wasp-yellow neon that ignited the black waters off the pier. She'd made a couple of new friends. They were huddled and shaking, clutching each other, sitting on the boardwalk with their backs to a shuttered concession stand. She didn't have to tie them up; they were too afraid to try to run.

"You know what?" I said. "You're right. I just came back from a long trip, I'm tired, and I have dinner waiting at home. And by 'dinner' I mean cocaine. You need to let these people go. Then you need to go back to the hospital."

"I don't like cocaine," she said.

Good. Meaning she wasn't on any. When Damsel did coke, people around her had a habit of vibrating until their skin burst open. I still wasn't sure what she'd scored this time around. There were pink elephants whirling through the air by the police cordon, holding the cops back, and I kept seeing sparkles and glowing pink trails at the corners of my vision. I hoped it wasn't acid. The only thing worse than a bad acid trip was standing at ground zero when Damsel's brain gave her hallucinations teeth, claws, and hunger. This I knew from personal experience.

And I still couldn't shake the feeling of trouble on my heels. Tonight had gone smooth as silk until now, but a stray thought banged around the back of my skull like a fly trying to get out through a closed window. *Something is very wrong here.*

"You're scaring these people," I said. "You don't want to scare anyone, do you?"

She never wanted to, not intentionally. The problem with Damsel wasn't talking her down; it was doing it before she managed to break her victims' brains beyond repair. My brow was wet and sticky and the aroma of spicy cinnamon wreathed my head like a tainted halo; I'd inscribed the lesser banishing hexagon of Malkuth on my forehead with anointing oil to keep her out of my head while I worked.

Faust considers the role of the ego when it comes to occult operations. A strong sense of self is often the only thing that keeps a mortal mind from fracturing into splinters when exposed to reality-altering magic.

I frowned. Where had that thought come from? Sounded like something from one of my books, back at the office, but I couldn't place it. I knew it was something I'd read recently, though.

"I discovered something tonight," Damsel said. She leaned back, her hair flowing in a cold and salt-tinged wind. "I'm a psychopomp. That's a conductor. Not a choo-choo conductor, though."

I knew the meaning of the word, of course. A guide for dead souls. All the same, it registered wrong, like that wasn't what she meant. More words flitted through my mind, joining my sense of disquiet. Paladin, Enemy, Witch, Knight, Psychopomp, Thief—

Thief.

Damsel was wearing ballet slippers with her hospital gown. No idea who she stole them from. She stood en pointe, heels arched high, and raised one wobbly arm above her head.

"You're displaced." She spun into a sleepy, loping pirouette. "You don't even know how you got here, do you?"

Of course I did. I'd gotten the call from the chief, then I'd...

...it was a blur. I had hung up the phone, grabbed my hat on my way out, and found myself staring into Damsel's kaleidoscope eyes. Not the first time that had happened tonight. The bullet train home from Stettle was more of a vague impression than a solid memory.

She froze in mid-twirl, bent back impossibly far, one leg extended as she balanced on the toes of a single foot. Our eyes locked.

"Who are you?" she asked me.

That was easy. I was...names. Names cascaded through my mind, spilling like stray pages from an overstuffed binder. Billowing around me, spinning in a chaotic whirlwind. I grabbed at them, my fingers snatching nothing but air.

a strong sense of self is often the only thing

Where had I been? I remembered a dark office, no lights, the book I'd been paid to snatch lying out in plain sight. Who was the client? I couldn't remember taking the job. I couldn't remember yesterday.

that keeps a mortal mind from fracturing into splinters

This wasn't my city. This wasn't my anything. I was coming apart, colors at the corners of my eyes stretching, smearing like oil paint. This wasn't Damsel's doing. It was me, the lack of me, the nothing I was below the surface.

when exposed to reality-altering magic

I needed something familiar to latch on to, a life preserver in the tempest. I remembered talking to Melanie. (*Melanie? Who the hell was Melanie?*) "Sex appeal is easy," I told her, then tapped the side of my head. "Ego appeal is powerful."

Ego could mean sense of self. Ego could mean conceit. I didn't consider myself a conceited woman, maybe a little vain about my image, but—

There it was. The chaos wave broke on a shore of crystal clarity. I almost laughed. It was something I'd said once in a careless moment of bravado and the name had chased me ever since, a constant irritation. In the end, that irritation had dug deep enough under my psychic skin to follow me across the wheel of worlds. I'd traveled light-years with a pebble in my shoe.

"I know exactly who I am," I told her. "I'm...*the guy*."

40.

I blasted through the office doors, cradling my prize under my arm.

In the wrong direction. I hadn't left the Enemy's darkened lair. I'd returned to it. I jolted to a stop in mid-run, resting one palm against the glass desk while I caught my breath. My heart was pounding in a mad stampede and my hands shook as I slapped the book down. I ripped the cover open.

Paper fluttered, opening to the exact spot where I'd left off. Fresh stage directions appeared on the half-filled page.

FAUST returns to his original body, it read, *and as his senses come back to him, he is gifted with two realizations. Firstly, the reliquary will not allow itself to be taken from this room. Secondly, he has no idea how much time has passed in his own world. The meeting downstairs may be ending or already over. The Enemy may be on his way back upstairs even as he reads these very words.*

Faust must run, or die.

So I ran. Through the labyrinth, doubling back and following corridors that bent and overlapped, only vague memory to guide me. They weren't the same hallways. The Enemy's lair rearranged itself by deranged whim. I wondered how much of it was due to his reality-bending experiments and how much was caused by the presence of the reliquary, like radiation seeping from a nuclear reactor.

A reliquary that, thanks to my screwup, had Ada's and Harmony's names. All I could do now was get out of here, fast, and warn them both before Fleiss and a kill team kicked their doors in. *Asshole*, I thought. Enough. I could beat myself up about it later, on my own time. Right now I had a hat full of stolen relics and a job to finish.

I found the elevators. I hit the down button and hid around the corner, lurking out of sight until the doors rumbled open on an empty glass cage. The coast was clear, for the moment. I still had a little time before the Enemy returned. Maybe just enough time.

I took the elevator down to thirty-six. Into room 3603, through the dangling plastic tarp, embraced by the soft crooning of a Perry Como tune on the vintage radio. Marcel's sterile prison was just the way I'd left it, with his shrunken and mutilated body lying still under a gauzy tent. The impossible window had changed; instead of Paris, now it looked out over the Seattle skyline, with the first stains of a dirty orange sunset on the horizon.

My fingers brushed the stiff cardboard train ticket, nestled in my shirt pocket. Hope. In a few minutes I'd either be free of the Thief's curse and the cycle of the first story, or I wouldn't be.

"Do you know who I am?" I asked Marcel.

His scarred, puckered face gave a little twitch. No. He had no idea. I wondered if he even knew who *he* was, or why the Enemy had done this to him. I pulled back the plastic flap of his tent so I could look straight in his one good eye.

"I want you to know this isn't personal," I told him. "Another time, another place, we might have worked together. I could have learned a thing or two."

The corner of his mouth, a pinwheel of twisted burn tissue, shivered. He was trying to talk. Just two words, and I read them on his lips as his breath wheezed out: *do it*.

I snatched the pillow from under his head, pressed it against his face, and shoved down with both hands.

He bucked under me. The gnarled stump of his arm pushed feebly at my chest, trying to force me back. It doesn't matter how badly a man wants to die: self-preservation is a primal instinct. I leaned in, putting all my weight into the job. The nubs of his amputated legs hammered the hospital bed, a desperate frenzy as his air ran out and his brain began to starve.

His body heaved under me, twice. Then he went limp.

I wasn't sure what I was expecting. A sensation, a sign, something to show that either the curse had lifted or that it was still with me. I felt exactly the same. Time would have to tell, at least until we figured out a way to be certain.

Marcel was light, for dead weight. Losing most of his limbs had done that. I heaved his corpse over my shoulder and lugged him to the closet. Then I dumped him inside and shut the door, leaving him in the dark.

Funny how things worked out.

Marcel Deschamps had been the greatest cat burglar in the world once. Then he took the wrong job from the wrong man and this was the end of his story: mutilated, broken, smothered, and dead, dumped to rot in a broom closet. Then again, if he was the professional I imagined he was, he knew that pulling one last job and retiring to a tropical beach only happens in the movies. Getting into the life means signing up for the whole ride: the highs, the lows, and the short hard drop at the very end.

When my time was up, I'd probably end up facedown in a ditch somewhere. If I were lucky, I wouldn't see it coming.

I went back to the elevators, rode down one more floor, and stepped into a quiet alcove. My phone finally had a signal. I sent a quick text to Teddy: OK?

In position, he replied. Good. One last step. I called the front desk.

"Thank you for calling Northlight," the receptionist said. "How may I direct your call?"

"I have planted two bombs somewhere inside your building. They detonate in twenty minutes. Good luck."

I was on the elevator back to the thirty-sixth floor, coasting upward in a cage of glass, when the klaxon of a fire alarm split the air.

They had procedures for this sort of thing. No time to ask

questions, no time to investigate: the Enemy's handpicked "jaguar teams" would be scrambling into position, ready to evacuate Marcel and the Canton relics. I was scrambling too, back to the sterile prison, clambering into Marcel's empty bed. I pulled the thin, starchy sheets over my head and went fetal, flattening the top hat and clutching the brim against my chest.

I listened for the stampede of steel-toed boots. They arrived with a radio squawk and a blast of panicked chatter riding on static.

"—no, bomb squad and EMS are on their way, but they're saying we need to clear the building—"

"Is this a drill?" a gruff voice asked. "Can someone confirm?"

Hands grabbed the sheets. They hoisted me into the air and onto the waiting gurney, my curled form shrouded under the tangled linens. Then I was moving, rolling fast down a hallway.

"Doesn't matter," said another voice, shouting over the fire alarm's electronic shriek. "We don't have time to—"

"Team one, team one," blurted the walkie-talkie. "Confirm you have the patient?"

A rough hand shook my shoulder through the sheets. I curled my legs tighter and played comatose.

"On our way to extraction. Why?"

"We have a problem on thirty-seven. The collection is gone."

"Repeat, Jaguar Two?"

I heard the rumbling hiss of a freight elevator's doors. The gurney's wheels bucked against a bump in the floor.

"—*gone*," came the reply, washed out in a squeal of static. "We're assuming Ms. Fleiss had it relocated, but we can't get ahold of her—"

"Jesus," breathed a voice beside me. "If she didn't—"

"Not our problem. Stay focused."

The lobby acoustics caught the fire alarm and bounced it off the polished granite walls, adding a warbling echo to its ear-piercing wail. There were footsteps, moving fast, a swirling confusion of voices. The gurney rolled down a concrete ramp, turning hard. I smelled rotting trash, the stench of an overflowing dumpster.

"Who the hell are you two?" a voice demanded. "Where's Jim?"

"Rotated out," Teddy said, shouting over the alarm. "I don't know, man, some kind of payroll screwup at the home office. Staff schedules got shuffled overnight and nobody knows why. Ms. Fleiss just told us to come down here and get the medevac prepped. That's the patient, right? We're supposed to drive him to off-site Alpha? No problem, we'll take it from here."

"Should we call it in?" one of the guards asked. I could barely hear his partner's response, his voice pitched low as they leaned over my huddled body.

"You want to be standing here arguing if it turns out those bombs are real? Let's get the hell out of here." He turned back to Teddy, louder now. "You'll take *us* to the off-site facility. Let's go."

Double doors slammed shut, and the engine of an ambulance revved to life.

* * *

I played possum for a while. Long enough to chance a peek from under my swaddled sheets and get the lay of the land. The ambulance plowed through traffic with Pecos behind the wheel, hitting the siren and lights to clear a path at every intersection. This was a refit model, an oversize van converted to a medical unit, with no partition between the driver's compartment and the back. Teddy sat beside Pecos up front, eyes forward, his fingers nervously drumming his lap. I could see why. We hadn't planned for company, and the one jaguar-team guard I could see had a wheelgun on his hip big enough for bear hunting. His partner was somewhere behind me, and I had to assume he was carrying, too.

The guard I could see was on his radio. A stream of nonstop chatter poured in, voices talking over each other.

"—no, it wasn't relocated, it's gone. Gone as in stolen—"

"—looking at the door right now. There's no damage. I'm telling you, somebody had the access code—"

"We are so screwed," muttered the guard behind my gurney.

"We did our jobs," his partner said. "Not our problem."

I squirmed enough to ease my phone out of my pocket. Huddled tight, I shot off a quick text to Teddy: *I've got this. Signal me when a hard turn is coming up.*

Through my narrow crack in the sheets, I saw him look at his phone. He showed the screen to Pecos.

"Looks like smooth sailing, boys," she said, breezy and casual. "We're past the worst traffic, think I can speed us up a little."

"Team one," said a familiar voice on the radio. "This is Fleiss. Report."

The guard in my sights put the radio to his lips. "Yes, ma'am. We're with the replacement driver, en route to off-site Alpha with the patient. Everything's fine here, over."

"*What* replacement driver?"

"The one you..."

He trailed off, staring at Pecos and Teddy. His hand slowly dropped to his holster.

Pecos wrenched the wheel and stomped on the brakes. The ambulance veered down a side road and I rolled with the turn, tumbling off the gurney and slamming into the guard. I pulled him down with me, both of us hitting the floor. His partner jumped on my back and hooked a beefy arm around my throat. I wrestled his buddy for the gun, grabbing his wrist, pounding his knuckles against the floor of the van until his skin split and he let go. Pecos hit the gas and the wheelgun went sliding, spinning out of reach.

His partner hauled on my throat until black spots blossomed in my vision. I threw an elbow into his gut and he let go with a grunt, staggering back. The first guard only had eyes for the gun. He scrambled for it on his bloody hand, reaching, and another screeching right turn sent the three of us tumbling against the gurney. It fell hard and we crashed into it together, cold metal rattling my spine. I shook off the pain and threw a punch and the guard with the gun howled louder than the ambulance's siren as his nose shattered. We clinched and his hot blood spattered across my cheek, painting the air in frenzied arcs.

His buddy went for the defibrillator. I got turned around in the clinch, an arm hooking mine, yanking my wrist behind my back as he lunged in with the shock paddles high. I turned on my heel, threw all my weight into it, and shoved the guard with the busted nose. There was an electric *pop* and then he was down on the ground, flopping like a gutted fish as the ambulance filled with the stench of his empty bowels.

A playing card leaped to my fingertips. A second later the other guard went down with a cherry-red line welling along his throat, a scalpel-perfect slice from ear to ear.

I leaned against the wall as the ambulance swayed, catching my breath while I waited for the corpses to stop twitching. I was caked in sweat and another man's blood, back muscles burning like they were on fire. I felt eyes on me. Pecos was watching the road, professional, disinterested in the carnage behind her. Teddy was staring, though. Staring at me like I was a stranger.

This was the part of my job I never wanted him to see. Too late to take it back now.

"They didn't give me much of a choice," I told him.

"It's not that," he said.

"What, then?"

He looked to the bodies at my feet, then back to me.

"You don't...feel anything, do you?"

I didn't know what to tell him. I wasn't going to lie to my brother, and the truth wouldn't make him feel any better. I bent down and scooped up the fallen top hat. And the radio. Fleiss was on the air, demanding an update.

"Hey there," I said.

She didn't answer right away. Finally she came back on the air, her voice dripping with venom.

"*What did you do?*"

"I thought your boss's collection of Canton memorabilia was really cool. So cool, in fact, that I decided to start my own. Thank him for the donation?"

"Where," she hissed, "is Marcel Deschamps?"

"Check the closet in his room. If my hunch is right, Marcel just reincarnated as a newborn baby...somewhere, on any of a few thousand possible parallel worlds. Good luck finding him."

I only hoped I was telling the truth. According to the first story, the Thief is killed by his lover after a successful heist. Given the fact that I had a magical hat filled to the literal brim with Canton's legacy, a host of relics intended to arm the Paladin and save the world, jobs didn't get much more successful than this.

She went silent for a while. The radio hissed, a roil of static.

"My lord has a message for you," she said.

"I'm all ears."

"He says to thank *you*. For the Paladin's name."

My sweat ran cold.

"Maybe I was lying," I said.

"We'll find out," she said. "Won't we?"

After that, she had nothing left to say. Neither did I.

The ambulance careened down a country road, leaving the city far behind. Out on the edge of nowhere, I opened the back doors and shoved the bodies out one at a time, watching them bounce and roll in the dirt. Night had fallen over us, pulling a dark blanket across the sky. It was rustic out here, peaceful, and we followed the rough bend of the road along a riverbank as it rose to a bridge.

"Pecos?" I said, calling back over my shoulder as I watched the road behind us.

"Yeah, Dan?"

"I don't want to question your navigation skills, but I don't think this is the way to the rendezvous point."

"No, Dan," Teddy said. "It sure isn't."

I turned. Teddy had picked up the dead man's revolver. It sat cradled in his hand. Easy, casual, and pointed right at me.

41.

The ambulance pulled over to the side of the road, at the lip of a trestle bridge.

"Teddy," I said, "what...what is this?"

He held the gun on me and nodded to the open back doors.

"Overdue is what it is," he said. "Out."

I got out. He came around and met me, and Pecos circled the other way. I couldn't read her face. The three of us stood in the scarlet glow of the ambulance's taillights, at the bridge's edge. Cold waters ran below, burbling in the dark.

Pecos reached into my jacket and took my deck of cards. She dropped them into the top hat.

"And the wand," Teddy said. "Don't forget the wand."

I stared down the muzzle of the gun.

"You sure you want that?" I asked him.

He snickered. "C'mon, are you really trying to bluff me right now? I know all your tricks. And *hers*. Louise Canton's wand won't defend the person who wields it, remember? It only protects the innocent. And, uh...no innocent people here. Just us."

"Just us," I said.

I flexed my wrist and the wand dropped into my hand. No last-minute miracles; it was dormant, powerless as Pecos plucked it from my fingertips. She stepped back and stood at Teddy's shoulder.

"What did I tell you?" she said. "You shouldn't take scores with blood in the mix. That's a good way to get hurt."

"Getting stabbed in the back by *you*, that I could imagine." I shook my head. "But my own brother? What are you doing, Teddy?"

"Do you really think any of this happened by accident? Think about it. The Network approached the Enemy about an alliance. Never did make much sense, did it? Odd bedfellows. But then Elmer Donaghy cooked up his scheme to plant geas-roaches in a batch of politicians. A little subtle prodding and Mayor Seabrook hires Tall Pines Security to protect her from the threat. And lo and behold, your long-lost brother is freshly transferred and promoted, suddenly in the perfect place to come back into your life."

"Oh, that's not the strange coincidence," Pecos said, playing along. "The *really* strange coincidence is how that exact same company provides security at Northlight Tower. Almost guaranteeing that Daniel would approach his brother for help with the heist. That part confuses me, though."

"Oh?" Teddy said. "How so?"

"Well, considering his brother would be in horrible danger, what kind of person would do that?"

"The kind who uses people," Teddy said, shooting me a look. "The kind who doesn't care who gets hurt, as long as he gets what he wants."

I wagged an open hand, keeping them both up and visible.

"Can I join in, or is this a conversation for two?"

"Feel free," he said.

I saw how the pieces were landing. I didn't like the pattern, but I couldn't change the facts. Time to face them down.

"You're a Network agent," I said. "You're a fucking Network agent. This was about screwing over the Enemy and stopping him from burning down the worlds *you're* trying to take over."

"Ooh." Teddy winced. He gave Pecos a sidelong glance. "Check out Sherlock over here. Sorry, bro, swing and a miss. I answer to a higher power. See, you and me, we're more alike than you think."

He held up his free hand and snapped his fingers.

One of my cards leaped from Canton's hat. It spun around his fingertips and danced at his command. Then he snapped a second time, and it ignited. The card flared like a firefly then crumbled away. A cold wind caught the embers, washing them over the bridge's edge, down to the currents below where they faded and died.

"I started young," he told me. "See, there I was, living with the old man. They pressured me into lying on the witness stand, you got sent away—"

"I never blamed you for that," I said.

"He never—" Teddy stared at me. He looked to Pecos. "He never blamed me. Do you believe this shit? Am I actually hearing this?"

"I never lied to you, Teddy. I never blamed you."

His nostrils flared and as the gun shook in his hand, his finger tight on the trigger, I realized how wrong I'd gotten it.

"*I blamed you.*" He said, seething. "You were my big brother. You were supposed to protect me. You were supposed to protect me from the monsters, and I had to live with one. Alone. With you gone, the old man beat me enough for both of us."

"What was I supposed to do? I was locked up—"

"You got out." He looked to Pecos again. "And he never came around. Never checked on me. See, he says he didn't blame me for sending him away, but...I'm thinking maybe my brother's better at lying to himself than he thinks."

"I tried to protect you," I told him. "I tried my best. I'm sorry it wasn't good enough."

"'Sorry,' he says. The great Daniel Faust. Saved the world once. Now here he is, on another grand crusade, off to do it again." I saw the glint in my brother's eyes as his voice quavered. "But you never saved *me.*"

"You found your savior," Pecos said.

"That I did," he said. "That I did. See, Dan, I walked the same road as you. Funny how that happened. But I didn't waste my time with card tricks. I needed real power. I opened a door, down in the dark, and called out for help. And help came for me."

At first, I thought it was a trick of the light. Pecos stood in the crimson glow of the ambulance's taillights, her face washed in blood. Her skin seemed to darken, turning olive by shades as her hair went inky black.

Not that kind of trick. She was changing. Her face becoming sharper, cheekbones higher, shoulders back as she rose in height. She rested one hand on my brother's shoulder and her nails grew, turning green as polished jade.

"I came for him," Naavarasi said. "Such a fine young man. How could I refuse him in his hour of need?"

My psychic tendrils snapped out, washing over her. I fumbled for words, something to say, but they all died on my lips. She wasn't there. Invisible, like glass. She savored my confusion like a fine wine.

"Oh, Daniel, how many times do I have to teach you this lesson? I am the mistress of illusion. Your eyes see what I command them to see. And that includes your *third* eye."

Naavarasi had been working a long con from the moment we crossed paths. She played the puffed-up fool for over a year, convincing us that she was incapable of doing anything without bragging about it, that she'd spoil her own plans for a taste of the spotlight she coveted. We considered her a minor threat, exactly like she wanted us to. And Caitlin and I found out, almost too late, that it was all a trick: the woman was whip-smart, deadly, and her most important cards had always been held close to her chest.

But that was a trick that would only work once. I felt more confident after that. Just like I was confident that she could never sneak up on us by changing her shape again. See, I knew her magical scent.

"Every time," I breathed. "Every single time you came around wearing someone else's face. You were faking it. You projected a fake psychic imprint, over and over again, and you made damn sure I recognized it. You were *training* me to recognize it."

"And thanks to you, all of your closest friends—and your dear lover Caitlin—are convinced they can spot a rakshasa from a mile away." Her jade-painted lips curled, feline and smug. "I've been so intimate with you all, Daniel. So close you can't imagine. I've been in your homes. I've stood over you while you slept. Tell me, do you remember the first time we met? I tried to recruit you to my service."

It came back to me in a flash. Naavarasi casually dropping my ex-girlfriend's name, details about my life. Things she had no business knowing. *Oh, I know all about you, Daniel. I've been watching you for years, from afar. Not constantly, just...checking in now and again.*

I didn't understand it then.

"And what did I say to you when you asked how I knew so much about you?"

I can't tell you that. It would ruin the surprise.

"You knew about me because of him." I looked to my brother, to the gun in his hand. "You two were already working together."

"For years," Teddy said. "You didn't save me. But Baron Naavarasi did. When you walked into her restaurant it was like kismet. Almost perfect luck."

"I wanted you both," Naavarasi added. "You should have bent your knee to me, Daniel. We wouldn't be in this situation if you had."

Teddy nodded, fervent. A true believer. I had no idea what she'd done to my brother, but she'd had years to sink her claws in and mix him up any way she wanted.

"For the record," he said, "I lied. Dad didn't die of pneumonia."

"Do tell," I said.

"He died choking on his own blood, with my fingers wrapped around his shriveled black heart. I wish you'd been there. The look on the old man's face..."

Naavarasi scratched behind Teddy's ear like he was a well-behaved dog. "And we *feasted* that night. Your brother's first taste of human meat. Like I always say, nothing makes you stronger than the flesh of your own kind."

I had to hold it together. I had to pretend my heart wasn't

breaking. I'd found my brother, a family I didn't know I had, a human connection, and now it was all crumbling down like a citadel built on sour dirt.

"So that was your master plan? Manipulate me into pulling the heist at Northlight, then swoop in and steal the score out from under me?"

Naavarasi's smile gleamed, pearly in the dark. "Actually, no. That was lucky happenstance. I had spent an incredible amount of time and effort already, working my way into Fleiss and the Enemy's...well, I won't say *trust*, because they're not the trusting kind, but establishing myself—and your brother, my loyal servant—as reliable assets in their employ."

"The whole Tall Pines gig was for me," Teddy said. "Eventually, once we figured out how to pull it off and get away clean, *I* was supposed to steal the Canton relics. We just couldn't find the right angle. Then you came along and solved the problem for us. We take the relics, you take the blame. Probably shaved months off the timetable, too."

"Timetable?" I said.

Naavarasi's hand curled tighter on my brother's shoulder.

"The grand design," she said.

Sometimes I hate being right. Everyone thought Naavarasi's endgame, all her manipulations and tricks, was aimed at putting Caitlin on a leash. I didn't buy it. I knew she was up to something even bigger than that.

"Nice plan, but you're forgetting something. I'm a knight in Prince Sitri's court, remember? The rules say I can't attack you directly, and you can't attack me. I'm pretty sure this hijacking is a violation of infernal law."

"So is murdering you," Naavarasi replied, "but you should know the most fundamental tenet of demonic politics: if no one witnesses the crime, there *is* no crime. I've enjoyed you as a sparring partner, Daniel, but it's time to remove you from the chessboard. My work will proceed much more smoothly in a world without you in it."

She wasn't bluffing. I looked to Teddy, swallowing down my rising desperation.

"You're my *brother*. You can't let her do this."

"I'm not," he said. Then he thumbed back the hammer on his revolver. "I'm going to do it for her."

"Such a faithful servant," Naavarasi purred. Her jade fingernails stroked the nape of his neck.

I locked eyes with Teddy.

"It's funny," he said. "I read up on, you know, families like ours. We're an anomaly. The fact is, most children of abuse grow up to be caring, nurturing adults. What were the odds of both of us turning out fucked up and damned?"

"We've got free will, Teddy. We're all free to make our own choices. And you're making a real bad one."

"Choices?" He gave me a humorless smile. "I was born a monster. It's in my blood, same as yours. That's fate. You can't fight fate."

"There's no such thing as fate," I told him.

"Are those really the last words you want to go out with?"

"No," I said. "You want some last words to remember me by? Here's three: watch your back."

"Pithy," he said. "I'll write it on your tombstone."

I still didn't believe he'd pull the trigger. Not until the wheelgun roared, flashing in the dark, and the first bullet hit me in the chest.

It plowed through my dress shirt, through the stiff cardboard of the train ticket, tore through skin and bone like a red-hot poker and crumpled in my heart. The second bullet turned a rib to powdered splinters and ripped a hole in my lung. I was stumbling backward and then I was falling, wind whistling in my ears as I pitched over the edge of the trestle bridge.

My fingers brushed something cold, hard, and a spark of magic, not mine, bristled to angry life. A clock ticked in my ears, slow and thunderous. My ruptured heart slowed, then stopped.

My body hit the ice-cold water. I was gone before the splash.

Epilogue

A pickup truck sat at the edge of another lonely backwoods road, silent, waiting as the sky went dark. Jennifer paced in the dirt, kicking stray rocks.

"They shoulda been here by now," she said.

Caitlin reclined in the driver's seat, door open to let the cool evening breeze wash in. She checked her phone. Still no word. They had confirmation that Northlight Tower had evacuated over an hour ago. A spotter had seen the ambulance roll out, on its way to their rendezvous. Everything had gone according to plan.

And then, nothing.

Caitlin slammed her door shut and started the ignition. Jennifer jumped in beside her, hitting her speed dial.

"Pixie? Hey, sugar, it's Jen. Can you do me a favor real quick? We might have a situation here. I just need you to ping Dan's phone and tell us where he's at..."

She was able to narrow it down to a stretch of road thirty minutes away in the wrong direction. According to the cell-tower logs, his phone hadn't moved for an hour. They rolled up on the ambulance, doors open, abandoned with the engine cold.

The toe of Jennifer's boot nudged a tire track.

"This is all kinds of wrong," she murmured.

Caitlin's eyes shifted in the shadows. They whirled with motes of copper, turning to molten metal. She could hunt in the dark. Her nose twitched as she sniffed for the scent of blood on the air. Then she glanced down the grassy embankment, down to the river's edge.

And to the body, floating facedown in the shallow water.

* * *

The crash cart blasted through the operating room doors. Shears sliced through Daniel's clothes, peeling away bloody and soaked fabric as a mask clamped down over his nose and mouth.

"Vitals dropping—"

"Dr. Harris wants him in OR Three, prepped and ready. *Now,* people!"

"Pulse is—" A nurse's voice dropped to a whisper. "Can someone explain what I'm seeing here? How the hell is this guy still alive?"

* * *

He spent fourteen hours in surgery.

Caitlin and Jennifer waited, and paced like lionesses in the waiting room. Three hours in, Bentley and Corman arrived at the hospital, fresh from their flight. Margaux was next, and Melanie and her mother, Emma, weren't far behind. Emma pulled Caitlin into a tight embrace, holding her for a moment, speechless.

When Emma spoke, her teeth bore jagged points, like the maw of a great white shark. She growled a one-word question: "*Who?*"

"We don't know yet," Caitlin said. "But we will."

Bentley was pale, leaning into Corman's protective arms. "What do we know? About Daniel?"

"It's touch and go," Jennifer said. "But he's holding strong, somehow. By all rights, he should have died before he hit the water. They can't explain it."

"What happened out there?" Melanie asked.

Caitlin took a deep breath.

"Near as we can tell, there was an ambush. Daniel was shot, and we don't know what happened to his brother or the getaway driver. Their bodies could still be out there somewhere."

"Or they were in on it," Jennifer said. Her eyes narrowed to serpentine slits. "It was a proper bushwhack, no matter who did the deed. Knew who they were up against, too; the orderly showed us what Dan had on him. No hat, no cards, and his sleeve holster was empty. All he had was his wallet, and this."

She held up Canton's pocket watch. The hands were frozen at nine seconds to midnight.

"Can...can I see that?" Melanie asked.

She cradled it between her hands. Stretching out her senses the way Daniel had taught her, her mind extended like the tendrils of neon-pink anemones. She sifted through symbols, parting signal from psychic noise.

Caitlin tilted her head, watching her. "What do you know?"

"This is Louise Canton's watch. Canton's Hibernation—that's how Daniel was going to hide himself when he got smuggled into Northlight." Melanie's brow furrowed. "You said they can't explain how he survived?"

"Miracle, considerin' how much of a beating he took, not to mention how long he was bleeding out and suckin' down river water," Jennifer said.

Melanie's fingernail tapped the face of the pocket watch.

"I think maybe, just maybe, using this was the last thing he did. From what he told me, it's not an illusion, not exactly. Canton's Hibernation puts you in a state of...suspended animation, basically. You're dead, but not. You're frozen somewhere in between."

"So if the enchantment stops working..." Margaux said.

Melanie's knuckles went white, her hands squeezing the watch. "We can't let that happen. If he's in hibernation and he snaps out of it before his wounds heal—"

"We got more problems than that," Jennifer said. "For starters, hospitals got to report gunshot wounds. Soon as he's out of surgery, if he pulls through, we're gonna have Seattle's finest up in here asking questions. If they take his prints and figure out who 'Paul Emerson' really is, Dan's going to finish convalescin' in a prison infirmary."

Caitlin folded her arms. "That's not even the last of it. By now, the Enemy doubtless knows his treasures have gone missing—and likely has a good idea who took them. And here we are, in the heart of his city."

"And then there's Ada and the Redemption Choir," Melanie said. "I mean, they were following the same trail we were."

"We better get ready for a goddamn firefight," Jennifer said.

* * *

"It's important that you keep your expectations reasonable," the balding surgeon told them.

Caitlin had flashed a black credit card, whisking Daniel to a private room. One of the orderlies made noises about "visits from immediate family only," and Jennifer hit him with a graveyard stare. He didn't challenge her twice.

Daniel was motionless, silent, with a tube up his nose and another running down his throat. The outlines of more tubes, more wires, wound under the sterile white sheet. Machines chimed softly all around him.

"Define 'reasonable,'" Caitlin said.

"Honestly? He's alive in the most technical sense of the word. And we don't know how." The surgeon hugged his clipboard like a shield. "We were able to start his pulse again and repair the worst of the damage to his heart and lung, but he can't breathe without assistance. It's possible he never will again."

Canton's pocket watch sat out on the bedside table. Its hands were still frozen, counting down the seconds to midnight.

"And the rest?" Caitlin asked.

"He's comatose. Minimal brain activity. Regardless of the bullet wounds, he was completely starved of oxygen for...longer than anyone should be able to survive. If he ever wakes up, and I would consider that an incredible long shot, you can expect severe brain damage."

Caitlin stared at Daniel's body.

"Thank you, Doctor," she said. Then she fell silent until he left, the door swinging shut behind him.

Emma stood at Caitlin's side, down by the foot of the bed. Copper motes swirled in her eyes.

"You see it," she murmured.

Caitlin nodded.

Bentley and Corman were at Daniel's bedside, hands held tight, focused on their son. Across from them, Margaux perked up, suddenly suspicious. She met Jennifer's gaze and gave her a subtle nod, directing her attention.

"I was hoping I was wrong," Melanie whispered. Her mother put an arm around her shoulder and pulled her close.

Jennifer put her hands on her hips.

"Dish," she said. "*Now.*"

Everyone turned her way. She pointed from Caitlin to Emma to Melanie.

"Sorry, couldn't help but notice that the three demons in the room are all staring at something the rest of us can't see. Fill us in."

"It's his soul," Melanie said.

"What about it?"

Her voice was barely a whisper, as if speaking it out loud would cement the truth, make it undeniable.

"It's...*gone*. His body is...like the doctor said, his body is technically alive, but his soul..." Melanie shook her head. "It's gone."

Caitlin raised her chin. She took a deep, steadying breath. Then she spoke.

"Daniel is counting on us, and the next few hours are crucial. Margaux, Bentley, Corman, I want this room warded with every defensive spell you can muster. Make it vanish from the world. Jennifer, find out who the hospital has called. If they've already contacted the police about the gunshot wounds, we'll need to plan our response."

"And if they haven't?"

"Make sure they understand the virtue of silence. Pay them in gold or pay them in fear, whatever works. Emma, call the home office. We can anticipate a siege, either from the forces of the Enemy, the Redemption Choir, or both. I want assault teams on site before that happens."

Caitlin turned on her heel and strode to the door.

"Where are you going?" Melanie asked.

"Let's not fool ourselves. If his soul is missing—if it came dislodged, if he briefly died before the hibernation spell could net him, however it happened—there's only one place he could possibly be."

She paused in the doorway, giving his body one last glance.

"Daniel is in hell," she said. "I'm going down there, and I'm going to bring him back."

Afterword

For some time now, readers have been asking — since we've been just about everywhere else in Daniel Faust's universe — when we'd actually get a look at hell. You can probably imagine how hard it was to keep a straight face as I played innocent, usually responding with some variation on "When we're going there, you'll know it."

Now you know.

(And that's to say nothing of how I had to sit on the truth all this time about Naavarasi's cryptic comments from way back in *Redemption Song*. I'm a strong believer in plotting a series way out in advance, but it makes for serious temptation when it comes to spoilers...)

Suffice to say there's one heck of a big, weird adventure coming down the pike, with some old familiar faces involved. You won't be waiting long; the day I wrote the final page of this book, I opened a fresh document and laid down the first lines of the next one. We're on a one-way ride to the end of the world, here. Maybe all the worlds. We'll see how things go.

Thanks for riding along with me. And thanks to everyone who helped make this book possible: my editor Kira Rubenthaler, cover designer James T. Egan, audiobook narrator Adam Verner, and my assistant Morgan Blake. They're a top-notch crew, and I'm proud to work with them. Speaking of work, I'd better get back to it. Seems like Daniel's in a bit of a fix. That said, I have a feeling he's still got a few tricks up his sleeve...

Want to know what's coming next? Head over to http://www.craigschaeferbooks.com/mailing-list/ and hop onto my mailing list. Once-a-month newsletters, zero spam. Want to reach out? You can find me on Facebook at http://www.facebook.com/ CraigSchaeferBooks, on Twitter as @craig_schaefer, or just drop me an email at craig@craigschaeferbooks.com.

Made in the USA
San Bernardino, CA
13 January 2020

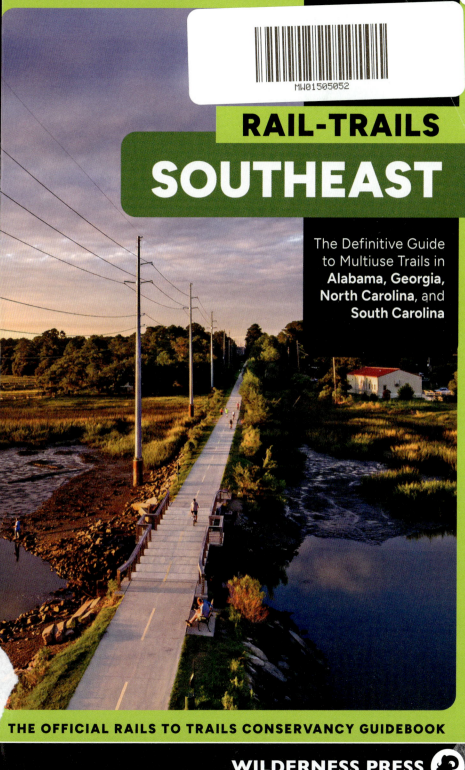

RAIL-TRAILS

SOUTHEAST

The Definitive Guide to Multiuse Trails in **Alabama, Georgia, North Carolina,** and **South Carolina**

THE OFFICIAL RAILS TO TRAILS CONSERVANCY GUIDEBOOK

WILDERNESS PRESS

Rail-Trails: Southeast
1st Edition © 2006
2nd Edition © 2024

Copyright © 2024 by Rails to Trails Conservancy
Cover and interior photographs copyright © 2024 by Rails to Trails Conservancy

Project editor: Kate Johnson
Content editors: Laura Stark and Amy Kapp
Maps: Derek Strout, Lohnes+Wright; map data © OpenStreetMap contributors
Cover design: Jon Norberg
Book design and layout: Hilary Harkness
Proofreader: Emily Beaumont
Indexer: Potomac Indexing

Cataloging-in-Publication data is on file with the Library of Congress.

ISBN 978-1-64359-106-3 (pbk.) | ISBN: 978-1-64359-107-0 (ebook)

Published by: 🐾 **WILDERNESS PRESS**
An imprint of AdventureKEEN
2204 First Ave. S., Ste. 102
Birmingham, AL 35233
800-678-7006; fax 877-374-9016

Visit **wildernesspress.com** for a complete listing of our books and for ordering information. Contact us at our website, at **facebook.com/wildernesspress1967,** or at **x.com/wilderness1967** with questions or comments. To find out more about who we are and what we're doing, visit **blog .wildernesspress.com.**

Manufactured in the United States of America
Distributed by Publishers Group West

Front cover photo: South Carolina's Spanish Moss Trail (see page 259); photo courtesy Friends of the Spanish Moss Trail.
Back cover photo: Georgia's Jekyll Island Trail (see page 93); photographed by TrailLink user mlawlor72

SAFETY NOTICE Although Wilderness Press and Rails to Trails Conservancy have made every attempt to ensure that the information in this book is accurate at press time, they are not responsible for any financial or other loss, damage, injury, or inconvenience that may occur to anyone while using this book. You are responsible for your own safety and health while on the trail. The fact that a trail is described in this book does not mean that it will be safe for you. Be aware that trail conditions can change from day to day. Always check local conditions, know your own limitations, and consult a map.

About Rails to Trails Conservancy

Headquartered in Washington, D.C., Rails to Trails Conservancy (RTC) is the largest trails, walking, and biking advocacy organization in the United States, working to build a nation connected by trails. RTC reimagines public spaces to create safe ways for everyone to walk, bike, and be active outdoors. With a grassroots community more than 1 million strong, RTC is committed to ensuring a better future for America made possible by trails and the connections they inspire. Learn more at **railstotrails.org.**

Railways helped build America. Spanning from coast to coast, these ribbons of steel linked people, communities, and enterprises, spurring commerce and transforming the nation. Over time, many of these routes have fallen into disuse, leaving corridors in disrepair and presenting an opportunity to create new public spaces to bring communities together.

When RTC opened its doors in 1986, the rail-trail movement was in its infancy. Most projects, created for recreation and conservation, focused on single, linear routes in rural areas. RTC sought broader protection for the unused corridors, incorporating rural, suburban, and urban routes.

Year after year, RTC's efforts to protect and align public funding with trail building created an environment that allowed trail advocates in communities across the country to initiate trail projects. These ever-growing ranks of trail professionals, volunteers, and RTC supporters have built momentum for the national rail-trails movement. As the number of supporters has multiplied, so have the rail-trails.

Americans now enjoy more than 25,000 miles of open rail-trails, and they flock to the trails to connect with family members and friends, enjoy nature, and access places in their local neighborhoods and beyond. And thanks to the foundation of rail-trails across the country, connected trail networks are being developed in every state in the nation—maximizing the benefits this infrastructure can bring to the well-being of people, places, and the planet.

TrailLink, the free trail-finder website and mobile app from RTC, can be used as a companion resource to the trails in this guidebook; it includes detailed descriptions, interactive maps, photo galleries, and firsthand ratings and reviews. When RTC launched the website in 2000, our organization was one of the first to compile such detailed trail information on a national scale. Today, TrailLink continues to play a critical role in both encouraging and satisfying the country's growing need for opportunities to use trails for recreation or transportation.

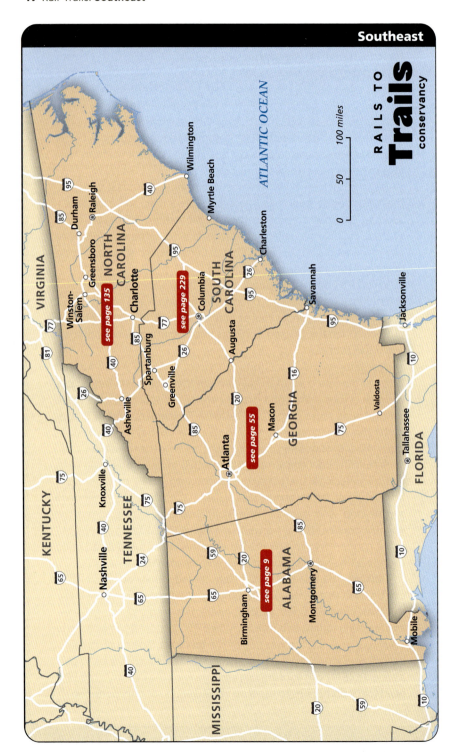

Table of Contents

SOUTH CAROLINA   229

Foreword

Welcome to the *Rail-Trails: Southeast* guidebook, a comprehensive companion for discovering the region's top rail-trails and multiuse pathways. This book will help you uncover fantastic opportunities to get outside on trails in Alabama, Georgia, North Carolina, and South Carolina—whether for exercise, transportation, or just pure fun.

Rails to Trails Conservancy's (RTC's) mission is to build a nation connected by trails. We reimagine public spaces to create safe ways for everyone to walk, bike, and be active outdoors. We hope this book will inspire you to experience firsthand how trails can connect people to one another and to the places they love, while also creating connections to nature, history, and culture.

Since its founding in 1986, RTC has witnessed a massive growth in the rail-trail and active-transportation movement. Today, more than 40,000 miles of multiuse trails provide invaluable benefits for people and communities across the country. We hope you find this book to be a delightful and informative resource for discovering the many unique trail destinations throughout the region.

I'll be out on the trails, too, experiencing the thrill of the ride right alongside you. Be sure to say hello and share your #TrailMoments with us on social media. You can find us @railstotrails on Facebook, Instagram, and X (formerly known as Twitter). Participate in our Trail Moments initiative by sharing your stories of resilience, joy, health, and connection on the trail at **trailmoments.org.**

Enjoy the journey,

Ryan Chao, President
Rails to Trails Conservancy

Acknowledgments

Special acknowledgment is owed to Laura Stark and Amy Kapp, editors of this guidebook, and to Derek Strout and Bart Wright (with Lohnes+Wright) for their work on the creation of the trail maps included in the book. Rails to Trails Conservancy also thanks Amy Ahn, Cindy Barks, Gene Bisbee, and Amy Grisak for their assistance in writing and editing content.

We also appreciate the following staff contributors, as well as local trail managers, who helped us ensure that the maps, photographs, and trail descriptions are as accurate as possible.

Quinton Batts

Ryan Cree

Peter Dean

Cindy Dickerson

Andrew Dupuy

Kate Foster

Brandi Horton

Brian Housh

Joe LaCroix

Isabelle Lord

Suzanne Matyas

Kevin Mills

Yvonne Mwangi

Anya Saretzky

Summary of Trails

Trail Number/Name	Page	Mileage	Walking	Cycling	Wheelchair Accessible	In-line Skating	Mountain Biking	Fishing	Horseback Riding
ALABAMA									
1 Aldridge Creek Greenway	11	5.5	•	•	•	•			
2 Big Cove Creek Greenway and Flint River Greenway	13	4.9	•	•	•	•		•	
3 Chief Ladiga Trail	17	33	•	•	•	•			•
4 Five Mile Creek Greenway	21	8.25	•	•					
5 High Ore Line Trail	23	3.1	•	•	•	•			
6 Historic Bridgeport Walking Trail	27	0.8	•		•				
7 Hugh Kaul Trail, Railroad Park Rail Trail, and Rotary Trail	29	4	•	•	•	•			
8 Hugh S. Branyon Backcountry Trail	33	23.4	•	•	•	•		•	
9 Indian Creek Greenway	37	3.8	•	•	•	•		•	
10 Old Railroad Bridge Trail	39	1.6	•	•	•	•			
11 Richard Martin Trail	43	10.2	•				•		•
12 Shades Creek Greenway	45	2.6	•	•	•	•			
13 Sunset Drive Trail	49	3.7	•	•	•	•		•	
14 Yoholo Micco, The Creek Indian Trail	51	3.2	•	•	•	•		•	
GEORGIA									
15 AdventHealth Redmond ECO Greenway	57	16	•	•	•				
16 Arabia Mountain PATH	61	12.4	•	•	•				
17 Atlanta BeltLine	63	20.8	•	•	•	•			
18 Augusta Canal National Heritage Area Trails	67	7.9	•	•	•	•		•	
19 Big Creek Greenway	71	27.8	•	•	•	•			
20 Bill and Dustie MacKay Trail	73	1.7	•	•	•	•		•	
21 Carrollton GreenBelt	77	19	•	•	•	•		•	
22 Columbus Fall Line Trace	81	10.5	•	•	•	•		•	
23 Cricket Frog Trail	83	13.6	•	•	•	•			
24 Douglas Greenway Trail	87	4.4	•	•	•	•			
25 Euchee Creek Greenway	89	6.1	•	•	•	•			
26 Jekyll Island Trail	93	24.8	•	•	•	•		•	
27 Man O' War Railroad Recreation Trail	95	13.5	•	•	•	•			
28 Noonday Creek Trail	99	8.6	•	•	•	•			

Trail Number/Name	Page	Mileage	Walking	Cycling	Wheelchair Accessible	In-line Skating	Mountain Biking	Fishing	Horseback Riding
29 PATH400 Greenway	101	5.6	•	•	•	•		•	
30 Rockdale River Trail	105	9.5	•	•	•	•		•	
31 Silver Comet Trail	107	61.5	•	•	•	•			•
32 Simms Mountain Trail	111	4.1	•				•		•
33 South Peachtree Creek Trail	115	2.6	•	•	•				
34 South River Trail	117	13.5	•	•	•	•			
35 Suwanee Creek Greenway	121	3.1	•	•	•	•			
36 The Thread Trail	123	13	•	•	•	•			
37 Tom White Linear Park	127	7.2	•	•	•	•			
38 Truman Linear Park Trail	131	3.1	•	•	•	•		•	
NORTH CAROLINA									
39 American Tobacco Trail	137	22.2	•	•	•	•		•	•
40 Atlantic & Yadkin Greenway	141	7.8	•	•	•	•		•	
41 Bicentennial Greenway	143	14.5	•	•				•	
42 Boone Greenway Trail*	147	4.3	•	•	•			•	
43 Cape Fear River Trail	151	7.5	•	•		•		•	
44 Catawba River Greenway	155	3.8	•	•	•	•		•	
45 Charlotte Rail Trail	159	3.5	•	•	•				
46 City of Lenoir Greenway	161	10	•	•	•	•			
47 Dunn-Erwin Rail-Trail	165	7.2	•	•	•				
48 Elkin & Alleghany Rail-Trail	167	1.2	•	•	•			•	
49 Estatoe Trail	171	5.6	•	•	•	•			
50 French Broad River Greenway and Wilma Dykeman Greenway	173	4.3/ 2.2	•	•	•	•			
51 Irwin Creek Greenway and Stewart Creek Greenway	177	4.2	•	•	•	•			
52 Little Sugar Creek Greenway	181	16.4	•	•	•	•			
53 Little Tennessee River Greenway	185	4.7	•	•	•	•		•	
54 Marcia H. Cloninger Rail-Trail	189	1.7	•	•	•	•		•	
55 Muddy Creek Greenway	191	4	•	•	•	•			
56 Neuse River Greenway Trail	195	29.8	•	•	•	•		•	
57 Oklawaha Greenway	199	3.5	•	•	•	•			
58 Point Lookout Trail	201	3.6	•	•					
59 Rocky Branch Trail	205	3.8	•	•	•	•			

* Offers cross-country skiing

continued on next page

Trail Number/Name	Page	Mileage	Walking	Cycling	Wheelchair Accessible	In-line Skating	Mountain Biking	Fishing	Horseback Riding
60 Salem Creek Greenway	207	5.2	•	•	•	•			
61 Salem Lake Trail	211	7	•		•		•	•	
62 South Tar River Greenway	215	4.7	•	•	•	•		•	
63 Thermal Belt Rail Trail	219	13.6	•	•	•	•			
64 White Oak Creek Greenway	221	7.4	•	•	•	•			
65 Yadkin River Greenway	225	8.2	•	•	•	•		•	
SOUTH CAROLINA									
66 Doodle Rail Trail	231	8.5	•	•	•	•			
67 Florence Rail Trail	233	3.2	•	•	•	•	•		
68 Heritage Trail	237	2.5	•	•	•	•			
69 Lindsay Pettus Greenway	239	2	•	•	•				
70 Mary Black Foundation Rail Trail	243	1.9	•	•	•	•			
71 North Augusta Greeneway	245	9	•	•	•	•		•	
72 Peak to Prosperity Passage	249	10.8	•			•	•	•	
73 Piedmont Medical Center Trail	251	3.4	•	•	•	•			
74 Prisma Health Swamp Rabbit Trail	255	28.2	•	•	•	•			
75 Spanish Moss Trail	259	10.2	•	•	•	•		•	
76 Three Rivers Greenway	261	19.4	•	•	•	•		•	
77 Waccamaw Neck Bikeway	267	13.6	•	•	•	•		•	
78 West Ashley Greenway and Bikeway	269	10.9	•	•	•	•		•	
79 Wonders' Way	273	2.7	•	•	•				

Introduction

Of the more than 2,400 rail-trails across the United States, 130 thread through Alabama, Georgia, North Carolina, and South Carolina. These routes relate a two-part story: The first speaks to the early years of railroading, while the second showcases efforts by Rails to Trails Conservancy (RTC), other groups, and their supporters to resurrect these unused railroad corridors as public-use trails. This guidebook highlights 79 of the region's top trails, including dozens of rail-trails and other multiuse pathways.

One of the premier trail experiences in the South is the Hall of Fame pair of Georgia's Silver Comet Trail (page 107) and Alabama's Chief Ladiga Trail (page 17); seamlessly connected and spanning 94 miles, together they offer one of the longest paved rail-trail routes in the country.

Alabama, the most biodiverse state east of the Mississippi River, is also home to the sugar-white beaches of the Gulf Coast area, Talladega National Forest, river deltas, and open prairies—with the state's robust system of trails offering access to it all. One of its largest cities, Birmingham, is also the hub for the vast Red Rock Trail System, a developing 750-mile trail network featuring urban attractions and historic sites along routes like the Railroad Park Rail Trail (page 29) and the High Ore Line Trail (page 23).

In neighboring Georgia, trail networks like the Atlanta BeltLine (page 63) and Columbus' Dragonfly Trails (Fall Line Trace, page 81) are a testament to the growing status of the Peach State in the trails movement. From urban settings bursting with cultural attractions to tranquil wildlife-rich areas like the Jekyll Island Trail (page 93) on the coast or the Bill and Dustie MacKay Trail (page 73) in the state's northern forests, Georgia's trails offer access to an exciting and diverse mix of landscapes.

North Carolina abounds in its own natural beauty, from its Appalachian Mountains terrain to its scenic Atlantic coastline. On the outskirts of Raleigh, the Neuse River Greenway Trail (page 195)—one of the state's longest paved pathways—offers a picturesque journey along the waterway and through wetlands. In the southwestern corner of the state, the Thermal Belt Rail-Trail (page 219), with its textile-industry roots, connects a handful of rural towns where travelers will find mom-and-pop eateries, charming B&Bs, and historic downtowns.

At the doorstep to the Blue Ridge Mountains of South Carolina, the Prisma Health Swamp Rabbit Trail (page 255) has become so integrated into the culture of its trailside towns—for active transportation and physical activity—that its iconic rabbit has become the mascot for the entire community. Many of the local businesses include a nod to the trail in their name; visitors will find a Swamp Rabbit Café, Swamp Rabbit Brewery, and Swamp Rabbit Inn, among others. This passion for access to the outdoors can be found throughout the state, reflected in projects like the cross-state Palmetto Trail and the Carolina Thread Trail, connecting North and South Carolina by multiuse pathways.

No matter which routes in *Rail-Trails: Southeast* you choose, you'll experience the unique history, culture, and geography of each, as well as the communities that have built and embraced them.

What Is a Rail-Trail?

Rail-trails are multiuse public paths built along former railroad corridors. Most often flat or following a gentle grade, they are suited to walking, running, cycling, mountain biking, wheelchair use, in-line skating, cross-country skiing, and horseback riding. Since the 1960s, Americans have created more than 25,000 miles of rail-trails throughout the country.

These extremely popular recreation and transportation corridors traverse urban, suburban, and rural landscapes. Many preserve historic landmarks, while others serve as wildlife conservation corridors, linking isolated parks and establishing greenways in developed areas. Rail-trails also stimulate local economies by boosting tourism and promoting trailside businesses.

What Is a Rail-with-Trail?

A rail-with-trail is a public path that parallels a still-active rail line. Some run adjacent to fast-moving, scheduled trains, often linking public transportation stations, while others follow tourist routes and slow-moving excursion trains. Many share an easement, separated from the rails by fencing or other barriers. Nearly 450 rails-with-trails exist in 47 states across the country.

What Is Rails to Trails Conservancy's Hall of Fame?

rails to trails conservancy
Hall of Fame
In 2007, RTC began recognizing exemplary rail-trails around the country through its Hall of Fame program. Inductees are selected based on merits such as scenic value, high use, trail and trailside amenities, historical significance, excellence in management and maintenance of facility, community connections, and geographic distribution. In 2023, RTC expanded the Hall of Fame eligibility criteria beyond rail-trails to include the breadth of multiuse trails that are fundamental to our vision of a future where trails connect everyone, everywhere.

The Southeast region boasts a Hall of Fame pair: the seamlessly connected Silver Comet Trail (see page 107) in Georgia and the Chief Ladiga Trail (see page 17) in Alabama; they are indicated in this book with a special blue icon. For the full list of Hall of Fame trails, visit **railstotrails.org/halloffame.**

How to Use This Book

Rail-Trails: Southeast provides the information you'll need to plan a rewarding trek on a rail-trail or other multiuse trail in the region. With words to inspire you and maps to chart your path, it makes choosing the best route a breeze. Following are some of the highlights.

Maps

You'll find three levels of maps in this book: an overall regional map, state locator maps, and detailed trail maps.

The trails in this book are located in Alabama, Georgia, North Carolina, and South Carolina. Each chapter details a particular state's network of trails, marked on locator maps in the chapter introduction. Use these maps to find the trails nearest you, or select several neighboring trails and plan a weekend excursion. Once you find a trail on a state locator map, simply flip to the corresponding trail number for a full description. Accompanying trail maps mark each route's access roads, trailheads, parking areas, restrooms, and other defining features.

Key to Map Icons

parking

drinking water

restrooms

featured trail

connecting trail

active railroad

Trail Descriptions

Trails are listed in alphabetical order within each state chapter. Each description begins with a summary of key facts about the trail, including possible uses, trail endpoints and mileage, a roughness rating, and the trail surface.

The map and summary information list the trail endpoints (either a city, street, or more specific location), with suggested start and finish points. Additional access points are marked on the maps and mentioned in the trail descriptions. The maps and descriptions also highlight available amenities, including parking; restrooms; and area attractions such as shops, services, museums, parks, and stadiums. Trail length is listed in miles, one way, and includes only completed trail; the mileage for any gaps in the trail will be noted in its description.

Each trail description includes a **roughness rating** from 1 to 3. A rating of 1 indicates a smooth, level surface that is accessible to users of all ages and abilities. A 2 rating means the surface may be loose and/or uneven and could pose a problem for road bikes and wheelchairs. A 3 rating suggests a rough surface that is recommended only for mountain bikers and hikers. Surfaces can range from asphalt or concrete to ballast, boardwalk, cinder, crushed

3

stone, gravel, grass, dirt, sand, and/or wood chips. Where relevant, trail descriptions address alternating surface conditions.

All trails are open to pedestrians. Bicycles are permitted unless otherwise noted in the trail summary or description. The summary also indicates whether the trail is wheelchair accessible. Other possible uses include in-line skating, mountain biking, horseback riding, and fishing.

Trail descriptions themselves suggest an ideal itinerary for each route, including the best parking areas and access points, where to begin, direction of travel, and any highlights along the way.

Each trail description also lists a local website for further information. Be sure to check these websites for updates and current conditions before you set out. **TrailLink** is another great resource for updated content on the trails in this guidebook.

Parking Waypoints

In the Parking section for each trail, we've included GPS coordinates for the main parking waypoints. These latitude and longitude coordinates can be used on a GPS device or with online mapping programs to locate parking areas. If you have a smartphone, you can use this guidebook along with Rails to Trails Conservancy's TrailLink app—available from the App Store and Google Play—which provides driving directions at the tap of a waypoint.

Hays Nature Preserve in Alabama offers views of open fields and wooded riparian habitat (*see Trail 2, page 13*).

Trail Use Guidelines

Rail-trails are popular destinations for a range of users, which makes them busy places to enjoy the outdoors. Following basic trail etiquette and safety guidelines will make your experience more pleasant.

➤ **Keep to the right,** except when passing.

➤ **Pass on the left, and give a clear, audible warning:** "On your left!"

➤ **Be aware of other trail users,** particularly around corners and blind spots, and be especially careful when entering a trail, changing direction, or passing so that you don't collide with traffic.

➤ **Respect wildlife and public and private property.** Leave no trace and take out litter.

➤ **Control your speed,** especially near pedestrians, playgrounds, and congested areas.

➤ **Travel single file.** Cyclists and pedestrians should ride or walk single file in congested areas or areas with reduced visibility.

➤ **Cross carefully at intersections.** Always look both ways, and yield to through traffic. Pedestrians have the right-of-way.

➤ **Keep one ear open and your headphone volume low** to increase your awareness of your surroundings.

➤ **Wear a helmet and other safety gear** if you're riding a bicycle or in-line skating.

➤ **Consider visibility.** Wear reflective clothing, use bicycle lights, and bring a flashlight or helmet-mounted light for tunnel passages or twilight excursions.

➤ **Keep moving and don't block the trail.** When taking a rest, exit the trail on the right-hand side. Groups should avoid congregating on or blocking the trails. If you have an accident on the trail, move to the right as soon as possible.

➤ **Bicyclists yield to all other trail users.** Pedestrians yield to horses. If in doubt, yield to all other trail users.

➤ **Dogs are permitted on most trails,** but some trails through parks, wildlife refuges, or other sensitive areas may not allow pets; it's best to check the trail website before your visit. If pets are permitted, keep your dog on a short leash and under your control at all times. Place dog waste in a designated trash receptacle.

➤ **Teach your children these trail essentials** and be diligent in keeping them out of faster-moving trail traffic.

➤ **Be prepared, especially on long-distance and rural trails.** Bring water, snacks, maps, a light source, matches, and other equipment you may need. Because some areas may not have good reception for mobile phones, know where you're going and tell someone else your plan.

E-Bikes

Electric bicycles, commonly called e-bikes, feature a small electric motor to assist the rider by adding power to the wheels. A three-tiered system has been developed to classify e-bikes based on speed capacity and other factors; many states allow Class 1 (up to 20 mph; requires pedaling) and Class 2 (uses a throttle) e-bikes to operate on trails, but not Class 3 (up to 28 mph). However, these rules vary by local jurisdiction, so if you would like to ride an e-bike on one of the trails listed in this book, please visit the website listed for the trail or contact the local trail manager to determine whether the use of e-bikes is permitted. Learn more at **rtc.li/rtc-ebikes.**

Bicycle Rules

In Alabama, Georgia, and North Carolina, state laws require all bicyclists under the age of 16 to wear a helmet. For more information on Alabama's bicycle laws, visit **rtc.li/alabama-public-health;** for Georgia, visit **georgiabikes.org;** and for North Carolina, visit **rtc.li/north-carolina-dot.** South Carolina does not have a helmet law; visit **scdps.sc.gov/bicyclesafety** for information on the state's bicycle safety policies.

Wherever you explore, remember to #SharetheTrail (**railstotrails.org/share -the-trail**) and #RecreateResponsibly (**recreateresponsibly.org**), as multiuse trails are used by people of every age, ability, and mode. Together, we can help make every trip safe and fun for everyone.

Travel Precautions

When planning a trail excursion in the South, check risk levels for severe weather events, such as hurricanes and tornadoes, before you go. Visit the website listed for the trail or contact the local trail manager to see if there are any weather-related restrictions in the area you plan to visit. You can also check national resources, such as the Storm Prediction Center (**spc.noaa.gov**) or National Weather Service (**weather.gov**), for current risk assessments.

State-specific resources include: the Alabama Emergency Management Agency (**ema.alabama.gov**), the Georgia Emergency Management and Homeland Security Agency (**gema.georgia.gov**), North Carolina Emergency Management (**readync.gov**), and the South Carolina Emergency Management Division (**scemd.org**).

Key to Trail Use Icons

| walking | cycling | wheelchair access | in-line skating | mountain biking | fishing | horseback riding |

Learn More

To learn about additional multiuse trails in your area or to plan a trip to an area beyond the scope of this book, visit **TrailLink,** the free trail-finder website and mobile app from Rails to Trails Conservancy with more than 40,000 miles of mapped rail-trails and multiuse trails nationwide.

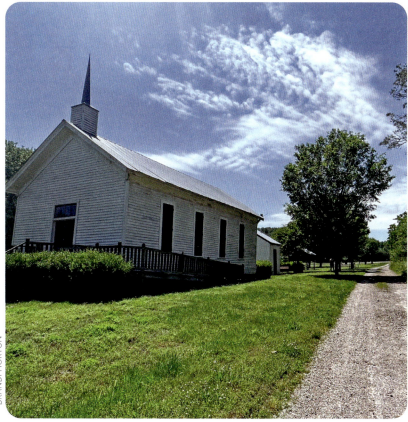

BRANDI HORTON

An old schoolhouse adorns the northern end of Alabama's Richard Martin Trail in Veto near the Tennessee border (*see Trail 11, page 43*).

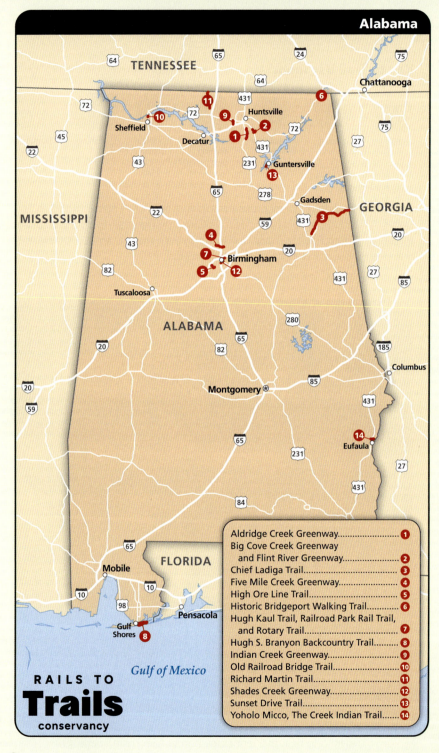

TENNESSEE

Chattanooga

Sheffield

Huntsville

Decatur

Guntersville

Gadsden

GEORGIA

MISSISSIPPI

ALABAMA

Tuscaloosa

Birmingham

Montgomery

Columbus

Eufaula

Mobile

FLORIDA

Pensacola

Gulf
Shores

Gulf of Mexico

RAILS TO
Trails
conservancy

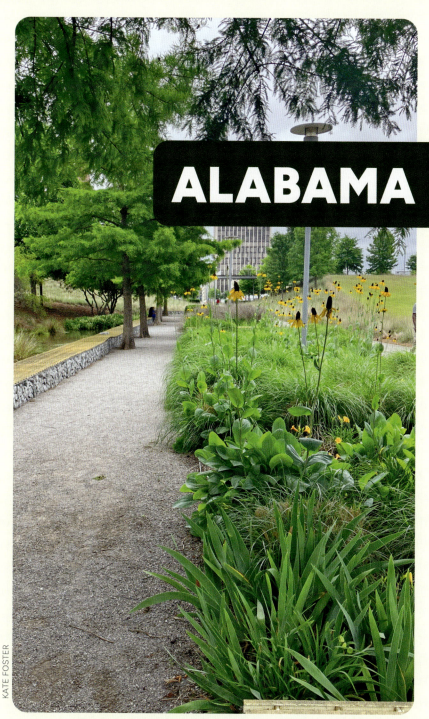

ALABAMA

KATE FOSTER

The Railroad Park Rail Trail offers a pleasant linear route
through downtown Birmingham (*see* Trail 7, *page 29*).

9

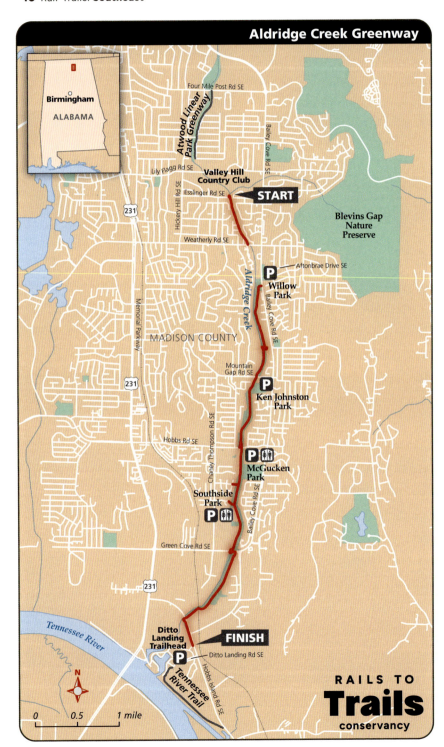

Aldridge Creek Greenway

Birmingham
ALABAMA

Four Mile Post Rd SE

Atwood Linear Park Greenway

Lily Flagg Rd SE

Bailey Cove Rd SE

Valley Hill Country Club

Hickery Hill Rd SE

Esslinger Rd SE

START

231

Weatherly Rd SE

Blevins Gap Nature Preserve

Aldridge Creek

P
Willow Park

Aftonbrae Drive SE

Bailey Cove Rd SE

MADISON COUNTY

Memorial Parkway

Mountain Gap Rd SE

P
Ken Johnston Park

Chaney Thompson Rd SE

231

Hobbs Rd SE

P
McGucken Park

Bailey Cove Rd SE

Southside Park
P

Green Cove Rd SE

231

Ditto Landing Trailhead

FINISH

P
Ditto Landing Rd SE

Tennessee River

Hobbs Island Rd SE

Tennessee River Trail

N

0   0.5   1 mile

RAILS TO Trails conservancy

Aldridge Creek Greenway

This paved community greenway winds along Aldridge Creek, providing a pleasant, semirural trail experience in Huntsville. Trail users who keep their noise down and pay attention are likely to spot shorebirds and other wildlife in or around the creek. Multiple sidewalk connections into adjacent neighborhoods make the trail easily accessible for area residents. A community dog park with a trailside gate at Southside Park also offers easy access to the trail.

Paralleling Bailey Cove Road Southeast, the trail runs north–south from Esslinger Road Southeast, just south of the Valley Hill Country Club, to Ditto Landing Road Southeast in Huntsville. There is a 0.6-mile gap between Weatherly Road Southeast and the southern end of Willow Park, where the trail picks back up on the west side of Bailey Cove Road Southeast. Willow Park is also your first option to find parking. Those wanting to walk or ride the entire length of the trail should be prepared to use the sidewalk and cross a major intersection at Weatherly Road Southeast and Bailey Cove Road Southeast in this gap.

County
Madison

Endpoints
Esslinger Road SE, 0.1 mile east of Willow Hill Dr. SE (Huntsville); Weatherly Road SE, 350 feet east of Cascade Cir. SE (Huntsville); Bailey Cove Road SE, south of Willow Park (Huntsville); Tennessee River Greenway at Ditto Landing (Huntsville)

Mileage
5.5

Type
Greenway/Non-Rail-Trail

Roughness Rating
1

Surface
Asphalt, Concrete

BRANDI HORTON

Near Ditto Landing, the trail runs beneath a trestle supporting an active rail line.

The trail segment that runs under Hobbs Road Southeast—2.1 miles south of the Willow Park Trailhead—is close to the creek and is prone to flooding after heavy rains. A bridge over the creek provides access to McGucken Park, which contains restrooms, fields and courts, and parking. Near Ditto Landing, the trail runs beneath a train trestle supporting an active rail line, adding a fun element for train enthusiasts and children. Mostly flat, this greenway makes an ideal trail for a stroll or casual bike ride. There is minimal shade, however, so be prepared for full sun for most of the trail.

Trail users looking for a longer ride may continue south onto the 0.9-mile Tennessee River Greenway, which begins at the southern terminus of the Aldridge Creek Greenway at Ditto Landing.

CONTACT: rtc.li/huntsville

PARKING

Parking areas are located within Huntsville and are listed from north to south. *Indicates that at least one accessible parking space is available.*

WILLOW PARK TRAILHEAD*: Willow Park at Aftonbrae Dr. SE (34.6411, -86.5386).

KEN JOHNSTON PARK*: Ken Johnston Park at Mountain Gap Road SE (34.6238, -86.5393).

MCGUCKEN PARK*: 13020 Bailey Cove Road SE (34.6075, -86.5417).

SOUTHSIDE PARK*: 16159 Chaney Thompson Road SE (34.5997, -86.5458).

DITTO LANDING*: Younger Road at Wheeler Lake, between W. Eugene Morgan Road and Ditto Landing Road SE (34.57693, -86.55891).

Big Cove Creek Greenway and Flint River Greenway

2

Together, the Big Cove Creek Greenway and Flint River Greenway form a seamless, nearly 5-mile paved route that quickly transports you from the suburbs of Huntsville to the immersive experience of North Alabama's floodplains and the Hays Nature Preserve.

While most will begin their trip heading south on the Big Cove Creek Greenway from the Old Highway 431 trailhead at Wade Road, starting at the northern terminus at Cranfield Road Southeast offers connections to several neighborhoods and Hampton Cove Elementary and Middle Schools. From the Cranfield Road terminus, you'll reach the school campus in 0.9 mile. Where the trail forks, stay right to continue on Big Cove Creek Greenway. Immediately following the Old Highway 431 underpass, loop around to the left to continue on the Big Cove Creek Greenway. (Heading right connects you to the Little Cove Road Greenway and several shopping areas.)

The trail continues approximately 1.5 miles, paralleling Big Cove Creek and treating visitors to wetlands and woodlands along the way. The crown jewel of the journey is where the trail meets the Flint River Greenway—within Hays Nature

A footbridge over the Flint River in the Hays Nature Preserve connects the two greenways.

BRANDI HORTON

County
Madison

Endpoints
Dead end of Cranfield Road SE, 0.2 mile west of Featherstone Lane SE (Huntsville); SE Old Hwy. 431, 0.6 mile northwest of Cherry Tree Road (Huntsville)

Mileage
4.9

Type
Greenway/ Non-Rail-Trail

Roughness Rating
1

Surface
Asphalt, Concrete

Big Cove Creek Greenway and Flint River Greenway

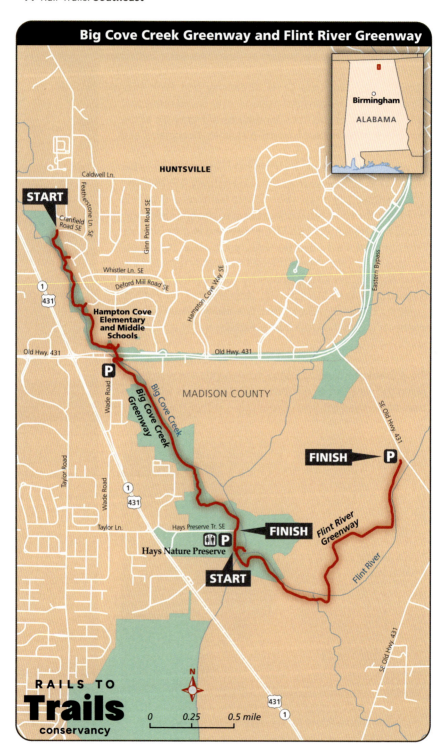

HUNTSVILLE

Birmingham
ALABAMA

Caldwell Ln.

START

Cranfield
Road SE

Featherstone Ln. SE

Ginn Point Road SE

Whistler Ln. SE

Deford Mill Road SE

1
431

Hampton Cove Way SE

**Hampton Cove
Elementary
and Middle
Schools**

Old Hwy. 431

Old Hwy. 431

Eastern Bypass

P

Wade Road

MADISON COUNTY

Big Cove Creek
Greenway

SE Old Hwy. 431

Taylor Road

Wade Road

FINISH **P**

1
431

Flint River
Greenway

Taylor Ln.

Hays Preserve Tr. SE

FINISH

Flint River

P

Hays Nature Preserve

START

SE Old Hwy. 431

**RAILS TO
Trails
conservancy**

N

0   0.25   0.5 mile

431
1

Preserve. Miles of hiking trails can be found here, and the area is a local favorite for fishing (be sure to note signs for designated fishing areas and license requirements). The preserve is also part of the North Alabama Birding Trail, with habitat for green and great blue herons and belted kingfishers along the river and numerous other species at the edges of the wooded areas.

Cross the Flint River on the footbridge adjacent to the Hays Nature Preserve parking lot to continue on the Flint River Greenway, taking in the spectacular change in scenery as you leave the woodlands and meet open wildflower meadow. The refreshing change in vistas is a reminder of the richness of the geography and habitat found along Alabama's waterways.

The Flint River Greenway continues to weave in and out of woodlands and open fields and offers opportunities to create loops to head back to the preserve. To get to the eastern terminus at Southeast Old Highway 431, turn left on the trail after approximately 1.5 miles. The trail ends at a large parking lot with a trail kiosk.

In some areas along these trails, you will see flooded oak groves and the unique ecosystem of a floodplain, evidence that the trails are subject to flooding; take caution after storms.

CONTACT: rtc.li/huntsville

PARKING

Parking areas are located within Huntsville and are listed from north to south. *Indicates that at least one accessible parking space is available.*

BIG COVE CREEK GREENWAY TRAILHEAD*: 327 Old Hwy. 431 (34.6595, -86.4794); parking lot entrance off Wade Road.

HAYS NATURE PRESERVE*: Enter at 7161 US 431, go east 0.5 mile on Hays Preserve Trail SE, then turn right to parking (34.6441, -86.4732).

FLINT RIVER GREENWAY TRAILHEAD*: 7153 SE Old US 431 (34.6518, -86.4493).

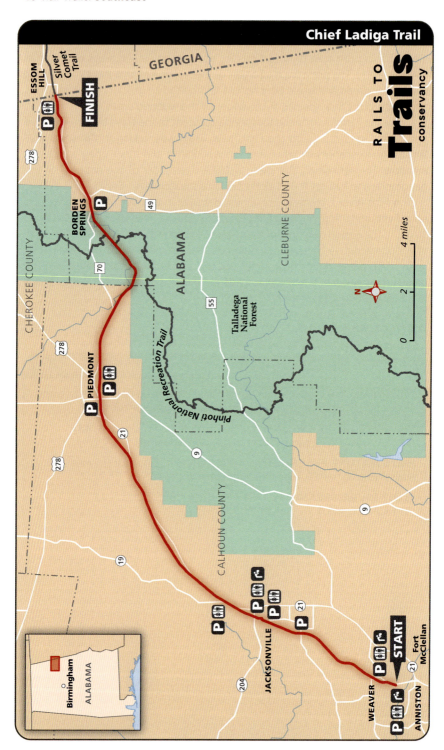

Chief Ladiga Trail

The Chief Ladiga Trail is steeped in history and nature—traversing the historic Alabama communities of Anniston, Weaver, Jacksonville, and Piedmont as it weaves through the countryside, forests, and wetlands of Calhoun and Cleburne Counties. The paved pathway is a celebration of northeast Alabama's rich and beautiful natural landscapes, from pastoral views to mountainous terrain, and of the hundreds of species of plants and wildlife that call it home, including the red-tailed hawk and blue-gray gnatcatchers that dance with you as you move along the trail.

In 1988, the 61.5-mile Silver Comet Trail (see page 107) began to take shape in Georgia—representing one of the first formal rail-trail development efforts in the South. Alabama's 33-mile Chief Ladiga Trail began to develop shortly after, in the 1990s. In 2008, the two trails were connected, creating one of the longest rail-trails in the country and an example of interstate connectivity, stretching from the outskirts of Atlanta to Anniston, Alabama.

BRANDI HORTON

Enjoy passage through Talladega National Forest and along creeks and wetlands.

Counties
Calhoun, Cleburne

Endpoints
Weaver Road and Holley Farm Road (Anniston); Silver Comet Trail at the Alabama–Georgia state line (Piedmont)

Mileage
33

Type
Rail-Trail

Roughness Rating
1

Surface
Asphalt

The rail-trail is named for Chief Ladiga (pronounced la-dye-ga), the leader of the Muscogee (Creek) Nation who signed the 1832 Treaty of Cusseta, which surrendered the tribe's remaining land in the area to the United States. It is built along the former Seaboard Air Line Railroad, which connected Atlanta to Birmingham. Today, the Chief Ladiga Trail runs for 33 miles along that route between Anniston and the Georgia state line, where it connects to the 62-mile Silver Comet Trail (see page 107).

Together, the two trails entered Rails to Trails Conservancy's Hall of Fame in 2009. The Chief Ladiga Trail is celebrated as Alabama's first rail-trail project and has served as an example as the state's trail network has been developed. Restored depots in Piedmont (Piedmont Museum, 198 N. Center Ave., by appointment only) and Jacksonville (650 Mountain St. NW) serve as historical markers and provide insight into the region's railroad past.

If you're seeking a longer adventure, your best bet is to head out from Anniston. Even though the trail is remarkably flat, you'll gain around 700 feet in elevation. In Cleburne County, at the eastern end of the trail, some equestrian use is allowed. For those who want a shorter trek, there are ample access points along the trail between Anniston and Piedmont; after Piedmont, trail access becomes more limited. Water and resources are also limited past this point, as you pass through the more rural communities surrounding Talladega National Forest; however, there are many amenities along the trail before Piedmont, so stock up if you plan to go farther.

Heading northeast from Anniston, in 1 mile you'll reach Weaver, your first stop to pick up snacks and water from local shops. When you enter Jacksonville, after another 3.2 miles, the trail passes through Jacksonville State University. With ample parking, water, and restrooms, this is another good place to refresh before heading farther east. Germania Springs Park in Jacksonville offers a playground, shelters, and shade, as well as restrooms and parking.

Just before entering Piedmont (9.6 miles after exiting Germania Springs Park), the trail crosses the Old Cherokee Indian Boundary, which marked the divide between the Creek and Cherokee Nations until the signing of the Treaty of Cusseta. Piedmont, a community with several trail access points, is the final stop for refreshments and restrooms.

Exiting Piedmont, about 13 miles remain until trail's end at the Alabama–Georgia state line, where you can seamlessly connect to the Silver Comet Trail. Note that the trail quickly becomes more rural and remote, and cell phone service is limited. Also, take note of areas where the trail surface is bumpier because of root damage.

This section of the trail through Talladega National Forest and the southern foothills of the Appalachian Mountains is awe-inspiring, offering vistas that give way to impressive rock formations revealed by the construction of the Seaboard Air Line Railroad a century ago. Along the way, you are treated to various views of Dugger Mountain, the second-highest peak in Alabama, as well as glimpses of Mount Cheaha, the highest peak in the state. Approximately 7 miles from the Georgia line, the trail intersects with the 335-mile Pinhoti National Recreation Trail. A trailhead accessible for hikers is available for both the Pinhoti and Chief Ladiga Trails several hundred feet north of the trail.

A planned extension of the Chief Ladiga Trail will connect the western-most trailhead in Anniston to the Anniston Multi-Modal Center, adding 6.5 miles and furthering the city's goals for economic development and tourism supported by cycling. The project is anticipated to be completed in late 2024.

CONTACT: rtc.li/jacksonville, rtc.li/piedmont, and rtc.li/anniston

PARKING

Parking areas are listed from west to east. *Indicates that at least one accessible parking space is available.*

ANNISTON*: Michael Tucker Park, 6514 Weaver Road at the intersection of Holley Farm Road (33.7379, -85.8181).

WEAVER*: Elwell Park, 500 Anniston St. (33.7488, -85.8132).

JACKSONVILLE*: Chief Ladiga Landing, 7201 Alexandria-Jacksonville Hwy. (33.7971, -85.7802).

JACKSONVILLE: Ladiga Trail Park Gardens, 916 Francis St. W. (33.8164, -85.7740).

JACKSONVILLE*: Jacksonville State University on Miller St., 465 feet south of Village St. (33.8211, -85.7712).

JACKSONVILLE*: Jacksonville State University on Miller St., 100 feet north of Pelham Road (33.8239, -85.7705).

JACKSONVILLE*: Germania Springs Park, 540 Roy Webb Road (33.8476, -85.7570).

PIEDMONT: W. Ladiga St., 0.1 mile northeast of Memorial Dr. (33.9221, -85.6205).

PIEDMONT*: Seaboard Blvd. and S. Center Ave. (33.9227, -85.6117).

PIEDMONT*: Eubanks Welcome Center, 202 Dailey St. (33.9226, -85.6070).

CLEBURNE COUNTY*: CR 70 and CR 225 (33.9291, -85.4707)

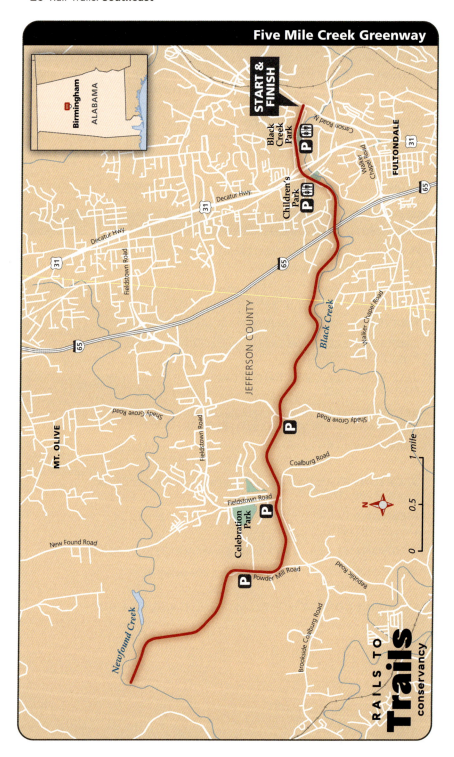

4

Five Mile Creek Greenway

To fully experience Five Mile Creek Greenway, head west from Fultondale's Black Creek Park, where there is a sizable parking lot, restrooms, and rain shelters, as well as community baseball fields and green space to enjoy. The rail-trail follows the route of the former Birmingham Mineral Railroad, originally constructed in the late 1800s to serve mining operations across the region.

The 8.25-mile trail, which is part of a regional plan to protect the Five Mile Creek watershed, delivers a rustic journey through densely wooded terrain where you are immersed in the sounds and smells of Alabama's woodlands. The shaded trail delivers relief from the Southern sun year-round as it follows the path of Black Creek, which can often be spotted through the foliage.

The crushed-stone surface can be loose in spots, so if you are planning to bike, a hybrid or mountain bike will serve you well. The trail is best experienced as an out-and-back trip from Black Creek Park, as there is no current trail access or parking at Newfound Creek in Brookside. There are few

BRANDI HORTON

Largely tucked into woodlands, Five Mile Creek Greenway offers an inviting space to recreate.

County
Jefferson

Endpoints
Carson Road N. overpass, 100 feet north of Yarbrough Road (Fultondale); Newfound Creek, 1.9 miles northwest of where the trail crosses Powder Mill Road (Brookside)

Mileage
8.25

Type
Rail-Trail

Roughness Rating
2

Surface
Crushed Stone

The pathway meanders through natural green space north of Birmingham.

amenities along the way, with trailheads every few miles but limited restrooms and water.

When you return to Black Creek Park, there are trails that loop around the park complex, and you can continue heading eastward 0.6 mile to a disused railroad bridge.

Future plans call for extending the trail to Graysville for a total of 16.5 miles, which will make it the longest rail-trail in Jefferson County. The trail is part of Alabama's developing Red Rock Trail System, which will connect more than 750 miles of trails in and around Birmingham.

CONTACT: rtc.li/five-mile-creek and fultondale.com/parks

PARKING

Parking areas are listed from east to west. *Indicates that at least one accessible parking space is available.*

FULTONDALE*: Black Creek Park, 777 Yarbrough Road (33.6216, -86.7947).

FULTONDALE*: Children's Park, 2408 Stouts Road (33.6192, -86.8022).

MT. OLIVE: 2262 Fieldstown Road (33.6304, -86.8655).

MT. OLIVE: 4250 Powder Mill Road (33.6357, -86.8790).

High Ore Line Trail

5

Opened in 2016, the High Ore Line Trail is located in the southwestern outskirts of Birmingham, sometimes called the Pittsburgh of the South for its industrial history. The original pathway is a flat, elevated rail-trail offering a convenient and pleasant transportation option along the former High Ore Line Railroad. The Tennessee Coal, Iron and Railroad Company used the rail corridor to transport iron ore from a former Red Mountain mining camp in the community of Wenonah to steelworks in Fairfield and Ensley.

The High Ore Line Trail is designated as a U.S. Civil Rights Trail. For a majority of the route, trees surround the trail, providing shade and making it a welcoming place to explore views of Valley Creek, active train lines, and the surrounding area.

The trail begins near the county health department's Western Health Center in Midfield and heads 0.3 mile northeast to the former rail line, crossing over US 11/AL 5/Bessemer Super Highway. The rail-trail next goes over scenic Valley Creek. Continuing through the West Brownville

Trainspotters can enjoy the trail's elevated vantage points over active railroads.

County
Jefferson

Endpoints
Dr. Martin Luther King Jr. Dr. and Etheridge Dr. (Midfield); Red Mountain Park, Venice Road entrance (Birmingham)

Mileage
3.1

Type
Rail-Trail

Roughness Rating
1

Surface
Asphalt

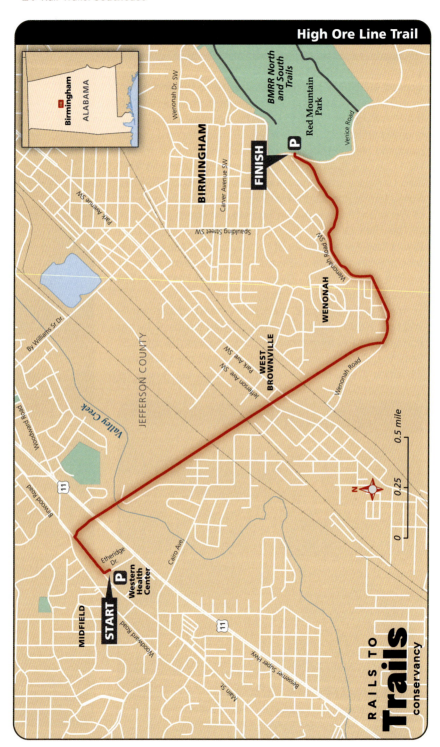

High Ore Line Trail

neighborhood, it passes over three active railroads and onto a bridge over Jefferson Avenue Southwest.

After a rolling trail section that includes a steep hill, the trail ends at Venice Road, which you must cross to reach the parking area, located at the western entrance to Red Mountain Park. At 1,500 acres, this park is one of the largest urban parks in the country. Its namesake mountain was the source of the rich iron ore deposits that made the city an industrial powerhouse in the late 1800s. The Birmingham Mineral Railroad (BMRR) North and South Trails form the backbone of the park's network of hiking and biking pathways, which, along with the High Ore Line Trail, are part of the Red Rock Trail System, a developing 750-mile network of multiuse trails in Jefferson County that connect important destinations throughout the region.

CONTACT: freshwaterlandtrust.org

PARKING

Parking areas are listed from west to east. Additionally, Birmingham's public transit system, the Metro Area Express (MAX), provides convenient access to the trail; visit **maxtransit.org** to plan your trip. *Indicates that at least one accessible parking space is available.*

MIDFIELD*: Western Health Center at Dr. Martin Luther King Jr. Dr. and Etheridge Dr. (33.4525, -86.9249); located 0.3 mile from the western terminus by sidewalk.

BIRMINGHAM*: Red Mountain Park, 2019 Venice Road (33.4417, -86.8873); parking is located 0.2 mile east of the eastern terminus by sidewalk.

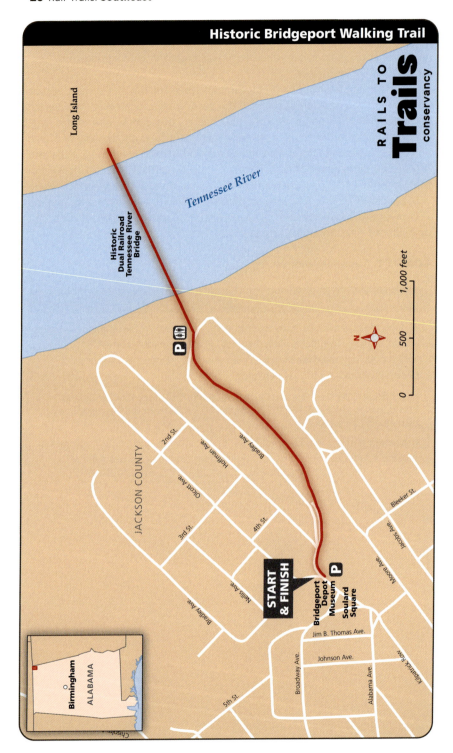

Historic Bridgeport Walking Trail

RAILS TO
Trails
conservancy

Long Island

Tennessee River

Historic
Dual Railroad
Tennessee River
Bridge

N

0   500   1,000 feet

JACKSON COUNTY

2nd St.

Hoffman Ave.

Olcott Ave.

Bradley Ave.

3rd St.

4th St.

Bleeker St.

Jacobs Ave.

Moore Ave.

Nellis Ave.

Bradley Ave.

**START
& FINISH**

Bridgeport
Depot
Museum

Soulard
Square

Jim B. Thomas Ave.

Broadway Ave.

Johnson Ave.

Alabama Ave.

Kilpatrick Row

5th St.

Chisolm

Birmingham
ALABAMA

Historic Bridgeport Walking Trail

6

Tucked into the northeast corner of Alabama, the Historic Bridgeport Walking Trail begins at the restored Bridgeport Depot Museum and heads 0.5 mile to the Tennessee River, which it crosses on a historic bridge. History, rail, and genealogy buffs should leave extra time before or after the walk to visit the museum, which houses local artifacts, railroad memorabilia, and a historical research library.

A steep, short incline (less than 75 yards) begins the trail, but the remainder of the walk is flat. Continue east on Bradley Avenue, keeping right at the fork. Roughly 200 yards from the beginning, turn right onto a gravel path with Bradley Avenue to your left and the railbed to your right. In another 575 yards, you will find restrooms, parking, and a trailhead. Follow signs indicating where the path travels over active railroad tracks (near the dead end of Bradley Avenue). At the 0.5-mile mark, head onto the paved Historic Dual Railroad Tennessee River Bridge.

At the shoreline at the start of the bridge is a historical marker about the Trail of Tears. The marker acknowledges

County
Jackson

Endpoint
Bridgeport Depot Museum at Soulard Square and Bradley Ave. (Bridgeport); east end of the Historic Dual Railroad Tennessee River Bridge (Long Island)

Mileage
0.8

Type
Rail-with-Trail

Roughness Rating
1–2

Surface
Asphalt, Concrete, Gravel

MATTHEW NICHOLS

Begin your journey at the Bridgeport Depot Museum, which houses local artifacts and railroad memorabilia.

the 1,070 Cherokees who were forced to travel on foot for a 230-mile segment near this very spot in June 1838, when the Tennessee River became too low to navigate. Each September since 1994, Bridgeport has acted as the starting place for the Trail of Tears Commemorative Motorcycle Ride, which travels across northern Alabama from Bridgeport to Waterloo.

During the Civil War, the railroad bridge became a focal point because of its connection between Alabama and Tennessee. It was destroyed and rebuilt twice. Following the war, it was used for train travel until 1998, when CSX built a new railroad bridge paralleling the old one. The town of Bridgeport kept the original bridge, which now serves as a pedestrian bridge ending at Long Island in the middle of the Tennessee River.

While the first half-mile segment to the start of the bridge is shaded, the 0.3-mile walk across the bridge is in the sun. Enjoy views of the shore in the distance, the river beneath you, and possibly even a freight train passing on the parallel tracks, which continue past Long Island. At the end of the pedestrian bridge is a small white enclosure with a bench.

Back at the start of the bridge, in a parking lot on Bradley Avenue, you will find a trailhead for the 12-mile River Mont Cave Historic Trail, a hiking trail ending at Russell Cave National Monument.

CONTACT: rtc.li/bridgeport-depot

PARKING

Parking areas are located within Bridgeport and are listed from west to east.
Indicates that at least one accessible parking space is available.

BRIDGEPORT DEPOT MUSEUM*: 116 Soulard Square
(34.9488, -85.7120).

HISTORIC DUAL RAILROAD TENNESSEE RIVER BRIDGE*:
101 Bradley Ave. (34.9522, -85.7058).

Hugh Kaul Trail, Railroad Park Rail Trail, and Rotary Trail

7

Downtown Birmingham's Hugh Kaul Trail, Railroad Park Rail Trail, and Rotary Trail weave their way through the city's Central Business District. Part of the Freshwater Land Trust's planned 750-mile Red Rock Trail System, these urban trail segments provide a nearly contiguous trail that will eventually connect to a planned 36-mile loop linking Fairfield, Birmingham, Homewood, and Irondale.

Beginning at the southwestern end of Railroad Park, the **Railroad Park Rail Trail** leads into downtown's stunning park, a creative redesign of a former rail viaduct that cut through the heart of the business district. Roughly a third of the park is made up of water features, including a pond, streams, a rain curtain, and a wetland area. Benches constructed from materials found on-site during park construction are incorporated throughout. Native plant–infused landscaping flanks the trail, beautifying the park and attracting birds, butterflies, and other insects.

Although there are many meandering paths throughout the park that can be enjoyed on foot, the rail-trail offers a direct route through the park for pedestrians, wheelchair users, and

County
Jefferson

Endpoints
Railroad Park Rail Trail: 14th St. S., between Morris Ave. and First Ave. S. (Birmingham); 18th St. S. and Powell Ave. S. (Birmingham) *Rotary Trail:* 20th St. S. and First Ave. S. (Birmingham); 24th St. S. underpass and First Ave. S. (Birmingham) *Hugh Kaul Trail:* 25th St. S. and First Ave. S. (Birmingham); 38th St. S. and Second Ave. S. (Birmingham)

Mileage
4.0 total (*Hugh Kaul Trail:* 1.9; *Railroad Park Rail Trail:* 1.7; *Rotary Trail:* 0.4)

Type
Rail-Trail

Roughness Rating
1

Surface
Asphalt, Concrete

BRANDI HORTON

Nestled in a railway cut, the Rotary Trail
is flanked by lush landscaping.

Hugh Kaul Trail, Railroad Park Rail Trail, and Rotary Trail

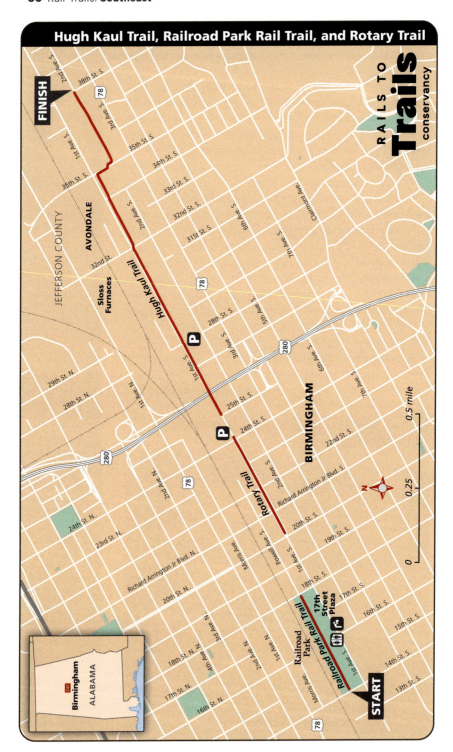

bicyclists. It passes an expansive field and playground before passing a rain curtain and wetland area. Restrooms and water fountains are located in the 17th Street Plaza under a pavilion about halfway down the trail, where trail users will also find seating and food vendors. Additional retail and restaurant options are nearby.

The Railroad Park Rail Trail ends at 18th Street. Those who would like to continue to the **Rotary Trail** should proceed two blocks east along First Avenue South to the beginning of the trail at the corner of First Avenue South and 20th Street South. A tall, arched gateway announcing ROTARY TRAIL IN THE MAGIC CITY marks the beginning of this 0.4-mile pedestrian-only trail. (*Note:* Bicyclists wishing to ride to the Hugh Kaul Trail should use the cycle track on First Avenue South or ride low-traffic side streets, as bicycles are not allowed on the Rotary Trail.)

Following the path of a narrow, below-grade railway, the Rotary Trail is flanked by lush landscaping and sculptures and has ample benches and picnic tables along its length. The trail passes through a below-street tunnel where lampposts provide illumination.

Starting at the eastern end of the Rotary Trail, the 1.9-mile **Hugh Kaul Trail** runs through a light industrial area into the Avondale neighborhood. This flat, paved trail is almost all in full sun and gets hot in the summer months. Breweries and restaurants are plentiful along the trail or within a few blocks for those wanting refreshments or to make a stop.

Of interest along the trail is Sloss Furnaces, a National Historic Landmark. Founded in 1880 by Col. James Withers Sloss, the site was once one of the largest manufacturers of pig iron in the world. Today, it is home to a museum, an event space, and an educational center for metal arts. Just past Sloss Furnaces at 32nd Street is a bike repair station.

Near the end of the trail lies a large sculpture made of rail steel, a nod to the trail's past life as a railroad corridor. The last trail segment travels an unmarked, two-block, on-street connection before ending at the historic Continental Gin building.

CONTACT: freshwaterlandtrust.org and railroadpark.org

PARKING

Parking areas are located within Birmingham and are listed from southwest to northeast. Street parking is also available along First Ave. S., from 16th St. S. to 28th St. * *Indicates that at least one accessible parking space is available.*

FIRST AVE. S. AND 24TH ST. S.: (33.5146, -86.7981).

FIRST AVE. S. AND 28TH ST.: (33.5170, -86.7928).

Hugh S. Branyon Backcountry Trail

Orange Beach City Hall

Rattlesnake Ridge Trail

Catman Road Trail

Cotton Bayou Trail

Twin Bridges Trail

ORANGE BEACH

START & FINISH

Orange Beach Sportsplex Trailhead

Catman Road Trail

Little Lake

Rosemary Dunes Trail

Perdido Beach Blvd.

N

1 mile

0

Gulf Oak Ridge Trail

Gulf State Park

Middle Lake

Gulf of Mexico

Lake Shelby

Coyote Crossing

GULF SHORES

BALDWIN COUNTY

180

59

Fort Morgan Road Trail

W. 2nd St.

180

59

182

ALABAMA

Birmingham

RAILS TO Trails conservancy

Hugh S. Branyon Backcountry Trail

8

The paved, ADA-accessible Hugh S. Branyon Backcountry Trail is a network of multiuse trails offering visitors a chance to experience the natural beauty and diverse ecosystems of Gulf State Park on Alabama's Gulf Coast. Designated a National Recreation Trail in 2010, it is part of Alabama's Coastal Connection National Scenic Byway and Coastal Birding Trail. In 2023, *USA Today* named it the country's best recreational trail.

The trail system spans more than 23 miles, connecting the cities of Orange Beach and Gulf Shores. Trail users may encounter rare and threatened indigenous plants, birds, and other wildlife, such as the Alabama beach mouse. In addition to the seven trails highlighted below, many other trails exist within the Hugh S. Branyon Backcountry Trail network, ranging from 0.1 mile to 2.2 miles with varied surfaces, including boardwalk, dirt, and sand. To learn more about each trail, visit **alapark.com/parks/gulf-state-park/trails.**

From the Orange Beach Sportsplex Trailhead, travel southwest on the 3.2-mile Gulf Oak Ridge Trail through a maritime forest of ancient, moss-covered live oaks and

County
Baldwin

Endpoints
Orange Beach Sportsplex Trailhead (Orange Beach); Orange Beach City Hall (Orange Beach); W. Second St. and AL 180/W. Fort Morgan Road (Gulf Shores)

Mileage
23.4

Type
Greenway/Non-Rail-Trail

Roughness Rating
1

Surface
Asphalt, Boardwalk

ROBERT ANNIS

Explore Gulf State Park's diverse ecosystems via its interconnected trail system.

palmettos to State Park Road 2. This coastal corridor was used by Indigenous peoples, explorers, settlers, and soldiers from nearby Fort Morgan. With many benches throughout and a bluff overlooking the valley below, the trail is a popular spot for bird-watching and wildlife photography.

From the western end of the Gulf Oak Ridge Trail, you can pick up the newest addition to the trail system: Coyote Crossing, which travels 2.2 miles west from the western Gulf Oak Ridge Trailhead to AL 59/Gulf Shores Parkway. There, a crosswalk allows access to the paved, 5.6-mile Fort Morgan Road Trail (separate from this trail system) traveling through Gulf Shores.

Alternatively, if you head east from the sports complex, you'll travel on the mile-long Twin Bridges Trail, which includes a parkour course and crosses two timber bridges, a pine savannah environment, a unique wet prairie, and an impressive pitcher plant bog. At the end of the Twin Bridges Trail, you can connect with two more trails in the network. First, you'll reach the 2-mile Rattlesnake Ridge Trail, home to the eastern diamondback rattlesnake and other reptiles. This trail heads east, ending at Orange Beach City Hall.

Just 150 feet south of the Rattlesnake Ridge Trail juncture, the Twin Bridges Trail dead-ends at the 1.9-mile Catman Road Trail, which follows a former roadway through coastal scrubland and wet pine flatwoods. The trail, named for a legendary half-man/half-panther creature that supposedly haunts these forests, heads west past Little Lake and east to AL 161/Alabama's Coastal Connection. As the trail travels east, it meets the mile-long Cotton Bayou Trail, 0.4 mile from the juncture with the Twin Bridges Trail. The Cotton Bayou Trail traverses coastal wetlands, offering opportunities to see waterfowl and wading birds and providing access to a primitive campsite with canvas-walled tents available for rent (call 251-948-7275).

Near the intersection of these trails is Boulder Park, which offers a children's climbing area, as well as a butterfly garden and nature pavilion. Heading west from Boulder Park, you'll be on the 1.6-mile Rosemary Dunes Trail, which navigates a relict dune scrub ecosystem featuring a variety of marsh wildlife, including alligators, the endangered Alabama beach mouse, and the gopher tortoise. Sharp-eyed viewers can also spot an eagle's nest. The Rosemary Dunes Trail ends at Perdido Beach Boulevard, which is lined with beach resorts and shops, as the roadway is just a block from Romar Beach Access.

Additional trails in Gulf State Park connect to a nature center, a beach pavilion, campgrounds, a lodge, a fishing pier, and Lake Shelby.

CONTACT: alapark.com/parks/gulf-state-park/trails and backcountrytrail.com

PARKING

Select parking areas for the trail are listed clockwise, beginning from the Orange Beach Sportsplex Trailhead at the north-central point of the loop. For a detailed list of parking areas and other waypoints, consult **TrailLink™.** For information about parking fees at Gulf State Park, visit **alapark.com/parks/gulf -state-park.** *Indicates that at least one accessible parking space is available.*

ORANGE BEACH*: Orange Beach Sportsplex Trailhead, 4385 William Silvers Pkwy. (30.2816, -87.6133).

ORANGE BEACH*: Orange Beach City Hall, 4099 Orange Beach Blvd. (30.2838, -87.5829).

ORANGE BEACH*: Catman Road Trailhead at Catman Road/Marina Road and AL 161/Alabama's Coastal Connection (30.2805, -87.5819).

ORANGE BEACH*: Cotton Bayou Trailhead at Cotton Bayou Trail and AL 161/Alabama's Coastal Connection (30.2731, -87.5851).

ORANGE BEACH*: Rosemary Dunes Trailhead at Perdido Beach Blvd./ AL 182/Alabama's Coastal Connection (30.2584, -87.6339).

GULF SHORES*: Gulf State Park Interpretive Center, 22250-A E. Beach Blvd. (30.2555, -87.6425).

GULF SHORES*: Lake Shelby Picnic Area Dog Pond (30.2526, -87.6620).

GULF SHORES*: Gulf State Park headquarters, 20115 State Park Road (30.2665, -87.6818).

GULF SHORES*: Lakeview Trailhead at State Park Road 2/Eagle Connector/Fort Morgan Road (30.2660, -87.6715).

ORANGE BEACH*: Gulf Oak Ridge Trailhead West at the dead end of State Park Road 2/County Road 2/Fort Morgan Road (30.2716, -87.6556).

Indian Creek Greenway

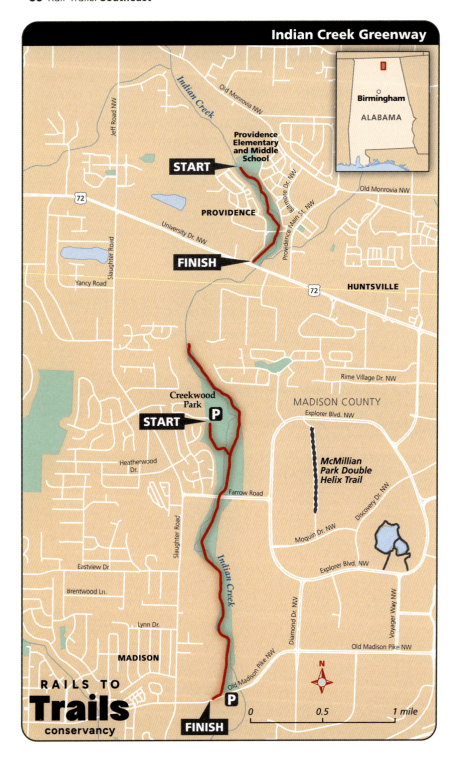

Birmingham
ALABAMA

Jeff Road NW

Indian Creek

Old Monrovia NW

Providence
Elementary
and Middle
School

START

72

PROVIDENCE

University Dr. NW

Providence Biltmore Dr. NW

Providence Main St. NW

Old Monrovia NW

FINISH

72

HUNTSVILLE

Slaughter Road

Yancy Road

Rime Village Dr. NW

MADISON COUNTY

Creekwood
Park

P

START

Explorer Blvd. NW

*McMillian
Park Double
Helix Trail*

Discovery Dr. NW

Heatherwood
Dr.

Farrow Road

Moquin Dr. NW

Slaughter Road

Indian Creek

Explorer Blvd. NW

Eastview Dr.

Voyager Way NW

Brentwood Ln.

Diamond Dr. NW

Old Madison Pike NW

Lynn Dr.

Old Madison Pike NW

MADISON

Old Madison Pike NW

N

P

FINISH

0   0.5   1 mile

RAILS TO
Trails
conservancy

Indian Creek Greenway

9

The Indian Creek Greenway, currently open in two disconnected sections, runs along the border of Madison and Huntsville, or Rocket City. The trail provides connections to residential developments, a high school, and Cummings Research Park, the second-largest research park in the United States, which is home to a massive rocket-building plant.

Currently, the trail's 0.8-mile northern segment begins just south of Providence Elementary School and travels south to US 72/AL 2/University Drive Northwest/Lee Highway. The pathway runs through a heavily wooded area with spurs leading out to residential areas, restaurants, and shops in the Providence community. Note that there is no designated trail parking available for this segment.

The primary segment of the greenway meanders south along its namesake creek for a leisurely 3 miles, through farmland and woods and over several bridge crossings. This scenic segment runs through the popular 72-acre Creekwood Park. Near the northern end of the park, a parking area at Harvestwood Court includes a large playground, an 18-hole disc golf course, covered picnic pavilions, restrooms, and a

County
Madison

Endpoints
Battery St. NW and Meeting St. (Huntsville); Hillcrest Ave. NW and US 72/AL 2/University Dr. NW/Lee Hwy. (Huntsville); northern tip of Creekwood Park (Madison); Old Madison Pike, 0.3 mile east of Slaughter Road (Huntsville)

Mileage
3.8

Type
Greenway/Non-Rail-Trail

Roughness Rating
1

Surface
Asphalt, Concrete

COURTESY CITY OF HUNTSVILLE

Meander through woods, farmland, and popular Creekwood Park on the greenway.

fenced-in dog park. Those interested in fishing may catch bass, catfish, and bluegill in the creek. Keep an eye out for turtles, great blue herons, and rabbits in the woods, as well as cows and horses grazing in the farmland portions.

Those seeking to extend their overall mileage have several nearby options. Nearly halfway through the park, at 1.2 miles, the trail passes beneath Farrow Road, where sidewalks on either side give greenway users the chance to take a detour east to HudsonAlpha Institute for Biotechnology's McMillian Park, part of Cummings Research Park. Here, users can find the unique Double Helix Trail, complete with an educational and interactive Genome Walk. Take the park's outer paved loop for a 1.2-mile circuit or the double helix–shaped inner path for a 1.3-mile course. Just east of here, another paved trail encircles a small lake at the Adtran building. Driving a bit farther east will bring you to hiking and biking trails behind the U.S. Space & Rocket Center.

Back on the greenway, the trail heads another 1.4 miles to its southernmost endpoint at Old Madison Pike. Plans call for extending the trail farther south from here, extending the northern segment farther north to Old Monrovia Road Northwest in the West Ridge neighborhood, and connecting the two disconnected segments, for an eventual total of 6 miles.

CONTACT: huntsvilleal.gov/locations/indian-creek-greenway

PARKING

Parking areas are located within Huntsville and are listed from north to south. *Indicates that at least one accessible parking space is available.*

CREEKWOOD PARK*: 360 Harvestwood Court (34.7351, -86.7030).

OLD MADISON PIKE*: 7488 Old Madison Pike (34.7100, -86.6999).

Old Railroad Bridge Trail

10

The Old Railroad Bridge Trail in northwestern Alabama is part of the 17-mile Muscle Shoals National Recreational Trail system, a network of paved and primitive trails and bikeways within the Tennessee Valley Authority's (TVA's) Muscle Shoals Reservation. The trail system features Wilson Dam, limestone bluffs, underwater caves, a native plant garden, and the 1,580-foot-long, double-decker Old Railroad Bridge.

The Old Railroad Bridge Trail, also known as the TVA Nature Loop, offers a short connection between Sheffield on the south side of the Tennessee River and Patton Island (near Florence) on the river's north bank. The paved trail travels through a pleasantly wooded area and offers spectacular views as it crosses the river on the Old Railroad Bridge. Along the way, you may enjoy sightings of pawpaw trees, as well as waterfowl, wading birds, gulls, raptors, bluebirds, great crested flycatchers, and Baltimore or orchard orioles.

Originally opened as a toll bridge in 1840 by the Florence Bridge Company, this historic landmark was transformed

LAUREN V. THOMAS

The trail's highlight is the double-decker bridge over the Tennessee River between Sheffield and Florence.

County
Colbert

Endpoints
Ashe Blvd.,
0.2 mile west
of US 43/US
72 (Sheffield);
Patton Island
(Florence)

Mileage
1.6

Type
Rail-Trail

**Roughness
Rating**
1

Surface
Asphalt,
Boardwalk

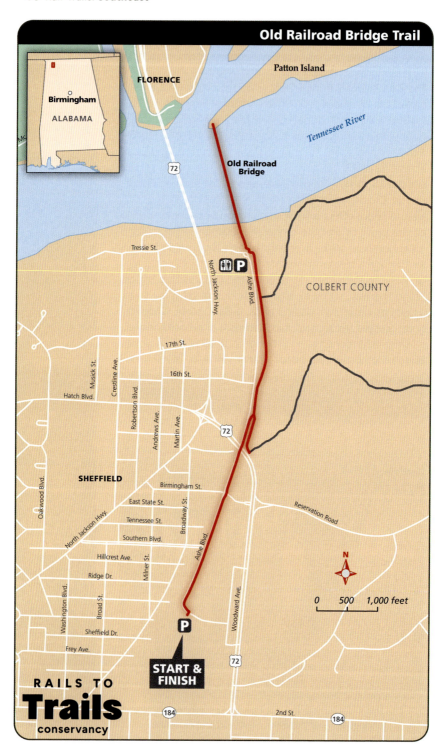

Old Railroad Bridge Trail

FLORENCE

Patton Island

Birmingham

ALABAMA

Tennessee River

72

Old Railroad
Bridge

Tressie St.

P

COLBERT COUNTY

North Jackson Hwy

Ashe Blvd.

17th St.

16th St.

Musick St.

Crestline Ave.

Hatch Blvd.

Robertson Blvd.

Andrews Ave.

Martin Ave.

72

SHEFFIELD

Oakwood Blvd.

Birmingham St.

East State St.

Tennessee St.

Broadway St.

Reservation Road

North Jackson Hwy.

Southern Blvd.

Hillcrest Ave.

Milner St.

Ashe Blvd.

Ridge Dr.

Washington Blvd.

Broad St.

N

Sheffield Dr.

Woodward Ave.

0   500   1,000 feet

Frey Ave.

72

P

**START &
FINISH**

RAILS TO
Trails
conservancy

184

2nd St.

184

into a double-decker bridge in 1858. The lower deck was used as a toll road for trains, wagons, and livestock, while the upper deck was used to transport freight and passengers by local passenger train service and, eventually, by streetcars.

Norfolk Southern Railroad stopped using the railroad in 1988 and five years later donated it to the Old Railroad Bridge Company, a group dedicated to the preservation, restoration, and development of Alabama's oldest historical bridge. The wooden-deck bridge no longer goes completely across the Tennessee River, stopping right before the westernmost tip of Patton Island.

The trail has a linear south–north course, spanning 1.6 miles one-way; note that there is no outlet at the northern end, so you'll have to return the way you came. Trail parking lots are located at the southern end on Ashe Boulevard and just before the bridge; the latter has restrooms.

CONTACT: rtc.li/tva and oldrailroadbridge.com/old-railroad-bridge-landmark

PARKING

Parking areas are both located in Sheffield and are listed from south to north. *Indicates that at least one accessible parking space is available.*

ASHE BLVD.*: US 72 and E. Second St., 0.2 mile west of US 43/US 72 (34.7636, -87.6701).

ASHE BLVD.: South of the Old Railroad Bridge (34.7794, -87.6671).

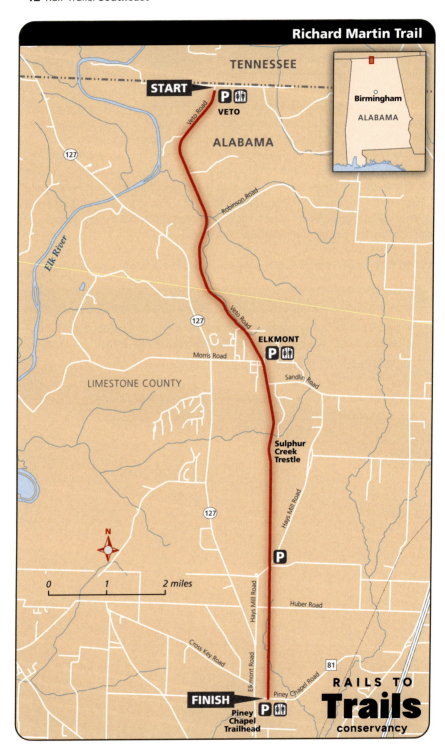

Richard Martin Trail

TENNESSEE

START

VETO

ALABAMA

Birmingham

ALABAMA

127

Robinson Road

Elk River

Veto Road

127

ELKMONT

Morris Road

Sandlin Road

LIMESTONE COUNTY

Sulphur
Creek
Trestle

Hays Mill Road

127

N

Hays Mill Road

Huber Road

0   1   2 miles

Cross Key Road

Elkmont Road

81

FINISH

Piney
Chapel
Trailhead

Piney Chapel Road

RAILS TO
Trails
conservancy

Richard Martin Trail

11

This rail-trail is named for local advocate Richard Martin, who continues to rally for the improvement and extension of the trail. Until 1986, the Tennessee & Alabama Central Railroad (TA&C) line brought in mail and supplies to area communities and carried away cotton, a mainstay of the local economy. The trail is dotted with historical markers, providing users the chance to learn more about the area's former inhabitants.

The northern trailhead is located just south of the Tennessee line in the historic community of Veto, where an old schoolhouse and a nearby covered picnic area and restrooms form a gateway to the trail. The rough gravel trail winds south through wooded areas and wetlands.

For RV travelers, there is a trailside RV park at mile 2. You likely will encounter horses along the trail, as it is a favorite among equestrians. Horseback riding is allowed along the entire trail; horseback riders must travel on the far-right side and yield to other trail users. If you intend to bike the route, take a mountain bike or hybrid, as the rough terrain will give you—and your tires—a workout. Also be sure to

BRANDI HORTON

In Elkmont, you'll be greeted by
a colorful railcar and historic depot.

County
Limestone

Endpoints
Veto Road at Tennessee–Alabama state line (Elkmont); County Road 81/Piney Chapel Road, 0.3 mile east of AL 127/Elkmont Road (Athens)

Mileage
10.2

Type
Rail-Trail

Roughness Rating
2

Surface
Gravel

bring food and drink, as Elkmont is the only place to purchase refreshments along the route.

About halfway through the trail, you'll find Elkmont's historic depot (it's used for community activities), a refurbished railcar, a few places to eat, and retail options for those wanting to make a side trip. The Elkmont Trailhead has restrooms at the southern end of the depot, as well as a small parking area, making it a good place to access the trail.

A mile south of Elkmont, a sign marks the location of the Sulphur Creek Trestle, the tallest bridge on this former rail line, which served as a major transport artery for Union troops and supplies heading to the Civil War's Southern front. A plaque commemorates the 1864 Battle of Sulphur Creek Trestle, during which a TA&C supply train moving Union Army troops and goods from Nashville to Atlanta came under attack. More than 200 soldiers were killed during the ensuing firefight.

A small gravel parking lot off of County Road 55/Hays Mill Road provides another access point, although there is room for only two to four cars. The southern portion of the trail continues through wooded areas and features a charming covered bridge before ending at the Piney Chapel Road Trailhead, where you will find ample parking, a covered picnic area, and restrooms.

CONTACT: rtc.li/limestone-county

PARKING

Parking areas are listed from north to south. *Indicates that at least one accessible parking space is available.*

VETO*: 30600–30898 Bob Coffman Road (34.9941, -86.9885).

ELKMONT*: Elkmont Depot Trailhead at Railroad St. and CR 49/Upper Fort Hampton Road (34.9288, -86.9734).

ELKMONT: CR 55/Hays Mill Road at CR 80/Carey Road and Railroad Lane (34.8802, -86.9699); limited parking available.

ATHENS*: Piney Chapel Road Trailhead, 19779 Piney Chapel Road (34.8488, -86.9691).

Shades Creek Greenway

12

Shades Creek Greenway, a popular trail that winds through Homewood (a suburb south of Birmingham), creates connections to neighborhood destinations, including schools, a shopping center, and office buildings, while providing direct access to the impressive nature that surrounds the area. This short trail delivers an outsize experience as it shows off the ecosystem and wildlife habitat of Shades Creek.

Drinking water, parking, and bike repair stations are available at the trailheads on either end of the paved pathway. Departing from the western trailhead at South Lakeshore Drive and Columbiana Road on the outskirts of Birmingham, the trail follows Shades Creek as it meanders northeast, passing Homewood High School and Samford University at the halfway point.

Besides offering a safe walking and biking route for exercise and recreation, the trail is also a slice of Alabama's beautiful outdoors. Because of the moisture the creek delivers to the soil, the habitat resembles that of a riverside forest. The creek is lined with impressive American sycamore and box elder trees, among other species. Part of the Alabama

KATE JOHNSON

Follow the wooded banks of Shades Creek through Homewood, a suburb south of Birmingham.

County
Jefferson

Endpoints
Columbiana Road, 0.1 mile south of Lakeshore Dr. (Birmingham); Brookwood Blvd., 0.2 mile south of Shades Creek Pkwy. (Homewood)

Mileage
2.6

Type
Greenway/ Non-Rail-Trail

Roughness Rating
1

Surface
Asphalt, Concrete

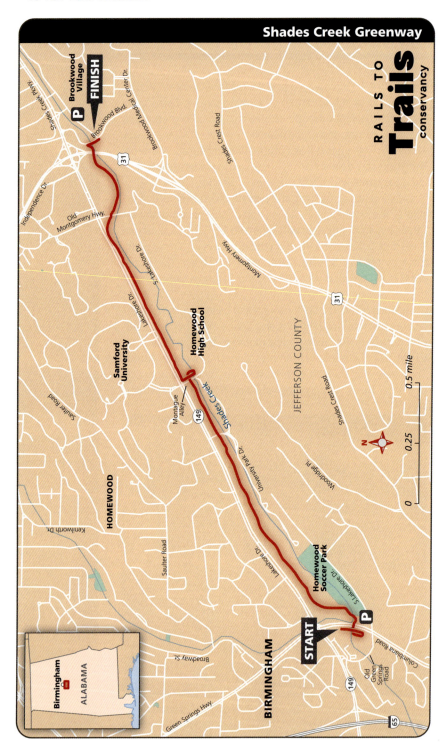

Shades Creek Greenway

Birding Trail, the corridor is also home to pileated woodpeckers, green herons, yellow-crowned night herons, and belted kingfishers. At different times of the year, you'll be treated to lush blankets of wildflowers and the sight of butterflies and beetles.

When you arrive at the trail's eastern terminus at busy Brookwood Boulevard, use the signals to cross to the other side, where you'll find parking about 0.1 mile ahead on the left by Shades Creek. On your right is Brookwood Village, a commercial district with shopping and a coffee shop (note that the once popular Brookwood Mall, straight ahead at the east end of the village, closed in 2022 and at press time was not open to the public).

If you wish to continue your journey, you can connect to the Jemison Park Greenway via a nearly 1-mile sidewalk connection that continues east to this recently renovated, 54-acre natural oasis in the city of Mountain Brook. To get there, follow the sidewalk heading east from the trailhead at Brookwood Village. Take the first bridge on the left to pass over Shades Creek and use the crosswalk to access the sidewalk on the far side of the creek. In 0.3 mile, use the crosswalk at Windsor Drive (the last bridge over Shades Creek) to cross Shades Creek Parkway and continue east on the sidewalk. After another 0.4 mile, at Cahaba Road, use the crosswalks to cross Shades Creek Parkway again and connect with the Jemison Park Greenway as you continue east.

Shades Creek Greenway is part of Jefferson County's developing 750-miles-plus Red Rock Trail System. Plans to extend the trail from its western end are taking hold in 2024 with the planned opening of a 1.4-mile extension heading west from Columbiana Road. This new trail segment will go behind the Wildwood shopping area and will intersect with the Wildwood Preserve.

Cautionary note: As you explore the trail, be aware that some areas would benefit from surface improvements. Given its proximity to the creek, flooding is also a possibility, so take caution after storms.

CONTACT: freshwaterlandtrust.org

PARKING

Parking areas are listed from west to east. *Indicates that at least one accessible parking space is available.*

BIRMINGHAM*: 1710 S. Lakeshore Dr. (33.4498, -86.8106).

HOMEWOOD*: Brookwood Village, 601 Brookwood Blvd. (33.4684, -86.7748).

Sunset Drive Trail

START

431

P

Hill Ave

Taylor St.

Gunter Ave

Blount Ave

Lake Guntersville Park Dr.

227

Lusk St.

GUNTERSVILLE

Gilbreath St.

Ringold St.

Lurleen B. Wallace Pavilion

Lusk St.

Rotary Park

Henry St.

Rayburn Ave

Obrig Ave

Gunter Ave

MARSHALL COUNTY

P

P

Civitan Park

Ogletree Park

Tom Jackson Park

P

P

Guntersville Recreation Center

Forest Dr.

Sunset Dr.

Patterson St.

1

P

Willow Beach Road

Sunset Drive Sandy Beach Area

FINISH

P

Sunset Drive Parking Lot

Guntersville Lake

69

0.5 mile

N

0.25

0

Birmingham

ALABAMA

RAILS TO **Trails** conservancy

Sunset Drive Trail

13

The rolling, paved Sunset Drive Trail follows the shoreline of Lake Guntersville, at the southernmost point of the Tennessee River. The views across the lake are fabulous, especially at sunset. The trail is well maintained and well used, with restrooms, drinking water, and parking all along the route.

The trail is a gathering place for the community of Guntersville, a designated Alabama Community of Excellence. The trail is open in two sections alongside Sunset Drive, divided by busy AL 69/Henry Street. Park and begin your journey at the trail's northernmost endpoint—the Lake Guntersville Chamber of Commerce, just west of US 431 and the City Harbor—so you can explore the city's historic downtown before or after your trip. From here, the trail makes its way 1.2 miles west to the Guntersville Farmers Market at Rotary Park, hugging the shore of Alabama's largest lake.

Another 0.4 mile brings you past a middle school and into Civitan Park, followed by Ogletree Park and Tom Jackson Park. Together, the parks include a playground, several baseball fields, an amphitheater and bleacher seating, a pavilion, a floating dock, the Civitan Park Pier, a dog park,

County
Marshall

Endpoints
Lurleen B. Wallace Dr., across from the Lake Guntersville Chamber of Commerce (Guntersville); Tom Jackson Park at AL 69/ Henry St. and Sunset Dr. (Guntersville); Guntersville Recreation Center at Sunset Dr. (Guntersville); Sunset Dr., 0.2 mile north of Willow Beach Road (Guntersville)

Mileage
3.7

Type
Greenway/ Non-Rail-Trail

Roughness Rating
1

Surface
Asphalt, Concrete

KATE FOSTER

Tracing Alabama's largest lake, the trail offers spectacular waterfront views.

and a public boat ramp. Civitan Park serves as a venue for local concerts and festivals, as well as bass fishing tournaments, 5K runs, and corporate picnics. This segment ends in another 0.3 mile at the end of the parks.

The southern segment begins at the Guntersville Recreation Center, across from a shopping center at AL 69/Henry Street and Sunset Drive, and heads 1.5 miles south. Exercise caution when crossing AL 69/Henry Street and passing through the parking lot of the recreation department and senior center, as the connection lacks a curb cut and navigational signage. The southern segment provides access to a public sandy beach and fishing spot 0.7 mile south of the recreation center. From the beach, head another 0.8 mile to the southernmost terminus, just north of a water plant. The trail includes some hills but plenty of flat areas as well. Enjoy the ample shade of pine trees, charming views of Guntersville's historic homes, and glimpses of eagles and waterfowl such as mallards, Canada geese, and great blue herons.

If you have time after your trip, drive 20 minutes east to the 6,000-acre Lake Guntersville State Park, where you'll find a championship golf course, more fishing, and 36 miles of hiking and biking trails.

CONTACT: guntersvilleal.org/departments/parks-recreation

PARKING

Parking areas are located within Guntersville and are listed from north to south. Select parking areas for the trail are listed below; for a detailed list of parking areas and other waypoints, consult **TrailLink™**. *Indicates that at least one accessible parking space is available.*

LAKE GUNTERSVILLE CHAMBER OF COMMERCE: 200 Gunter Ave. (34.3637, -86.2912).

LURLEEN B. WALLACE PAVILION*: Sunset Dr., 0.1 mile north of Ringold St. (34.3630, -86.3057).

ROTARY PARK: Sunset Dr., 0.2 mile west of Ringold St. (34.3612, -86.3091).

CIVITAN PARK*: 1130 Sunset Dr. (34.3573, -86.3145).

TOM JACKSON PARK*: Henry St. and Sunset Dr. (34.3540, -86.3155).

GUNTERSVILLE RECREATION CENTER*: 1500 Sunset Dr. (34.3512, -86.3182).

SUNSET DR. SANDY BEACH AREA: Sunset Dr. and Forest Dr. (34.3442, -86.3226).

SUNSET DR. PARKING LOT*: Sunset Dr., 0.2 mile north of Willow Beach Road (34.3361, -86.3283).

Yoholo Micco, The Creek Indian Trail

14

In southeastern Alabama, nature lovers, bird-watchers, and history buffs will enjoy the many hidden gems that Yoholo Micco, The Creek Indian Trail, has to offer, many of which are tucked away on dirt side trails marked with rustic signs. Less-hidden sights along the paved rail-trail include views of Lake Eufaula; welded folk art sculptures by a local artist; and railroad paraphernalia, such as original crossties, salvaged rails, a railcar scale, and railroad crossing signs. Benches and exercise stations can be found throughout the trail.

The trail incorporates many of the region's habitat types, including grassy meadows, mixed woodlands, hardwood forests, and shoreline. It is also part of Alabama's Wiregrass Birding Trail, offering bird-watchers the chance to spot nesting bald eagles and ospreys, common ground doves, pileated woodpeckers, winter wrens, common loons, and more.

The rail-trail lies along the right-of-way of the former Montgomery and Eufaula Railroad, incorporated in 1860 to connect Montgomery, Alabama, with the Chattahoochee River at Eufaula. The southern end of the trail is at the Eufaula Barbour County Chamber of Commerce in the heart of downtown Eufaula—a city boasting the second-largest

County
Barbour

Endpoints
Eufaula Barbour County Chamber of Commerce at E. Broad St. and N. Livingston Ave. (Eufaula); Lake Eufaula Campground at dead end of W. Chewalla Creek Dr. (Eufaula); Old Creek Town Park on Lake Dr. (Eufaula)

Mileage
3.2

Type
Rail-Trail

Roughness Rating
1

Surface
Asphalt

COURTESY EUFAULA BARBOUR COUNTY CHAMBER OF COMMERCE

The trail's name and signage honors Yoholo, a Creek leader.

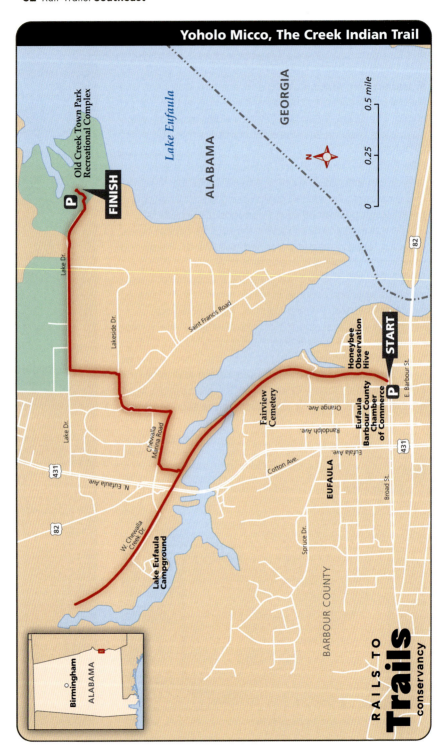

Yoholo Micco, The Creek Indian Trail

Lake Eufaula

GEORGIA

ALABAMA

Old Creek Town Park
Recreational Complex

FINISH

Lake Dr.

Lakeside Dr.

Saint Francis Road

N

0   0.25   0.5 mile

82

START

Honeybee
Observation
Hive

E. Barbour St.

Fairview
Cemetery

Eufaula
Barbour County
Chamber
of Commerce

Orange Ave.

Randolph Ave.

Lake Dr.

Chewalla
Marina Road

Eufala Ave

Cotton Ave.

431

EUFAULA

N. Eufaula Ave.

Broad St.

82

W. Chewalla
Creek Dr.

Spruce Dr.

**Lake Eufaula
Campground**

BARBOUR COUNTY

Birmingham
ALABAMA

RAILS TO
Trails
conservancy

historic district in the state. Casual dining options are located downtown, which makes this the perfect place to begin and end your journey.

The trail is considered easy for most users, though there are steep hills within the first 0.4 mile as the trail heads north. An unusual feature just 0.1 mile from the chamber of commerce is the City of Eufaula's Honeybee Observation Hive, an active, glassed-in beehive allowing trail users to watch honeybees at work. Around 0.4 mile are signs for side trails to Waterfall Trail and Tree Hugger Park, a popular picnic spot. At the 0.6-mile mark, the trail passes the historic Fairview Cemetery, where one of several nature trails has been created off the main trail. The path heads over an old (inactive) railroad trestle across Lake Eufaula at the 1-mile mark.

At 0.2 mile from the trestle, you'll reach a Y-juncture in the trail. The left fork of the Y heads 1 mile northwest toward Lake Eufaula Campground, going under US 431/US 82/North Eufaula Avenue and up to the dead end of West Chewalla Creek Drive. Alternatively, take the right fork of the Y, heading toward Chewalla Marina Road, then follow the trail through a residential section of the city.

The trail ends at Old Creek Town Park, the former site of a Creek village. The trail, once known as the Eufaula Rail-Trail, was renamed the Yoholo Micco in honor of Yoholo, the Creek leader of Old Eufaula Town (*micco* is the Muskogean word for chief). He and his people were driven from this area in 1836 and forced to follow the Trail of Tears to Oklahoma.

The 205-acre Old Creek Town Park Recreational Complex features a picnic shelter and pavilions, restrooms, sports fields, a fishing pier, a boat landing, and the community-built Playground of Dreams, all overlooking Lake Eufaula.

CONTACT: eufaulaalabama.com/173/yoholo-micco-the-creek-indian-trail and eufaulachamber.com

PARKING

Parking areas are located within Eufaula and are listed from south to north. Street parking is also available in downtown Eufaula. *Indicates that at least one accessible parking space is available.*

EUFAULA BARBOUR COUNTY CHAMBER OF COMMERCE*: 333 E. Broad St. (31.8926, -85.1406).

OLD CREEK TOWN PARK RECREATIONAL COMPLEX*: Lake Dr., 0.3 mile east of Lakeside Dr. (31.9164, -85.1258).

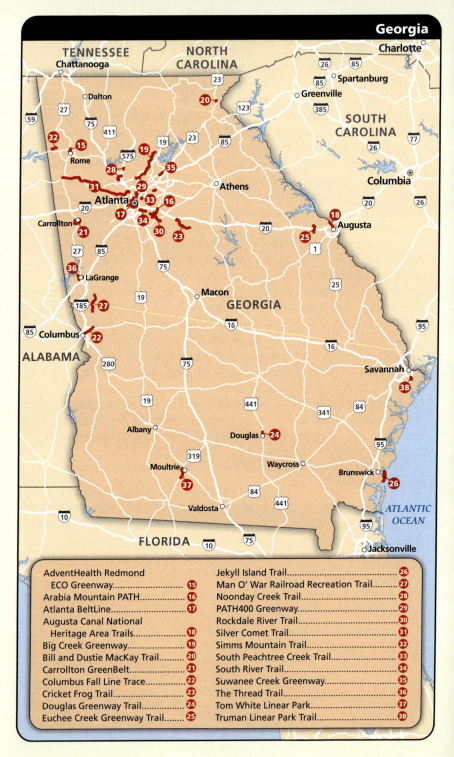

Georgia

TENNESSEE
Chattanooga
NORTH CAROLINA
Charlotte
Dalton
Spartanburg
Greenville
SOUTH CAROLINA
Rome
Columbia
Atlanta
Athens
Carrollton
Augusta
LaGrange
Macon
GEORGIA
Columbus
ALABAMA
Savannah
Albany
Douglas
Moultrie
Waycross
Brunswick
ATLANTIC OCEAN
Valdosta
FLORIDA
Jacksonville

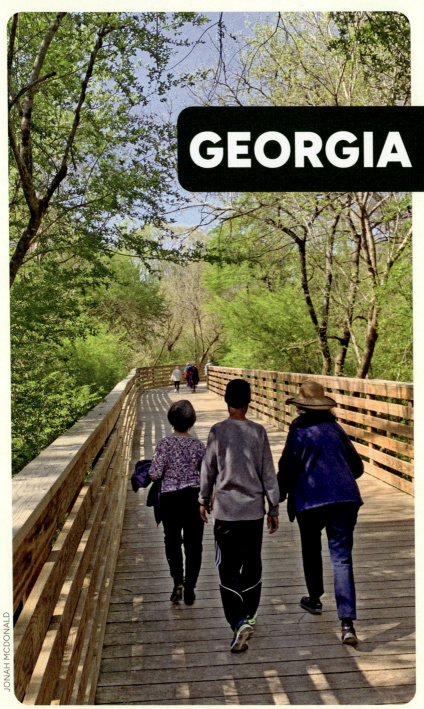

GEORGIA

A stretch of the South Peachtree Creek Trail along Burnt Fork Creek offers an elevated boardwalk enveloped in trees (*see Trail 33, page 115*).

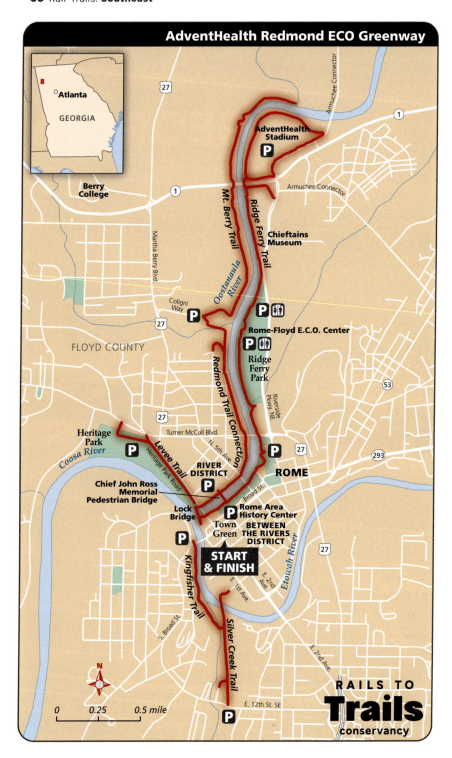

AdventHealth Redmond ECO Greenway

GEORGIA
○ Atlanta

Berry
College

AdventHealth
Stadium
🅿

Mt. Berry Trail

Ridge Ferry Trail

Armuchee Connector

Chieftains
Museum

Oostanaula River

Coligni
Way
🅿

FLOYD COUNTY

🅿 🚻

Rome-Floyd E.C.O. Center

🅿 🚻

Ridge
Ferry
Park

Redmond Trail Connection

Riverside Pkwy. NE

Heritage
Park
🅿

Coosa River

Levee Trail

Turner McCall Blvd.

Heritage Park Road

N. 5th Ave.

RIVER
DISTRICT
🅿

🅿

ROME

Chief John Ross
Memorial
Pedestrian Bridge

Broad St.

Lock
Bridge

🅿

🅿 Rome Area
History Center

Town
Green

**BETWEEN
THE RIVERS
DISTRICT**

🅿

**START
& FINISH**

Kingfisher Trail

E. 1st Ave.

E. 2nd Ave.

Etowah River

Silver Creek Trail

S. Broad St.

E. 2nd Ave.

0   0.25   0.5 mile

N

E. 12th St. SE

🅿

RAILS TO
Trails
conservancy

AdventHealth Redmond ECO Greenway

15

All trails lead to Rome on the AdventHealth Redmond ECO Greenway, a mostly flat, interconnected system of six trails in an otherwise hilly North Georgia city. The greenway's name represents the three rivers—the Etowah, Coosa, and Oostanaula—that run through the city.

The greenway grew out of the city's desire to connect short pieces of trail that followed old railroad lines and rivers that historically contributed to the city's economic growth. The result is a 16-mile trail system that runs mostly along both banks of the Oostanaula River, but also along parts of the Etowah and Coosa Rivers.

Starting in downtown Rome and rolling clockwise in a loop on a seamless trail route, visitors will encounter the Ridge Ferry Trail, the Levee Trail (a loop), the Redmond Trail Connection, and the Mt. Berry Trail, and then return to the Ridge Ferry Trail. At the southern base of that 13-mile round-trip, there are short on-street connections to the Kingfisher Trail and the Silver Creek Trail. Historical markers and interpretive signs explain the city's growth and culture along the way.

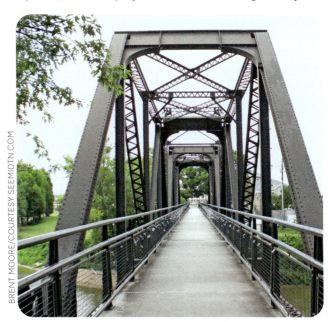

Rome's Lock Bridge, known for the padlocks that lovers place here, spans the Oostanaula River downtown.

BRENT MOORE/COURTESY SEEMIDTN.COM

County
Floyd

Endpoints
E. 12th St. SE, between Silver St. and Cedar Ave. SW (Rome); Braves Blvd. NE/Armuchee Connector at AdventHealth Stadium (Rome) *Full list of endpoints in the description*

Mileage
16

Type
Greenway, Rail-Trail

Roughness Rating
1

Surface
Asphalt, Concrete

The endpoints for each trail are as follows:

➤ *Ridge Ferry Trail*: W. First St. and Bridgepoint Plaza (at the confluence of the Etowah and Oostanaula Rivers); Braves Blvd. NE/Armuchee Connector at the northeast corner of AdventHealth Stadium

➤ *Levee Trail (loop):* Lock Bridge at Heritage Park Road and N. Second Ave. NW

➤ *Redmond Trail Connection:* N. Fifth Ave. just east of N. Fourth Ave. SW; Oostanaula Dr. and Ave. B; Coligni Way just east of US 27/Martha Berry Blvd. NE

➤ *Mt. Berry Trail:* Coligni Way just east of US 27/Martha Berry Blvd. NE; Oostanaula River (north bank) across river from AdventHealth Stadium

➤ *Silver Creek Trail:* E. 12th St. SE, between Silver St. and Cedar Ave. SW; 0.1 mile southwest of intersection of E. Fourth St. and E. First St.

➤ *Kingfisher Trail:* S. Broad St. and Branham Ave. SW

Town Green, overlooking the Oostanaula River in downtown Rome's Between the Rivers District, is considered the main trailhead for the Ridge Ferry Trail. The park's splash pad and fountain are welcome features on hot summer days. The free Rome Area History Center is located across Tribune Street.

Heading southwest from the green, you come to a T-junction in 0.2 mile. A left takes you across the Etowah River on Broad Street to join the Kingfisher Trail, which rolls along the heavily wooded Etowah River shoreline for 0.6 mile, ending at a junction with the Silver Creek Trail. A right turn on the Silver Creek Trail goes 0.4 mile to the county health department and local cafés, while a left turn crosses back over the river on an old railroad trestle to East Fourth Street. A left onto East First Avenue here leads to the Levee Trail in 0.4 mile.

If you take the right fork at the Ridge Ferry Trail's T-junction, you'll cross the river on a 1905 Central of Georgia Railway swing span, known locally as the Lock Bridge because lovers attach padlocks on the span to signify their devotion to each other. You'll arrive at the Levee Trail at the northern foot of the bridge. If you head straight onto Heritage Park Road, you can make a 1.2-mile loop on the road and Levee Trail through the park overlooking the Coosa River.

The Levee Trail then passes under the Lock Bridge into Rome's River District, an ambitious downtown redevelopment area. It sits directly across the Oostanaula River from Town Green, connected by the Chief John Ross Memorial Pedestrian Bridge.

The Levee Trail transitions to the Redmond Trail Connection under the North Fifth Avenue bridge and continues up the Oostanaula River's west bank to the Mt. Berry Trail, named for the nearby private Berry College, founded in 1902. The trail follows the wooded shoreline of the river for about 3 miles. A recently completed connection to the pedestrian shoulder of the Armuchee Connector bridge allows users to cross the river to AdventHealth stadium, home to the Rome Braves minor-league baseball team.

From the stadium, the Ridge Ferry Trail heads south along the eastern shore of the Oostanaula River through a shady hardwood forest that's a destination for leaf peeping in the fall. In 1.2 miles, you'll arrive at Chieftains Museum/Major Ridge Home, a National Historic Landmark that's the former home of a prosperous leader of the Cherokee Nation who signed a treaty with the U.S. government, the Treaty of New Echota, that led to disastrous results for him and his people, who were forced to relocate. You'll also pass through Ridge Ferry Park and the environmental study facility at the Rome-Floyd E.C.O. Center on this 3-mile section before returning to Town Green.

CONTACT: ecogreenway.org

PARKING

Parking areas are located within Rome and are listed clockwise, starting at Town Green downtown. *Indicates that at least one accessible parking space is available.*

THIRD AVE. PARKING DECK*: 131 W. First St. (34.2541, -85.1736); fee charged after 1 hour.

FLOYD COUNTY HEALTH DEPARTMENT: 16 E. 12th St. SE (34.2380, -85.1738).

MYRTLE HILL CEMETERY: Branham Ave. SW and Broad St. (34.2518, -85.1771).

HERITAGE PARK*: 1 Shorter Ave. (34.2606, -85.1837).

RIVER DISTRICT: 300 W. Third St. (34.2571, -85.1750); on-street parking.

MT. BERRY TRAILHEAD: 1420 Martha Berry Blvd. (34.2710, -85.1771).

ADVENTHEALTH STADIUM*: 755 Braves Blvd. NE (34.2861, -85.1645).

RIDGE FERRY PARK: 473 Riverside Pkwy. NE (34.2709, -85.1707); gravel lot.

ROME-FLOYD E.C.O. CENTER: 393 Riverside Pkwy. NE (34.2685, -85.1718).

SARA HIGHTOWER LIBRARY: 205 Riverside Pkwy. NE (34.2588, -85.1692).

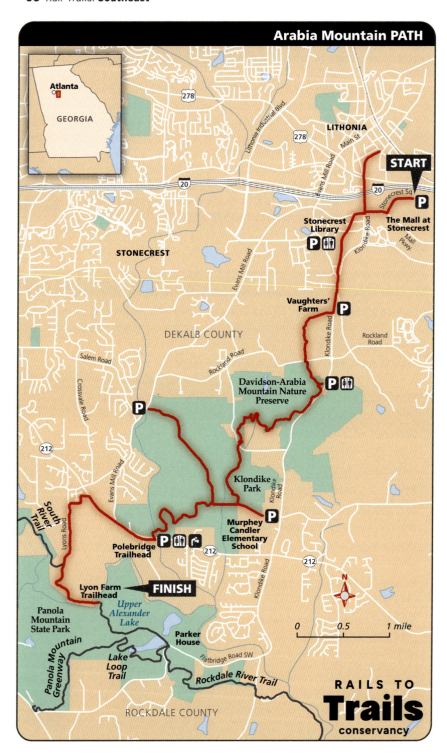

Arabia Mountain PATH

Arabia Mountain PATH

Southeast of Atlanta, the Arabia Mountain PATH winds through Stonecrest and a beautiful natural oasis, including giant rock outcrops, rushing creeks, dense woodlands, and wildflower meadows. Because the route includes steep hills and some sharp turns that require low speeds, the experience may be challenging for some trail users.

Begin at the trail's northern end at The Mall at Stonecrest, where plentiful parking is available. From the lot, you'll head southwest along the concrete pathway paralleling Stonecrest Square and make a right turn on Mall Parkway in 0.4 mile. The trail follows the parkway for 0.2 mile, then splits, with a 0.8-mile spur heading north to Lithonia and the majority of the trail heading south into the woods at the intersection of Mall Parkway and Klondike Road.

In 0.3 mile on the southern route, you'll reach a connection to the Stonecrest Library, which provides your first opportunity for restrooms. Continuing south, you'll see an old white barn to your right in 0.7 mile; this is Vaughters' Farm, a remnant from the time when DeKalb County was

Counties
DeKalb, Rockdale

Endpoints
The Mall at Stonecrest at Stonecrest Square and Mall Ring Road (Stonecrest); Johnson St., between Magnolia St. and Council St. (Lithonia); Murphey Candler Elementary School at the dead end of S. Goddard Road (Stonecrest); Evans Mill Road, 0.4 mile south of Rockland Road (Stonecrest); Rockdale River Trail at the South River crossing (Stonecrest)

Mileage
12.4

Type
Rail-Trail

Roughness Rating
1–2

Surface
Boardwalk, Concrete

BOB MARTILOTTA

The pathway winds through a natural oasis, including rock outcrops, woodlands, and meadows.

the dairy capital of Georgia. Its former cow pasture now offers nature trails on which you might spot deer, turkey, or other wildlife.

After the farm, you'll reach the Davidson-Arabia Mountain Nature Preserve in 1.2 miles. Enjoy the picturesque surroundings of wetlands, pine and oak forests, streams, and lakes across its 2,550 acres, and visit its nature center to participate in ranger-led educational programming. Heading south, you'll wind past Klondike Park and, in 2.6 miles, reach a T-intersection. Turn right to stay on the main trail; turning left puts you on a short spur to Murphey Candler Elementary School and Arabia Mountain High School.

In 0.3 mile, you'll reach another fork in the trail. Take a left to stay on the main trail. If you turn right, you'll take a 1.4-mile spur to a trailhead on Evans Mill Road. Heading southwest on the main trail, you'll be enveloped by trees and reach the Polebridge Trailhead in 1.2 miles, where there is a portable toilet, benches, a drinking fountain, and the southernmost parking lot on the trail. In 2 miles, you'll reach the Lyon Farm Trailhead, the site of a historic rural homestead, and have the opportunity to hop on the South River Trail (see page 117), which heads northwest along the river to Martin Luther King Jr. High School. From this juncture it's 0.9 mile to the Arabia Mountain PATH's end at the South River and a connection to the Rockdale River Trail (see page 105), which continues southeast through Panola Mountain State Park.

CONTACT: pathfoundation.org/arabia-mountain-path

PARKING

Parking areas are located within Stonecrest and are listed from north to south. Select parking areas for the trail are listed below; for a detailed list of parking areas and other waypoints, consult **TrailLink™**. *Indicates that at least one accessible parking space is available.*

THE MALL AT STONECREST*: 2929 Turner Hill Road (33.7002, -84.0982).

STONECREST LIBRARY*: 3123 Klondike Road (33.6947, -84.1102).

VAUGHTERS' FARM TRAILHEAD*: 3366 Klondike Road (33.6839, -84.1138); large gravel lot with two paved accessible spaces.

DAVIDSON-ARABIA MOUNTAIN NATURE PRESERVE: 3787 Klondike Road (33.6723, -84.1161); gravel lot.

EVANS MILL ROAD TRAILHEAD: 4028 Evans Mill Road (33.6687, -84.1502).

POLEBRIDGE TRAILHEAD*: 6262 Browns Mill Road (33.6493, -84.1480).

Atlanta BeltLine

17

In Georgia's capital, the ever-evolving Atlanta BeltLine is a rail-trail rock star for both the state and the South. Since 2008, segments of the planned 22-mile multiuse loop have opened up in neighborhoods all across the city, connecting dozens of parks, mass transit stations, schools, and businesses. Outlined here are eight of the BeltLine's open segments, which are concrete-surfaced except where noted.

Begin at Piedmont Park on the eastern side of the Atlanta BeltLine to take a clockwise route. This crown jewel of the city's park system offers plentiful recreational amenities, including an aquatic center, a playground, gardens, nature trails, athletic facilities, and eateries. You'll also have access to parking, restrooms, and drinking fountains in the 185-acre park. The BeltLine's 3.6-mile **Eastside Trail** begins at the southeast corner of the park at Monroe Drive NE and 10th Street NE in Midtown and heads southeast to the Cabbagetown and Reynoldstown neighborhoods. Due to the popularity of this section, it can be difficult to navigate by bike on crowded weekends.

County
Fulton

Endpoints
(All in Atlanta) *Northeast and Eastside Trails:* Monroe Dr. NE and 10th St. NE; dead end of Mayson St. NE just north of I-85 *Westside Trail:* Washington Park Tennis Center at Lena Ave. *West End Trail:* Westview Cemetery *Westside BeltLine Connector:* Northside Dr. and Ivan Allen Jr. Blvd.; Marietta Blvd. NW and Huff Road NW *Southwest Connector Trail:* Westwood Ave. SW and Handley Ave. SW; Lionel Hampton Trail in Lionel Hampton Park; Beecher Hills Elementary School *Northside Trail:* Ardmore Park; Bobby Jones Golf Course at S. Colonial Homes Cir. NW

Mileage
20.8

Type
Greenway/Non-Rail-Trail, Rail-Trail

Roughness Rating
1

Surface
Concrete, Gravel

The Westside BeltLine Connector begins in downtown Atlanta and traverses commercial, residential, and industrial areas.

BRIAN HOUSH

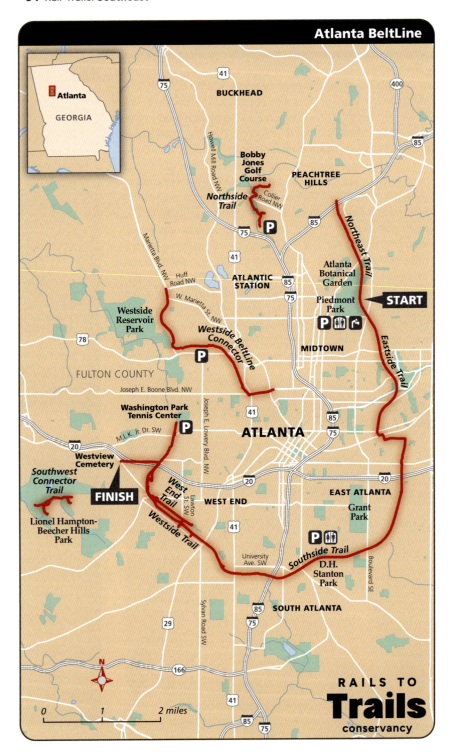

Atlanta BeltLine

From Piedmont Park, you'll arrive at a connection to the 20-mile Stone Mountain Trail in 1.4 mile, just after the John Lewis Freedom Parkway underpass; that trail heads west to downtown Atlanta and east to Stone Mountain Park. The Eastside Trail ends at Glenwood Avenue Southeast and Bill Kennedy Way Southeast, shortly after crossing I-20 on a protected bike lane.

The developing **Southside Trail** picks up where the Eastside Trail ends and provides a 3.9-mile route through the city's southern neighborhoods from Glenwood Park to Oakland City. (*Note:* While this section is open, most of the route has a gravel surface that may prove challenging for some trail users. Improvements for the Southside Trail are planned for 2024; during construction, detour routes can be found at **beltline.org.**) After 1.2 miles, you'll reach a signaled crossing of Boulevard Southeast. You could turn right (north) here and follow the sidewalk paralleling the street for 0.3 mile to reach popular Grant Park, which houses Zoo Atlanta. Continuing west from Boulevard, you'll reach a connection to D.H. Stanton Park on your right in 0.9 mile. The park includes a playground, a splash pad, a picnic pavilion, restrooms, and drinking fountains. In another 1.8 miles, after passing under I-85, the Southside Trail ends and the Westside Trail begins.

The **Westside Trail** picks up near University Avenue SW and provides a 3.6-mile, tree-lined route through some of the city's oldest neighborhoods along the former Louisville and Nashville Railroad. As you approach the Lawton Street underpass in 1.1 miles, you can follow the ramp and signs to jump over to the similarly named **West End Trail.** The 2.3-mile West End Trail parallels the Westside Trail until reaching Gordon White Park. At the park, a crosswalk will guide you to the left and back onto the Westside Trail. (Just after the I-20 underpass, the West End Trail deviates and heads west, ending at the Westview Cemetery, which is on the National Register of Historic Places.)

If you stay on the Westside Trail, you'll continue traveling northwest, reaching a colorfully painted tunnel under Lucile Avenue Southwest in 1.2 miles. The Westside Trail ends in another 1.3 miles at the Washington Park Tennis Center on Lena Avenue.

A future extension of the Westside Trail, which will connect to the **Westside BeltLine Connector,** is under construction and expected to be completed in 2025. This 3.1-mile segment begins in downtown Atlanta at Ivan Allen Jr. Boulevard Northwest and Luckie Street Northwest, across from the Georgia Aquarium. The trail begins with an elevated portion over city streets as it takes a northwesterly course through a mix of commercial, residential, and industrial areas. In 1.4 miles, you'll reach a trail parking lot at Bedford Street Northwest and Joseph E. Lowery Boulevard Northwest. From there, the trail heads east toward Marietta Boulevard Northwest, then parallels that roadway north just east of Westside Reservoir Park (also known as Westside Park), Atlanta's largest green space. The trail ends where the boulevard intersects Huff Road NW in another 1.7 miles.

The **Southwest Connector Trail,** a 1.1-mile disconnected segment of the BeltLine, begins farther west at Westwood Avenue Southwest and Handley Avenue Southwest. From there, it heads west, winding through a 54-acre hardwood forest linking Beecher Hills Park and Lionel Hampton Park (collectively referred to as Lionel Hampton–Beecher Hills Park). In 0.4 mile, a 0.3-mile spur leads south to Beecher Hills Elementary School.

The lushly wooded 1.2-mile **Northside Trail** begins in Buckhead at Ardmore Park. Heading north, at 0.1 mile, you'll pass under a trestle. Over the next 0.4 mile, you'll traverse Tanyard Park (which offers parking and features a historical marker about the Civil War Battle of Peachtree Creek) and approach Collier Road Northwest. In another 0.7 mile, you'll arrive at the southern end of the Bobby Jones Golf Course and the end of the trail.

After a gap of about 3.5 miles where a planned Northwest Trail is still in the design phase, you can pick up the **Northeast Trail** at the dead end of Mayson Street Northeast just north of I-85. From here, the developing trail is paved and heads south through residential neighborhoods for 2 miles. It ends at the southeast corner of Piedmont Park, where a 0.9-mile segment is under construction on the eastern edge of the park. Detouring around, you'll be back where you began your journey on the Eastside Trail.

CONTACT: beltline.org

PARKING

Parking areas are located within Atlanta and are listed clockwise. Select parking areas for the trail are listed below; for a detailed list of parking areas and other waypoints, consult **TrailLink™.** You can also reach the trail via MARTA, Atlanta's bus, rail, and streetcar system; visit **itsmarta.com** for more information. *Indicates that at least one accessible parking space is available.*

PIEDMONT PARK*: 1345 Piedmont Ave. NE (33.7892, -84.3727); the parking lot is 1 mile north of the start of the trail, which begins at the southeast corner of the park at Monroe Dr. NE and 10th St. NE.

WASHINGTON PARK TENNIS CENTER*: 1125 Lena St. NW (33.7569, -84.4246).

WESTSIDE BELTLINE CONNECTOR TRAIL PARKING LOT*: Bedford St. NW and Joseph E. Lowery Blvd. NW (33.7750, -84.4166).

TANYARD PARK: Collier Road NW and Overbrook Dr. NW (33.8105, -84.4030).

Augusta Canal National Heritage Area Trails

18

Taking a trek through Augusta's industrial past is as easy as hopping on the towpath and the Mill Village Trail. They form a nearly 8-mile level track nestled between the Savannah River and the Augusta Canal and create a backbone for a network of trails in the Augusta Canal National Heritage Area, designated by Congress in 1996.

Completed in 1845, the canal carried commercial traffic and harnessed the river's energy to power local textile mills, which helped establish the city as one of the South's few manufacturing centers by the Civil War. Today, the waterway is the nation's only intact industrial canal still in operation. Along the trail, you'll view renovated textile mills and the chimney of the Confederate Powder Works, which was operational between 1862 and 1865.

The trail—mostly hard-packed dirt—runs along the old towpath from the canal headgates at Savannah Rapids Park north of Augusta to the Old Turning Basin at 13th St. in the town's central business district. The trail surface is suitable for bicycles and is wheelchair accessible. Fishing is a popular pastime along the trail, as long as you follow the rules—don't feed the alligators!

The Augusta Canal Trail parallels the oldest continuously operating hydropower canal in the United States.

Counties
Columbia, Richmond

Endpoints
Augusta Canal headgates at Savannah Rapids Park, just northeast of 3300 Evans to Locks Road (Martinez); 13th St. and Walton Way (Augusta)

Mileage
7.9

Type
Canal

Roughness Rating
1

Surface
Concrete, Packed Dirt

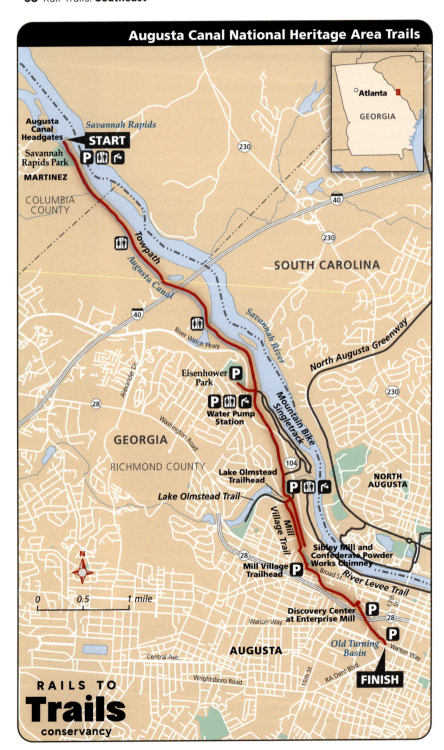

Augusta Canal National Heritage Area Trails

Atlanta
GEORGIA

Savannah Rapids

Augusta
Canal
Headgates
START

Savannah
Rapids Park

MARTINEZ

COLUMBIA
COUNTY

Towpath

Augusta Canal

Savannah River

SOUTH CAROLINA

North Augusta Greenway

River Watch Pkwy.

Alexander Dr.

Eisenhower
Park

Washington Road

Water Pump
Station

Mountain Bike Singletrack

GEORGIA

RICHMOND COUNTY

Lake Olmstead
Trailhead

Lake Olmstead Trail

**NORTH
AUGUSTA**

Mill Village Trail

Sibley Mill and
Confederate Powder
Works Chimney

River Levee Trail

Mill Village
Trailhead

Broad St.

Discovery Center
at Enterprise Mill

13th St.

Walton Way

Walton Way

*Old Turning
Basin*

FINISH

AUGUSTA

Central Ave.

Wrightsboro Road

15th St.

RA Dent Blvd.

N

0   0.5   1 mile

**RAILS TO
Trails
conservancy**

Beginning your visit at the northern end, you will find plenty of parking at the headgates trailhead in Savannah Rapids Park, where bicycle and kayak rentals are available. After crossing the 1875 gatehouse and locks at the head of the canal, you'll head south on the towpath on a narrow, wooded strip of land between the canal and the river. In about 2.5 miles, a clearing provides a spot to picnic or wade into the river.

While you can watch Augusta's skyline emerge as you head south, the first trailside buildings arise in another mile at the pump station, which has been drawing drinking water from the canal since 1899. This is also the junction with the 2.5-mile Mountain Bike Singletrack and a pedestrian bridge crossing the canal to parking and ballfields.

Another 1.3 miles brings you to the Lake Olmstead Trailhead, where you'll cross a bridge to continue on a paved main trail (the Mill Village Trail). You can also continue south for 0.5 mile on the old towpath or take excursions on the Lake Olmstead and River Levee Trails, which meet here.

In 0.6 mile, you'll reach the Mill Village Trailhead, after which the remaining trail is paved. Just south of the trailhead, you'll find the old redbrick Confederate Powder Works chimney and Sibley Mill. In another mile, the trail crosses back to the north side of the canal and passes the Enterprise Mill, a former textile factory that houses historical exhibits in the Discovery Center. The trail ends in 0.4 mile at the Old Turning Basin, formerly a wide spot where canal boats could turn around.

CONTACT: augustacanal.com

PARKING

Parking areas are listed from north to south. *Indicates that at least one accessible parking space is available.*

MARTINEZ*: Savannah Rapids Park, 3300 Evans to Locks Road (33.5503, -82.0401).

AUGUSTA: Eisenhower Park, park access road 0.2 mile southeast of Eisenhower Dr. (33.5133, -82.0057).

AUGUSTA: Lake Olmstead Trailhead, Lakeshore Loop at Milledge Road (33.4946, -81.9973).

AUGUSTA*: Mill Village Trailhead, Pearl Ave. and Eve St. (33.4877, -81.9950).

AUGUSTA*: Discovery Center at Enterprise Mill, 1450 Greene St. (33.4766, -81.9816).

AUGUSTA: Old Turning Basin Trailhead, 13th St. and Fenwick St. (33.4726, -81.9784).

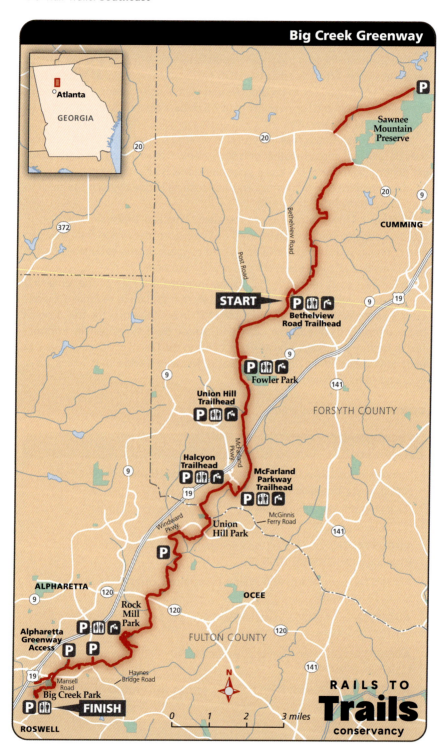

Big Creek Greenway

GEORGIA

Atlanta

Sawnee Mountain Preserve

CUMMING

START
Bethelview Road Trailhead

Fowler Park

Union Hill Trailhead

FORSYTH COUNTY

Halcyon Trailhead

McFarland Parkway Trailhead

McGinnis Ferry Road

Union Hill Park

ALPHARETTA

Rock Mill Park

OCEE

FULTON COUNTY

Alpharetta Greenway Access

Haynes Bridge Road

Mansell Road

Big Creek Park

FINISH

ROSWELL

0   1   2   3 miles

RAILS TO
Trails
conservancy

Big Creek Greenway

Big Creek Greenway follows a leisurely course through the fast-growing suburbs of the northeastern Atlanta metro area. It traces the woodsy floodplain of Big Creek, a tributary of the Chattahoochee River, and bypasses Cumming before passing through Alpharetta and arriving in Roswell.

The route offers shade in the summer and colorful foliage in the fall. The 12-foot-wide trail sections are smooth enough for in-line skating and wheelchair use. Although busy roads crisscross the corridor, most pass overhead on bridges, so there are long stretches where you don't have to physically cross a road. In some cases, the greenway parallels roads as a side path. There are some road crossings, however, where trail users should exercise caution. The overall slope trends downhill as the greenway heads south, but there are a few climbs. The boardwalks can be slippery when wet.

In the north, an isolated section of greenway starts at Forsyth County's Sawnee Mountain Preserve, which has 11 miles of nature trails, an overlook, and interpretive exhibits. That section ends in 2.5 miles at Canton Highway/ GA 20, a busy road with no shoulders, and then resumes after a mile-long gap on GA 20 (where there is no parking). Until that gap is closed, it is recommended that you begin at the Bethelview Road Trailhead, about 5 miles south.

BRIAN HOUSH

Boardwalks carry visitors over low, swampy wetland areas.

Counties
Forsyth, Fulton

Endpoints
Spot Road and Twin Lakes Road (Cumming); Spot Road Connector and Canton Hwy./GA 20 (Cumming); Canton Hwy./ GA 20 between Crestbrook Dr. and Tower Road (Cumming); Big Creek Park, 0.4 mile north of Old Alabama Road (Roswell)

Mileage
27.8

Type
Greenway/ Non-Rail-Trail

Roughness Rating
2

Surface
Asphalt, Boardwalk, Cinder, Concrete

Following the trail south, you'll pass numerous access paths to subdivisions that have sprung up near Big Creek, and signs identify many native plants, such as the flowering dogwood tree. Keep an eye out for deer, wild turkeys, herons, and other creekside inhabitants—including venomous copperhead snakes.

About 3.6 miles south of the Bethelview Road Trailhead, you'll come to Fowler Park, which has a skate park and athletic fields. As at other regularly spaced trailheads along the route, you'll find restrooms, drinking water, and parking here.

Passing into Alpharetta and Fulton County at McGinnis Ferry Road, you'll notice more housing and commercial areas. About 2 miles from the greenway's southern endpoint, you can exit the trail to the right at the Haynes Bridge Road junction and head north into a congested shopping and restaurant district around North Point Mall with plenty of choices for dining.

About 1 mile south, the trail splits right before Mansell Road in Roswell, with the left fork following the Roswell Greenway for 1.2 miles to parking at the trailhead in Big Creek Park. The right fork takes Big Creek Greenway to a cul-de-sac on Beaver Creek Road with no services.

CONTACT: parks.forsythco.com/parks/big-creek-greenway

PARKING

Parking areas are listed from north to south. *Indicates that at least one accessible parking space is available.*

CUMMING*: Sawnee Mountain Preserve Trailhead, 4075 Spot Road at Twin Lakes Road (34.2555, -84.1395).

CUMMING*: Bethelview Road Trailhead, 5120 Bethelview Road (34.1816, -84.1942).

CUMMING*: Fowler Park Trailhead, 4110 Carolene Way (34.1516, -84.2103).

CUMMING*: Union Hill Trailhead, 5259 Union Hill Road (34.1352, -84.2148).

ALPHARETTA*: Halcyon Trailhead, 6265 Cortland Walk (34.1097, -84.2221).

ALPHARETTA*: Union Hill Park, 1590 Little Pine Trail (34.0975, -84.2345).

ALPHARETTA*: Rock Mill Park, 3100 Kimball Bridge Road (34.0524, -84.2709).

ALPHARETTA*: Haynes Bridge Road Access, 10801 Haynes Bridge Road (34.0450, -84.2846).

ALPHARETTA*: Alpharetta Greenway Access, 6698 N. Point Pkwy. (34.0436, -84.2959).

ROSWELL*: Big Creek Park, 0.4 mile north of Old Alabama Road, between Holcomb Woods Pkwy. and Crabtree Dr. (34.0303, -84.3110).

The Bill and Dustie MacKay Trail at Tallulah Gorge State Park in North Georgia is one of those rare level paths passing through otherwise rugged terrain. Previously known as the Shortline Trail and, before that, the Tallulah Falls Rail-Trail, the 1.7-mile paved asphalt trail follows the Tallulah River, which it crosses on a scenic suspension bridge. State lawmakers renamed the trail for volunteers William and Dustie MacKay in recognition of the many years the couple spent maintaining the trail and ensuring the safety of visitors.

The trail follows a short segment of the Tallulah Falls Railway, which launched in 1871 and reached Tallulah Falls by 1882. It eventually ran between Cornelia, Georgia, and Franklin, North Carolina, until 1961. Tourists flocked to the Victorian resort town of Tallulah Falls by the turn of the 20th century to experience the area's waterfalls, forests, and 1,000-foot chasm. Outdoor adventurers still visit Tallulah Gorge State Park to camp, kayak, fish, hike, and rock climb.

The southern trailhead is on Terrora Circle at the north end of the state park, about a mile northwest of Tallulah Falls' central business district. The pilings from an old railroad trestle still stand in a slack water portion of the river here. The trail

KELLY VERDECK/WANDERLAND.XYZ

The trail follows the scenic Tallulah River and crosses it via a suspension bridge.

County
Rabun

Endpoints
Terrora Cir., 0.2 mile west of US 441/US 23/ GA 15 via Jane Hurt Yarn Road (Tallulah Falls); Terrora Cir. at Y Camp Road (Tallulah Falls)

Mileage
1.7

Type
Rail-Trail

Roughness
1

Surface
Asphalt, Dirt

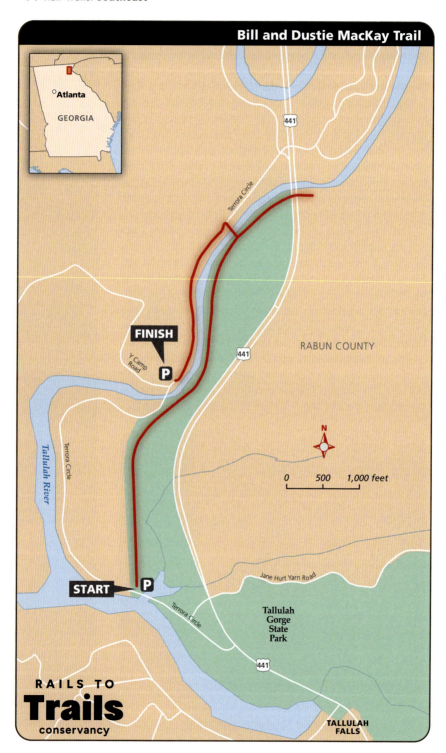

Bill and Dustie MacKay Trail

Atlanta

GEORGIA

Terrora Circle

441

FINISH

P

Y Camp Road

441

RABUN COUNTY

Tallulah River

Terrora Circle

N

0   500   1,000 feet

START

P

Jane Hurt Yarn Road

Terrora Circle

Tallulah Gorge State Park

441

RAILS TO

Trails

conservancy

TALLULAH FALLS

can be a cool diversion on a hot day, as water seeping out of rocky railroad cuts evaporates to chill the air.

In about 0.5 mile, you can see the Tallulah River through the woods. The river above the dam here is too shallow for paddle sports, but fishing is allowed with a license. At 0.9 mile, you'll reach a trail fork. To the right is a dirt trail that continues on the old railbed for a quarter mile before ending at the US 441 overpass. The left leg follows the main trail across a 230-foot-long suspension bridge built in 1998 that provides views as much as 20 feet above the river.

On the other side of the river, the trail heads back south, running between river and road for 0.4 mile before it ends at a trailhead on another part of Terrora Circle. Then you can either retrace your steps back to the main trailhead or continue south along the sinuous Terrora Circle for 0.9 mile to return to your starting point for a 2.5-mile loop. Look to your right as you ride along Terrora Circle, and through a break in the trees you'll spy across the river the historic Terrora Hydro Plant, which entered service in 1925 and is still operating.

CONTACT: gastateparks.org/tallulahgorge

PARKING

Parking areas are within Tallulah Gorge State Park and are listed from south to north. There is a $5 parking fee. *Indicates that at least one accessible parking space is available.*

SOUTH TRAILHEAD: Terrora Cir., 0.2 mile west of US 441/US 23/GA 15 via Jane Hurt Yarn Road (34.7429, -83.4036).

NORTH TRAILHEAD: Terrora Cir., 0.6 mile southwest of US 441/US 23/ GA 15/Old 441 S. intersection (34.7510, -83.4013).

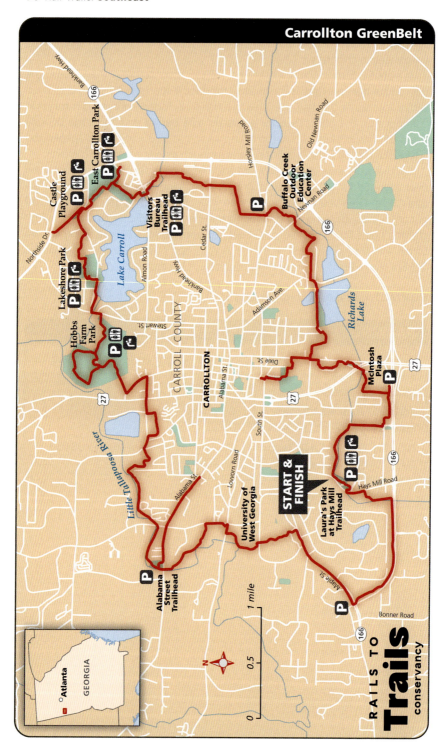

Carrollton GreenBelt

Castle Playground

East Carrollton Park

Lakeshore Park

Hobbs Farm Park

Lake Carroll

Little Carroll

Visitors Bureau Trailhead

Cedar St.

Buffalo Creek Outdoor Education Center

Pea St.

Horsley Mill Rd.

Old Newnan Road

Newnan Road

166

Almon Road

Stewart St.

Bankhead Hwy.

Adamson Ave.

Richards Lake

CARROLL COUNTY

CARROLLTON

Alabama St.

Dixie St.

27

McIntosh Plaza

27

Little Tallapoosa River

27

South St.

166

Northside Dr.

Bankhead Hwy.

166

University of West Georgia

Lovvorn Road

START & FINISH

Laura's Park at Hays Mill Trailhead

Hays Mill Road

166

Alabama Street Trailhead

Alabama St.

Maple St.

Bonner Road

166

GEORGIA

Atlanta

N

1 mile

0.5

0

RAILS TO Trails conservancy

Imagine walking or biking completely around your hometown on a paved trail separated from traffic. That's what folks in Carrollton can do whenever the mood strikes them. The Carrollton GreenBelt is a 19-mile trail—the longest paved loop in the state—that completely encircles the West Georgia town. Along the way, it passes the University of West Georgia, the city schools complex, parks, and shopping and employment centers.

Trail users can find themselves crossing rolling terrain through woodlands and pastures dotted with grazing cattle, then passing alongside a lake or crossing a bridge over a stream before entering a busy commercial area.

The idea for a loop trail got its start with the birth of the Friends of the Carrollton GreenBelt in 2011. Construction of the first mile launched that year. Various sections were installed over the years, with the main loop being officially completed in spring 2017. Several short spurs extend the GreenBelt's reach into the city.

A tour of the trail can start from anywhere, but drinking water, restrooms, and picnic facilities can be found at six

COURTESY MARTYNA GRIFFIN AND FRIENDS OF CARROLLTON GREENBELT

The Carrollton GreenBelt encircles its namesake town, offering access to schools, parks, and commercial areas.

County
Carroll

Endpoints
East Carrollton Park at Lake Dr. and Northside Dr. (Carrollton); Maple St., 400 feet west of Commons Blvd. (Carrollton)

Mileage
19

Type
Greenway/ Non-Rail-Trail

Roughness Rating
1

Surface
Concrete

The trail includes several picturesque crossings of Buffalo Creek and Curtis Creek.

trailheads—Laura's Park at Hays Mill, Hobbs Farm Park, Lakeshore Park, Castle Playground, East Carrollton Park, and Visitors Bureau (parking can be found at these and other locations; see Parking, opposite).

A convenient place to start your journey in the southwest corner of the loop is the Laura's Park at Hays Mill Trailhead (480 Hays Mill Road). A right turn heading south begins a clockwise route around the city, which was founded in 1829 and remained a small rural town until the arrival of the railroad in the 1870s. In 2.3 miles, pass through the campus of the University of West Georgia, which got its start as an agricultural and mechanical school in 1906.

About a mile past the Alabama Street Trailhead, near the northwest corner of the loop, you'll pass beneath a railroad bridge over the Little Tallapoosa River. In 2 more miles, you'll arrive at Hobbs Farm Park. On a 0.7-mile loop around the farm park, you can see where beavers have been active near the river.

Another mile reveals access to Lake Carroll, a 160-acre artificial lake where fishing and swimming are allowed. East Carrollton Park—a former airfield site in the northeast section of the loop—sits just beyond the eastern shore of the lake. The trail skirts North Lakeshore Drive for a few hundred feet and then turns right to loop around a historic log cabin—which now serves as the Carrollton Police Department's Eastside Precinct—just before crossing Bankhead Highway. (*Note:* Although this is the Visitors Bureau Trailhead, the precinct is not an official visitor center and is not always open. However, when someone is there, trail users are welcome to stop in to see the inside of the cabin or grab a bottle of water.)

At the Newnan Road crossing in about 2 miles, in the southeast section of the loop, the Buffalo Creek Outdoor Education Center features a bird sanctuary and demonstration gardens. Heading east, visitors take a causeway across an arm of Richards Lake before entering a light-industrial and shopping district. In the final couple of miles, you'll pass through the campuses of multiple schools in the Carrollton school system and discover a waterfall on Buffalo Creek before returning to Laura's Park.

CONTACT: carrolltongreenbelt.com

PARKING

Parking areas are located within Carrollton and are listed clockwise from the Laura's Park at Hays Mill Trailhead in the southwest area of the loop. *Indicates that at least one accessible parking space is available.*

LAURA'S PARK AT HAYS MILL TRAILHEAD*: 480 Hays Mill Road (33.5641, -85.0922).

MAPLE ST.*: Maple St. and Commons Blvd. (33.5631, -85.1098).

ALABAMA ST. TRAILHEAD*: Alabama St./Mt. Zion Road, 0.1 mile east of Skinner Road (33.5888, -85.1051).

HOBBS FARM PARK TRAILHEAD*: 500 Believers Way; entrance at 1145 Rome St. (33.5979, -85.0736).

N. LAKESHORE DR.: N. Lakeshore Dr. and Stewart St. (33.5988, -85.0652).

LAKESHORE PARK TRAILHEAD*: N. Lakeshore Dr. and Lumpkin Dr. (33.5977, -85.0601).

EAST CARROLLTON PARK/CASTLE PLAYGROUND*: N. Lake Dr., between Lake Terrance Ct. and Northside Dr. (33.6009, -85.0503).

EAST CARROLLTON PARK*: 300 Northside Dr. (33.5967, -85.0454).

FIRE STATION 24*: 150 Fire Station Dr. (33.5952, -85.0427).

VISITORS BUREAU TRAILHEAD*: 102 N. Lakeshore Dr. (33.5922, -85.0470).

OLD NEWNAN ROAD TRAILHEAD*: 515 Old Newnan Road (33.5750, -85.0496).

MCINTOSH PLAZA*: 1129 S. Park St. (33.5585, -85.0758).

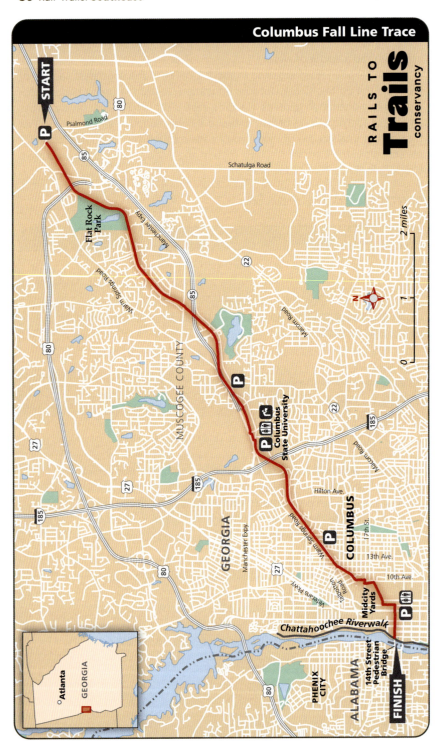

Columbus Fall Line Trace

RAILS TO **Trails** conservancy

Columbus Fall Line Trace

22

Outdoors enthusiasts often fall for the Columbus Fall Line Trace on their first visit. The paved, mostly flat rail-trail runs from the outskirts of Columbus to the Chattahoochee Riverwalk, a promenade that follows the river through the historic downtown area.

The trail is part of the 33.5-mile Dragonfly Trails system, a growing network of interconnected trails that will eventually cover 60 miles. Because the dragonfly indicates clean water, the name symbolizes the efforts to clean up pollution in the Chattahoochee River. Today the river is a popular tourist draw as an urban whitewater course and for its adjacent 13-mile paved river walk.

The Fall Line Trace is named after Georgia's so-called fall line, the transition between the hilly Piedmont of northern Georgia and the Upper Coastal Plain in the south. The drop in elevation energizes the Chattahoochee River, and entrepreneurs once harnessed that power to operate the gristmills and textile mills that made this city on the Georgia–Alabama border an industrial center of the South in the 19th century.

COURTESY DRAGONFLY TRAIL NETWORK

The trail runs from the woodsy outskirts of Columbus through its bustling downtown to the Chattahoochee Riverwalk.

County
Muscogee

Endpoints
Psalmond Road, 0.2 mile southeast of Warm Springs Road (Columbus); 14th St. Pedestrian Bridge at Front Ave. (Columbus)

Mileage
10.5

Type
Rail-Trail

Roughness Rating
1

Surface
Asphalt, Concrete

The trail follows a former corridor of the Central of Georgia Railway, one of the railroads that—coupled with commerce on the Chattahoochee—made Columbus a transportation hub. The Norfolk Southern Railway eventually acquired the railroad, and the city bought the disused rail line and opened the trail in 2011.

A good place to start is the trailhead on Psalmond Road in northeast Columbus, which has about a dozen parking spaces. Passing beneath a brick archway, the trail proceeds through a woodsy area and arrives at a popular fishing hole at Flat Rock Park. Although you reach the developed outskirts of Columbus soon after, a line of trees screens the trail until nearly mile 4.8, where Manchester Expressway/GA 85 runs alongside.

In another mile, you'll arrive at a large rest area with parking, restrooms, drinking water, and a bike shop. Next comes the bustling Columbus State University campus, founded in 1958. After another 1.5 miles, the trail starts to run adjacent to various city streets as it makes its way into downtown. Along the way, you can check out the redeveloped industrial area of Midcity Yards (located on the short stretch of trail paralleling Fifth Avenue, just before 14th Street), which features a brewery, a barbecue restaurant, and shops.

Finishing the last leg on 14th Street, you'll find the site of the Civil War Battle of Columbus and a plaque for the Columbus pharmacist who whipped up the formula for Coca-Cola. At the end of the trail at 14th Street and Front Avenue, you can connect to the Chattahoochee Riverwalk, which rolls 3.7 miles north to a dam, or 8 miles south to Fort Moore (formerly Fort Benning) and its 20 miles of paved trails through the base. You can also cross the 14th Street Pedestrian Bridge into Alabama.

CONTACT: pathfoundation.org/columbus-dragonfly-trail and moore.armymwr.com/programs/parks-ponds-trails

PARKING

Parking areas are located within Columbus and are listed northeast to southwest. *Indicates that at least one accessible parking space is available.*

FALL LINE TRACE TRAILHEAD*: 7324 Psalmond Road (32.5552, -84.8623).

MANCHESTER EXPY. PARK AND RIDE*: 3690 Manchester Expy. (32.5082, -84.9356).

COLUMBUS STATE UNIVERSITY: Walden Soccer Complex, 3600 Algonquin Dr. (32.5030, -84.9461).

FIRST AVE.: Along First Ave., north and south of 14th St. (32.4725, -84.9918); street parking.

Cricket Frog Trail

23

Anyone wanting a breath of fresh country air can hop on over to the Cricket Frog Trail in rural Newton County, about 40 miles east of Atlanta. The paved rail-trail is named for a quarter-size amphibian that is native to this part of Georgia and is acclaimed for its jumping prowess.

The trail follows a Central of Georgia Railway spur installed in 1893. The trail is split into two sections. The western 5.4-mile segment runs between the county seat of Covington and a closed, dilapidated railroad trestle over the Alcovy River. The 8.2-mile eastern segment proceeds from the river to a park between Mansfield and Newborn. Both sections are paved.

The nearest parking in western Covington is Turner Lake Park, about 0.3 mile west of the trail via a pedestrian path on Clark Street. Once on the Cricket Frog Trail, you'll find the actual starting point 0.6 mile south, at Turner Lake Circle Southwest. From there, you'll head north and then east, soon entering the downtown area, which is listed on the National Register of Historic Places. Many eateries cater to county office workers and others doing business in the county seat.

GREG MILLER

The trail offers a scenic jaunt through Georgia's rural Newton County.

County
Newton

Endpoints
Turner Lake Road, just south of Turner Lake Cir. SW (Covington); East End Road and east bank of Alcovy River (Covington); west bank of Alcovy River (Covington); Zeigler Road, 0.1 mile south of CR 213 (Mansfield)

Mileage
13.6

Type
Rail-Trail

Roughness Rating
1

Surface
Asphalt, Concrete

Cricket Frog Trail

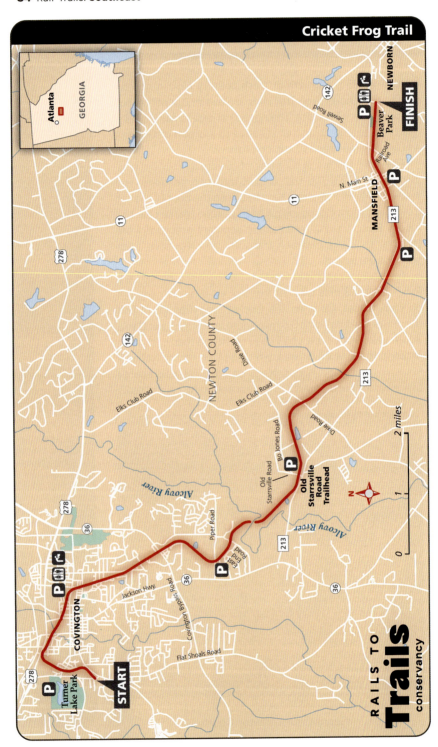

GEORGIA

Atlanta

NEWBORN

FINISH

Beaver Park

Railroad Ave

N. Main St

MANSFIELD

213

Sewell Road

142

11

11

278

142

NEWTON COUNTY

Dixie Road

Elks Club Road

Elks Club Road

Dixie Road

Bo Jones Road

Old Starrsville Road

Old Starrsville Road Trailhead

213

Alcovy River

Alcovy River

2 miles

N

1

0

278

36

Piper Road

East End Road

213

Jackson Hwy.

Covington Bypass Road

36

36

COVINGTON

Flat Shoals Road

278

Turner Lake Park

START

RAILS TO **Trails** conservancy

While checking out the sights, you can be forgiven for a sense of déjà vu, as things like the circa 1884 courthouse may seem familiar. That's because the downtown has been the location of nearly 70 films and TV shows, from early episodes of *The Dukes of Hazzard* to *My Cousin Vinny* and *The Walking Dead*.

Leaving downtown, the trail enters a large residential area with homes dating from the mid-1800s to the 1940s. Vegetation that has grown up along the rail line provides screen and shade. The paved trail ends at East End Road, about half a mile from Alcovy Bridge, an unsafe trestle that is slated for renovation.

The on-road connection to the nearest trailhead on the east side is not recommended, as the road is heavily trafficked with a very narrow shoulder. Instead, begin this section about 5 miles east of downtown Covington at the Old Starrsville Road trailhead near an old brick warehouse. The area is listed on the National Register of Historic Places and has been farmed for generations.

You can backtrack on the paved trail for 1.5 miles to the river, or head east through shady woodlots and former cotton fields for 6 miles to Mansfield, which has several cafés and an old depot at Railroad Avenue and GA 11. The trail ends in another 1.3 miles at Zeigler Road, just past Beaver Park, where you'll find parking, drinking water, and restrooms.

CONTACT: newtontrails.org/cricketfrogtrail

PARKING

Parking areas are listed from west to east. *Indicates that at least one accessible parking space is available.*

COVINGTON: Turner Lake Park, 6185 Turner Lake Road NW, 0.3 mile west of trail via a pedestrian path (33.6006, -83.8786).

COVINGTON*: Parking garage, 1166 Elm St., NE (33.5981, -83.85832).

COVINGTON*: Legion Field–Fairgrounds, 3173 Mill St. NE (33.5983, -83.8509).

COVINGTON*: Academy Springs Park, 3120 Conyers St. SE (33.5934, -83.8530).

COVINGTON: Sunbelt Pkwy. and Piper Road (33.5603, -83.8437).

COVINGTON: Old Starrsville Road, 300 feet north of County Road 213 (33.5394, -83.8192).

COVINGTON: County Road 213, 0.4 mile west of Gaithers Road (33.5143, -83.7560); small gravel lot with 5–6 spaces.

MANSFIELD*: City Hall Parking, 3146 GA 11 (33.5167, -83.7344); the designated accessible parking space is at the front of the building.

MANSFIELD*: Beaver Park, County Road 213, 0.4 mile east of Sewell Road (33.5207, -83.7192).

Douglas Greenway Trail

Coffee High School

Premier Sports Complex

J.C. Adams Municipal Park

FINISH

Chariot Tr.
Borwell Royal Road

Van Davis Road

441

Herbert Batten Road

Douglas-Broxton Hwy.

206

206

Industrial Blvd. N.

Twenty Mile Creek

441

COFFEE COUNTY

Chester Ave.

206

W. Walker St.

Leon St.

E. Walker St.

E. Jefferson St.

32

W. Gordon St.

N. Peterson St.

N. Madison Ave.

E. Gordon St.

E. Franklin St.

E. Peachtree St.

Ocilla Road

W. Jackson St.

Heritage Station Museum

W. Ward St.

E. Ashley St.

E. Ward St.

DOUGLAS

E. Bryan St.

W. Phillips St.

Railroad St.

W. Cherry St.

N
S

Manilla Ave.

Baker St

E. Baker Hwy.

0   0.25   0.5 mile

W. Baker Hwy.

South Georgia State College

N. Madison Ave.

S. Peterson Ave.

E. College Park Dr.

McDonald Road

353

Tiger Road

P

P

START

S. Wheeler Ave.

Pope Dr.

Trojan Ln.

441

Bowens Mill Road SE

221

RAILS TO
Trails
conservancy

Atlanta

GEORGIA

Douglas Greenway Trail

24

A railroad corridor that was once used to ship locally grown produce out of this rural county seat in southern Georgia now serves Douglas residents as a paved recreational and commuting trail across town.

The 4.4-mile Douglas Greenway Trail sits atop the old railbed of the Wadley and Mount Vernon Railway, which was incorporated into the Georgia & Florida Railroad in 1907. Running from Augusta, Georgia, to Madison, Florida, it eventually operated 321 miles of rail line to connect towns in the heavily agricultural region. Later bought by Norfolk Southern Railway, the corridor was acquired by the City of Douglas in 2000 to create today's trail.

You can discover more about the railroad and the agricultural history of the town at the Heritage Station Museum, housed in the circa 1905 railroad depot between West Ward and West Irwin Streets. Here you'll learn that the Douglas area was once a major tobacco producer, as well as a center for corn and cotton. Across the trail sits a renovated caboose that you can explore during museum hours. (Check hours at **cityofdouglasga.gov/125/heritage-station-museum.**)

BOB DECAMP

Traveling north–south through Douglas, you'll have access to many city destinations.

County
Coffee

Endpoints
Trojan Lane, 300 feet west of Peterson Ave. S./ US 441 (Douglas); Van Davis Road, between Herbert Batten Road and Chariot Trail (Douglas)

Mileage
4.4

Type
Rail-Trail

Roughness
1

Surface
Asphalt, Concrete

The trail runs north–south across town. You'll find plenty of restaurants and cafés within one or two blocks of the route as it passes through downtown. The trail is level and fairly exposed, but a few shady spots with benches provide refreshing rest areas.

A good place to start is the trailhead at the southern end with parking at a shopping district on the west side of Peterson Avenue South/US 441 at Trojan Lane. Heading north, in 0.2 mile you'll enter the campus of South Georgia State College. Founded in 1927 as the first state-supported junior college in Georgia, it now offers four-year programs. The campus is on the National Register of Historic Places, and a circular roadway on the main campus just west of the trail passes many historic buildings.

Beyond, the trail passes an eclectic mix of suburban homes, old farm-houses, mobile homes, and warehouses. You'll come to a jog in the trail on sidewalks in 0.9 mile; take a left onto West Cherry Street, right onto South Manilla Avenue, and right onto West Phillips Street to return to the trail.

You'll pass the old railroad depot and caboose in 0.2 mile, just two blocks west of the county courthouse and town center. Heading north, there are fewer cross streets as the trail enters an area with aromatic pines. Just north of Chester Avenue, you'll cross a pedestrian bridge spanning Twenty Mile Creek.

From the creek, it's another 1.4 miles across grasslands and meadows on a newly opened segment to the athletic fields at the Premier Sports Complex on Van Davis Road. Across the road, you'll find parking near the high school football stadium on Bonwell Royal Road/Chariot Trail; Coffee High School is another 0.4 mile down this road. The J.C. Adams Municipal Park, about 0.1 mile west on Van Davis Road, provides a picnic shelter, pond, and playground.

CONTACT: cityofdouglasga.gov/324/walking-trails-and-tracks

PARKING

Parking areas are located within Douglas and are listed from south to north.
Indicates that at least one accessible parking space is available.

TROJAN LANE: Park in the shopping district at Trojan Lane and Peterson Ave. S./US 441 (31.4921, -82.8520).

SOUTH GEORGIA STATE COLLEGE*: Tiger Road, 0.1 mile south of W. College Park Dr. (31.4957, -82.8526).

JARDINE STADIUM AT COFFEE HIGH SCHOOL*: Bonwell Royal Road/ Chariot Trail, 200 feet north of Van Davis Road (31.5475, -82.8596).

25

Euchee Creek Greenway

Grovetown's Euchee Creek Greenway elevates visitors across the soggiest sections of this verdant route in East Georgia on a series of boardwalks. Located in metropolitan Augusta, the trail follows a creek named for the Indigenous Yuchi people (also spelled Euchee and Uchee) who lived here in the 17th and 18th centuries, before they were forced to relocate to Oklahoma in the 1830s.

The Columbia County greenway is divided into two segments. The 5-mile northern section was completed in 2019 and runs from Patriots Park recreation area to the Canterbury Farms development. The 1.1-mile southern segment is known as the Grovetown Trails at Euchee Creek and connects to a paved trail around a lake.

Upon opening, the northern section immediately saw heavy use, as it predated by only a few weeks the onset of the COVID-19 pandemic, which led many people to seek more outdoor recreation opportunities. Long-range plans call for a connection with the southern segment, more trails into northern Columbia County, and an extension to

Elevated boardwalks provide enchanting views in the wooded Euchee Creek area.

TRAILLINK USER RPF

County
Columbia

Endpoints
Northern section: William Few Pkwy., 0.2 mile south of Laurel Dr. (Grovetown); Stone Meadows Ct. and Palamon Dr. (Grovetown) *Southern section:* Wrightsboro Road/GA 223 and Deer Hollow Run (Grovetown); Harlem Grovetown Road between Urial Dr. and Ashland Way (Grovetown)

Mileage
6.1

Type
Greenway/Non-Rail-Trail

Roughness Rating
1

Surface
Asphalt, Concrete, Boardwalk

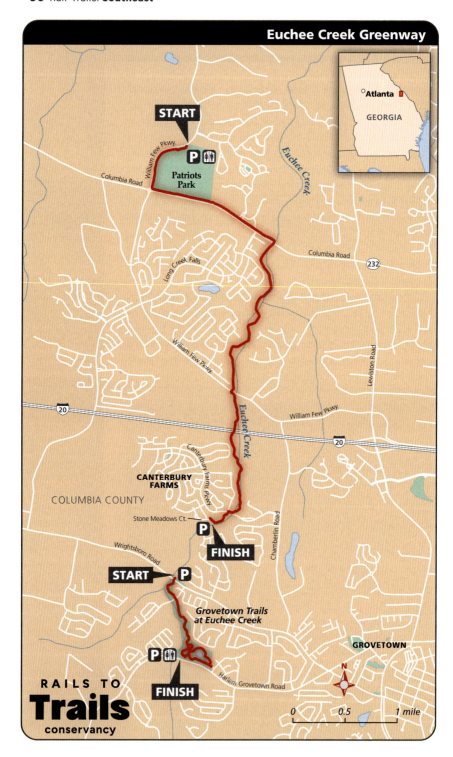

Euchee Creek Greenway

GEORGIA

Atlanta

START

P

Patriots Park

Columbia Road

William Few Pkwy.

Long Creek Falls

Euchee Creek

Columbia Road

232

William Few Pkwy.

Lewiston Road

20

William Few Pkwy.

Euchee Creek

20

Canterbury Farms Pkwy.

CANTERBURY FARMS

COLUMBIA COUNTY

Stone Meadows Ct.

P

FINISH

Chamberlin Road

Wrightsboro Road

START

P

Grovetown Trails at Euchee Creek

GROVETOWN

P

FINISH

Harlem Grovetown Road

N

0   0.5   1 mile

RAILS TO
Trails
conservancy

the Evans to Locks Multi-Use Trail, which connects to the Augusta Canal National Heritage Area Trails (see page 67).

The Euchee Creek Greenway is paved in asphalt and concrete, although several sections—where the route meanders through the creek's floodplain—are elevated above ground level on a boardwalk with side rails. It is mostly flat, although westbound travelers will find a steep climb where the trail ascends out of the floodplain and runs as a side path along Columbia Road/GA 232. The slope in this section may prove challenging for some people.

Starting in the north, the trail emerges from Patriots Park, a county recreation facility that features athletic fields, disc golf, and restrooms. The trail runs east alongside Columbia Road for 1.3 miles before descending into the floodplain and heading south.

For the next 3.2 miles, the trail follows a route through woodlands that separate housing developments scattered across the landscape. The trail crosses only one road—William Few Parkway—on this stretch, as all the other highway crossings are overhead. Ending at the Canterbury Farms development, trail users will find several access points to residential streets.

About a mile south, the southern section begins at a trailhead on Wrightsboro Road. This segment follows the creek for nearly a mile to a loop around a lake on Harlem Grovetown Road.

CONTACT: rtc.li/columbia-co-eucheecreekgw and rtc.li/cityofgrovetown-rec

PARKING

Parking areas are located within Grovetown and are listed from north to south. *Indicates that at least one accessible parking space is available.*

PATRIOTS PARK: William Few Pkwy. between Columbia Road and Laurel Dr. (33.5234, -82.2300); access the parking lot 0.2 mile southwest of Laurel Dr.

PATRIOTS PARK*: 5445 Columbia Road (33.5198, -82.2297); located at the park administration building.

PATRIOTS PARK*: 5445 Columbia Road (33.5177, -82.2306); located just inside the park entrance.

CANTERBURY FARMS: Stone Meadows Ct. at Palamon Dr. (33.4744, -82.2264); on-street parking.

GREENWAY TRAILHEAD*: Wrightsboro Road at Deer Hollow Run (33.4666, -82.2320).

GROVETOWN TRAILS TRAILHEAD*: Harlem Grovetown Road between Urial Dr. and Ashland Way (33.4563, -82.2312).

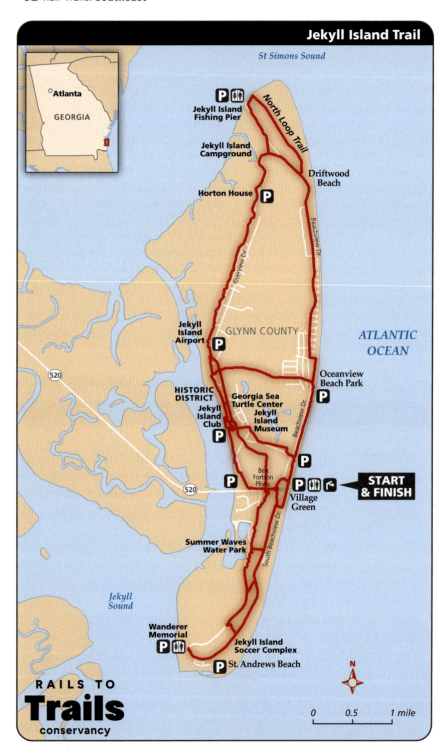

Jekyll Island Trail

St Simons Sound

Atlanta
GEORGIA

North Loop Trail

Jekyll Island
Fishing Pier

Jekyll Island
Campground

Driftwood
Beach

Horton House

Beachview Dr.

Riverview Dr.

Jekyll
Island
Airport

GLYNN COUNTY

ATLANTIC
OCEAN

520

HISTORIC
DISTRICT

Georgia Sea
Turtle Center

Jekyll
Island
Museum

Oceanview
Beach Park

Jekyll
Island
Club

Beachview Dr.

520

Ben
Fortson
Pkwy.

START
& FINISH

Village
Green

Summer Waves
Water Park

South Beachview Dr.

Jekyll
Sound

Wanderer
Memorial

Jekyll Island
Soccer Complex

St. Andrews Beach

N

RAILS TO
Trails
conservancy

0   0.5   1 mile

At more than 24 miles long, the Jekyll Island Trail carries visitors through a landscape they're unlikely to encounter elsewhere in Georgia. As the last outpost before the Atlantic Ocean, the 7-mile-long barrier island features sandy beaches, live oaks draped in Spanish moss, and the historic vacation homes of the early 20th century's rich and famous.

The mostly paved, interconnected trail system encircles the island, a popular destination for sunbathers, campers, and golfers. It stretches from Driftwood Beach in the north, where ghostly remnants of a forest march into the surf, to the growing southern beach. Although the trail is paved, side trails may be dirt or packed sand. Wildlife, such as deer or terrapins, is often seen on the trail; visitors are asked to report sightings of invasive species, such as feral hogs or coyotes.

The island, a former plantation, is now owned by the state. Several buildings of the historic Jekyll Island Club still stand, and visitors can walk where the Vanderbilts, Rockefellers, and Morgans once played.

A central starting point for the 16-mile main loop is the Village Green at the eastern end of Ben Fortson Parkway/ GA 520, which crosses the East River from the mainland. Heading north, the trail passes numerous hotels overlooking the beach. Boardwalks cross the dunes to access the beach.

The trail allows for exploration of Jekyll Island's sandy beaches, stands of live oak, and historic district.

TRAILLINK USER MLAWLOR72

County
Glynn

Endpoints
Jekyll Island Fishing Pier at Clam Creek Road (Jekyll Island); S. Beachview Dr. and Riverview Dr. (Jekyll Island)

Mileage
24.8

Type
Greenway/ Non-Rail-Trail

Roughness Rating
1

Surface
Asphalt, Boardwalk, Concrete, Crushed Stone, Dirt

In 1.7 miles, the trail veers one block inland as a side path along Beach View Drive. In 2.3 miles, turn right to connect to the North Loop Trail, which passes through marshes and the eerie Driftwood Beach. The trail turns left in 1.4 miles at a fishing pier and begins its southern journey through a shady forest.

In 1.3 miles, after passing the 200-site campground, you'll find the remains of the circa 1743 Horton House, one of the oldest surviving structures in the state. This route through a forest at the edge of a marsh ends at the airport in 2.3 miles; the trail enters the historic district in less than 1 more mile. The well-manicured lawns of the old Jekyll Island Club are home to "cottages" that look more like mansions. The historic district also houses the Georgia Sea Turtle Center, where injured turtles are rehabilitated and studied, and the Jekyll Island Museum.

The route around the southern section of the island crosses the parkway and heads south, passing Summer Waves Water Park in a mile. In 2 miles, the trail—which sometimes takes the form of a side path and sometimes a crushed-stone path—reaches St. Andrews Beach. This is the site of the *Wanderer* Memorial, commemorating the survivors of one of the last illegal slave ships to cross the Atlantic. Head north on the trail next to South Beachview Drive to return to the Village Green in 3 miles.

CONTACT: goldenisles.com/listing/jekyll-island-trail-system/165

PARKING

Parking areas are located within Jekyll Island and are listed from north to south. *Indicates that at least one accessible parking space is available.*

FISHING PIER*: Clam Creek Road, 0.7 mile north of Beach View Dr. N. (31.1162, -81.4178).

HORTON HOUSE: 1147 Riverview Dr. (31.1021, -81.4145).

JEKYLL ISLAND AIRPORT: Riverview Dr. and Old Plantation Road (31.0726, -81.4266).

OCEANVIEW BEACH PARK*: 549 Beachview Dr. N. (31.0633, -81.4049).

HISTORIC DISTRICT PIER*: N. Riverview Dr. and Pier Road (31.0580, -81.4228).

GREAT DUNES PARK*: Beachview Dr. N. and Shell Road (31.0530, -81.4090).

CAUSEWAY PARKING: Jekyll Island Causeway and N. Riverview Dr. (31.0476, -81.4193).

ST. ANDREWS PICNIC AREA*: Beach View Dr. and S. Riverview Dr. (31.0210, -81.4335).

SOCCER COMPLEX*: S. Beachview Dr., 2.1 miles south of Ben Fortson Parkway/GA 520 (31.0184, -81.4253).

The 13.5-mile Man O' War Railroad Recreation Trail zips across Harris County like a speeding locomotive. In fact, the rail-trail was named for a high-speed diesel passenger train that ran between Atlanta and Columbus from 1947 to 1970. The train, in turn, was named for a thoroughbred considered the fastest racehorse of all time.

The paved rail-trail runs along the former Central of Georgia Railway corridor from the town of Pine Mountain to south of Hamilton, the county seat of Harris County. Long-range plans call for connecting the Man O' War trail to the Columbus Fall Line Trace (see page 81) to complete an off-road route to the Chattahoochee River at the Alabama state line.

Harris County acquired the rail corridor in 2008; work on the trail was started 10 years later and completed in 2023. The 10-foot-wide trail roughly follows US 27 and features six trailheads with parking.

In addition to connecting two towns—Pine Mountain and Hamilton—filled with cafés and other services, the trail also runs past Callaway Gardens, a 2,500-acre resort complex

TRAILLINK USER SCROTZ1

The trail roughly follows US 27.

County
Harris

Endpoints
North end of McDougald Ave., 0.1 mile north of Chipley St. (Pine Mountain); Mulberry Creek Bridge west of US 27 (Hamilton)

Mileage
13.5

Type
Rail-Trail

Roughness Rating
1

Surface
Asphalt

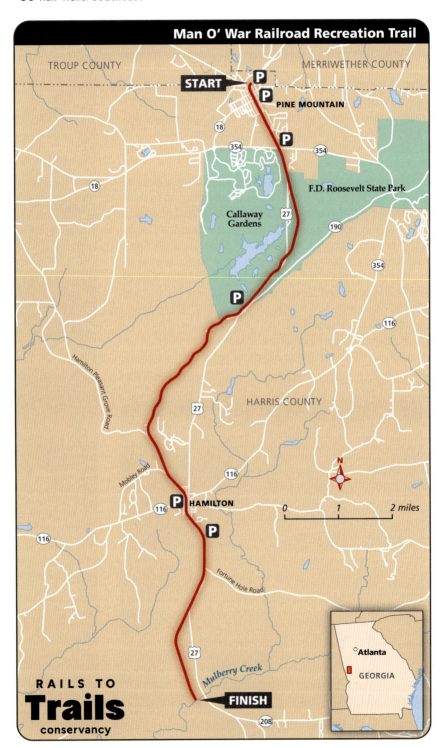

that features sprawling azalea gardens, a butterfly conservatory, a lodge, a spa, and more. F.D. Roosevelt State Park, named for the 32nd president, is to the east. FDR sought therapy in nearby Warm Springs for a debilitating illness and found solace in the hills here.

The trail starts just south of the county line in the town of Pine Mountain, where you can park in the colorful downtown district amid restaurants, boutiques, and a bicycle shop. In 1.2 miles, the trail reaches Callaway Gardens, but there is no direct link from the trail to the private resort.

You'll notice a slight but steady slope beginning about 1.4 miles past GA 354. It's worth the effort if, after crossing US 27 on an old railroad bridge, you stop at a country store and restaurant near the top with sweeping views of the valley below. You'll summit the ridge in about a mile and enjoy a slight downhill slope for the rest of the trail.

The trail returns to forests for 3 miles until it meets and runs alongside Hamilton Pleasant Grove Road and Mobley Road. More than a mile later, it enters Hamilton, which boasts many dining establishments. Leaving town, the trail follows the west side of US 27 for 3.5 miles to its current end at Mulberry Creek. Work on the remaining 8 miles to the county line is scheduled to begin in 2027.

CONTACT: rtc.li/man-o-war-trail

PARKING

Parking areas are listed from north to south. *Indicates that at least one accessible parking space is available.*

PINE MOUNTAIN*: Chipley Trailhead, McDougald Ave., 0.1 mile north of Chipley St. (32.8687, -84.8555).

PINE MOUNTAIN*: Broad St. between N. Commerce Ave. and McDougald Ave. (32.8660, -84.8546).

PINE MOUNTAIN*: Hood Trailhead, US 27 at GA 354 (32.8524, -84.8459).

PINE MOUNTAIN: Callaway Country Store Trailhead, D St. and US 27 (32.8108, -84.8553).

HAMILTON*: Hamilton Square Trailhead, Dogwood Lane between Hamilton Square St. and US 27 (32.7586, -84.8754).

HAMILTON*: South Hamilton Trailhead, 184 Old College St./US 27 (32.7502, -84.8699).

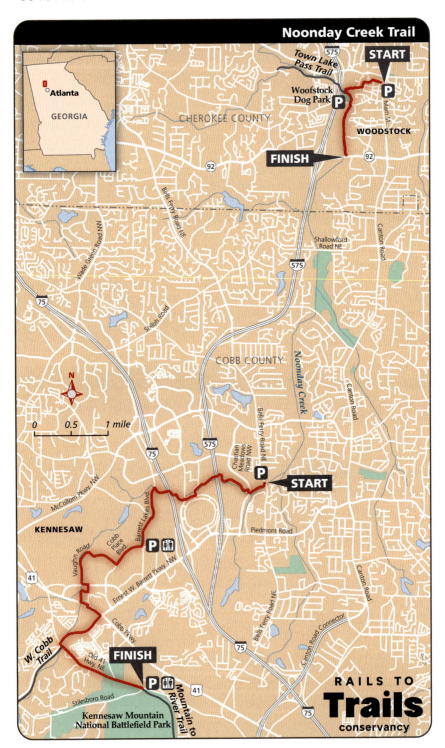

Noonday Creek Trail

START

Town Lake
Pass Trail

Woofstock
Dog Park

WOODSTOCK

FINISH

Atlanta

GEORGIA

CHEROKEE COUNTY

Wade Green Road NW

Bells Ferry Road NE

Shallowford
Road NE

Canton Road

Shiloh Road

COBB COUNTY

Noonday Creek

Bells Ferry Road NE

Canton Road

N

0   0.5   1 mile

Chastian
Meadows
Road NW

START

McCollom Pkwy NW

Piedmont Road

KENNESAW

Barrett Lakes Blvd

Cobb Place Blvd

Vaughn Road

Ernest W. Barrett Pkwy. NW

Bells Ferry Road NE

Canton Road Connector

Canton Road

Cobb Pkwy.

W. Cobb
Trail

Old 41
Hwy. NE

FINISH

Mountain to
River Trail

Stilesboro Road

Kennesaw Mountain
National Battlefield Park

RAILS TO
Trails
conservancy

Any time of day is a good time to visit the Noonday Creek Trail in the northern Atlanta metropolitan area. The paved trail, separated into two parts, runs along the stream's partly wooded and partly kudzu-covered floodplain in Cherokee and Cobb Counties.

The northern segment runs for 2 miles through Woodstock, a fast-growing suburban area. The southern segment runs for 6.6 miles through Town Center's bustling shopping area, ending at the doorstep of Kennesaw Mountain National Battlefield Park in Kennesaw.

Efforts are underway to link the two trails. Construction to lengthen the northern Woodstock section from GA 92 to the Cherokee–Cobb county line, about a half mile north of Shallowford Road, was to begin in late 2023. Meanwhile, Cobb County officials were meeting with residents to find the best route through the floodplain from the trailhead on Bells Ferry Road to Woodstock's trail extension.

In the north, the trail starts at a large parking lot at Market and Elm Streets in Woodstock and meanders behind some businesses for about 0.7 mile to Woofstock Dog Park and

Counties
Cherokee, Cobb

Endpoints
Northern segment: Market St. at Elm St. (Woodstock); GA 92/Alabama Road, 0.1 mile east of Pkwy. 575 (Woodstock) *Southern segment:* Bells Ferry Road NE, 0.2 mile north of Rock Bridge Road NE (Marietta); Old 41 Hwy. NW and Stilesboro Road NW (Kennesaw)

Mileage
8.6

Type
Greenway/Non-Rail-Trail

Roughness Rating
1

Surface
Asphalt, Cement

SHAWN TAYLOR/COURTESY ATLNATURE

Sections of the paved pathway follow the woodsy Noonday Creek in the northern Atlanta metropolitan area.

the junction with the Town Lake Pass Trail, another element in Woodstock's trail system. It runs alongside Noonday Creek for another 0.9 mile to GA 92.

Until the future extension closes the gap, the Cobb County segment starts at the Bells Ferry Road Northeast trailhead. Although this segment runs through the floodplain, much of the forest cover has been removed. The trail rolls past Town Center's sprawling mall and many other commercial and light-industrial areas.

After passing beneath I-75, you'll leave the creek and turn left onto Barrett Lakes Boulevard and take a side path on Cobb Place Boulevard and Vaughn Road before returning to the creek for a short stretch. It's back on a side path at Cobb Parkway/US 41 where you'll follow US 41 and turn right onto Ernest West Barrett Parkway Northwest. In 1.2 miles, turn left onto Old 41 Highway Northwest (the West Cobb Trail continues south). Follow the side path for 1.3 miles to Stilesboro Road at the entrance to the Civil War battlefield site and visitor center.

Bicycles are allowed in the park only on paved roads but are prohibited from Kennesaw Mountain Drive on weekends and holidays. At the visitor center, the Noonday Creek Trail junctions with the Mountain to River Trail, which meets the 61-mile-long Silver Comet Trail (page 107) in Smyrna.

CONTACT: towncentercid.com/parks-trails and woodstock.recdesk.com/community

PARKING

Parking areas are listed from north to south. *Indicates that at least one accessible parking space is available.*

WOODSTOCK*: 117 Elm St. (34.1003, -84.5205).

WOODSTOCK*: Woofstock Dog Park, 150 Dupree Road (34.0972, -84.5295).

MARIETTA*: Noonday Creek Trailhead, 3001 Bells Ferry Road NE (34.0231, -84.5490).

KENNESAW*: Aviation Park, 2659 Barrett Lakes Blvd. (34.0135, -84.5779).

KENNESAW*: Kennesaw Mountain National Battlefield Park Visitor Center, 900 Kennesaw Mountain Dr. (33.9834, -84.5787).

PATH400 Greenway

29

The PATH400 Greenway seeks out wooded nooks and crannies in the otherwise bustling Buckhead area, one of the wealthiest commercial and residential neighborhoods in the South, on Atlanta's north side. The paved greenway runs alongside a six-lane highway and mass-transit corridor, while at the same time unfolding into a tree-lined path ideal for a short bike ride or walk. Taking its name from the adjacent GA 400, it also passes close to three MARTA rapid-transit stations—Lindbergh Center, Lenox, and Buckhead. A variety of murals complement the trail experience, including the Buckhead Wall, the Railroad Bridge Mural, and installations from Buckhead Elementary School students. A wide variety of restaurant and lodging options are also directly accessible from the trail.

The greenway arose from grassroots efforts in 2013 by nonprofits Livable Buckhead and the PATH Foundation, which is linking trails throughout the Atlanta area. Long-range plans call for extensions north to Sandy Springs and south to the Atlanta BeltLine (see page 63).

County
Fulton

Endpoints
Adina Dr. at Piedmont Road NE (Atlanta); Wieuca Road NE between Ivy Road NE and Statewood Road NE (Atlanta); Roxboro Road at E. Paces Ferry Road NE (Atlanta)

Mileage
5.6

Type
Greenway/ Non-Rail-Trail

Roughness Rating
1

Surface
Concrete

BRIAN HOUSH

The greenway aims to add and connect green spaces throughout the Buckhead neighborhood.

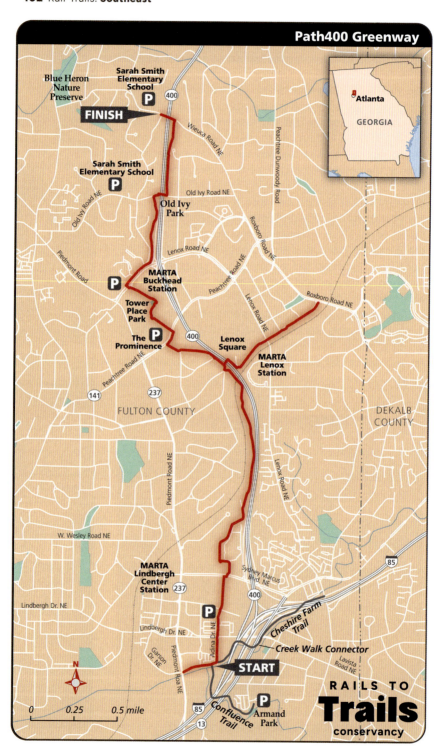

Starting on Adina Drive in southern Buckhead, PATH400 immediately passes a junction with two trails: the Confluence Trail, which crosses South Fork Peachtree Creek to Armand Park in 1.5 miles, and the Creek Walk Connector, which follows North Fork Peachtree Creek for 0.3 mile to the 0.5-mile Cheshire Farm Trail.

PATH400 itself heads left (north) as a side path between midrise buildings along Adina Drive for 0.5 mile to Sidney Marcus Boulevard. Over the next 1.4 miles, it follows a shady route between apartments and condominiums, then runs between GA 400 and MARTA until the rail corridor crosses overhead. At a trail junction just ahead, you can choose between continuing north on PATH400 or taking a pedestrian bridge across GA 400 to a 0.7-mile spur that passes the tony Lenox Square shopping district.

After the junction, PATH400 veers away from GA 400 by following a route along Highland Drive Northeast, then begins a 0.6-mile segment through Buckhead's high-rise downtown core on Peachtree Road, Tower Place Drive, and Buckhead Loop to pick up the trail on the north side of Lenox Road.

The trail enters a wooded area next to GA 400 for the final 0.9 mile to its endpoint on Wieuca Road. About halfway, the trail passes through the small Old Ivy Park. In 2023, work began on a two-year project to extend PATH400 north for 0.7 mile to Loridans Park on Loridans Drive.

CONTACT: path400greenway.org

PARKING

Parking areas are located within Atlanta and are listed from south to north. *Indicates that at least one accessible parking space is available.*

ARMAND PARK: 2177 Armand Road NE (33.8147, -84.3598); limited on-street free parking at end of Confluence Trail/Armand Greenspace Trail.

ADINA DRIVE: Adina Drive and Garson Dr. NE (33.8182, -84.3656); on-street free public parking.

THE PROMINENCE IN BUCKHEAD*: 3475 Piedmont Road NE (33.8508, -84.3750); free during trail hours.

SARAH SMITH ELEMENTARY SCHOOL*: 360 Old Ivy Road NE (33.8575, -84.3758); available outside of school hours.

SARAH SMITH ELEMENTARY SCHOOL*: 4141 Wieuca Road NE (33.8654, -84.3712); available outside of school hours.

Rockdale River Trail

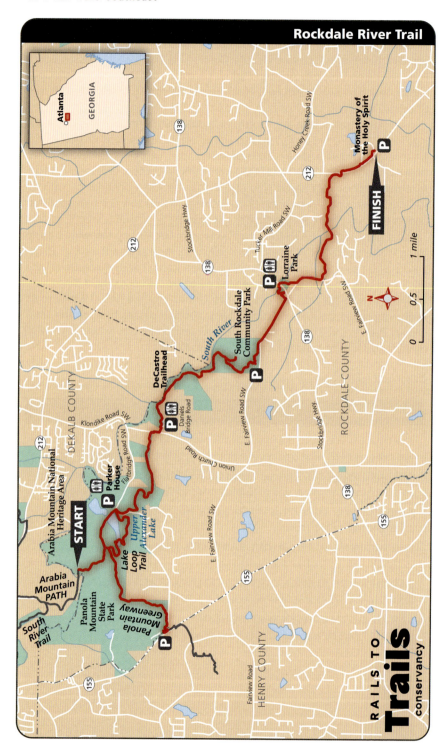

GEORGIA

Atlanta

FINISH

Monastery of the Holy Spirit

Honey Creek Road SW

Tucker Mill Road SW

Lorraine Park

212

138

Stockbridge Hwy.

South Rockdale Community Park

South River

DeCastro Trailhead

E. Fairview Road SW

Daniels Bridge Road

Klondike Road SW

Union Church Road

E. Fairview Road SW

DEKALB COUNTY

ROCKDALE COUNTY

E. Fairview Road SW

138

Stockbridge Hwy.

155

Parker House

Arabia Mountain National Heritage Area

START

Upper Alexander Lake

Lake Loop Trail

Arabia Mountain PATH

Panola Mountain State Park

South River Trail

Panola Mountain Greenway

E. Fairview Road SW

155

155

Fairview Road

HENRY COUNTY

N

1 mile

0.5

0

RAILS TO Trails conservancy

Rockdale River Trail

30

Although located in the Atlanta suburbs only a short drive from the city, the Rockdale River Trail and other connected trails in Panola Mountain State Park and the broader Arabia Mountain National Heritage Area feel a world away. Steep hills and dense woods might make trail users imagine that they're deep in the Appalachians.

The Rockdale River Trail roughly follows the drainage of the South River for 9.5 miles. It also connects to a larger network of more than 30 miles of paved trails in the Arabia Mountain PATH system that meander throughout the isolated granite mountains, wetlands, and pine and oak forests in the National Heritage Area.

The Rockdale River Trail starts where it meets the Arabia Mountain PATH (see page 61) on a bridge spanning the South River at the northern border of 1,635-acre Panola Mountain State Park. The Arabia Mountain PATH heads north for 12 miles to Lithonia, also connecting with a 3-mile segment of the South River Trail (see page 117).

Heading southeast for 0.6 mile, visitors come to a junction with Panola Mountain Greenway. This trail heads to the state park campground and visitor center in 1.7 miles and continues into Henry County for another mile. Travelers pass

ANDREW DUPUY

Journey through a forested landscape on a winding route through Rockdale County.

County
Rockdale

Endpoints
Arabia Mountain PATH, 1.1 miles northwest of the dead end of Flat Bridge Road SW (Stonecrest); Monastery of the Holy Spirit, GA 212/Scott Hwy. near Susong Road (Conyers)

Mileage
9.5

Type
Greenway/Non-Rail-Trail

Roughness Rating
1

Surface
Concrete

a 100-acre granite outcrop along the way, which is accessible only on ranger-led hikes (**gastateparks.org/panolamountain** for reservations). The greenway also accesses the 1.3-mile Lake Loop Trail, which overlooks the southern shore of Upper Alexander Lake, one of two fishing lakes in the state park.

Visitors experience a hilly route through the park, with turnouts for mountain biking labeled for beginner, intermediate, and advanced riders. The only restroom and drinking water are located at the trailhead for Alexander Lake and the Parker House. Built in 1822, the historic home was the center of a cotton plantation where more than 20 people were enslaved.

The Rockdale River Trail leaves the park about 1.7 miles past the lake and crosses Union Church Road. Go about 350 feet and turn left (unsigned) onto Daniels Bridge Road. This begins a section of on-and-off road travel for about a mile alongside the South River.

The final 5.5 miles of trail reflect the hilly, wooded, remote terrain found in the state park. The difference is that there are more trailheads, restrooms, drinking fountains, and recreational facilities along this segment, boosting accessibility for visitors.

After passing through South Rockdale Community Park and Lorraine Park, the trail crosses Scott Highway/GA 212 on a covered pedestrian bridge before arriving at the serene grounds of the Monastery of the Holy Spirit. Trappist monks moved to the site in 1944 and built the monastery, which opened in the 1950s. Today it doubles as a place of worship and a popular tourist attraction.

Long-range plans call for extending the trail about 3 miles from the monastery to connect with the city of Conyers via the Conyers Trail.

CONTACT: rockdalecountyga.gov/parks-and-trails

PARKING

Parking areas are listed from north to south. *Indicates that at least one accessible parking space is available.*

STOCKBRIDGE*: Panola Mountain State Park–Alexander Lake, 5015 Flat Bridge Road SW (33.6317, -84.1460); $5 state park fee.

STOCKBRIDGE: DeCastro Trailhead, 300 feet east of Union Church Road on Daniels Bridge Road (33.6236, -84.1294).

STOCKBRIDGE*: South Rockdale Community Park, 3909 E. Fairview Road (33.6058, -84.1154).

STOCKBRIDGE*: Lorraine Park, 3465 Stockbridge Hwy./GA 138 (33.6008, -84.1001).

CONYERS*: Monastery of the Holy Spirit, 2625 Scott Hwy./GA 212 (33.5839, -84.0698).

Silver Comet Trail

The Silver Comet Trail is a long-distance paved trail from the Atlanta suburb of Smyrna to the Alabama state line, where it connects to the Chief Ladiga Trail (see page 17). The Chief Ladiga Trail runs another 33 miles and, by late 2024, is expected to be extended 6.5 miles to downtown Anniston, Alabama, at which point the combined trails will provide a 101-mile paved route. The two trails joined Rails to Trails Conservancy's Hall of Fame together in 2009.

The rail-trail follows the bed of the old Seaboard Air Line. From 1947 to 1969, the shiny *Silver Comet* passenger train provided luxury service between New York and Birmingham. Today, three trestles and a railroad tunnel integrated into the design hint at some of the corridor's past glories. The eastern half of the rail-trail runs through suburban residential areas and is heavily used for local recreation and transportation. The western half provides a rural trail experience, winding through forest and farmland

CLARA WILLIAMS

The 700-foot-long Brushy Mountain Tunnel offers
a nod to the Silver Comet Trail's railroad past.

Counties
Cobb, Paulding, Polk

Endpoints
Mavell Road Trailhead (Smyrna); Georgia–Alabama state line at the beginning of the Chief Ladiga Trail (Cedartown)

Mileage
61.5

Type
Rail-Trail

Roughness Rating
1

Surface
Asphalt, Concrete

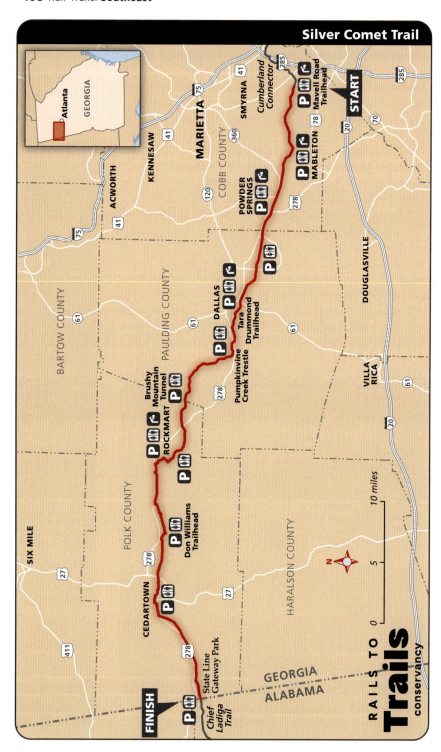

Silver Comet Trail

In 1988, the 61.5-mile Silver Comet Trail began to take shape in Georgia—representing one of the first formal rail-trail development efforts in the South. Alabama's 33-mile Chief Ladiga Trail (see page 17) began to develop shortly after in the 1990s. In 2008, the two trails were connected, creating one of the longest rail-trails in the country and an example of interstate connectivity, stretching from the outskirts of Atlanta to Anniston, Alabama.

and over rolling hills with some considerable inclines. There are numerous trail connections to residential areas and points of interest.

The eastern end of the Silver Comet Trail is in Smyrna, with mile 0 located at the Mavell Road Trailhead. In 9.6 miles, you'll arrive at a large playground at Linear Park in Powder Springs. There are wetlands around mile 12, following a trailhead at Florence Road. At mile 22.7, the Pumpkinvine Trestle stands 100 feet high and 700 feet long. Standing atop the trestle, you can almost picture the *Comet* streaking past in a silver blur. Forested sections within the 25,707-acre Paulding Forest Wildlife Management Area begin around mile 26, after a trailhead and parking area at McPherson Church Road. At mile 30.3, the Brushy Mountain Tunnel sounds a spooky note with 700 feet of damp, dark corridor.

Around mile 44, the Don Williams Trailhead in Rockmart gives access to the Fish Creek Disc Golf Course. A small platform off the trail just west of the disc golf course overlooks a wetland area ideal for viewing birds and other wildlife. Camp Comet, a primitive camping spot with no water or restrooms, is just west of the course. Around mile 50.7, the Cedartown Welcome Center features a restored train depot.

The Silver Comet Trail offers numerous amenities and accommodations. There is ample parking at many access points, and most are ADA accessible. Quite a few trailheads offer restrooms, and the trail has mile markers and signage. Benches are provided at reasonable intervals, some with scenic overlooks and others with covered roofs. Bicycle repair stations are provided at some trailheads (including Tara Drummond, Rockmart, and the Cedartown Welcome Center), and there is a trailside bicycle shop at Floyd Road in Mableton at mile 4.3. Services become less frequent in the western section, so bring plenty of water.

Overall, the trail is very well maintained by the counties along the route. However, in the western half, there are a few spots where repairs are needed. Cyclists should be aware that wooden plank bridges in the Fish Creek area are in need of repair, and a few isolated spots have missing or broken planks. Horseback riders should note that equestrian use ends at mile 36, near Rockmart, where trail signs instruct riders to dismount and exit the trail.

Exciting plans are afoot for the PATH Foundation to extend the eastern end of the Silver Comet Trail in Smyrna to downtown Atlanta via the Silver Comet Connector, a project that is anticipated to be completed by 2026. Another trail linkage emanating from the same starting point is already open; the Cumberland Connector begins at the eastern trailhead of the Silver Comet Trail and heads northeast, providing access to neighborhood amenities like Oakdale Park and Cumberland Mall.

CONTACT: pathfoundation.org/silver-comet-trail

PARKING

Parking areas are listed from east to west. Select parking areas for the trail are listed below; for a detailed list of parking areas and other waypoints, consult **TrailLink™**. *Indicates that at least one accessible parking space is available.*

SMYRNA*: Mavell Road, south of Nickajack Elementary School (33.8417, -84.5176).

MABLETON*: Floyd Road Trailhead, 4342 Floyd Road SW (33.8469, -84.5856).

POWDER SPRINGS*: Silver Comet Linear Park/Kids Park at Richard D. Sailors Pkwy., across from Villa Springs Cir. (33.8616, -84.6729).

HIRAM*: Hiram Trailhead at Seaboard St. and Seaboard Ave. (33.8823, -84.7549).

DALLAS*: Rambo Trailhead, 25 Tucker Blvd. (33.9153, -84.8689); 0.6 mile east of the Pumpkinvine Trestle.

ROCKMART: Coot's Lake Beach Trailhead at Coots Lake Road (33.9770, -85.0041).

ROCKMART*: Rockmart/Seaborn Jones Memorial Park, 100 E. Church St. (33.9976, -85.0532).

ROCKMART*: Don Williams Trailhead, 201 Hendrix Road, 0.4 mile south of US 278/GA 6/Rockmart Hwy. (33.9972, -85.1548).

CEDARTOWN*: Cedartown Welcome Center, 609 S. Main St. (34.0090, -85.2542).

CEDARTOWN: Esom Hill Trailhead, 92 Hardin Road (33.9523, -85.3888); gravel parking lot.

Simms Mountain Trail

32

Fear not: the trail's namesake mountain is a prominent ridge overlooking the trail, not one that the trail climbs. Except for a slope over a low pass, the 4.1-mile rail-trail runs fairly level at the southern end of the Appalachian foothills.

The mostly gravel-and-ballast trail follows the old corridor of the Central of Georgia Railway as it plowed north from the Georgia coast to the big railroad yards in Chattanooga. This segment of railbed passed through Rome about 11 miles east, then swung north along GA 100/Holland Road.

The stretch that became the Simms Mountain Trail was acquired by Floyd County and converted to a rail-trail in the 1990s. The trail is ideal for hiking, mountain biking, and horseback riding, as well as being a colorful destination for leaf-peeping in the fall.

The trail currently has no amenities, such as restrooms or drinking water, but there are benches at the trailheads, and crews regularly clear the trail of kudzu overgrowth and fallen trees. There's room for one or two cars to park at road

SCOTT McCORD/COURTESY TRAILS FOR RECREATION AND ECONOMIC DEVELOPMENT

Cross picturesque Cabin Creek on an old railroad bridge.

County
Floyd

Endpoints
Huffaker Road, 0.2 mile east of Big Texas Valley Road NW (Rome); GA 100/Holland Road NW, 0.2 mile south of County Line Road (Rome)

Mileage
4.1

Type
Rail-Trail

Roughness Rating
2–3

Surface
Ballast, Gravel

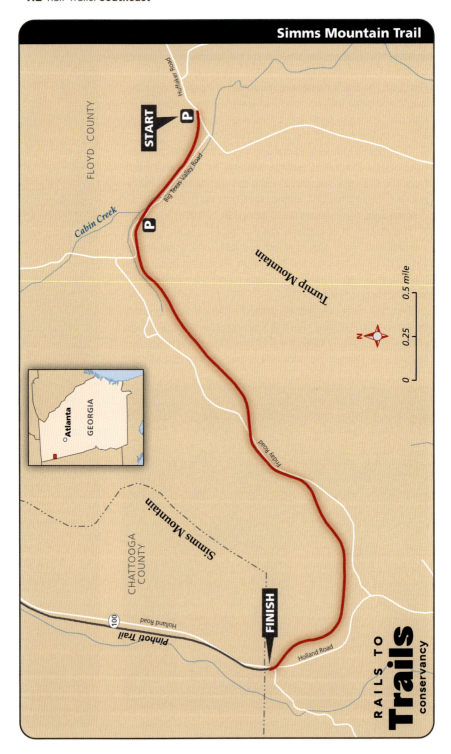

Simms Mountain Trail

FLOYD COUNTY

Huffaker Road

START P

Big Texas Valley Road

P

Cabin Creek

Turnip Mountain

0.5 mile

0.25

N

0

GEORGIA

Atlanta

Friday Road

CHATTOOGA COUNTY

Simms Mountain

Pinhoti Trail

100

Holland Road

FINISH

Holland Road

RAILS TO **Trails** conservancy

crossings. Also, be aware that unleashed dogs that patrol some remote homes in the area can be menacing.

The trail does double duty as section 18 of the 335-mile Pinhoti Trail, an on- and off-road route that runs across the southern Appalachians from Alabama to Georgia's Springer Mountain, the trailhead for the Appalachian Trail.

Starting at the easternmost trailhead on Huffaker Road, the Simms Mountain Trail heads west through dense woods for about half a mile to an old railroad bridge that crosses Cabin Creek, a small brook rushing over rocks and boulders.

In a short distance, you'll cross Big Texas Valley Road, and in another 1.5 miles, you'll cross Friday Road. Both of these are lightly traveled. Previous logging in this area opens up views of the surrounding landscape, including Turnip Mountain. The trail emerges from the woods in 1.8 miles, where it crosses GA 100/Holland Road on a crosswalk.

The Simms Mountain Trail ends at the Chattooga County line, but the Pinhoti Trail continues north as a gravel-and-dirt track next to GA 100 for 5.1 miles to the small crossroads of Holland—once a stop on the Central of Georgia Railway—and beyond.

CONTACT: Rome-Floyd Parks and Recreation, 706-291-0766

PARKING

Parking areas are within Rome and are listed from east to west. *Indicates that at least one accessible parking space is available.*

SIMMS MOUNTAIN TRAILHEAD: 3534 Huffaker Road NW, 0.2 mile east of Big Texas Valley Road NW (34.2926, -85.3406).

BIG TEXAS VALLEY ROAD: 0.6 mile northwest of Huffaker Road NW (34.2972, -85.3516); roadside parking at trail crossing.

HOLLAND ROAD: GA 100/Holland Road, 0.2 mile south of County Line Road (34.2851, -85.3966); parking at trail crossing 1.6 miles north of GA 20.

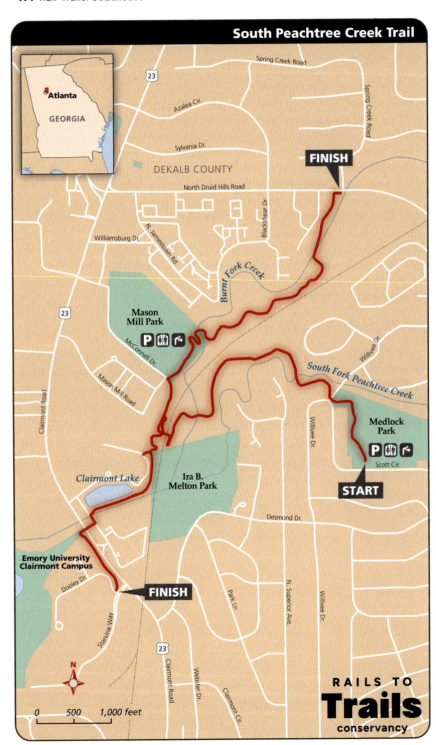

South Peachtree Creek Trail

South Peachtree Creek Trail

33

Spanning 2.6 miles with a concrete surface interspersed with boardwalk sections through natural areas, the South Peachtree Creek Trail provides a pleasant and easy way to navigate Atlanta's northeastern suburb of Decatur. Connecting to Emory University's Clairmont Campus and providing access to major parks, the tree-lined trail traverses relatively flat terrain and offers a bounty of recreational amenities and active-transportation options for residents, students, and visitors.

Begin your journey on the trail's eastern end at Medlock Park, where you'll have access to plentiful parking, restrooms, drinking fountains, and a picnic shelter. From the parking lot, follow the trail northwest past baseball fields and a community garden to reach the only road crossing, at Willivee Drive (a quiet residential street with a crosswalk), in 0.2 mile. From there, you'll wind through the woodlands along South Fork Peachtree Creek, taking a bridge over an active railroad in 0.7 mile.

If you wish to reach Emory University, turn right (south) at the fork 250 feet past the end of the bridge. In 400 feet,

JONAH MCDONALD

With boardwalk sections through natural areas, the trail provides a pleasant way to navigate Decatur.

County
DeKalb

Endpoints
Medlock Park on Scott Cir., 0.2 mile southeast of Willivee Dr. (Decatur); Emory University's Clairmont Campus at Dooley Drive and Starvine Way (Decatur); N. Druid Hills Road and Spring Creek Road (Decatur)

Mileage
2.6

Type
Greenway/ Non-Rail-Trail

Roughness Rating
1

Surface
Boardwalk, Concrete

you'll reach another fork; turn left to stay on the main trail (continuing straight will take you on a short spur to an apartment complex). You'll skirt Clairmont Lake and reach the Clairmont Road underpass in 0.3 mile. From the underpass, the trail's end is 0.2 mile away at Dooley Drive and Starvine Way on the Clairmont Campus.

Alternatively, continue straight at the trail fork by the bridge to reach Mason Mill Park in 0.1 mile. If you have some time to spend, the 120-acre park offers a plethora of facilities for fun, including a playground, tennis courts, a recreation center, a community garden, and a public library. You'll also find restrooms, drinking water, and parking.

From Mason Mill Park, you'll experience a scenic stretch of trail meandering north along Burnt Fork Creek on an elevated boardwalk enveloped in trees. The mix of woodlands and wetlands here provides a great opportunity for bird-watching and spotting deer, turtles, rabbits, and other wildlife. The trail's end arrives in 0.8 mile at the intersection of North Druid Hills Road and Spring Creek Road. This is an optional out-and-back, as there is a bus stop (but no dedicated trail parking).

CONTACT: dekalbcountyga.gov/parks/mason-mill-park and pathfoundation.org/south-peachtree-creek-trail

PARKING

Parking areas are located within Decatur and listed from east to west.
Indicates that at least one accessible parking space is available.
MEDLOCK PARK*: 951 Scott Cir. (33.8027, -84.2965).
MASON MILL PARK*: McConnell Dr. and Mason Mill Road (33.8065, -84.3051).

South River Trail

34

Part of the 300-mile PATH Foundation trail network (path foundation.org), the South River Trail currently consists of two separate segments totaling 13.5 miles that will eventually be connected into a seamless trail between the suburbs of Atlanta and Stonecrest. The shorter (3.5-mile) "East Trail" provides further links to the 12-mile Arabia Mountain Trail; the 2.8-mile Panola Mountain Greenway; and the 9.5-mile Rockdale River Trail, which heads south into Stockbridge. This trail network provides access to a variety of recreational venues, including the Davidson-Arabia Mountain Nature Preserve and Panola Mountain State Park, as well as shopping and restaurants in the Stonecrest Mall area. Scenic river views and wooded areas are primary features of this mostly flat and shaded trail.

The longer (10-mile) "West Trail" technically begins at Intrenchment Creek Park on Fayetteville Road Southeast, but as of 2023, this segment has been closed due to dangerous conditions, and trail users are advised to start at the trailhead in Gresham Park by Barack H. Obama Elementary

Counties
DeKalb, Rockdale

Endpoints
Western segment: Constitution Road SE, 0.3 mile west of West Side Pl. (Atlanta); Waldrop Road between Waldrop Cliff Lane and Robin Point Dr. at the South River (Atlanta) *Eastern segment:* Martin Luther King High School at Snapfinger Road, 0.1 mile east of Dogwood Farms Road (Stonecrest); Lyons Road, 0.7 mile south of Browns Mill Road (Stonecrest)

Mileage
13.5

Type
Greenway/ Non-Rail-Trail

Roughness Rating
1

Surface
Asphalt, Boardwalk

BRIAN HOUSH

Watch for deer along the trail's eastern section, which tends to be less crowded.

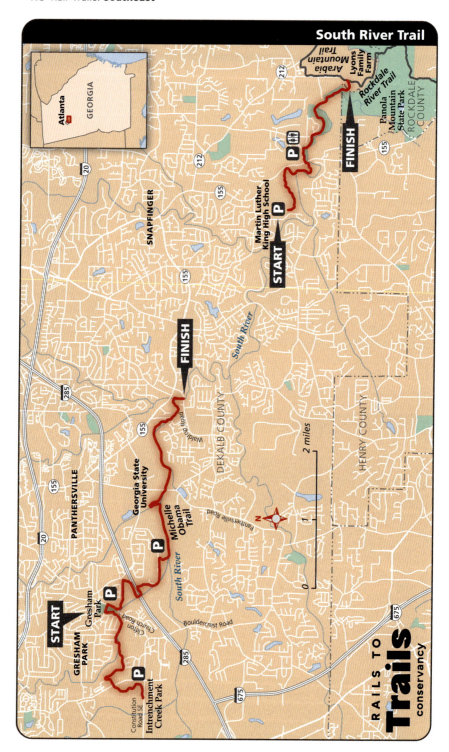

South River Trail

GEORGIA

Atlanta

GEORGIA

SNAPFINGER

PANTHERSVILLE

GRESHAM PARK

Gresham Park

Georgia State University

Michelle Obama Trail

Intrenchment Creek Park

Constitution Road SE

Clifton Church Road

Bouldercrest Road

Panthersville Road

South River

Waldrop Road

DEKALB COUNTY

HENRY COUNTY

ROCKDALE COUNTY

Martin Luther King High School

Arabia Mountain Trail

Lyons Family Farm

Rockdale River Trail

Panola Mountain State Park

START

START

FINISH

FINISH

2 miles

1

0

RAILS TO **Trails** conservancy

Magnet School of Technology. Heading west, you'll follow a 3.8-mile section of trail known as the Michelle Obama Trail past Georgia State University's (GSU's) Perimeter College campus. Along the way, you'll pass several parks, as well as GSU's Native Plant Botanical Garden, on a mostly tree-lined route, making it a great option for hot days. The trail ends somewhat abruptly by the South River at busy Waldrop Road in a residential area of Decatur.

The South River Trail's eastern section tends to be less crowded than the western section, so wildlife interactions are likely, and you'll see several DEER CROSSING signs along the route. Begin the 3.5-mile trail at Martin Luther King Jr. High School in Stonecrest (accessible from Snapfinger Road), after which you'll follow a winding southeasterly route to farmland along Lyons Road. Interpretive signage allows for learning more about the Arabia Mountain National Heritage Area, which encompasses the route, and its impressive history. Note that this segment is somewhat hilly; it's advised to start at the western end of this segment in the parking lot closest to the start point of the trail.

CONTACT: pathfoundation.org/south-river-trail

PARKING

Parking areas are listed from west to east. *Indicates that at least one accessible parking space is available.*

ATLANTA*: Intrenchment Creek Trailhead, 3301 West Side Pl. (33.6905, -84.3223).

ATLANTA*: Gresham Park Recreational Center, 3113 Gresham Road (33.6969, -84.3033).

DECATUR*: GSU Perimeter Campus/Panthersville Complex, 2401 Wildcat Road (33.68517, -84.29021).

STONECREST: Martin Luther King High School, 3991 Snapfinger Road (33.6589, -84.1999); designated accessible parking spots are located in the strip of parking north of the tennis courts. This section of the trail is hilly.

STONECREST*: Panola Shoals Trailhead, 4435 Panola Road (33.6544, -84.1865).

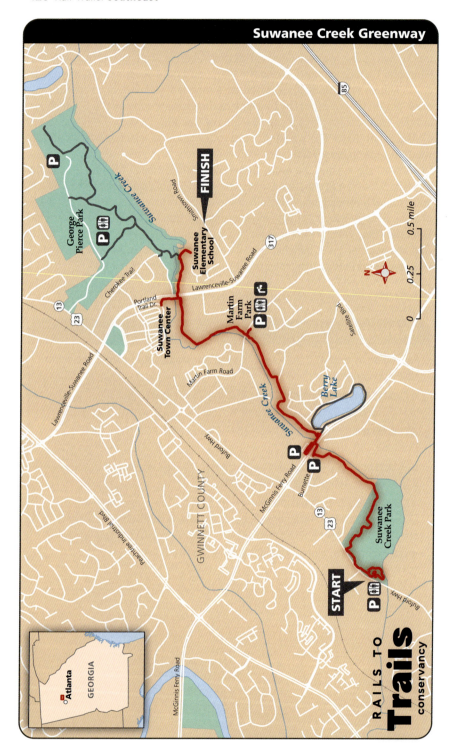

Suwanee Creek Greenway

Suwanee Creek Greenway

35

What's the best route between two parks? If you're on a bike or walking in the Atlanta suburb of Suwanee, then it's the Suwanee Creek Greenway. The 3.1-mile trail runs from Suwanee Creek Park on cement pavement and boardwalk to the southern section of George Pierce Park.

Suwanee Creek is a tributary of the Chattahoochee River, which flows along the western city limits. The town was once a village of the Shawnee and later the Cherokee and Creek peoples. European settlement started in the early 1800s, and the town further grew and developed with the arrival of the railroad. Its population has exploded in the past 40 years.

The city is known for its parks, and the greenway connects two nicely wooded ones. Suwanee Creek Park, an 85-acre city-operated facility, features an 18-hole disc golf course and a 19-point orienteering course. The county-managed George Pierce Park covers 304 acres with sports fields, a fishing pond, and a senior center. Both have restrooms.

The greenway is popular not only for its natural setting but also for crossing traffic only once along its length. Much of the route is swampy, which is why there are segments

County
Gwinnett

Endpoints
Suwanee Creek Park, access road at US 23/GA 13/ Buford Hwy., 100 feet west of Swiftwater Park Dr. (Suwanee); Suwanee Elementary School on Smithtown Road (Suwanee)

Mileage
3.1

Type
Greenway, Non-Rail-Trail

Roughness
1

Surface
Boardwalk, Cement

TRAILLINK USER KEITHWALTON2

Much of the greenway includes boardwalk over swampy areas.

on boardwalks. You may see deer along the edge of the forest, turtles sunning themselves on logs, or small fish in the shallow water.

Starting at either of the Suwanee Creek Park lots, the trail leaves the park but stays in the woods as it picks up the north side of the creek. It crosses a couple of wet areas on a boardwalk before it passes beneath McGinnis Ferry Road in about a mile. Immediately after the underpass, you'll climb a ramp up to McGinnis Ferry Road, cross the creek on the bridge, then descend to the south side of the creek on another ramp. You can take a 1-mile loop around Berry Lake on a connecting trail after returning to the Suwanee Creek Greenway.

Rolling on, the greenway takes another boardwalk through a swampy section of woods and crosses Martin Farm Road in 0.8 mile. After another 0.6 mile of forest, the greenway passes beneath GA 317/Lawrenceville-Suwanee Road. Just before the underpass, a spur trail heads north to Portland Trail Drive and Suwanee Town Center, which boasts restaurants, a performance stage and amphitheater, and a large fountain. The city's Suwanee Fest occurs here on the third weekend of September.

Emerging from the underpass, the greenway heads east for 0.2 mile to a junction. The right fork finishes the greenway behind an elementary school in 0.1 mile. The left fork crosses the creek into George Pierce Park, where it meets a multiuse trail that continues 0.8 mile to an array of sports fields.

CONTACT: suwanee.com/explore-suwanee/parks

PARKING

Parking areas are located in Suwanee and are listed from southwest to northeast. *Indicates that at least one accessible parking space is available.*

SUWANEE CREEK PARK*: 1170 Buford Hwy. (34.0349, -84.0870); turn right after park entrance, and go 0.2 mile to parking.

SUWANEE CREEK PARK*: 1170 Buford Hwy. (34.0352, -84.0830); go straight at park entrance for 0.2 mile to parking.

BURNETTE ROAD*: 3572 Burnette Road (34.0393, -84.0760).

MCGINNIS FERRY ROAD: 3583 McGinnis Ferry Road (34.0401, -84.0753).

MARTIN FARM PARK: 3562 Martin Farm Road (34.0447, -84.0631).

SUWANEE ELEMENTARY SCHOOL*: 3875 Smithtown Road (34.0484, -84.0558); parking is available on weekends and after 4 p.m. on weekdays.

The Thread Trail

36

The Thread Trail sews together many educational, recreational, historical, and cultural facets of the old textile town of LaGrange in a neat 13-mile package. Currently in two separate sections, the 12-foot-wide paved path runs alongside streets and through open space in the community. Plans call for extending the trail to 31 miles, which will close the gap and expand its reach.

The idea of a greenway through this Georgia city with a French-sounding name arose from a public-private effort launched in 2015. The city council approved the plan in 2016 with funding from a local option tax and fundraising by Friends of The Thread. The first mile was completed in 2017 in Granger Park, with more sections completed year after year. The trail is enhanced with public art, as well as interpretive signs and kiosks providing information on the natural environment, history, and landmarks.

Granger Park is a good, central location to start. It's a busy 46-acre park with athletic fields, a playground, plentiful

COURTESY VISIT LAGRANGE

The pathway provides access to a handful of parks in the community.

County
Troup

Endpoints
(All in LaGrange)
Western segment: Granger Park; Hollis Hand Elementary School at County Club Road and Pinetree Dr.; Murphy Ave. and Hunnicutt St.; 0.2 mile southwest of Peachtree St. and Douglas St.; Sweetland Amphitheatre
Eastern segment: Calumet Park at Union St. and Baugh St.; Mike Daniel Recreation Center on GA 109/Lafayette Pkwy.

Mileage
13

Type
Greenway/Non-Rail-Trail

Roughness
1

Surface
Asphalt, Boardwalk, Concrete

The Thread Trail

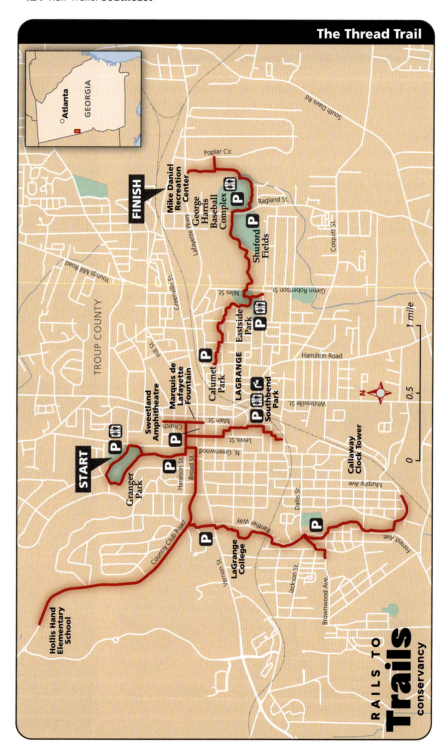

GEORGIA

Atlanta

TROUP COUNTY

FINISH

Mike Daniel Recreation Center

George Harris Baseball Complex

Shuford Fields

Poplar Cir.

Ragland St.

Colquitt St.

South Davis Rd.

Lafayette Pkwy.

Greenville St.

Niles St.

Glenn Robertson St.

Hamilton Road

Eastside Park

Whitesville St.

LAGRANGE

Calumet Park

Marquis de Lafayette Fountain

Sweetland Amphitheatre

Church St.

Main St.

Lewis St.

N. Greenwood

Southbend Park

START

Granger Park

Hill St.

Youngs Mill Road

Haralson St.

Broad St.

County Club Road

Vernon St.

LaGrange College

Panther Way

Dallis St.

Jackson St.

Brownwood Ave.

Callaway Clock Tower

Murphy Ave.

Forrest Ave.

Hollis Hand Elementary School

N

1 mile

0.5

0

RAILS TO Trails conservancy

COURTESY VISIT LAGRANGE

The Thread Trail connects open space, neighborhoods, and commercial areas within LaGrange.

parking, and restrooms. From the park, the greenway heads south through open space for 0.4 mile to West Haralson Street, where you turn left (east) to reach the first of three trail junctions.

At the first junction, turn right to head one block south on Greenwood Street to Broad Street, where you'll then head right (west) for 0.6 mile to a split. The right leg heads 1.4 miles northwest along Country Club Road to Hollis Hand Elementary School. (Some of the trail's roughly 500 feet of boardwalk is found here.) The left leg follows Panther Way south through LaGrange College (founded in 1831 and the oldest private college in the state) and open space to end at Murphy Avenue and Hunnicutt Street in a residential area.

Back on Haralson Street, the second right heads south on Lewis Street toward the historic downtown. You'll pass within a block of the prominent Marquis de Lafayette Fountain on Broad Street. A replica of a 19th-century fountain in France, it was cast in 1974 and later installed here. The city of LaGrange is named for the country estate of the Revolutionary War hero's wife. Continuing south along Lewis Street, you'll end up at Southbend Park, featuring a playground and skate park, in less than a mile. From the playground, the trail ends in 0.2 mile, just past the intersection of Peachtree and Douglas Streets. Plans call for completing a loop from Southbend to the Murphy Avenue neighborhood. Along the future 1.5-mile route, the trail would pass the soaring Callaway Clock Tower, built in 1929 as a tribute to local textile tycoon

Fuller E. Callaway, and the Mulberry Street Cemetery, where Union and Confederate soldiers are buried.

Back on Haralson Street, the third leg heads left (north) on Church Street for two blocks to the 2,500-seat Sweetland Amphitheatre, which regularly hosts big-name performers.

The disconnected eastern section of The Thread starts at Calumet Park on Union Street and heads east for 2.5 miles. This stretch passes through more open space and several large sports parks, namely Eastside Park, Shuford Fields, and the George Harris Baseball Complex, and ends at the Mike Daniel Recreation Center on GA 109/Lafayette Parkway.

CONTACT: thethreadtrail.org

PARKING

Parking areas are located within LaGrange. *Indicates that at least one accessible parking space is available.*

Western segment (north to south):

HUNNICUTT PLACE PARKING*: Granger Park, Hunnicutt Pl. and N. Greenwood St. (33.0469, -85.0354).

HARALSON ST. TRAILHEAD*: W. Haralson St., between N. Greenwood St. and Gordon St. (33.0410, -85.0358).

BROAD & VERNON PARKING DECK*: 109 Broad St. (33.0393, -85.0328).

PANTHER WAY PARKING*: LaGrange College Campus, 343–297 Panther Way (33.0386, -85.0453).

SOUTHBEND PARK*: 109 Cherry St. (33.0323, -85.0320).

COLEMAN CENTER*: Washington St., between Dallis St. and Brownwood St. (33.0257, -85.0466).

Eastern segment (west to east):

CALUMET PARK TRAILHEAD*: 109 Union St. (33.0378, -85.0242).

EASTSIDE PARK*: Niles St., between Belk St. and Revis St. (33.0341, -85.0153).

GEORGE HARRIS BASEBALL COMPLEX*: 131 Ragland St. (33.0356, -85.0041).

MIKE DANIEL RECREATION CENTER*: 1220 Lafayette Pkwy. (33.0406, -85.0004).

Tom White Linear Park

37

Tom White Linear Park runs for 7.2 miles through Moultrie's historic downtown to a municipal airport, providing examples of why this South Georgia county seat celebrates itself as The City of Southern Living. The tree-lined trail passes within two blocks of Colquitt County's historic courthouse and restaurants that serve such Southern specialties as shrimp and grits with sweet tea. Along the route are parks, an athletic stadium, an arts center, peaceful cemeteries, churches, and schools.

The 10-foot-wide paved trail follows a former CSX railway corridor, just one of the railroads that served this timber and agriculture center. For railroad fans, an old steam locomotive from a competing rail line, the Georgia Northern Railway, is displayed a few blocks from the northern terminus, at the corner of First Avenue SE and Fourth Street SE.

Completed in 2002, the trail is named for beloved former assistant football coach and dedicated runner Tom "Babe" White. The trail features shady shelters, park benches, and

TRAILLINK USER MAPLOVER2

The tree-lined trail follows a former railway corridor serving the agricultural hub of Moultrie.

County
Colquitt

Endpoints
First Ave. NW, 475 feet west of US 319 Bus. (Moultrie); Airport Dr., 300 feet southeast of Sunset Dr. (Moultrie)

Mileage
7.2

Type
Rail-Trail

Roughness
1

Surface
Asphalt

Tom White Linear Park

water fountains. It even incorporates a circular, 200-foot-long United Way Born Learning Trail to help educate toddlers.

In the north, parking is available at Wesley Ball Memorial Park at the corner of Second Avenue NW and First Street NW. The trail starts at the south end of the park, on First Avenue NW, and heads southwest. The picturesque courthouse is two blocks east of the trail on West Central Avenue, at the center of a collection of restaurants, grills, barbecue pits, bars, and coffeehouses.

Heading south into the residential neighborhoods, you'll be slowing frequently for crosswalks over the northern portion of the trail. In 0.7 mile, you'll pass one of the regular destinations for local trail users: the Willie J. Williams Middle School and its Tharpe Stadium. After passing baseball fields, the trail trends southeast and enters a woodsy section for 1.5 miles to just past Lower Meigs Road, a centrally located parking lot for the trail and site of the Born Learning Trail.

In the next 2.5 miles, the trail (with an adjacent crushed-gravel track for runners) rolls alongside GA 33/South Main Street past a golf course, a YMCA, a cemetery, and shopping districts to the four-lane US 319. The trail crosses this busy intersection at a stoplight and continues south on the east side of US 319.

The next 1.1 miles is an exposed stretch next to the highway, while the final 1.2 miles passes through shady woodlots on the way to the trail's terminus at the dual-runway Moultrie Municipal Airport.

CONTACT: mccpra.com/parks-facilities

PARKING

Parking areas are located in Moultrie and are listed north to south. *Indicates that at least one accessible parking space is available.*

WESLEY BALL MEMORIAL PARK*: First St. NW and Second Ave. NW (31.1816, -83.7902).

LOWER MEIGS ROAD: 0.1 mile west of GA 33/S. Main St. (31.1517, -83.7905).

MOULTRIE MUNICIPAL AIRPORT*: 194 Airport Dr. (31.0860, -83.8080).

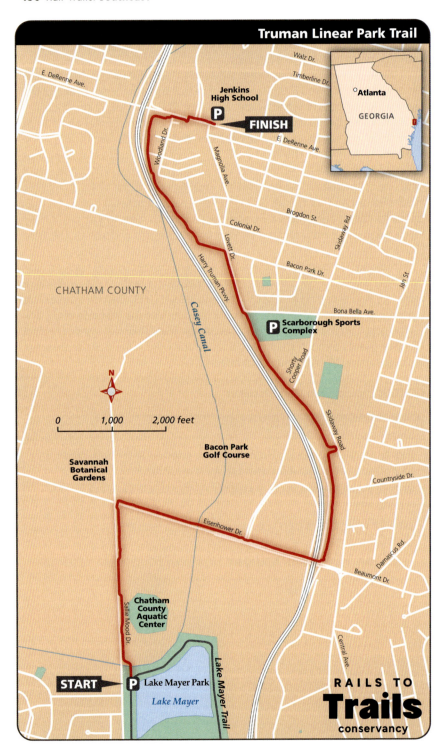

Truman Linear Park Trail

Jenkins High School

FINISH

Atlanta

GEORGIA

Walz Dr.

Timberline Dr.

E. DeRenne Ave.

E. DeRenne Ave.

Woodland Dr.

Magnolia Ave.

Brogdon St.

Skidaway Rd.

Colonial Dr.

Lovett Dr.

Harry Truman Pkwy.

CHATHAM COUNTY

Bacon Park Dr.

Bona Bella Ave.

Casey Canal

Scarborough Sports Complex

Shorty Cooper Road

Skidaway Road

Countryside Dr.

N

0   1,000   2,000 feet

Bacon Park Golf Course

Savannah Botanical Gardens

Eisenhower Dr.

Damascus Rd.

Beaumont Dr.

Chatham County Aquatic Center

Sallie Mood Dr.

Central Ave.

START   Lake Mayer Park

Lake Mayer Trail

Lake Mayer

RAILS TO
Trails
conservancy

Truman Linear Park Trail

38

Flanked by ecologically rich saltwater marshes, the Truman Linear Park Trail provides an opportunity to explore this picturesque area of south Savannah. The 3.1-mile paved trail runs along Harry S. Truman Parkway and Casey Canal most of the way between busy Lake Mayer Park and DeRenne Avenue in the Magnolia Park/Blueberry Hill neighborhood.

The Truman Linear Park Trail is the first step in Tide to Town, a local alternative-transportation project that seeks to connect all of Savannah's neighborhoods with an urban trail system. The figure-eight route would run from the Savannah Historic District, the largest National Historic Landmark District in the country, and the Victorian District, listed on the National Register of Historic Places, to more recent growth areas south of downtown.

Parking for the south end of Truman Linear Park Trail can be found on Sallie Mood Drive at the northwest corner of Lake Mayer. This is also a junction for the paved 1.5-mile Lake Mayer Trail, which encircles the lake. The loop connects by bridge to the Lake Mayer Community Park on an

The trail starts out heading north along Sallie Mood Drive.

TRAILLINK USER POINTWEST36

County
Chatham

Endpoints
Lake Mayer Park (Savannah); DeRenne Ave. (Savannah)

Mileage
3.1

Type
Greenway/ Non-Rail-Trail

Roughness Rating
1

Surface
Boardwalk, Concrete

The trail provides a pleasant route through southern Savannah, connecting athletic facilities, businesses, and residential neighborhoods.

island that features additional parking, tennis courts, a fishing pier and boat launch, and other amenities.

From the trailhead, the Truman trail heads north across a creek and runs alongside Sallie Mood Road for 0.5 mile. It passes the Chatham County Aquatic Center and two sets of ball fields that sit at the edge of the wooded Bacon Park neighborhood. Crossing Eisenhower Drive at a stoplight, the trail passes the Savannah Botanical Gardens and the Bacon Park Golf Course as it heads east along Eisenhower for 0.7 mile to an underpass at Harry S. Truman Parkway.

Crossing a ramp to the parkway, the trail heads north through an isolated area tucked between the parkway and Skidaway Road. In 1 mile, the trail passes Bona Bella Avenue and more athletic fields, then reaches East DeRenne Avenue in 0.9 mile. It heads east a short way on DeRenne Avenue, ending at Jenkins High School.

Plans call for extending the trail northward via an extension along Truman Parkway to 52nd Street and for incorporating the 0.6-mile Police Memorial Trail on its way to Daffin Park and its 1.5-mile loop around a swimming pool and athletic fields. The final product would be a 6-mile trail that connects Daffin Park to Lake Mayer Park as it traverses 18 neighborhoods, 13 schools, and more than 800 acres of public land.

CONTACT: trumanlinearparktrail.com

PARKING

Parking areas are located within Savannah and are listed from south to north. Also check the Chatham Area Transit (CAT) website at **catchacat.org** for transit information to Lake Mayer Park, Scarborough Sports Complex, or Jenkins High School. *Indicates that at least one accessible parking space is available.*

LAKE MAYER COMMUNITY PARK*: E. Montgomery Cross Road, between Truman Pkwy. and Sallie Mood Dr. (31.9906, -81.0877).

TRUMAN LINEAR PARK TRAILHEAD*: Lake Mayer Community Park on Sallie Mood Dr., 0.4 mile north of E. Montgomery Cross Road (31.9956, -81.0903).

SCARBOROUGH SPORTS COMPLEX*: Skidaway Road, 400 feet south of Bona Bella Ave. (32.0116, -81.0806).

TERRY WEBB BASEBALL FIELD AT JENKINS HIGH SCHOOL*: 1800 E. DeRenne Ave. (32.0219, -81.0842).

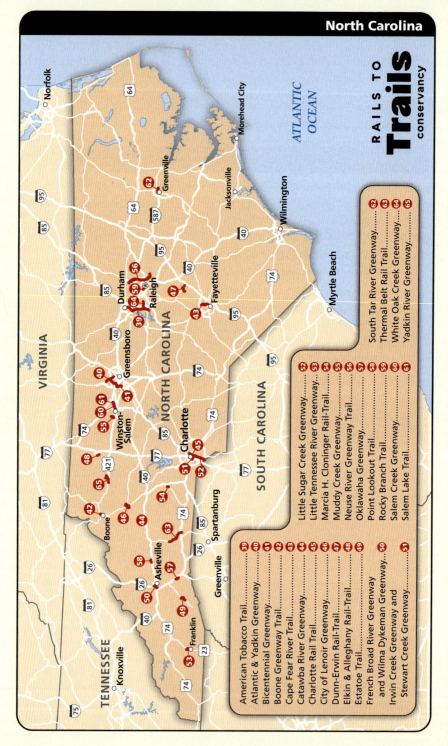

RAILS TO Trails conservancy

ATLANTIC OCEAN

Norfolk
Morehead City
Greenville
Jacksonville
Wilmington
Myrtle Beach
Fayetteville
Durham
Raleigh
Greensboro
Winston-Salem
Charlotte
Boone
Asheville
Spartanburg
Greenville
Franklin
Knoxville

VIRGINIA
NORTH CAROLINA
SOUTH CAROLINA
TENNESSEE

American Tobacco Trail.............................39
Atlantic & Yadkin Greenway......................40
Bicentennial Greenway...............................41
Boone Greenway Trail.................................42
Cape Fear River Trail..................................43
Catawba River Greenway...........................44
Charlotte Rail Trail......................................45
City of Lenoir Greenway.............................46
Dunn-Erwin Rail-Trail.................................47
Elkin & Alleghany Rail-Trail........................48
Estatoe Trail...49
French Broad River Greenway
and Wilma Dykeman Greenway..........50
Irwin Creek Greenway and
Stewart Creek Greenway......................51

Little Sugar Creek Greenway.....................52
Little Tennessee River Greenway..............53
Marcia H. Cloninger Rail-Trail...................54
Muddy Creek Greenway.............................55
Neuse River Greenway Trail.......................56
Oklawaha Greenway...................................57
Point Lookout Trail.....................................58
Rocky Branch Trail......................................59
Salem Creek Greenway..............................60
Salem Lake Trail...61

South Tar River Greenway..........................62
Thermal Belt Rail Trail................................63
White Oak Creek Greenway........................64
Yadkin River Greenway...............................65

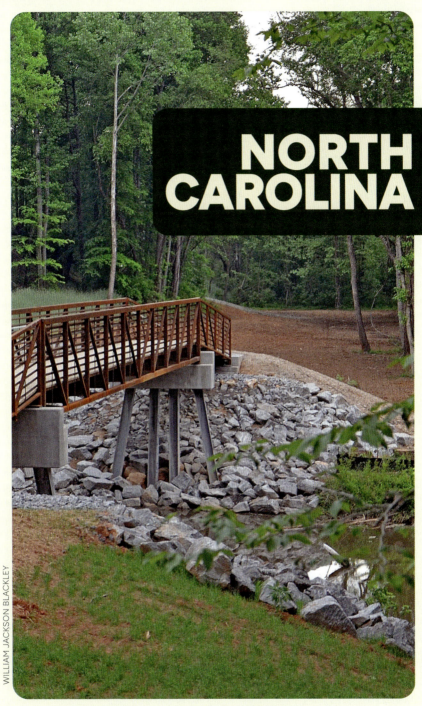

NORTH CAROLINA

WILLIAM JACKSON BLACKLEY

The Elkin & Alleghany Rail-Trail includes two crossings over
Big Elkin Creek (*see Trail 48, page 167*).

135

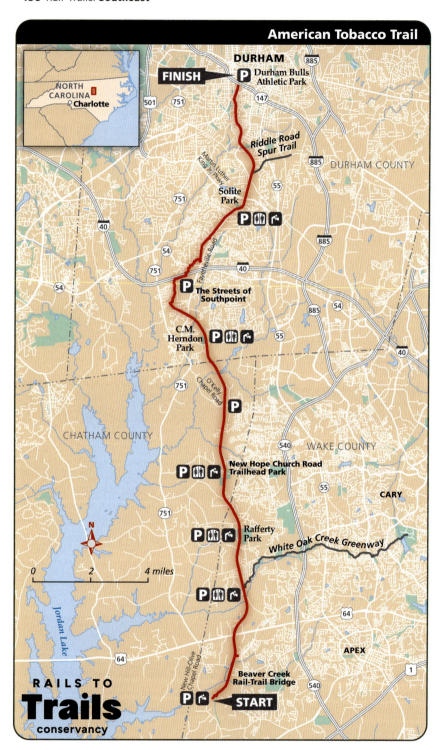

American Tobacco Trail

American Tobacco Trail

39

Spanning more than 22 miles, the American Tobacco Trail is one of the longest greenways in North Carolina and one of the most heavily used, connecting Durham with its southern suburbs and extending to the more rural and wooded exurbs of Chatham and Wake Counties. As the population of the Research Triangle region expands, new housing developments and amenities are being built with direct access to the trail as a feature. For much of its route, the trail offers a wide, low-grade, tree-lined corridor. Steeped in local history and intrinsically linked with its namesake, the American Tobacco Company (founded by James B. Duke, an inescapable name in the state's history), the trail is well maintained and offers access to amenities throughout its length.

The trail follows a rail line built to service the American Tobacco Company's Lucky Strike production facilities in Durham. After the closure of the Lucky Strike factory in the late 1980s, the rail corridor fell into disuse. It was used

JOE LACROIX

The trail journeys from Durham through its southern suburbs and into rural Chatham and Wake Counties.

Counties
Chatham, Durham, Wake

Endpoints
New Hill–Olive Chapel Road, 0.6 mile south of Tody Goodwin Road (Apex); Durham Bulls Athletic Park at Morehead Ave. and Blackwell St. (Durham)

Mileage
22.2

Type
Rail-Trail

Roughness Rating
1

Surface
Asphalt, Crushed Stone

JOE LACROIX

Relish views of a beautiful wetland area from the Beaver Creek Rail-Trail Bridge.

informally as a trail by locals before the Triangle Rails to Trails Conservancy was formed to help facilitate the formal development of the trail; the North Carolina Department of Transportation began purchasing segments of the corridor and leasing the land to the three managing counties in the 1990s. The trail is now an integral resource for the local communities, both for recreation and transportation.

Beginning from the southern trailhead on New Hill–Olive Chapel Road, west of Apex in Wake County, the trail offers a 12-foot-wide, crushed-stone surface nestled in a heavily wooded environment suitable for bikes of all types, equestrians, and pedestrians. This portion of the trail does have some mild grades that may make wheelchair accessibility difficult. After 0.8 mile, you'll reach the Beaver Creek Rail-Trail Bridge, a picturesque boardwalk highlighting the beautiful wetlands of the area and a great place to stop and observe the scenery and wildlife. Along the length of the trail, keen eyes may be able to spot a number of old tobacco barns, which were used by local farmers to cure crops before sending them along the railway for processing.

After traveling 3.1 miles from the bridge, you'll find a connection to the 7-mile White Oak Creek Greenway (see page 221), which gives Cary residents access to the American Tobacco Trail. Trail users needing accessible facilities are advised to begin their journey at the New Hope Church Road Trailhead Park in Cary, 3.8 miles north of the juncture with the White Oak Creek Greenway. It has ample parking, water, and year-round restroom facilities.

From the New Hope Church Road Trailhead Park, continue north 4.4 miles to C.M. Herndon Park, which offers a plethora of athletic facilities, as well as a playground, picnic tables, restrooms, and drinking water. In another 2.7 miles, you'll reach The Streets of Southpoint, a lively mall with a movie theater, restaurants, and stores.

At Scott King Road, around mile marker 14 (markers count up from Durham as you head south), the trail offers a side-by-side dual surface—10 feet of paved asphalt beside 6 feet of stone-dust shoulder—to accommodate all types of users. The crushed-stone surface ends 10 miles south of Durham—and equestrians are advised not to attempt those final 10 miles. As you near the Durham city limits, the environment becomes increasingly urbanized, with more road crossings and shorter straightaways. A highlight of this northern section of trail is the impressive bridge spanning I-40, which was completed in 2014 and serves as a vital connection between two previously disjointed sections of the trail.

The trail ends in downtown Durham, just south of the old American Tobacco Factory, which has been repurposed as a mixed-use development with offices, living spaces, shops, restaurants, and community amenities such as basketball courts and a concert green—a truly lovely space to end your journey and get a taste of a revitalized section of the city.

CONTACT: triangletrails.org/american-tobacco-trail, dprplaymore.org/263/american-tobacco-trail, and rtc.li/wake-county

PARKING

Parking areas are listed from south to north. Select parking areas are listed below; for a detailed list of parking areas and other waypoints, consult **TrailLink™**. *Indicates that at least one accessible parking space is available.*

APEX*: New Hill Parking Area, 1309 New Hill–Olive Chapel Road (35.7152, -78.9436); unpaved lot that is large enough for equestrian trailers to negotiate.

CARY*: New Hope Church Road Trailhead Park, 2575 New Hope Church Road; 100 parking spaces (35.8171, -78.9265).

DURHAM*: The Streets of Southpoint, 6910 Fayetteville Road (35.9058, -78.9453).

DURHAM*: Solite Park, 4704 Fayetteville Road (35.9355, -78.9107).

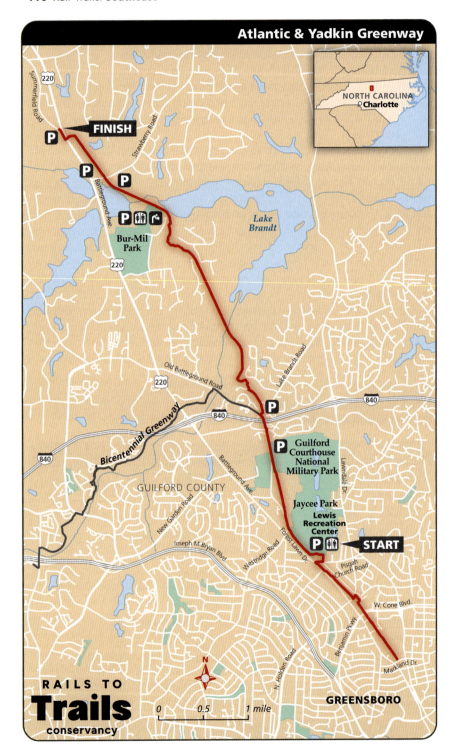

Atlantic & Yadkin Greenway

NORTH CAROLINA
Charlotte

P **FINISH**

Summerfield Road

220

Strawberry Road

P

P

Battleground Ave

P

Bur-Mil Park

220

Lake Brandt

Old Battleground Road

220

Bicentennial Greenway

840

P

840

Lake Branch Road

P

Guilford Courthouse National Military Park

Battleground Ave

GUILFORD COUNTY

New Garden Road

Lawndale Dr.

Jaycee Park

Lewis Recreation Center

P **START**

Joseph M. Bryan Blvd.

Westridge Road

Forest Lawn Dr.

Pisgah Church Road

W. Cone Blvd.

N. Holden Road

Benjamin Pkwy.

Markland Dr.

GREENSBORO

RAILS TO Trails conservancy

0   0.5   1 mile

Atlantic & Yadkin Greenway

40

The Atlantic & Yadkin Greenway spans a nearly 8-mile portion of a rail corridor that once stretched nearly 250 miles from Wilmington on the Atlantic Coast to Mount Airy in the Piedmont plateau region. Today, this rail-trail serves as a top recreational and commuting route from northwestern Greensboro to Summerfield, just beyond the sprawling Bur-Mil Park along Lake Brandt.

The greenway is planned to one day extend farther out in both directions: by roughly 2 miles to the Downtown Greenway in Greensboro on its southern end (with the extension estimated for completion in 2026) and to the Summerfield Community Park on its northern end. It's also part of North Carolina's Mountains-to-Sea Trail, a long-distance trail network connecting the Great Smoky Mountains to the Outer Banks.

Although the trail begins at Markland Drive in Greensboro, there are no amenities there, so we recommend starting your journey 1.7 miles farther north at the Lewis Recreation Center in Jaycee Park, which serves as a trailhead. Here, you'll find parking and restrooms among the park amenities,

County
Guilford

Endpoints
Markland Dr., 300 feet east of Battleground Ave./US 220 (Greensboro); Summerfield Road and Battleground Ave./US 220 (Summerfield)

Mileage
7.8

Type
Rail-Trail

Roughness Rating
1

Surface
Asphalt, Concrete, Crushed Stone

RYAN CREE

The Weaver Bridge offers spectacular views over Lake Brandt.

which also include hiking trails, recreational fields, and a science center. In the park, you'll pick up the trail on the west side of Forest Lawn Drive; the pathway parallels the roadway heading north.

In 1.3 miles, you'll reach Guilford Courthouse National Military Park. Pause here to visit monuments marking where generals Charles Cornwallis and Nathanael Greene clashed in one of the major battles of the Revolutionary War.

A bridge passes over busy I-840 in 0.5 mile, taking you to the intersection of Lake Brandt Road and Old Battleground Road, where the trail meets the 14.5-mile Bicentennial Greenway (see page 143). Turn right on the northern side of Lake Brandt Road, then turn left to continue on the Atlantic & Yadkin Greenway. The pathway heads into quiet, tree-lined neighborhoods that lead to the forests surrounding Lake Brandt, the second-largest reservoir in Greensboro, with many recreational opportunities. The pathway intersects with popular hiking and mountain biking trails, such as the Owl's Roost Trail and the Palmetto Trail, and provides access to the lake for boating. Bridges across the lake provide breathtaking views and chances to spot bald eagles, herons, and other wildlife.

On the northern end of the lake, Bur-Mil Park offers parking, restrooms, water fountains, fishing access, and other amenities. The pathway continues north for 1.6 miles, crossing under Battlefield Avenue/US 220 and ending at Summerfield Road.

CONTACT: greensborotrails.org

PARKING

Parking areas are listed from south to north. Select parking areas for the trail are listed below; for a detailed list of parking areas and other waypoints, consult **TrailLink™**. *Indicates that at least one accessible parking space is available.*

GREENSBORO*: Lewis Recreation Center Trailhead, 3110 Forest Lawn Dr. (36.1180, -79.8361).

GREENSBORO*: Guilford Courthouse National Military Park, Old Battleground Road and New Garden Road (36.1336, -79.8459).

GREENSBORO*: Frank Sharpe Jr. Wildlife Education Center, Bur-Mil Park, 5834 Bur-Mill Club Road Ext. (36.1691, -79.8670).

SUMMERFIELD*: Strawberry Road, 0.1 mile east of Battleground Ave./ US 220 (36.1757, -79.8795).

SUMMERFIELD*: Anna Long Marshall Wayside on Battleground Ave./ US 220, 0.1 mile north of Strawberry Road (36.1776, -79.8822).

SUMMERFIELD: Summerfield Road and Battleground Ave./US 220 (36.1836, -79.8887).

Bicentennial Greenway

41

This cherished multiuse trail winds along the western edge of—and into—Greensboro. The trail's development and maintenance is a collaborative effort between Guilford County and the City of Greensboro. Currently, 14.5 miles are complete and open, with plans in development to close the trail's gaps, creating a nearly 20-mile contiguous route.

The southern trailhead on Penny Road in High Point offers a serene starting point, as the pathway closely follows the forested shore of High Point Lake from here. From the parking lot, you will find a gorgeous boardwalk bridge that connects to High Point City Lake Park. Heading north on the trail, in 0.3 mile, you'll arrive at the Piedmont Environmental Center, which offers access to other wooded hiking trails and educational programming (open daily, 9 a.m.–5 p.m.).

Winding along the shaded edges of the lake, this portion of the trail features gentle hills that might present challenges for some trail users. There are also a number of steeper sections where bike riders will need to dismount to climb stairs, though these stairs do feature bike tracks. The greenway connects several regional parks and neighborhoods,

JOE LACROIX

The greenway weaves through hardwood and pine forests, parks, and natural areas.

County
Guilford

Endpoints
High Point City Lake at Penny Road and Lakeview Heights Dr. (High Point); Burnt Poplar Road and Boulder Road (Greensboro); W. Market St. and Swing Road (Greensboro); dead end of Fleming Terrace Road, 300 feet west of Fox Chase Road (Greensboro); Fox Chase Road, 400 feet west of Fleming Road (Greensboro); Old Battleground Road and Lake Brandt Road (Greensboro)

Mileage
14.5

Type
Greenway/Non-Rail-Trail

Roughness Rating
1–2

Surface
Asphalt, Concrete, Gravel

Bicentennial Greenway

NORTH CAROLINA
Charlotte

FINISH

220

Old Battleground Road

P

P

840

Kernodle
Middle
School

P

Atlantic &
Yadkin Greenway

Battleground Road

840

73

73

68

Horsepen Creek

N. Garden Road

Joseph M. Bryan Blvd.

Leonard
Recreation
Center

P

GREENSBORO

W. Friendly Ave.

W. Friendly Ave.

Piedmont
Triad
International
Airport

840

68

W. Market St.

Western Guilford
High School

P

GUILFORD COUNTY

W. Market St.

40

Burnt Poplar Road

W. Wendover Ave.

Gallimore Dairy Road

S. Chimney Rock Road

73

40

Piedmont Pkwy.

40

68

P

P

W. Wendover Ave.

73

P

Gibson
Park

Guilford College Road

73

Jamestown
Park

P

High
Point
Lake

85

Piedmont
Environmental
Center

P   **P**

JAMESTOWN

N

High Point
City Lake Park

START

HIGH POINT

0   1   2 miles

RAILS TO
Trails
conservancy

including Jamestown Park, which you'll reach 1.5 miles from the environmental center. The park has parking, restrooms, a playground, and picnic shelters. Continuing, you'll have picturesque views of the water, including a wetlands observation deck in 1.3 miles. In another 0.6 mile, you'll reach Gibson Park, which pays homage to the area's 19th-century rifle-making industry, complete with a cabin estimated to have been built in the early 1800s. The park includes amenities such as parking, restrooms, and drinking water.

The next section of the trail requires some navigation; while it provides a useful transportation route through Greensboro, it does not have the same relaxing feeling and pleasant scenery as the previous portion. From Gibson Park, you'll reach the intersection of Gallimore Dairy Road and South Chimney Rock Road in 3 miles. From here, the route follows a sidewalk, closely paralleling roadways with heavy tanker-truck traffic adjacent to petroleum facilities. The sidewalk ends at Burnt Poplar Road with roughly a 2-mile gap before the trail picks up again next to Western Guilford High School and reenters a parklike setting.

From the high school, the trail continues northward along a mostly wooded, off-road path with a few small gaps that require traveling on neighborhood streets and sidewalks. In 1.9 miles, you'll reach Leonard Recreation Center, which offers parking and restrooms. In another mile, the trail empties out onto a cul-de-sac at the end of Fleming Terrace Road. Navigate a short on-road gap by taking your first left on Fox Chase Road, a quiet residential street; follow the

From the southern trailhead, a boardwalk bridge
connects to High Point City Lake Park.

roadway for 0.5 mile, turning left on Fleming Road. Take the sidewalk paralleling busy Fleming Road north (and under I-73) for 0.2 mile until you reach the crosswalk to Bledsoe Drive on your right; follow Bledsoe Drive to the next segment of trail in 0.3 mile.

After 0.4 mile along the trail, you'll need to cross busy Horse Pen Creek Road at a crosswalk without a traffic light. Shortly thereafter, the surface of the trail changes; those on wheels should be prepared for the section of the trail following Horsepen Creek; narrow and unpaved, with a gravel surface, it's more like a hiking trail. The paved surface resumes as the trail approaches Drawbridge Parkway.

On the northern end of the trail, the route travels into northwest Greensboro, ending on the shaded Old Battleground Road with direct access to the Palmetto Trailhead of the Atlantic & Yadkin Greenway (see page 141).

CONTACT: greensborotrails.org and guilfordcountync.gov/our-county /county-parks/trails

PARKING

Parking areas are listed from south to north. *Indicates that at least one accessible parking space is available.*

HIGH POINT: High Point City Lake, 1102 Penny Road (36.0004, -79.9547).

HIGH POINT: Piedmont Environmental Center, 1220 Penny Road (36.0041, -79.9544).

JAMESTOWN*: Jamestown Park, 7041 E. Fork Road (36.0129, -79.9491).

JAMESTOWN*: Gibson Park, 5207 W. Wendover Ave. (36.0300, -79.9438); after turning off Wendover, follow Wintergreen Ct. around to the far end of the park.

HIGH POINT: 4160 Mendenhall Oaks Pkwy. (36.0467, -79.9548).

GREENSBORO: 4125 Piedmont Pkwy. (36.05368, -79.9537).

GREENSBORO: Western Guilford High School, 409 Friendway Road (36.0839, -79.9070).

GREENSBORO: Leonard Recreation Center, 6324 Ballinger Road (36.1033, -79.9101).

GREENSBORO*: Kernodle Middle School, 3600 Drawbridge Pkwy. (36.1320, -79.8805).

GREENSBORO*: Palmetto Trailhead, Old Battleground Road, 0.6 mile east of Battleground Ave./US 220 (36.1436, -79.8585); limited spaces available.

GREENSBORO: Nat Greene Trailhead, 4463 Old Battleground Road (36.1424, -79.8559); limited parking spaces available.

Boone Greenway Trail

42

Following and crossing the winding route of the South Fork of the New River in the Blue Ridge Mountains community of Boone, the Boone Greenway Trail features a mix of open meadows and dense forests. The 4.3-mile trail passes by a historic dam site and has plenty of benches for resting, picnic facilities, and interpretive signs that tell the story of the region's natural and human history. The greenway also boasts great bird-watching and wildflower-viewing.

The greenway begins at the Southgate Shopping Center, a busy commercial area and a convenient stop for lunch or dinner before or after your trail journey. Shortly after State Farm Road, the trail forks. You can loop back around, crossing a footbridge over the creek, to reach a field with baseball diamonds. On the western side of the creek, you'll reach a T-juncture facing the creek. Turn right to take a 0.1-mile route along the creek back toward the shopping area, or take a left to continue north along the trail.

If you head north, you'll reach Martin Luther King Jr. Street in 0.2 mile, and the National Guard Armory will appear on your right as you approach the street. Cross the street,

The Boone Greenway Trail features a mix of open meadows and dense forests.

BETH BRITTAIN

County
Watauga

Endpoints
Pride Dr., 150 feet north of Leola St. (Boone); Casey Lane, 200 feet south of New River Hills (Boone); dead end of Daniel Boone Dr. Ext., 0.2 mile from Daniel Boone Dr. (Boone)

Mileage
4.3

Type
Greenway/ Non-Rail-Trail

Roughness Rating
1

Surface
Asphalt, Boardwalk

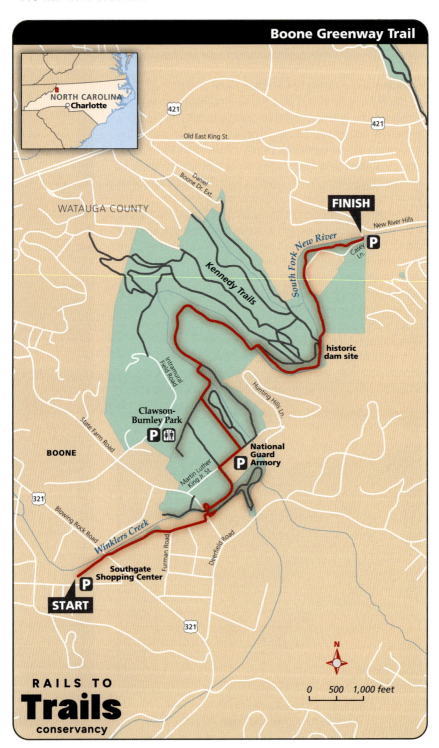

Boone Greenway Trail

NORTH CAROLINA
Charlotte

421

Old East King St.

Daniel Boone Dr. Ext.

WATAUGA COUNTY

FINISH

South Fork New River

New River Hills

P

Casey Ln.

Kennedy Trails

historic
dam site

Intramural Field Road

Hunting Hills Ln.

Clawson-
Burnley Park

P

State Farm Road

National
Guard
Armory

P

BOONE

Martin Luther King Jr. St.

321

Blowing Rock Road

Winklers Creek

Deerfield Road

Furman Road

Southgate
Shopping Center

P

START

321

N

0   500   1,000 feet

RAILS TO
Trails
conservancy

turn right, and follow it northeast 450 feet to the entrance of Clawson-Burnley Park on your left. In the park, you'll find informative signs about the region's plant and animal life, as it's a popular spot for birding and soaking up nature. It features an ADA-accessible picnic shelter, covered picnic tables, restrooms, and benches. This is also a great alternative parking location.

From the entrance to the park, you'll head northwest, reaching a T-juncture in the trail in 0.2 mile. Turning left at this juncture takes you 0.2 mile south to the Watauga County Industrial Fields Complex's ball fields and tennis and basketball courts, as well as a parking lot on Complex Drive.

If you instead turn right at the T-juncture, you'll head north/northeast for 0.1 mile before reaching a covered bridge over the South Fork New River. Take a left after you cross the bridge to stay on the main trail; turning right will take you to Hunting Hills Lane. From the bridge, it's 0.8 mile to a historic dam site and stone ruins of a hydroelectric-power station that produced the first electricity in Boone in the early 1900s. The station served the Appalachian Training School, now Appalachian State University, and early homes. Sitting in the midst of the densest forest along the greenway, the site features a view of the wood dam that still remains in the river. Continuing 0.5 mile northeast, you'll come to the end of the trail at the Casey Lane trailhead, located along the South Fork New River.

The greenway's mostly flat grade and smooth asphalt surface make it a natural fit for a relaxing bike ride or walk through nature. Those looking for a more

TRAILLINK USER RADHA ANANDA

Enjoy colorful foliage in the fall as you take a relaxing bike ride or walk on the mostly flat, smooth greenway.

challenging experience can connect to a network of gravel and dirt trails called the Kennedy Trails at the bridge over the South Fork New River about 0.75 mile northeast of Clawson-Burnley Park. This connector is marked by a large sign. The Kennedy Trails are also accessible across an adjacent sports field along Intramural Field Road just north of the Appalachian Field Hockey Stadium.

Looking into the future, the community is studying an extension that would connect the greenway with the Appalachian State University campus to the northwest. A feasibility study is in the early stages to determine a route for connecting the greenway from Pride Drive at the southern end for about 1.7 miles to the university campus. A projected completion date is yet to be determined.

CONTACT: townofboone.net/facilities/facility/details/greenwaytrail-27

PARKING

Parking areas are located in Boone and are listed from southwest to northeast. Select parking areas for the trail are listed below; for a detailed list of parking areas and other waypoints, consult **TrailLink™**. *Indicates that at least one accessible parking space is available.*

SOUTHGATE SHOPPING CENTER*: Pride Dr., 150 feet north of Leola St. (36.1987, -81.6596).

CLAWSON-BURNLEY PARK*: Martin Luther King Jr. St., 0.1 mile northeast of Complex Dr. (36.2051, -81.6510).

CASEY LANE TRAILHEAD*: Casey Lane, 200 feet south of New River Hills (36.2145, -81.6446).

Cape Fear River Trail

43

Featuring a blend of leafy trees, thick undergrowth, and occasional spectacular views of the Cape Fear River, the Cape Fear River Trail winds for 7.5 miles in north Fayetteville. The 10-foot-wide asphalt trail attracts a range of activities, including walking, jogging, and bicycling.

Trail users will find a scenic landscape of marshes and wetlands as the trail roughly follows the course of the Cape Fear River in a mostly north–south route. Along the way, the trail passes over more than a half dozen bridges, including quaint wooden structures and a covered bridge. A 0.2-mile boardwalk takes trail users through a wetlands area, and the trail also features playgrounds, benches, and birdhouses. Some sections of the trail are steep and hilly, and bicycles are required to maintain speeds of less than 15 miles per hour and yield to pedestrians.

You will find plentiful parking at the Clark Park Nature Center, where the trailhead is named in honor of Moses Mathis, who was known in the community for his Christmas bicycle giveaway to children in need. The nature center features a natural woodland area that is dedicated to preserving the

COURTESY CITY OF FAYETTEVILLE

Experience a serene setting of leafy trees along the trail in north Fayetteville.

County
Cumberland

Endpoints
N. Eastern Blvd., 0.4 mile northeast of the Riverside Dog Park (Fayetteville); Jordan Soccer Complex on Treetop Dr. (Fayetteville)

Mileage
7.5

Type
Greenway/ Rail-with-Trail

Roughness Rating
1–2

Surface
Asphalt, Boardwalk

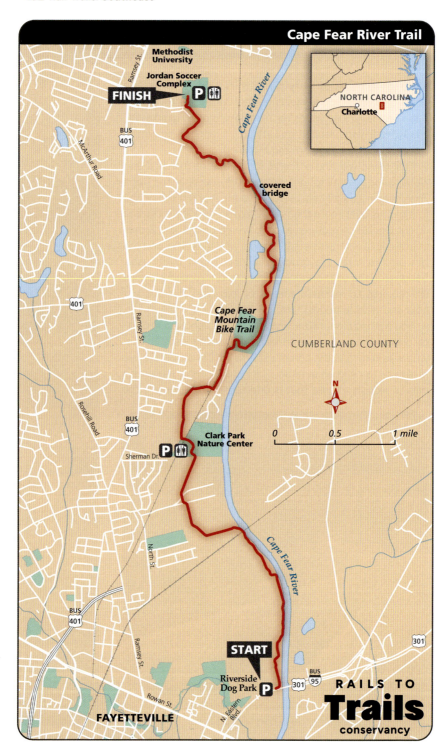

environment and educating the community about local plants and wildlife. You can view live animals at the nature center and walk along an "outdoor storybook" featuring changing stories on the trail near the playground before picnicking in spots overlooking the woods. Another option is to start at the Riverside Dog Park, 2.3 miles to the south, which is linked to the Cape Fear River Trail via a connector route. Limited parking is available at the dog park.

Begin at the trail's southern terminus on North Eastern Boulevard, adjacent to the US 301 underpass. (Note that parking is available nearby at the Riverside Dog Park, 0.4 mile southwest along North Eastern Boulevard.) From the terminus, you'll head north-northeast as the route winds along the river with scenic boardwalks. In 2.75 miles, you'll arrive at a pedestrian railroad crossing and then enter the grounds of the Clark Park Nature Center.

After meandering in a mostly northerly route for 3.1 miles (with the last 2 miles along the river), the trail comes to a picturesque covered bridge with a railroad trestle above it and a small waterfall flowing nearby. The trail then continues another 0.9 mile to the north/northwest until it reaches the Jordan Soccer Complex on the north end.

The Cape Fear Mountain Bike Trail, which is accessible off the Cape Fear River Trail 1 mile north of the Clark Park Nature Center, offers about 11 miles of woodland dirt trail suitable for mountain bikers and hikers. Restroom facilities are available at the Jordan Soccer Complex, as well as at the Clark Park Nature Center.

COURTESY CITY OF FAYETTEVILLE

The trail traverses a wooded landscape
on its way north to the Jordan Soccer Complex.

Interpretive signs are spaced along the trail describing the abundant wildlife that includes frogs, lizards, turtles, and deer, as well as 150 species of birds. Signs also explain the diverse plant life of more than 700 species of plants and a variety of hardwood trees. The thick trees and undergrowth offer shade along much of the trail during the spring and summer and offer changing colors in the fall.

The Cape Fear River Trail is a part of the East Coast Greenway, a growing network of multiuse trails connecting 15 states and 450 cities and towns on a 3,000-mile route between Maine and Florida.

CONTACT: fcpr.us/parks-trails/trails/cape-fear-river-trail

PARKING

Parking areas are located in Fayetteville and are listed from south to north. *Indicates that at least one accessible parking space is available.*

RIVERSIDE DOG PARK: 555 N. Eastern Blvd. (35.0558, -78.8623); limited parking.

CLARK PARK NATURE CENTER*: 631 Sherman Dr. (35.0878, -78.8710).

JORDAN SOCCER COMPLEX*: 445 Treetop Dr. (35.1293, -78.8694).

Catawba River Greenway

44

Located in Morganton, the paved Catawba River Greenway follows the meandering course of the Catawba River and offers sweeping river views along much of its 3.8-mile length. A portion of the trail passes through thick native forestland, while other sections traverse meadow terrain. The 10-foot-wide greenway's smooth asphalt surface and gentle grade of no more than 5% make it popular for a range of uses. Along with many joggers, walkers, and cyclists, the greenway attracts paddlers who are able to launch at a number of spots along the trail.

The route also highlights the area's history, including its proximity to a Revolutionary War battle site, and, as part of the Overmountain Victory National Historic Trail, it features plaques that commemorate the region's role in the war. The Catawba River Greenway is also part of the North Carolina Birding Trail and the Fonta Flora State Trail.

Beginning at the Catawba River Soccer Complex, on the trail's southwestern end, you'll head east for about a quarter mile. A canoe and kayak launch is located near this trailhead. The 0.6-mile Freedom Greenway branches off to the north,

County
Burke

Endpoints
Catawba River Soccer Complex at Greenlee Ford Road, 0.2 mile north of Carbon City Road/ US 70 (Morganton); Rocky Ford Access at Lenoir Road/US 64/ NC 18 (Morganton)

Mileage
3.8

Type
Greenway/ Non-Rail-Trail

Roughness Rating
1

Surface
Asphalt

COURTESY CITY OF MORGANTON

Closely following the Catawba River, the greenway offers river views along much of its length.

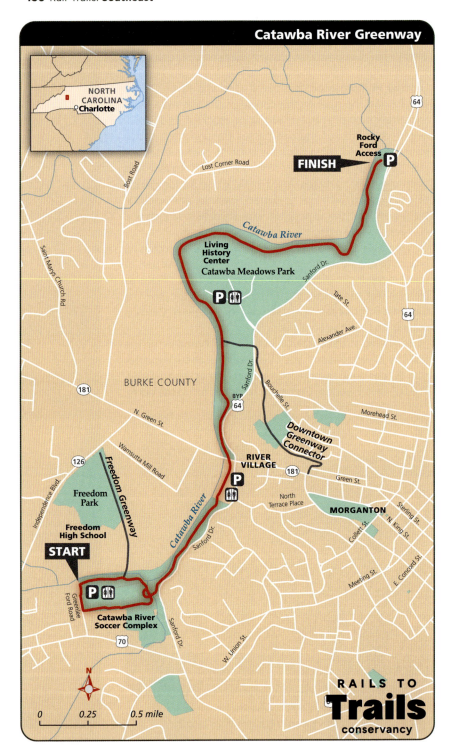

Catawba River Greenway

providing access to Freedom Park and Freedom High School; it's reached via a pedestrian bridge over the river.

Continuing on the Catawba River Greenway, you'll follow the river to the north/northeast, passing through the River Village commercial area in 0.8 mile and Catawba Meadows Park in another 0.1 mile. The 230-acre park features softball and baseball facilities, an 18-hole disc golf course, sand volleyball courts, picnic facilities, and canoe and kayak launch sites. The park is also home to the Living History Center, an interactive interpretive center located at the site of a 16th-century Catawba Indian village. The center, developed by the Exploring Joara Foundation in partnership with the City of Morganton, features replica 16th-century buildings that were re-created based on information found in excavations of the site.

The Morganton Downtown Historic District, which features buildings dating back to the late 1800s, is located about 1 mile southeast of the park and is within easy reach via the Downtown Greenway Connector.

From Catawba Meadows Park, the greenway continues east and north along the river before ending at the Rocky Ford Access, a gravel parking area above the Catawba River with a rugged dirt road leading down to the water and a launch point for paddlers.

CONTACT: rtc.li/morganton-greenway-system

PARKING

Parking areas are located in Morganton and are listed from southwest to northeast. *Indicates that at least one accessible parking space is available.*

GREENLEE FORD TRAILHEAD*: Greenlee Ford Road and Carbon City Road/US 70 (35.7404, -81.7180).

RIVER VILLAGE SHOPPING CENTER TRAILHEAD*: Sanford Dr. and N. Green St. (35.749079, - 81.704846).

CATAWBA MEADOWS TRAILHEAD*: Sanford Dr./Bypass US 64 and Catawba Meadows Dr./Alexander Ave. (35.7607, -81.7061).

ROCKY FORD TRAILHEAD*: Catawba River Soccer Complex, Lenoir Road/US 64/NC 18, 0.4 mile north of Sanford Dr./Kirksey Dr. (35.7710, -81.6916).

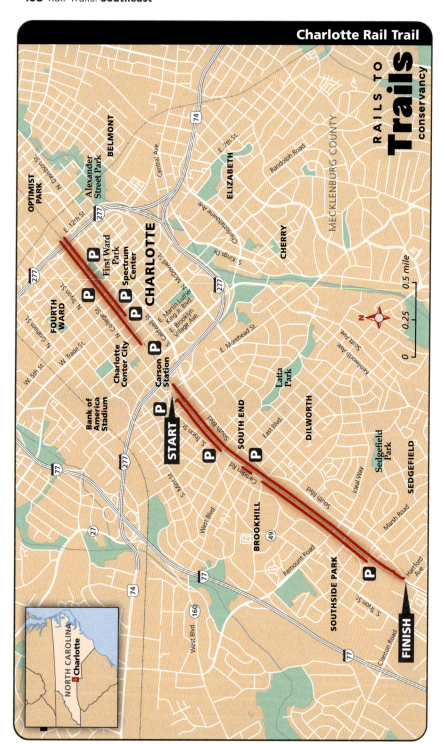

Charlotte Rail Trail

45

Once no more than a humble maintenance path along a trolley line, the Charlotte Rail Trail now offers a vibrant pathway extending 3.5 miles from Charlotte's Center City to the South End. Flanking both sides of the LYNX Blue Line light rail, this rail-with-trail provides numerous opportunities to move from one side of the tracks to the other—something you're practically guaranteed to do as a retail shop or eatery catches your eye.

Bicycles are allowed on the trail, but due to the large volume of trail users, it may be preferable to either walk the path (perhaps riding the light rail on the return trip) or rent an electric scooter from one of the companies servicing the city. The trail is also easily accessed by public transportation, with nine trailside train stations.

While the route technically begins at East 12th Street and Alpha Mill Lane, just north of the light rail's Ninth Street Station, a recommended starting point is 1.2 miles south at East Carson Boulevard (adjacent to the Carson Station), where the trail widens out, becomes fully paved,

SCOTT STARK

Through Charlotte's South End, residential housing and well-trimmed landscaping line the rail-trail.

County
Mecklenburg

Endpoints
E. 12th St. and Alpha Mill Lane (Charlotte); South Blvd., 450 feet north of Hartford Ave. (Charlotte)

Mileage
3.5

Type
Rail-with-Trail

Roughness Rating
1

Surface
Asphalt, Brick, Concrete

and traverses the thriving mixed-use neighborhood of South End. (*Note:* The northern portion of the trail is narrower and has a brick surface.)

On your way to the southern endpoint at South Boulevard in 2.3 miles, the trail is frequently dotted with public art, including brightly colored murals and sculptures. Well-trimmed bushes and trees line the pathway, and with condos and apartments lining the corridor, you're bound to see residents using the trail to catch the train, walk their dogs, or get to nearby destinations.

Currently, there is a gap in the middle of the trail (navigated via sidewalks), just north of Carson Station—where you began the route described here— with I-277 splitting the trail into two noncontiguous sections. As it stands now, trail users coming from the rail-trail's northern end must exit the protected pathway at East Martin Luther King Jr. Boulevard (adjacent to the Charlotte Convention Center). To navigate the gap, turn left at East Martin Luther King Jr. Boulevard and, in two blocks, turn right on South Caldwell Street, following the sidewalk along the busy roadway over the interstate to reach the southern half of the trail. A pedestrian bridge is planned (with an anticipated opening in 2025) that will continue to parallel the LYNX Blue Line across the interstate and provide a seamless experience for trail users.

CONTACT: charlotterailtrail.org

PARKING

While the trail doesn't have dedicated parking, paid parking can be found throughout downtown Charlotte. The trail is also easily accessed from nine adjacent LYNX Blue Line light rail stations, listed from north to south:

NINTH ST. STATION: 239 E. Ninth St. (35.2296, -80.8350).

SEVENTH ST. STATION: 260 E. Seventh St. (35.2273, -80.8381).

CHARLOTTE TRANSPORTATION CENTER/ARENA STATION: 303 E. Trade St. (35.2253, -80.8409).

THIRD ST. STATION: 305 E. Third St. (35.2238, -80.8431).

BROOKLYN VILLAGE STATION: 260 E. Brooklyn Village Ave. (35.2213, -80.8470).

CARSON STATION: 218 E. Carson Blvd. (35.2188, -80.8508).

BLAND ST. STATION: 1511 Camden Road (35.2158, -80.8553).

EAST/WEST BLVD. STATION: 1821 Camden Road (35.2121, -80.8591).

NEW BERN STATION: 129 New Bern St. (35.1998, -80.8691).

City of Lenoir Greenway

46

The 10-mile City of Lenoir Greenway provides access to major parks and other attractions in a community nestled in the foothills of North Carolina's Blue Ridge Mountains. The greenway is currently open in a handful of disconnected segments, but its main 7-mile section features a wide, smooth asphalt surface bordered by terrain that is mostly wooded, interspersed with some open areas. Although largely flat, the greenway includes some hilly areas as well.

Starting from the parking area off Zacks Fork Road in the northwest, the paved main greenway heads south. In just 230 feet, you'll reach a juncture with a short connector leading to the Lenoir Aquatic & Fitness Center, where you will find indoor and outdoor pools, a weight room, exercise classes, and access to the Zacks Fork Mountain Bike Trails, which offer 3.3 miles of off-road trails for mountain biking. Continuing on the main greenway, you'll soon pass the Lenoir Rotary Soccer Complex. In another 0.3 mile, the trail heads east and loops around the T. Henry Wilson Athletic Park. The municipal facility features ball fields and open space.

The northeast stretch of the greenway loops through wooded neighborhoods.

TRAILLINK USER SHARONBATES50

County
Caldwell

Endpoints
Zacks Fork Road and Roundabout Road (Lenoir); Severt Cir. and Cottrell Hill Road (Lenoir); Westbrook St. NW, 150 feet south of Pennton Ave. NW (Lenoir); T.H. Broyhill Walking Park (Lenoir); Morganton Blvd./US 64 (Lenoir); N. Main St. and Old North Road NW (Lenoir); Mulberry Recreation Center (Lenoir); Lenoir Optimist Park (Lenoir)

Mileage
10

Type
Rail-Trail, Greenway/Non-Rail-Trail

Roughness Rating
1

Surface
Asphalt

City of Lenoir Greenway

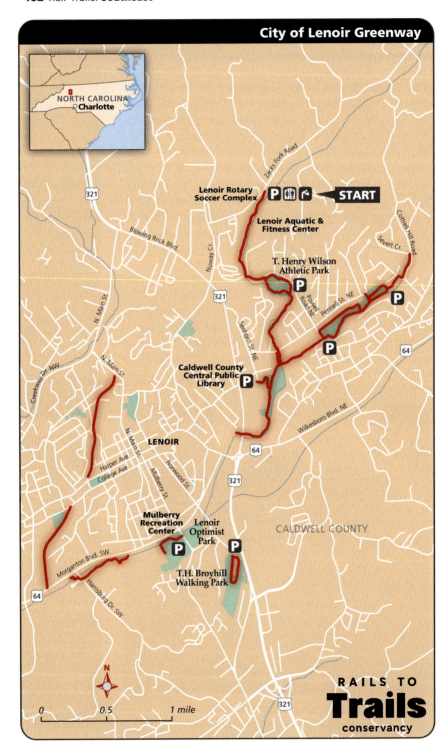

NORTH CAROLINA
Charlotte

Lenoir Rotary
Soccer Complex

START

Zacks Fork Road

Cottrell Hill Road

Lenoir Aquatic &
Fitness Center

Severt Cr.

Blowing Rock Blvd.

Nuway Ct.

T. Henry Wilson
Athletic Park

321

Powell
Road NE

Pennell St. NE

321

Seehorn St. NE

64

Creekway Dr. NW

N. Main St.

N. Main St.

Caldwell County
Central Public
Library

Wilkesboro Blvd. NE

N. Main St.

LENOIR

64

Harper Ave.
College Ave.

Mulberry St.

Norwood St.

321

Mulberry
Recreation
Center

Lenoir
Optimist
Park

CALDWELL COUNTY

Morganton Blvd. SW

T.H. Broyhill
Walking Park

64

Harrisburg Dr. SW

N

0   0.5   1 mile

321

RAILS TO
Trails
conservancy

From the southeastern end of the park, the greenway continues southwest before it reaches a well-marked crossing of Pennell Street Northeast in 0.5 mile. After crossing the roadway, you'll find a Y-juncture in the trail. Continue straight to take a northeasterly stretch of the greenway that continues for 1.5 miles to Severt Circle and Cottrell Hill Road, passing through neighborhoods and taking loops through greenways along the way.

Back at the Y-juncture, turning right takes you south to the Caldwell County Central Public Library in 0.5 mile. You'll arrive at the trail's southwest terminus in 0.6 mile after the turnoff for the library. A number of businesses are located within walking distance from the trail in this area for convenient access to dining and refreshments.

In addition to the main section, the greenway features a 0.4-mile loop in the T.H. Broyhill Walking Park and a 1.5-mile segment beginning at Morganton Boulevard/US 64 that follows an old Carolina & Northwestern Railway line northeast to North Main Street and Old North Road Northwest. The line was discontinued through Lenoir in 2007, and paving of the rail-trail started in 2019. Part of the multistate Overmountain Victory National Historic Trail, the rail-trail runs along the edge of downtown Lenoir and passes through wooded areas and commercial districts. A disconnected 0.3-mile segment beginning just east of the rail-trail connects the Mulberry Recreation Center and Lenoir Optimist Park, where you'll find ball fields, a playground, and picnic shelters.

CONTACT: cityoflenoir.com/410/lenoir-greenway

PARKING

Parking areas are located in Lenoir and are listed from north to south. Select parking areas are listed below; for a detailed list of parking areas and other waypoints, consult TrailLink ™. *Indicates that at least one accessible parking space is available.*

LENOIR ROTARY SOCCER COMPLEX*: 1050 Zacks Fork Road NE (35.9431, -81.5219).

T. HENRY WILSON ATHLETIC PARK*: 1010 Powell Road NE (35.9333, -81.5194).

POWELL ROAD PARKING LOT*: 710 Powell Road NE (35.9273, -81.5138).

CALDWELL COUNTY PUBLIC LIBRARY*: 120 Hospital Ave. NW (35.9218, -81.5229).

MULBERRY RECREATION CENTER*: 720 Mulberry St. SW (35.9051, -81.5329).

T.H. BROYHILL WALKING PARK*: 945 Lakewood Cir. SW (35.9034, -81.5254).

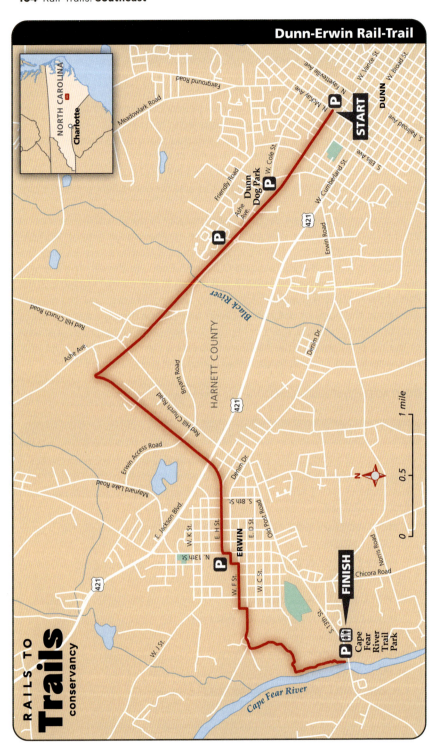

Following the route of a historic rail line that once serviced a coal plant and denim textile mills in Erwin, the Dunn-Erwin Rail-Trail passes through wooded terrain interspersed with open farmland and cotton fields. While the original rail-trail runs for about 5 miles, an extension along a non-rail-trail section to the Cape Fear River Trail Park (not to be confused with the similarly named trail in Fayetteville) brings the total length to 7.2 miles.

The rail-trail section connects the two central North Carolina towns of Dunn and Erwin, which lie between the metropolitan areas of Fayetteville and Raleigh. The Aberdeen and Rockfish rail line (previously Durham & Southern Railway) once served the towns of Dunn, known for cotton production, and Erwin, known for cotton and denim textile mills. The disued rail line opened as a rail-trail in the early 2000s.

Surfaced in crushed stone, the Dunn-Erwin Rail-Trail is ADA accessible. Its comfortable, flat surface makes for an easy and relaxing experience. Although the trail intersects with streets in multiple locations, the crossings are well

CARL DAVIS

On its eastern end, the trail passes through a largely wooded former rail corridor.

County
Harnett

Endpoints
N. McKay Ave., between W. Vance St. and W. Carr St. (Dunn); Cape Fear River Trail Park (Erwin)

Mileage
7.2

Type
Rail-Trail, Greenway/ Non-Rail-Trail

Roughness Rating
1

Surface
Concrete, Crushed Stone

marked. Trail users will find a series of signs that feature maps and information about points of historical interest.

Beginning just north of downtown Dunn, the rail-trail heads northwest, passing the Dunn Dog Park in 1.1 miles before heading into the flat farmland that makes up the countryside of Harnett County. The trail crosses the Black River in 0.7 mile, before reaching the approximate halfway point, where you'll encounter an abrupt left turn that you'll take to head southwest toward Erwin.

The flat, open terrain continues for 1.2 miles until the trail passes under US 421 and enters Erwin. There, you'll find a small-town setting and the trail occasionally lined with trees. Streetside parking is available near the greenway in Erwin. After the rail-trail portion ends, at the intersection of East H Street and 13th Street, the route continues for 2.2 miles to the south/southwest, first on a well-marked concrete pathway that meanders through downtown Erwin, quiet neighborhoods, and industrial areas, and then transitioning to a crushed-stone trail along remote forestland. The extension ends at a trailhead with restrooms and parking at Cape Fear River Trail Park on the Cape Fear River. The park also offers nature trails, scenic overlooks, canoe access, and a picnic shelter.

The rail-trail is part of the East Coast Greenway, a 3,000-mile trail network that runs from Maine to Florida, connecting 15 states and 450 cities and towns along the way.

CONTACT: harnett.org/parkrec/dunnerwin-rail-trail.asp

PARKING

Parking areas are listed from east to west. Select parking areas for the trail are listed below; for a detailed list of parking areas and other waypoints, consult **TrailLink™**. *Indicates that at least one accessible parking space is available.*

DUNN: Trailhead near N. McKay Ave. and W. Carr St. (35.3142, -78.6118); streetside parking.

DUNN: Dunn Dog Park, 701 N. Ashe Ave., near the intersection with Ponderosa Dr. (35.3240, -78.6261).

DUNN: Near Powell St. and Ashe Ave. (35.3265, -78.6307).

ERWIN: 1002 S. 13th St. and Cape Fear River Trail Park entrance (35.3134, -78.6916).

Elkin & Alleghany Rail-Trail

48

As part of the Mountains-to-Sea Trail (a hiking route across North Carolina), as well as the multistate Overmountain Victory National Historic Trail, the 1.2-mile Elkin & Alleghany Rail-Trail holds a significant place in the history and landscape of the region. The rail-trail follows the route of the Elkin & Alleghany short-line railroad, which was abandoned in 1931; the corridor was rediscovered and refurbished as a trail in the early 2000s.

The rail-trail's surface is crushed, compacted granite, and the route is mostly flat, although it has a slightly uphill grade as it heads toward the Blue Ridge Mountains to the northwest. The rail-trail supports a range of uses, including walking, running, and bicycling. Hatchery-supported trout fishing is also available in the creek all along the trail and is a popular activity.

The main trailhead is located at Elkin Municipal Park and Recreation Center, although the trail technically begins at North Front Street, 0.1 mile south of the park. From the park, the trail heads northwest, running parallel to the scenic Big Elkin Creek. A 0.3-mile section of the trail borders

WILLIAM JACKSON BLACKLEY

From Elkin Municipal Park, the trail heads northwest along wooded Big Elkin Creek.

County
Surry

Endpoints
N. Front St., 450 feet north of W. Market St. (Elkin); 0.8 mile west of Collins Road and CC Camp Road (Elkin)

Mileage
1.2

Type
Rail-Trail

Roughness Rating
1

Surface
Crushed Stone

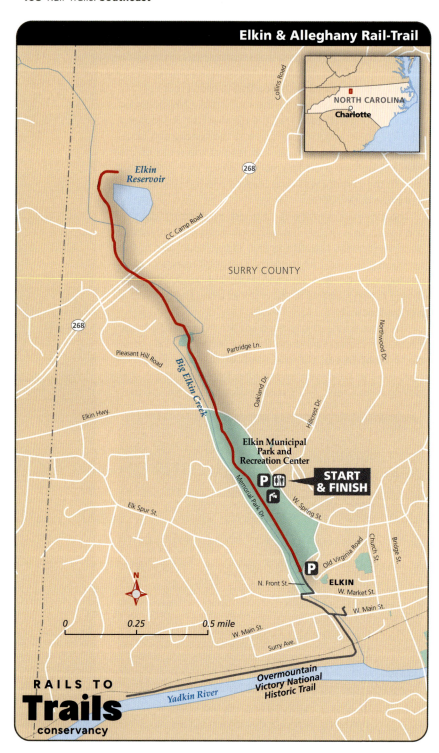

the park, which offers recreational activities such as swimming and tennis, plus restrooms, drinking water, and parking.

With old-growth trees providing shade, you'll cross two scenic bridges over the creek and ascend a hill just north of Elkin Reservoir, a small body of water that is visible from the trail. Along the way, the trail passes by a popular stopping point at a concrete dam and waterfall, located 0.3 mile from the municipal park, that dates back to the late 1800s. The dam is a remnant of the shoe and textile industries that once operated in Elkin. Other rail-trail highlights include educational displays and a "dog watering" spring that emerges from the rocks along the trail.

The trail ends at a split-rail fence at the property line near the reservoir. (Water recreation is not allowed because the reservoir serves as a municipal water source.)

For more adventure, about 7 miles of mountain-biking trails branch off the rail-trail, offering a more challenging option. Additionally, a section of the 330-mile Overmountain Victory National Historic Trail starts in Elkin Municipal Park and heads south before turning west and following the route of the Yadkin River.

The rail-trail is also part of a larger effort to connect Elkin with Stone Mountain State Park about 20 miles northwest. A projected completion date for the entire connector trail has yet to be determined, although small sections of the trail have been completed in rural areas as rights-of-way have become available. In total, about 9.5 miles of the route are open, including the rail-trail.

CONTACT: elkinvalleytrails.org/e-a-rail-trail

PARKING

Parking areas are located in Elkin and are listed from south to north. *Indicates that at least one accessible parking space is available.*

N. FRONT ST.: Just south of Elkin Municipal Park (36.2456, -80.8569).

ELKIN MUNICIPAL PARK*: 399 NC 268 W. (36.2494, -80.8596).

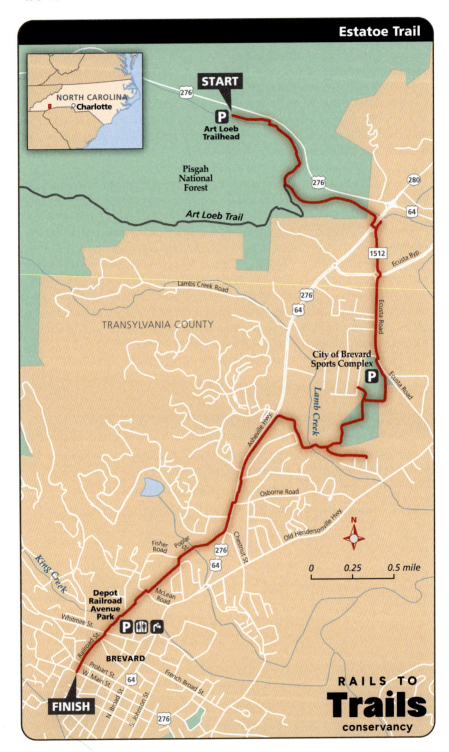

Estatoe Trail

START

276

P
Art Loeb
Trailhead

Pisgah
National
Forest

Art Loeb Trail

276

280

64

1512

Ecusta Byp.

Lambs Creek Road

276

64

TRANSYLVANIA COUNTY

City of Brevard
Sports Complex

P

Ecusta Road

Lamb Creek

Ecusta Road

Asheville Hwy.

Osborne Road

Old Hendersonville Hwy.

N

Fisher
Road

Poplar St.

276

64

Chestnut St.

0   0.25   0.5 mile

King Creek

Depot
Railroad
Avenue
Park

McLean Road

P

Whitmire St.

BREVARD

Probart St.

64

French Broad St.

FINISH

W. Main St.

N. Broad St.

S. Johnson St.

Railroad St.

276

NORTH CAROLINA
Charlotte

RAILS TO
Trails
conservancy

Estatoe Trail

The Estatoe Trail traverses 5.6 miles through Brevard. Some may want to forgo the northernmost segment between the Art Loeb Trailhead and NC 280/US 64, which has a rough gravel surface unlike the rest of the trail, which has a paved surface. The trailhead provides a connection to the Art Loeb Trail, a 30-mile hiking trail through Pisgah National Forest.

Begin the main, paved section of the Estatoe Trail on the east side of NC 280/US 64, where the highway meets County Road 1512/Ecusta Road. Head south, paralleling the roadway. In 0.2 mile, you'll hit a busy traffic circle, where you'll need to use caution. From the traffic circle, it's 0.5 mile to the City of Brevard Sports Complex, which provides playing fields, a skate park, and parking. If arriving by car, the complex may be the best location to begin your trip. The complex also includes the Jameson's Joy Memorial Fitness Park and a "story walk" for younger visitors.

Beyond the sports complex, you will be rewarded with a more nature-based experience, as well as a crossing over

ANYA SARETZKY

A beautiful native-plant garden along the trail serves as a Monarch Waystation.

County
Transylvania

Endpoints
Art Loeb Trailhead at Sycamore Cir. and Davidson River Campground Dr. (Pisgah National Forest); W. Main St., between Galloway St. and S. Oaklawn Ave. (Brevard)

Mileage
5.6

Type
Rail-Trail

Roughness Rating
1–2

Surface
Asphalt, Boardwalk, Concrete, Gravel

Lamb Creek. The corridor has been designated part of the North Carolina Birding Trail. Information is posted about the numerous species that make use of the local habitat, including turkey vultures, black vultures, peregrine falcons, ospreys, barred owls, and red-tailed hawks.

After this short reverie, you will find yourself back on a busy road—US 276/ US 64/Asheville Highway. Less than a mile after leaving the sports complex, the trail continues across the highway, so be sure to use caution. A number of businesses are present here if you need refreshments or supplies. The trail skirts behind this commercial landscape and transitions into a short boardwalk surrounded by a sliver of nature.

Next, the trail is routed briefly on-road through a quiet residential neighborhood. Take Poplar Street for one block, make a left onto County Road 1356/ Fisher Road, and turn right to get back on the trail. Cross CR 1356/McLean Road and continue on the trail as it parallels Railroad Avenue. Here you will find Depot Railroad Avenue Park, the highlight of the trail. The park incorporates elements of the original depot, which was demolished in 1981 after railroad traffic subsided in the 1970s. Today, the park serves as an excellent rest station for trail users, including shaded seating, restrooms, water fountains, parking, and a beautiful native-plant garden that serves as a Monarch Waystation. Enjoy the pleasant bridge crossing over King Creek. After the park, cross Railroad Avenue to continue through an industrial but quiet section of the route.

The trail ends at West Main Street, a few blocks from downtown Brevard. Plans are in the works to extend the trail from here to several unconnected segments, for a future total of roughly 7.5 miles. Plans include connecting the trail to the new Mary C. Jenkins Community Center, the Cadence Point neighborhood, and a 1-mile existing segment along CR 1118/Gallimore Road that was built in 2010 using a Safe Routes to School grant to connect Brevard's elementary and high schools.

CONTACT: conservingcarolina.org/friends-of-brevard-area-trails

PARKING

Parking areas are listed from north to south. *Indicates that at least one accessible parking space is available.*

PISGAH NATIONAL FOREST: Art Loeb Trailhead at Sycamore Cir. and Davidson River Campground Dr. (35.2820, -82.7215).

BREVARD*: City of Brevard Sports Complex, 324 Ecusta Road (35.2600, -82.7060).

BREVARD*: Depot Railroad Avenue Park, 390 Railroad Ave. (35.2410, -82.7334).

Located in the Land of the Sky, along the west bank of one of the oldest rivers in the world, is the French Broad River Greenway. The river is estimated to be 260–325 million years old and winds more than 200 miles, linking to the Holston, Mississippi, Ohio, and Tennessee Rivers. Though the paved greenway does not follow the river across the state line, its 4.3-mile route provides access to the waterway as well as other natural spaces, all within the city of Asheville. For information on the French Broad River, including access points and water quality updates, visit **riverlink .org/french-broad-river** or **frenchbroadpaddle.com.**

From the trail's southern end, visitors can begin in Hominy Creek River Park, with plenty of shade, river access for boaters, and places to picnic. Approximately 1 mile north, the trail reaches a riverfront RV park, where the route of the public path is outlined on the asphalt surface and marked so users can avoid wandering onto private property. Within a quarter mile, trail users are greeted by the 30-acres-plus Carrier Park, one of the city's premier parks, with volleyball courts; a large play area; multiuse fields; a roller hockey rink; parking; restrooms; a pavilion; an interpretive wetland area; and, uniquely, a velodrome, or cycling track. The oval

County
Buncombe

Endpoints
French Broad River Greenway: Hominy Creek River Park at Hominy Creek Road (Asheville); Craven St. and CR 1338/Emma Road (Asheville) *Wilma Dykeman Greenway:* NC 251/Riverside Dr. and NC 251/ Hill St. (Asheville); Lyman St. and Amboy Road (Asheville)

Mileage
French Broad River Greenway: 4.3 *Wilma Dykeman Greenway:* 2.2

Type
Greenway/ Non-Rail-Trail

Roughness Rating
1

Surface
Asphalt

SUZANNE MATYAS

The French Broad River Greenway offers access to Hominy Creek Park, Carrier Park, and the RiverLink.

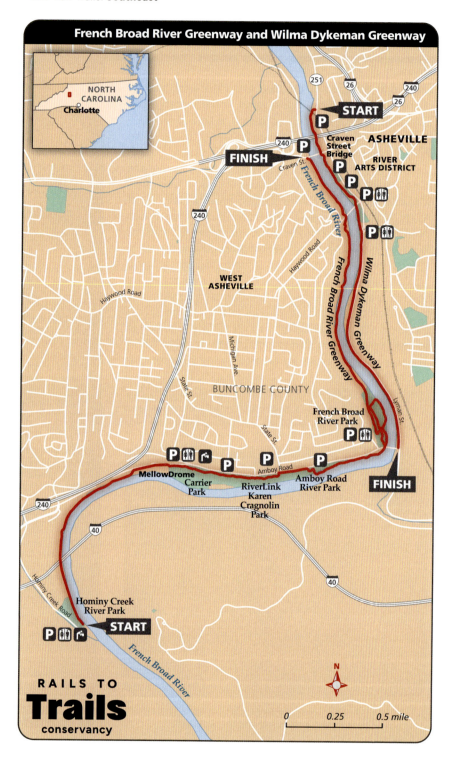

French Broad River Greenway and Wilma Dykeman Greenway

NORTH CAROLINA

Charlotte

START

Craven
Street
Bridge

ASHEVILLE

RIVER
ARTS
DISTRICT

FINISH

Craven St.

French Broad River

240

WEST
ASHEVILLE

Haywood Road

French Broad River Greenway

Wilma Dykeman Greenway

Haywood Road

Michigan Ave.

BUNCOMBE COUNTY

State St.

Lyman St.

State St.

French Broad
River Park

FINISH

MellowDrome

Carrier
Park

Amboy Road

RiverLink
Karen
Cragnolin
Park

Amboy Road
River Park

240

40

Hominy Creek Road

Hominy Creek
River Park

START

French Broad River

40

RAILS TO
Trails
conservancy

N

0   0.25   0.5 mile

track—nicknamed the MellowDrome—rests on the former Asheville speedway, which was a stock car racing track from 1960 to 1999, until the land was donated to the city. Signage and a memorial remind visitors of the velodrome's past. In addition to cycling, it also offers dedicated lanes for pedestrians, scooter riders, and in-line skaters.

Following Carrier Park is RiverLink Karen Cragnolin Park, an approximately 5-acre green space that used to be a junkyard. It's named in honor of the founder of RiverLink, a nonprofit that focuses on the economic and environmental vitality of the French Broad River watershed and supports several other projects along the river. After traveling 0.5 mile, users will approach French Broad River Park, which provides more tree-lined shade, parking, restrooms, recreational facilities, and a fenced-in dog park.

The trail continues to trace the west bank of the river as it proceeds north, passing power lines and encountering some slight inclines, until it reaches the turnoff to a trailside brewery. Just beyond is the greenway's endpoint at Craven Street, where there is parking for bikes and cars, educational signage, and a timeline display that highlights the history of the river and its role in the community.

The French Broad River Greenway is a part of Asheville's growing system of greenways, which includes the neighboring 2.2-mile Wilma Dykeman Greenway. This paved path runs along the east bank of the river and the edge of Asheville's colorful River Arts District. While not connected, the two greenways parallel each other and are both accessible via a sidewalk over the Craven Street bridge.

Wilma Dykeman was an Asheville-area native who was a celebrated author, activist, speaker, and teacher. Her award-winning first book, *The French Broad*, published in 1955, shared stories of the French Broad River's past and examined its relationship with economic development and pollution, a controversial topic at the time.

Decades of serving as an industrial and trade hub for the region contributed to the degradation of the river's health. By the 1980s and 1990s, however, efforts to restore the river began to gain momentum. Dykeman's message about economic opportunity through stewardship is often credited as a catalyst for this change. In 2004, the city approved the Wilma Dykeman RiverWay Plan, which was designed to redevelop the urban corridor between the French Broad and Swannanoa Rivers. In 2015, the city announced its River Arts District Improvement Project, which brought significant investment to revamping the area, including its greenways.

Officially opened and dedicated to Wilma Dykeman in 2021, the greenway provides visitors a way to experience nature as well as the restaurants, art studios, and other businesses of the River Arts District via an accessible, lighted, well-signed route. This short but sweet trail offers several parking areas. Users may prefer to begin their trip at the one beneath I-240/I-26, as it provides plenty of space to park cars and bikes. From here, a quick quarter-mile trip brings visitors to the greenway's northern endpoint, where waterside eateries can be found. Venturing south, visitors can experience the greenway's public art, benches and rest areas, educational pollinator garden, river access via a boat ramp and steps, and two-way protected bike lane. Plans are underway to extend the Wilma Dykeman Greenway and connect it to other local trails.

CONTACT: ashevillenc.gov/service/enjoy-greenways

PARKING

Parking areas are located within Asheville. *Indicates that at least one accessible parking space is available.*

French Broad River Greenway (south to north):

HOMINY CREEK RIVER PARK*: 220 Hominy Creek Road (35.5547, -82.5910).

CARRIER PARK (MELLOWDROME)*: Amboy Road, 0.2 mile west of Short Michigan Ave. (35.5662, -82.5822).

CARRIER PARK*: Amboy Road and Short Michigan Ave. (35.5660, -82.5777).

RIVERLINK KAREN CRAGNOLIN PARK: Amboy Road and Midnight Dr. (35.5668, -82.5714).

AMBOY ROAD RIVER PARK*: 180 Amboy Road (35.5674, -82.5692).

FRENCH BROAD RIVER PARK*: Riverview Dr. and Amboy Road (35.5699, -82.5652).

CRAVEN ST.*: Craven St. and CR 1338/Emma Road (35.5895, -82.5727).

Wilma Dykeman Greenway (north to south):

BENEATH I-240/I-26*: Riverside Dr. (35.5909, -82.5716).

RIVERSIDE DR. AND CRAVEN ST.*: 199 Riverside Dr. (35.5894, -82.5708).

RIVERSIDE DR., BETWEEN CRAVEN ST. AND HAYWOOD ROAD: 117 Riverside Dr. (35.5878, -82.5698).

Irwin Creek Greenway and Stewart Creek Greenway

51

The Irwin Creek and Stewart Creek Greenways connect a handful of parks and other popular recreational amenities in Charlotte's West End. Currently, this greenway system is open in two disconnected segments that together offer 4.2 miles of paved pathway. The greenways are also part of the Carolina Thread Trail, a developing trail network that will span more than 1,600 miles across the Carolinas.

To access the slightly longer, northern segment, begin at Ray's Splash Planet, a public indoor water park and recreational facility with available parking. From there, you'll travel on the Irwin Creek Greenway through a leafy corridor along the Irwin Creek, tunneling under major streets for

County
Mecklenburg

Endpoints
Irwin Creek Greenway: Ray's Splash Planet at N. Sycamore St. and W. Sixth St. (Charlotte); S. Cedar St., between W. First St. and Westmere Ave. (Charlotte); Freedom Dr. and Woodruff Pl. (Charlotte); Seversville Neighborhood Park at State St., 125 feet west of S. Turner Ave. (Charlotte) *Stewart Creek Greenway:* Revolution Park Dr. and West Blvd. (Charlotte); Clanton Park at Clanton Road and Golden Ridge Lane (Charlotte)

Mileage
4.2

Type
Rail-Trail/ Greenway/ Non-Rail-Trail

Roughness Rating
1

Surface
Asphalt, Concrete

SCOTT STARK

The Irwin Creek Greenway traces a leafy corridor along the creek.

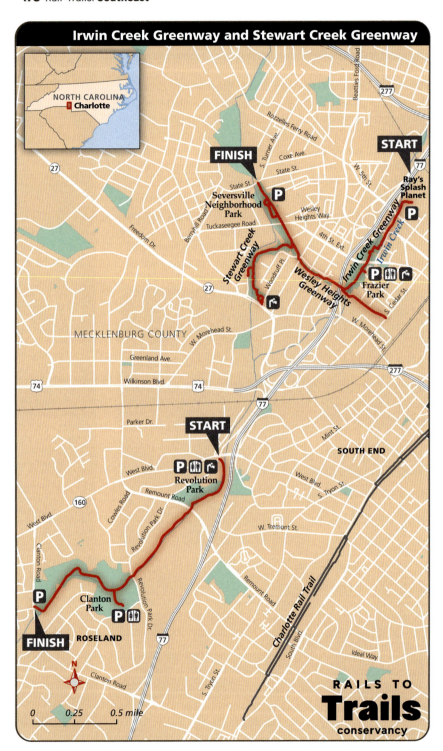

Irwin Creek Greenway and Stewart Creek Greenway

NORTH CAROLINA
Charlotte

FINISH

START

Ray's
Splash
Planet

Seversville
Neighborhood
Park

Berryhill Road
Freedom Dr.

Tuckaseegee Road

Stewart Creek
Greenway

Wesley Heights
Greenway

Irwin Creek Greenway

Frazier
Park

S. Turner Ave.
Coxe Ave.
State St.
State St.
Rozzelles Ferry Road
Beatties Ford Road
277
77
W. 5th St.
Wesley
Heights Way
4th St. Ext.
S. Cedar St.
Woodruff Pl.

MECKLENBURG COUNTY

W. Morehead St.
W. Morehead St.

Greenland Ave.

Wilkinson Blvd.

74
74
277
77

Parker Dr.

START

Revolution
Park

West Blvd.
West Blvd.
Remount Road
Cowles Road
Revolution Park Dr.
Revolution Park Dr.

160

West Blvd.

Clanton Road

Clanton
Park

FINISH

ROSELAND

SOUTH END

Mint St.
W. Tryon St.
S. Tryon St.
W. Tremont St.
Remount Road
South Blvd.
Ideal Way

Charlotte Rail Trail

Clanton Road

S. Tryon St.

N

0   0.25   0.5 mile

RAILS TO
Trails
conservancy

safe, easy commuting. In 0.3 mile, you'll reach the entrance to Frazier Park at a pedestrian bridge crossing the creek. The park offers basketball and tennis courts, athletic fields, picnic benches, and a dog park, plus drinking fountains and another parking lot. A unique feature here is a children's memorial park, which includes sculptures of children at play and a brick walkway inscribed with the names of children who have died in the city.

In 0.4 mile, the trail splits at the I-77 underpass. Turn left to take a 0.3-mile spur southeast, mostly following a large parking lot, to a commercial corridor along South Cedar Street with a view of the city's stadium in the distance. Or keep going along the main path and you'll head through the Wesley Heights Greenway, named for the neighborhood it traverses. Cutting through a utility corridor, this section is more open than other parts of the trail; turn around for views of the city skyline behind you. A disused CSX railroad track also parallels the trail to your right. Along the way, you'll cross a handful of lightly trafficked streets with well-marked crosswalks.

In 0.4 mile, you'll reach a juncture with the Stewart Creek Greenway on the left. This wooded, 0.5-mile spur leads to a trailhead with benches, a bike rack, and a drinking fountain at the intersection of Freedom Drive and Woodruff Place. If you instead continue straight at the juncture, you'll travel 0.4 mile northwest through Seversville Neighborhood Park on a route dotted with public art and picnic benches, reaching the trail's end at State Street.

In the Wesley Heights neighborhood, the greenway
offers views of the Charlotte skyline.

SCOTT STARK

To access the southern segment of the greenway, begin at Revolution Park, about 2 miles away from the northern segment, just northeast of where Revolution Park Drive intersects with Brentwood Place. At the park, you'll find plentiful parking, restrooms, and drinking fountains. From the parking lot, the pathway immediately splits; keep right to head southwest and experience the majority of this trail segment. (A short, 0.3-mile section of trail is to your left, heading north to the intersection of Revolution Park Drive and West Boulevard, but the only amenity at this end of the trail is a drinking fountain.)

Heading southwest, you'll pass under Remount Road and follow the paved pathway through the wooded Irwin Creek valley, past athletic fields and a golf course, with only one street crossing at Revolution Park Drive. In 1.2 miles, you'll enter Clanton Park in Charlotte's Roseland neighborhood. The park offers a playground and athletic facilities, including several basketball courts, as well as restrooms and parking. In another 0.7 mile, you'll reach the trail's end at Clanton Road.

CONTACT: parkandrec.mecknc.gov/places-to-visit/greenways

PARKING

Parking areas are located within Charlotte and are listed from north to south. *Indicates that at least one accessible parking space is available.*

RAY'S SPLASH PLANET*: 215 N. Sycamore St. (35.2377, -80.8522).

FRAZIER PARK: Greenleaf Ave., 300 feet southwest of Westbrook Dr. (35.2319, -80.8572).

SEVERSVILLE NEIGHBORHOOD PARK*: 530 S. Bruns Ave. (35.2390, -80.8663).

REVOLUTION PARK*: 2433 Revolution Park Dr. (35.2146, -80.8764).

CLANTON PARK (DOROTHY DOORES WADDY PAVILION)*: 3132 Manchester Dr. (35.2055, -80.8845).

CLANTON PARK*: 1520 Clanton Road (35.2075, -80.8924).

Little Sugar Creek Greenway

52

Spanning more than 16 miles from the heart of bustling Charlotte, through the suburbs south of the city, and on to the state border between North and South Carolina, Mecklenburg County's Little Sugar Creek Greenway serves as both a recreational gem and a major transportation route. The greenway has a key place in the regional Cross Charlotte Trail, which stretches 30 miles across the county from Pineville at the state line to neighboring Cabarrus County in the north. It also plays a role in the expansive Carolina Thread Trail, a developing trail network that will span more than 1,600 miles across the Carolinas.

Connecting nearly a dozen parks, the trail has no shortage of access points, though to experience its full length, the best place to begin is in Charlotte's Cordelia Park, on

SCOTT STARK

The trail provides a rural feeling south of Charlotte, where you're likely to spot deer.

County
Mecklenburg

Endpoints
N. Brevard St., 300 feet southwest of Jordan Pl. (Charlotte); North Carolina–South Carolina state line, 100 feet east of Gilroy Dr. and Barclay Ct. (Pineville)

Mileage
16.4

Type
Greenway/Non-Rail-Trail

Roughness Rating
1

Surface
Asphalt, Concrete

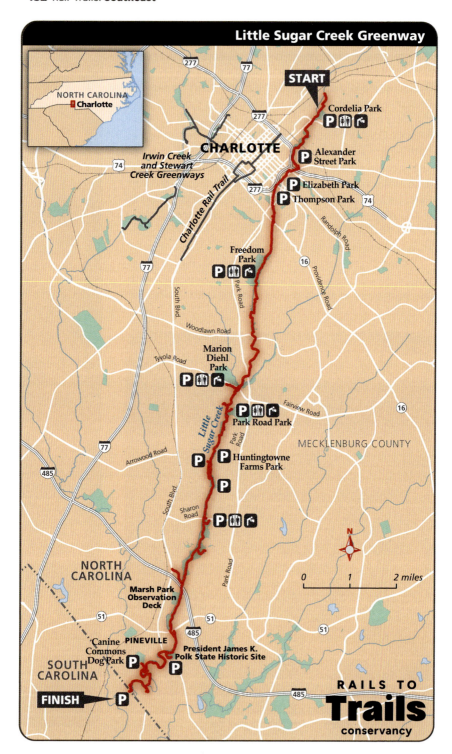

Little Sugar Creek Greenway

START

Cordelia Park

Alexander Street Park

Elizabeth Park

Thompson Park

CHARLOTTE

Irwin Creek and Stewart Creek Greenways

Charlotte Rail Trail

Freedom Park

Randolph Road

Providence Road

South Blvd

Woodlawn Road

Park Road

Tyvola Road

Marion Diehl Park

Little Sugar Creek

Park Road Park

Fairview Road

Park Road

MECKLENBURG COUNTY

Arrowood Road

Huntingtowne Farms Park

South Blvd

Sharon Road

NORTH CAROLINA

Marsh Park Observation Deck

PINEVILLE

Canine Commons Dog Park

President James K. Polk State Historic Site

SOUTH CAROLINA

FINISH

NORTH CAROLINA
Charlotte

0   1   2 miles

RAILS TO
Trails
conservancy

the northern end of the trail, where you'll find parking, drinking fountains, and restrooms, plus a public pool open in the summer months. (While the trail technically ends 0.4 mile farther north at North Brevard Street, there are no amenities available for trail users there.)

From Cordelia Park, you'll head southwest on a well-maintained, paved pathway in a parklike setting with residential housing, businesses, and city skyline views just beyond the trees. After 1.2 miles, you'll reach a short on-road section spanning about 800 feet. Beginning at the dead end of Cross Trail Drive—where a colorful piece of public art marks the end of this trail section—you'll take your first right onto Prospect Street, following the bright-green bike-route markings on the road. In one block, you'll take another right onto busy Central Avenue. You'll follow the marked bike lane separated from traffic by plastic bollards for one block, reaching the trail again after crossing East Seventh Street.

Within moments of getting back on the trail, you'll be greeted by the first of several trailside statues of historical figures from the past 250 years. Part of the city's Trail of History program (**charlottetrailofhistory.org**), their stories and contributions to the region are shared on plaques adjacent to the life-size figures.

Another highlight of the route occurs 1.8 miles farther, when you reach Freedom Park, centered around a 7-acre turquoise-blue lake. The park offers a vibrant place to enjoy the outdoors, with wide grassy fields, a large pavilion, and a bike-share station, plus restrooms, drinking fountains, and parking. At the southern end of the park, you'll exit onto Jameston Drive and take a 0.4-mile well-marked route along little-trafficked streets until you pick up the next section of trail at Irby Drive and Westfield Road.

For the next 2.3 miles to the Tyvola Road underpass, you'll be traveling through tree-filled suburban neighborhoods with occasional glimpses of Little Sugar Creek, which parallels the trail. After passing under Tyvola Road, you'll reach a short spur leading to Park Road Park with amenities for trail users and a plethora of athletic facilities.

For the final leg of your journey, the trail provides a peaceful, more rural feeling, and you're likely to spot deer in the underbrush. From Park Road Park, you'll reach the I-485 underpass and enter Pineville in 3.9 miles. Just beyond the underpass (in another 0.8 mile), you'll arrive at the Marsh Park Observation Deck; take a moment to look for birds and other wildlife in this beautiful wetland area. If you need a place to refresh and refuel, the Centrum Shopping Center, directly across from Marsh Park, offers a handful of restaurants.

For history buffs, a mile south of the observation deck you'll find a short spur to the left that will take you to the President James K. Polk State Historic Site (open Tuesday–Saturday). From there, the final 2.5 miles of trail twist and turn through the lushly wooded creek valley before ending in a parking lot on Gilroy Drive in a residential community at the (unmarked) state line.

CONTACT: parkandrec.mecknc.gov/places-to-visit/greenways

PARKING

Parking areas are listed from north to south. Select parking areas are listed below; for a detailed list of parking areas and other waypoints, consult **TrailLink™**. *Indicates that at least one accessible parking space is available.*

CHARLOTTE*: Cordelia Park, 600 E. 24th St. (35.2371, -80.8156).

CHARLOTTE*: Alexander Street Park, 739 E. 12th St. (35.2281, -80.8274).

CHARLOTTE*: Elizabeth Park, 101 N. Kings Dr. (35.2183, -80.8330).

CHARLOTTE*: Thompson Park, 1129 E. Third St. (35.2166, -80.8332).

CHARLOTTE*: Freedom Park, 1908 East Blvd. (35.1958, -80.8392).

CHARLOTTE*: Park Road Park, 6220 Park Road (35.1501, -80.8554).

CHARLOTTE*: Huntingtowne Farms Park, 2203 Huntingtowne Farms Lane (35.1364, -80.8634).

PINEVILLE*: Canine Commons Dog Park, 181 Lake Dr. (35.0762, -80.8936).

PINEVILLE: North Carolina–South Carolina state line, 100 feet east of Gilroy Dr. and Barclay Ct. (35.0679, -80.8988).

Little Tennessee River Greenway

53

From woods to wetlands to meadows, the 4.7-mile Little Tennessee River Greenway passes through a variety of habitats as it follows the scenic banks of the Little Tennessee River. Part of the North Carolina Birding Trail, it meanders along the river as it makes its way through the small city of Franklin. A network of dirt trails off the path offers a more strenuous experience for mountain bikers and hikers. Other features include a disc golf course, exercise stations, a monarch butterfly garden, a playground, and a splash pad. Plans call for adding about 1.5 miles to the greenway on its southern end to reach the Macon County Recreation Center.

Most sections of the greenway have Cherokee names to honor the Indigenous peoples who lived in three ancient villages that were located along the banks of the river. Other historical features include a section of the early-20th-century Tallulah Falls Railroad, as well as a section of an abandoned airport runway. In addition, a section called the Tartan Trail recalls early settlers from the 1700s.

Starting at the south end behind the Macon County Public Library, where restrooms are available, the trail passes by

COURTESY RITA C. ST. CLAIR

You'll experience a variety of habitats along the riverside trail.

County
Macon

Endpoints
1.1 miles southwest of Siler Road (Franklin); Arthur Drake Road and Riverview St. (Franklin)

Mileage
4.7

Type
Rail-Trail, Greenway/Non-Rail-Trail

Roughness Rating
1

Surface
Asphalt

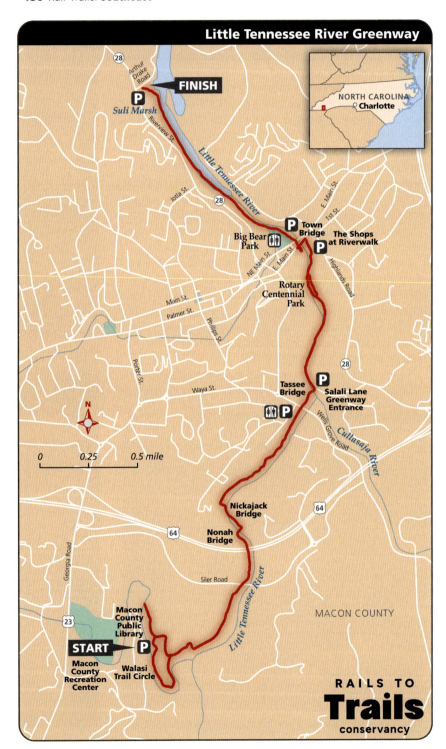

Little Tennessee River Greenway

the open meadow of the Walasi Trail Circle, where you'll be treated to sweeping views of the river and wildflowers in the field. Moving north on the Tartan Trail, the greenway passes by a community garden and part of the disc golf course before crossing the covered Nonah Bridge in 1.4 miles. Just 0.2 mile farther, you'll cross the river again on the 1890s steel-truss Nickajack Bridge.

Next up is a section of the Tallulah Falls Railroad Trail, which follows a train route that carried passengers between Franklin and Cornelia, Georgia, from 1907 to 1946. In 0.8 mile, you'll come upon the 120-foot-long wooden Tassee Bridge, which offers a picture-perfect view of the confluence of the Little Tennessee River and its tributary, the Cullasaja River. Restrooms are available at the Tassee Shelter. Here, the greenway heads north on the Old Airport Trace—a section consisting of about 2,700 feet (0.5 mile) of an old north–south airport runway used from 1946 to 1968.

As the greenway approaches The Shops at Riverwalk entrance, which is located 250 feet south of Main Street, Rotary Centennial Park offers exercise stations, a shelter, and a butterfly garden. After crossing back over the river on the Town Bridge, you'll come to the shelter, playground, splash pad, wetlands, and restrooms at Big Bear Park off Main Street. The final destination to the north—reached 1.1 miles after Big Bear Park—is the boardwalk of Suli Marsh, located at Arthur Drake Road and Riverview Street, where you'll find another parking area. *Suli* is the Cherokee word for vulture, and you might spot the imposing birds perched in the trees there on some mornings.

CONTACT: littletennessee.org

PARKING

Parking areas are located in Franklin and are listed from south to north. Select parking areas for the trail are listed below; for a detailed list of parking areas and other waypoints, consult **TrailLink™**. *Indicates that at least one accessible parking space is available.*

MACON COUNTY PUBLIC LIBRARY*: 149 Siler Farm Road (35.15982, -83.38231).

TASSEE SHELTER*: 803 Ulco Dr. (35.1738, -83.3720).

SALALI LANE GREENWAY ENTRANCE*: 0.3 mile west of Fox Ridge Road and Highlands Road (35.1755, -83.3699).

THE SHOPS AT RIVERWALK*: Highlands Road, 250 feet south of Main St. (35.1854, -83.3703).

FRIENDS OF THE GREENWAY HEADQUARTERS*: 573 E. Main St. (35.1857, -83.3722).

SULI LANE GREENWAY ENTRANCE*: Arthur Drake Road and Riverview St. (35.1967, -83.3871).

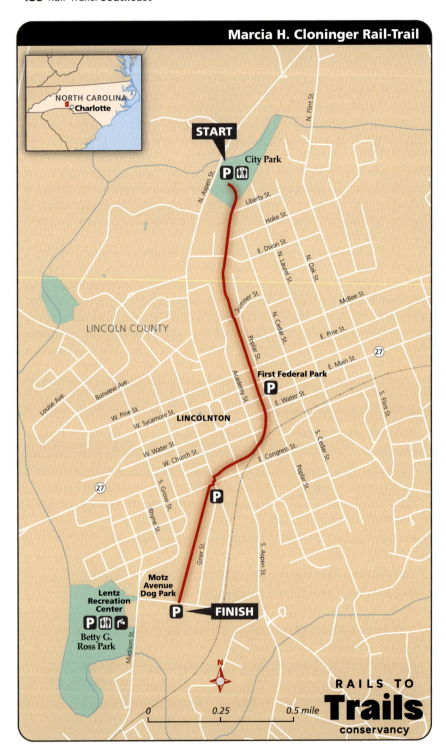

Marcia H. Cloninger Rail-Trail

NORTH CAROLINA

Charlotte

START

City Park

Liberty St.

Hoke St.

N. Flint St.

E. Dixon St.

N. Laurel St.

N. Oak St.

N. Aspen St.

Sumner St.

McBee St.

E. Pine St.

LINCOLN COUNTY

Poplar St.

N. Cedar St.

E. Main St.

27

Academy St.

First Federal Park

Louise Ave.

Bonview Ave.

E. Water St.

S. Flint St.

W. Pine St.

W. Sycamore St.

LINCOLNTON

E. Congress St.

S. Cedar St.

W. Water St.

Poplar St.

W. Church St.

27

S. Grove St.

Rhyne St.

Grier St.

S. Aspen St.

Motz Avenue Dog Park

Lentz Recreation Center

Madison St.

FINISH

Betty G. Ross Park

N

0   0.25   0.5 mile

RAILS TO

Trails

conservancy

Known locally as the Lincolnton Rail-Trail, the Marcia H. Cloninger Rail-Trail offers a chance to explore the heart of this small Southern town, highlighted by its stately courthouse, model Main Street, thriving arts scene, and nearby lakes and mountains. The former Norfolk Southern Railroad corridor is now the pride and joy of "Lovable Lincolnton." Paved the entire way, relatively flat, and with benches lining the route, the trail invites you to take in this enchanting town at a gentle pace.

Established in 2013, the trail was named in memory of Marcia Cloninger, the Lincolnton supporter who championed its cause and was instrumental in securing the funds to build it. The trail connects four city parks and is part of the Carolina Thread Trail, an expansive network that will eventually connect more than 1,600 miles of trails, greenways, and blueways across North and South Carolina.

Traveling north to south, the trail begins at City Park, where parking and restrooms are available. The first part of the trail primarily runs through neighborhoods, crossing East Dixon and Sumner Streets, both low-volume residential

COURTESY CITY OF LINCOLNTON

Paved the entire way and relatively flat, the trail offers a pleasant route through Lincolnton.

County
Lincoln

Endpoints
City Park at
N. Aspen St.
(Lincolnton);
Motz Avenue
Dog Park at Motz
Ave. (Lincolnton)

Mileage
1.7

Type
Rail-Trail/
Rail-with-Trail

**Roughness
Rating**
1

Surface
Asphalt

roads with crosswalks. In 0.6 mile, you'll reach First Federal Park, which offers a splash pad in the summer.

South of First Federal Park, you'll find highly detailed murals depicting railroad scenes on a few buildings between East Sycamore and South Academy Streets. The Catawba pottery tradition is also on display throughout downtown with large and whimsical face jugs. For those who wish to explore the rich history of Lincolnton, the Lincoln County Historical Association offers a self-guided walking tour of the downtown area on its website (**lincolncounty history.com/historic-walking-tour-of-lincolnton**).

A block south of East Sycamore Street, the trail heads under East Main Street. On the ceiling of the tunnel, an eagle soars, while butterfly wings adorn its walls. Up top, the street offers access to downtown shops and restaurants. South of East Main Street, the trail passes under East Water Street and South Aspen Street. In this section, the trail also briefly shares its corridor with an active CSX railroad line. The route continues through a wooded area from West Congress Street to its end at the Motz Avenue Dog Park.

Additional amenities, including a fishing pier, are available in Betty G. Ross Park, near the trail's southern end. From the dog park, travel west 0.2 mile along Motz Avenue (on the street or on the sidewalk) and cross Madison Avenue to reach the park, which has a recreation center, picnic areas, a swimming pool, basketball and tennis courts, and a disc golf course, as well as drinking fountains, parking, and restrooms.

CONTACT: ci.lincolnton.nc.us/550/our-parks-facilities

PARKING

Parking areas are located within Lincolnton and are listed from north to south.
Indicates that at least one accessible parking space is available.

CITY PARK*: 1000 N. Aspen St. (35.4823, -81.2567).

FIRST FEDERAL PARK*: 201 N. Poplar St. (35.4733, -81.2547).

W. CONGRESS STREET: 208 W. Congress St. (35.4677, -81.2573).

MOTZ AVENUE DOG PARK: 493 Motz Ave. (35.4624, -81.2595).

BETTY G. ROSS PARK*: 800 Madison St. (35.4620, -81.2627).

Muddy Creek Greenway

The Muddy Creek Greenway offers a fantastic opportunity west of Winston-Salem for visitors to explore 2.9 miles along the main paved route, as well as another mile of unpaved connecting spurs to five neighborhoods. Traveling from north to south, the trail gradually drops 62 feet over the nearly 3-mile distance, making for a nearly imperceptible downhill trip.

Jefferson Elementary School anchors the northern end of the trail. Here, you can take a brief side excursion following the blue paw prints found in the gravel parking lot next to the school's yellow gate. They'll take you to the Little Pet Chapel, where you'll find special spaces memorializing beloved pets with notes, photos, and cherished mementos. Pet treats are also often left by local animal lovers.

LYNN BYRD

On the north end of the trail, you can visit the Little Pet Chapel, next to Jefferson Elementary School.

County
Forsyth

Endpoints
Jefferson School Lane, 0.4 mile north of Robinhood Road (Winston-Salem); 200 feet southwest of Gramercy St. and Brookberry Dr. (Winston-Salem)

Length
4

Type
Greenway/
Non-Rail-Trail

Roughness Rating
1

Surface
Asphalt, Dirt

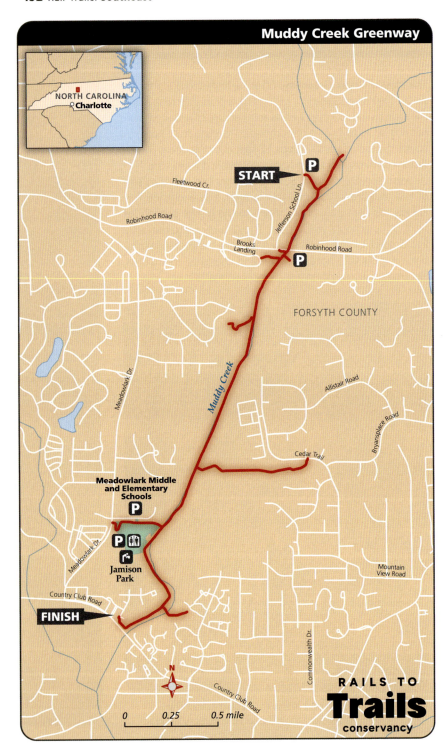

Muddy Creek Greenway

From the parking area along Jefferson Elementary School Lane, you'll travel south on the Muddy Creek Greenway, reaching an intersection in approximately 100 yards. The trail branching to the left (northeast) leads to privately owned trails for the Summerfield Community subdivision; keep right (heading south) to continue on the greenway.

Paralleling Muddy Creek, the trail is 10 feet wide and well shaded, providing a sense of seclusion that makes it easier to savor quiet moments. Look for year-round birds such as cardinals, chickadees, and woodpeckers. Trailside bluebird boxes also welcome nesting Eastern bluebirds in the spring. Wild turkeys occasionally appear in the fields among the treed landscape, too, particularly along the southern half of the greenway. Bridges cross the water multiple times, and flood prevention measures taken by the City of Winston-Salem have greatly reduced the amount of water on the trail.

In 0.4 mile, the greenway travels under Robinhood Road; 250 feet beyond this point, a connecting spur heads west to the Brooks Landing neighborhood. Continuing along the wooded area past this connector, it's approximately 0.3 mile to the next side trail leading west to another neighborhood. Within 0.5 mile, there is another connector leading east to Cedar Trail (a roadway).

In the final mile, there are two more connecting trails. One heads west to Jamison Park, which offers a spacious parking area, as well as restrooms, drinking fountains, picnic areas, and a dog park; this side trail also reaches Meadowlark Middle and Elementary Schools. Beyond Jamison Park, there is another connecting trail that leads southeast over a bridge crossing Muddy Creek and into residential neighborhoods. The greenway ends in the Brookberry Park neighborhood adjacent to Country Club Road.

CONTACT: cityofws.org/1014/muddy-creek-greenway

PARKING

Parking areas are located within Winston-Salem and are listed from north to south. *Indicates that at least one accessible parking space is available.*

JEFFERSON SCHOOL LANE: Jefferson School Lane, 0.4 mile north of Robinhood Road (36.1240, -80.3483).

ROBINHOOD ROAD*: 4600 Robinhood Road (36.1177, -80.3497).

JAMISON PARK*: 285 Meadowlark Dr. (36.0990, -80.3637).

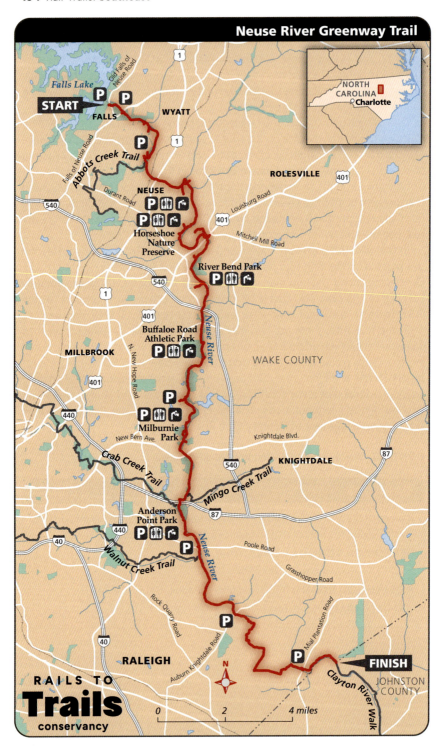

Neuse River Greenway Trail

NORTH CAROLINA

Charlotte

Falls Lake

Old Falls of Neuse Road

START

FALLS

WYATT

ROLESVILLE

Abbots Creek Trail

Falls of Neuse Road

NEUSE

Durant Road

Louisburg Road

Horseshoe Nature Preserve

Mitchell Mill Road

River Bend Park

Neuse River

Buffaloe Road Athletic Park

MILLBROOK

N. New Hope Road

WAKE COUNTY

Milburnie Park

New Bern Ave.

Knightdale Blvd.

Crab Creek Trail

KNIGHTDALE

Mingo Creek Trail

Anderson Point Park

Walnut Creek Trail

Poole Road

Neuse River

Grasshopper Road

Rock Quarry Road

Mial Plantation Road

RALEIGH

Auburn Knightdale Road

N

FINISH

Clayton River Walk

JOHNSTON COUNTY

RAILS TO
Trails
conservancy

0   2   4 miles

56

The Neuse River Greenway Trail runs along its namesake river for nearly 30 miles, from Falls Lake Dam in Wake Forest until it meets the Clayton River Walk at the Wake–Johnston county line. The trail follows the tree-lined banks with boardwalks, bridges, river access, and scenic views of the waterway.

The greenway is part of North Carolina's Mountains-to-Sea Trail, a long-distance trail network connecting the Great Smoky Mountains to the Outer Banks and Raleigh's Capital Area Greenway System. A portion of the trail, from Raleigh to Clayton, is also part of the East Coast Greenway, a growing network of multiuse trails connecting 15 states and 450 cities and towns on a 3,000-mile route between Maine and Florida.

Begin your journey at the Falls Lake Dam and take in the views of the river spilling out of the barrier as it makes its

RYAN CREE

Winding along the Neuse River, the trail traces the northeastern outskirts of Raleigh.

County
Wake

Endpoints
Old Falls of Neuse Road and Pleasant Union Church Road (Wake Forest); Clayton River Walk at the Wake–Johnston county line (Clayton)

Mileage
29.8

Type
Greenway/Non-Rail-Trail

Roughness Rating
1

Surface
Asphalt, Boardwalk, Concrete

way toward the Pamlico Sound on the Atlantic Coast. This is a popular recreational area with fishing, birding, and river access for canoes and kayaks. For those on bikes, a repair shop is just steps away from the main parking lot at the base of the dam.

Traveling south, you'll immediately follow the Neuse River, its forested banks providing shade in the summer heat. The trail passes under roadways and highways with ample opportunities for seeing deer and other wildlife. Occasional well-marked side paths connect to nearby neighborhoods, giving trail access to local recreation seekers and commuters.

After 2.8 miles, the trail intersects with the Abbots Creek Trail, which heads west. From that trail juncture, you'll reach a covered underpass beneath a rail bridge in 0.6 mile and, shortly thereafter, pass under Capital Boulevard (US 1).

The trail traces a sweeping oxbow between the 6- and 8-mile mark. Restrooms and water are available at the WRAL Fields recreational area to the right and at the Horseshoe Nature Preserve. Visit this gorgeous nature preserve by way of a suspension bridge and short side path to explore the natural and cultural heritage of the region. The greenway continues south under Louisburg Road (US 401). Side paths connect to several parks with restrooms, water fountains, and other amenities, including River Bend Park, Buffaloe Road Athletic Park, Milburnie Park, and Anderson Point Park.

Near mile marker 16, the trail passes by a site steeped in history. These rapids were an important fishing resource for Indigenous tribes dating back at least 8,000 years. Later, the site would house mills that were critical to the formation of Raleigh. The remains of the Milburnie Mill and Dam, which brought electricity to Raleigh in the early 1900s, can be seen at a viewing area just off the trail. A bridge takes you to River Beach, a popular recreational area with river access.

The greenway connects to the wider Capital Area Greenway Network by way of the Crab Creek Trail at Anderson Point Park (just past mile marker 17) and the Walnut Creek Trail (at mile marker 19). The pathway continues south under the cover of the riparian forest until just past Auburn Nightdale Road (approximately mile marker 22), where the trail diverges from the river along open farm fields and meadows before rejoining the river near the trail's southern endpoint at the Wake–Johnston county line. There, the trail seamlessly connects to the Clayton River Walk, which continues south along the Neuse River.

Closure Notice: During 2024, several sections of trail will be closed due to highway and utility projects and will include major detours. Be sure to get the latest updates at **raleighnc.gov/greenway-alerts.**

CONTACT: raleighnc.gov/parks/places/neuse-river-greenway-trail

PARKING

Parking areas are listed from north to south. Select parking areas are listed below; for a detailed list of parking areas and other waypoints, consult **TrailLink™.** *Indicates that at least one accessible parking space is available.*

WAKE FOREST*: Pleasant Union Church Road and Old Falls of Neuse Road (35.9401, -78.5806).

WAKE FOREST*: Falls of Neuse Canoe Launch, 12101 Old Falls of Neuse Road (35.9391, -78.5754).

RALEIGH*: Bedfordtown Dr. and Settle In Lane (35.9201, -78.5597).

RALEIGH*: 6100 Thornton Road (35.9020, -78.5402).

RALEIGH: WRAL Fields, 7700 Perry Creek Road (35.8858, -78.5433); the easternmost parking lot at the dead end of McGuire Dr. is closest to the trail.

RALEIGH*: Buffaloe Road Athletic Park, 5812 Buffaloe Road (35.8406, -78.5342); two parking lots are available near the trail on the eastern end of the park by baseball diamonds.

RALEIGH*: Buffaloe Road Aquatic Center, 5908 Buffaloe Road (35.8376, -78.5353).

RALEIGH*: 2900 Abington Lane (35.8158, -78.5429).

RALEIGH*: Milburnie Park, 5428 Allen Dr. (35.8013, -78.5409).

RALEIGH*: Anderson Point Park, 20 Anderson Point Dr. (35.7725, -78.5416).

RALEIGH*: Poole Road Park, 1721 Riverview Road (35.7548, -78.5335).

RALEIGH*: 3021 Auburn Nightdale Road (35.7255, -78.5146).

CLAYTON*: 6008 Mial Plantation Road (35.7040, -78.4780).

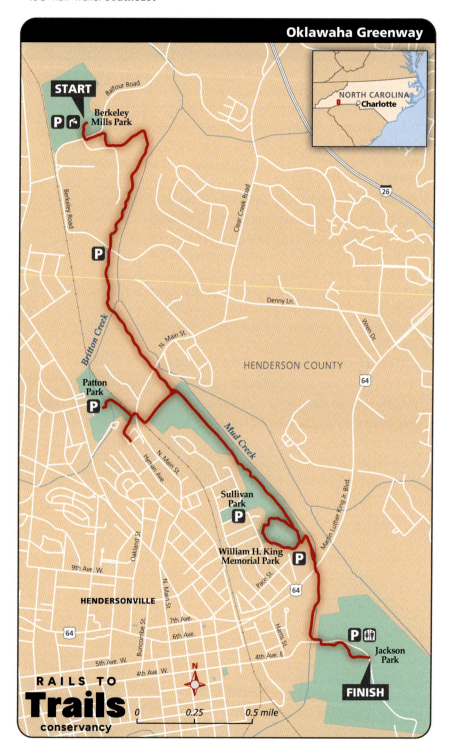

Oklawaha Greenway

START

Berkeley
Mills Park

Balfour Road

NORTH CAROLINA

Charlotte

26

Berkeley Road

Clear Creek Road

Denny Ln.

Wren Dr.

P

Britton Creek

N. Main St.

HENDERSON COUNTY

64

Patton
Park

P

Mud Creek

Hyman Ave.

N. Main St.

Sullivan
Park

P

William H. King
Memorial Park

P

Martin Luther King Jr. Blvd.

Pace St.

64

Oakland St.

9th Ave. W.

N. Main St.

HENDERSONVILLE

7th Ave.

6th Ave.

Buncombe St.

Harris St.

P

Jackson
Park

64

5th Ave. W.

4th Ave. W.

4th Ave. E.

FINISH

RAILS TO
Trails
conservancy

N

0   0.25   0.5 mile

Oklawaha Greenway

57

The Oklawaha Greenway gets its name from the Cherokee word *oklawaha,* meaning "slowly moving muddy waters." This is an accurate description, as the greenway runs along none other than the gently flowing Mud Creek. The 3.5-mile paved trail connects Berkeley Mills Park, Patton Park, and Jackson Park, all of which include parking and serve as good starting points for your journey. Jackson Park has the largest parking lot of the three.

Starting at Berkeley Mills Park, you will find an accessible parking lot with bike parking, a bike repair station, and a water fountain. The winding trail is smooth asphalt with a yellow stripe down the middle to guide visitors traveling from opposite directions and facilitate safe passing. Helpful signage directs visitors to the various parks along the route, and mile markers signal how far you are from each park. Educational signage along the trail teaches visitors about pollinator meadows, rain gardens, invasive species, and swamp forest habitats. Soon, three popular birding hot spots will be marked as well. Before crossing the bridge

ISABELLE LORD

Beginning from Berkeley Mills Park, the first mile of the greenway is surrounded by lush greenery.

County
Henderson

Endpoints
Berkeley Mills Park (Hendersonville); Jackson Park (Hendersonville)

Mileage
3.5

Type
Greenway/Non-Rail-Trail

Roughness Rating
1

Surface
Asphalt

above Britton Creek, you can read what the City of Hendersonville is doing to restore the creek bank.

After you cross the creek, a red kiosk pops up around the 1-mile mark. Take a moment to admire the labeled native-plant garden dedicated to Wes Burlingame in honor of his work with these plant species. The kiosk provides a map, benches, and a dog waste station. From here, you can leave the primary trail and head right toward Patton Park (note that a section of this route exceeds an 8% grade and may not be suitable for all trail users). If you continue toward Patton Park, you will need to cross North Main Street, then turn right by the automotive building.

If you decide to keep heading toward Jackson Park from the red kiosk, you will reach an optional loop that takes you around William H. King Memorial Park and puts you right back on the trail. Once finished with the loop, turn left at Seventh Avenue East, walk along the bridge, and cross Seventh Avenue East at the crosswalk to access the remainder of the trail.

After passing under US 64, you will need to cross Fourth Avenue East. This last section of the trail toward Jackson Park exceeds an 8% grade. Once you reach Jackson Park, you will find a parking lot, tennis courts, disc golf, baseball, and an inclusive playground.

CONTACT: friendsofoklawaha.org

PARKING

Parking areas are located within Hendersonville and are listed from north to south. *Indicates that at least one accessible parking space is available.*

BERKELEY MILLS PARK*: 69 Balfour Road (35.3484, -82.4697).

BERKELEY ROAD*: 415 Berkeley Road (35.3417, -82.4687).

PATTON PARK*: 59 E. Clairmont Dr. (35.3324, -82.4673).

WILLIAM H. KING MEMORIAL PARK*: 810 Robinson Terr. (35.3246, -82.4524).

JACKSON PARK*: 640 Glover St. (35.3185, -82.4466).

Point Lookout Trail

58

Located approximately 25 miles east of the vibrant city of Asheville, the Point Lookout Trail offers visitors the opportunity to be enveloped by nature as they travel through the dense woods of the Pisgah National Forest. The more than 500,000 acres of national forest are home to waterfalls, the country's first school of forestry, a variety of wildlife, and the highest peak of the Appalachian Mountains: Mount Mitchell.

The trail follows part of the route of the Old NC 10 (Central Highway)/Old US 70 West, which served as a main link between the Asheville area and the rest of the state before the road was closed to vehicular traffic in 1982. Years later, the North Carolina Department of Transportation funded converting the road into a paved greenway. Although most of the trail falls within the domain of the U.S. Forest Service, a small portion is clearly marked as private property; please respect these boundaries and do not stray from the trail in this area.

Visitors seeking a more physically strenuous journey can begin at the trail's eastern terminus in Old Fort, as the trail ascends more than 900 feet in elevation over its 3.6 miles. Those who are more interested in experiencing the trail with

SUZANNE MATYAS

Be enveloped by nature on a route through the Pisgah National Forest.

County
McDowell

Endpoints
CR 1407/Mill Creek Road/ Old US 70 W. (Ridgecrest); CR 1400/ Old US 70 W. (Old Fort)

Mileage
3.6

Type
Greenway/ Non-Rail-Trail

Roughness Rating
1

Surface
Asphalt

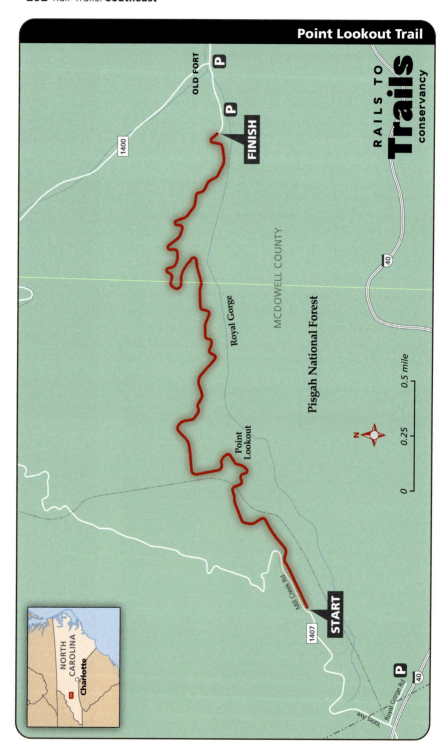

Point Lookout Trail

RAILS TO **Trails** conservancy

OLD FORT

1400

FINISH

McDOWELL COUNTY

Royal Gorge

Pisgah National Forest

N

0.5 mile

0.25

0

Point Lookout

START

1407

Mill Creek Rd

Royal Gorge Rd

Yates Ave

40

NORTH CAROLINA

Charlotte

the assistance of gravity, however, should start uphill at the western terminus in Ridgecrest.

At the Ridgecrest terminus, a gate blocks unauthorized motor vehicles, but hikers, walkers, runners, and bicyclists can go around it. From there, the trail descends through lush hardwood forest, punctuated with breaks in the trees that grant glimpses of sweeping vistas of the surrounding verdant slopes.

After approximately three-quarters of a mile, the trail encounters a Norfolk Southern railroad corridor stretching below, providing an over-the-shoulder view of rail tracks approaching a tunnel. Soon after, the trail opens up to its most noteworthy stop: Point Lookout. In addition to the dazzling overlook, you'll find benches to rest and informational signs detailing the point's history as a tourist destination.

The remainder of the trail continues to wind downhill, treating you to more views of the Royal Gorge and the natural beauty of the mountains. The Point Lookout Trail is part of the Fonta Flora State Trail, a developing 100-mile trail system that will connect the cities of Morganton and Asheville and provide access to other destinations and trail networks.

CONTACT: rtc.li/mcdowell-county

PARKING

Parking areas are listed from west to east. *Indicates that at least one accessible parking spot is available.*

RIDGECREST: Kitsuma Trail parking lot, 209 Royal Gorge Road (35.6212, -82.2685). The parking lot is 1 mile from the upper gate of the Point Lookout Trail. To reach the trail from the parking lot, follow Royal Gorge Road west to its intersection with Yates Avenue; turn right on Yates Avenue, which becomes Mill Creek Road, and follow the roadway to the trail entrance. Use caution as there are no bike lanes on these roads.

OLD FORT: CR 1400/Old US 70 W. (35.6347, -82.2235); the parking lot is shared with the Piney Grove Baptist Church, so parking is limited during church services on Sunday.

OLD FORT: Old Fort Picnic Grounds, 2415 CR 1400 (35.6354, -82.2192).

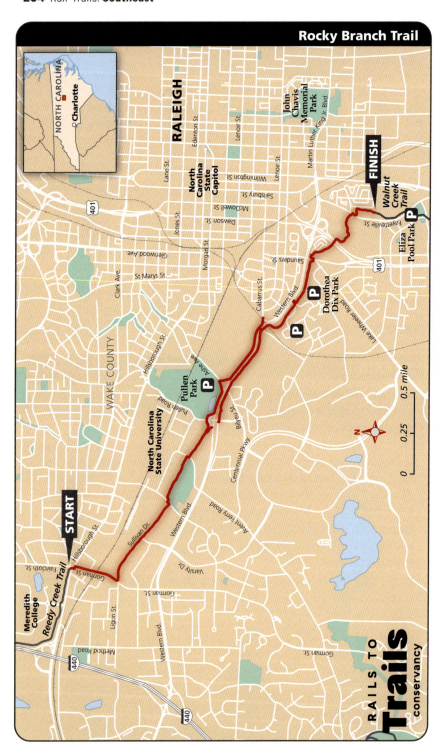

Rocky Branch Trail

Rocky Branch Trail

59

Running through the heart of North Carolina State University, the Rocky Branch Trail serves as a commuter route for the 35,000-student campus, the largest in the state. Although less than 4 miles long, the paved trail extends its reach as one of 28 trails in the Capital Area Greenway System, which covers more than 100 miles in the Raleigh area along protected stream corridors. Connections with the greenway system can be found at the junction with the Reedy Creek Trail in the west and the Walnut Creek Trail in the east. It also makes up a short section of the East Coast Greenway, a growing network of multiuse trails connecting 15 states and 450 cities and towns on a 3,000-mile route between Maine and Florida.

The trail roughly follows Rocky Branch from Meredith College, a private women's undergrad college and coed grad school, in the west to a cemetery south of downtown Raleigh. Along the way, it passes several athletic fields associated with NC State, as well as two large public parks. The trail is ADA accessible, with a slight but steady downhill slope from west to east.

RYAN CREE

The trail provides a pleasant route through Raleigh largely following the wooded corridor of Rocky Branch.

County
Wake

Endpoints
Reedy Creek Trail at Hillsborough St., Gorman St. and Faircloth St. (Raleigh); Walnut Creek Trail between Keeter Center Dr. and Fayetteville St. (Raleigh)

Mileage
3.8

Type
Greenway/Non-Rail-Trail

Roughness Rating
1

Surface
Asphalt

Starting in the east at Reedy Creek Trail, the trail crosses the intersection of Hillsborough Street at Faircloth Street and continues south as a side path along Gorman Street for 0.3 mile to a left turn at Sullivan Drive into the NC State campus, founded in 1887. The trail continues for 1.3 miles across campus, first adjacent to Sullivan Drive, then as a greenway past the college baseball field, dorms, gymnasium, intramural athletic fields, and Paul Derr Track Facility.

At Pullen Road, the trail leaves the campus and begins a segment along both the north and south sides of Western Boulevard. The segment on the northern side traces the border of Pullen Park for 0.3 mile. The 66-acre public park was also founded in 1887 and over the years served as an amusement park. In addition to picnic shelters, a performance venue, and an aquatic center, the park features a miniature train, paddleboats, kiddie boats, and a historic carousel.

The segment of the trail on the south side of Western Boulevard runs through the more than 300-acre Dorothea Dix Park. Dix, an advocate for the mentally ill, lobbied for construction of a hospital that opened here in 1856. The facility closed in 2012, and the city acquired a portion of the sprawling grounds for use as a park. You can take a guided walking tour here and participate in seasonal events.

The trail concludes with a 0.7-mile stretch through a wooded section that ends after passing the Mt. Hope Cemetery, a historic African American cemetery. At Keeter Center Drive, the trail meets the 18-mile Walnut Creek Trail, which runs east–west.

CONTACT: raleighnc.gov/places/rocky-branch-greenway

PARKING

Parking areas are located within Raleigh and are listed from east to west. *Indicates that at least one accessible parking space is available.*

PULLEN PARK*: 520 Ashe Ave. (35.7790, -78.6628).

DOROTHEA DIX PARK: Tate Dr., 225 feet east of S. Boylan Ave. (35.7709, -78.6529); small lot.

DOROTHEA DIX PARK: Richardson Dr., 0.3 mile southwest of Western Blvd. on Tate Dr. to Richardson Dr. (35.7712, -78.6561).

Salem Creek Greenway

60

Connecting downtown Winston-Salem to historical points of interest in town, as well as more natural settings, the 5.2-mile Salem Creek Greenway is a favorite experience among residents and visitors. The trail is fully paved and, for the most part, has a gentle grade with a gradual climb of approximately 210 feet when traveling from west to east. There is a notable hill, however, which increases nearly 100 feet over a mile, at Salem Lake on the trail's eastern end.

The west end of the trail begins at the Marketplace Mall parking lot and, in 0.4 mile, arrives at the 75-acre Washington Park. With parking, restrooms, drinking fountains, a dinosaur-themed playground, and a dog park, Washington Park is also an excellent place to start your journey along the greenway.

From the park, you'll arrive at the Gateway Nature Preserve, an oasis on the edge of town, in 0.5 mile. After passing the information kiosk, you'll find a "story circle," which is

Between Reynolds Park and Salem Lake,
the greenway traverses a densely wooded area.

TRAILLINK USER K8MKC2MD6R

County
Forsyth

Endpoints
Northeast corner of the Marketplace Mall parking lot, 0.3 mile northeast of Peters Creek Pkwy. (Winston-Salem); Salem Lake Park (Winston-Salem)

Mileage
5.2

Type
Greenway/Non-Rail-Trail

Roughness Rating
1

Surface
Asphalt

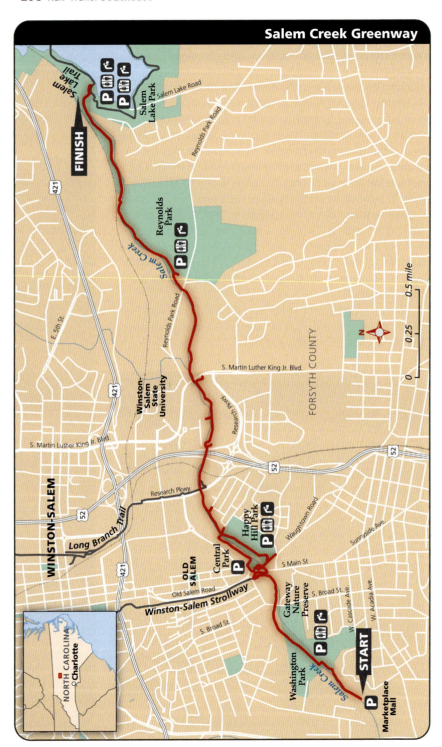

Salem Creek Greenway

a gathering spot for presentations, on the right-hand side of the greenway; on your left is the Forest Discovery Trail. Just beyond the Forest Discovery Trail, another side trail on the right leads to a sandy beach along Salem Creek. It's definitely worthwhile to stop and explore this beautiful area, including visiting the pollinator garden on the eastern edge of the preserve.

As you leave the Gateway Nature Preserve, the trail crosses South Broad Street and reaches a small roundabout near an apartment complex in 0.3 mile. From here, there is an option to turn left and head northwest, following the Winston-Salem Strollway, a 1.2-mile trail that travels through Old Salem and quiet neighborhoods. Another option is to cross the pedestrian bridge on your right to reach South Main Street. To stay on the Salem Creek Greenway, continue straight at the roundabout. The trail will arrive at another traffic circle in 0.1 mile; turn right at the circle, traveling south along South Main Street until you come to an underpass that safely takes you beneath the busy street.

After the South Main Street underpass, the trail enters Happy Hill Park, the oldest Black neighborhood in Winston-Salem, which is now a regional park. The site was originally used as the town plantation and slave quarters until its people were freed in 1836. After the Civil War, the first school for Blacks in Winston-Salem was established in 1867 and, by the early 1870s, freed slaves made Happy Hill their home. Today, visitors can enjoy the children's play area, recreation area, splash pad, and picnic shelters at Happy Hill Park. Restrooms, drinking fountains, and parking are also available here.

On the north side of Happy Hill Park, there is a side trail heading northwest toward Central Park on the other side of Salem Creek, where there are tennis courts and a parking area. Exiting Happy Hill Park and continuing east, the Salem Creek Greenway arrives at an underpass for Research Parkway in 0.3 mile. About 250 feet beyond the underpass, there's an option to connect with the Long Branch Trail, a 1.7-mile rail-trail that traverses the Wake Forest Innovation Quarter, a live-work-play district with more than 100 companies and five academic institutions.

Continuing east another 0.1 mile, the greenway passes under the John Gold Memorial Expressway/US 52 and travels through a wooded area north of Winston-Salem State University's football field. Exiting the campus, the trail heads under South Martin Luther King Jr. Drive and reaches Reynolds Park Road in 0.6 mile. On the east side of the road, Reynolds Park offers a parking area with restrooms and drinking fountains, as well as a playground, a swimming pool, and picnic areas.

Beyond Reynolds Park, the greenway traverses a wooded area for another mile before ending on the west side of Salem Lake. Just before reaching the lakeshore, you'll be able to connect with the Salem Lake Trail (see page 211), which offers outstanding views of the lake on a 7-mile loop around it. Parking, restrooms, and drinking fountains are available at the Salem Lake Marina Center and Salem Lake Playground.

Caution: The eastern end of the trail, between Reynolds Park and Salem Lake, is prone to flooding during extreme rain events, so call the Salem Lake Marina Center (336-650-7677) to check trail conditions before you head out.

CONTACT: cityofws.org/827/recreation-parks

PARKING

Parking areas are located within Winston-Salem and are listed from west to east. Select parking areas for the trail are listed below; for a detailed list of parking areas and other waypoints, consult TrailLink ™. *Indicates that at least one accessible parking space is available.*

MARKETPLACE MALL*: 2101 Peters Creek Pkwy. (36.0721, -80.2539).

WASHINGTON PARK*: Dead end of Bond St., 0.3 mile west of S. Broad St. (36.0770, -80.2489).

CENTRAL PARK*: 801 Salem Ave. (36.0822, -80.2403).

HAPPY HILL PARK*: 1230 Alder St. (36.0829, -80.2361).

REYNOLDS PARK*: Reynolds Park Road, 0.1 mile east of Peachtree St. (36.0879, -80.2091).

SALEM LAKE PARK*: 1001 Salem Lake Road (36.0948, -80.1932).

Salem Lake Trail

61

Originally created in 1911, the 365-acre Salem Lake offers a recreational haven on Winston-Salem's east side. Holding approximately a billion gallons of water, the lake provides a third of the drinking water for the city, as well as exceptional recreational opportunities. Those who love to fish, boat, kayak, bird-watch, or simply stretch their legs can enjoy the 1,400-acre park surrounding the lake.

Following the perimeter of the lake, the Salem Lake Trail offers a lush, mostly shaded 7-mile loop on a primarily natural-surface trail for mountain biking, running, or walking. There is a wheelchair-accessible section of approximately a mile near the lake's marina and playground area. Mile markers are visible for those traveling counterclockwise, which is the easiest direction to travel due to the trail's grade.

Begin at the Salem Lake Marina Center, where there is a large parking lot, as well as restrooms in the marina office. Boat rentals and fishing supplies are also available here. Fishing for crappie, bream, bass, catfish, or perch is permitted from a boat or from the main pier; a fee is charged. Keep in mind that the gate to Salem Lake is locked every evening at 7:30 p.m., so park outside the gate if you don't think you'll make it back in time.

COURTESY VISIT WINSTON-SALEM

The 7-mile loop around Salem Lake provides spectacular views and access to the surrounding 1,400-acre park.

County
Forsyth

Endpoint
Salem Lake
Marina Center
(Winston-Salem)

Mileage
7

Type
Greenway/
Non-Rail-Trail

**Roughness
Rating**
1–2

Surface
Asphalt, Dirt

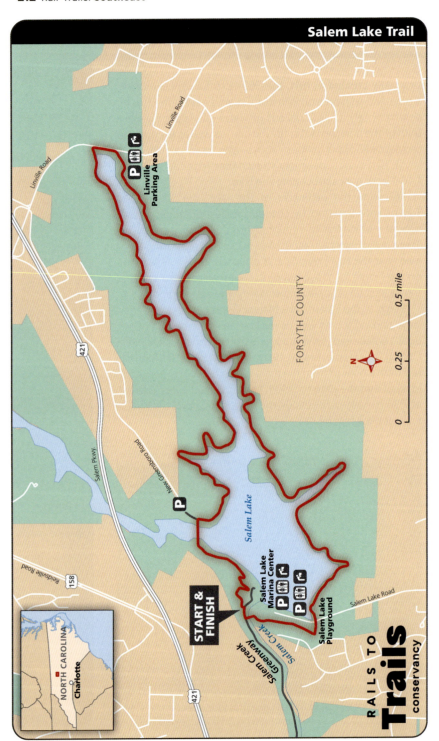

Salem Lake Trail

Linville Road

Linville Parking Area

Linville Road

FORSYTH COUNTY

0.5 mile

0.25

0

N

421

New Greensboro Road

P

Salem Lake

Salem Lake Marina Center

P

P

Salem Lake Playground

Salem Lake Road

START & FINISH

Salem Pkwy.

Reidsville Road

158

Salem Creek Greenway

Salem Creek

421

NORTH CAROLINA

Charlotte

RAILS TO **Trails** conservancy

In 0.3 mile, the expansive and brightly colored Salem Lake Playground comes into view. This area also offers parking, restrooms, and drinking fountains. Be aware of a hill that climbs 35 feet at an 8% grade at roughly the 1-mile mark from the marina—though it does give you a great view of the area with a bench at the top.

From the playground, you'll reach the Linville Parking Area on the east end of the lake in 3.4 miles (about the halfway point of your trip). There is another restroom and drinking fountain available here. About 200 feet from the end of the parking lot, the trail begins to parallel Linville Road over the water. Continuing along the north side of the lake, mature trees envelop the trail.

From Linville Road, in 2.5 miles you'll reach a small bridge that provides a terrific vantage point for picturesque views of the lake and bird-watching. In 0.5 mile, you'll experience an elevation gain on either side of the spillway where Salem Creek meets the lake. A nearly mile-long stretch of pavement begins just before the dam, allowing for a smooth ride up and coast down that continues back to the marina at trail's end. At the Salem Creek juncture, you can extend your journey by connecting with the Salem Creek Greenway (see page 207), which heads west 5.2 miles to Marketplace Mall.

CONTACT: cityofws.org/2151/salem-lake-trail-information

PARKING

Parking areas are located within Winston-Salem and are listed counterclockwise from the Salem Lake Marina Center. *Indicates that at least one accessible parking space is available.*

SALEM LAKE MARINA CENTER*: 815 Salem Lake Road (36.0946, -80.1933).

SALEM LAKE PLAYGROUND*: Salem Lake Road, 0.6 mile north of Reynolds Park Road (36.0926, -80.1927).

LINVILLE PARKING AREA: Linville Road, 0.4 mile south of Salem Pkwy. (36.1047, - 80.1598).

NEW GREENSBORO ROAD PARKING: New Greensboro Road, 0.3 mile from Forest Knolls Cir. SE; a spur trail from the parking lot leads to the Salem Lake Trail (36.1024, -80.1824).

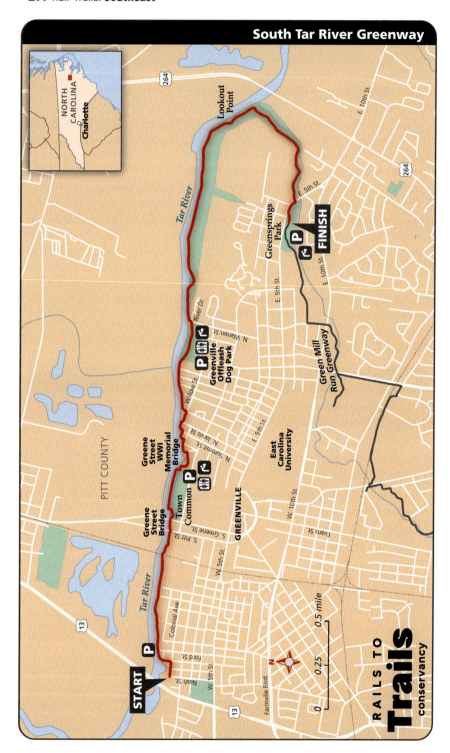

South Tar River Greenway

South Tar River Greenway

62

Meandering for nearly 200 miles, the Tar River empties into the Pamlico Sound, the largest lagoon along the East Coast. More than two centuries ago, steamboats plied the river, transporting cotton, tobacco, lumber, and other materials to the coast, while the regional longleaf pines provided turpentine for shipbuilding.

The paved, mostly flat South Tar River Greenway travels 4.7 miles along the river, with the water in sight for much of the route. Shaded the majority of the way and wide enough to comfortably accommodate multiple users, it's a pleasant way to experience Greenville and offers opportunities to fish, paddle, and bird-watch.

On its western end, the trail begins in a residential neighborhood at Nash Street and Colonial Avenue; the closest available parking is 0.2 mile farther east at the north end of Fairfax Avenue, off Ford Street. The trail follows the tree-lined south shore of the Tar River, and you won't arrive at a street crossing until South Pitt Street, 0.9 mile into your journey. After crossing South Pitt Street, followed immediately by North Greene Street, you'll enter the vibrant Town

AARON HINES/COURTESY CITY OF GREENVILLE

In Greenville's Town Common, the trail crosses the WWI Memorial Bridge.

County
Pitt

Endpoints
Nash St. and Colonial Ave. (Greenville); Greensprings Park at E. Fifth St., 200 feet south of Cemetery Road (Greenville)

Mileage
4.7

Type
Greenway/ Non-Rail-Trail

Roughness Rating
1

Surface
Asphalt

The Tar River is in sight throughout most of the route.

Common, where you'll find ample parking and amenities, including a playground, restrooms, and drinking fountains, as well as a river access point. This area was the homeland of several Indigenous tribes for thousands of years, and an educational marker in the park shares details of this heritage.

On the east end of the Town Common, the trail crosses the WWI Memorial Bridge, a pedestrian bridge that empties out onto Avery Street. Trail users should turn left on Avery Street, following the roadway north and then east to pick up the trail again in 450 feet. The trail crosses North Summit Street, then continues to the intersection of North Jarvis Street and Willow Street. Follow Willow Street on-road for 340 feet before turning left on River Drive, which dead-ends into the trail (look for the kiosk at the entrance). From the River Drive entrance, you'll reach Ash Street in 0.4 mile. Turn right on Ash Street to reach the Greenville Offleash Dog Park, which offers parking, restrooms, and a drinking fountain. Here, you'll also find the Friends of Greenville Greenways Shade Garden, with a large picnic shelter, picnic tables, access to the river, and walkways meandering through the native plants and flowers.

After crossing Ash Street, the trail takes River Drive for 365 feet, then turns left (north) at North Warren Street. Lush vegetation encompasses both sides of the trail here, and numerous unpaved side trails lead to the river for visitors who want to fish. There are also several small ponds in this section for fishing and catching a glimpse of turtles, great blue herons, and other wildlife.

On the southeast end of the trail, there is a small unnamed pond. In this area, Lookout Point is a tiny loop trail off the main route with a picnic table and views of the river. From Lookout Point, travel roughly 1 mile to the trail's end at East Fifth Street. Cross the street to connect to the Green Mill Run Greenway, which continues another 3.1 miles, ending at J.H. Rose High School at Arlington Boulevard and Evans Street. There is a parking area for these two connected trails in Greensprings Park (at East Fifth Street and Beech Street), which features a picnic shelter and tables, as well as drinking water.

The South Tar River Greenway is also a designated part of the East Coast Greenway, a growing network of multiuse trails connecting 15 states and 450 cities and towns on a 3,000-mile route between Maine and Florida.

CONTACT: greenvillenc.gov/government/recreation-parks/greenville -greenways and froggs.org

PARKING

Parking areas are located within Greenville and are listed from west to east. *Indicates that at least one accessible parking space is available.*

FAIRFAX AVE.*: Dead end of Fairfax Ave., off Ford St. (35.6174, -77.3878).

TOWN COMMON*: 100 E. First St. (35.6150, -77.3683).

GREENVILLE OFF-LEASH DOG AREA*: 200 N. Ash St. (35.6134, -77.3553).

GREENSPRINGS PARK*: 2500 E. Fifth St. (35.6061, -77.3433).

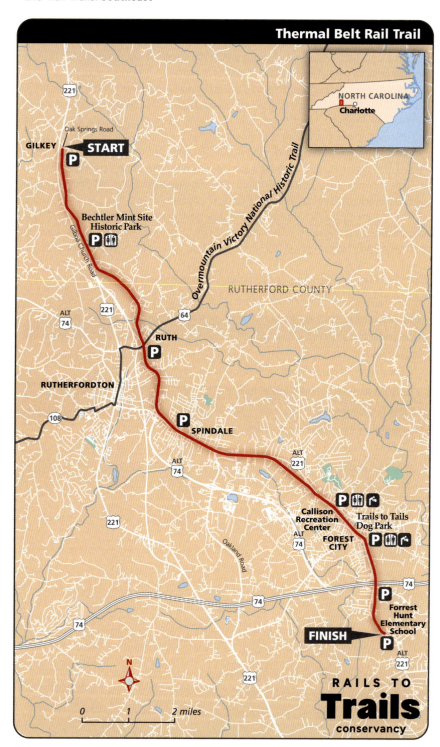

Thermal Belt Rail Trail

NORTH CAROLINA

Charlotte

221

Oak Springs Road

GILKEY   **START**

P

Bechtler Mint Site
Historic Park

P

Gilboa Church Road

ALT
74

221

RUTHERFORD COUNTY

Overmountain Victory National Historic Trail

64

RUTH

P

RUTHERFORDTON

108

P

SPINDALE

ALT
74

ALT
221

221

Callison
Recreation
Center

P

Trails to Tails
Dog Park

P

ALT
74

FOREST
CITY

Oakland Road

P

74

74

74

ALT
221

FINISH

Forrest
Hunt
Elementary
School

P

N

0   1   2 miles

R A I L S   T O
Trails
conservancy

Thermal Belt Rail Trail

63

Named after the temperate climate of the region's isothermal belt, the Thermal Belt Rail Trail spans 13.6 miles and traverses four municipalities in Rutherford County along a corridor that originally served the Wilmington, Charlotte and Rutherford Railroad, which was chartered prior to the Civil War. In 2001, the first segments of the trail were constructed.

The trail starts in the community of Gilkey and heads south through lush forest. At mile 2.1, make a quick pit stop at the Bechtler Mint Site Historic Park to learn about the North Carolina gold rush of the early 1800s. The park features remnants of Christopher Bechtler's 1838 home and mint, where more than $2.2 million in gold was minted. Peer into a mysterious tunnel that may have been the entrance to the gold mine.

Near mile 5.5, the trail intersects the Overmountain Victory National Historic Trail, a 330-mile route that was used by the American Patriot militia in 1780 during the Kings Mountain campaign of the Revolutionary War. At this trail connection in Ruth, you'll reach US 64; take heed while crossing this busy, unsignalized intersection.

ANYA SARETZKY

Stop for a workout at Forest City's outdoor fitness course along the trail.

County
Rutherford

Endpoints
Oak Springs Road between US 221 and Rucker Road (Rutherfordton); Forrest W. Hunt Dr. and entrance of Forrest Hunt Elementary School at Alt. US 221 (Forest City)

Mileage
13.6

Type
Rail-Trail

Roughness Rating
1

Surface
Asphalt

Mile 7 brings you to the heart of downtown Spindale, which is full of shops, restaurants, and the American Dairy Goat Association headquarters. The original rail line serviced Spindale's textile industry, and the Stonecutter Mill—the last mill to have operated in Spindale before it closed in 1999—is located right along the trail. If your on-trail journey is not demanding enough, stop at mile 11 for a workout at Forest City's outdoor fitness course. The Trails to Tails Dog Park is across the trail from the fitness course. Historic downtown Forest City is just a block away and boasts many small businesses and restaurants. If visiting during the holidays, be sure to see Main Street's Hometown Holidays celebration, which has been happening for almost 100 years.

For the grand finale of the trail, cross the bridge over US 74, made from the steel of the original 1906 bridge. The trail ends soon after, at the entrance to Forrest Hunt Elementary School.

CONTACT: thermalbeltrailtrail.com

PARKING

Parking areas are listed from north to south. *Indicates that at least one accessible parking space is available.*

RUTHERFORDTON*: Oak Springs Road between US 221 and Rucker Road (35.4418, -81.9808).

RUTHERFORDTON*: Bechtler Mint Site Historic Park, 342 Gilboa Church Road (35.4136, -81.9705).

RUTHERFORDTON*: Alt. US 74/Railroad Ave. and Southern St. (35.3826, -81.9475).

SPINDALE*: Steward St., west of County Road 1546/Spindale St. (35.3574, -81.9304).

FOREST CITY: Callison Recreation Center, Clay St. and Harris St. (35.3382, -81.8757).

FOREST CITY*: 209 Park Square Cir., across from the outdoor fitness course (35.3322, -81.8662).

FOREST CITY*: Pine St. and Heritage Ave. (35.3149, -81.8564).

FOREST CITY*: Forrest W. Hunt Dr. and Alt. US 221 (35.3005, -81.8530).

Take a break from traffic on this greenway that meanders among suburban housing developments surrounding Cary, about 15 miles west of Raleigh. The 10-foot-wide asphalt trail runs 7.4 miles from Fred G. Bond Metro Park to the American Tobacco Trail (see page 137) with a gentle climb along the way to Davis Drive Park.

The eastern part of the trail is in the city limits of Cary, a tech center whose population has doubled in the 21st century. The entire trail is part of Cary's greenway system, a 50-miles-plus system of nearly 40 trails that the city has been augmenting since the 1980s. The White Oak Creek Greenway is also part of the East Coast Greenway, a growing network of multiuse trails connecting 15 states and 450 cities and towns on a 3,000-mile route between Maine and Florida.

A good place to start is the Fred G. Bond Metro Park, a 300-acre facility that contains an artificial lake. Roughly in the center of the city limits, it serves as a hub for a half dozen greenways. In addition to ample parking and restrooms, it also offers kayak and paddleboat rentals. Traveling west from White Oak Creek Greenway's junction with the Paw

The greenway offers access to parks and greenspace on a route connecting Cary and Apex.

JOE LACROIX

County
Wake

Endpoints
Paw Paw Trail and Black Creek Greenway, 0.1 mile southwest of Metro Park Dr. in Fred G. Bond Metro Park (Cary); American Tobacco Trail at Weddington Community Pool on Cloverdale Road, 0.1 mile southwest of Weddington Park Lane (Apex)

Mileage
7.4

Type
Greenway/ Non-Rail-Trail

Roughness Rating
1

Surface
Asphalt, Boardwalk

White Oak Creek Greenway

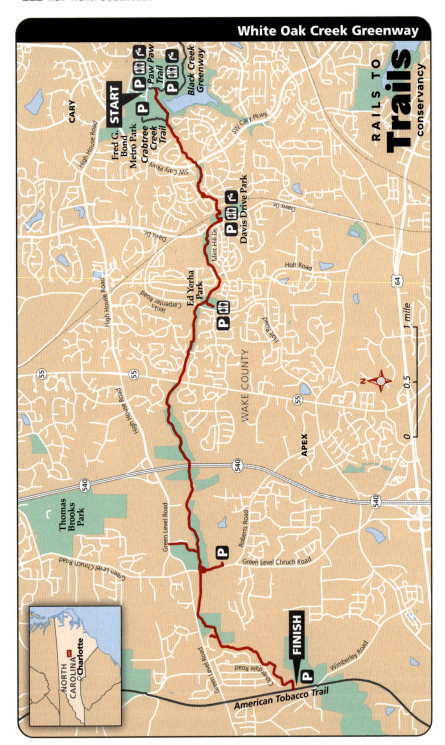

RAILS TO **Trails** conservancy

CARY

START

Fred G. Bond Metro Park

Crabtree Creek Trail

Paw Paw Trail

Black Creek Greenway

SW Cary Pkwy.

SW Cary Pkwy

Davis Dr.

Davis Drive Park

Mint Hill Dr.

Davis Dr.

Holt Road

US 64

Ed Yerha Park

Jenks Carpenter Road

High House Road

High House Road

1 mile

0.5

0

N

55

55

55

WAKE COUNTY

Holt Road

APEX

540

540

Thomas Brooks Park

Green Level Road

Green Level Chruch Road

Green Level Chruch Road

Roberts Road

Wimberley Road

FINISH

Green Level Road

Cloverdale Road

American Tobacco Trail

NORTH CAROLINA
Charlotte

Paw Trail and Black Creek Greenway here, the trail goes through some partially shaded parkland and into a greenbelt nestled between housing.

Passing through a tunnel under Cary Parkway, the trail rolls past a neighborhood garden and then crosses MacArthur Drive on a crosswalk before reaching Davis Drive Park, roughly the high point on the trail at milepost 1.5. Cross Davis Drive and follow it north for 0.1 mile to continue on the greenway. In about a half mile, the greenway enters the wooded stream corridor of White Oak Creek, which it follows for the final 5 miles.

In 0.8 mile past Davis Drive, you'll come to one of the many connector trails along the greenway; this one goes to the facilities at Ed Yerha Park on Jenks Carpenter Road. Over the next mile, the trail passes several ponds that in the fall reflect the colorful surrounding foliage.

After an underpass at Triangle Expressway/NC 540, the greenway runs through wetlands for the final 3 miles. Be careful on the 1,700 feet of boardwalk here in rainy weather, as the surface is slippery when wet. The last section features 450 acres set aside for wetland conservation, offering a stark contrast to the woodsy views at the trail's start. The route finishes at a connection with the American Tobacco Trail.

CONTACT: rtc.li/white-oak-creek-greenway

PARKING

Parking areas are listed from east to west. *Indicates that at least one accessible parking space is available.*

CARY*: Fred G. Bond Metro Park Community Center, 150 Metro Park Dr. (35.7844, -78.8247).

CARY*: Fred G. Bond Metro Park, Bond Park Dr., 0.4 mile south of High House Road (35.7814, -78.8249).

CARY*: Crabtree Creek Greenway Trailhead, Metro Park Dr., 0.2 mile west of Maury Odell Place (35.7847, -78.8293).

CARY*: Davis Drive Park, 1610 Davis Dr. at Park Village Dr. (35.7738, -78.8456).

CARY*: Ed Yerha Park, 1216 Jenks Carpenter Road (35.7746, -78.8599).

CARY*: White Oak Creek Trailhead, 8232 Green Level Church Road (35.7741, -78.9014).

APEX: American Tobacco Trailhead, 1017 Wimberly Road, (35.7609, -78.9209).

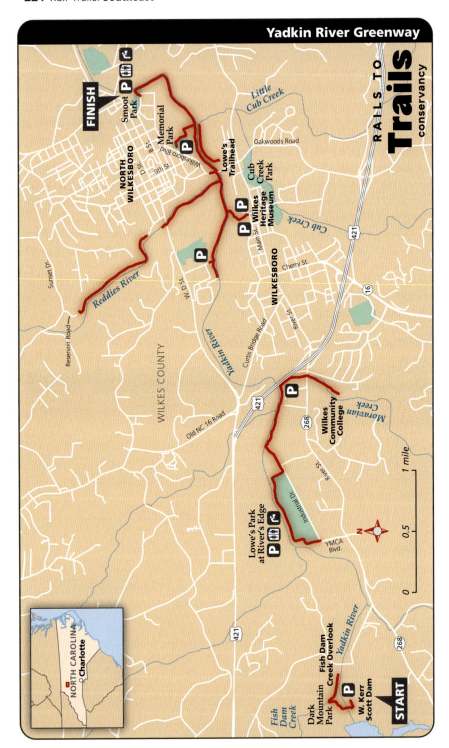

Yadkin River Greenway

RAILS TO **Trails** conservancy

FINISH

Smoot Park

NORTH WILKESBORO

Memorial Park

Lowe's Trailhead

Little Cub Creek

Oakwoods Road

Cub Creek Park

Wilkes Heritage Museum

Cub Creek

WILKESBORO

Cherry St.

16

Reddies River

Reservoir Road

Sunset Dr.

W. D St.

Curtis Bridge Road

River St.

WILKES COUNTY

Yadkin River

421

Old NC 16 Road

421

268

Wilkes Community College

Moravian Creek

River St.

1 mile

N

0.5

Lowe's Park at River's Edge

Industrial Dr.

YMCA Blvd.

0

268

Fish Dam Creek Overlook

Yadkin River

NORTH CAROLINA
Charlotte

Fish Dam Creek

Dark Mountain Park

W. Kerr Scott Dam

START

Yadkin River Greenway

65

Currently made up of a handful disconnected sections, the Yadkin River Greenway offers 8.2 miles of trail stretching from the W. Kerr Scott Dam, through Wilkesboro and North Wilkesboro, to Smoot Park. With connections to parks, fitness areas, river-based activities, and recreational facilities, the trail provides numerous opportunities to pursue an active and healthy lifestyle. Even though it's not fully connected yet, the route is also recognized as part of the Overmountain Victory National Historic Trail commemorating the march of the American Patriot militia, who in 1780 camped in what is now Smoot Park and ultimately defeated British troops in the Revolutionary War battle of Kings Mountain.

The westernmost section of the greenway begins near the W. Kerr Scott Reservoir and the western tip of the Yadkin River. Start at the W. Kerr Scott Trailhead parking area,

County
Wilkes

Endpoints
W. Kerr Scott Trailhead (Wilkesboro); Lowe's Park at River's Edge at YMCA Blvd. and Industrial Dr. (Wilkesboro); Wilkes Community College at S. Collegiate Dr. and Carolina Realty Lane (Wilkesboro); West Park Fitness Zone (North Wilkesboro); D St./US 421 Bus. underpass (North Wilkesboro); Smoot Park (North Wilkesboro); 13th St. and F St. (North Wilkesboro); dead end of NW Reservoir Road (North Wilkesboro); Wilkesboro Ave., 0.6 mile north of E. Main St.

Mileage
8.2

Type
Greenway/Non-Rail-Trail

Roughness Rating
1–2

Surface
Asphalt, Crushed Stone, Dirt

COURTESY EXPLORE WILKESBORO

With connections to parks and river-based activities, the trail provides numerous opportunities to enjoy the outdoors.

on the south side of the Yadkin River. The trail heads west out of the parking lot, then north, curving around the river. In 0.2 mile, you'll reach a bridge over Fish Dam Creek, then finish the rest of your journey paralleling the north side of the river. Although this section spans only 0.6 mile, it provides access to Dark Mountain Park, which offers hiking and mountain biking trails that wind through the hilly, wooded area on the north side of the reservoir.

After a gap, the next section of trail begins on the western outskirts of Wilkesboro at YMCA Boulevard and Industrial Drive, just north of the Wilkes Family YMCA. This segment traces the perimeter of Lowe's Park at River's Edge, which includes a skate park, a dirt bike track, and river access for fishing and paddle sports, plus parking, restrooms, and drinking fountains. Exiting the east end of the park, the trail heads east 0.3 mile to the Yadkin River, then makes a right turn to follow the river southeast for 0.5 mile until reaching Moravian Creek. The trail heads south for 0.2 mile, with the tree-lined creek on one side and a commercial area on the other, until reaching NC 268. From there, the trail goes under the highway and continues another 0.4 mile to Wilkes Community College.

After another gap, the next section begins at the West Park Fitness Zone, a public space with outdoor workout equipment, adjacent to the Wilkes Express YMCA. It offers 1.9 miles of trail along the tree-lined Yadkin and Reddies Rivers. In 0.4 mile, you can turn right to cross a footbridge over the Yadkin River to reach West North Street, just a block from the Wilkes Heritage Museum (where you can learn about local history, including Daniel Boone), as well as shops and restaurants along Wilkesboro's Main Street.

If you continue straight along the greenway instead of crossing the Yadkin River footbridge, you'll parallel the north side of the river for 0.3 mile until reaching a bridge across the Reddies River. If you cross the Reddies River, you'll soon head under Wilkesboro Avenue and, in 0.1 mile, be able to access the avenue at street level. From Wilkesboro Avenue, you can continue your journey east along the Yadkin River to access Memorial Park and then Smoot Park, where this segment of trail ends and where you'll find a skate park and playground, plus restrooms, drinking fountains, and parking.

If you turn left at the Reddies River bridge (instead of crossing the river) you'll be on a short spur heading north along the Reddies River for 0.6 mile until just past the D Street/US 421 Business underpass in North Wilkesboro.

On the opposite side of the Reddies River, the northernmost disconnected section of the greenway, known as the Historic Jefferson Turnpike, traces the eastern bank of the river for 1.3 miles. It begins adjacent to a picturesque dam near the intersection of 13th Street and F Street in North Wilkesboro and heads northwest, enveloped in trees, to the dead end of Northwest Reservoir Road. Stop to read the interpretive signs along the way to envision the Giant Lumber Company's 24-mile log flume, which ran along this route until it was destroyed by a flood in 1916.

Spanning 0.4 mile, another section of tree-lined trail parallels the south side of the Yadkin River from Cornerstone Church at the dead end of Wilkesboro Boulevard to Cub Creek. An extension anticipated for completion by 2025 or 2026 will connect the trail to Cub Creek Park, which features a sports complex, mountain biking trails, a dog park, community gardens, and picnic areas.

CONTACT: yadkinrivergreenway.com

PARKING

Parking areas are listed from west to east. Select parking areas for the trail are listed below; for a detailed list of parking areas and other waypoints, consult **TrailLink™**. *Indicates that at least one accessible parking space is available.*

WILKESBORO*: W. Kerr Scott Dam/Fish Dam Creek, 860 NC 268 (36.1353, -81.2235).

WILKESBORO*: Lowe's Park at River's Edge, 1608 Industrial Dr. (36.1427, -81.1933).

WILKESBORO: N. Collegiate Dr., 400 feet east of Golden Needles St. (36.1441, -81.1789).

NORTH WILKESBORO*: West Park Fitness Zone, 1467 West Park Lane (36.1534, -81.1596).

WILKESBORO: 129 W. North St. (36.1492, -81.1526).

WILKESBORO: Wilkes Heritage Museum, 104 Broad St. (36.1491, -81.1514).

NORTH WILKESBORO*: Memorial Park, 119 Wilkesboro Ave. (36.1582, -81.1430).

NORTH WILKESBORO*: Smoot Park, 106 Chestnut St. (36.1627, -81.1363).

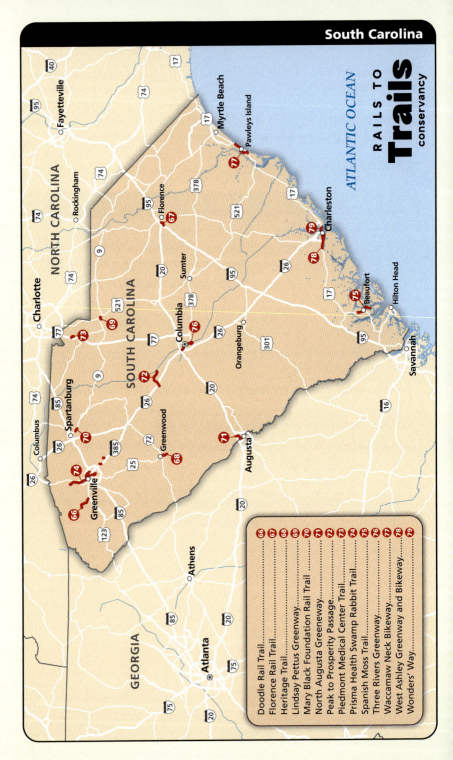

RAILS TO
Trails
conservancy

ATLANTIC OCEAN

NORTH CAROLINA

SOUTH CAROLINA

GEORGIA

Fayetteville
Rockingham
Charlotte
Columbus
Spartanburg
Greenwood
Greenville
Athens
Atlanta
Columbia
Sumter
Florence
Myrtle Beach
Pawleys Island
Charleston
Beaufort
Hilton Head
Savannah
Orangeburg
Augusta

Doodle Rail Trail.................................... 66
Florence Rail Trail................................ 67
Heritage Trail....................................... 68
Lindsay Pettus Greenway...................... 69
Mary Black Foundation Rail Trail.......... 70
North Augusta Greeneway..................... 71
Peak to Prosperity Passage................... 72
Piedmont Medical Center Trail.............. 73
Prisma Health Swamp Rabbit Trail........ 74
Spanish Moss Trail................................ 75
Three Rivers Greenway.......................... 76
Waccamaw Neck Bikeway...................... 77
West Ashley Greenway and Bikeway...... 78
Wonders' Way....................................... 79

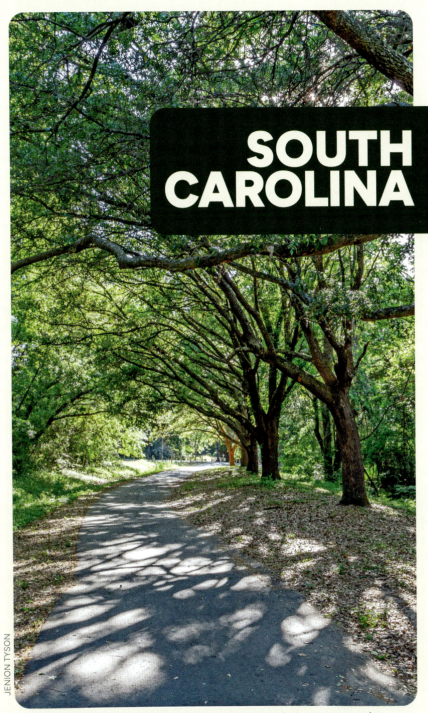

SOUTH CAROLINA

The West Ashley Bikeway provides a tree-canopied route connecting several western Charleston neighborhoods (*see Trail 78, page 269*).

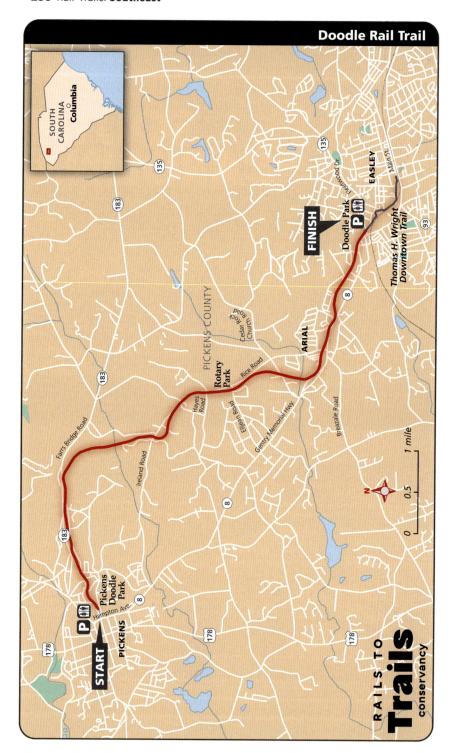

Doodle Rail Trail

Doodle Rail Trail

66

The Doodle Rail Trail connects the towns of Pickens and Easley in the northwest corner of South Carolina. The paved trail follows a former railbed for 8.5 miles and includes two wooden bridges. The railway began passenger and freight service in 1898 and was called the "Doodle" because it ran backwards like a doodlebug between Pickens and Easley due to its inability to turn around.

The Pickens trailhead is located at Pickens Doodle Park with amenities evoking the area's railroading history, including a building and shelter styled like a train depot, brightly colored murals of the train, and an actual engine and car that once ran the Doodle line.

From there, you will find that the landscape shifts as the trail meanders; sometimes the path runs right alongside a road, while at other times it's tucked behind the trees. Single-family homes give way to thickly wooded corridors and lush rolling pastures where cattle languidly pass the time. Remnants of the Upstate's industrial past are also apparent in the shuttered plants. Painted on the asphalt are 0.1-mile markers to help you track your progress.

Discover a train engine and railcar at Pickens Doodle Park.

County
Pickens

Endpoints
Railroad St., 350 feet east of Hampton Ave. (Pickens); Main St. and S. First St. (Easley)

Mileage
8.5

Type
Rail-Trail

Roughness Rating
1

Surface
Asphalt

At about the halfway mark (near Elljean Road), you will come upon a hidden gem—Rotary Park—which was jointly erected by the Rotary Clubs of Pickens and Easley. The small, semicircular space is nestled between the trees and provides seating, a bike repair station, a trail map, and bike parking. If you pause to take in the serenity of the park, you may hear the sounds of birds chirping, leaves rustling, and squirrels and bunnies scurrying in the brush.

While the route does have an abundance of road crossings, they are well marked with striping, tactile paving, and stop signs for trail users. Even if the road seems fairly empty, do not be tempted to rush across; visibility is sometimes poor, and a car may appear without much warning.

After 8.5 miles navigating the trail's gradual inclines, you will appreciate the sight of Easley's Doodle Park as you emerge onto Fleetwood Drive. Like its counterpart in Pickens, this park also features train cars as decoration. These are also functional, however, with one of them housing the park's restrooms. From the park, you can also pick up the roughly 1-mile Thomas H. Wright Downtown Trail Connector; to access the connector trail, cross busy Fleetwood Drive, then meander through neighborhoods and the local cemetery (a steep section of the route) before emerging into downtown Easley, which boasts a wide range of restaurants.

CONTACT: cityofpickens.com and cityofeasley.com

PARKING

Parking areas are listed from west to east. Street parking is also available in downtown Easley. *Indicates that at least one accessible parking space is available.*

PICKENS*: Pickens Doodle Park, 124 Railroad St. (34.8838, -82.7018).

EASLEY*: Doodle Park, 514 Fleetwood Dr. (34.8359, -82.6174).

Florence Rail Trail

67

The Florence Rail Trail lies on a former railway used during the Civil War. Today, the popular trail acts as an important community connector within Florence—a city striving to connect conservation areas to parks, neighborhoods, and urban street trails to encourage exercise and interaction with nature. The rail-trail serves as a transportation alternative to access restaurants, retail establishments, hotels, the local high school, and residential neighborhoods. Pine and sweet gum trees line the trail throughout this urban forest, their thick canopy providing respite from the hot summer sun.

In 2003, the South Carolina Governor's Council on Physical Fitness recognized the Florence Rail Trail Committee with a community award for its work on the well-loved trail. Local individuals and groups of walkers, runners, cyclists, and in-line skaters flock here for their daily fitness routines, and visitors are welcome to join them.

The rail-trail connects to a network of urban connector trails as well. Leaving west from Ebenezer Park is the Live Oak Connector, which uses sidewalks on Pine Needles Road to connect to a popular trail in the Live Oak neighborhood.

TRAILLINK USER SUSANCNETT

The Florence Rail Trail is lined with pines, sweet gums, and honeysuckle.

County
Florence

Endpoints
Old Ebenezer Road, 480 feet north of Harvard Way; SC S-21-13/ Hoffmeyer Road and N. Beltline Dr. (Florence)

Mileage
3.2

Type
Rail-Trail

Roughness Rating
1–2

Surface
Asphalt, Boardwalk, Dirt

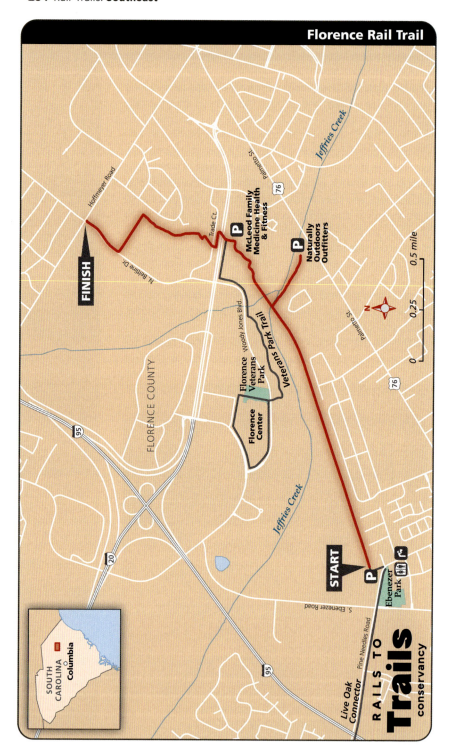

Florence Rail Trail

Another connection at Trade Court uses sidewalks to lead to the city's Florence Veterans Park and the Florence Center—a convention, entertainment, and exhibition facility. A much-anticipated future extension will travel to the 80-acre Florence Soccer Complex, located about a mile southwest of Ebenezer Park.

Replica railroad crossing gates mark the rail-trail's western endpoint and trailhead just east of Ebenezer Park. In the park, you'll find restrooms, drinking fountains, and parking, as well as picnic tables, shelters, a playground, and sports fields. From the park, the trail continues past pines, sweet gums, honeysuckle, and grape vines that attract birds and other wildlife.

After traveling 1.4 miles from Ebenezer Park, you'll reach a spur on the right leading to an outdoors outfitter and a bicycle shop. Just after the spur, a bridge carries the trail over Jeffries Creek and marks a drastic change in surfaces, from asphalt to a mix of dirt and boardwalk over wetlands. The wooded trail continues east to cut through the grounds of McLeod Family Medicine Health & Fitness. Stroll the fitness center's half mile of packed-dirt trails, spurs, and boardwalks over small streams before rejoining the rail-trail at Trade Court. From Trade Court, head 0.9 mile behind a shopping complex to the trail's eastern terminus at Hoffmeyer Road.

CONTACT: cityofflorence.com/city-florence-trail-system and scgreatoutdoors.com/park-florencerailtrail.html

PARKING

Parking areas are located within Florence and are listed from west to east. *Indicates that at least one accessible parking space is available.*

EBENEZER PARK: Old Ebenezer Road, 480 feet north of Harvard Way (34.1765, -79.8493); gravel lot.

NATURALLY OUTDOORS OUTFITTERS AND PHIL'S BICYCLE WORLD*: 2519 W. Palmetto St. (34.1811, -79.8219).

MCLEOD FAMILY MEDICINE HEALTH & FITNESS*: 2437 Willwood Dr. (34.1866, -79.8188); parking available at the front of the fitness center.

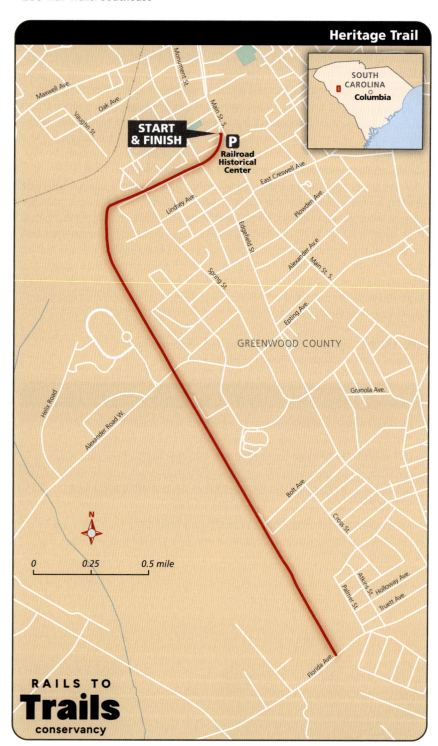

Heritage Trail

START & FINISH

Railroad Historical Center

SOUTH CAROLINA
○ **Columbia**

Maxwell Ave.
Oak Ave.
Vaughn St.
Monument St.
Main St. S.
Lindsey Ave.
East Creswell Ave.
Plowden Ave.
Edgefield St.
Alexander Ave.
Main St. S.
Spring St.
Epting Ave.

GREENWOOD COUNTY

Granola Ave.

Helix Road
Alexander Road W.

Bolt Ave.
Cross St.

Atkins St.
Palmer St.
Holloway Ave.
Truett Ave.

Florida Ave.

N

0   0.25   0.5 mile

RAILS TO
Trails
conservancy

Heritage Trail

68

There is no better place to take in Greenwood's industrial and railroading past than along the aptly named Heritage Trail, which extends 2.5 miles from the town center south to outlying countryside in the South Carolina foothills. Throughout the mid-20th century, five railroads ran through town, crisscrossing and paralleling one another. The busy junction was dubbed Hobo Jungle because the rails attracted a population of transients. Though trains no longer use the rail corridor, the legacy of the Georgia & Florida Railroad lives on through the Heritage Trail.

For most of the trail, the surrounding vegetation (including kudzu-draped pine and hardwood trees) makes you forget how close you are to downtown. The trail is mostly flat as it heads through isolated swamps, pastureland, and mill relics. Benches are provided along the route, but there are no restrooms or water fountains, so plan accordingly.

A commemorative brick plaza marks the northern terminus in downtown Greenwood, at the Railroad Historical Center. The plaza centers on a turntable once used by railroad workers, two at a time, to manually turn steam locomotives

The trail's surrounding pine and hardwood trees make you forget how close you are to Greenwood's downtown.

JIM SCHMID

County
Greenwood

Endpoints
Railroad Historical Center at Main St. S./ SC 34 (Greenwood); Florida Ave. between Chalmers Park Road and Palmer St. (Greenwood)

Mileage
2.5

Type
Rail-Trail

Roughness Rating
1

Surface
Asphalt

for their return trips. The trailhead also features interpretive signs and a pair of passenger cars from the early 1900s. Heading south from Main Street South, the trail passes through a residential area. After a tree-lined half mile, look right to see an old Coca-Cola building, where soda was bottled through the 1950s. In the early 20th century, a circus set up tents in the adjacent field, and the rail line was used to transport animals and equipment for a downtown parade.

Farther down the trail are the century-old Panola and Mathews Mills, part of the nationwide Abney Mill and Greenwood Mills textile companies. Other monikers for the trail include the Railroad and Mill Village Heritage Trail and the Greenwood Mill Village and Railroad Heritage Trail.

On the western side of the trail, Grede Foundries used to cast automobile parts and other products. The paved, mostly shaded trail ends amid open fields and scattered homes. There is no parking at the southern terminus, so you will need to head back the way you came.

CONTACT: rtc.li/greenwood and gwdparks.org/projects

PARKING

Indicates that at least one accessible parking space is available.

GREENWOOD*: Railroad Historical Center, 908 Main St. S./SC 34 (34.1847, -82.1583).

Lindsay Pettus Greenway

69

Running through the city of Lancaster (known as the Red Rose City), the Lindsay Pettus Greenway is a hard-surface, ADA-compliant multiuse trail that connects neighborhoods, schools, and local businesses, all while providing access to a wooded natural area full of wildlife. A large portion of the trail runs through land held for permanent conservation by the Katawba Valley Land Trust. Permanent art installations throughout the trail, made possible through a partnership with the Lancaster County Council of the Arts, highlight the beauty of the region's natural resources. The trail meanders along Gills Creek, which eventually connects to the Catawba River.

Restrooms, trail kiosks, benches, trash cans, and dog waste stations are available at both ends of the trail. There is only one parking lot with designated accessible parking spaces; it's located at the Forest Drive Trailhead on the west end of the trail. The trail has a few ramps up to street level with grades that may be challenging for some.

Start your journey on the east end of the trail at the Founders Federal Credit Union Trailhead behind the Barr

LAUREN V. THOMAS

A nature pavilion at the Comporium Communications Trailhead beckons you into an environmental education area.

County
Lancaster

Endpoints
Barr Street Learning Center on N. Ferguson St. (Lancaster); Gillsbrook Road and Forest Dr. (Lancaster)

Mileage
2

Type
Greenway/ Non-Rail-Trail

Roughness Rating
1

Surface
Asphalt, Boardwalk, Concrete, Crushed Stone

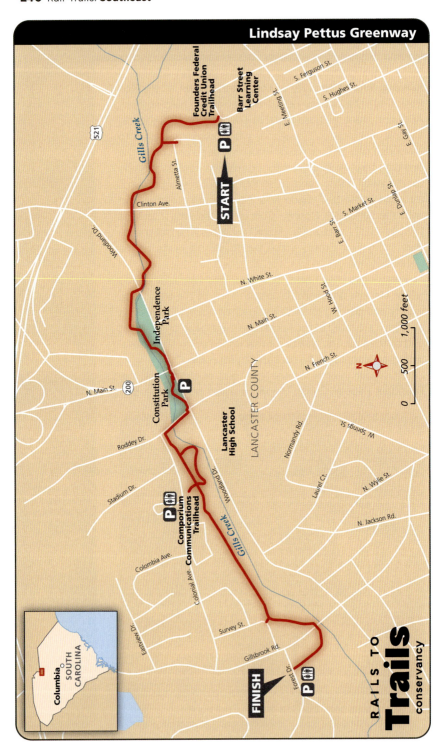

Street Learning Center. The trailhead has a family-friendly rest area that includes a Little Free Library, an art sculpture, a TRACK Trail nature brochure kiosk, and a covered bike rack. Near the 0.7-mile marker, look for an art installation at the Woodland Drive tunnel underpass.

After the tunnel, you will head onto a pedestrian bridge on Roddey Drive. Continue west to the Comporium Communications Trailhead, next to the Lancaster County Chamber of Commerce. From here to the western endpoint at Gillsbrook Road and Forest Drive, you will pass through the Katawba Valley Land Trust's environmental education area. The area includes interpretive panels, wetlands overlooks, pollinator gardens, and a 0.3-mile crushed-stone loop with views of Gills Creek.

In addition to the Founders Federal Credit Union and Comporium Communications Trailheads, there is neighborhood and downtown access to the trail (but no parking) from Almetta Street, Clinton Avenue, Independence Park, Colonial Avenue and Roddey Drive, and Survey Street.

Phase 1 of the greenway was completed in 2020. Plans include extending the trail to increase community connectivity, with the goal being more than 6 miles of total trail mileage. The greenway is also planned to be part of the Carolina Thread Trail, a developing regional network of greenways, trails, and blueways in North and South Carolina, with more than 260 miles of trails open to the public.

CONTACT: lindsaypettusgreenway.org

PARKING

Parking areas are located within Lancaster and are listed from east to west. *Indicates that at least one accessible parking space is available.*

FOUNDERS FEDERAL CREDIT UNION TRAILHEAD: 610 E. Meeting St. (34.7276, -80.7643); public parking is available behind the Barr Street Learning Center.

CONSTITUTION PARK: Roddey Dr. and Woodland Dr. (34.7294, -80.7771).

COMPORIUM COMMUNICATIONS TRAILHEAD: 459 Colonial Dr. (34.7292, -80.7816); free public parking is available at the Lancaster High School football stadium visitor lot.

FOREST DRIVE TRAILHEAD*: Gillsbrook Road and Forest Dr. (34.7251, -80.7886). Very limited parking (two spaces) is reserved for the greenway at an apartment complex; these spaces are recommended only for trail users who need accessible parking.

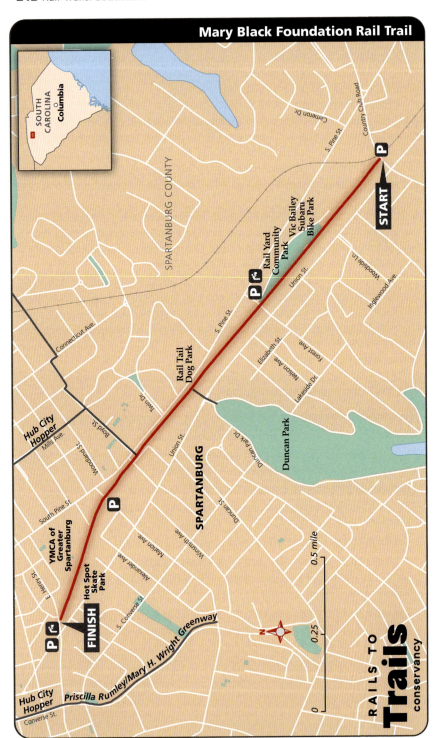

Mary Black Foundation Rail Trail

SOUTH CAROLINA

Columbia

SPARTANBURG COUNTY

START

Country Club Road

Cameron Dr.

S. Pine St.

Vic Bailey
Subaru
Bike Park

Rail Yard
Community
Park

Union St.

Woodside Ln.

Inglewood Ave.

Rail Tail
Dog Park

S. Pine St.

Elizabeth St.

Nelson Ave.

Forest Ave.

Lakeside Dr.

Duncan Park

Duncan Park Dr.

Twin Dr.

Hub City
Hopper

Mills Ave.

Connecticut Ave.

Boyd St.

Woodland St.

Union St.

SPARTANBURG

Winsmith Ave.

Duncan St.

YMCA of
Greater
Spartanburg

South Pine St.

FINISH

Hot Spot
Skate
Park

E. Henry St.

Marion Ave.

Alexander Ave.

S. Converse St.

Priscilla Rumley/Mary H. Wright Greenway

Hub City
Hopper

Converse St.

N

0.5 mile

0.25

0

RAILS TO
Trails
conservancy

Mary Black Foundation Rail Trail

70

Spanning 1.9 miles, the Mary Black Foundation Rail Trail is part of Spartanburg's 50-mile urban trail network known as the Daniel Morgan Trail System (The Dan). It is also part of the larger Palmetto Trail, a developing trail stretching across South Carolina that will span 500 miles once complete.

Beginning at the Country Club Road trailhead on the southeastern end, you are greeted by a wide, flat asphalt path and the remains of Norfolk Southern Railroad tracks from a bygone era. Originally called the Spartanburg & Union Railroad, the line saw more than a century of service before closing in the late 1990s. Now it is a refreshing linear park with an industrial feel, thanks to the warehouses lining it on one side. In fact, Spartanburg is nicknamed Hub City because of the many rail lines that met there.

The Vic Bailey Subaru Bike Park is an early highlight of the trail. Next to it is a fitness station providing equipment for those seeking an extra workout. The bike park is part of the Rail Yard Community Park, another access point. The park contains a picnic shelter, a water fountain, an amphitheater, a trolley pavilion, and a Panthers NFL Play 60 Challenge

YVONNE MWANGI

From the trail's northwestern end, you can continue onto the Hub City Hopper, which takes you downtown.

County
Spartanburg

Endpoints
Country Club Road and SC 56/Union St. (Spartanburg); E. Henry St. and SC 56/Union St. (Spartanburg)

Mileage
1.9

Type
Rail-Trail

Roughness Rating
1

Surface
Asphalt

Course for kids. Continuing, you will come to Forest Avenue, the first of several neatly marked road crossings. At the threshold of the trail are bright-yellow swinging benches on either side of the crossing.

As the trail continues, the tree cover thickens in parts, making for a cooler trip on a warm day. Those visiting the trail with their furry friends can visit the newly renovated Rail Tail Dog Park. The YMCA of Greater Spartanburg is also located along this route, with direct access to the trail. Restaurants and cafés are located on or close to the trail.

At the western end, the East Henry Street trailhead offers parking, water, benches, bike repair, and more. From here, you can turn around and return the way you came or continue onto the recently built 0.6-mile segment of the Hub City Hopper, which begins on the other side of East Henry Street and takes you downtown and into Barnet Park. On the east side of the rail-trail, another 7-mile extension is underway that will eventually connect to Glendale Shoals Preserve and Clifton Beach. The rail-trail also provides access to Duncan Park, the Cottonwood Trail at Edwin M. Griffin Nature Preserve, and the Priscilla Rumley/Mary H. Wright Greenway via signed bike or pedestrian routes.

CONTACT: palspartanburg.org/mary-black-foundation-rail-trail

PARKING

Parking areas are located in Spartanburg and are listed from southeast to northwest. *Indicates that at least one accessible parking space is available.*

PALMETTO TRAIL HUB CITY PASSAGE AND CEDAR SPRINGS PASSAGE PARKING*: Country Club Road/SC S-42-47 and Union St./SC 56 (34.9319, -81.8952).

RAIL YARD COMMUNITY PARK*: 353 Forest Ave. (34.9366, -81.9015).

E. HENRY ST.*: 295 E. Henry St., southeast of E. Henry St. and Union St./SC 56 (34.9475, -81.9213).

Following the former right-of-way of the Central of Georgia Railway, the paved North Augusta Greeneway meanders 9 miles through the riverfront community of North Augusta and is touted as the city's most popular recreational activity. Known to locals as simply the Greeneway, the rail-trail is named for the late Thomas W. Greene, former mayor and trail champion.

Despite the dense suburban setting, the trail's careful design transports users into a surprisingly quiet natural environment. Buffering much of the route is a 100-foot-wide, wooded corridor that provides a significant amount of shade, as well as habitat for native birds, deer, and other wildlife. Trees hide the more developed surroundings along the trail, while new bridges and culvert tunnels whisk users beneath and over busy road crossings. Such conscientious environmental planning helped the trail earn its designation as a National Recreation Trail.

Begin at the southern endpoint at The River Golf Club on the Savannah River. The trail heads 0.6 mile west from the clubhouse to Riverside Boulevard, where you'll find a

At Riverside Boulevard, a preserved segment of track gives a nod to the trail's railroad past.

County
Aiken

Endpoints
Clubhouse at The River Golf Club, 0.4 mile east of Riverside Blvd. (North Augusta); Riverside Blvd. and SC 125/ E. Buena Vista Ave. (North Augusta); Mayfield Dr., between Devon Ct. and Bonnie Brook Dr. (North Augusta)

Mileage
9

Type
Rail-Trail

Roughness Rating
1

Surface
Asphalt

TRAILLINK USER OLDTERRY

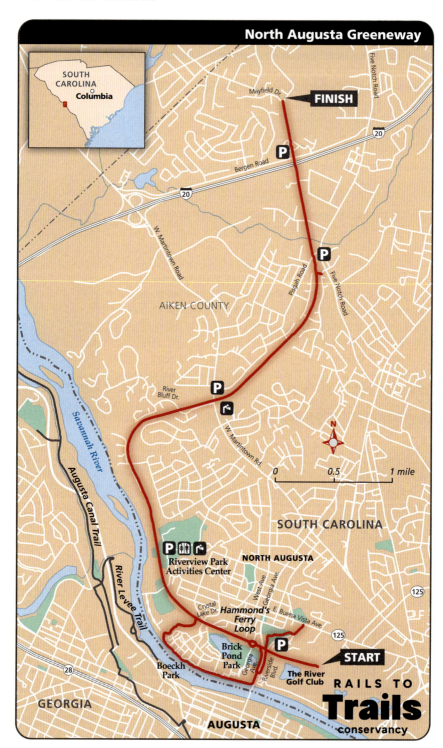

North Augusta Greeneway

preserved segment of railroad track and a parking lot for the trail. From here, you can go 0.5 mile northeast to SC 125/East Buena Vista Avenue, where this segment ends.

Back at the parking lot at Riverside Boulevard, head right (west) into a tunnel beneath US 25 Business/Georgia Avenue. After the tunnel, you can either continue straight for a shorter trip or, for views of the Savannah River, turn left (south) onto a 1.6-mile extension known as Hammond's Ferry Loop. In 0.1 mile, the loop passes through Brick Pond Park, a 40-acre nature conservation area. In another 0.7 mile, you'll reach Boeckh Park, which includes a pavilion and floating dock. The trail turns northeast, away from the river, following Crystal Creek through the woods and over a 90-foot flatbed railcar serving as a bridge before rejoining the main path just west of Crystal Lake Drive.

From this trail juncture at the end of the Hammond's Ferry Loop, turn left and continue 0.7 mile northwest to the Riverview Park Activities Center and the Riverview Park Trailhead, where a fishing pier on the Savannah River is just a short walk away. From here, the next 4.5 miles will take you under River Bluff Drive via tunnel, over SC 230/West Martintown Road via pedestrian bridge, and across busy Pisgah Road via signalized crossing. Note that the trail's uphill grade heading north is gradual yet noticeable. The northern terminus, at Mayfield Drive, is 0.5 mile north of the last parking area at Bergen Road, just north of I-20.

Within the next five years, a new bridge on 13th Street/Georgia Avenue crossing the Savannah River will connect the Greeneway to Georgia's Augusta Canal National Heritage Area Trails (see page 67).

CONTACT: rtc.li/north-augusta-greeneway and northaugustaforward.org /friends-of-greeneway

PARKING

Parking areas are located in North Augusta and are listed from south to north. *Indicates that at least one accessible parking space is available.*

THE RIVER GOLF CLUB*: 306 Riverside Blvd., opposite the entrance driveway to the golf club (33.4878, -81.9714); this is the best parking area to access Hammond's Ferry Loop.

RIVERVIEW PARK TRAILHEAD*: 101 Riverview Park Dr., in front of the Riverview Park Activities Center (33.5001, -81.9873).

RAPIDS SUBDIVISION: West of SC 230/W. Martintown Road (33.5174, -81.9805).

PISGAH ROAD*: 500 feet west of SC 45/Five Notch Road (33.5346, -81.9654).

BERGEN ROAD*: 1.6 mile east of Bergen Road and SC 230/W. Martintown Road (33.5466, -81.9684).

Peak to Prosperity Passage

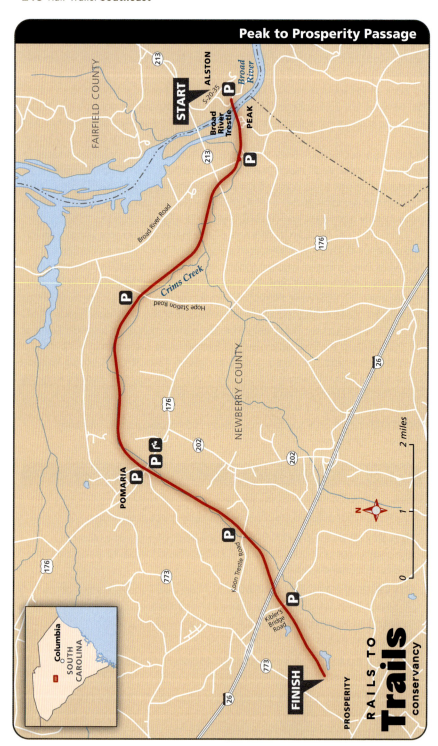

About 30 miles northwest of Columbia, the Peak to Prosperity Passage offers a scenic, shaded route along the right-of-way of a former Norfolk Southern Railroad corridor. Popular with dog walkers, hikers, and bird-watchers, the trail provides ample opportunities for wildlife sightings and beautiful views from its 20 numbered, historic converted trestles—including 17 wooden-decked trestles spanning the meandering Crims Creek. This area was home to many German immigrants in the 1730s and is known as the Dutch Fork of South Carolina.

The first 6.5 miles of the passage opened in 2009 after two volunteers, Charles Weber and Furman Miller, cleared and decked eight trestles. While the rail-trail is flat, the natural surface would make for a rough ride for road bicycles, so mountain bikes are recommended. Users must also traverse wooden stairs to access several of the trestles.

The trail heads west from the Alston Trailhead in Fairfield County. Here, you can find parking, picnic tables, a picnic shelter, a campsite—including a grill and fire pit—and

SETH BERRY

See beautiful views from the trail's 20 converted trestles.

Counties
Fairfield, Newberry

Endpoints
Alston Trailhead at SC S-20-35 (Alston); 1.1 miles southwest of the Kibler's Bridge Trailhead (Prosperity)

Mileage
10.8

Type
Rail-Trail

Roughness Rating
2

Surfaces
Crushed Stone, Dirt, Grass, Sand

access to the Broad River for canoeing, kayaking, and fishing. Four other camp-sites are also located along the Peak to Prosperity Passage, but the Alston site is the only one with parking. For more information on these primitive campsites, visit **palmettoconservation.org.**

From the Alston Trailhead, the trail immediately crosses the 1,100-foot Broad River trestle. Originally constructed in 1848 and opened to rail traffic in 1851, the bridge was flooded and rebuilt before being burned down during the Civil War. The current steel structure was built in 1904. The trestle is the crown jewel of the trail, providing spectacular views of the water, bald eagles, and turtles.

Across the river in Newberry County, the rail-trail skirts the town of Peak and cuts an easy swath through Piedmont forests, across the town of Pomaria, and toward Prosperity. At 6.5 miles, near the center of the route, a trailhead, park-ing, a water fountain, and a grocery store are available in Pomaria. In 2 miles, the trail crosses Koon Trestle Road, where you'll find a small parking lot before the Koon trestle. Roughly 500 feet beyond the trestle is a campsite and picnic area. Another 1.2 miles after that is a trailhead and parking area just after Kibler's Bridge Road (the last parking area for the trail). If you like, you may continue another 1.1 miles southwest to the trail's western terminus before making the journey back.

The Peak to Prosperity Passage is one of 31 passages making up the develop-ing Palmetto Trail, with usage data showing it as the most heavily trafficked. As South Carolina's longest pedestrian and bicycle trail and largest trail construc-tion project, the Palmetto Trail will span 500 continuous miles once complete.

CONTACT: palmettoconservation.org/passage/peak-to-prosperity-passage

PARKING

Parking areas are listed from east to west. *Indicates that at least one acces-sible parking space is available.*

ALSTON: Alston Trailhead at SC S-20-35, between the railroad tracks and the Broad River (34.2437, -81.3178); dirt lot.

PEAK: River St. Trestle (Trestle 3), 0.5 mile south of Broad River Road and SC 213/Parr Road, on the eastern bank of Crims Creek (34.2419, -81.3324).

POMARIA: Hope Station Road Trailhead, 1.4 miles north of Hope Station Road and US 176 (34.2634, -81.3681); small day-use parking area (two spots).

POMARIA: Pomaria Trailhead at Anjella St. beside Wilson's Grocery, 225 feet north of US 176 (34.2627, -81.4134).

PROSPERITY: Kibler's Bridge Trailhead, south of the Mid Carolina Club at Kibler's Bridge Road and SC 773 (34.2305, -81.4501).

73

Closely following the Catawba River, the Piedmont Medical Center Trail (formerly called the Riverwalk Trail) offers a pleasant, 3.4-mile jaunt along the wooded riverbank in Rock Hill, South Carolina, about 20 miles from the state border with North Carolina. It's named for a hospital that's been serving the community for more than three decades. Although the trail is fully paved, note that there are hilly sections throughout the route.

Begin at the River Park Trailhead at the trail's southern end off Red River Road/SC 50, where plentiful parking and restrooms are available. If you are up for more adventure after your excursion on the Piedmont Medical Center Trail, you can experience more trails (both paved and unpaved) in the 70-acre park.

After traveling 0.7 mile along the pathway, you will have a wow moment as a massive Norfolk Southern train trestle crosses the river above you. A historical marker adjacent to the bridge shares information about the importance of this region, including that it was once the heart of the Catawba Nation. A swinging bench here (one of a few along the trail)

SCOTT STARK

Closely following the Catawba River, the trail offers a relaxing jaunt along the wooded riverbank.

County
York

Endpoints
River Park at Quality Cir. (Rock Hill); Herrons Ferry Road and Rapid Run Road (Rock Hill)

Mileage
3.4

Type
Greenway/Non-Rail-Trail

Roughness Rating
1

Surface
Asphalt

Piedmont Medical Center Trail

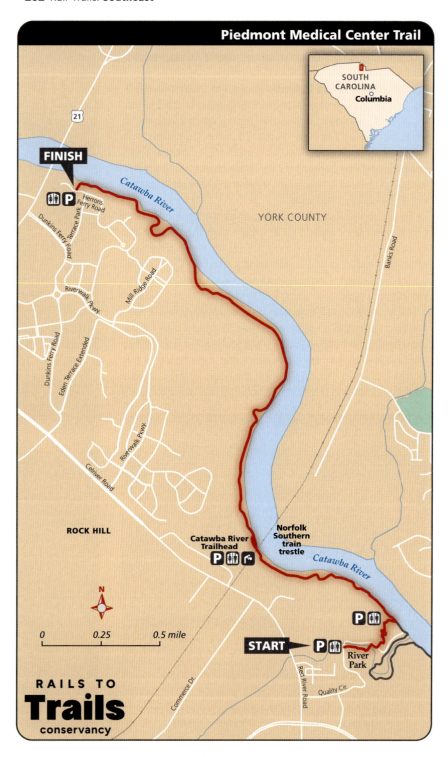

provides a nice spot to enjoy the view. At the bench, you'll find a trail juncture with a 0.1-mile spur leading to the Catawba River Trailhead, which has restrooms, a drinking fountain, and more parking.

With its picturesque backdrop and access to the river for canoeing, kayaking, and tubing, the trail is a lively place on weekends and widely used by runners, dog walkers, and families with young children. On the north end of the trail, you'll pop out of the parklike setting onto Herrons Ferry Road and into the mixed-use neighborhood of Riverwalk. A parking area and temporary restrooms are available across the street. Nearby, you'll see the towering Pump House, a popular restaurant in a converted industrial building that once delivered water to a nearby factory.

The Piedmont Medical Center Trail is part of a larger regional effort called the Carolina Thread Trail, a developing trail network that will span more than 1,600 miles across the Carolinas.

CONTACT: rtc.li/rockhill

PARKING

Parking areas are located within Rock Hill and are listed from south to north. *Indicates that at least one accessible parking space is available.*

RIVER PARK*: 1782 Quality Cir. (34.9565, -80.9504); follow the road to the right, then take the access road to the right to reach the park trailhead.

CATAWBA RIVER TRAILHEAD*: 100 Celriver Road/SC 50 (34.9600, -80.9601).

HERRONS FERRY ROAD PARKING AREA: Herrons Ferry Road, 0.2 mile north of Dunkins Ferry Road (34.9840, -80.9739); follow the RIVER USER PARKING signs to the parking area.

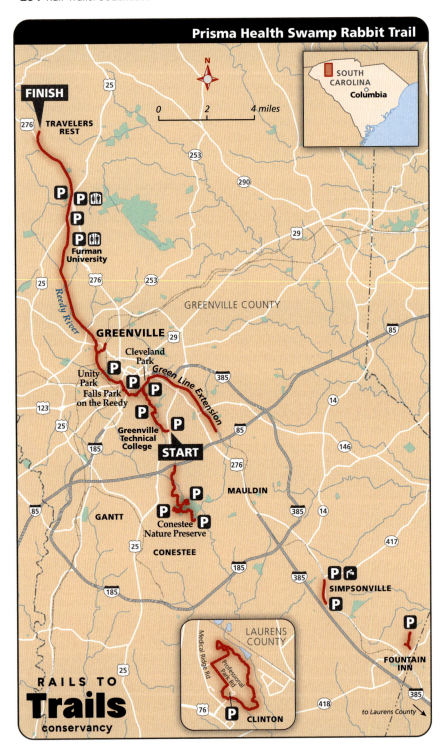

Prisma Health Swamp Rabbit Trail

Prisma Health
Swamp Rabbit Trail

74

With the perfect mix of cityscapes and natural views, the Prisma Health Swamp Rabbit Trail is a Southern gem. The trail was named for the former Greenville and Northern Railroad, nicknamed the Swamp Rabbit because its route took it through the wetlands of the upper Reedy River.

To date, the 28.2-mile rail-trail has three short, disconnected segments in Clinton, Fountain Inn, and Simpsonville; a 5.7-mile segment connecting Conestee Nature Preserve to Greenville's Cleveland Park; a 0.6-mile segment through Hampton Station; and one 17.7-mile continuous segment, which is described on the next page. The trail is segmented into Green, Orange, and Blue Lines, which will be like subway lines as the trail system expands, creating a community-wide transportation element.

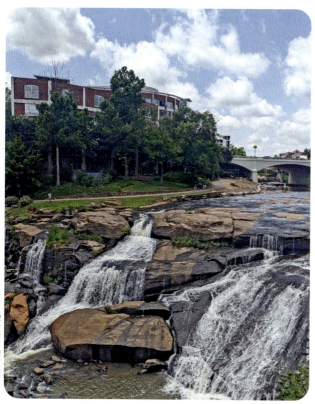

A highlight of the trail is Greenville's Falls Park on the Reedy.

YVONNE MWANGI

Counties
Greenville, Laurens

Endpoints
Southernmost: Professional Park Road, 0.2 mile north of US 76 (Clinton) *Northernmost:* Tate Road south of CR 59/White Horse Road Ext. (Travelers Rest) *Full list of endpoints in the description*

Mileage
28.2

Type
Rail-Trail

Roughness Rating
1

Surface
Asphalt, Boardwalk

As of early 2024, endpoints for the completed sections are as follows, from south to north:

➤ **Loop starting and ending at Professional Park Road,** 0.2 mile north of US 76 (Clinton)

➤ **Duckett St. and CR 891/Mt. Zion Dr.** (Fountain Inn); CR 234/ Hellams St. and SC S-23-889 (Fountain Inn)

➤ **Plain St. and CR 55/S. Main St.** (Simpsonville); SC 417/SC 14/ SE Main St. and Curtis St. (Simpsonville)

➤ **Spanco Dr.** at Conestee Nature Preserve, 500 feet north of Conestee Road (Greenville); Parkins Mill Road at the I-85 underpass (Greenville)

➤ **SC 147/W. Washington St.,** 0.3 mile north of CR 105/E. Bramlett Road (Greenville); Buncombe Road, 500 feet east of Old Buncombe Road (Greenville)

➤ **Verdae Blvd.,** 0.4 mile east of SC 276/Laurens Road (Greenville); Tate Road south of CR 59/White Horse Road Ext. (Travelers Rest)

To travel the 17.7-mile continuous trail segment from Greenville to Travelers Rest, start at Greenville Technical College and head northwest to East Faris Road. Use caution as you continue along the Reedy River toward Travelers Rest, as this section of the trail is subject to flooding. When you reach Cleveland Park Drive, you may either continue toward downtown Greenville by turning left or explore the Cleveland Park Spur, which wraps around the park. The spur marks the beginning of the 4-mile Green Line Extension, completed in the summer of 2023, which features two bridges over multilane roads and South Carolina's first diagonal pedestrian crossing with a bike signal. The freshly paved trail heads through lush greenery and passes Holland Park, where you can find ropes courses and good food. The extension ends at Verdae Boulevard.

If you decide to forgo the new extension and continue toward downtown Greenville, you will pass Cancer Survivors Park and the beautiful Falls Park on the Reedy, featuring a pedestrian bridge over the Reedy River. The next section of the paved trail includes rubberized asphalt for runners. Continuing, you will turn left at Linky Stone Park under US 123/South Academy Street and follow signage through downtown to Unity Park, featuring eateries, a huge playground, and a splash pad.

The remainder of the trail is quiet and scenic as you continue north along the Reedy River under a canopy of trees and past Furman University. At the end of your journey, you will find yourself in the growing town of Travelers Rest, where a bicycle shop offers rentals and repairs.

CONTACT: greenvillerec.com/swamprabbit

PARKING

Parking areas are listed from south to north. Select parking areas for the trail are listed below; for a detailed list of parking areas and other waypoints, go to **TrailLink™.** *Indicates that at least one accessible parking space is available.*

GREENVILLE*: 720 S. Pleasantburg Dr. (34.8208, -82.3702).

GREENVILLE*: YMCA of Greenville, 721 Cleveland St. (34.8356, -82.3852).

GREENVILLE*: Cleveland Park, 130 Woodland Way (34.8409, -82.3858).

GREENVILLE*: Cleveland Park, 150 Cleveland Park Dr. (34.8460, -82.3871).

GREENVILLE*: Cancer Survivors Park, 52 Cleveland St. (34.8413, -82.3974).

GREENVILLE*: Prisma Health Welcome Center at Unity Park, 111 Welborn St. (34.8524, -82.4117).

GREENVILLE: Paladin Stadium at Furman University, 3300 Poinsett Hwy. (34.9199, -82.4376).

GREENVILLE*: 905 Roe Ford Road (34.9365, -82.4425).

TRAVELERS REST*: 2623 S. Main St. (34.9533, -82.4400).

TRAVELERS REST: Trailblazer Park, 235 Trailblazer Dr. (34.9556, -82.4429).

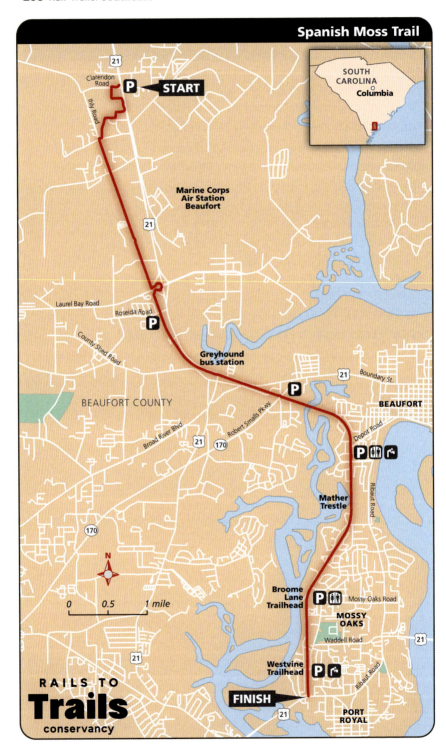

Spanish Moss Trail

75

This developing 12-foot-wide Spanish Moss Trail offers spectacular salt marsh vistas and coastal wildlife viewing as it meanders through neighborhoods and beautiful wetlands. There are historical points of interest along the rail-trail, bringing together the natural beauty of the Low Country landscape with the area's past.

Open year-round, sunrise to sunset, the trail attracts more than 100,000 people a year. It was named one of the country's 10 Best Urban Walking Trails by *Outside* magazine and the Best Hiking Trail in the Palmetto State by *Parade* magazine. The Spanish Moss Trail is part of the developing 3,000-mile East Coast Greenway, a network of trails extending from Maine to Florida.

Many visitors begin their journey by spending a night in the Beaufort–Port Royal area. Beaufort is the second-oldest city in South Carolina, with a large National Historic Landmark District to explore. The area offers wonderful local restaurants; shopping; and outdoor recreational experiences, including boating, paddleboarding, kayaking, fishing, and carriage tours.

COURTESY FRIENDS OF THE SPANISH MOSS TRAIL

The trail's Mather Trestle is a popular fishing spot and sunset-viewing destination.

County
Beaufort

Endpoints
Clarendon Road and US 21/ Trask Pkwy. (Beaufort); US 21/Ribaut Road, between Drayton Dr. and Rahn Lane (Port Royal)

Mileage
10.2

Type
Rail-Trail

Roughness Rating
1

Surface
Concrete

For the full experience of the trail, begin by parking at Clarendon Road—currently the northernmost trailhead. From Clarendon Road, the trail weaves through wooded neighborhoods. You may hear the buzz of fighter jets overhead, as the Marine Corps Air Station Beaufort is located nearby. There is one small tunnel under a commercial driveway that may be challenging to navigate due to its steepness. It is located directly across from Beaufort's Greyhound bus station, 4.7 miles south of the Clarendon Road Trailhead. Otherwise, the trail is flat.

From the tunnel, you'll reach the most populated segment of the trail in 2.3 miles when you arrive at the Depot Road Trailhead, which passes through an iconic 1901 warehouse structure. A half mile south of that trailhead, you'll cross the Mather Trestle, a popular fishing and sunset-viewing spot. Continuing south 1.2 miles to the Broome Lane Trailhead, the path meanders through neighborhoods full of Spanish moss–draped live oaks and other tidal views. You'll then travel 1.1 miles to the Westvine Trailhead. The trail continues south from there into the town of Port Royal, ending in 0.3 mile at US 21/Ribaut Road. An extension estimated for completion by 2030 will continue the trail south to Sands Beach.

In 2024, another important connection will be made from the Depot Road Trailhead into the historic downtown Beaufort area. By 2030, the Spanish Moss Trail will be a 16-mile scenic pathway extending north to a county park at the Whale Branch River—connecting the communities of Seabrook, Grays Hill, Burton, Beaufort, and Port Royal.

CONTACT: spanishmosstrail.com

PARKING

Parking areas are listed from north to south. *Indicates that at least one accessible parking space is available.*

BEAUFORT*: Clarendon Road Trailhead, Clarendon Road and US 21/Trask Pkwy. (32.4934, -80.7426).

BURTON*: Roseida Road Trailhead, Roseida Road, 500 feet west of US 21 (32.4530, -80.7342).

BEAUFORT*: Beaufort Plaza, 11 Robert Smalls Pkwy./SC 170 (32.4391, -80.7041).

BEAUFORT*: Depot Road Trailhead, Depot Road and Middleton St. (32.4275, -80.6922).

BEAUFORT*: Broome Lane Trailhead, 2824 Broome Lane (32.4030, -80.7013).

PORT ROYAL*: Westvine Dr. Trailhead, Westvine Dr., 250 feet east of Battery Park Dr. (32.3883, -80.7020).

Three Rivers Greenway

76

Located at the confluence of the Broad, Congaree, and Saluda Rivers, the Y-shaped Three Rivers Greenway offers a series of disconnected pathways in Columbia, West Columbia, and Cayce. The greenway provides a taste of wildlife within the state's capital and views of Southern hardwood forests and the remains of canal locks. There are numerous opportunities to fish, as well as access points for tubing and paddle sports. The trails are lighted, making them perfect for cool evening strolls.

As of early 2024, endpoints for the completed sections are as follows:

➤ *Riverfront Park:* Northern tip of the Columbia Canal and Riverfront Park North (Columbia); Gist St. and Senate St. (Columbia)

➤ *Saluda Riverwalk:* North of Saluda River, just south of overpass between US 76/I-126 and I-26 (West Columbia); Sanctuary at Boyd Island (Columbia)

Counties
Lexington, Richland

Endpoints
Northernmost:
Northern tip of the Columbia Canal and Riverfront Park North (Columbia); *Southernmost:* Cayce Tennis & Fitness Center (Cayce) *Full list of endpoints in the description*

Mileage
19.4

Type
Greenway/ Non-Rail-Trail

Roughness Rating
1

Surface
Asphalt, Boardwalk, Concrete

ROBERT ANNIS

Enjoy picturesque views of the greenway's namesake: the Broad, Congaree, and Saluda Rivers.

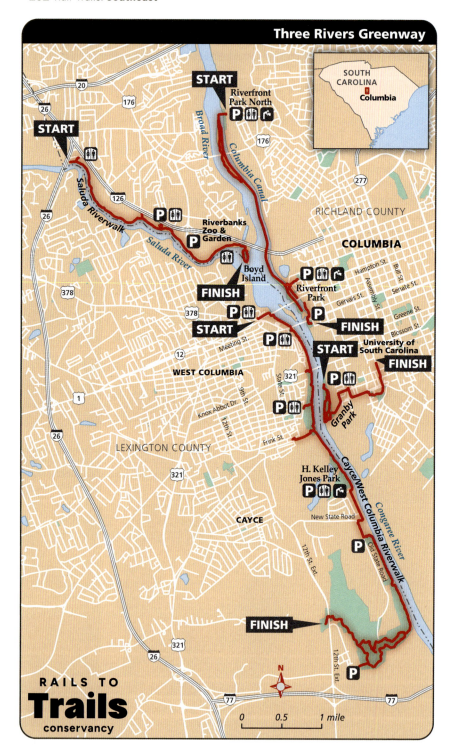

Three Rivers Greenway

SOUTH CAROLINA

Columbia

START
Riverfront
Park North

START

RICHLAND COUNTY

COLUMBIA

Riverbanks
Zoo &
Garden

Boyd
Island

Riverfront
Park

FINISH

FINISH

START

University of
South Carolina

FINISH

START

WEST COLUMBIA

Granby
Park

LEXINGTON COUNTY

H. Kelley
Jones Park

CAYCE

New State Road

FINISH

RAILS TO
Trails
conservancy

0   0.5   1 mile

➤ *Cayce/West Columbia Riverwalk and Amphitheater:* Riverside Dr., northwest of US 378/Sunset Blvd. and SC 12/Jarvis Klapman Blvd. (West Columbia); Cayce Tennis & Fitness Center (Cayce)

➤ *Granby Park and Mill Village Riverlink:* Granby Park at Catawba Cir. (Columbia); Lincoln St., 0.1 mile north of Catawba St. (Columbia)

Columbia's 4-mile Riverfront Park segment—the northeastern leg of the greenway's Y—follows the towpath of the historic Columbia Canal. The park is also part of the developing 500-mile Palmetto Trail, South Carolina's longest pedestrian and bicycle trail. This segment includes a bike-share station, a picnic shelter, overlooks with benches, and views of a canal diversion dam. From the starting point, you'll immediately cross the canal to a strip of land separating the canal from the Broad River. Shortly thereafter, the trail splits, with one side continuing to follow the canal south and the other side hugging the Broad River. In 0.8 mile, the two reconnect at a stairway. From there, you'll continue 1.5 miles to another crossing of the canal at the park's amphitheater. If you cross the canal, you'll reach the Laurel Street parking area and a visitor center in 0.2 mile. If you don't cross the canal, you'll continue 0.2 mile south to this segment's end.

The 3-mile Saluda Riverwalk, a mix of lighted concrete path and timber boardwalk, comprises the northwestern leg of the Y and follows the Saluda River between I-26 and I-126. From its northernmost parking area on Candi

The greenway provides access to forested areas and green space within the Columbia metro region.

Lane, you could head north for just over a mile along the tree-lined waterfront (note that there is no parking at the end of the trail). Alternatively, head south from Candi Lane and follow the riverwalk past the Riverbanks Zoo & Garden in 0.6 mile. In another 0.9 mile, the trail ends with a half-mile loop around the Sanctuary at Boyd Island, a 7-acre oasis featuring metal sculptures, picnic tables, and an observation deck. Plans are in place to connect this riverwalk to the Riverfront Park segment with a bridge.

Along the 8-mile Cayce/West Columbia Riverwalk and Amphitheater segment, you can fish for striped bass in the Congaree River, have lunch at the picnic pavilion, learn about the area's history through historical markers, and zigzag through dogwood and oak trees. The trail begins at a parking lot for the riverwalk on Riverside Drive. From there, you'll follow the western bank of the river, reaching the West Columbia Riverwalk Park and Amphitheater in 0.6 mile, then enter Cayce in another half mile as you approach the US 321 underpass. You'll find restrooms and a drinking fountain in 1.7 miles at H. Kelley Jones Park. From there, the trail parallels the river another 1.5 miles before heading west and meandering along Congaree Creek to the trail's end at the Cayce Tennis & Fitness Center.

The Granby Park segment begins on the eastern bank of the Congaree River in Columbia and provides an easy, deeply shaded 0.5-mile path through the park with overlooks of the river, a picnic area, benches, birding opportunities, and signs describing local flora. Exiting the park on Gist Street, the trail deviates from the river, traveling through residential neighborhoods and connecting to the 1.5-mile Mill Village Riverlink at Heyward Street. The Riverlink offers a quiet walk or ride on city streets and sidewalks as it passes old mill buildings and traverses Olympia Park, ending at Lincoln Street and the University of South Carolina's Greek Village.

CONTACT: riveralliance.org/project/three-rivers-greenway

PARKING

Parking areas are listed from north to south. Select parking areas are listed below; for a detailed list of parking areas and other waypoints, consult **TrailLink™.** *Indicates that at least one accessible parking space is available.*

Riverfront Park segment:

COLUMBIA: Riverfront Park N., 0.5 mile north of US 176/River Dr. (34.0326, -81.0682).

COLUMBIA: Riverfront Park at 312 Laurel St. (34.0049, -81.0509).

Saluda Riverwalk segment:

COLUMBIA*: 650 Candi Lane (34.0137, -81.0821).

COLUMBIA*: Riverbanks Zoo & Garden, Red Lot on Candi Lane (34.0106, -81.0764); fee.

Cayce/West Columbia Riverwalk and Amphitheater segment:

WEST COLUMBIA*: 100 Riverside Dr. (33.9972, -81.0599), just off Jarvis Klapman Blvd./SC 12.

WEST COLUMBIA*: West Columbia Riverwalk Park and Amphitheater at Alexander Road, between Oliver St. and Congaree Park Dr. (33.9947, -81.0530); follow signs for Riverwalk parking, then park by the amphitheater.

CAYCE: 201 Naples Ave. (33.9809, -81.0498).

CAYCE: Old State Road and Taylor Road (33.9578, -81.0354).

CAYCE*: Cayce Tennis & Fitness Center at 1120 Fort Congaree Trail (33.9339, -81.0394).

Granby Park segment:

COLUMBIA: Granby Park, at dead end of Catawba St./Catawba Cir. (33.9834, -81.0444).

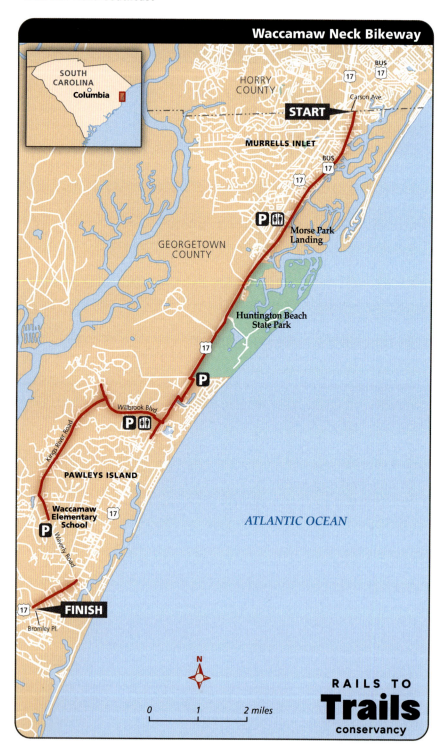

Waccamaw Neck Bikeway

SOUTH CAROLINA
Columbia

HORRY COUNTY

BUS 17

17

Carson Ave.

START

MURRELLS INLET

BUS 17

17

P

Morse Park Landing

GEORGETOWN COUNTY

Huntington Beach State Park

17

P

Willbrook Blvd.

P

Kings River Road

PAWLEYS ISLAND

Waccamaw Elementary School

17

P

Waverly Road

17

FINISH

Bromley Pl.

ATLANTIC OCEAN

N

0   1   2 miles

RAILS TO Trails conservancy

Waccamaw Neck Bikeway

77

The developing Waccamaw Neck Bikeway parallels US 17 and Kings River Road from Murrells Inlet to Pawleys Island. While a good portion is along roads and the sounds of traffic are frequently in the background, nature abounds as the trail traverses Huntington Beach State Park.

Starting at Murrells Inlet just south of the Horry–Georgetown county line, the first section heads south from Carson Avenue via 5-foot-wide bike lanes on either side of US 17 Business—the only portion of the trail that is not off-road. There are road crossings up and down US 17, but they are all well signed. In 2.7 miles, you'll arrive at a trailhead at Morse Park Landing, complete with maps, restrooms, a boat landing, and parking. In just under a mile, the trail merges onto an off-road trail before going over a small bridge known as the Bike Bridge. Just after the bridge is Huntington Beach State Park, a sprawling, 2,500-acre natural oasis of maritime forest and pristine wetlands. Watch out for the numerous twists and turns weaving along the densely wooded path, as well as tree roots that have led to some cracking in the asphalt.

You can explore the state park from its paved causeway, a stretch of road near the park's entrance with a brackish

TRAILLINK USER MARYDEGANGE

The stretch along Kings River Road
includes this pretty waterfront view.

County
Georgetown

Endpoints
US 17 Bus. and
Carson Ave.
(Murrells Inlet);
US 17 and
Bromley Pl.
(Pawleys Island)

Mileage
13.6

Type
Greenway/
Non-Rail-Trail

**Roughness
Rating**
1–2

Surface
Asphalt,
Concrete

pond on one side and salt marsh on the other. Other sites include a beach; campsites; hiking and interpretive trails; wildlife-viewing boardwalks in a salt marsh and freshwater lagoon; picnic shelters; a nature center; and Atalaya Castle, a National Historic Landmark. Popular activities include bird-watching and fishing in the surf or from the jetty. For park fees, parking, fishing licenses, and other information, visit **southcarolinaparks.com/huntington-beach.**

Roughly 1.7 miles from the state park, the off-road trail crosses the four-lane US 17 via a signalized crossing on the south side of Willbrook Boulevard/County Road S-22-362, weaving across the front of a golf resort. After crossing US 17, the trail parallels Willbrook Boulevard/CR S-22-362 to the Reserve Community—the only segment of trail where golf carts from neighboring clubs are permitted. The trail turns left onto Kings River Road around 1.5 miles from the US 17 crossing, then travels 2.5 miles southwest.

The trail turns left onto Waverly Road/CR S-22-46 and heads 0.5 mile to Waccamaw Elementary School. A 1.3-mile concrete bike path, anticipated to be completed by mid-2024, will travel from the school to the intersection of US 17 and Waverly Road/CR S-22-46/North Causeway Road. From here, the final open segment of trail runs 1.1 miles along US 17 to just south of Bromley Place in Pawleys Island.

Plans are underway to lengthen the bikeway—initially known as the Bike the Neck project—for a total of 27 miles down to the Waccamaw Neck Peninsula. The trail is part of the East Coast Greenway, a growing network of multiuse trails connecting 15 states and 450 cities and towns on a 3,000-mile route between Maine and Florida.

CONTACT: gtcounty.org/389/waccamaw-bikeway

PARKING

Parking areas are listed from north to south. There are many places to park in Huntington Beach State Park for a nominal park admission fee. *Indicates that at least one accessible parking space is available.*

MURRELLS INLET*: Morse Park Landing, 4939 US 17 Bus. (33.5392, -79.0507).

NORTH LITCHFIELD*: Huntington Beach State Park, US 17 and Trace Dr./CR S-22-362 (33.4962, -79.0858); this paved, 12-spot parking lot is just south of the state park.

PAWLEYS ISLAND*: Waccamaw Neck Branch Library, 41 St. Paul's Pl. (33.4864, -79.1000).

PAWLEYS ISLAND*: Waccamaw Elementary School, 1364 Waverly Road (33.4554, -79.1360).

West Ashley Greenway and Bikeway

78

A favorite of local bikers and joggers, the West Ashley Greenway takes you on an 8.2-mile trip from Albemarle Road, near the Ashley River, through suburban Charleston to the scenic Low Country wetlands that surround this charming city. Nearly halfway through the greenway, you can connect to the 2.7-mile West Ashley Bikeway via a short on-road connection. Note that there are no restrooms along either trail, so plan accordingly.

The greenway and bikeway are part of the city's system of 42-plus miles of interconnected, off-street multiuse paths. The West Ashley Greenway also forms a component of the East Coast Greenway, a growing network of multiuse trails connecting 15 states and 450 cities and towns on a 3,000-mile route between Maine and Florida.

The greenway begins on the eastern edge of the Charleston neighborhood of West Ashley at Albemarle Road and Croghan Spur Road, where you'll find a historical marker for the Atlantic Coast Line Railroad's Croghans Branch, which once served as the eastern end of the main line from Savannah to Charleston. However, you may prefer to start your journey 0.4 mile west at the Folly Road Boulevard Trailhead, as parking is available there and you can avoid the busy

This unique bridge, designed by Clemson University students, links the West Ashley Bikeway with Forest Park Playground.

JENION TYSON

County
Charleston

Endpoints
West Ashley Greenway: Albemarle Road and Croghan Spur Road (Charleston); McLeod Mill Road near Main Road/SC S-10-20 (Charleston) *West Ashley Bikeway:* Higgins Pier at the Ashley River (Charleston); Wappoo Road and US 17 (Charleston)

Mileage
10.9

Type
Rail-Trail

Roughness Rating
1–2

Surface
Asphalt, Gravel

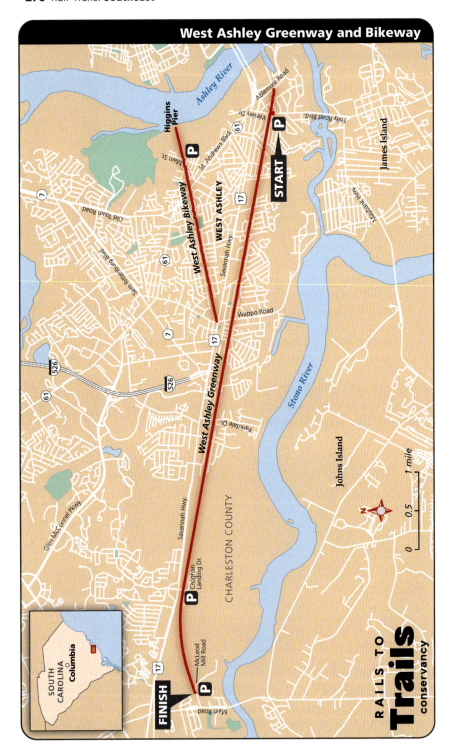

West Ashley Greenway and Bikeway

intersection of Folly Road Boulevard and Wesley Drive. The partially paved greenway continues west through the former rail corridor.

At the Wappoo Road crossing—3.2 miles from the eastern endpoint—you have the option to travel north on narrow sidewalks for 0.2 mile, crossing US 17, to hop on the paved West Ashley Bikeway, which heads northeast. In 1.8 miles, the bikeway reaches the four-lane St. Andrews Boulevard/SC 61. Trail users must cross the busy road without the benefit of a light or crosswalk, so use caution. From there, the bikeway continues 0.9 mile northeast to its end at Higgins Pier on the Ashley River.

Back at Wappoo Road, you could also continue west on the West Ashley Greenway. In 1.3 miles, at Parkdale Drive, the trail switches to a compacted gravel surface, then travels 2.3 miles to Croghan Landing Drive. The final 1.4-mile section, from Croghan Landing Drive to the western terminus at McLeod Mill Road, features a causeway along marsh and creek—a popular spot for crabbing, fishing, and wildlife-viewing. Broad wetlands flanking the trail present magnificent views and rewarding coastal bird sightings. If your timing is right, you may catch sight of the tidal flow that carved these lacework channels.

CONTACT: charleston-sc.gov/251/parks

PARKING

Parking areas are located within Charleston and are listed from east to west. *Indicates that at least one accessible parking space is available.*

FOLLY ROAD BLVD. TRAILHEAD: Windermere Blvd. and Folly Road Blvd. (32.7773, -79.9745); park beside the trailhead on the north side of South Windermere Center.

HIGGINS PIER PARKING: Main St. and Chickadee Ave. (32.7947, -79.9838); small gravel lot.

CROGHAN LANDING DR.: Croghan Landing Dr. and US 17 (32.7956, -80.0814); small gravel lot.

MCLEOD MILL ROAD: McLeod Mill Road and West Ashley Greenway, 0.2 mile east of Main Road/SC S-10-20 (32.7936, -80.1044); dirt lot.

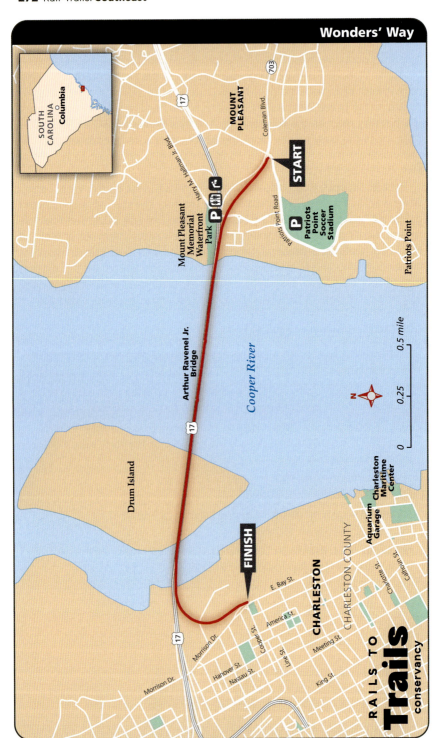

Wonders' Way

79

Stretching 2.5 miles, the Arthur Ravenel Jr. Bridge is the longest bridge in South Carolina and has a clearance of 186 feet to allow for Cooper River port traffic below. It connects the town of Mount Pleasant and downtown Charleston via eight lanes of vehicular traffic along US 17. Thanks to the work of a persistent grassroots advocacy effort, it also includes a dedicated multiuse path. The Wonders' Way trail adds an additional 0.2 mile with the lead-up to the bridge in Mount Pleasant and the ramp to it in Charleston. The trail is named for Garrett Wonders, a cyclist who was killed in a bike–car collision near Charleston in 2004.

The trail's eastern endpoint is at Patriots Point Road and Coleman Boulevard/SC 703 in Mount Pleasant, but because there is no official trail parking there, many people park underneath the bridge and begin their journey at Mount Pleasant Memorial Waterfront Park. The park includes a visitor center, an art center, a café and gift shop, restrooms, a playground, and a pedestrian pier with panoramic views of the harbor.

A short access path under the bridge leads to the trail from Harry M. Hallman Jr. Boulevard. Follow signs for Wonders' Way as you make your way onto the south side of the Ravenel Bridge, heading west over the Cooper River. The

DENNIS HAWKINS

With dedicated lanes for trail users, the Ravenel Bridge offers views of the Cooper River and Charleston Harbor.

County
Charleston

Endpoints
Patriots Point Road and Coleman Blvd./SC 703 (Mount Pleasant); E. Bay St. and Cooper St. (Charleston)

Mileage
2.7

Type
Greenway/Non-Rail-Trail

Roughness Rating
1

Surface
Asphalt

12-foot-wide, paved path is separated from vehicular traffic by a low concrete wall and has separate lanes for cyclists and pedestrians. Be prepared for a gradual slope ascending to the center of the bridge, which can be challenging against the wind.

From a viewing area at the top of the bridge, enjoy expansive Low Country views of the Cooper River, the Charleston skyline and harbor, and even Folly Beach and Isle of Palms in the distance. Continue on Wonders' Way to its end-point at East Bay Street and Cooper Street in Charleston. There is no official parking on this end of the trail, though metered street parking is available.

Wonders' Way is also part of the developing East Coast Greenway, a growing network of multiuse trails connecting 15 states and 450 cities and towns on a 3,000-mile route between Maine and Florida.

CONTACT: visit-historic-charleston.com/arthur-ravenel-bridge.html

PARKING

The parking area is located in Mount Pleasant on the east end of the trail.
Indicates that at least one accessible parking space is available.

MOUNT PLEASANT MEMORIAL WATERFRONT PARK*: US 17 and Harry M. Hallman Jr. Blvd. (32.8006, -79.9019); free parking is available underneath the Ravenel Bridge on both sides of Harry M. Hallman Jr. Blvd. A short access path leads to the start of Wonders' Way.

Index

Support Rails to Trails Conservancy

Rails to Trails Conservancy (RTC) is a nonprofit organization working to build a nation connected by trails. We reimagine public spaces to create safe ways for everyone to walk, bike, and be active outdoors. Since 1986, RTC has worked from coast to coast, helping to transform unused rail corridors and other rights-of-way into vibrant public places, ensuring a better future for America made possible by trails and the connections they inspire.

We know trails improve lives, engage communities, create opportunities, and inspire movement. And we know these opportunities are possible only with the help of our passionate members and supporters across the country. Learn how you can support RTC, and discover the benefits of membership at **railstotrails.org/support.**

Rails to Trails Conservancy is a 501(c)(3) nonprofit organization, and contributions are tax-deductible.

FIND YOUR TRAIL

TrailLink

California's Crystal Springs Regional Trail | Photo by Joe LaCroix

Trail
moments

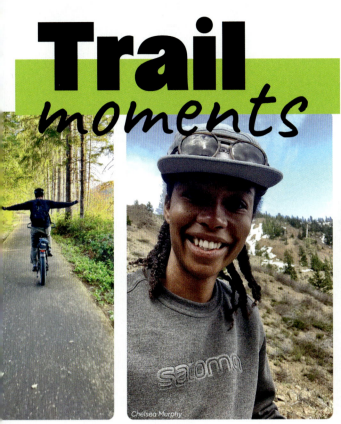

Chelsea Murphy

Bree Corbin

Trail stories that inspire.

In neighborhoods across America, trails are essential—creating space for us to walk, bike and be active outside. Trails are places where we connect with friends and family, log daily steps, safely commute to the places we need to go or simply take some time for ourselves. The moments we make in these spaces are limitless, but across the board, **trail moments make our everyday moments better**.

View the Trail Moments collection or share your own story! railstotrails.org/trailmoments

#TrailMoments

RAILS TO
Trails
conservancy

Our members make trails happen.

Join the movement! Become a member and help us build a nation connected by trails.

Give $18 or more to become a member. Your yearlong membership includes an exclusive member T-shirt, a subscription to our quarterly flagship magazine and reduced prices on trail guidebooks and gear!

Get even more benefits by becoming a monthly donor or auto-renewal member, or by joining the Trailblazer Society.

SUPPORT THE TRAILS YOU LOVE
railstotrails.org/membership

West Virginia's Caperton Rail Trail | Photo by Renee Rosensteel